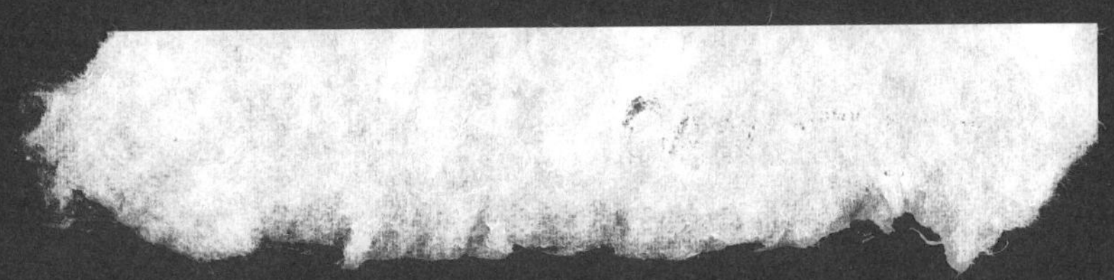

D0506206

¡COMRADES!

ALSO BY PAUL PRESTON

Editor, *Spain in Crisis: Evolution and Decline of the Franco Regime*
(Harvester Press, 1976)

The Coming of the Spanish Civil War: Reform, Reaction and Revolution in the Second Spanish Republic 1931–1936
(Macmillan, 1978)

(with Denis Smyth) *Spain, the EEC and NATO*
(Royal Institute of International Affairs & Routledge and Kegan Paul, 1984)

Editor, *Revolution and War in Spain 1931–1939*
(Methuen, 1984)

Las derechas españolas en el siglo veinte: autoritarismo, fascismo, golpismo
(Editorial Sistema, Madrid, 1986)

The Triumph of Democracy in Spain
(Methuen, 1986)

The Spanish Civil War 1936–1939
(Weidenfeld & Nicolson, 1986)

Salvador de Madariaga and the Quest for Liberty in Spain
(Clarendon Press, 1987)

The Politics of Revenge: Fascism and the Military in Twentieth Century Spain
(Unwin Hyman, 1990)

Editor (with Frances Lannon) *Elites and Power in Twentieth Century Spain: Essays in Honour of Sir Raymond Carr*
(Clarendon Press, 1990)

Franco
(HarperCollins, 1993)

A Concise History of the Spanish Civil War
(HarperCollins, 1996)

Editor (with Ann Mackenzie) *The Republic Besieged: Civil War in Spain 1936–1939*
(Edinburgh University Press, 1996)

¡COMRADES!

Portraits from
The Spanish Civil War

PAUL PRESTON

HarperCollins*Publishers*

HarperCollins*Publishers*
77–85 Fulham Palace Road,
Hammersmith, London W6 8JB

1 3 5 7 9 8 6 4 2

First published in Great Britain by
HarperCollins*Publishers* 1999

ISBN 0 00 215392 0

Set in Janson by
Rowland Phototypesetting Ltd,
Bury St Edmunds, Suffolk

Printed and bound in Great Britain by
Caledonian International Book Manufacturing Ltd, Glasgow

For Miguel Dols and Hilari Raguer

CONTENTS

LIST OF ILLUSTRATIONS

The author and publishers would like to thank the Spanish publishers of this book, Plaza y Janés, who kindly granted us permission to reproduce these photographs.

Between pages 174 and 175

Between pages 270 and 271

Julián Besteiro and the 1917 strike committee with their lawyer.
Besteiro in the carriage of the President of the Republic.
Besteiro announces the creation of the anti-Communist Junta de Defensa.
Besteiro in 1940 in the prison at Carmona.
Azaña casts his vote in Madrid in the elections for the Constituent Cortes.
Azaña in La Coruña on 21 September 1932.
Azaña with the Papal Nuncio, Monsignor Federico Tedeschini.
General Franco accompanies José María Gil Robles during manoeuvres.
Azaña addresses his followers after the victory of the Popular Front in 1936.
Prieto, in conversation with Manuel Portela Valladares.
Headlines announce the military coup of Miguel Primo de Rivera.
Santiago Casares Quiroga, Azaña and Prieto.
Franco escorts Diego Hidalgo during military manoeuvres in Mallorca.
Dr Juan Negrín.
Dolores Ibárruri digging trenches.
Pasionaria surrounded by admirers.
Dolores Ibárruri's and Francisco Antón.
Dolores and José Díaz watch Jesús Hernández.
Andreu Nin.
A Communist pamphlet containing a speech by Dolores Ibárruri.

ACKNOWLEDGEMENTS

In the course of writing this book, I incurred a number of debts. I am immensely grateful to those who shared with me their memories, either as protagonists of the Spanish Civil War and/or as relatives or friends of the nine people whose portraits make up the bulk of this volume. Coming from different parts of the ideological spectrum, they all represent the three Spains of this book. Given that the book is the fruit of many years dedicated to the study of the war, some of the conversations to which I refer took place more than a quarter of a century ago, and sadly a number of my interlocutors have since died. I learned much from them all, both from their humanity and from their thoughtful reflections on the recent history of Spain. For that, I would like to thank: Santiago Alvarez, the late Ignacio Arenillas de Chaves, the late Manuel Azcárate, Rosa María Carrasco i Azemar, Santiago Carrillo, the late Fernando Claudín, Irene Falcón, Marisa Laporta Girón, Shevawn Lynam, Isabel de Madariaga, Mabel Marañón, José Prat García, Miguel Primo de Rivera y Urquijo, Miquel Roca Junyent, Mercedes Sanz Bachiller, Ramón Serrano Suñer, Jorge Semprún, the late Francisco Tomás y Valiente and Fernando Urbaneja.

I would also like to record my warm thanks to friends and colleagues who kindly read and commented on all or part of the manuscript and/or helped me to locate documents and books: Michael Alpert, Beatriz Anson, Sebastian Balfour, Nicolás Belmonte, Rafael Borràs Betriu, Angela Cenarro, Elías Díaz, Sheelagh Ellwood, Moris Farhi, Nina Farhi, Nigel Glendinning, Jerónimo Gonzalo, Helen Graham, Peter Hennessy, Santos Juliá, Marisa Maldonado Blanco, Aurelio Martín Naquera, Enrique Moradiellos, Alberto Reig Tapia, Margarita Rivière, Ismael Saz, Herbert Southworth, Robert Stradling. I am especially grateful to my wife Gabrielle for her perceptive psychological insights into the protagonists of this book.

I was extremely fortunate during the production process of this book. Robyn Marsack was a sensitive and creative copy editor. My friend and editor, Philip Gwyn Jones of HarperCollins, once again managed to find time in a hectic schedule to make perceptive comments on my manuscript and to provide unfailing encouragement.

The book is dedicated to two friends, Miguel Dols and Hilari Raguer. Both are men of exemplary rectitude, generosity and loyalty. Miguel Dols is the inspiration behind the Vicente Cañada Blanch Foundation whose work has done so much for research on Spain in the United Kingdom. The encouragement and support which he has unstintingly provided for my academic enterprises has been of great importance to me in good and bad moments. Dom Hilari Raguer, as well as being prodigal with his help in terms of advice and documents, has profoundly altered my thinking on the Spanish Civil War. The influence of his biographies of Manuel Carrasco y Formiguera and General Domingo Batet is present on every page of this book, which I hope is worthy of his example. I am deeply aware of my good fortune in being able to include them both among my friends.

CHRONOLOGY

1870	21 September	Birth of Julián Besteiro Fernández in Madrid
1879	5 July	Birth of José Millán Astray in La Coruña
1880	17 January	Birth of Manuel Azaña Díaz in Alcalá de Henares
1883	30 April	Birth of Indalecio Prieto Tuero in Oviedo
1886	23 July	Birth of Salvador de Madariaga Rojo in La Coruña
1892	4 December	Birth of Francisco Franco Bahamonde in El Ferrol
1895	9 December	Birth of Dolores Ibárruri Gómez in Gallarta
1898		Defeat of Spain by USA; loss of Cuba, Puerto Rico and Philippines
1903	24 April	Birth of José Antonio Primo de Rivera in Madrid
1907	4 November	Birth of Pilar Primo de Rivera in Madrid
1917	August	Socialist general strike – Besteiro arrested and sentenced to death
1923	13 September	Military coup led by General Primo de Rivera
1930	30 January	Primo de Rivera replaced by General Dámaso Berenguer
1931	14 March	Foundation of fascist newspaper *La Conquista del Estado* by Ramiro Ledesma Ramos
	14 April	Departure of King Alfonso XIII and the foundation of the Second Republic
		Provisional government under premiership of Niceto Alcalá Zamora with Manuel Azaña as Minister of War, Indalecio Prieto as Minister of Finance
	26 April	Foundation of Catholic authoritarian party Acción Popular
	10 October	Foundation of fascist party Juntas de Ofensiva Nacional-Sindicalista by Onesimo Redondo and Ramiro Ledesma Ramos
	14 October	Alcalá Zamora resigns as prime minister, replaced by Azaña
	11 December	Alcalá Zamora elected President of the Republic

	14 December	Azaña forms new government, retaining Ministry of War; Prieto moves to Ministry of Public Works.
	15 December	Foundation of Alfonsine monarchist society and journal *Acción Española*
1932	10 August	Failed military coup by General José Sanjurjo
1933	8 January	Police and Civil Guard massacre anarchist villagers at Casas Viejas (Cádiz); Azaña is blamed
	28 February	Acción Popular unites with other legalist rightist groups to form the CEDA – Confederación Española de Derechas Autónomas
	1 March	*Acción Española* creates political front organization, Renovación Española
	29 October	José Antonio Primo de Rivera launches Falange Española
	19 November	Election victory for coalition of Radicals and CEDA
	12 December	Alejandro Lerroux forms an exclusively Radical government with the parliamentary support of Gil Robles's CEDA
1934	11 February	Falange Española merges with the Juntas de Ofensiva Nacional-Sindicalista to become FE de las JONS
	4 October	Lerroux forms a new cabinet including three CEDA ministers
	6 October	General strike, left-wing uprising in Asturias and brief declaration of Catalan independence, both crushed by army
1935	6 May	Radical–CEDA coalition government under Lerroux with Gil Robles as Minister of War, Luis Lucia as Minister of Communications
1936	16 February	Popular Front wins elections
	19 February	Manuel Azaña forms Left-Republican government without Socialist participation
	14 March	FE de las JONS outlawed and its leadership, including José Antonio Primo de Rivera, arrested
	7 April	Niceto Alcalá Zamora removed from the Presidency of the Republic
	10 May	Azaña elected President of the Republic

11 May	Largo Caballero uses his control of the PSOE parliamentary group to prevent Prieto accepting an invitation from Azaña to form a government
12 May	Azaña's party colleague, the weak Santiago Casares Quiroga, forms a government
1 June	José Antonio Primo de Rivera commits the Falange to the military uprising
5 June	José Antonio Primo de Rivera transferred to Alicante prison
13 July	Assassination of monarchist leader José Calvo Sotelo
17 July	Military uprising in Spanish Morocco
18 July	Military uprising on Spanish mainland; Civil War starts; Franco flies from Canary Islands to Morocco to lead Army of Africa
19 July	José Giral forms Republican cabinet
29 July	Italian and German transport planes begin airlift of African Army from Morocco to Seville
2 August	Franco's African columns leave Seville to start their march on Madrid
19 August	Assassination of Federico García Lorca in Granada
4 September	Francisco Largo Caballero forms a Popular Front government with participation of Republicans, Socialists and Communists
27 September	March on Madrid interrupted for Franco to relieve the siege of the Alcázar of Toledo
28 September	In Salamanca, the rebel generals elect Franco 'Head of the Government of the Spanish State'
6 October	Franco's march on Madrid resumed
19 October	With rebel troops on the outskirts of Madrid, Azaña evacuated to Barcelona
4 November	Four Anarchist ministers join Largo Caballero government
6 November	Largo Caballero government evacuated to Valencia; defence of Madrid left to Junta de Defensa under General José Miaja
mid-November	Fierce fighting in Madrid's University City and northern suburbs

	20 November	Execution in Alicante of José Antonio Primo de Rivera
	23 November	Franco abandons his attack on Madrid
	15 December	Franco tries to close the besieging circle around Madrid with attacks on Boadilla del Monte
1937	22 January	General Batet executed by the Nationalists
	6 February	Beginning of Battle of Jarama; Republicans and International Brigaders withstand, at great loss, a Nationalist offensive to the north east of Madrid
	8 February	Málaga falls to the Nationalists
	8–19 March	Republican victory over Nationalists and Italians in Battle of Guadalajara
	31 March	General Mola begins assault on Basque Country
	19 April	Franco forcibly unites Falange, Carlists, CEDA and Renovación Española into Falange Española Tradicionalista y de las JONS and suppresses the radical Falangists under Hedilla
	26 April	Luftwaffe destroys Guernica, the Basque spiritual capital
	3–9 May	'May Days' – Republican and Communist forces crush anarchist and Trotskyist revolt in Barcelona
	17 May	Juan Negrín forms government of Socialists, Communists and Republicans, with Prieto as Minister of National Defence
	19 June	Nationalists take Bilbao
	6–26 July	Republican counter-offensive at Brunete near Madrid to divert Nationalists from their advance in the north ends in stalemate at enormous cost to both sides
	23 August	Republican counter-offensive at Belchite near Zaragoza fails to divert Nationalists from attack on Santander
	26 August	Santander taken by Nationalists
	21 October	Nationalist capture of Gijón (Asturias) concludes war in the north
	15 December	With Franco poised to attack Madrid, the Republic launches counter-offensive on Teruel
1938	7 January	Teruel falls to Republicans

1938	22 February	Nationalists recapture Teruel
	9 March	Franco launches massive offensive through Aragón and western Catalonia towards the Mediterranean
	5 April	Negrín reshuffles cabinet, dropping Prieto as too defeatist, and himself taking over the Ministry of National Defence
	6 April	Franco ignores an ill-defended Catalonia to launch a great push southwards against Valencia
	9 April	Franco ignores Vatican pleas for clemency and executes Manuel Carrasco i Formiguera
	15 April	Nationalist troops reach Mediterranean coast at Vinaroz and split Republican zone in two
	25 July	Republic launches last-ditch counter-offensive across the River Ebro near Gandesa, the beginning of a four-month bloodbath
	29 October	Negrín withdraws International Brigades
	15 November	Republicans retreat back over Ebro
	23 December	Franco launches major attack on Catalonia
1939	26 January	Nationalists enter Barcelona
	6 February	Azaña crosses frontier into France
	27 February	Azaña resigns as President of the Republic
	5 March	Anti-Negrín coup in Madrid as Besteiro announces the creation of the Junta de Defensa under Colonel Segismundo Casado. Mini civil war unleashed in Republican zone
	28 March	Nationalists enters Madrid
	1 April	End of Civil War
1940	23 October	Franco meets Hitler at Hendaye
	27 September	Besteiro dies in prison at Carmona
	3 November	Azaña dies in Montauban
1954	1 January	Millán Astray dies in Madrid
1962	1 February	Indalecio Prieto dies in Mexico City
1975	20 November	Franco dies in Madrid
1978	14 December	Salvador de Madariaga dies in Locarno
1989	12 November	Dolores Ibárruri dies in Madrid
1991	17 March	Pilar Primo de Rivera dies in Madrid

Prologue: In Extremis

'Españolito que vienes/al mundo,/te guarde Díos./
Una de las dos Españas/ha de helarte el corazón'
(Little Spaniard coming into the world,/may God protect you./
One of the two Spains/will freeze your heart)

– ANTONIO MACHADO

The Spanish Civil War of 1936–9 lives in the popular memory as a conflict of extremes in which cruelty and passionate fanaticism abounded. At the time, too, it was often described in simple terms: communism against fascism, Christian civilization against the barbaric hordes of Moscow, good against evil. In fact, far from being a conflict between two monolithic blocks, it was not one but many wars. It was a war of landless peasants against rich landowners, of anti-clericals against Catholics, of regional nationalists against military centralists, of industrial workers against factory-owners. It is not difficult to find, in the years preceding 1936, the embittered conflicts which seemed to make war inevitable. In mid-July 1936 they were subsumed within days into a war fought to the death between two Spains. Latent hostilities were encouraged by many aspects of the confrontation. In any war, normally repressed bloodlusts are unleashed. This was especially the case in Spain, since the military uprising saw the breakdown of the apparatus of the state. Structures of law and order were replaced in the rebel zone by the Army, the Church and the Falange and in the Republican zone by party and syndical militias and people's committees. In both zones, long-standing resentments found an opportunity for reprisals. The consequent atrocities, together with battlefield deaths, provoked desire for revenge among the families and comrades of the victims.

The Spanish conflict is thus remembered not for its kaleidoscopic complexities but for its bloodshed and atrocities: the murder of the poet Federico García Lorca, the mass assassination of priests and nuns, the bombing of Guernica. Even after the war was over, there was no place for reconciliation. One of General Franco's central objectives after 1939 was to maintain a festering division of Spain between the victorious and the vanquished, the privileged 'authentic Spain' and the castigated 'anti-Spain'. For the Caudillo, the defeated constituted the *canalla* (scum) of the Jewish-Masonic-Communist conspiracy. On 27 August 1938 he declared: 'the Spanish war . . . is the struggle of the *Patria* [the fatherland] against the *anti-Patria*, of national unity against separatism, of morality against iniquity, of the spirit against materialism. It can have no other outcome than the triumph of pure and eternal principles over bastard, anti-Spanish ones.'[1] In various post-war speeches, he referred to the vanquished Republicans as 'undesirables', as 'true common criminals who, after bloodying Spain with their terror squads, tortures and murders, fled abroad with their booty'.[2]

Franco's stance, given widespread currency by the propaganda machinery of his regime, reinforced the popular assumption that, in 1936, the entire Spanish nation was divided into two blocks identified with the one or other set of extremisms. On both left and right, there were many who saw the Civil War as the occasion to resolve by violence conflicts which had been intensifying over the previous five years. A significant minority was responsible for outbursts of blind hatred and irresponsible bloodletting all over Spain. On both sides, there were *sacas* (enemies being 'taken out'). Class and religious hatreds fuelled appalling atrocities in both zones. They were often carried out by those who preferred to assassinate civilians in the rearguard rather than face the harsher existence of the battle front. The often careless nature of such extremism is captured in an anecdote recounted to me by the Catalan politician, Miquel Roca Junyent. It concerned his maternal grandfather, Miquel Junyent i Rovira, a leading figure in the Catalan Carlist movement (ultra-conservative monarchists). On 22 July 1936, a group of militiamen of the anarchist FAI (Federación Anarquista Ibérica) appeared at Junyent's house and demanded that he accompany them. Since he was a prominent right-winger, there could be no doubting that their intentions were hostile. In fact, he was beyond their reach, having died of a heart attack the day before. When informed of this by the housekeeper, the *milicianos* suspected subterfuge and insisted on seeing the body. She led them to the open coffin where, faced by the incontrovertible evidence of Junyent's demise, one of them turned to the others and said 'Bollocks. I told you we should have come yesterday.'[3] An equally representative act of thoughtless cruelty may be found in an anecdote from the rebel zone. At dawn on a bitter winter's day in 1936, a truck was conducting some Republicans to their execution. One of them, shivering in his shirtsleeves, made an attempt to talk to the Civil Guards, the Falangists and the priest in the lorry: 'I never realized it could be so cold!' The priest looked at him with contempt and said brusquely 'Well, it's much worse for us. We've got to make the return trip!'[4]

The uncontrolled and callous sectarianism which lay behind a thousand outrages shows how hard-liners saw the other side as less than human or less human than themselves. The violence of the *incontrolados* was something that the Republican authorities in Catalonia and the rest of Spain worked hard to eliminate – with varying degrees of success. In the rebel zone, however, extermination of the 'enemy' was a more deliberate instrument of policy. The problem faced by Republican politicians was that the military rebellion had created a power vacuum which permitted violence to flourish. For the rebels, there was no equivalent to that intrinsic weakness of the Republican state. That was largely because of the power of the Army and the Church which, between them, imposed a fierce physical and ideological discipline. Soldiers and prelates were thrown into each other's arms by the popular revolution which had partially defeated the uprising and unleashed a massacre of clergy. Such was the millenarian hatred visited upon the clergy that it was hardly surprising that the ecclesiastical hierarchy ended up blessing the military. At that point, in the eyes of the Church, the war ceased to be a Civil War and became a crusade. In such a manichean vision, it was simply a confrontation between the crusaders for Christian civilization and the marxist and anarchist barbarians. This lay behind a rhetoric of racial extermination which was used to justify executions of Republicans. In towns such as Salamanca and Valladolid, the consequent killings were turned into a public spectacle attended by educated members of the middle classes.[5]

For Franco, the entire population of the Republican zone constituted the anti-Patria. Without differentiation or nuance, the anti-España covered a spectrum from neutral pacifists, intellectuals like Salvador de Madariaga and Julián Besteiro, through advocates of a negotiated peace such as the bookish Republican President Manuel Azaña, life-long democrats like the Socialist Indalecio Prieto, right through to Communists, anarcho-syndicalists and beyond, to the perpetrators of anti-clerical atrocities and to common criminals. Yet the blood-stained clash of extremisms was not something which involved all of those who took part in the war. There were many – probably the majority of the population, and even of the political class – who regarded the war with horror. Of those who did not relish the thought of partisan interests being resolved by bloodshed, a few who had either the financial means or the professional skills to enable them to live abroad went into immediate exile. The rest were pulled into the war with fear and repugnance. They were involved in many different ways, whether passively as victims of air raids or the reprisals of occupying troops, or more actively, as soldiers – either as volunteers or conscripts – or else engaged in other forms of war work. They believed simply that they must do their duty, or at least do what was necessary to survive. Clearly, their unwilling or unenthusiastic wartime involvement makes it difficult to think of such people as belonging to the commonplace categories of extremism associated with the Spanish Civil War.

This book is an attempt to provide a different perspective on the complexity of the Spanish Civil War by studying the lives of nine of its most prominent protagonists. The first, General José Millán Astray, the founder of the Spanish Foreign Legion, was a formative figure in the development of General Francisco Franco. In Africa, Millán Astray elaborated the ideas of redemption through blood which would inspire Franco's pursuit of victory. Franco himself personified the rebel war effort and perpetuated his victory through a highly personal autocratic rule thereafter. José Antonio Primo de Rivera, the founder of the Spanish Fascist Party, the Falange, was a key figure in the spiral of violence and reprisal which contributed to the breakdown of social order in the spring of 1936. By the time that he was executed in the Republican zone, his views had evolved dramatically. The posthumous object of a cult of personality in the Franco regime, José Antonio was far from being an admirer of Franco. His sister, Pilar, was devastated by his death and that of another brother, Fernando. She sublimated her grief into her leadership of the Falange's Sección Femenina which wielded enormous influence over millions of Spanish women during and after the war. Salvador de Madariaga was one of Spain's best-known intellectuals who stood aside from the conflict, was condemned to exile and devoted the remainder of his life to the thankless task of reconciliation.

Altogether more tragic was the fate of Madariaga's friend, Julián Besteiro, a professor of logic, at one time President both of the Spanish Socialist Party and General Union of Workers, and of the Republican parliament. Despite this identification with the left, he stood aside from the conflict until, in the last weeks of the war, in a misguided attempt to accelerate progress towards an armistice, he took part in Colonel Casado's military coup against the Republic. Franco, the beneficiary of this betrayal, rewarded Besteiro with life imprisonment. Manuel Azaña, successively Prime Minister and President, is widely recognized as incarnating the Republic every bit as much as his adversary Franco represented the Nationalist side. Although appalled by the war, Azaña remained at his post out of a profound sense of civic duty. His experience was not dissimilar to that of his friend, Indalecio Prieto, the leader of the moderate faction of the Socialist Party. Prieto devoted his life to the establishment of the Republic as the crucial step on the road to the modernization of Spain. Convinced that the outbreak of war could end only in long-term defeat for the nation as a whole, he was deeply defeatist yet squandered his health in a titanic effort to keep the Republican war effort alive. In contrast, the feisty Communist orator, Dolores Ibárruri, 'Pasionaria', threw herself with energy and enthusiasm into mobilizing popular support for the Republic. In the process, she came to be a symbol of the Republic's resistance for Spaniards and foreigners alike.

The chapters in this book concern individuals in extreme situations but they are not confined to the period 1936–9. The lives of its nine central characters offer an illuminating insight into the calamitous process of the breakdown of peace, the course of the war, and its appalling consequences. The Spanish Civil War broke out in 1936 but it did not start then. To understand the way in which politicians and soldiers responded to the crisis situation of 1936, it is necessary to look at their earlier lives. The hostilities of the Spanish Civil War ended formally on 1 April 1939 but the war went on, in the form of guerrilla struggle until 1948 and a resistance movement until 1977. Accordingly, it is necessary also to look at their later lives. To differing degrees, all nine had a part in the gestation of the hostilities. Each played a significant role within the conflict. In its turn, the war had a dramatic impact on the lives of every one. Two of them would die as a direct consequence. Four would be forced into a wretched exile. Three would be the beneficiaries of victory.

In each of the nine lives recounted here, the attempt to relate the personal life of the individual to his or her political role has put into starker relief the sadness, the distress and the suffering of the Civil War. With the exception of Franco and Millán Astray, who relished the use of violence and terror as deliberate instruments of their own ambition, the political role of each of the figures studied encapsulates a personal catastrophe. Indeed, the lives of the individuals discussed in this book provoke reflection on the depth of the calamity that befell the entire Spanish people. The war blighted seven of the lives recounted here. Millán Astray and Franco were convinced of the efficacy of terror and, as advocates of the idea that a nation can be redeemed by blood, were quite ready to sacrifice the lives of their fellow countrymen. In that sense, it might be argued that their lives had already been blighted by the colonial wars which had formed them. All of the remaining seven protagonists, to varying degrees, suffered mental and emotional agonies, tormented by doubts about the war. All nine are representative figures of the Spanish tragedy.

In most of the literature about the Spanish Civil War there is little or no place for individuals. It is recalled as a war of 'isms', of collectivities and of masses. Outside Spain, Franco became a household name, but few knew the name of the head of state of the Republic, Manuel Azaña. Much is remembered about the attempts to build a new world through the experiment of collective farms and collectivized industries. 'We carry a new world in our hearts' said the anarchist leader Buenaventura Durruti in a memorable interview shortly before his death at the Madrid front. A large part of the emotional charge still carried by the Spanish Civil War is about the destruction of that dream. Newsreel footage of the defeated Republican army trudging across the French frontier still retains its intense pathos. Yet few of the thousands of books written about the war convey a sense of the plight of individuals facing extreme circumstances. On both sides, for many ordinary people, the war meant the loss of loved ones and was a source of hatred and desire for vengeance. Those in the political élite experienced most of the same emotions. However, they had to deal with them while facing momentous responsibilities.

The choice of the nine principal protagonists of this book was, to some extent, arbitrary. There were others, equally representative, on whom I worked at length but, in the last resort, did not include. On the Republican side, the most notable omissions were the anarchist leader Buenaventura Durruti, the wartime prime minister Juan Negrín, Prieto's Socialist adversary Francisco Largo Caballero, and the Catalan President Lluis Companys; on the rebel side, the 'radio general' Gonzalo Queipo de Llano, the co-ordinator of the military coup, General Emilio Mola, and the brains behind Franco's political system, Ramón Serrano Suñer. Azaña and Franco, the two heads of state of the warring Spains, perhaps chose themselves. José Antonio Primo de

Rivera, the founder of the Spanish fascist party and Dolores Ibárruri, the visible head of the Communist Party, were also unavoidable choices. With all of the others, and indeed with those inevitable four, there was an element of personal choice. All the characters of this book struck a chord of some kind.

Over thirty years and several books devoted to the study of twentieth-century Spain, I have always been fascinated by the relationship of individuals to great social and political problems. With some of those individuals, I found myself engaging more intensely than with others. Sometimes, as was the case with the sheer surrealistic lunacy of Millán Astray, the individual leapt out of the general picture. Sometimes – as was true of Azaña and Prieto – their personal tragedy seemed particularly poignant to me. My work on the Second Republic and the Civil War has brought me into regular contact with both, and knowledge of their flaws has only increased my admiration for the essential humanity which both enhanced and inhibited their political careers. My engagement with Dolores Ibárruri was rather different. In the course of research on the Spanish Communist Party, I did not develop a particularly favourable impression of her. However, in the mid-1970s, seeing her, in her eighties, speak at political rallies gave me a glimpse of the impact of her stirring wartime oratory. I was fortunate enough to meet her and was overwhelmed by her warmth and vitality. Those brief contacts with a truly extraordinary woman left me determined to investigate the relationship between the legend and the reality. In another case, that of Pilar Primo de Rivera, I was initially drawn to her simply because nothing of significance seemed to be known about the human being within the leader of the Falange's women's section. It was perplexing that someone who wielded such power could seem to be an automaton. I was moved to discover that a life's work which benefited Franco's regime had been imbued with the pain of the loss of her brothers, which had cast a dark shadow over her entire life. In the cases of Besteiro and José Antonio Primo de Rivera, I was fascinated by their apparently contradictory behaviour in their last days.

Whether my decision to write each biographical portrait derived from a strong personal empathy or antipathy, in all cases I hoped to understand the human person within the political personage. To write a biography successfully requires that the writer experience the illusion of knowing his protagonists. Whether that illusion can be passed on to the reader is another matter. I achieved a sense of having known the protagonists and the experience was obviously different in each of the nine cases. Nonetheless, I found writing every one of these nine lives a moving and a chastening experience. The lives included here, and indeed those on which I had embarked but finally had to omit, revealed, or rather reinforced, something obvious, but so often forgotten, about the Spanish Civil War. The conflict was not a tidy split between right and left, between the forces of evil and the forces of good. It was a messy and appallingly painful amalgam of intertwined hostilities and hatreds. Being reminded of that was a salutory experience for the historian of the Spanish Civil War. I hope that these portraits might convey to the reader some sense of the complexity and the tragedy of the Spanish Civil War.

1

The Bridegroom of Death: Millán Astray

José Millán Astray y Terreros was perhaps the individual who had the most influence over the moral and ideological formation of Francisco Franco. Sanctified in his own lifetime as '*el glorioso mutilado*', he made a unique contribution to the violent ethos of the Spanish extreme right through his creation of the Tercio de Extranjeros (the Foreign Legion). Through it, he institutionalized and preached the brutal and brutalizing values by which Franco fought and won the Spanish Civil War. He was instrumental in Franco's rise to fame, appointing him second-in-command and field commander of the Legion, a force soon celebrated for its efficacy and bravery. Millán was also influential in the nomination of the future Caudillo as Director of the Academia Militar General de Zaragoza and certainly his views prevailed in the type of military education inculcated there under Franco. Throughout the Civil War, he was tireless in the elaboration and dissemination of Franco's image as an invincible saviour. More specifically, he played a crucial role in the machinations in the last week of September 1936 which led to Franco's elevation as Head of State. All of this partially explains a curious fact. Millán Astray was the only significant figure who had once had Franco under his orders yet with whom the Caudillo maintained cordial relations after reaching the zenith of his power. In this, he differed dramatically from Generals Sanjurjo and Cabanellas, Franco's superior officers in Morocco, or José María Gil Robles, leader of the Catholic authoritarian CEDA and Minister of War in 1935, who were the later targets of Franco's resentment.[1] It is a measure of the contradictions at the heart of Millán Astray's character that the intrepid founder of the Legion managed to maintain the Caudillo's goodwill because he made it abundantly clear that he was happy to devote himself to the constant and most servile inflation of Franco's standing.

Millán Astray was born in La Coruña on 5 July 1879, the son of José Millán Astray and Pilar Terreros Segade. His father was a lawyer and civil servant, and a would-be writer. He had wanted to be a soldier but had been forced by his own father to study law. José Millán Astray senior was a kindly man and encouraged the young José to read; he devoured the heroic adventure stories which later influenced his own career.[2] The fact that, when he was old enough to do so, the future hero chose to use his father's matronymic Astray, with its starry connotations, as against that of his mother, Terreros, redolent of the lowly and earth-bound, suggests a burning ambition. Together with the fact that he opted for a military career, it strongly indicated the extent to which he identified with his father. He entered the Infantry Academy in Toledo on 30 August 1894. By dint of taking a shortened course and frenetic cramming, he graduated as a second lieutenant at the end of February 1896, at the age of sixteen. For six months, he served with an infantry regiment stationed in Madrid where he stood out as obsessive about the cleanliness of his uniform and those of his men. Buckles, belts and bayonets had to shine brightly. On 1 September 1896, he entered the Escuela Superior de Guerra to study for the much-prized general staff diploma.

After two months, however, he volunteered for active service in the repression of the nationalist rebellion which had broken out in the Philippines. He arrived there on 3 November 1896. As would be the case throughout his career, he quickly began to accumulate important awards for bravery. Within a month, at the age of seventeen, his defence of the village of San Rafael with thirty men against two thousand rebels converted him into a national hero and won him the Cross of María Cristina, at that time Spain's highest award for bravery. This was followed a month later by the Cruz Roja de Mérito Militar and shortly after the Cruz Primera Clase de Mérito Militar.[3] There has been speculation that his obsession with spit and polish, and indeed his bravery, were efforts to wipe out a perceived stain on the family honour for which his father was responsible. His father had been Director of the Cárcel Modelo in Madrid where, for a price, prisoners were allowed to leave the prison for short periods. During one such absence, a prisoner was involved in a notorious murder which led to the trial of Millán Astray senior.[4] Acts of bravery and heroism, risk-taking and the cult of violence and death could all in some way have been part of an effort to obscure the anything but heroic behaviour of his father, who had acted dishonourably in a quest for a comfortable existence.

In June 1897, Millán Astray returned as a thrice-decorated war hero to the Escuela Superior de Guerra where he remained for a year and a half. Thereafter, he was posted to various infantry regiments of the peninsula. He reached the rank of captain in January 1905. On 2 March 1906, he married Elvira Gutiérrez de la Torre, daughter of General Gutiérrez Cámara. Immediately after the wedding, his bride timidly informed him that she had made an unbreakable vow of life-long chastity. It was perhaps indicative of autoerotic or homosexual tendencies that Millán Astray did not take the opportunity to have the marriage annulled but decided to live with Elvirita, as he called her, in a 'fraternal' relationship. She, for her part, assumed the role of handmaiden to the great man and devotedly looked after him until his death.[5] After his 'honeymoon', he returned to the Escuela Superior de Guerra for a further three years' study. In the summer of 1910, he was invited to join the staff of the Infantry Academy of Toledo where he taught military history, geography and tactics. His war service, his technical preparation and his marriage to the daughter of a senior officer had given Millán Astray a curriculum vitae to reckon with. He was a potential general staff officer with a brilliant future. However, when he was formally invited to join the General Staff, he declined, saying that he wished to fight in Africa. Hungry for adventure, and convinced that in the slow life of the mainland he would never achieve the glory or the rapid promotions that he longed for, he requested a transfer to Spanish Morocco. It was finally granted in August 1912 when he was sent to serve with the recently created Regulares Indígenas.[6]

From 1913 onwards, Millán Astray built a reputation as a brave, determined officer. It was at this time that he initiated the practice of motivating his men by means of fervent harangues before they went into action. Mentions in despatches and medals for bravery became frequent occurrences until, in July 1914, he was promoted to Major 'por méritos de guerra' (for distinction on the battlefield). For another three years he continued in Africa, consolidating his reputation for bravery and success, until, in April 1917, he was posted to Madrid.[7] In 1918, Millán Astray began to propound the idea that Spain needed a mercenary force if public opinion were not to put a stop to her African adventures – 'if Spaniards join the suggested corps, they will do so willingly; if foreigners do so, they will be doubly useful since they will provide a soldier and save a Spaniard'.[8] One of his early converts was the then Major Francisco Franco-Bahamonde, whom he met in November 1918 while on a marksmanship course for majors at Valdemoro in the province of Madrid.[9]

Millán Astray was a sufficiently distinguished officer to be taken seriously and he was able to gain an audience with the Minister of War, General Antonio Tovar Marcoleta, and persuade him of the possibilities of his idea. It was decided in September 1919 to send him for three weeks to study the French Foreign Legion in Algeria. He first visited the Spanish High Commissioner in Morocco, General Dámaso Berenguer, to receive instructions. Arriving just as a major attack on the rebel leader, El Raisuni, was about to be launched, he seized the opportunity to request permission to take part and was seconded to the General Staff. He served in the column of Colonel José Sanjurjo until setting out for Algeria in early October. He visited the headquarters of the French Foreign Legion at Sidi-Bel-Abbés and also a regiment in Tremecen. He was especially impressed by the system of lavish rewards and savage punishments.[10] In the meantime, his persuasive lobbying in Madrid had borne fruit. By royal decree of 28 January 1920, Millán Astray, promoted to Lieutenant Colonel three weeks earlier, was named head of the Foreign Legion or Tercio de Extranjeros (*Tercio*, or third, was the name used in the sixteenth century for regiments in the Army of Flanders which had been composed of three groups, pikemen, crossbowmen and arquebusiers). When established formally on 31 August 1920, it was projected that the Legion would eventually have three battalions known as *banderas* ('colours' or 'flags'). Millán Astray disliked the name *Tercio* and always insisted on calling the new force 'the Legion'.

Invited to join him as second-in-command, Franco, after some hesitation, agreed. Millán Astray undertook, virtually single-handed, to establish recruiting offices in Madrid, Zaragoza, Barcelona and Valencia. By dint of determination and improvisation, he set up headquarters in Ceuta and equipped the new recruits, combatting the early morale problems posed by inadequate funds with rousing speeches.[11] When those first mercenary recruits of the *primera bandera*, under the command of Franco, arrived in Ceuta on 10 October 1920, a motley band of misfits and cut-throats, some tough, some pitiful, Millán Astray greeted them with a stark message: 'You have lifted yourselves from among the dead – for don't forget that you were dead, that your lives were over. You have come here to live a new life for which you must pay with death. You have come here to die.'[12] 'Since you crossed the Straits, you have no mother, no girlfriend, no family; from today all that will be provided by the Legion.' '¡Viva la muerte!' He seemed to have an instinctive feeling of how to get the best out of the ragbag of desperadoes, outcasts and malcontents that appeared, ranging from criminals on the run to First World War veterans unable to adjust to peacetime existence and anarcho-syndicalists fleeing the repression in Barcelona. He offered them a social nexus with some kind of human warmth and comradeship. In return, he demanded blind obedience and a readiness to die. His romantic notion that the Legion would offer its outcast recruits redemption through sacrifice, discipline, hardship, violence and death was transmitted to Franco and runs through Franco's diary of its first two years, *Diario de una bandera*, a bizarre blend of sentimentalized adventure-story romanticism and cold insensitivity in the face of human bestiality. Together, Millán and Franco elaborated a brutal routine which converted the recruits into automatons who followed orders without thought. Indeed, Millán Astray always placed the irrational over the rational. The hymn of the Legion was 'the wedding march of those who married death', the Legionarios themselves 'los novios de la muerte' (the bridegrooms of death).[13]

Millán Astray's obsession with death was reflected in the Legionario's Credo in which he stated 'Death in combat is the greatest honour. You die only once. Death arrives without pain and is not so terrible as it seems. The most horrible thing is to live as a coward.'[14] This reflected his interest in samurai literature and his belief that only through death could life's sins be redeemed. Millán Astray recruited for the Legion on the basis that there was no prior sin which could not be cleansed by death. His bible in this regard was a book published in 1895 by a Japanese, Inazo Nitobé, *Bushido. The Soul of Japan*. Its Spanish translation – from Nitobé's own English rendition – was allegedly the work of Millán himself, although there is no evidence of his knowing either English or Japanese.[15] Nor is there much evidence that the drunken sadists of the Legion followed the austere Japanese Bushido. The idea served, none the less, to give dignity to a unit whose rank-and-file were treated as expendable cannon fodder. Millán Astray and Franco together imbued the Legion with an ethos of ruthless savagery. There was also a sense of camaraderie and exclusivity symbolized by the idea that any Legionarios within earshot would always come to the aid of a comrade who shouted '¡A mí la Legión!' whether in the thick of battle or in a bar-room brawl. Millán Astray was an amiable commander who would often invite his officers to a drink and had a weakness for telling jokes.[16]

The Socialist writer, Arturo Barea, who served in the Moroccan Army in the 1920s, found that his own critical faculties were swept aside by the mass hysteria generated by the histrionic performance of the Head of the Legion. 'Millán Astray's entire body underwent an hysterical transfiguration. His voice thundered and sobbed and howled. He spat into the faces of these men all their misery, their shame, their filth, their crimes, and then he dragged them along in fanatical fury to a sense of chivalry, to a renunciation of all hope, beyond that of dying a death which would wash away the stains of their cowardice in the splendour of heroism.'[17] This rhetoric hid a multitude of sins. The psychopaths, drunkards and outcasts of the Legion were treated brutally and, in return, given free rein to indulge their own bloodlusts. 'When it attacked, the *Tercio* knew no limits to its vengeance. When it left a village, nothing remained but fires and the corpses of men, women and children. Thus, I witnessed the villages of Beni Arós razed to the ground in the spring of 1921. Whenever a legionary was murdered on a lonely cross-country march, the throats of all the men in the neighbouring villages were cut unless the assailant came forward.'[18] Despite the fierce discipline in other matters, no limits were put by Millán Astray or by Franco on the atrocities which were committed against Moorish villages. Prisoners were decapitated and their severed heads exhibited as trophies. The Duquesa de la Victoria, a philanthropist who organized a team of volunteer nurses, was welcomed by the Legion with a basket of roses in the centre of which lay two severed Moorish heads. When the Dictator General Primo de Rivera visited Morocco in 1926, he was appalled to find one battalion of the Legion awaiting inspection with heads stuck on their bayonets.[19]

Millán and Franco came to revel in the grim reputation of their men, manifesting a fierce pride in their brutality. The notoriety of the Legion was a powerful instrument of colonial repression. Franco learnt thereby powerful lessons about the exemplary function of terror. With the Legion in Africa and during the Civil War, Franco permitted and encouraged the killing and mutilation of prisoners. The years spent amidst the inhuman savagery of Millán Astray's Legion contributed to a dehumanizing of Franco which was to be a source of strength to him in later life.[20] In October 1934, for instance, entrusted with supervising the repression of the left-wing insurrection in Asturias, he sent in the Legion. 'This is a frontier war', he commented to a journalist, 'against socialism, communism and whatever attacks civilization in order to replace it with barbarism.'[21] He regarded left-wing workers with the same racialist contempt with which he had regarded the tribesmen of the Rif. The terror unleashed in Asturias was to be repeated in the south of Spain in 1936. The advance of the Army of Africa towards Madrid generated a paralysing terror. After each town or village was taken by the African columns, there would be a massacre of prisoners and women would be raped.[22] Intimidation and the use of terror, euphemistically described as *castigo* (punishment), were a deliberate and explicit tactic. Franco was building on the heritage of Millán Astray.

In 1921, Arturo Barea witnessed an extraordinary scene which both revealed Millán Astray's violent personality and set the tone for life in the Legion. Inspecting the troops,

> he stopped in front of a mulatto with fat lips, his immense eyes bloodshot and yellowish. 'Where are you from, lad?' 'What the devil is that to you?' replied the man insolently. Millán Astray went rigid, staring into his eyes. 'You think you're very brave, don't you? Look, the Chief here is me. When the likes of you speaks to me, he stands to attention and says "At your orders, Lieutenant Colonel. I prefer not to say where I'm from." And that's fine. You are perfectly within your rights not to mention your country, but you do not have the right to speak to me as if I was your equal.' 'And what have you got that makes you more than me?' was spat back from lips dripping with saliva and as red as the sex of a bitch on heat. There are times when men can howl. At times they can pounce as if their muscles were made of rubber and their bones rods of steel. 'I . . . ?' roared the commander. 'I am more than you! Much more of a man than you!' He leapt on the other and seized him by the shirt collar. He lifted him off the ground, threw him into the centre of the circle and beat his face horribly with both fists. It took only two or three seconds. They hit each other like men in the jungle must have done before the first axe was made. The mulatto lay on the ground blood pouring from him. Millán Astray, more stiff, more horrific than ever, epileptic in a furious homicidal madness, screamed 'Attention!' The eight hundred Legionarios – and I – responded like automatons. The mulatto got up, scraping the earth with his hands and his knees. His nostrils poured blood

> mixed with dust like an urchin's snotty nose. His lip, split open, was fatter than ever, misshapen. He clicked his heels and saluted. Millán Astray clapped him on his huge shoulders. 'Tomorrow I need brave men at my side. I suppose I'll see you near me.' 'At your orders, Lieutenant Colonel.' His eyes, more bloodshot than ever, more yellow with jaundice, flared with fanaticism.

On the following day, Barea witnessed a reckless Millán Astray on horseback, in the midst of the battle, standing up in the saddle, raising a bloodstained arm and crying '*¡A mí la Legión!* Fix bayonets!' and leading a successful but costly charge.[23] According to Barea, Millán Astray often 'advertised his own death-defying bravery in advance, with much shouting and waving of arms'.[24]

In a devastating report on the behaviour of officers of the Moroccan army, written after the notorious disaster of July 1921 at Annual, Colonel Domingo Batet wrote that the much-vaunted bravery of the officers of the Regulares and the Tercio was inspired by alcohol, cocaine or morphine and characterized by a high degree of boastful pretence. Specifically, he wrote of 'the theatrical clown Millán Astray who trembles when he hears the whistle of bullets and flees his post'.[25] It might be argued that Millán Astray, unlike Franco who never knew fear, was an ordinary man who could be scared in battle and, despite suffering greatly in consequence, overcame his terror and confronted danger. Whatever he felt, his exploits led to him becoming a great favourite of King Alfonso XIII, who made him Gentilhombre de Cámara (Gentleman of the Chamber) on 18 September 1921.[26] In consequence, he was invited to a party at one of the royal palaces. He let the King know that he did not possess an evening suit. Alfonso XIII responded by sending him one of his own. When Millán Astray later returned it, he requested permission to keep the shirt. Thereafter, he always wore it in battle and, after each action, would cable the Palace with the news.[27] The King's interventions on his behalf led to tension with Niceto Alcalá Zamora, then Minister of War.[28]

Millán Astray was brave, irresponsibly so, in the earlier part of his career, yet there was probably an element of calculation about it. Certainly, from the time of the foundation of the Legion, the hallmark of his behaviour was ever more histrionic excess. On one occasion in 1922, he visited a military hospital in Tetuán. An eye-witness, the later founder of Spanish surrealism, Ernesto Giménez Caballero described him entering the surgical ward 'like a whirlwind', shouting 'Let me see my Legionarios! Where are my jackals? I am your chief! Legionarios, long live Spain, long live the King, long live the Legion!'. The wounded jackals hobbled over or sat up in bed. Millán Astray, constantly indicating an arm in a sling, passed among them, muttering 'this neuritis is killing me!' He went from one to another, asking them 'What's up with you, my son?' – 'A bullet-wound here.' 'A bullet-wound! And you, lad?' 'Well, I've got one in the head.' 'Another bullet-wound! And you, son?' 'I've got two wounds.' 'Two bullet-wounds!' As he went around, they told him of the lack of food and he would turn to his aide and get him to note down chickens, ham, bottles of wine, although it is to be assumed that nothing more was ever heard of the promised victuals.[29]

Millán Astray's recklessness on the battlefield wreaked a fierce toll on his person. His wounds led to him being described as the general 'rebuilt out of hooks, bits of wood, string and glass' (*recompuesto de garfios, maderas, cuerdas y vidrios*).[30] He carried a huge scar on his chest. It was a relic of a wound received on 17 September 1921, sustained while discussing tactics and observing the enemy positions through binoculars near Nador, with Major Francisco Franco and his cousin, Captain Francisco Franco Salgado-Araujo. He fell, wounded by a sniper's bullet, shouting '¡Me han matado! ¡Me han matado!' (they've killed me) then '¡Viva España! ¡Viva el rey! ¡Viva la Legión!'[31] In his own inflated account, tinged with eroticism, 'I had the honour to be hit in the chest by an enemy bullet and I am proud that it was the strong and well-formed arms of Franco that, together with a captain also called Francisco Franco, held me with fraternal affection.'[32] Despite the fact that his wound was not properly healed, he returned to action three weeks later. On 10 January 1922, he was badly wounded in the leg. Among his many decorations, he received in the autumn of 1922, the 'medalla de sufrimientos por la patria' (medal for suffering undergone for the fatherland).[33] A bullet went through his left elbow on 26 October 1924 at Fondak in Morocco, and two days later he had to have the arm amputated after gangrene had set in. He lost one eye and afterwards bore a terrible scar from a bullet which, on 4 March 1926, entered his cheek, shattered his right eye-socket, split his jaw-bone and knocked out many of his teeth. He was apparently delighted to receive a telegram from one of his subordinates, Joaquín Ríos Capapié: 'Congratulations on your fourth wound STOP I impatiently await the fifth STOP'.[34] He was as gaunt as an El Greco figure although his wild surviving left eye had something Goyesque about it. He purchased a glass eye in Germany but rarely wore it, preferring a more romantic black patch.[35]

In behaviour and, after a while, in appearance too, Millán Astray resembled the Italian poet/adventurer Gabrielle D'Annunzio. The Italian's frenetic determination to live as a Nietzschean superman had many echoes in the life of Millán Astray. He was aware of the parallel and once asked the Spanish right-wing poet José María Pemán, 'Is it true that I resemble D'Annunzio?' The poet replied that, although he had never seen the Italian, he did not doubt that 'his bald pate like a renaissance dome and his one eye make you quite like him'.[36] The Falangist intellectual, Dionisio Ridruejo, who knew Millán Astray during the Spanish Civil War, concluded many years later that his extreme behaviour was partly an effort to emulate D'Annunzio.[37]

Millán Astray's buccaneering attitude to military life was reflected in his fanatical belief in the efficacy of song in lifting morale during combat:

> my war cry is 'Legionarios to fight, Legionarios to die'. And when we Legionarios fight and we see death nearby, we sing the 'Hymn of the Legion' and when we are happy and content, we also sing it because in the 'Hymn of the Legion' can be found the purest essences of our soul: not just in the words but in the music, in the singing of the rhythm and in the vibrant notes of the bugles. That is why, when I undergo painful treatment for my wounds in hospital, I place a piano in the next room and have a Legionario play the 'Hymn of the Legion' and 'El Novio de la Muerte' so as not to feel the pain. Once, when they had just amputated my arm, the wounded Legionarios who were in the hospital threw themselves from their beds, whether they could walk or not, and with the latter dragging themselves along the floor, they all came to my room to sing me the 'Hymn of the Legion'. I also jumped out of bed and, standing rigidly to attention, I sang with them. Another time, when I was being taken on a stretcher from one hospital to another, wounded by a cruel bullet which had gone through my temple, as we went through Riffien where the Legion has its headquarters, everyone came out to sing the 'Hymn of War' and I jumped from the stretcher and I sang with them. And when we bury a Legionario, we

> sing, and when we win, we sing and when we challenge the enemy, we sing because the song, at certain times, is a threat and a challenge. And when there is the greatest danger in battle and death draws near, the Legion – because it never surrenders – sings in the face of death . . . That is the song which gives us encouragement in combat.[38]

Millán Astray was more than a well-known hero of battle. He also had a political role – although his political interventions, like his heroism, were driven by an obsession with being in the limelight.[39] As the most prominent figure within the colonial wing of the army, Millán Astray took an active part in the ongoing conflict between the Africanistas and the professional organization known as the 'Juntas de Defensa'. The more liberal members of the Juntas, dominated by officers from the artillery and engineers corps stationed in mainland Spain, opposed the principle of battlefield promotion which was dear to the hearts of the Africanistas. In May 1922, Millán Astray became the focus of their hostility when he resigned, with some publicity, from the Juntas.[40] In the autumn, he attracted further attention. The King agreed to take part in a public tribute in Seville to Spain's Moorish mercenary police force, the Regulares Indígenas. Although the Legion was not involved, Millán Astray arranged for every Legionario to make a contribution to the purchase of a jewel to be presented to the Queen at the ceremony. The celebration, held on 14 October 1922, was boycotted by the Juntero infantry officers of the Seville garrison. Millán Astray's intervention had significantly augmented his popularity among the Africanistas. On 20 October, virtually the entire officer corps of the Madrid garrison, many of whom had fought in Africa and were favourites of the King, appeared at the railway station to send off Millán Astray when he left for the south *en route* to Melilla.[41]

However, in his bid for royal favour, Millán Astray was soon to overreach himself. On 7 November 1922, he committed a blatant act of self-publicity, writing an open letter to the King offering to resign his commission in protest at the influence of the Junteros. He issued a dramatic manifesto to the nation, appealing to 'mayors, members of parliament, senators, generals and officers' to support him. Young rightists demonstrated in the streets in his favour and officers from the Madrid garrison visited his home to leave their calling cards. Franco sent a telegram expressing the unanimous solidarity of the Legion's officers. Alfonso XIII did not refuse his resignation and thereby deliver a public demonstration of royal favour. Instead, the Junteros having demanded that Millán Astray's resignation be accepted, the King compromised by permitting him to be replaced in his command of the Legion by Lieutenant Colonel Rafael Valenzuela. The reason given for his replacement was the extent of his wounds. The hostility against him among the Junteros was such that he was unwelcome in many other corps and was the object of regular humiliations.[42] Finally, he secured a posting to the Regimiento de Pavia in San Roque (Cádiz) in mid-February 1923, but on 28 June he was sent to Paris to study French military organization. When General Miguel Primo de Rivera became Dictator in September 1923, the King was able to persuade him to have Millán Astray attached first to the Military Academy at Saint-Cyr in January and February of 1924, and then to the Infantry Academy at Saint-Maixent from March.

Millán Astray returned to a Spanish regiment in Alicante in July 1924. In late October 1924, he was attached to the staff of the High Commissioner in Morocco and promoted to full Colonel. On 26 October, driving to Fondak, he found the road cut by Moorish insurgents. He got out of his car, strode to where some Spanish troops were fighting, and had just begun to harangue them when he was hit in the arm. In consequence, he had to have the amputation for which he was subsequently celebrated.[43] Valenzuela was killed on 5 June 1923 and Franco was rapidly promoted to Lieutenant Colonel in order that he could take command of the Legion. He remained at the head of the Legion until 5 December 1925 when he was promoted to Brigadier General and thus became too senior to command the Legion. Millán Astray, after more than a year of convalescence, was on the point of being transferred to the Cuerpo de Inválidos when Franco and Sanjurjo intervened on his behalf with the Dictator. On 9 February 1926, he was named to fill the vacancy at the head of the Legion created by Franco's departure. This required a change in the regulations concerning invalids which caused considerable resentment among the Junteros. Despite, or perhaps because of this, Millán Astray was careless of his personal safety and, on 4 March 1926, was hit in the face and lost his right eye. Within four months, he was back in action. On 18 June 1927, he was promoted to Brigadier General and was thus obliged to leave the Legion. On 1 October 1927, he was made permanent honorary colonel of the Legion, a position which he was to use to the full during the Spanish Civil War.[44]

In fact, prior to this, and partly on the basis of his sojourn in

France, it was widely anticipated that he would be named head of the Infantry Academy at Toledo as a reward for the sacrifices that he had made in Africa. In the spring of 1925, Millán Astray was invited to speak of his French experiences in a lecture on military organization at the military club in Madrid, El Centro del Ejército y de la Armada. Such was the dislike of the Junteros for this symbolic Africanista that their outcry forced the cancellation of the lecture and the shelving of his nomination to the directorship of the Academy.[45] Gossip now suggested that Millán Astray would be named Director of the newly revived Academia General Militar in Zaragoza. Again, opposition from the Junteros ensured that the proposal did not prosper. It is possible, however, that the nomination of Franco as second choice was the consequence of a suggestion from Millán Astray.[46] In any case, his ideas were to be the essence of the military education imparted by his disciple Franco and other Africanistas who acted as teachers.[47]

Millán Astray's last active post was as general commanding the Ceuta–Tetuán district for most of 1928 and 1929. On 15 January 1930, he was attached to the Ministry of War. It was from there that he anxiously followed the triumph of Republican candidates in the municipal elections of 12 April 1931. He telephoned Franco on the morning of 14 April to discuss the fact that General Sanjurjo, Director General of the Civil Guard, had advised the King to leave Spain.[48] As a protégé of Alfonso XIII and a militarist, he was distressed by the coming of the Republic. Many of the Junteros against whom he felt the greatest antipathy now found positions of prominence as advisers to the new Minister of War, Manuel Azaña. Despite being left without an active post and thus, in February 1932, transferred to the reserve, he managed at first to avoid confrontation with the new regime. He was rumoured to be complicit in the various military plots against Azaña. Certainly, his restlessness got the better of him in mid-June 1932, when he took a tram to the Army School of Marksmanship (Escuela de Tiro) in Carabanchel, asked for a horse, formed up the various cadets from the military academies, and had them parade past him.[49] He seems to have been on the fringes of the Sanjurjo plot of 10 August 1932 but was inhibited from active participation by Franco's firm decision not to be involved. However, his links with the plot were certainly behind the decision made by the Ministry of War on the very day of the coup to transfer him to the reserve.[50]

During the Republic, Millán Astray began to manifest a deference to Franco which eventually became servile sycophancy during the Spanish Civil War. Although regarded as a malcontent, his determination not to be out of step with Franco seems to have kept him out of more trouble.[51] In late 1934, when his time in the reserve was drawing to a close and there was again pressure for him to be invalided out of the army, his career was rescued by the amnesty for those involved in the Sanjurjada. The Prime Minister, the corrupt leader of the Radical Party, Alejandro Lerroux, had taken over the Ministry of War after his more liberal colleague, Diego Hidalgo, had been obliged to resign in mid-November 1934. Lerroux had been a friend of Millán Astray's father. To keep him on the active list, he gave him a meaningless but prestigious bureaucratic post in the Ministry of War as Secretario del Consejo Supremo (Secretary to the Supreme War Council – a rarely convened committee of senior generals).[52] Millán Astray maintained this position under both Gil Robles and, briefly, his successor after the Popular Front elections in February 1936, General Nicolás Molero.[53] However, the return of Manuel Azaña to government, and to the Ministry of War, saw Millán Astray passed to the Cuerpo de Inválidos.[54]

With no remunerated post to keep him in Spain, on 19 March 1936 Millán Astray set off on a well-paid lecture tour of Argentina. He also appeared on radio talking of his exploits in Morocco and showed off his scars in the drawing-rooms of the rich. On hearing of the military uprising, he is said to have shouted to his wife Elvira, 'Elvirita, the radio says that the Legion has risen. That for me is the same as hearing the cry of '¡A mí la Legión!' He rapidly booked a passage on a ship for Spain but the early news that he received on board, of the death of Sanjurjo and the failures of Fanjul in Madrid and Goded in Barcelona, inclined him to wait on events before deciding which side to join.[55] His hesitation was compounded by the fact that General Emilio Mola, the 'director' of the military conspiracy, had not kept him informed. Mola despised Millán for his theatricality and had grave doubts about his discretion. In his turn, Millán Astray deeply resented Mola.[56]

Millán Astray reached Lisbon at the end of the first week of August. Conversations with Franco's agents there, his brother Nicolás and the Catholic politician José María Gil Robles, resolved his doubts and he then sailed on to Cádiz, determined to trade on his greatest asset, the prestige accruing to the founder of the Legion. He made a speech on the dockside claiming that he had come from South America because he had heard the cry of '¡A mí la Legión!'[57] Within days of arriving in Seville, Franco had set up an embryonic staff including a propaganda service in the form of the Gabinete de Prensa established on 9 August under the journalist Juan Pujol, with Joaquín Arrarás (the future Generalísimo's friend and first biographer) as his assistant.[58] Franco swiftly concluded that Millán Astray's white-hot rhetoric could be pressed into service to propagate his cause throughout the Nationalist zone. He was quickly installed at Franco's side along with his immediate staff in the Palacio de Yanduri in Seville.[59] Millán's first major public appearance was alongside Franco and Queipo de Llano on 15 August in Seville at the ceremonial adoption of the monarchist flag by the military rebels. Gesticulating like a man possessed, he screamed, 'We are not afraid of them. Let them come, let them come and they will see what we are capable of under the shadow of this flag.' He was interrupted by a by-stander shouting '¡Viva Millán Astray!' at which he shouted back 'What's that? Let no one shout *viva* Millán Astray! Let everyone shout with me, with all the force of which you are capable *¡Viva la muerte! ¡Viva la muerte! ¡Viva la muerteee!*' As the crowd cried out their *vivas*, he screamed 'Now let the reds come. They will all die!' Then he threw his cap with a manic gesture into the crowd.[60]

Franco's headquarters had moved on to Cáceres at this time and he immediately put Millán Astray in charge of a more ambitious propaganda operation. He went on tour to Valladolid, Vigo, La Coruña and other cities. Completely without self-consciousness, he set the pseudo-medieval crusader tone which was to characterize subsequent Nationalist image-building. On 21 August, he spoke in Pamplona, the home of the ultra-traditionalist Carlist movement, which was committed to the re-establishment of a medieval military monarchy far more reactionary than anything contemplated by Franco. On the balcony of the Círculo Carlista, gesticulating wildly, he shouted, 'Navarra, Pamplona! With profound reverence, I salute you. You are the Covadonga of the Reconquest of Spain and of the Faith. You are the cradle of national heroism. You are NAVARRA!'[61] Earlier on the same day, he had taken part in an equally bizarre – and perhaps consciously orchestrated – scene in the Military Hospital in Pamplona. Standing by the body of Lieutenant Colonel Ricardo Ortiz de Zárate, an officer of the Legion, Millán Astray addressed the corpse: 'Brother! Now you have found her [death]! Now she is yours! How many times did you run after her on the battlefields of Africa . . . Now she is yours; forged in an embrace, you lie together . . .' After rambling on in this vein for some time, he suddenly stopped and, after a few moments of silence, said, 'Now, brother, in your honour, I will sing our hymn for you.' In a broken and tuneless voice, he began to sing 'Soy valiente y leal legionario . . .'[62]

Wherever he went, he sang the glories of Franco, in some way as if the more he exaggerated the more some would rub off on himself.[63] In fact, Millán Astray manifested an unqualified admiration for Franco bordering on slavish servility while always managing to insinuate that the new saviour was his discovery. As he told Giménez Caballero, 'I made Franco in Africa and yet there is something that is missing from my quadrant which Franco has. I don't know what it is, but it is decisive.'[64] Even at this early stage, he insisted on the crucial role of Franco, who was still no more than a member of the Junta de Burgos. He expressed his total conviction that Franco's lucky star (*buena estrella*) which guided him in all his works was the best guarantee of eventual victory. Dramatically reminding his listeners of the crucial role of the Legion, he would always end his harangues with a thunderous '¡Viva la muerte!'[65] One of his many services to Franco was the invention of the slogan 'Una Patria, Un Estado, Un Caudillo', based on the Nazi 'Ein Volk, ein Reich, ein Führer'.[66]

Along with General Alfredo Kindelán, Nicolás Franco, General Luis Orgaz and Colonel Juan Yagüe, Millán Astray played an important role in a kind of political campaign staff committed to the elevation of Franco to commander-in-chief and then to the headship of State. Franco was cautious throughout, fearful of gambling the position that he had already gained. His hesitations had the effect of making it seem as if he were being obliged, for the good of the Nationalist cause, to accept reluctantly a position that was being forced upon him.[67]

The first meeting of senior generals to choose an overall commander-in-chief was held at an airfield near Salamanca on 21 September. When it became clear that there was hesitation within the High Command, Millán Astray assumed the role of publicizing the 'need' for Franco, of both generating and expressing 'popular' pressure. In particular, he personified the determination of the Legion, with which he was irrevocably associated, that Franco be named single commander. In this regard, on the evening of 27 September 1936, he skilfully choreographed the scenes of popular rejoicing in Cáceres which greeted news of the relief of the siege of the Alcázar of Toledo.

When the generals met for their second meeting on the next morning, they succumbed to the pressure of the Legion and named Franco both Generalísimo and, somewhat ambiguously, 'Head of the Government of the Spanish State'.[68]

On 4 October, three days after Franco became Head of State, Millán Astray proclaimed that the Caudillo was 'the man sent by God to lead Spain to liberation and greatness', 'the man who saved the situation during the Jaca rising' and the 'greatest strategist of the century'.[69] Millán's adulation and his eccentricities stood out even among the gallery of bizarre and grotesque figures gathering in Salamanca. In the chill autumn of 1936, Franco now replaced Pujol with his one-time mentor. Millán was placed in official charge of the expanded Oficina de Prensa y Propaganda in its improvised offices in the Instituto Anaya, an old palace which housed the Faculty of Sciences of the University of Salamanca. There too were the scientists who were endeavouring to produce toxic gas for the Nationalists. Elsewhere in the building was a Hindu alchemist called Sarvapoldi Hammaralt. Hammaralt had turned up in Salamanca offering to make all the gold that Franco needed to win the war. He had been interviewed by Franco's brother Nicolás and had assured him that he possessed the formula for the manufacture of gold, 'a formula which can be used only if the gold created is used in a good cause'. Hammaralt declared that he considered the Nationalist cause to be 'noble and holy'. On the recommendation of Nicolás, the Generalísimo had Salamanca University's chemistry laboratories put at Hammaralt's disposal. While he worked at his alchemy, Hammaralt helped Nicolás in numerous small ways including the provision of chemicals which permitted the censorship office to read the letters written in invisible ink by German and Italian agents. He also carried out experiments on corpses collected from the battlefields. As rumours of these activities leaked out, alarmed Catholics were reassured by an announcement that Hammaralt's experiments were conducted only on already dismembered Moors. Eventually, never having produced any gold, he fled, suspected of being a British agent.[70] In the Palacio Anaya, Millán Astray gathered around him some of the most extravagant figures of a city bursting at the seams with oddities – ranging from the great wit Agustín de Foxá, via the deranged surrealist Ernesto Giménez Caballero to Captain Gonzalo Aguilera y Yeltes, an aristocrat who attributed all Spain's problems to the introduction of sewers.[71]

Millán Astray ate most evenings in the dining-room of the Gran

Hotel in Salamanca. An American correspondent in Salamanca, Charles Foltz, witnessed bizarre scenes: 'when the spirit moved him he would order everybody in the room, foreign diplomats included to rise and sing *Legionario*, the hymn of the Legion. He kept time with his pistol, which sometimes went off.' On one occasion, he kept the entire, and thoroughly bemused, company standing with arms outstretched in the fascist salute until they had sung the anthems of the Falange, of the Carlist Requeté, of the Legion, the Nazi *Horst Wessel Lied*, the Fascist hymn *Giovinezza* and the German, Italian and Portuguese national anthems.[72]

Fuelling the eccentricities was a barely contained violence. As one observer put it, 'his angry and rancorous bearing kills any compassion his mutilations might have inspired'.[73] One day, having gone to Lugo to make a speech, he caused an incident in a restaurant on a *día sin postre* (a day without pudding), one of various austerity measures adopted in the Nationalist zone. Being a Gallego, he was singing the praises of Gallego cuisine and asked the waiter to bring him *queso de tetilla* (a soft, mild cheese in the form of a woman's breast). Wrongly suspecting a test, the waiter reminded him that it was a *día sin postre*. 'Do you know who I am?' thundered the *glorioso mutilado*. 'Yes, Your Excellency, General Millán Astray.' 'Then bring me immediately a *queso de tetilla*!' When the waiter hesitated, the general lost control of himself and began to hit the unfortunate man about the head.[74] On another occasion, on one of his visits to a hospital, there was a similar scandal. As Millán Astray and his escort of Legionarios went around the wards, he would ask each wounded man for details of the action in which he had been hit. As they told him, he would say to his aide, 'Note down, this man is to be given one hundred pesetas!' 'That man is to be given two hundred pesetas!' Finally, he came to a soldier who could produce no heroic incident – he had been thrown from a motorcycle sidecar. Beside himself with fury, Millán Astray brutally beat the patient.[75] His prejudices also got the better of him on another occasion when he was distributing medals. Unbeknownst to Millán Astray, the heroic recipient happened to be a Catalan. On asking his name in the familiar jovial manner, the answer 'Vidal–Ribas' and the accent gave the game away. Millán Astray turned away gravely, saying 'What a pity you're a Catalan'.[76]

He was deeply superstitious, telling Franco's cousin that God always gave bad luck to his enemies, 'generals A and B were shot by the reds, colonel so-and-so died at the front, another in an accident.

I never hate anyone and I like to forgive my enemies. What is infallible is that they all soon die.'[77] On 29 September 1936, shortly after the relief of the Alcázar de Toledo, Franco hosted a lunch for the hero of the siege, Colonel José Moscardó, at the Hotel Castilla along with General Varela, Millán Astray and various other officers. When Millán Astray realized that there were thirteen at the table, he grabbed a passing messenger-boy and obliged the terrified young man to join the company and eat with them.[78]

Shortly after taking up his position as Franco's image-maker, Millán Astray played a part in an incident which did much to characterize the Franco regime for the outside world. He clashed with the Rector of the University of Salamanca, the seventy-two-year-old philosopher and novelist, Miguel de Unamuno, on the occasion of the celebration in the Great Hall (Paraninfo) of the *Día la Raza*, 12 October 1936, the anniversary of Christopher Columbus's 'discovery' of America. Millán Astray had arrived complete with his escort of Legionarios armed with machine-guns – an affectation that he was to maintain throughout the war. A series of speakers trotted out the usual Nationalist clichés about anti-España. An outraged Unamuno, who had not been planning to speak, had furiously jotted down some notes and then rose to make a passionate speech:

> Much has been said here about the international war in defence of Christian civilization; I have done the same myself on other occasions. But no, our war is only an uncivil war . . . To win [*vencer*] is not to convince [*convencer*], and it is necessary to convince and that cannot be done by the hatred which has no place for compassion . . . There has been talk too of Catalans and Basques, calling them the anti-Spain. Well, with the same justification could they say the same of you. Here is the Bishop, himself a Catalan, who teaches you Christian doctrine which you don't want to learn. And I, who am a Basque, I have spent my life teaching you the Spanish language, which you do not know . . .

At that point Millán Astray began to shout, 'Can I speak? Can I speak?' His escorts readied their guns and someone in the audience shouted '¡Viva la muerte!' In what Ridruejo saw as a coolly calculated bid for the limelight,[79] Millán Astray spoke: 'Catalonia and the Basque Country, the Basque Country and Catalonia, are two cancers in the body of the nation! Fascism, Spain's remedy, comes to exterminate them, slicing healthy, living flesh like a scalpel.' He worked himself up into a frenzy until he could speak no more. Gasping for breath, he stood to attention while cries of '¡Viva España!' rang out. A deathly silence fell and anxious eyes turned to Unamuno. With a grimace of distaste, the philosopher rose again to speak:

> I have just heard the senseless and necrophiliac cry of *¡Viva la muerte!* To me this is the same as crying Death to Life! And I, who have spent my life creating paradoxes which annoyed those who did not understand them, I have to tell you, as an authority on the subject, that this outlandish paradox seems to me to be repellent. Given that it was shouted in tribute to the last speaker, I take it that it was directed to him, if in a rather twisted and excessive form, as a testimony to the fact that he himself is a symbol of death. And another thing! General Millán Astray is a war invalid. It is not necessary to say this in a whisper. Cervantes was too. But extremes cannot be taken as the norm. Unfortunately, today there are too many invalids. And soon there will be more if God does not help us. It pains me to think that General Millán Astray might dictate the norms of mass psychology. An invalid who lacks the spiritual grandeur of Cervantes, who was a man, not a superman, virile and complete despite his mutilations, an invalid, as I said, who lacks that superiority of spirit, is often made to feel better by seeing the number of cripples around him grow . . . General Millán Astray would like to create a new Spain in his own image, a negative creation without doubt. And so he would like to see a mutilated Spain . . .

Millán Astray, now apoplectic with rage, screamed '¡Muera la inteligencia!' The poet José María Pemán tried to take the edge off the proceedings by shouting 'No! *¡Viva la inteligencia!* Death to bad intellectuals!' Undeterred, Unamuno concluded, 'This is the temple of intelligence! I am its high priest! You are profaning its sacred precincts. I have always been, no matter what the proverb says, a prophet in my own country. You will win [*venceréis*] but you will not convince [*no convenceréis*]. You will win because you have more than enough brute force; but you will not convince, because to convince means to persuade. And to persuade you need something that you lack: reason and right in the struggle. It seems to me useless to beg you to think of Spain.' Millán Astray was able to gain sufficient control of himself to bark at Unamuno, pointing at Franco's wife, 'Take the Señora's arm!' He did so and this prevented further tragic incident.[80]

Later that evening, there was a dinner in honour of the Nationalist poet José María Pemán, given by the Guardias Cívicos de Salamanca (municipal police) and hosted by the Alcalde (mayor). On his return to the Gran Hotel, Millán Astray appeared in the lobby and, before a perplexed public, embraced Pemán and offered him his 'Medalla de sufrimientos por la Patria'. Pemán cleverly sidestepped the embarrassment by kissing the medal reverently and giving it back to Millán Astray.[81] It is not clear whether Millán was trying to neutralize the possibly negative effects of his attacks on the intelligentsia or was merely looking to ingratiate himself with a hugely influential writer.

As far as Franco was concerned, Millán Astray had behaved as he should in his confrontation with Unamuno.[82] That such a man could command respect and admiration and be the recipient of preferment from Franco himself reflects much upon the nature of the Caudillo and his court. Franco gave him a vague overall responsibility for the morale of the Nationalist troops in which capacity he regularly toured the front and visited military hospitals.[83] Certainly, as one of the Generalísimo's closest collaborators, he was usually present at the late-night meeting (*tertulias*) at which the Generalísimo discussed the progress of the war with his Chiefs of Army, Navy and Air Force Staff, Colonel Francisco Martínez Moreno, General Alfredo Kindelán and Admiral Juan Cervera.[84] He had unhindered access to Franco.[85] He was also often present when Lieutenant Colonel Lorenzo Martínez Fuset brought Franco sheafs of death penalties for confirmation.[86] Even after Franco recognized that the growth of his propaganda machine required a bureaucratic apparatus for the management of which Millán Astray was perhaps not the best man, he was often used as a kind of tour guide for visiting dignitaries. On one occasion, before ushering in a delegation of French extreme rightists to meet Franco, he warned them that they were about to enter the presence of 'the voice of God'.[87]

Millán Astray remained in charge of propaganda for some time after the confrontation with Unamuno. Indeed, he soon acquired a worthy assistant. On 4 November 1936, Ernesto Giménez Caballero, the ultra-right-wing surrealist, arrived in Salamanca. He was one of the few characters capable of matching Millán Astray's eccentricity. In the lobby of his hotel he met the founder of the Legion whom he had not seen since their encounter in the military hospital in Tetuan in 1922. Giménez Caballero stood to attention, saluted and introduced himself. Completely unimpressed, Millán Astray replied 'So what?', to which Giménez Caballero rejoined, 'I am one of the ideological founders of Falangism.' Millán Astray then ordered one of the Legionarios of his escort to take his name, investigate and report back. In the meanwhile, Giménez Caballero visited the Palacio Episcopal where in a large room divided up by screens Franco's embryonic government worked, each 'Ministry' established at a separate table. At the 'Ministry' of Foreign Affairs, the portly José Antonio Sangróniz, who slept in a small side-room concealed by a screen, introduced him to Nicolás Franco. Through his intervention, Giménez Caballero was received by the Caudillo himself on 7 November. Having read one of his books, the extraordinary panegyric of fascist mysticism, *Genio de España*, Franco was keen to use him as part of his propaganda operation and instructed him to talk to Millán Astray. On the following morning, one of Millán Astray's Legionarios ordered him to present himself to the great man. Since there was no budget, Millán Astray offered one month's wages and Giménez Caballero borrowed a thousand pesetas from his brother Angel to buy paper. They requisitioned typewriters, roped in some Falangist friends of Giménez Caballero – Juan Aparicio and Victor de la Serna – and set up a press office in the Palacio de Anaya. Each day, as he had done in the Legion, Millán Astray would summon the journalists with a whistle and form them up in lines to listen to his daily harangue.[88]

Millán Astray's greatest ambition was fulfilled when Franco permitted him to set up a radio station to broadcast his propaganda. Giménez Caballero managed to get hold of the necessary equipment and, on the evening of the first planned broadcast, on 22 November 1936, Millán Astray arrived with his escort and his wife, Elvira. He barked out an order, 'Elvirita! Go over there and don't talk. Everyone silent!' While Millán Astray got ever more impatient, the symptom of which was a trembling in the stump of his amputated arm, Giménez Caballero checked the microphone only to discover that it was dead. Rather than face the wrath of the hero of the Legion, he launched into an adulatory introduction which was quickly followed by Millán Astray's harangue to the people of the Republican zone. It was a plea to the Republicans to lay down their arms and submit to Franco's love, nobility and humanity.

Giménez Caballero's subterfuge might not have been discovered had it not been for the fact that, in the early hours of the following morning, a Republican bomber, perhaps trying to hit Franco's headquarters, dropped a bomb on the Palacio Anaya. As he staggered from the basement shelter, Giménez Caballero was brusquely summoned to Millán Astray's presence. Accompanied by the Nationalist air ace, Joaquín García Morato, Millán Astray began to shout, 'Stand to attention! Caballero! I'm going to have you shot. Prepare yourself. You know I'm not joking.' – 'General, may I know my crime?' stammered Giménez Caballero. 'You still have to ask?' barked Millán Astray. 'To no one but you would it occur to introduce me on the radio and mention the Palacio de Anaya. The enemy has thus located me and tried to finish me off. A crime of the gravest imprudence.' Giménez Caballero opted for a mischievous humility. 'General, as always, you are right and are just. I deserve a serious punishment, yes, I deserve a severe punishment, even death. But not for the crime of letting the Reds hear us but for a much more serious blunder – the crime that they didn't hear you when you spoke so marvellously! The radio wasn't working and I didn't dare miss out on one of Millán Astray's harangues delivered just for me . . . ah! and also for Elvirita, who was crying with pleasure.' A grinning Millan Astray just shouted, 'And now get out of my sight!'[89]

Much of Millán Astray's time was devoted to tours of the Nationalist zone, raising morale with his famous harangues. On the flimsiest excuse, he would often stop someone in the street and launch into a spontaneous diatribe which often drew a crowd around him. It reached a point where many who knew him took evasive action when they saw him coming.[90] In May 1937, he spoke in Salamanca at the Gran Hotel where he excited a demonstration of protesters against the Republican bombing of the German cruiser *Deutschland* (the dead were buried with full military honours in Gibraltar).[91] One evening, at the start of a meeting before a large crowd in Ceuta, he lost his voice. Unperturbed, he addressed the meeting in a spontaneously invented sign-language of wild gesticulations which won him a standing ovation.[92] Not all his oratory was so well received. On one occasion he spoke to a group of Alféreces Provisionales, acting second lieutenants, rapidly trained in order to meet the Nationalists' urgent need for officers. To the consternation of the recently graduated officers, he opened his speech with a resounding '¡Alféreces Provisionales de hoy! ¡Cadáveres efectivos de manãna!' (acting second lieutenants of today, full corpses of tomorrow).[93] Many broadcast harangues were directed to the

Republican zone and consisted of the most outrageous lies. He systematically denied, for instance, that the advancing Nationalist columns killed civilians and affirmed Franco's commitment to be 'the liberator of the poor' bringing a regime of 'justice and love'.[94] Towards the end of the Spanish Civil War, he was employed at the Madrid front, addressing the Republican lines through a loudspeaker, urging them to surrender and claiming that Franco offered them 'bread, forgiveness and justice'.[95]

When not engaged in propaganda, Millán Astray was often delegated to be Franco's representative on occasions both public and private. When General Mola was killed in an air crash on 3 June 1937, Franco himself presided over the funeral service held in Burgos when the coffin arrived there. However, knowing of Mola's contempt for Millán Astray, with characteristically malicious humour, he delegated the founder of the Legion to represent him at the more solemn ceremonies when the body was taken to Pamplona for burial.[96] Franco also used Millán Astray at times as an intermediary. For instance, in December 1936, he sent him to see the Falangist leader, Manuel Hedilla, and request that, with a view to the formation of 'Brigadas Mixtas' which would include Italian volunteers, he provide 15,000 men.[97] Similarly, in February 1937, during the most difficult moments of the Battle of Jarama, he sent Millán Astray to see the Italian High Command to request that they hasten a diversionary attack.[98] In April 1937, he was one of the emissaries sent by Franco to secure the collaboration of Manuel Hedilla in the forced unification of the Falange and the Carlist movement.[99]

Millán Astray was, incidentally, an avid admirer of the Falange and formally proclaimed his membership after the *Unificación*, thereby giving publicity to the decree incorporating all members of the armed forces into the Falange Española Tradicionalista y de las JONS.[100] The step from *Africanista* to *fascista* was a short one. As he had said in his speech attacking Unamuno, he saw fascism as 'the remedy for Spain'. On 1 January 1938, he proclaimed 'there is only one road to salvation: the awakening of the great nations in which Caudillos are emerging, the great Caudillos of the present moment in the life of humanity: Mussolini, Hitler, Hiro-Hito, Oliveira Salazar, FRANCISCO FRANCO BAHAMONDE.'[101]

In July 1938, he was invited by the Falangist poet, Dionisio Ridruejo, to make a speech at a Falangist rally in Valladolid to commemorate the second anniversary of the outbreak of the Spanish Civil War.

On the morning of the rally, Ridruejo, still in his pyjamas, was called urgently to Millán Astray's hotel room. Stark naked, the General received Ridruejo in his bath, the stump of his arm jerking as it often did when he was nervous. He was helped by his wife Elvira and his usual escort of Legionarios. They dried him and he put on his underpants. He then took Ridruejo aside, and said, 'I really like you and besides I'm very grateful that you remembered me for this meeting. That will have done you no harm. And I want to repay you with a favour. I have to tell you that your name doesn't go down well among the top brass. They regard you as a rebel and untrustworthy. I'm ready to vouch for you but, for that, we must swear the oath of the Legion right here and now.' In a squalidly homoerotic scene, Millán Astray, still clad only in his underpants, made Ridruejo stand to attention with one hand on an imaginary cross and the other holding an imaginary flagpole flying the Legion's standard, and swear the oath.[102]

In late 1937, there was an opportunity for Franco to reward Millán Astray. The large number of those mutilated in the war required some form of government action and so a Dirección General de Mutilados was created and Millán Astray given the post of Director General del Benemérito Cuerpo de Mutilados de Guerra por la Patria. His inaugural speech was as fanatical as all the others. 'And now, mutilated one and all, be prepared to receive at any moment the order or the cry of "To me the mutilated!" in order that, just like Legionarios, on hearing the cry of "To me the Legion!", we all pull together so that with the limbs which we have left and with our hearts, that keep on beating with the same ardour, we can form the Tercio de Mutilados.' He threw himself into the organization of the new corps with his usual manic enthusiasm, declaring that he would be 'the Army's first stretcher-bearer'. He arranged pensions for the disabled on a sliding scale which reached its apogee of generosity for generals.[103] After the Civil War, a decree was passed which allotted to the Dirección General de Mutilados a proportion of posts as doormen, commissionaires and receptionists in public buildings, as well as a number of guaranteed places in competitive examinations for senior positions in the civil service.[104]

Millán Astray considered himself still the spiritual head of the Legion. The fact that he was able to sport an escort of Legionarios indicated that he was still conceded a certain authority within the corps. His offices in Salamanca were referred to as his *Estado Mayor* and he inspected units in such a capacity. On one occasion in early December 1938, he visited the Cuarta Bandera under the command of Major Carlos Iniesta Cano. Iniesta Cano was later to be one of the prominent *generales azules* of late Francoism and a worthy disciple of Millán Astray.[105] His unit was in the village of Guijuelo in Salamanca, resting and reorganizing after its efforts in the Battle of the Ebro. Millán Astray asked Iniesta how many casualties the Cuarta Bandera had suffered since the beginning of the war. On hearing the figure of nearly 8000 (equivalent to the entire strength of the Legion at the beginning of the war), Millán Astray jumped to attention, saluted Iniesta and barked out, 'At your orders, Major!' He then invited the officers to a drink in the Casino of the village and, to their embarrassment, asked if any of them needed any money. Faced with their silence, he asked if anyone present hailed from Seville. When a Lieutenant Piñero stepped forward, Millán Astray said to Iniesta, 'Send him to my headquarters in Salamanca to collect 2000 pesetas which I haven't got on me.' The money was duly collected, was spent on wine and duly enhanced the myth of Millán Astray within the Legion.[106]

At one point during the occupation of Salamanca by the Francoist circus, Millán Astray had occasion to visit a dentist. Accompanied as always by an escort of Legionarios, Falangists and Carlist Requetés, heavily armed with rifles and machine-guns, he went to see Dr José García de la Cruz, who was also treating the Franco family. One section of the escort occupied the pavement outside the dental clinic, another guarded the doors to the consulting room. Like Franco himself, and indeed most Spanish officers who had fought in Morocco where dental treatment was non-existent, Millán Astray needed root extractions. On one visit to the surgery, Millán Astray had one of his sergeants injected in order to ensure that the anaesthetic was not poisoned. On other visits, one of his bodyguards would check the capsule with the anaesthetic before he would permit himself to be injected. When Dr García de la Cruz came to make the injection, Millán Astray gripped the dental chair as if he were being electrocuted. On seeing this, his escort formed up and began to sing the hymn of the Legion as they had done in the Moroccan wars to help the bridegroom of death through his ordeal: '¡Soy valiente y leal legionario/ Soy soldado de brava legión/Pesa en mi alma doliente calvario/que en el fuego busca redención/mi divisa no conoce el miedo/mi destino tan solo sufrir/mi bandera luchar con denuedo/hasta conseguir/vencer o morir.'* When the extraction was successfully accomplished, the chorus of Legionarios fell silent, Millán Astray sat up and said, 'That wasn't too bad, now I want you to make me a complete set of false teeth in gold.'

Since there was an acute shortage of gold and the Francoist hierarchy was not in the habit of paying bills, Dr García stammered out that there was no gold to be had in Nationalist Spain, particularly for dentists, and that, unless the General could get hold of some, his ambitions for a spectacular dental plate could not be fulfilled. Noticing a photograph of Franco's daughter Carmen on the wall, Millán Astray said, 'I see that you treated Carmencita', and asked how much she had been charged. Understandably, in wartime Salamanca, the dentist had not dared to send a bill to Franco and he replied truthfully, 'Nothing, I just asked her to give me a signed photograph.' In a burst of generosity, Millán Astray announced, 'Well, I'm going to do the same. I'm going to give you a photo of me and with that we're quits.' Some years later, Millán Astray appeared at Dr García's consulting rooms to show off a mouth full of gold which led the dentist to assume that he had taken advantage of a dentist with a Republican past anxious to ingratiate himself with the new regime.[107] In fact, he was much given to distributing signed photographs of himself. In the early summer of 1937, with his escort, he was awaiting an audience with Franco in the Palacio Episcopal of Salamanca. He was greeted by the son of an old military friend. After asking after the father, he said, 'I want you to have a picture of me in memory of this day', called over his aide and pulled a handful of photographs from his briefcase and asked 'Which do you like best? Pick any one you like.'[108]

In May 1938, he visited Italy with a group of Francoist intellectuals including Ridruejo and Pemán to take part in a propaganda tour. The tour ended with an 'Italo–Spanish Solidarity Day' at which speeches were made in the Teatro Adriano in Rome. During this event, in his capacity as Director General del Benemérito Cuerpo de Mutilados de Guerra por la Patria, he was introduced to his Italian equivalent, Carlo Delcroix, President of the Associazione Nazionale Mutilati e Invalidi di Guerra. Millán Astray was momentarily nonplussed to discover that the Fascist war hero had lost both arms and both eyes in a bomb

* 'I am a valiant and loyal legionaire. I am a soldier of the brave Legion. A painful calvary weighs down my soul which seeks its redemption in the fire of battle. My badge knows no fear. My destiny is just to suffer. My flag is to fight with daring until I meet victory or death.'

explosion in 1917. After a brief hesitation, however, Millán Astray recovered his usual confident theatricality, embraced Delcroix and tearfully declared, 'O happy art thou, brother, whose fatherland demanded of thee two eyes, while mine called for only one of mine; O happy art thou, brother, whose fatherland took from thee two hands, while mine left me with one.' It was assumed by the wildly enthusiastic audience that Millán Astray had lost his arm and his eye fighting in the Spanish Civil War. He did not disabuse them.[109] Millán Astray and Pemán had lunch with the Italian Foreign Minister, Count Galeazzo Ciano, who spoke to them in inflated terms of the Duce's Herculean capacity for work. Millán Astray, who was convinced, quite wrongly, that he could speak Italian, was not to be outdone. Speaking a comically italianized Spanish, he declared, 'Pues il nostro Caudiglio pasa cuatorce hores in la mesa de trabaglio e non se levanta ni pere meare' (Well, our Caudillo spends fourteen hours at his desk and doesn't get up even to piss).[110]

Millán Astray was a fervent believer in his own popularity. In a wartime broadcast to the soldiers of both sides, he said:

> Why are you dying? I will tell you. I, Millán Astray, founder of the Legion. So beloved of all soldiers. Held so dear by the humble, by fascists, by Carlists, by anarchists, by Socialists, by prisoners, by the helpless. I have the right to speak to each and every one of you. On 19 March of this year of 1936 when I was leaving for South America, the railway-workers of Seville beseeched me in the station 'Stay with us'. The dockworkers in Cádiz, on the same day, in the tavern with the public telephone, embracing me with tears in their eyes, said 'General, don't go to America and stay with us'. You can check. Those of you who can hear me in Madrid can find out who I am from the waiters in the cafés, from the shoeshine boys, from the tram-drivers, from all the taxi-drivers (who all know me), the newspaper-vendors, the poor, the needy, those on the run from justice, the odd hit-man whose father, a railway-worker, came to my house, the prisoners in the jails, even the sister of *La Libertaria*. And they will all say that I have always spoken to everyone about the fatherland; that they all knew that I was the founder of the Legion, that I am a Legionario, but all, when I say goodbye, embrace me.[111]

He believed hardly less fervently in his own sexual attractiveness. He boasted of kissing every woman he met, including nine cloistered nuns and three abbesses.[112] Whenever introduced to a woman, he would ask 'Married or single?' and if the reply was the latter, immediately kiss her twice. He was particularly effusive with Dr García's dental nurse.[113] At the end of his speeches, he would order that men and women in the audience kiss one another, thereby scandalizing the clergy present. If it happened to be an evening event, he would order the lights to be switched off. Sometimes, while passing through the Plaza Mayor of Salamanca, he would shout for those around him to embrace and kiss.[114] On the other hand, he was notably prurient. The semi-naked protagonist of the scene with Ridruejo and the imaginary flagpole declared that he would have nothing to do with tailors on the grounds that, when they took measurements for trousers, they brushed their clients' genitals.[115] He asked Republican listeners to his broadcasts: 'What do you feel, those of you who have honour and a sense of shame, when you see young women wearing mechanic's overalls who, when the zip slides down, are completely naked, showing everything that a woman's modesty forbids?'[116]

By way of making a public declaration of his own sexual potency, he adopted the great sex-symbol of Francoist Spain, the Argentinian musical comedy singer–actress Celia Gámez, as his protégée and, by implication, lover. When she married on 1 July 1944, in the Church of San Jerónimo el Real in Madrid, he appeared as her *padrino* (to give her away). Since she had had many lovers, most of them illustrious in one way or another, she decided to invite them all to her wedding, thinking to give the occasion more prestige. However, a group of them paid some urchins to throw a bag of horns (the symbol of cuckoldry) at the feet of the couple. In the resulting tumult, the priest was unable to impose order. Millán Astray blew his whistle, shouted '¡A mí la Legión!' and the four armed Legionarios of his escort appeared. Millán Astray then bellowed, 'If you cannot respect the Church, at least show respect for me!' When silence was reimposed, the Legionarios formed a small square in which the couple and the priest were able to continue the ceremony.[117]

Life after the Spanish Civil War was an inevitable anti-climax for Millán Astray. To an extent, he had been able to fight the war vicariously and relive the adulation that he had enjoyed in Morocco. For a while, he continued to make propaganda tours keeping alive the memory of the war. In the summer of 1939, he visited a Jesuit seminary in Granada. As he often did, he enthused his audience by speaking both of the glories of the recent 'crusade' and also of the empire to come. He ended his performance ordering the young theology students to make the fascist salute and sing along with him. They sang the hymn of the Legion, then the Falange's *Cara al sol* and finally, saying, 'now the hymn of your St Ignatius of Loyola, the captain, but also with arms outstretched', he led them in a fervent rendition of 'Now let us sing to the love of all loves'. As he left, a student came up and said, 'General, I saw you once from the trenches. I fought for all three years of the war. At your orders!' Millán Astray pulled out his wallet, gave him a thousand pesetas and said 'Take this to get drunk with!'[118]

The prospect of a new African empire for Spain filled Millán Astray with joy. During the Second World War, he followed the progress of the Axis with avid enthusiasm and then bitter disappointment. Franco's enthusiastic response to the German invasion of the Soviet Union had led to the hasty recruitment of a volunteer force, known as the Blue Division, to fight on the Eastern Front. When its first commander, General Agustín Muñoz Grandes, left for Germany on 14 July 1941, Millán Astray was at the aerodrome of Barajas to bid him farewell. Muñoz Grandes had fought in the Legion and Millán Astray's warm embrace for his one-time subordinate emphasized that in part the expedition was a continuation of the Legion's role in the Spanish Civil War. When the first contingents of weary soldiers returned on leave, Millán Astray was in the welcoming committee of Francoist dignitaries at the Estación del Norte bedecked with Falangist, Nazi and Italian Fascist flags.[119] The defeat of the Axis caused Millán Astray considerable distress. He was outraged in May 1950 when Marshal Rodolfo Graziani, Mussolini's Chief of Staff during the Second World War and in the Repubblica di Salò, was condemned for collaboration with the Germans and deprived, by order of the Minister of Defence, Randolfo Pacciardi, of the right to wear his medals for bravery and for being wounded. Alerted to the possibilities for publicity by the news that Pacciardi had been commander of the Garibaldi battalion of the International Brigades during the Spanish Civil War, Millán Astray sent Graziani his own 'Medalla de sufrimientos por la Patria', which fourteen years earlier he had offered to José María Pemán. The gesture led to Millán Astray being front-page news in Italy.[120]

Franco rewarded Millán Astray's fidelity in 1943 when he named him as Procurador in Cortes, a lucrative sinecure.[121] However, after the Second World War, Millán Astray found it difficult to withdraw from public life. During the period of Spain's international ostracism, he would regularly visit the Caudillo's cousin and private secretary, Pacón (General Francisco Franco Salgado-Araujo), to make known his views on domestic and foreign policy. He would also regularly make the rounds of the embassies of the democratic powers endeavouring to ascertain the current situation and, it is to be supposed, pontificating about his own vision of world affairs. Concerned that he might provoke misunderstandings during a period of singularly delicate relations, in 1949, the Minister of Foreign Affairs, Alberto Martín Artajo, requested the Minister of War, General Fidel Dávila, to order him to desist. Millán Astray was so mortified that, in a fit of self-pity, he decided to resign from the Army and go into exile. He visited Pacón at his office in the Palacio de Oriente, told him about Dávila's reprimand, said that he could not accept it and gave him a sheaf of papers sealed with sealing wax to be handed to the Caudillo. Pacón replied that he never handed sealed papers personally to Franco without knowing their contents and that, if Millán Astray insisted on handing it over sealed, it must go through the normal channels. Millán Astray then read out to him a formal petition requesting his separation from the Army and permission to live in Lisbon, and said that he would return within a week to hear Franco's reaction. Pacón, knowing him only too well, simply put the letter in a drawer and told the Caudillo nothing. A week later, a much chastened Millán Astray returned and asked timidly what Franco had said. Pacón told him that he was incapable of being the instrument of division between his two most admired senior officers and had therefore broken his promise to hand over the papers. A grateful Millán Astray tearfully embraced him saying, 'You are one of my most faithful friends. I was beside myself when I wrote that petition.'[122]

His life had changed in early 1941 when, at a bridge party at the home of Natalio Rivas, he met and fell in love with Rita Gasset. The daughter of Rafael Gasset, one-time Minister of the Economy, and the cousin of the philosopher Ortega y Gasset, Rita was young enough to be Millán Astray's daughter. She became pregnant and Millán Astray decided finally to annul his marriage to Elvira. He was informed that, in view of his wife's vow of chastity, there was no impediment to a canonical annulment. However, always deferential to Franco, he informed the Caudillo of his intentions. Franco, who was obsessively sensitive to any hint of sexual impropriety, exploded. 'You will not create a scandal. I forbid you to do this.' Millán Astray went to Lisbon with Rita Gasset where their daughter, Peregrina, was born on 23 January 1942. Elvira treated her affectionately as her niece.[123]

After a lengthy bout of cardiac illness, Millán Astray died on 1 January 1954, largely forgotten.[124] Spain was on the verge of losing her Moroccan empire. The foundation of the Legion was the central pillar of the Africanista ideology which, mixed with Falangism, had become the peculiar philosophy behind Franco's cruel and violent war effort. In the Spain of the 1950s, all of that mattered little. Nevertheless, in death, Millán Astray maintained some of the theatricality that had characterized him in life. He left instructions that there were to be no flowers at his burial and that he was not to receive the military honours corresponding to his rank and decorations. Instead, a simple ceremony with his escort of Legionarios replicated the battlefield burials of the Legion.[125] His obituary in *ABC* rightly claimed that he was the man who had created what it called 'la escuela de 1936'. Fittingly, among those present were some of the most prominent Africanistas and Francoists, Generals Agustín Muñoz Grandes, Camilo Alonso Vega and Francisco Franco Salgado-Araujo, as well as his biographer, General Carlos Silva. A telegram of condolence was sent to Elvira Gutiérrez in the name of the Caudillo but Franco did not attend the funeral. Now seeking to present himself to the world as the ally of President Eisenhower, Franco did not wish to be associated with Millán Astray.[126]

2

The Discreet Charm of a Dictator: Francisco Franco

Franco spent the first forty-five years of his life getting to the top. A ferocious ambition drove him to the summit of the military profession by 1934 when he became a *general de división* (major general) and, shortly afterwards, Jefe del Estado Mayor (Chief of General Staff). During the Spanish Civil War, he put every effort into ensuring first of all that he would be recognized as sole military commander of the Nationalist zone. This he achieved on 21 September 1936. Within one week, he had increased his power to that of Head of State. Seven months later, he had overcome all political rivals through the forced unification of parties in Salamanca in April 1937. Thereafter, his main concern was to hold onto the power that he had secured. This involved winning the Civil War, then surviving the Second World War and the international hostility which he had earned by his closeness to the Axis. The peak of his success came in September 1953, when the Pact of Madrid was signed with the United States. Franco's fascination lies in the contrast between the skills and qualities required to achieve such successes and his startling intellectual mediocrity and a personal timidity which led many who met him to comment just how unlike their image of a dictator he really was.

The fascination and the difficulty of comprehending Franco is increased by the way in which he himself interpreted his actions to create myths which were then eagerly propagated by his admirers. There is Franco the tireless, vigilant and omniscient watchman: 'I am the sentry who is never relieved; the one who receives the unwelcome telegrams and dictates the solutions; the one who is watchful while others sleep.'[1] There is Franco the brilliant diplomat, who kept Spain out of the Second World War by dint of his supposed *hábil prudencia* in outwitting Hitler. There is Franco the benefactor of all Spaniards, the bestower of the so-called 'social peace'. Yet, the ceaseless vigil was increasingly interrupted for long hunting and fishing jaunts, as well as interminable sessions in front of cinema – and later, television – screens. The idea that he cunningly deceived Hitler is unsustainable in the face of overwhelming evidence that Franco was anxious to be part of a future fascist world order and was prevented from joining the Axis war effort only by obstacles beyond his control: Spain's economic and military weakness and his own tense relationship with Hitler. The twenty-five years of peace and prosperity for the victors was achieved at the cost of forced labour camps, mass exile, prisons, torture and executions among the defeated.

Contradictions abound and are complicated by Franco's sheer longevity. The straightforward and impetuous soldier of 1916 is virtually unrecognizable in the cunning power-broker of the 1940s and seems to have nothing to do with the man who surrounded himself with the trappings of royalty in the 1950s. The difficulties of explanation are compounded by Franco's own efforts at obfuscation. In maturity, he cultivated an impenetrability intended to ensure that his intentions were indecipherable. His chaplain for forty years, Father José María Bulart, made the ingenuously contradictory comment that 'perhaps he was cold as some have said, but he never showed it. In fact, he never showed anything.'[2] The key to his art was an ability to avoid concrete definition. One of the ways in which he did that was by constantly keeping his distance, both politically and physically. At innumerable moments of crisis throughout his years in power, Franco was simply absent, usually uncontactable while hunting in some remote sierra.

The mature Franco was a chameleon. In the power struggle of the 1940s between army officers and Falangists, for instance, this ability to remain apart, ostensibly committed to nothing, was central to his survival. He would tell prominent Falangists that their proposals for social revolution were being blocked by reactionary army officers, as if he were powerless to stop them, conveniently forgetting that he was Generalísimo of the armed forces. At the same time, when conservative generals protested to him about Falangist excesses, he would reply conspiratorially that he and they had to be wary of Falangist hotheads, neatly overlooking the fact that he was Jefe Nacional of the Falange.

The strength derived from Franco's cool and detached calculation was a corollary of the fact that he lacked both the manic genius of Hitler and the reckless impetuosity of Mussolini. That is not to say that he did not have passions and enthusiasms and obsessions: his hatred of freemasonry was pathological; his quest for pleasure on the hunting field was unquenchable. Like the Duce and the Führer, Franco had the power and conviction that come from neurosis. However, there was less about him, certainly after his elevation to supreme power, that was charismatic. Indeed, when in the spotlight as a political leader, he sometimes showed an unexpected shyness, and was often inhibited and ill-at-ease on public occasions.

This apparent modesty contrasted with a delight in adulation and a frequent resort to self-glorification. This had numerous manifestations but none quite so self-indulgent as his major literary achievement, *Raza*. In late 1940, when his propagandists would have us believe that Franco was keeping a lonely and watchful vigil to prevent Hitler pulling Spain into the World War, he found the time and emotional energy to write a novel-cum-filmscript. *Raza* was transparently autobiographical. In it, and through its heroic central character, he put right all of the frustrations of his own life.[3] The plot relates the experiences of a Galician family, totally identifiable with Franco's own, from Spain's imperial collapse in 1898 to the political instability of the first third of the twentieth century and the Civil War. The pivotal character in the book is the mother figure, Doña Isabel de Andrade. Alone, with three sons and a daughter to bring up, like Franco's mother Pilar Bahamonde y Pardo de Andrade, the pious Doña Isabel is a gentle yet strong figure. Pilar was abandoned by Francisco's dissolute, gambling, philandering father. In contrast, in the novel, the hero's father is a naval hero and Doña Isabel is widowed when he is killed in the Cuban war. In his many writings and speeches, in his unfinished memoirs and in many interviews, Franco often remodelled aspects of his past to aggrandize his own role but never so sweepingly and revealingly as here.

In private life and in power, Francisco would implacably reject all the things he associated with his father, from the pleasures of the flesh to the ideas of the left. An intense, indeeed schizoid, identification with his mother's suffering at the hands of his promiscuous father may be read into the fact that his attitudes to women and sex were fraught with difficulty. In the Legion, he was famed for having no need for women and songs were written about his readiness to leave his bride in order to fight in Africa.[4] His public references to matters sexual were rare and odd. On a visit to the Zaragoza Military Academy in 1942, he told one of the staff that an additional bed should be put in rooms that had two 'to avoid marriages'.[5]

In 1937, he discussed with his brother-in-law the death of the young founder of the Falange, José Antonio Primo de Rivera. José Antonio was not only a potential political rival but, as a handsome aristocrat, he was also the object of Franco's jealousy and resentment. Despite indisputable evidence that the Falangist leader had been executed by the Republic, the Caudillo revealed more than he intended when he asserted that José Antonio was in the hands of the Russians, 'who have probably castrated him'.[6] In November 1937, speaking to the correspondent of *La Prensa* of Buenos Aires, he said: 'visit Asturias and you will find girls of 15 and 16 years old, if not younger, violated and pregnant: you will find constant examples of free love, girls requisitioned for such and such a Russian officer, and an infinity of other proofs of barbarism'.[7] In the 1950s, he urged a delegation from the Spanish Society of Authors to emulate the gloomy, guilt-ridden tragedies of the seventeenth century dramatist, Pedro Calderón de la Barca, which showed how to restore family Honour with the 'detergent of blood'.

Franco's repudiation of his father was matched by a deep identification with his mother, something which might perhaps be seen in many aspects of his personal style, a gentle manner, a soft voice, a propensity to weep, an enduring sense of deprivation. A tone of self-pitying resentment runs through his speeches as Caudillo and was one of the motivating forces of his drive to greatness. Several anecdotes from his years in power are redolent of the hard-done-by little boy that he must have been. A solid trencherman, he complained one day with regard to his favourite meat stew, 'because I'm Chief of State, they serve me the stew with lots of meat, but I like potatoes as well'. Nothing would have been simpler than to ask waiters for more potatoes, yet he could not bring himself to do so.[8] One day in the early 1960s, he admired a pair of shoes worn by his brother-in-law and private secretary, Felipe Polo. On being told that they were imported from England and what they cost, Franco said, 'I couldn't afford to pay that much.'[9] This was not a joke. Franco wore heavy shoes sent him free of charge by one of Spain's leading manufacturers. They were entirely unsuitable and would cause him severe distress in later life.

Linked to the sense of deprivation and the self-pity was Franco's open sentimentality. Although he was implacably cruel with his enemies and icily distant with his subordinates, he could be easily moved, or easily move himself, to tears. He cried on the day of his first communion. He cried when talking about Alfonso XIII, despite the fact that he delayed the restoration of the Spanish monarchy for nearly forty years.[10] He cried when speaking of the help that he received during the Civil War from Portugal, Italy and Germany.[11] When he met Hitler, Mussolini, and Eisenhower he was visibly overcome with emotion, more with pride at being on equal terms with his heroes than out of gratitude for military assistance that he took for granted. His eyes filled with tears when he recalled Pétain's shame in having to sue for armistice, managing easily to forget how he had tried to exploit French weakness to take over part of France's North African empire.[12] He was overcome with emotion on the day that he received an honorary doctorate from the Universidad Pontificia of Salamanca.[13] Such emotion was in stark contrast with the coldness with which he could contemplate mass death sentences. Tearful gratitude for Portuguese help during the Civil War did not inhibit him from toying with the notion of absorbing Portugal into a greater Spain.

Many aspects of Franco's demeanour – the eyes, the soft voice, the apparent outer calm – seemed to commentators to be somehow feminine. John Whitaker, the distinguished American journalist who met him several times during the Civil War, commented on the almost feminine tone of his voice. 'A small man, his hand is like a woman's and always damp with perspiration. Excessively shy, as he fences to understand a caller, his voice is shrill and pitched on a high note which is slightly disconcerting since he speaks very softly – almost in a whisper.'[14] The femininity of Franco's appearance was frequently, and inadvertently, underlined by his admirers. 'His eyes are the most remarkable part of his physiognomy. They are typically Spanish, large and luminous with long lashes. Usually they are smiling and somewhat reflective, but I have seen them flash with decision and, though I have never witnessed it, I am told that when roused to anger they can become as cold and hard as steel.'[15] 'The eyes are the man. Under longish lashes, his dark eyes are neither hard nor stern nor truculent. They are memorable for their extreme kindness.'[16] 'It is the eyes that will strike you first. They have a remarkable animation and seem to look straight at you and take you in at a glance. They are penetrating but very human.'[17] 'His dark luminous eyes stared at me with that "long enquiring look" which other visitors have remarked upon.'[18]

Rejecting the father who brought so much pain to his mother, he identified with her in many ways to the detriment of his own developing personality. That would be manifest in the olympian self-regard which became apparent once he had reached prominence in Africa, a reflection of his capacity, at its most extreme in *Raza*, to create for himself successive public personae that could cope with the difficulties of life. The security provided by these personae permitted Franco almost always to seem contained and composed. Everyone who came into contact with him remarked on his affably courteous, but always distant, manner. Neither anger nor hilarity disturbed his self-control. He took pride in having the hill shepherd's patience and sense of the unimportance of time. The notion of time being on his side was something that Franco felt and indeed used as a weapon. That was possible because he was also an unsinkable optimist.[19] During the Civil War, at bleak moments for the Nationalists, he would raise morale by categoric affirmations of what he called his 'blind faith'. His serenity was revealed repeatedly in his uncanny ability to ride out damaging storms, at the most difficult moments of international isolation at the end of the Second World War and during the Cold War, sitting tight when his advisors were convinced that the end was in sight.

After his childhood traumas, the great formative experience of Franco's life was the Army and, above all, his time as a colonial officer in Africa. After the insecurities of his childhood, the Army provided him with a framework of certainties based on hierarchy and command. He revelled in the discipline and the ability to lose himself in a military machine built on obedience and a shared rhetoric of patriotism and honour. In 1912 he went to Morocco, where he spent ten and a half of the next fourteen years. The bulk of his early career, culminating in promotion to brigadier general at the age of thirty-three, took place first with the fierce Moorish mercenaries of the so-called Regulares Indígenas (native regulars) and then with the brutalized shock troops of the ruthless Tercio Extranjero (Foreign Legion). As he told the journalist Manuel Aznar in 1938, 'My years in Africa live within me with indescribable force. There was born the possibility of rescuing a great Spain. There was founded the idea which today redeems us. Without Africa, I can scarcely explain myself to myself, nor can I explain myself properly to my comrades in arms.'[20] In Africa, he acquired the central beliefs of his political life: the right of the Army to be the arbiter of Spain's political destiny and, most importantly, his own right to command. Thereafter, he never perceived the Army as subject to any political sovereignty but responsible only to the

Patria. He was always to see political authority in terms of military hierarchy, obedience and discipline. He was a tough disciplinarian and men were frightened by his unwavering imposition of punishments for infractions of the rules.

One reason that men accepted Franco's ferocious discipline was the fact that he was extremely courageous. There is no record of Franco ever having manifested fear.[21] In part that derived from the fact that Franco the soldier was a creation, constructed to help him cope with his personal insecurities. By an effort of will, he turned the timid teenager from Galicia into the tough desert hero. It was the beginning of the process whereby Franco would mould reality to his own needs rather than adjust himself to it. He was seriously wounded only once, on 29 June 1916. That, together with the media adulation of which he was made the object from the 1920s onwards, gave him the self-regarding sense of being a man of destiny which was to characterize his later career. He is alleged to have said, somewhat portentously, 'I have seen death walk by my side many times, but fortunately, she did not know me.'[22] His coolness under fire and his practical competence as a field officer won him a series of rapid promotions which made him successively in 1916 the youngest captain, in 1917 the youngest major and in 1926 the youngest general in Europe. Ironically, it has been suggested that Franco had a real fear of death and for that reason systematically avoided either talking about it or attending funerals. He did not attend the burial of his father. His failure to attend the funeral of his Foreign Minister, the Conde de Jordana, in 1944 was widely commented upon.[23] Nor did he attend the burial of his life-long servant Admiral Luis Carrero Blanco.

His bravery as a young soldier cannot, however, be denied. Behind it, there was an icy sang-froid which would carry him through the darkest days of the Civil War, the World War and the Cold War and would permit him to preside over a machinery of terror. He showed only indifference in the face of complaints about the atrocities being committed in the areas under his control during the Civil War.[24] The scale of the repression in the Civil War and into the 1940s surprised Mussolini's emissaries, Count Ciano and Roberto Farinacci and even Heinrich Himmler.[25] His cruelty was facilitated by his lack of imagination. In power, for instance, he could not conceive that the opposition or discontent of others might have objective justification; he saw it simply as the work of foreign communist agitators and sinister freemasons. Such detachment from reality gave Franco a confidence not undermined by self-criticism. The conviction that he was always right gave him the flexibility endlessly to tack to changing domestic and international circumstances.

Nor was he restricted by any far-reaching ideological vision in the way that Hitler and Mussolini were. Instead, he had an idealized notion of a harmonious society in which opposition and subversion would not exist. It would be like a united family ruled over by a strong, all-seeing father. In so far as he had a political philosophy at all, it was extremely narrow, often negative and derived from his military background. Like most army officers of his generation, his overriding hatreds were separatism, communism and freemasonry. Irrespective of the human cost, he was determined to eradicate all three from Spain, along with socialism and liberalism. That came to mean the annihilation of the legacies of the Enlightenment, of the French Revolution and of the industrial revolution in order to return to the glories of medieval Spain. His most dearly held objectives were altogether more abstract, more spiritual than ideological in the modern sense. He wanted, by bloodshed, to 'redeem' the Spanish people of the burden of the centuries of failure since Felipe II when Spain's greatness began to crumble. In this regard, he was applying to an entire nation the ideas upon which Millán Astray had built the violent credo of the Legion.

For reasons that had no basis in rationality, he blamed the decline of Spain and all her subsequent misfortunes on freemasonry. He held freemasonry responsible for Napoleon's invasion of Spain, for the loss of the Spanish empire, for the civil wars of the nineteenth and twentieth century, for international efforts to impede his victory in the war of 1936–1939 and for the international ostracism to which he was subjected after 1945.[26] His obsession with freemasonry was unusually virulent, playing a part in his life akin to that played in Hitler's by anti-Semitism. His obsession was such as to lead him to suspect both the Moroccan independence movement of the 1950s and the Second Vatican Council of being masonic inspirations. The most likely reason for this hatred was the fact that his father was a free-thinker with considerable sympathy for freemasonry. It may also relate to the fact that his unconventional brother Ramón was a mason. Freemasonry thus became the target for his anger at his brother's wildness and the embarrassment that it caused him. It has also been suggested that he had applied to join masonic lodges in 1924 and 1932 and had been rejected because he had accepted promotions by merit when many officers had sworn not to do so. He believed himself, in retrospect, to have been the object of persecution by freemasons in the Army during the Second Republic. In response, he tended to accuse all cultured or educated critics of being freemasons.[27]

By freemasonry, Franco understood the flowering of liberal values in Spain or what he called 'the great invasion of evil'. Spanish history since Felipe II consisted only of three 'calamitous centuries' which brought decadence, corruption and freemasonry. His eternal delays in restoring the monarchy were excused on the grounds that the Bourbon dynasty was no longer capable of emulating the virile 'totalitarian' monarchy which had expelled the Jews and the Moriscos and conquered America.[28] To eliminate the historical legacy of the three awkward centuries of decadence, Franco endeavoured to create a uniquely Spanish political model based on a fusion of medieval absolutism and Axis totalitarianism. Accordingly, when his acolytes referred to Fernando el Católico as the first authentic Caudillo, or when Franco made references to the great medieval 'Caudillo kings', the clear implication was that he belonged to a line of great leaders that had been interrupted after Felipe II.[29] He considered himself, like them, to be a warrior of God against the infidels who would destroy the nation's faith and culture. The seed had been first planted in Franco's mind in the late 1920s. At that period, he spent time at a small Asturian estate owned by his wife known as La Piniella, situated near San Cucao de Llanera, thirteen kilometres from Oviedo. A particularly sycophantic local priest who fancied himself as the chaplain to the house was constantly telling both Doña Carmen and Franco himself that he was on the way to repeating the epic achievements of El Cid and the great medieval Caudillo Kings of Asturias. Franco's wife often reminded him of the priest's comments.[30]

Franco was particularly taken by the pseudo-medieval choreography which characterized many of the great public occasions in which he took part. The generalized portrayal of Franco as a warrior king or specifically as El Cid was both personally titillating to him and central to what passed for ideology in his dictatorship. In the posters and paintings, in the ceremonies of his regime, an impression was created of Franco's all-seeing omnipotence by projecting him as a saintly crusader entrusted with God's mission. The Church went along with the idea because many senior ecclesiastics longed to return to a period of greatness when Church and State had worked closely together. His immediate entourage went along with it because they knew that it pleased him immensely. For Franco himself, his projection as medieval champion, Caudillo by the grace of God, helped justify the idea that he was totally irreplaceable.[31]

Behind the public display, Franco remained intensely private. He was abundantly imbued with the inscrutable pragmatism or *retranca* of the Gallego peasant. Whether that was because of his origins as a native of Galicia, or the fruit of his Moroccan experiences is impossible to say. Whatever its origins in Franco, *retranca* may be defined as an evasion of commitment and a taste for the imprecise. This characteristic is illustrated by the tale of two Gallegos discussing the Falange when the single party seemed all-powerful in the 1940s. 'What do you really think about it?' asked the first. 'Well,' replied his friend, aware that anyone might be a police informer, 'in the first place, you know, and, in the second, what can I tell you?' Franco used his own *retranca* to confuse friends and enemies alike. When his doctor suggested that the Caudillo dictate his memoirs into a tape-recorder, for later transcription by a reliable typist, he was rebuffed by Franco whispering darkly, 'I don't think they'll let you.'

The silent politician contrasted with the affable soldier. There is an abyss between what the hagiographers and the critics make of Franco's military skills. General Sanjurjo, who admired him greatly, remarked in 1931 'he is hardly a Napoleon, but given what the others are like . . .'[32] He shared with Napoleon not much more than diminutive size and the fact that he became a general very young. That his style as a general could not have been further from that of Napoleon was made clear during the Civil War. His approach was the despair of his Axis allies, who condemned his strategy as over-cautious. He was obsessed with logistics and territorial control and unreceptive to contemporary notions of rapid, mechanized war. He made no secret of his political purpose: he wanted to conquer slowly in order to carry out 'the moral redemption' and 'spiritual conquest' of the areas occupied by his troops.[33]

The same calculated ruthlessness characterized the repression of the left during the war and after. After mass trials were held, Franco would flick through folders of death sentences, often while doing something else, and sign them. The scale of the repression – with perhaps as many as 1 million prisoners in labour camps and jails and 200,000 executions – served as a lesson for decades. Like Hitler, Franco had plenty of collaborators willing to undertake the detailed work of repression and, also like the Führer, he was able to distance himself from the process. None the less, since he was the supreme authority within the system of military justice, there is no dispute as to where ultimate responsibility lay. Moreover, in his speeches, Franco made no secret of his belief in the necessity of blood sacrifices. The story is told that when asked by his friend General Camilo Alonso Vega about the fate of an old comrade from the Moroccan wars (possibly General Agustín Gómez Morato, the military commander in Spanish Morocco who was executed for refusing to join the rising), Franco replied 'le fusilaron los nacionales' (the Nationalists shot him), for all the world as if it had nothing to do with him at all.[34] This was typical of his method of turning a blind eye, *dejar hacer*, while his subordinates became enmeshed in what has been called 'the covenant of blood'.[35] He seems to have been able to convince himself that the atrocities of his regime did not take place. He simply denied evidence put before him about the persecution of Basque priests or the atrocities which followed the capture of Malaga in February 1937. He took pride in telling the Nationalist poet, José María Pemán that, in Spain, the right had not followed the Italian Fascist practice of forcing their enemies to drink castor-oil. The clear implication was that they had not done worse things.[36] Apart from the fact that the Italian practice was frequently emulated, the scale of his bloody repression makes a bizarre irrelevance of the idea that failure to use castor-oil might be a mitigating factor.

On numerous occasions, with his characteristic capacity for self-deception, Franco denied that he was a dictator. In March 1947, he told Edward Knoblaugh of the International News Service that there was no dictatorship in Spain: 'I am not free, as it is believed abroad, to do what I want. I need, like every ruler on earth, the help and agreement of my government.'[37] In June 1958, he told a French journalist that 'for all Spaniards and for myself, to describe me as a dictator is simply childish. My prerogatives, my own powers are much less important than those granted by the Constitution of the United States to the President.'[38] In June 1961, he told William Randolph Hearst Jr that 'in Spain, there is no dictatorship' and that 'my powers as Chief of State are less than those of the Presidents of most Latin American States and the fact that the present laws forbid licentiousness [*libertinaje*] neither denies nor limits real liberty'.[39] At the end of April 1969, when General De Gaulle resigned after losing a referendum, Franco commented: 'Make no mistake, the fall of De Gaulle could be seen coming because he was always a dictator.'[40]

He could think of himself in such benevolent terms with total sincerity, believing in some way that a readiness to let his ministers talk interminably in cabinet meetings, which reflected poor chairmanship rather than anything else, more than compensated for the one-party state, the censorship, the prison camps and the apparatus of terror. Moreover, decisions which really mattered to him were often taken outside the council of ministers. For those in the charmed circles of the regime, there was freedom to do anything except oppose Franco. When they did, he would strike quickly. On 30 May 1968, an article on the May events in France by the Catholic intellectual Rafael Calvo Serer was published in his paper *Madrid*. It ran under the headline 'To Retire in Time: No to General de Gaulle'. Franco was furious at the hint and had the newspaper closed down.[41] The Caudillo was able simultaneously to act as a dictator and be convinced that he was not for several reasons. First of all, regarding himself as the saviour of Spain universally beloved by all but the sinister agents of occult powers, it was hardly surprising that Franco did not consider himself a dictator. In addition, he saw political power as an extension of military authority. He always referred to his power as *el mando* (command) and simply treated opposition as mutiny worthy of the severest punishment. It was always a power used cunningly – in general, it was only the defeated, the *anti-España*, of the left which suffered the consistently oppressive weight of the dictatorship. Those within his own establishment were given considerable leeway, although Franco always dangled over them the possibility of a swift and arbitrary punishment if they strayed too far. The device of *dejar hacer* was one of the reasons why Franco perhaps appeared less obviously tyrannical than he might have done. *Dejar hacer* was an effective means of absolutist control, particularly in the area of that most subtle form of repression, corruption.

Despite a reputation for strict personal austerity and puritanism, Franco never took action against corruption. His own image as an austere man was to a large extent spurious. In his personal habits, he was certainly abstemious, rarely drinking, other than to take a glass of sweet wine, and never smoking. However, at the State's expense, he indulged the most extravagant tastes, including having the yacht *Azor* built for deep-sea fishing. His hunting trips and fishing expeditions with destroyer escorts were immensely costly. He and his wife acquired considerable property. She already owned a country estate, La Piniella, in Oviedo and Franco himself inherited the family home in El Ferrol. His palace at El Pardo belonged to the State. In November 1937, José María de Palacio y Abarzuza, Conde de las Almenas, died childless. He expressed his gratitude to Franco for 'reconquering Spain' by leaving him in his will an estate in the Sierra de Guadarrama near El Escorial, known as Canto del Pico. Consisting of 820,000 square metres, it was dominated by a large mansion called the Casa del Viento. There was also the Pazo de Meirás in Galicia, another reward for his efforts in the Civil War, and his estate near Móstoles on the outskirts of Madrid known as Valdefuentes. In addition, Doña Carmen acquired an apartment building in Madrid after the Civil War and, in 1962, the magnificent Palacio de Cornide in La Coruña. The family also acquired a further fifteen properties.[42] In addition, it has been calculated that Franco received four thousand million pesetas (approximately £4,000,000/$7,500,000) worth of gifts during his rule.[43]

The Caudillo's family became extremely rich. In addition to landed property, Franco's wife amassed a considerable collection of antiques and jewellery. Her penchant for jewellery led to her acquiring the nickname 'Doña Collares' (Doña Necklaces).[44] Franco's sister Pilar was to be involved in financial scandals. She claimed disingenuously that her business success was the consequence of the fact that 'my name made a good impression' (*mi nombre caía bien*) and 'opened many doors'.[45] His brother Nicolás was involved in questionable business deals which made use of his influence with the Caudillo and benefitted from the protection of the regime when they ended in scandal and accusations of fraud. His activities ranged from the simple sale of letters of introduction to ministers to profitable participation in companies with official links. Three in particular came to difficult ends from the consequences of which Nicolás was saved by the benevolence of his brother.[46] The family of his son-in-law, Cristóbal Martínez Bordiu, made a fortune as a consequence of their perceived closeness to the Caudillo. The same was true of many senior figures in the regime who were enriched by directorships and other connections in industry and the banking world.[47]

Spectacular fortunes were made by some of Franco's henchmen through bureaucratic graft and government contracts. Fortunes were made by Falangists responsible for the repair of war damage. Many officials were involved, too, in the black market which sprang up in the 1940s.[48] Malpractices – ranging from the Argentinian wheat, sent in 1949 to relieve Spain's hunger and sold abroad before it arrived, to the monster Matesa machinery export swindle of 1969 – were benevolently overlooked by the Caudillo.

Turning a blind eye to corruption allowed Franco to keep control over potential opponents. On the occasion of his return to Spain after fighting in Russia with the volunteers of the División Azul, the idealistic Falangist Dionisio Ridruejo told Franco that, among his comrades, there was much criticism of the corruption in Spain. The Caudillo replied complacently that in other times, victors were rewarded with titles of nobility and lands. Since to do so was now difficult, he found it necessary to turn a blind eye to venality to prevent the spread of discontent among his supporters.[49] Franco never showed the slightest interest in putting a stop to graft as opposed to using knowledge of it to increase his power over those involved. Indeed, he often repaid those who informed him of corruption not by taking action against the guilty but by letting them know who had informed on them.[50] This is hardly surprising given that the ultimate source of the Caudillo's power lay in astutely playing off the *familias*, or power groups, of the coalition which won the Civil War. His devious insouciance enveloped them in Byzantine competitions for the spoils of power.

Franco was a supreme master at political manipulation yet he had little or no interest in the free interplay of political life. It was entirely without humour or irony that Franco advised one of his subordinates (Sebastián Garrigues) to 'be like me, don't get involved in politics', a remark that he would later repeat regularly. On one occasion, he said with total conviction, 'I am here because I don't understand politics, nor am I a politician. That is my secret.'[51] In fact, his attitude to his rule in Spain was roughly what it would have been to Morocco had he been High Commissioner. In other words, he considered himself a supreme colonial ruler governing by military means. This was one reason why, although he kept control of the broad lines of policy until the early 1960s at least, he took little interest in what his ministers did within their departments. Another was that their very freedom and its venal temptations made them more likely to compromise themselves, more anxious not to lose their enjoyment of the spoils of power, thus more dependent on him. One ex-Foreign Minister, José Felix Lequerica, commented that 'to be a minister of Franco is to be a little king who does whatever he feels like without restraint from the Caudillo'.[52] According to Manuel Fraga, 'Franco let his ministers get on with the job'.[53]

Of course, aware of their dependence on him, Franco could be brutal with his ministers and was openly contemptuous of the most cherished institutions of his regime. He often proclaimed that the so-called 'organic' democracy of his pseudo-parliament, the Cortes, with its hand-picked 'representatives' was infinitely superior to western democracy which was tainted by the fact of reflecting the will of the masses. Yet, on one occasion when his liberal Catholic Minister, Joaquín Ruiz Gimeñez, made some remark which suggested that he took seriously the farce of the Cortes, the Caudillo impatiently snapped 'and who do the Cortes represent?'[54] On another, when one of his generals voted against a law in the Cortes, Franco was outraged, commenting 'if he doesn't like the project, he may abstain but never vote against since he owes his seat to me by direct nomination'.[55] He once remarked to one of his ambassadors that the Movimiento, his single-party amalgam of the Falange and the Carlists, was 'the claque which accompanies me on my tours around Spain'.[56] In these disdainful remarks, Franco was inadvertently recognizing that the legal and institutional structure of his regime was merely a carefully constructed façade to cover his personal dictatorship.

There can be little doubt that the area in which Franco's political skills were truly masterly was in the manipulation of his equals and his subordinates. He had an uncanny capacity to spot the weakness of an opponent that he could meet face-to-face. In this respect, he was no doubt helped by his prodigious memory. Perhaps the weapon which he handled with the greatest skill was the embarrassing silence which would reduce his interlocutor to nervous babbling.[57] Silence was not just used to intimidate. Although not interested in constructive dialogue, Franco listened carefully and rarely interrupted. He would remain impassive, looking inquisitively at the speaker and often appearing to agree with what was said without in fact committing himself or even revealing his opinion.[58] The ability to calibrate almost instantly the weakness and/or the price of a man enabled him to know unerringly when a would-be opponent could be turned into a collaborator by some preferment, or even the promise of it – a ministry, an embassy, a prestigious military posting, a job in a State enterprise, a decoration, an import licence or just a box of cigars. 'His agile left hand', as this skill was called by the Catalan politician Francesc Cambó, was the basis of his success. 'He toys with men – especially his generals – with consummate skill: now he puts the most brilliant of his aides into the shade, without anyone saying a word; now he plucks a prestigious prize out of nowhere and brings him back from the shadows into the light. And all these games he plays with such dexterity that they affect only the person concerned thereby avoiding any joint action against himself.'[59] On the few occasions on which he came across incorruptible men, such as Dionisio Ridruejo or the austere monarchist General Alfredo Kindelán, he was at first baffled and then irritated.[60]

This cynical instrumentalization of appointments was starkly clear in his selection of collaborators. For most of his career, Franco appointed ministers and other senior functionaries without concern for their practical competence in a given area but rather as part of his own balancing act within the Francoist coalition. He never felt any particular loyalty or gratitude towards those who had served him. Indeed, he once commented to his brother-in-law, Ramón Serrano Suñer, who had asked him to do something for an ex-minister, 'it is necessary to get everything out of them that they've got, squeeze them like lemons'.[61] His ministers usually learned that they had been dismissed from a letter delivered by motorcycle despatch rider or by reading a newspaper.

It would be wrong to exaggerate Franco's deviousness and powers of manipulation particularly in his earlier career. There is little doubt that Franco learned as he went along. In a sense, he had to shake off the political disadvantages of his spectacularly successful military career. Serrano Suñer claims that, shortly before the meeting with Hitler at Hendaye, he feared that it would be an unequal contest given Hitler's practice in wheeling and dealing as against Franco's experience of commanding. 'He was a very military kind of soldier. Obviously, he was not in the habit of arguing with political antagonists and had no practice in controversy. He had always commanded. His mental and intellectual activity was unilateral.'[62] Serrano Suñer made the same point to the Portuguese Ambassador Pedro Theotonio Pereira on 6 November 1940: 'the Generalísimo is a simple man. It is just as well he didn't speak much with Hitler.' In conversation with the Italian Ambassador Francesco Lequio in early 1941, Serrano Suñer explained the Hendaye summit's failure to bear fruit: 'Franco who has a more military than political mentality was ill-prepared for the tight dialectical game to which the Germans subjected him.'[63] Franco would learn, adding the techniques of political manipulation to already considerable instinctive skills in that area.

From the time that he reached political pre-eminence, Franco leaned heavily on three people and learned much from them. The first was his brother Nicolás, who handled political matters for him from the early days of the Civil War until 1937. However, he suffered from the disadvantage that Franco's wife did not like him. Accordingly, she was happy to see him replaced in early 1937 by Ramón Serrano Suñer, her sister's husband. Serrano Suñer was probably the most talented collaborator that Franco ever had. Eventually, in September 1942, he dismissed him. Several factors played their part in that particular crisis, including the irritation of Carmen Polo that her brother-in-law was putting her husband in the shade and the advice of the man who was emerging from the shadows as the man who would be the Caudillo's close familiar for the rest of his life. The dour and deferential naval captain Luis Carrero Blanco could not have been further removed in style from the handsome, swashbuckling Serrano Suñer who saw Franco as an equal and treated him as such, giving him frank and often unwelcome advice at a time when the Caudillo was increasingly surrounding himself with sycophants. Serrano Suñer was ambitious; Carrero Blanco, in contrast, had no greater ambition in life than to serve Franco. In that sense, he was a Francoist second only to Franco himself and an ideal servant for the Caudillo once he had squeezed the juice out of Serrano Suñer.

Franco came to be surrounded by sycophants from the early 1940s onwards. He, his wife and daughter tended to remain in El Pardo, leaving only for official functions at which their supreme importance as a semi-royal family was built into the choreography. Their perception of the outside world and their own place in it came through the filter of adulation. The judgement of the dictator and his wife was inevitably distorted.[64] After 1945, at El Pardo, the Caudillo's wife restricted her friendships to a court of admirers. It consisted of the wives of his life-long friends General Camilo Alonso Vega and Admiral Nieto Antúnez, and a monumental snob, Pura de Hoces y Dorticós, the Marquesa de Huétor. From the mid-1950s, an ever more important role was played in the El Pardo court by the wider family of Franco's son-in-law, the so-called 'Villaverde clan'.[65] The last thirty years of Franco's life took place in a hermetic world shut off even from his apparently closest friends. In his detailed chronicles of their more than seventy years of friendship and almost daily contact, his devoted cousin and aide-de-camp, Francisco Franco Salgado-Araujo, 'Pacón', presents a Franco who issued instructions, recounted his version of events or explained how the world was threatened by freemasonry and communism. Pacón never saw a Franco open to fruitful dialogue or to creative self-doubt. Another lifelong friend, Admiral Pedro Nieto Antúnez, presented a similar picture. Like Franco born in El Ferrol, 'Pedrolo' was to be successively ADC to the Caudillo in 1946, Assistant Head of the Casa Civil in 1950, and Minister for the Navy in 1962. He was one of Franco's constant companions on the frequent and lengthy fishing trips on the *Azor*. When asked what they talked about during the long days together, 'Pedrolo' said: 'I have never had a dialogue with the General. I have heard very long monologues from him, but he wasn't speaking to me but to himself.'[66]

It is hardly surprising, then, that the Caudillo remains the least known of the dictators of the twentieth century. For many years, there were rumours in Spain to the effect that he wrote memoirs.[67] However, all that has come to light is a brief hand-written synopsis, a few dozen pages written in 1962 and the reminiscences taped shortly before his death in 1975 by Dr Vicente Pozuelo.[68] None of it is sufficient to explain the contradiction between the profound and worldly wise cynicism with which he manipulated his political allies and adversaries and his ingenuous views on many issues. He had a touchingly naïve faith in virtually magical 'wheezes' which would solve a particular problem. During the Civil War, he placed his trust in the alchemist called Sarvapoldi Hammaralt who had offered to make all the gold that he needed to win the war. In 1940, Franco claimed that Spain would soon be a rich petroleum-exporting country. He was the victim of an elaborate fraud by an Austrian confidence trickster, Albert Elder von Filek, who had convinced him that he had the formula for an instant synthetic petrol made from water and powdered herbs.[69] After the capture of Málaga in 1937, Franco was presented with the arm of Santa Teresa, a relic which had been stolen from the Carmelite convent of Ronda. He kept it with him for the rest of his life, believing firmly in its miraculous powers.[70]

Franco held ideas almost equally startling in the field of economic theory. He believed economics to be one of his specialities and, in the first half of his dictatorship, he intervened personally in economic policy. He was especially proud of the notion that gold reserves were an irrelevance as long as their absence was kept secret. This conviction was consolidated during the Civil War. At that time, when the peseta was dramatically overvalued, he overruled his economic advisers who wanted to devalue it by half. In retrospect, he praised his own clarity of vision in ensuring that the peseta remained at a high rate 'which was the first time that a nation at war had managed to sustain, without gold or foreign currency, the quotation of its currency'.[71] He believed that he could maintain Spain's foreign earnings by the device of inflating the value of the currency, unaware of its impact on the competitiveness of exports.

Towards the end of the Civil War, he began to express his confidence in Spain's self-sufficiency. He boasted that his policies during the Civil War would seriously alter the basic economic theories which the world had hitherto taken as dogma.[72] After the war, he arranged for José María Zumalacarregui, the Professor of Economics at Madrid University, to visit him weekly to discuss the economy. After a few weeks, the professor excused himself, unable to put up with the embarrassment of listening to Franco explaining to him the most abstruse problems of economic theory.[73] In 1955, despite the fact that Germany and Italy were beginning to show clear signs of their future growth, the Caudillo told his cousin that 'at the end of the war, the victorious powers did not want the defeated to recover quickly from their prostration. To make sure that they would not, the defeated were obliged to adopt the democratic system because the victors were convinced that, in that way, prosperity would never come their way.'[74]

The fact that Franco could hold such views was the measure of his lack of intellectual sophistication. His life-long friend and one-time minister, Juan Antonio Suanzes, commented that Franco aspired to Alfonso XIII's facility to make small talk on any subject, a facility in which the King had been trained since his youth. Franco, however, according to Suanzes, 'with no preparation whatsoever, comes out with nothing but simple and trivial remarks whether they are relevant or not'.[75] When relaxed, with his family and close collaborators, Franco was an inveterate talker, a garrulous windbag according to his cousin.[76] This unsophisticated simplicity in no way diminishes his talents as a careful and cynical power-broker. The cautious Franco was most apparent in his control over his own tongue. The conversations recorded in the memoirs of his cousin and of Doctors Soriano, Gil and Pozuelo reveal a shocking mediocrity. Nevertheless, there is no doubt that, when exercising his remarkable skills for verbal fencing in face-to-face conversation, he could be as vague, ambiguous or simply silent as the occasion demanded.

Public speaking, however, was a different matter. He spoke with noticeable hesitance; his high-pitched voice and slight speech impediment, an audible rush of air across his teeth as he breathed in, prevented his ever being an impressive orator.[77] Yet the lavish compliments of the sycophants on his staff and the near hysterical response of his audiences soon dispelled any doubts that he might have had about his abilities.[78] Franco often opened public occasions by saying 'I'm a man of few words' (*Sólo dos palabras porque soy muy poco amigo de ellas*).[79] That was certainly not true of the Caudillo in private nor, as the thousands of pages of his speeches attest, of the public man. The presence of a large enthusiastic audience occasionally led him to depart from the written texts of his speeches and to commit slips of the tongue. That he regretted them may be deduced from the fact that they were often omitted from subsequent printed collections. The most startling example was his speech in Madrid on 17 July 1941 when his enthusiasm for the German invasion of Russia led him to the brink of a public declaration of war on the Axis side. Despite the fact that his speeches were usually sprinkled with the Falangist rhetoric of social justice, on one occasion he blurted out a stark statement of the class nature of his rule: 'Our Crusade is the only struggle in which the rich who went to war came out richer than when they started.'[80]

Franco may have lacked sophistication but he had a prodigious capacity for hard work. During the Civil War, a period in which he aged noticeably, he worked interminable hours, overseeing the war effort, maintaining military and diplomatic relations with the Axis powers and manoeuvring within the labyrinthine political struggles of the Nationalist camp. His propagandists never ceased to stress his resistance to discomfort and his powers of endurance. During the Civil War, Millán Astray tried to impress Ciano by selecting from all Franco's achievements his ability to spend fourteen hours at his desk without needing to relieve himself.[81] His iron bladder-control in meetings or on hunting trips was legendary – something of which he was proud and yet another of the ways in which he marked distance between himself and his father.[82] When Franco left a cabinet meeting on 6 December 1968 in order to go to the lavatory, it was the first time that he had interrupted such a session in thirty years. His ability to remain impassive throughout long meetings was described by one of his ministers as the triumph of the continent over the incontinent.[83]

However, in addition to the hard-working Caudillo, there was also a *homo ludens* who was dogged in the pursuit of pleasure. After the Civil War, Franco indulged to the full his passion for hunting and, in the late 1940s, discovered the delights of deep-sea fishing. He fished for salmon in the deep rivers of northern Spain, and for bigger deep-sea fish in the Atlantic, particularly in the company of his friend

Max Borrell.[84] His main objective seemed to be to kill as much as possible, suggesting that hunting, like soldiering before it, was the outlet for the sublimated aggression of the outwardly timid Franco. How essential it became to him was indicated by the increasing amounts of time devoted to the chase in the 1950s and 1960s. On one occasion, indicating the files stacked on his desk, the telephone and huge appointments book, he commented to José María Pemán, 'Look, if it weren't for hunting or for fishing which give one back a bit of nature, I couldn't put up with all this.' The hunting trips became notorious as the occasions for the distribution of favours and government contracts. Important sums changed hands as aspirants to Franco's favour sponsored hunts in order to gain access to the fount of patronage.[85]

Franco began to play golf in 1936 and was recommending it to his generals in 1940.[86] By the end of the 1940s, he had the audacity to explain to the Duque de Alba, who was also the Duke of Berwick, James Fitz-James Stuart y Falcó, how to make a golf-course.[87] Franco was gratified in the 1950s to discover that what had become a passion gave him something in common with President Eisenhower. When not at the chase or on the golf-course, he spent considerable time playing cards (*mus* and *tresillo*) and dominoes with his inner circle of military friends, General Camilo Alonso Vega, Admiral Pedro Nieto Antúnez and General Pablo Martín Alonso. He enjoyed watching movies in his private cinema and televised football matches. He also liked the *corrida de toros* (bull-fighting) about which he was knowledgeable, having become an *aficionado* during his time as Director of the Military Academy in Zaragoza. As he got older, he watched ever more television and had innumerable sets placed around the Pardo.[88] The long hours which he spent immobile watching the 1974 World Cup were a contributing factor to the attack of thromboflebitis which he suffered shortly afterwards. He even did the pools (*quiniela*) every week, for a time signing his coupon (*boleto*) Francisco Cofran, and winning twice. It is difficult, somehow, to imagine Hitler or Mussolini doing the pools.[89]

From the late 1950s, he was able to abandon many of the cares of government, leaving much of the day-to-day administration in the hands of Carrero Blanco and his team of technocrats. That left him many routine duties which he fulfilled in the manner of a monarch, receiving large numbers of people in audience, inaugurating public works, presiding at the meetings of the council of ministers and, perhaps most importantly, attending religious services. Foreign and Spanish admiration of Franco hinged to a considerable extent on his Catholicism. Both the approval of the Vatican, which he assiduously courted, and his own ostentatious religiosity after 1936 were eagerly taken by his admirers as distinguishing him from Hitler and Mussolini. However, it is difficult to measure with certainty the real depth of his Catholic faith. Prior to 1936, the issue was entirely ambiguous; Franco's view of religion was that of any bluff soldier. His early attitude to institutional Catholicism, if not his spirituality, was revealed at a lunch which he attended in 1935. The conversation hinged on an audience given by Pope Pius XI to Alfonso XIII. The exiled King, following traditional protocol, had knelt to kiss the right foot of the Pontiff. Franco commented contemptuously, 'the fact is that the King has made us Spaniards look ridiculous, genuflecting to kiss the dirty sandal of an old priest'.[90] On the other hand, his mother was a pious Catholic and, at least, to avoid offending her, he was assiduous in his religious duties when living with, or later visiting, her. In the same way, after his marriage in 1923 to Carmen Polo, from a prominent and traditional Oviedo family, his apparent Catholic piety increased. The Polo family was not as illustrious as it had been, and in its decline it became more snobbish and ostentatiously religious.[91]

The lifelong devotion to the relic of St Teresa indicated some form of primitive religious faith.[92] After his elevation to the Headship of State on 1 October 1936, his propagandists built him up as a great Catholic crusader and his public religiosity intensified. The endorsement of the Church mattered to him in gaining both foreign and domestic support. From 4 October 1936 until his death, he had a personal chaplain, Father José María Bulart.[93] On the other hand, it was said that religious ceremonial bored him almost more than anything else and he suffered agonies when he had to receive the visitations of religious groups, commenting 'we're doing saints today' (*hoy estamos de santos*). His pious wife had a small chapel next to their bedroom where she was assiduous in her devotions to the Virgen del Carmen and San Francisco de Asís.[94] In later life his religiosity increased and he spent hours praying in the small chapel at El Pardo. As Head of State, Franco went on retreat every year, once under the direction of the founder of the Opus Dei, Monseñor Escrivá de Balaguer.[95]

Franco was not a cultured man. It is reasonable to dismiss the claims of his adulators that he was one of the greatest novelists, journalists, painters and architects of all time. More intriguing is his wife's suggestion in an interview in 1928 that Franco enjoyed the novels of Ramón del Valle-Inclán.[96] Given that Valle-Inclán harshly satirized the Spanish officer corps and its elaborate sense of honour, this is frankly difficult to believe and smacks more of a wife trying to say 'the right thing' in public. The exotic and grotesque *avant-garde* fantasies of Valle-Inclán seem unlikely reading material for a man whose main literary influence, on the basis of *Raza*, seems to have been P. C. Wren's *Beau Geste*. From the beginning of the years in power, he rarely read books, skimmed newspapers, and had little interest in culture or the arts. Indeed, there is no convincing evidence that at any time in his life he was seriously attracted by books.

In later life, he began to create for himself a past in which his every free moment had been spent poring over books on politics, economics, social problems and military science. He deliberately conveyed this image to three British journalists, S. F. A. Coles, Brian Crozier and George Hills, as well as developing it in his draft memoirs.[97] A Franco ravenously devouring works of political science, sociology and economics, even when on duty in Africa, is difficult to accept. There is not a word about reading in his diary of his first year in the Legion. Whatever his post, he invariably had a full professional timetable during the day, which he always observed thoroughly. At night, as the writings of his cousin and others who knew him have testified, he was given to long dinners and even longer after-dinner conversations with his cronies. During the Civil War, his readiness to chat well into the early hours was the despair of his staff, who feared for the effects on his health of the consequent lack of sleep. When his residence at El Pardo was opened to the public as a museum after his death, it was apparent that he had no library. Aside from the lurid anti-communist bulletins of the Entente Internationale contre la Troisième Internationale, to which he was a subscriber, Franco's only known literary passion was for books about Napoleon. In 1953, Franco talked knowledgeably to the English journalist S. F. A. Coles about Napoleon's letters and his marginal notes to Machiavelli's *The Prince*. Coles was told that Franco secured his now well-thumbed copy of the annotated edition of the *The Prince* during the Civil War by sending a special courier through the lines.[98]

If Franco's reading centred on Napoleon, his other cultural interests were even narrower. He occasionally claimed that he liked painting and particularly the work of Velázquez.[99] Certainly, the canvases that he painted himself reflect the influence of the great age of Spanish painting. Pemán recounts accompanying a group of Spanish film-producers at an audience with the Caudillo. Franco listened to their specific request and then complained to them that too many American films were shown all of which 'exalted divorce and ignored family values'. Instead, he offered them a series of suitable subjects for new Spanish movies: the great imperialist heroes Cortés and Pizarro; the great symbol of the struggle against the Napoleonic invasion; the Dos de Mayo; or the sentimental mid nineteenth-century *zarzuela* (operetta) *Marina* by the Basque composer Emilio Arrieta. Some weeks later, a delegation from the Society of Authors visited him. He expressed his outrage at the production of so many foreign plays, from which he passed on to say that French Vaudeville was concerned only with beds and marital infidelities. From there he went on to make his already quoted remark in praise of Calderón and the 'detergent of blood'. Finally, he again suggested that the whole sorry mess, as he saw it, of the theatrical world could be remedied by a revival of *Marina*, a second-rank, conservative and thoroughly Italianate *zarzuela* with a naïvely romantic plot.[100]

The only music which Franco is known with any certainty to have liked is the *zarzuela* and military marches. Otherwise, the musical–cultural pretensions of Hitler are entirely absent. During the preparations for the festival of the three thousandth anniversary of Cádiz, Franco received a delegation from the city, among whom were those responsible for mounting Manuel de Falla's unfinished cantata *Atlántida*, a work which had occupied the last eighteen years of the maestro's life. In an effort to give the Caudillo a sense of its importance, the composer Ernesto Halffter, who had been responsible for editing Falla's unfinished text, said 'There is no more important work in all of Spanish music. I would even go so far as to say that it is our *Parsifal*.' At that Franco turned away, muttering 'Our *Parsifal*? What an almighty bore that will be.' It is difficult to interpret the remark as indicating that Franco shared a not uncommon response to Wagner's religious music-drama, since it is unlikely that he was acquainted with the work in whole or even in part. When *Atlántida* was finally premiered, in November 1961 at the Liceo in Barcelona, Franco sent the twenty-three-year-old Prince Juan Carlos to represent the Jefe del Estado.[101]

He took up painting originally in the 1940s to emulate Hitler, although he was delighted to discover in the 1950s that it gave him something in common with Churchill and that Eisenhower was known to dabble too. Only a small selection of Franco's pictures have ever been published, most having been destroyed in a fire in 1978. Their authenticity has never been questioned, and assuming that they are genuinely his work, they show a competent amateur whose work is of more interest to the psychiatrist than to the art critic. The subject matter suggests a conservative, petty-bourgeois taste. The influences are unmistakably those of the Goya tapestry cartoons and the great age of seventeenth-century Spanish painting in landscapes, still-lives of dead game and guns, a bloodthirsty portrayal of a bear being attacked by a pack of dogs. One interesting exception is a Modigliani-like portrait of his daughter Carmen.[102] It is noteworthy that the few well-known pictures show a remarkable similarity of subject matter to paintings by Carrero Blanco. Apart from still-lives of game and guns, among Carrero's canvases was one of a bull being attacked by a pack of dogs. The differences lie in the fact that Carrero Blanco's paintings are almost invariably copies of classic Spanish and Dutch painters whereas Franco, although conservative and derivative in style, is somewhat more imaginative in his choice of subjects.[103]

Franco seems to have had a dry, oblique and muted sense of humour although it has been claimed that he often told jokes, especially slightly smutty ones, and enjoyed hearing them. His cousin related that when he told any story more than once, it was 'without changing a word as if he was reading them out'.[104] Certainly, the examples of his jests that have survived do not suggest irresistible talent as a humourist. According to his sister, he had a sense of humour but didn't practice it.[105] There are a few anecdotes about a teasing irony when relaxed and in the intimate circle of friends and family. Apparently, in cabinet meetings, he would occasionally display a degree of malicious sarcasm (*sorna*) almost *sotto voce* and looking away from his victim.[106]

There also exist a few examples of cruel barrack-room practical jokes. In the course of 1918, there took place in Oviedo a trivial incident which is nevertheless worth recounting. One day, Franco decided to play a crude practical joke on one of his friends from the Real Automóvil Club de Oviedo, Dr Ricardo Pérez y Linares Rivas. He and three captains from his battalion, including his cousin Pacón Franco Salgado Araujo, disguised as cut-throats, waited one night for Linares in the Park of San Francisco. When he appeared, Franco shouted, 'Get that one', they ostentatiously opened enormous jack-knives and a terrified Linares ran for his life. When he realized who they were, he apparently took the joke in good part. A few days later, a delighted Franco told Pacón that he had received a telegram from the Ministry of the Army stating that approval had been granted for him to be awarded the Cruz Laureada de San Fernando. He made a great point of not telling Linares because he thought him incapable of keeping a secret. Finally, he said to him that he had an important piece of news and that he would have told him had he not been such a gossip. To Franco's outrage, Linares replied that there was no need since he knew all about it. He had sent the telegram in revenge for Franco's practical joke. Franco was furious, declaring that there was no comparison between a little fright and the anxious hopes of a soldier awaiting a decoration. 'It's easy to see that you are not a soldier. As far as I am concerned, our friendship is over.' It was several days before they were on speaking terms.[107] The episode and its aftermath shows that despite his battlefield achievements and his seniority, the twenty-six-year-old Franco was still something of an adolescent. It also shows the severe limits of his sense of humour. Both jokes were cruel, the revenge by Linares perhaps especially so, but Franco's reaction also stressed the extent to which he regarded things military as totally sacrosanct.

Another example of Franco's cruel humour concerned his cousin Pacón, who had poor sea legs and a consequent horror of sailing. On one occasion in the summer of 1954, as Head of Franco's Military Household, he was accompanying Franco on his yacht *Azor* from San Sebastián to a regatta at Lequeitio. With the Generalísimo's complicity, a sailor handed the admiral in charge a sealed envelope with a bogus storm warning, which he then read out in order to discomfit Pacón.[108] On a hunting party at the Sierra de Gredos in Avila in 1958, a rare female goat had been shot by accident, contrary to all the rules of conservation. With Franco's knowledge, his life-long friend, the rather stiff General Camilo Alonso Vega, an expert shot and an unlikely culprit, was blamed and mercilessly taunted by Franco for the alleged offence to the near apoplexy of his victim.[109]

Franco had delusions of being a royal personage, his pride demanding that he could be succeeded only by someone of royal blood. He always rejected out of hand the possibility of being succeeded by a non-royal president.[110] Indeed, throughout his rule, he avoided the title of president, limiting himself to that of Jefe del Estado, and exercising the functions of a king, a role that he assumed as naturally as he had that of military hero earlier in his career. The sincerity of his monarchist convictions cannot be calculated. During the Primo de Rivera dictatorship, Franco had maintained to General Castro Girona that it was the duty of the soldier to show unconditional obedience to whatever the King wished.[111] That loyalty disappeared in 1931 when Franco pragmatically decided to serve the Republic. There was little of it left by the time of the Civil War, although he was happy enough to let it be assumed that he was fighting in order to restore the monarchy.[112] His brother-in-law wrote that 'never, not for a single instant, did Franco consider letting an institution with a flesh and blood king overshadow the authority of his own position in which he had concentrated all the powers of the State'.[113] Alfonso XIII allegedly said of him shortly before he died, 'I picked Franco out when he was a nobody. He has double-crossed and deceived me at every turn.'[114]

After the war, as his own self-regard grew, Franco consistently avoided opportunities to bring back the King. That is not surprising, given the scale of the adulation to which he was subjected. In May 1939, Alexander W. Weddell, the recently arrived American Ambassador, and his wife Virginia were in the main square of San Sebastián when a car carrying Franco and Doña Carmen swept in. 'Without a sound or a signal the thousands of Spaniards who were in the plaza knelt down until the car had driven away.'[115] In the 1940s, Franco antagonized monarchists with a decree that the Royal March should be played whenever his wife arrived at a state function, as it had for the Queen before 1931.[116] He shocked some members of the Church hierarchy by his unwavering insistence on the royal prerogative of having a canopy borne above him during major ecclesiastical ceremonies, a privilege rarely used even by Alfonso XIII.[117] Franco clashed with Cardinal Segura of Seville in 1948 when the prelate refused to accord royal protocol to Doña Carmen.[118]

By accident or design, Franco's style of government, particularly after 1945, resembled that of a seventeenth-century monarch. He left day-to-day administration to his ministers and, increasingly, relied on Carrero Blanco as if he were his Richelieu or Olivares. Nevertheless, like the competent absolutist he was, he kept a tight grip on power. His household, or Casa Civil, was often run by an aristocrat, such as the Marqués de Huétor de Santillán or the Conde de Casa Loja. The Jefe de la Casa Civil always held the post of administrator of the Patrimonio Nacional which consisted of all of the palaces, parks and art treasures belonging to the royal family. For thirty-five years, the

Franco family had exclusive use of them. Franco bestowed titles of nobility as if he were a king and, having no sons of his own, created a dynasty in 1954 by changing his first grandson's name to Francisco Franco. The arrogance behind his delay in restoring the monarchy was revealed in a conversation in the 1960s with Fraga and Pemán when he said, 'I have not taken the crown from anyone. I found it in the gutter and I am still cleaning it. I will return it, at the right moment, with the agreement of the Cortes and the Spanish people to whichever person can best wear it.'[119] When one of his granddaughters married a Bourbon in 1972, there were widespread rumours about Señora Franco's royal ambitions and the possibility that the Caudillo might alter plans for the monarchical succession.[120]

As early as September 1942, a somewhat jaundiced Hitler had noted the regal inclinations in the Caudillo. 'When Franco appears in public, he is always surrounded by his Moorish Guard. He has assimilated all the mannerisms of royalty, and when the King returns, he will be the ideal stirrup-holder.'[121] Franco would be careful not to let the King return but, until the late 1950s, wherever he went his car was indeed surrounded by his personal bodyguard of Moorish cavalry, resplendent in blue uniform and white cloaks. This reflected caution as well as royal delusions. Nevertheless, he delighted in receiving foreign decorations and was insistent on maximum pomp and splendour on public occasions.[122] Franco's regal pretensions could be discerned in his insistence on the niceties of etiquette – although it also indicated a mechanism for covering up unease or resentment. To visit him at any time, morning clothes (*chaqué*) were *de rigueur*. The Duque de Alba once called upon Franco wearing a lounge suit instead of morning clothes or diplomatic uniform, only to be told to go away and come back suitably dressed for an audience with his Excellency the Chief of State.[123]

Franco's haughtiness struck another close observer, the American diplomat, Willard L. Beaulac, who served in Madrid during the Second World War: 'He greeted people courteously but without warmth. He was aloof in the manner sometimes associated with royalty. This quality of Franco's infuriated the nobility who suspected, doubtless with abundant reason, that Franco considered himself at least as good as royalty and better than nobility.'[124] Pacón said of him that, from his earliest days, he could be affable but was always reserved, never allowing anyone to establish intimacy with him. Nevertheless, he would lavishly reward those who flattered him while never finding 'a word of gratitude, a gesture of sympathy' for those who served him quietly for a lifetime.[125] José Sanchiz, a frequent hunting companion for more than a decade, the administrator of his estate in Valdefuentes and uncle by marriage of his son-in-law, said to Franco: '*¿No le parece que hemos llegado al punto en que nos podríamos tutear?*' (Isn't it time we used the intimate form of address?), to which Franco replied glacially, '*El trato que me corresponde es "Excelencia"*' (The correct mode of address for me is 'Your Excellency').[126] Even a genuine friend of forty years standing, Max Borrell, was never released from the obligation to address Franco as *Excelencia*. The same was true of his political chief of staff for thirty-five years, Luis Carrero Blanco.

Franco was often ill-at-ease with those who served him. Even at the hunting parties to which he was addicted, he could sometimes be cold and distant.[127] The fiercely Francoist priest, Fray Justo Pérez de Urbel, noted critically that Franco never had a word of praise for anyone. During the building of the Valle de los Caídos, a project dear to Franco's heart and one which he visited with remarkable frequency, the mosaic expert Padrós put in millions of stones yet the Caudillo never once even said good day to him.[128] On receiving visitors, no matter how important they were, Eisenhower included, he did little to put them at their ease, but took a chair with his back to a large window, himself silhouetted, them bathed in light, a mild form of interrogation technique.[129] Interviewed by *Le Figaro* on 13 January 1958, Franco made the revealing statement that 'the most complete statesman, the one most worthy of respect, that I have known is Salazar. I regard him as an extraordinary personality for his intelligence, his political sense, his humanity. His only defect is probably his modesty.'[130] That was not a defect of which Francisco Franco could have been accused.

3

The Absent Hero: José Antonio Primo de Rivera

Sixty years after his death, José Antonio Primo de Rivera is virtually unknown among his countrymen. Yet, he was the founder of Spain's fascist party, the Falange Española, which was to be the political instrument with which Franco ruled Spain for nearly four decades. After his execution by a Republican firing squad on 20 November 1936, he was converted into a symbolic martyr, the fulfilment of whose alleged plans for Spain provided a spurious justification for almost every act of the Caudillo. The case for assessment of the career of José Antonio Primo de Rivera in life and in death is overwhelming and is not in any way diminished by the fact that the cult of his memory so cynically and deafeningly built up by the regime was already an obsolete irrelevance before the demise of the dictator. Indeed, the importance of José Antonio Primo de Rivera as both man and myth is underlined by the existence of several contradictory myths enthusiastically used by the adulators of Franco, by Falangist opponents of Franco and even by anti-Francoist democrats.

Although none of these myths correspond precisely to historical reality, all feed on different aspects of José Antonio's multi-faceted personality, the fascination of which cannot be gainsaid. The most elaborate montage was constituted by the official Francoist myths of José Antonio as the saintly predecessor of the Caudillo, a Christ-like martyr in *la Cruzada* (the crusade, as the right called its war effort). This reached its tasteless apogee in a best-selling book entitled *Via crucis* (the Way of the Cross). Its chapter headings, each from a station of Jesus Christ's ascent of calvary, recounted José Antonio Primo de Rivera's life as an echo of that of the Messiah.[1] Many streets and squares, schools, university halls of residence and other official buildings were named after him. Virtually every church in Spain, with the exception of the Cathedral of Seville, had painted or carved on its walls the words *José Antonio Primo de Rivera, ¡Presente!* – a reference to the practice in the early days of ending meetings by shouting out the names of the absent (*ausente*) Falangist dead. Alongside the vaguely religious symbolism, there was a more direct political objective to this myth. The legends of a romantic and poetic leader of a Falange which was both revolutionary and *franquista* were carefully cultivated by the Franco regime to provide a populist mask for its own commitment to traditional oligarchic interests. The regime thus cried crocodile tears at José Antonio's absence while deriving immense benefit from the fact that he could not be an irksome presence.

Altogether more subtle and still pervasive are the myths of José Antonio, agent of reconciliation, above parties, certainly not a fascist, concerned only with the welfare of all Spaniards. This José Antonio would have opposed Franco and carried out *la revolución pendiente*, the Falange's great unfinished revolution.[2] In support of this view, there exists José Antonio's own dismissal of his suitability as a populist leader. In his first political manifesto, as a candidate in the June 1931 elections, he said, 'God knows that my vocation is among my books, and to leave them to throw myself into the sharp vertigo of politics causes me real pain.'[3] He wrote to a friend: 'I could be anything but a fascist caudillo. The attitude of doubt and the sense of irony which never leaves those of us who have had some intellectual curiosity renders us incapable of making the robust and categoric statements needed by the leaders of the masses.'[4] His political partner, Ramiro Ledesma Ramos, shared this view, regarding José Antonio's suave, rational scepticism, 'with his polite temperament and his legal education', as inclining him to parliamentary politics rather than fascism.[5] The philosopher Miguel de Unamuno said that he was too aristocratic (*excesivamente señorito*), too refined and, deep down, too shy, to be a political leader, let alone a dictator, 'to which it should be added that one of the basic requirements for the head of a fascist party is to be an epileptic'.[6] Falangist opponents of Franco propagated the idea that the young Primo de Rivera represented Spain's great lost opportunity, that somehow he could have led a Spain free of both the divisiveness of the Republic and the brutality of Francoism. This view can also be found in the writings of the exiled Socialist leader, Indalecio Prieto. Musing on the transfer of the mortal remains of José Antonio from the monastery of El Escorial to Franco's great mausoleum at the Valle de los Caídos in 1959, he wrote: 'He was a good-hearted man, unlike the man who will be his bed-fellow in the tomb at Cuelgamuros. José Antonio has been condemned to dishonourable company, which he certainly does not deserve, in the Valle de los Caídos. He is dishonoured by being associated with the atrocities and corruptions of others.'[7]

Both sets of myths – his official posthumous role as the holy predecessor of Franco and the unofficial as the revolutionary reconciler – have grains of truth, but they should not obscure certain inconvenient facts about José Antonio Primo de Rivera's political activities and his personal relationship with Franco. A detailed examination of his role during the Second Republic suggests that he was neither so poetic nor so progressive as the myths imply. It is reasonable to assume that the extremely shrewd Prieto wrote in the way he did in the hope of intensifying further the existing tensions between Franco and part of the Falange. Even if Prieto's outrage on behalf of Franco's bed-fellow is deemed to have been sincere, to sustain his conclusion would require much counter-factual speculation. José Antonio Primo de Rivera would have to be exonerated from any connection with the role played by the Falange as the violent destabilizer of Republican legality and as the blood-stained auxiliary repressive force which freed the military from the task of politically purging conquered territory during the Spanish Civil War.[8]

José Antonio was undoubtedly an attractive figure, shy but witty, cultured, personally courageous, loyal to his friends and a wickedly amusing journalist.[9] The American Ambassador, Claude Bowers, found him 'courtly, modest and deferential' and the Engish journalist Henry Buckley wrote that 'soft-voiced, courteous José Antonio was one of the nicest people in Madrid'.[10] The son of the dictator General Miguel Primo de Rivera, his loyalty to the memory of his father and his bravery in defending it, was what pulled him into politics.[11] An elegant lawyer-about-town, his saturnine good looks made him the heart-throb of many young women in the high society of 1930s Spain.[12] He shared little of the buffoonery of Mussolini or of the loud vulgarity of Hitler, and the attractions of his personality have seduced more than one Anglo-Saxon scholar.[13] Equally, the dignity of his death at the age of thirty-three facilitated the subsequent Francoist invention of a cult of his memory.

The founder of the Falange contributed significantly to the atmosphere of political violence which preceded the military uprising of 1936. Behind José Antonio's polished exterior there lurked a violence which occasionally turned him into a cheap brawler and even found its way into his theoretical statements. As a student in the 1920s, he was often involved in violent altercations. On several occasions in the 1930s he was involved in fist fights and duels because he took criticisms of the dictatorship as personal insults to his father.[14] Jealous of his own dignity, he refused to permit anyone to call him by the usual diminutives associated with his name, to the extent of once declaring 'If anyone called me Pepe or Don Pepe, I believe that I would be capable of shooting them.'[15] On one occasion, he leapt the benches of the Cortes to get to Indalecio Prieto whom he perceived to have insulted the memory of his father. In the ensuing brawl, 'he functioned like a punching machine'. On another, he knocked down the Radical deputy for Cuenca, José María Alvarez Mendizábal. As his victim reeled backwards towards the government benches, José Antonio sneered, 'Thank me because I've helped you get to the front bench for once in your life, albeit rolling on the floor.'[16] It is likely, however, that the use of violence was, at least sometimes, coldly fabricated in search of an appropriately 'fascist' image. According to a perceptive monarchist observer, 'he made a show of a strong and violent attitude but, really, if he acted on it, it was because he believed it to be for the good of his organization. He was violent not because he was impulsive, incapable of reason and given to risking, because of his aggression, something for which he carried the responsibility. He was cold, moderate and of sound judgement.'[17] This view was shared by his friend José Finat y Escrivá de Romaní, the Conde de Mayalde, who said that he 'conceived and carried out violence with his surprisingly cold head'.[18] In such a spirit of calculation, in order to keep alive the idea that the Falange was at war, he refused to have his car repaired after its bodywork was damaged in a bomb attack on 10 April 1934.[19]

He seems to have derived some pleasure from what were called 'laxative sanctions', the forcing of castor-oil on the Falange's enemies and spoke of the 'joyful irresponsibility' necessary for assaults on newspaper kiosks.[20] His cult of violence facilitated the destabilization of the politics of the Second Republic. His blue-shirted militias, with their Roman salutes and their ritual chants of '¡*Arriba España*!' (Arise, Spain!) and '¡*España*! ¡*Una*! ¡*España*! ¡*Libre*! ¡*España*! ¡*Grande*!' (Spain – One, Free, Great), aped Nazi and Fascist models. From 1933 to 1936, Falange Española functioned as the shock-troops of the haute bourgeoisie, provoking street brawls and helping to generate the lawlessness which, exaggerated by the right-wing press, was used to justify the military rising. The intrinsic violence, personal and political, of José Antonio – whether calculated or spontaneous – undermines his posthumous image as an agent of reconciliation in November 1936.

Similarly, the notion of a progressive, left-wing José Antonio propounded by opposition Falangists is impossible to sustain.[21] To begin with, it is difficult to explain away the close links between José Antonio and the southern landowning oligarchy. He was born on 24 April 1903 into a distinguished and comfortably wealthy Andalusian military family. His great-uncle, Fernando Primo de Rivera y Sobremonte, was made Marqués de Estella for his part in the siege of that Navarrese town during the second Carlist war. On General Fernando Primo de Rivera's death, successive holders of the title, including José Antonio himself, had the status of 'grandes de España'. There were aristocratic connections too through his mother, Doña Casilda Sáenz de Heredia.[22] An instinctive snobbery *de señorito* rendered José Antonio an unlikely leader of Spain's hungry masses.[23] He frequented the best restaurants and bars, cultivated an exquisite elegance of dress, wearing only English suits, and collected English equine prints. He was often to be seen in the Ritz in evening dress, was a wine connoisseur and drove a red sports car. His great passions were horses, riding and hunting. In early 1934, two Falangists were assassinated. The first, Vicente Pérez Rodríguez, was killed on 27 January. The news reached José Antonio when he was at a ball at the fashionable Madrid country club at Puerta de Hierro. The second, Matías Montero, was killed on 9 February. José Antonio was late for the funeral because he had been out hunting.[24]

He regarded the ability to ride well as crucial. Accordingly, he discounted the monarchist leader José Calvo Sotelo as a potential caudillo because 'he couldn't ride' (*porque no sabía montar a caballo*). He commented that he never understood how 'it could be possible to be chief of anything of importance without being able to cut a dashing figure in the saddle astride a nervous and potent brute which must be dominated by one's thighs and knees, with one's ankles and with one's intelligence'.[25] This haughty disdain sat ill with the young Primo de Rivera's populist pretensions. In fact, José Antonio's first experience in politics was as vice-secretary general to the Unión Monárquica Nacional, a monarchist organization of ex-ministers and collaborators of his father. He also stood unsuccessfully as a monarchist candidate for Madrid in a by-election in October 1931.[26]

Indeed, the monarchist aristocrat José Antonio Primo de Rivera had little to do with the first pioneering efforts to create a Spanish fascism made by the deranged surrealist Ernesto Giménez Caballero, by the eccentric Dr José María Albiñana, by the would-be Nazi and translator of *Mein Kampf* Onésimo Redondo Ortega, or by the post-office functionary and energetic student of German philosophy, Ramiro Ledesma Ramos. Giménez Caballero was author of surrealist classics such as *Yo, inspector de alcantarillas* (Me, Sewer Inspector) and innumerable political works drenched in overt sexual metaphors which constitute a kind of erotico-fascism. During the Spanish Civil War, he became a slavish sycophant of Franco, producing panegyrics to the Caudillo along the lines of: 'Who has penetrated the innermost parts of Spain like Franco to the point where it is not clear if Spain is Franco or Franco is Spain? Oh Franco, our Caudillo, father of Spain!'[27] His contribution to the introduction of fascism into Spain derived from his love affair with Rome. In 1927, he founded the literary magazine *La Gaceta Literaria* through which he imported into Spain Italian fascist ideas. He was in many respects the principal ideological precursor of Spanish fascism, although Ledesma Ramos would eventually split with him precisely because of his excessive Italophilia.[28]

Albiñana, a Valencian neurologist and admirer of General Primo de Rivera, was the author of more than twenty novels and books on neurasthenia, religion, the history and philosophy of medicine and Spanish politics, and a number of mildly imperialist works about Mexico. In April 1930, he launched his Partido Nacionalista Español, 'Hispanic brotherhood of energetic action' with the aim of 'annihilating the internal enemies of the fatherland'. Its objectives were the defence of religious principles, of the political unity of Spain, of the monarchy and of the army. A fascist appearance was provided by a blue-shirted, Roman-saluting Legionarios de España, a 'citizen volunteer force to act directly, explosively and expeditiously against any initiative which attacks or diminishes the prestige of the fatherland'. Although he declared himself 'a new man' and announced the need for the seizure of power, Albiñana, for all his authoritarianism, nationalism and anti-Semitism, was essentially a conservative. Eventually, Albiñana linked up with the monarchists of Renovación Española.[29]

The first effort to create an overtly fascist party in Spain was launched in February 1931, when ten men met in a squalid room in an office block in Madrid. The light had not been connected and the only furniture was a table. They signed a manifesto composed by Ledesma Ramos called *La Conquista del Estado* (The Conquest of the State). José Antonio was not one of their number. An eleventh,

Giménez Caballero, telephoned his support from Barcelona. A newspaper of the same name was launched on 14 March and published over the next year, despite public indifference and police harassment.[30] Three months later, Onésimo Redondo, a functionary of the sugarbeet growers' association, founded a fascist group in Valladolid under the name La Junta Castellana de Actuación Hispánica. In October 1931, these two tiny organizations fused into Las Juntas de Ofensiva Nacional-Sindicalista (JONS), a penurious outfit whose greatest asset was their symbol, the yoke and the arrows. They could not pay the hundred pesetas per month rent on their modest Madrid headquarters and could barely afford to produce propaganda leaflets.[31] According to the Italian Ambassador Raffaele Guariglia, although they could fight university students, they were too weak to take on Socialist or Communist labour organizations in the streets.[32]

While these early attempts were being made to launch fascism in Spain, José Antonio Primo de Rivera was busy working for the Unión Monárquica. It was during this period that José Antonio first met General Franco. After the Falangist leader's death, the idea of Franco as the representative on earth of the absent José Antonio was built up assiduously by the regime. In fact there was considerable personal acrimony between them and, in power, Franco systematically ignored the legacy, such as it was, of Primo de Rivera's thought. Their first meeting took place in Zaragoza in the early 1930s. At the time, Franco was the Director of the General Military Academy in Zaragoza where he had become friendly with a brilliant lawyer, Ramón Serrano Suñer. When, in February 1931, Serrano Suñer married Zita Polo, the beautiful sister of Franco's wife, Carmen, in Oviedo, the bride was given away by her brother-in-law, Francisco Franco; the groom's witness was José Antonio Primo de Rivera.[33] Despite the encouragement of Serrano Suñer, the dour, hard-working general and the rising young lawyer did not become friends. Although both opposed the Second Republic, their style and attitudes could not have been more different. Even when involved in the creation of Falange Española, José Antonio remained a popular socialite and a witty journalist. He was the antithesis of the general ten years his senior, whose eminence owed nothing to the advantages of birth or verbal brilliance and everything to hard work and bravery. Exclusively concerned with safeguarding his military career in a hostile environment, and never a man to look backwards, Franco was not inclined to sympathize with José Antonio's efforts to defend his father.

It was not until 1933 that José Antonio, inspired by the success of Hitler, developed an interest in fascism. Along with his father's one-time collaborator, Manuel Delgado Barreto, editor of the conservative daily, *La Nación*, he was involved in an attempt to launch a paper called *El Fascio* in February 1933. They were joined by Giménez Caballero, Ledesma Ramos, Rafael Sánchez Mazas and Juan Aparicio, their 'adolescent eyes opened by the triumph of Hitler' and the Nazi victory marches portrayed on cinema screens. Only one issue of *El Fascio* ever appeared. It carried an article on the New State by José Antonio Primo de Rivera entitled 'Orientaciones' and signed 'E' (for Estella). As Juan Aparicio wrote later, 'The Marqués de Estella remained reluctant to give up the historic links of his family past.' Not that it mattered, since most copies were seized by the police. Nevertheless, the group continued to meet and was soon joined by the famous aviator Julio Ruiz de Alda and the young university professor and disciple of the philosopher José Ortega y Gasset, Alfonso García Valdecasas.[34] They formed a group called the Movimiento Español Sindicalista whose propaganda carried the subtitle '*Fascismo Español*'.[35]

José Antonio Primo de Rivera seems by this time to have decided that if there was ever to be a significant fascist option in Spain, he would have to supply it. During 1933 he therefore embarked on a three-pronged plan which involved seeking support from the traditional right, gaining the backing of Fascist Italy and finding ways of unifying the existing fascist embryos. The link with Fascist Italy was not simply a question of immediate finance but rather lay at the heart of José Antonio's imperialist project. The Falangist alternative to the class struggle was empire. However, an awareness that Spain alone would be unable to challenge the international hegemony of Britain and France led José Antonio and his followers to think in terms of an alliance with other powers anxious to overturn that hegemony. In José Antonio's sympathy for Italy and Germany can be seen the hope, shared by Franco, that, in conjunction with Fascists and Nazis, Falangist Spain could overthrow the possessing powers and seize an empire.[36] As Herbert Southworth has shown, the ambition of Franco was directed against Britain and France far more than against Soviet Russia.[37] Like Franco, José Antonio loathed the League of Nations. On one occasion, his friend Juan Antonio Giménez Arnau, *en route* for Switzerland, asked him, 'Is there anything I can do for you in Geneva?' José Antonio replied, 'If you have time, burn it down.'[38]

In search of links with like-minded groups, José Antonio Primo de Rivera entered into contact with the JONS and, through García Valdecasas, with Frente Español (Spanish Front), a group consisting of young followers of Ortega y Gasset, including the historian Juan Antonio Maravall. Having formed the Agrupación al Servicio de la República, Ortega had become disillusioned by the reality of democracy. Frente Español had emerged in March 1932 and never acquired more than the couple of dozen members who took turns waiting in vain at their offices for new recruits to turn up. Most of them would finally pull back from the prospect of creating a full-blown fascist organisation but García Valdecasas was convinced that the name Frente Español and particularly its initials (*FE* spells faith in Spanish) had a political value. He was open to the idea of fusing this moribund shell with the dynamic, but unstructured Movimiento Español Sindicalista – Fascismo Español. His erstwhile comrades from the organization opposed the use of its title for a new fascist group. The name Falange Española was chosen in an attempt to retain part of the original cachet and the statutes of the Falange were those of Frente Español.[39] José Antonio Primo de Rivera derived from Ortega y Gasset several of his central ideas: the nation as a community of destiny, the need to 'give Spain a backbone' (*vertebrar España*), the relation of the élite to the masses. However, he was never to forgive Ortega for failing fully to embrace Spanish fascism.[40]

The leadership of the new party Falange Española consisted of José Antonio and García Valdecasas, along with the aviator, Julio Ruiz de Alda, who had accompanied Ramón Franco on his historic transatlantic flight in 1926. At a meeting in San Sebastían in late August 1933, organised by the Basque extreme rightist, José María de Areilza, at the time linked to both Acción Española and the JONS, they tried unsuccessfully to secure the participation of Ledesma Ramos. The JONS leader, endlessly suspicious of the upper-class connections of Primo de Rivera, simply insisted that the newcomers join his party. Ledesma did, however, despite his suspicions of the haute bourgeoisie, accept from the monarchists of Acción Española the gift of a motorbike which he rode on his propaganda trips around Spain.[41] More successful was the agreement made in August 1933 by José Antonio Primo de Rivera with representatives of the Carlist organization the Traditionalist Communion and the monarchists of Renovación Española represented by Pedro Sainz Rodríguez and José Antonio de Sangróniz – the so-called Pacto de El Escorial. The monarchists undertook to finance the Falange to the tune of 10,000 pesctas per month in return for the Falange's not opposing the restoration of the monarchy and for an undertaking that the Falange would consult with them on major policy initiatives. Even before Falange Española was officially launched it was thus already tied to the most conservative sectors of the old patrician right. A cordial arrangement seems to have existed for some time thereafter with Sainz Rodríguez, nominated as the monarchist liaison with the Falange. Sainz Rodríguez even helped José Antonio in the drafting of the Falange's programme.[42]

Having secured the backing of the traditional right and gone some of the way to uniting the disparate fascist fragments, Primo de Rivera turned to his goal of securing Italian endorsement. He was fortunate that the Italian Ambassador in Madrid, Raffaele Guariglia, was a firm advocate of Rome's providing material help for the establishment of a Spanish fascist party. Armed with a letter of introduction from Guariglia, José Antonio Primo de Rivera went to Italy in mid-October 1933 'to obtain information about Italian Fascism and the achievements of its regime. And also to get, as far as possible, advice on the organization of a similar movement in Spain.' He was received by Mussolini on the evening of 19 October. A few minutes before the meeting, he told an Italian journalist, 'I am like a pupil about to see the teacher. How much good he could do, if he wanted and I am sure that he will want to, for me, for my movement and for my country. He was a friend of my father, he will surely help me.' The meeting itself was evoked by José Antonio in his introduction to the Spanish translation of Mussolini's *La Dottrina del fascismo*, a reverential piece in which he describes the Duce in a corner of his immense, cold, marble-clad office, working while Rome relaxed, 'watching over Italy, listening to her breathing as if to that of small daughter . . . the hero made father, beside the eternal lamplight, keeping vigil over the anxieties and the slumber of his people'. While in Rome, he visited the offices of the Partito Nazionale Fascista and was given all the information that he sought.[43] The Duce presented him with an autographed photograph that he hung thereafter in his office next to a portrait of his father.[44]

The creation of Falange Española was announced by José Antonio ten days later, during the election campaign of November 1933. Recruiting had started in early October. New militants were required to fill in a form which asked if they had a bicycle – a euphemism for pistol – and were then issued with a truncheon (*porra*). The formal launch took place on Sunday 29 October at the Teatro de la Comedia in Madrid. Defence squads around the building were organized by the chief of the Falange militias, Lieutenant Colonel Ricardo de Rada.[45] In his otherwise poetically flowery inaugural speech, José Antonio made much of his commitment to violence: 'if our aims have to be achieved by violence, let us not hold back before violence. Because who has ever said – when speaking in terms of "anything other than violence" – that the highest of moral values is to be found in amiability? Who has ever said that, when our feelings our insulted, rather than react like men, we are obliged to be amiable? The dialectic is all very well as a first instrument of communication. But the only dialectic admissible when justice or the Fatherland is offended is the dialectic of fists and pistols.'[46] Although violence was to become a commonplace of the politics of Spain in the 1930s, no politician incorporated the rhetoric of violence so lyrically into his oratorical repertoire. This was frequently evident at the funeral rituals which, in emulation of the practice of the Italian Fascist Squadristi, followed the participation of Falangists in street violence.[47] Paradoxically, after the meeting, José Antonio told his devoted biographer, Felipe Ximénez de Sándoval, 'The masses embarrass me. The idea of hundreds of eyes fixed on me causes me real distress . . . How I suffered on seeing the arms raised to salute me!'[48] This led to a lack of spontaneity which he covered by elaborate preparation. According to the Jonsista, Javier Martínez Bedoya, 'he was one of those orators who learn their speeches by heart, even down to the full-stops and commas, but he was prodigious in his diction, in his range of expression, in the elegance of his gestures . . .' According to his friend, Raimundo Fernández Cuesta, his speech at the Comedia had been carefully rehearsed – 'he hated improvisation and said that those speakers who stand up without knowing what they are going to say cheat their audiences'.[49]

Within four weeks of the party's foundation, García Valdecasas had disappeared on an interminable honeymoon with a wealthy aristocratic bride.[50] José Antonio also took advantage of all his conservative connections in running on a monarchist slate for a seat in the Cortes for Cádiz, where his family enjoyed enormous influence. Thanks to the electoral power of the local ultra-conservative landowners, he was elected with 49,028 votes, 18.5 per cent of the total cast, a figure far in excess of anything that he could have managed running as a Falangist. His decision reflected the financial weakness of the Falange although there is no reason to suppose that either he or the Cádiz monarchists were uncomfortable with the arrangement.[51] Indeed, he told the Italian chargé d'affaires, Geisser Celesia, of his disappointment that neither the leader of the Catholic authoritarian CEDA party, José María Gil Robles, nor the 'grandes de España' would finance the Falange. This was an unusually frank admission to Mussolini's representative and one which revealed the limitations of his desire to break free of conservative influences. For Celesia, José Antonio was a *señorito* who could never appeal to the masses precisely because he looked to the oligarchy for his finance.[52]

The appearance of a new fascist party to rival the JONS caused financial problems for both and stimulated thoughts of union. At first, Ledesma Ramos was reluctant to see the JONS join with the Falange, but some of his lieutenants, notably Francisco Bravo Martínez and Ernesto Giménez Caballero, persuaded him that the logic of eventual fusion was unavoidable.[53] The rich had not been prepared to fund Ledesma Ramos – when he managed to secure an interview at the Ritz with the Catalan millionaire Francesc Cambó, he was quickly seen off.[54] In contrast, monarchists had been prepared to finance the Falange as an instrument of political destabilization. José Antonio's credentials as a southern landowner, a 'grande de España', an eligible socialite, and above all as the eldest son of the late lamented military dictator, seemed to offer a guarantee to the upper classes that Spanish fascism would not get out of establishment control in the way of its German and Italian equivalents. Understandably therefore, monarchist enthusiasm for José Antonio diminished somewhat when, on 15 February 1934, he fused Falange Española with Ledesma's more radical Juntas de Ofensiva Nacional-Sindicalista. During negotiations which had taken place over the previous three days, José Antonio made numerous symbolic concessions in terms of the name and the flag but was adamant that the new FE de las JONS was to be ruled over by a three-man executive made up of two Falangists and one Jonsista.[55] The triumvirate consisted of Primo de Rivera, Ruiz de Alda and Ledesma Ramos. It was not long before José Antonio was able to please his new allies with a gesture which seemed to manifest some of the radicalism associated with the JONS. In May 1934, he rejected an attempt to join the Falange by José Calvo Sotelo, who had recently returned from exile after being amnestied. Ledesma Ramos fondly believed that Calvo Sotelo was excluded because José Antonio regarded him as too closely linked to the grand bourgeoisie. In fact, José Antonio felt a simmering hostility to the monarchist leader whom he believed had fled like a coward rather than defend the record of the Dictatorship. Thus patrician disdain and personal resentment, rather than any inclination to prevent the radicalism of the new party being tainted by Calvo Sotelo's conservatism, lay behind the rejection.[56] Nevertheless, the gesture did nothing to improve the Falange's relationship with its erstwhile backers.

The link with the JONS intensified the contradictions between José Antonio's aristocratic instincts and his populist ambitions. This was to have economic consequences. Partly in reaction to these financial difficulties, José Antonio began in early 1934 to fish for an invitation to Nazi Germany. There was also an element of sympathetic curiosity behind his visit – he had been an avid reader of *Mein Kampf* and Alfred Rosenberg's *Der Mythus der zwanzigsten Jahrhunderts* (The Myth of the Twentieth Century). He met Hitler in Berlin in May 1934 but the Germans had little interest in giving him financial assistance.[57] In some frustration, the Italian Embassy reported regularly throughout 1934 that the new party had financial problems and that its violent acts of retaliation against the left were clumsily handled. On one occasion, after a Falangist had been killed, a group of leading Falangists sat around a table spinning a pistol to see who would undertake the reprisal. In fact, no action was taken but, on leaving the meeting, José Antonio said, 'I wasn't born for this, I was meant to be an eighteenth-century mathematician.' Celesia attributed the party's lack of popular impact to the fact that José Antonio Primo de Rivera was a *señorito* and that his speeches had little appeal to the masses, since they were either theoretical disquisitions or defences of his father. Guariglia lamented that 'in this great political lunatic asylum that is called Spain' (*in questo immenso manicomio politico che si chiama la Spagna*), the new fascists could do nothing beyond issuing verbal statements and leave the hopes of the right in the Catholic CEDA.[58]

Accordingly, the FE de las JONS remained dependent on grudging monarchist charity. In April 1934, for a nominal rent, one of the party's few rich backers, Francisco Moreno y Herrera, the Marqués de La Eliseda, had permitted use of one of his Madrid houses, at Marqués de Riscal 12, as Falange headquarters.[59] Eliseda complained to Celesia in September 1934 that cash was tight, but recruitment booming, because the Falange was going towards the left. Eliseda abandoned the party two months later and endeavoured to evict the Falange from his property. José Antonio used every possible legal subterfuge to permit his men to go on using the premises. Eliseda retaliated by cutting off the gas and the electricity, which were surreptitiously and illegally reconnected. Always happier to direct violence against the left than the right, José Antonio then intervened to stop enraged comrades giving Eliseda a dose of castor-oil.[60]

The marriage of the two parties, financial difficulties aside, was never an easy one. Conflict derived from the different ambitions of José Antonio and Ramiro Ledesma Ramos, the one élitist, the other populist. Tensions were provoked in the summer of 1934 by the monarchist adventurer Juan Antonio Ansaldo. A well-known aviator and playboy, Ansaldo had joined the Falange in late April at the invitation of José Antonio. He was given the title of 'Jefe de Objetivos', a euphemism which covered his organization of terrorist squads. Although uneasy about his reactionary monarchism, Ledesma approved of the efficacy with which Ansaldo toughened up what was called the 'Falange de la Sangre' (the Falange of Blood):

> His presence in the party was of undeniable utility because he found a place for that active, violent sector which the reactionary spirit produces everywhere as one of the most fertile ingredients for the national armed struggle. Remember what analogous groups meant for German Hitlerism especially in its early stages.

During the summer, a plan to blow up the Casa del Pueblo of Madrid (the Socialist headquarters) reached an advanced stage. The followers of Ansaldo were disappointed that José Antonio did not throw greater weight into the terrorist destabilization of the Republic. There was even talk of a group of militia officials led by Ansaldo threatening him with expulsion from the leadership if he did not drop what was perceived as his policy of appeasement. Matters grew worse after the discovery by the police, on 10 July 1934, of large quantities of guns, ammunition, dynamite and bombs at the Marqués de Riscal headquarters. Eighty militants, mainly Jonsistas and members of Ansaldo's squads, were imprisoned for three weeks. During the days spent in prison, criticisms of Primo de Rivera's leadership surfaced. Moreover, Ansaldo and the militia leaders, together with the Jonsistas, were particularly incensed by José Antonio's evident enjoyment in participating in Cortes debates. They were even more outraged by the fact that, on 3 June 1934, José Antonio had crossed the chamber in order to shake Prieto's hand, after the Socialist leader had opposed the lifting of his parliamentary immunity and that of the Socialist Juan Lozano, parliamentary deputy for Jaén, which would have permitted their being tried for illicit possession of arms (*tenencia ilícita de armas*). The Ansaldo-inspired mutterings widened into a broader conflict between Falangistas and Jonsistas.[61]

When he found out what was happening, José Antonio immediately expelled Ansaldo before the end of July, commenting that the conspirators involved in this 'dirty intrigue' matched 'their felony with their imbecility'. Thereafter, the hit-squads continued to carry out reprisals against the left with equal frequency and efficiency, albeit with greater loyalty to José Antonio Primo de Rivera. With apparent reluctance, he then moved in September 1934 to abandon the triumvirate and assume sole leadership of the Falange.[62] He cannot have been unaware of the involvement of Ramiro Ledesma in Ansaldo's conspiracy. The Falange's student leader, Alejandro Salazar, wrote in his diary in the summer: 'For some time now Ramiro Ledesma is no longer one of ours.'[63] In fact, Ledesma Ramos was always resentful of Primo de Rivera's aristocratic background and his wealth. The resentment was intensified by the fact that he was prevented from ever matching José Antonio as a fascist orator by a speech defect – a defect cruelly mocked by José Antonio later.[64]

In the late summer of 1934, when left–right tension was reaching a peak, José Antonio took an initiative which substantiated the suspicions of Ledesma Ramos that he could never break free of his family background and aristocratic instincts. He wrote an hysterical letter to Franco. In an attempt to incline Franco to make a coup against the left, he claimed that Socialist victory was imminent and equivalent to 'a foreign invasion' since France would seize the opportunity to annex Catalonia. Franco did not deign to reply. Now well-established as a Major General and a favoured confidant of the Minister of Defence, Diego Hidalgo, Franco was not remotely interested in assuming the risks involved in association with small-time fascist organizations. Believing that only the Army had the right and the might to determine the political destiny of Spain, Franco can have felt little but disdain for the nascent Falange.[65]

The first meeting of the Consejo Nacional of the Falange, convened to ratify José Antonio's assumption of the role of Jefe Nacional, was held from 4 to 7 October in Madrid. The left-wing uprising in Asturias on 6 October 1934 took place while the Consejo was in session. During the proceedings, it was decided to adopt the blue shirt. The Jonsistas present opposed the move on the grounds that the adoption of an overtly fascist style would cut off the movement from the revolutionary masses that they hoped to recruit. On 7 October, José Antonio, uncharacteristically wearing a blue shirt with the sleeves rolled up, visited the Prime Minister, Alejandro Lerroux. He offered the help of the Falange and asked – unsuccessfully – for his followers to be armed.[66] He then led a demonstration from Falange headquarters to the Puerta del Sol. Climbing onto the scaffolding which surrounded the construction site for the new metro, he made a speech in support of the government which Ledesma Ramos regarded as feeble and inappropriate. In the provinces, Falangists appear to have acted as auxiliary forces of order.[67] In Madrid, there seems to have been little by way of anti-revolutionary initiatives beyond the impromptu speech and an act of bullying. Dining out one evening after one of the sessions of the Consejo Nacional, José Antonio, his friend Raimundo Fernández Cuesta and Julio Ruiz de Alda threatened to beat up the Catalan student leader Antonio María Sbert if he did not leave the fashionable restaurant where they had just taken a table. Sbert had been the leader of the student opposition to the dictatorship of Miguel Primo de Rivera.[68] Celesia reported sarcastically to Rome that Falangists could be heard boasting in Madrid of having fought the revolution by collecting the odd dust-bin or giving a lift to an army officer in their cars.[69] The Falange played some small role in the repression after the Asturian insurrection.[70] However, even after the crushing of the left after the rising, the Italians complained of the failure of the Falange to impose itself on the situation.

José Antonio's conservative inclinations and his awareness of his ultimate dependence on the oligarchy was most starkly seen in the elaboration of the programme of the new party which followed the Consejo Nacional. A first, and radical, draft was drawn up by Francisco Bravo and Ledesma Ramos on behalf of the Junta Política (the permanent executive committee of the Consejo Nacional) which he chaired. Ledesma naïvely hoped to use the programme to facilitate the alliance with the anarcho-syndicalist CNT. The final version was the work of José Antonio, who had not only improved the prose but also rendered the programme more abstract and altogether less radical. A struggle for power grew out of friction over the programme and Ledesma's dismay that the Falange's trade union organization, the Central Obrera Nacional Sindicalista, was marginalized.[71] In late November, Geisser Celesia informed Rome that Ledesma Ramos was about to leave the Falange. In this he was being encouraged by one of the most radical of the Jonsistas, the ex-anarchist Nicasio Alvarez de Sotomayor.[72] In consequence, on 14 January 1935, Ledesma, Alvarez de Sotomayor and Onésimo Redondo announced that they would be reorganizing the JONS outside the Falange. Rather than accept this split, José Antonio announced to the Junta Política two days later that Ledesma had been expelled because of persistent factionalism. After José Antonio, in an impeccably tailored grey suit and crisp white shirt, had addressed a hostile group of blue-shirted syndicalists, the bulk of the JONS, including Onésimo Redondo, remained within FE de las JONS.[73]

In his own accounts, Ledesma denied that he had been pushed out and claimed that he had left of his own initiative because of 'irresolvable differences' with José Antonio over the deradicalization of the 27-point programme. He accused José Antonio of undermining the revolutionary mission of the JONS – 'the national-syndicalism that Primo de Rivera claimed to defend was a naïve trick, an empty fiction'.[74] In his own version, José Antonio spoke contemptuously of the factionalism of a few lumpenproletariat mercenaries: 'a few people brought up in the lowest depths, revolutionaries for hire, are those who have had to leave the Falange de las JONS not to establish any unity of thought, but for reasons of hygiene.' So intense were the divisions that allegedly only the intervention of José Antonio prevented a Falangist assassination attempt on Ledesma Ramos.[75] None the less, José Antonio led a Falangist hit-squad to seize the offices occupied by the JONS in the Calle del Príncipe.[76] He also published a savage attack on Ledesma, ridiculing his speech defect.[77] Only a small number of Jonsistas accompanied Ledesma. He threatened legal action against José Antonio Primo de Rivera to regain the name of his party,[78] but his effort to start a new party eventually came to naught and he returned to his job in the Post Office, only to be shot as a fascist at the beginning of the Civil War.

The removal of radical elements did not endear the Falange to the middle and upper classes. Satisfaction with conservative governments in 1935 ensured that financial support remained exiguous. Efforts to create a daily newspaper foundered.[79] José Antonio used his own money and received a few gifts from friends but the total raised was still inadequate. The Falange in Gijón rented a flat which belonged to Franco's wife, Carmen. When the general found out the use to which it was being put, he instructed his brother-in-law Ramón Serrano Suñer to tell José Antonio to evict his followers.[80] By the end of 1934, the Falange could not pay its lighting and heating bills. Shivering members of the leadership held meetings by candlelight.[81]

Primo de Rivera was finally obliged to turn to Mussolini. At the end of April 1935, he visited Italy again and was received in Genoa by Eugenio Coselschi, one-time secretary to D'Annunzio, the head of the Comitati d'Azione per la Universalità di Roma. Mussolini's equivalent of the Nazi Auslandorganization, the CAUR was placed within the Italian Ministry of Press and Propaganda under the direction of its under-secretary, Galeazzo Ciano, the Duce's son-in-law. Mussolini himself authorized funds for José Antonio. Between June 1935 and January 1936, he received It. L50,000 per month (i.e. about ptas 30,000 of the day) – a significant sum – in money deriving from police slush funds. José Antonio collected the money himself in bi-monthly instalments during visits to Paris in June, August, November 1935 and January 1936, receiving it from Amadeo Landini, the energetic press attaché at the Italian Embassy in Paris. From February 1936, with Italy suffering a crisis in its foreign currency reserves, the amount was to be reduced by half. José Antonio Primo de Rivera was unable to collect his payments for February and March, due in March, because by then he was in jail.[82]

Perhaps it was Italian criticisms of Falangist weakness and indecision which impelled José Antonio to make the ill-advised move to armed struggle to overthrow the democratic regime. Alarmed at the moderate scale of the repression after the October insurrection, José Antonio was anxious to take action before the left could return to power.[83] The decision was taken at a meeting of the Junta Política held at the Parador de Gredos in mid-July 1935. José Antonio reported to his comrades on his contacts with sympathetic army officers. He then put forward a plan for an uprising against the government to take place near the Portuguese frontier at Fuentes de Oñoro in the province of Salamanca. An unnamed general, possibly Sanjurjo, was to have secured 10,000 rifles in Portugal which would then be handed over to Falangist militants. The initial coup would then be followed by a 'march on Madrid'.[84] It was fraught with risk. With the left recently defeated and suffering ongoing repression, with an authoritarian right-wing government in power, with the most right-wing elements of the military in positions of power, the timing could not have been more inappropriate. Accordingly, José Antonio seems to have presented the idea in a half-hearted manner, hoping perhaps that it would never get beyond the planning stage. Senior military encouragement was not forthcoming and, probably to José Antonio's relief, the idea was quickly dropped. The head of the Falangist student organization, Alejandro Salazar, wrote bitterly in his diary, 'We returned from Gredos with wild enthusiasm only to see it converted into disillusionment on finding out that all we had done there was pass the time.'[85] The main consequence of the decision to move to armed struggle was ultimately the establishment by José Antonio of contacts with the ultra-rightist Unión Militar Española in an unsuccessful quest for weapons.[86]

Presumably it was in the knowledge that funds were now forthcoming from Italy, that José Antonio felt able to make a rashly radical speech at the Cine Madrid on 19 May 1935. He declared that the monarchy was dead and dissociated the Falange from 'monarchist reaction'. He complained that the counter-revolutionary forces in Spain 'had hoped at first that we would be the vanguard of their endangered interests, and so they offered to protect and help us at that time, and even to give us some money. And now they are crazed with despair when they see that what they thought would just be the vanguard has turned into a whole independent army.' Confident of Italian funding, he could declare his belief in the miracle of eventual success despite the fact that the Falange was 'attacked on all sides, without money, without newspapers'.[87] However, his tone changed in the course of the year. In his closing address to the second Consejo Nacional of the Falange in the Cine Madrid on 17 November 1935, he spoke in horrified terms of the Soviet assault on family life and religious values. He described the Russian Revolution as the 'invasion of the barbarians'.[88] As Southworth has pointed out, José Antonio, recognizing that his party could go nowhere without the financial support of the oligarchy, was trying to create an ambience of fear which might induce its members to finance the Falange as a means of self-defence.[89] However, it was too late. The damage had been done and boats had been burned.

On 2 October 1935, José Antonio spoke up firmly in the Cortes in favour of the Italian attack on Ethiopia. He was to some extent expressing gratitude for the financial assistance that he was receiving from Mussolini but his words also reflected his hopes that the Duce might undo the Anglo-French hegemony that enslaved Spain. He used the occasion for a fervent reminder of the indignity of British occupation of Gibraltar.[90] Elsewhere, he wrote, in terms reminiscent of Mussolini's rhetoric about Italian servitude in the Mediterranean, 'in foreign policy, weakness, servility, forgetting Gibraltar and Tangier. In a nutshell: spiritual and material ruin. Shame!'[91]

Perhaps because more serious elements of the army had shown no interest in Falangist overtures, José Antonio Primo de Rivera took a singularly hare-brained step at the end of 1935. In mid-December 1935, in complex circumstances, the government of Joaquín Chapaprieta fell, and with it José María Gil Robles, the CEDA leader who had been Minister of War since May. Several right-wing politicians tried to persuade senior generals to intervene in order to prevent new elections being called. The view held by General Franco, that the relative success of the working class during the events of October 1934 did not bode well for a military coup, prevailed. However, on 27 December, taking up a suggestion by the Jefe Provincial de Toledo, José Sainz Nothnagel, the Jefe Nacional proposed that several hundred Falangist militants join the cadets in the Alcázar of Toledo to make a *pronunciamiento*. It was a ridiculous idea in itself and one member of the Junta de Mando, José María Alfaro, tried to dissuade him by pointing out that the enterprise could be defeated in Toledo's narrow streets by people dropping flowerpots on the insurrectionaries. Nevertheless, José Antonio was filled with enthusiasm for the idea, declaring 'we will place machine-guns in the Puerta Visagra. I will handle one of them.' He sent his lieutenants Raimundo Fernández Cuesta, Alfaro and Sainz Nothnagel to Toledo to put this ill-considered proposal to Colonel José Moscardó, military governor and Director of the Escuela Central de Gimnasia there (the Central School of Physical Education). Their departure was delayed until after a dinner held by a gourmet dining-club to which José Antonio and Alfaro belonged, along with a number of prominent monarchists. As soon as Alfaro changed out of his dinner-jacket, they set off at 2 a.m., spending the remains of the night in an hotel in Toledo. Moscardó, whom they saw early the next morning, was a third-rank figure at best which perhaps explains why he did not dismiss the idea out of hand. Instead, he drove to Madrid to discuss it with Franco. It was José Antonio's good fortune that Franco, having just turned down rather better supported proposals, rejected the scheme as impracticable and badly timed.[92] Franco resented what he regarded as premature initiatives from civilians.[93]

Franco and José Antonio met again in February 1936 at the home of Ramón Serrano Suñer's father and brothers, just before the Popular Front elections in mid-February. José Antonio argued passionately in favour of a military coup in order to establish a counter-revolutionary national government. His charm was lost on Franco, who was cautiously evasive and rambled interminably. Regarding him as a dangerous dilettante, Franco had no intention of getting involved in conspiracy with him but typically failed to say so clearly. José Antonio was bitterly disillusioned and irritated, saying, 'my father for all his defects, for all his political disorientation, was something else altogether. He had humanity, decisiveness and nobility. But these people . . .'[94]

Despite the efforts of José Antonio, who visited Gil Robles on three occasions, the Falange was unable to reach an agreement with the conservative right in the preparations for the elections of mid-February 1936. He wanted more safe seats than the Falange's exiguous electoral support seemed to Gil Robles to justify. José Antonio refused to accept a few token seats which would, he claimed, have taken the Falange's votes while depriving the party of any role other than that of the guerrilla forces of the conservatives.[95] Since the safest seats were the Galician rotten boroughs and the Andalusian fiefs controlled by the ultra-conservatives of Renovación Española, José Antonio believed that his exclusion was influenced by Calvo Sotelo seeking revenge for the rejection of his own attempt to join the Falange.[96] Had the Falange formed part of the broad right-wing front, it is likely that José Antonio would have been elected. Alone, and lacking substantial popular appeal, he had little chance.

José Antonio campaigned tirelessly but, for all the rhetoric about being neither of the left nor the right, his sympathies were clear. The Falangist dissident and poet, Dionisio Ridruejo, demolished the idea of a left-wing Falange when he described the fury of José Antonio on witnessing a working-class demonstration in Madrid shortly after the Popular Front electoral victory of February 1936. José Antonio commented, 'With a pair of good marksmen, a demonstration like that can be dissolved in ten minutes.' Ridruejo wrote: 'Such reactions were a useful way to persuade those who deny the necessarily and viscerally rightist or reactionary character of the Falangist movement that, "cold", kept its distance from the wider counter-revolutionary movement and even felt repulsion for it, but that, "in the heat of the moment" found itself helplessly pulled into its orbit.' His distaste for Calvo Sotelo aside, José Antonio was prepared to let the Falange act as the instrument of the upper classes. As he said to Ridruejo, 'Let's hope that they finally wise up. We are ready to take the risks [*dispuestos a poner las narices*], no? Well let them, at least, provide the money.'[97]

That the allegedly left-wing José Antonio sought money from bankers and industrialists is no more surprising than that the indisputably nationalist José Antonio accepted money from Mussolini. Both facts remind us of the reality so conveniently forgotten by Francoist apologists, that the scale of support enjoyed by the Falange in 1936 hardly boded well for its leader's chances of becoming a serious political option by legal means. It is worth remembering that, whereas the cerebral Azaña attracted hundreds of thousands of Spaniards to his meetings *en campo abierto* during 1935, José Antonio never hypnotized a mass audience. Geisser Celesia complained of the 'scholastic and philosophical mentality' revealed in speeches by José Antonio that he regarded as 'more technical than political'.[98] His attractions were most intense in the salon and the *tertulia* rather than in the mass arena. This was reflected in his electoral fortunes. In the elections of 19 November 1933, as a candidate for Cádiz as part of a broad right-wing platform, he had been elected with 18.5 per cent of the vote. In February 1936, he ran as an independent Falangist candidate and gained only 7499 votes, 4.6 per cent of the total, while the conservative Ramón de Carranza of Renovación Española gained 64,326 votes. The only other occasion when he gained sufficient votes for a parliamentary seat was also as part of a broad right-wing candidacy in the re-run elections at Cuenca in May 1936, a seat he would be prevented from occupying because of irregularities concerning his candidacy.

Despite his failure in the February elections, the changed circumstances after the victory of the Popular Front dramatically improved the Falange's chances. Perhaps as many as 15,000 members of the CEDA youth movement, the Juventud de Acción Popular, swung over to FE de las JONS.[99] Unfortunately, José Antonio Primo de Rivera was unable to capitalize on this change of conjuncture. Nevertheless, he took various other opportunities provided by his friend Ramón Serrano Suñer to make clear to senior military figures his interest in, and sympathy for, their conspiracy. He had an interview on 8 March with General Mola, apparently to offer the services of the Falange. Earlier on the same day, Mola had been designated 'El Director' of the projected military uprising by the principal conspirators, including General Franco. He also met Lieutenant Colonel Juan Yagüe, Mola's liaison with the lynch-pin of the rebellion, Spain's Moroccan Army.[100] The role of the Falange would be to carry out acts of terrorism to provoke left-wing reprisals, the two things combining to justify right-wing jeremiads about disorder.

In early March, there were numerous incidents in Madrid in which

Falangists and left-wingers fought in the streets. On 11 March, a Falangist law student, Juan José Olano, was shot dead. On the following day, as an act of reprisal, a three-man Falangist hit-squad, probably acting with the knowledge of José Antonio, attempted to assassinate Luis Jiménez Asúa, chosen because he was a distinguished professor of law and PSOE parliamentary deputy. Jiménez Asúa survived but his police bodyguard, Jesús Gisbert, was killed. His funeral saw major public order disturbances in Madrid. Two churches and the offices of *La Nación*, the newspaper of José Antonio's friend, Manuel Delgado Barreto, were set on fire. The consequence was that, on 14 March, having lost his parliamentary immunity in the recent elections, José Antonio Primo de Rivera, together with other members of the senior leadership of FE de las JONS, was arrested. As his involvement in the assassination could not be proved, he was detained on a technicality. However, it is likely that he approved of the attempt since his brother, Miguel, felt able to ask Juan Antonio Ansaldo to visit José Antonio to discuss ways of getting the three would-be assassins out of Spain. Ansaldo then saw José Antonio in his Madrid prison, the Cárcel Modelo, to refine the details of the plan to fly them across the French frontier. Ansaldo carried out the operation a few days later but the young men concerned were arrested in France and extradited back to Spain. On 8 April, the three gunmen were tried for the murder of Jesús Gisbert and the attempted murder of Luis Jiménez Asúa. Their leader, Alberto Ortega, was sentenced to twenty-five years imprisonment and his two accomplices to six years each. At the highest level of the Falange – which meant the imprisoned leadership – a decision was taken to respond with a revenge attack on the judge, Manuel Pedregal, who was shot dead on 13 April as a warning to judges in any future trials of Falangists.[101]

In the course of April and May, José Antonio made a number of court appearances within the Cárcel Modelo to defend himself against various charges aimed at keeping him in custody. In the second, on 30 April, the judge declared that there were no grounds for banning the Falange, although the judgement was not made public. At the last of these appearances, on 28 May, José Antonio was charged with illegal possession of arms. It was alleged that the police had found two pistols in his home six weeks after his arrest. Citing the many previous searches, he accused the police of planting the guns. When the court found against him, José Antonio Primo de Rivera, beside himself with rage, ripped off his lawyer's robes and wiped his feet on them, declaring that, if this was Spanish justice, he renounced its service. Shouting '*¡Arriba España!*', he and other Falangists tried to assault the bench and a brawl ensued.[102] In prison, he and his companions could receive visits both in the mornings and the afternoons, get up and go to bed when they wished and have food sent in from outside. He organized exercise programmes for his fellow prisoners and played centre-forward in the Falangist prisoners' football team,[103] but principally devoted his time to directing the Falangist strategy of tension. The party itself went underground and the scale of the bloody cycle of provocation and reprisal intensified dramatically.[104] He told his friend Felipe Ximénez de Sandoval, 'I don't want any more Falangists in jail. I will use all my authority as Jefe Nacional of the Falange to expel anyone who comes here without good reason, such as having killed Azaña or Largo Caballero.' As he wrote to the prominent monarchist Antonio Goicoechea on 20 May 1936, prison did not stand in the way of his organization of the Falange's role in the preparations for civil war. From prison, José Antonio was in touch with Carlists and with Renovación Española.[105] He remained in contact with Mola, offering him 4000 men as a shock force.[106]

There were isolated exceptions to José Antonio's commitment to the strategy of violence – in April, for instance, he prevented an assassination attempt against Largo Caballero in the hospital where he used to visit his dying wife.[107] In general, however, he was using the Falange in the role of street-fighting cannon-fodder so crucial to the political scenario of the military uprising. At the end of May 1936, he gave José Luis de Arrese responsibility for organizing the Falange in Granada. The three squads so organized played a crucial role in the repression in Granada that followed the July coup.[108] Other subordinates of José Antonio were sent as emissaries to the provinces to organize co-ordination between the Falange and the military. The dynamic José Sainz Nothnagel was active in New Castile, Zaragoza, Murcia, Albacete and Alicante. Manuel Hedilla was tireless in Santander and Galicia.[109] Rafael Garcerán was sent by José Antonio to Pamplona with a letter for General Mola containing details of the proposed participation of the Falange in the imminent rising.[110] In the meanwhile, however, Calvo Sotelo had emerged as the strong man of the Spanish right which was, in any case, placing its hopes in the Army.

Ironically, despite the efforts of Francoist propagandists to write a different story, José Antonio's relationship with Franco, far from the co-operation of two heroes, was one of mutual contempt. What really put the seal on their long-running antipathy was their involvement in the re-run elections in Cuenca in April 1936. After the Popular Front elections of 16 February 1936, the results had been declared null and void in certain provinces including Cuenca, where there had been falsification of votes. In the re-run elections scheduled for the beginning of May 1936, the united right-wing slate included both José Antonio Primo de Rivera and General Franco. The Falange leader was included in the hope of securing for him the parliamentary immunity which would ensure his release from jail where he had been since mid-March.[111] However, José Antonio Primo de Rivera made it known that he regarded the inclusion of Franco in the list as a 'crass error'. Believing that Franco would be a failure as a parliamentary orator, José Antonio said to Serrano Suñer: 'This is not what he's good at and, given that what is brewing is something more conclusive than a parliamentary offensive, let him stay in his territory and leave me where I have already proved myself.' In the event, the Cuenca election was declared at the last minute to be technically a re-run and, although José Antonio Primo de Rivera gained sufficient votes to win a seat, he was disqualified. He was not eligible to stand in the repeated election because, the first time around in February, he had not been a candidate for Cuenca, but for Cádiz.[112] However, Franco would never forgive the Falangist leader's part in what he regarded as a humiliation.[113]

If José Antonio Primo de Rivera had been freed from prison as a result of the Cuenca elections, we do not know how he would have behaved. His 'Carta a los Militares de España' (letter to the soldiers of Spain) of 4 May 1936 did little to suggest that he was a figure of peace, reconciliation or progressive ideals: 'when that which is permanent is itself in danger, you no longer have any right to be neutral. The time has then come in which your weapons have to come into play to save fundamental values.' This document was a logical sequel to José Antonio's advocacy of a military coup before the February elections – itself an instinctive resort to family traditions. He always believed in the necessity of military assistance; his concern was only that the Falange not be submerged by reactionary army officers.[114] He was also worried about their determination, saying, 'It is useless to rely on generals on active service. They are just mother-hens and Franco is the biggest mother-hen of the lot.'[115] On the other hand, his two circulars to the Jefes Provinciales on 24 and 29 June 1936 indicated his worries that the Falange would be destroyed even by a successful military uprising.

With the government fearing an escape bid, the Falangist leader was transferred, with his brother Miguel, from Madrid to Alicante during the night of 5 June. He protested loudly and violently, with what he himself, in a letter to a female 'comrade', described as a 'biblical rage'.[116] The small, dirty prison in Alicante came as a shock after Madrid. Nevertheless, the brothers were treated extremely well by the kindly, not to say irresponsibly tolerant, prison governor, Teodorico de la Serna. José Antonio wrote to Onésimo Redondo on 17 June that 'my new residence is pleasant and tranquil, and permits me to organize my time rather well'. He received the press, vast quantities of correspondence and over 1800 visitors without any official interference until 4 August, nearly three weeks into the war. So many people came to visit him that José Antonio had to ask the director of the prison to arrange for them to be admitted in groups of twenty and permitted to stay for only five or ten minutes at a time. On 8 July, his sister Carmen and his aunt María, known as Tía Ma, together with Miguel's wife, Margarita Larios ('Margot'), came to stay in Alicante in order to look after the two imprisoned brothers.[117]

The laxity of the prison regime ensured that, throughout June and the first half of July, José Antonio was able to play an active role in the preparation both of the uprising and of his own projected escape. He sent instructions to his brother, Fernando, who acted as link with the conspirators in Madrid, for Falangists in the capital to take to the streets with the military rebels. He was also in close contact with the military conspirators in Alicante. On 12 July, he wrote to Ernesto Giménez Caballero, 'by dint of keeping up contacts, I am completely abreast of everything effective that is likely to happen in Spain. So much so, that nothing can now be done without the Falange.' Confident of the outcome of the uprising, plans were made for José Antonio's escape by Fernando Primo de Rivera and the CEDA deputy for Toledo, his friend José Finat Escrivá de Romaní, the Conde de Mayalde. To this end, Mayalde smuggled two pistols into his cell on 14 July although the escape bid was continually put off, in large part because of confidence that they would be released by the successful uprising. Having heard of the death of José Calvo Sotelo on the previous day, José Antonio sent Mayalde to Pamplona with an imperious letter telling Mola to make haste with the uprising. In it, he declared, 'I am convinced that every minute of inaction is translated into an appreciable advantage for the government'. He also instructed Mayalde 'and tell him that if he doesn't make his mind up and start the movement, I will start it here'. In fact, when Mayalde reached Pamplona, Mola told him that he had already sent an officer to Alicante to give orders for the rising.[118] Informed by this officer of the precise date of the uprising, José Antonio wrote a manifesto, dated 17 July 1936, in which he expressed the Falange's unreserved participation in the rebellion which, he believed, would take place on that day. He spent the two days immediately before the outbreak of war tidying his voluminous papers and packing his suitcases, clearly under the impression that the coup would be successful in Alicante and that he would soon be leaving the prison. On the night of 17 July, the Primo de Rivera brothers drank wine with the twenty-seven Falangists in the prison and José Antonio made a toast to the triumph of the uprising. On the following day, the first news that he received of the military rebellion provoked considerable euphoria. He was sufficiently confident to send his sister, Carmen, his sister-in-law Margarita and his aunt María to Alcoy with instructions for the local Falange. On their return, they were arrested and would eventually be tried along with José Antonio. The news soon reached him that the military governor of Alicante, General José García Aldave, had not joined the rising and the left had taken power locally. It was a devastating blow and he was worried, not without reason, that the prison might be attacked by a left-wing mob. He and Miguel burned compromising letters and papers. Thereafter, in an atlas borrowed from the prison library, he followed closely the progress of Franco's African columns.[119]

An apparent transformation undergone by José Antonio over the next four months gave rise to the subsequently widespread idea that he was the great lost opportunity to bring together both sides in the Spanish Civil War. The notion was based firstly on the fact that, in the prison in Alicante, after the uprising had failed and more particularly after he had himself been condemned to death, he expressed an interest in reconciliation; secondly, on a reasonable supposition that he could not have co-existed politically with Franco and, finally, on a much-exaggerated mutual sympathy between him and the Socialist Indalecio Prieto. On 9 August 1936, José Antonio Primo de Rivera wrote to the President of the Cortes, Diego Martínez Barrio, requesting an audience. Martínez Barrio sent an intermediary to whom José Antonio unsuccessfully pleaded to be sent to the Nationalist zone in order to work to bring an end to the war. He gave his word of honour that, if released for this mission, he would return to prison, which was an implicit, if not cynical, recognition of the legitimacy of the Republic. Given the circumstances, the Republican authorities could not accept his offer. In any case, Martínez Barrio was, sensibly, convinced that a peace mission, even one consisting of the Jefe Nacional of the Falange, could have had little impact on the military rebels.[120]

There has been speculation about the possible outcome had one of the pre-18 July escape bids succeeded, or José Antonio Primo de Rivera somehow reached the Nationalist zone in the earliest days of the Civil War. After all, when he was sent to Alicante from Madrid, some of his fellow-prisoners had been sent to Vitoria and Huelva, both of which quickly fell to the Nationalists. Whether he would have been willing or able to moderate the behaviour of the Falange during the Civil War can be a matter only for speculation. José Antonio's supervision of the terrorist activities of the Falange's *primera línea* (front-line squads) during the spring of 1936 and the scene narrated by Ridruejo sow serious doubts as to whether he would have objected to a greatly expanded Falange, flooded with newcomers, becoming one of the instruments of state terror which annihilated the left in the Nationalist zone. It does, however, seem reasonable to suppose that he would have regarded with disgust its subsequent incorporation into the Movimiento Nacional, Franco's bureaucratic claque. Moreover, it is difficult to believe that he would have approved of the way in which Falange Española, once converted into Falange Española Tradicionalista y de las JONS, deteriorated into a parasitical organization whose main function was to provide jobs in the Organización Sindical and elsewhere for its members. On the other hand, there is little evidence to support the belief that he could have done something to put a stop to the orgy of killing in which the Falange quickly became involved.

It was presumably in the hope of sowing discord in the Francoist camp that, after the death of José Antonio Primo de Rivera, Prieto sent copies of his prison writings to his two executors (*albaceas*), Ramón Serrano Suñer and Raimundo Fernández Cuesta.[121] The alleged sympathy between Prieto and Primo de Rivera rested on only three flimsy premises. There had been their celebrated handshake in June 1934. The second connection was the fact that, in prison in Madrid, Primo de Rivera wrote an article in response to Prieto's famous speech on 1 May 1936, during the Cuenca election campaign. Then, in mid-August 1936, Prieto intervened to prevent José Antonio, his brother Miguel and his sister-in-law Margot being shot without trial by the revolutionary Comité de Orden Público in Alicante. The Civil Governor discovered that, on the pretext of transferring them to the prison in Cartagena, local anarchists intended to murder them *en route*. Through the mediation of Prieto, a prestigious local Socialist, Antonio Cañizares, managed to persuade the Comité de Orden Público to abandon its scheme. As a result, new and more efficient prison officials were appointed who discovered the pistols brought by Mayalde. The brothers claimed that they had been planted.[122]

José Antonio's article, entitled 'Prieto se acerca a la Falange' (Prieto draws near to the Falange), was published in the obscure Falangist journal *Aquí Estamos* in Palma de Mallorca on 23 May. Prieto did not see it until after José Antonio's death and, when finally he wrote a response in late December 1938, he protested that, far from 'drawing near to the Falange', he had said nothing that he had not been saying for the previous twenty-five years. However, Prieto was sufficiently moved by José Antonio's article to write, 'Perhaps in Spain, we have not calmly compared ideologies to find out where they coincide, perhaps in the fundamentals, and measure the divergencies, which are probably secondary, with a view to finding out if these differences can be resolved only on the battlefield.'[123]

That Prieto himself might have considered that José Antonio could have been a serious inconvenience for Franco indicates why so little was done in Salamanca to facilitate attempts to save him from execution. Once he was dead, of course, Franco had no scruples about allowing his death to be mythologized into martyrdom as a means of attracting supporters. The man who once declared that 'We want a happy and short-skirted Spain' (*Nosotros queremos una España alegre y faldicorta*) was hardly likely to be to Franco's taste.[124] His execution was a gross political error on the part of the Republic.[125] Since he had been in jail since mid-March, four months before the military uprising, he was to an extent being tried as much for what it was assumed that he might have done had he been at liberty as for his, undeniable, part in the preparation of the rising.

An escape bid or a prisoner exchange, although clearly hazardous, had not been entirely out of the question. Several prominent Nationalists crossed the lines. José Antonio's close friend Raimundo Fernández Cuesta was officially exchanged for a minor Republican figure, Justino de Azcárate. His brother Miguel was eventually exchanged for the son of the Republican General Miaja. Among the more significant escapees was José Antonio's other close friend, Ramón Serrano Suñer. Although ultimately rejected, the notion of an exchange of José Antonio for the son of the Republican Prime Minister Francisco Largo Caballero was mooted.[126] Obviously, given the pre-eminence of José Antonio Primo de Rivera, his release or escape would be far from easy. Yet there were attempts to liberate him. The first had been the work of isolated groups of Falangists in Alicante. Then in early September, when the Germans had come to see the Falange as the Spanish component of a future world political order, more serious efforts were made, largely under the auspices of their Consul in Alicante, Hans Joachim von Knobloch. A band of Falangists led by José Antonio's cousin, the twenty-four-year-old Agustín Aznar, arrived on a German torpedo boat on 17 September. However, their plans for a *coup de main* were changed into an attempt to get Primo de Rivera out by bribery, which failed when Aznar was caught and only narrowly escaped himself. In October, von Knobloch and Aznar continued their efforts but came up against a less than enthusiastic backing from the newly elevated Head of State.[127]

This was hardly surprising. Franco needed the Falange both as a device for the political mobilization of the civilian population and as a way of creating a spurious identification with the ideals of his German and Italian allies. If the charismatic José Antonio Primo de Rivera were to have turned up at Salamanca, it would have made it significantly more difficult for Franco to have dominated and manipulated the Falange as he wished. It was certainly the case that José Antonio Primo de Rivera's disappointing encounters with Franco before the war, and his personal acquaintance with many generals, had left him cautious about too great a co-operation with the Army lest the Falange simply be used as cannon-fodder and political trimming for the defence of the old order. He revealed some of his thoughts on this when he gave his last ever interview to the American journalist Jay Allen, on 3 October 1936. It was published six days later in the *Chicago Daily Tribune*. The Falangist leader spoke in terms of outrage because the defence of oligarchical interests had swamped his party's rhetorical ambitions for sweeping social change. He also told an incredulous Jay Allen that his responsibility for political violence in Madrid could not be proven.[128] The Nationalists 'will throw Spain into the abyss'. Even taking into account the possibility that José Antonio was exaggerating his revolutionary aims to curry favour with his jailers, the implied clash with the political plans of Franco was clear. Jay Allen found José

Antonio's attitude anything but conciliatory and he felt obliged to terminate the interview 'because of the astounding indiscretions of Primo'.[129]

At his trial, José Antonio Primo de Rivera was to deny that he had played any part in the preparation of the uprising. In the circumstances of civil war, there can be little doubt that his active participation in co-ordinating the Falange's role in the uprising justified his being charged, along with his brother Miguel and his sister-in-law Margot, with conspiracy and military rebellion. The judicial process began on 3 October 1936. On 16 November, the brothers were brought before a People's Court, presided over by three magistrates, and with a fourteen-man jury that was allowed to cross-examine witnesses and the accused. In such cases of rebellion against the state, the code of military justice applied – to be found guilty meant a firing squad. Fighting for his life, José Antonio responded evasively to the prosecutor's interrogation. When asked about his involvement with monarchists in the preparations for the uprising, he replied that he would not collaborate with groups that he had fought against for the previous two years – which, in the light of his contacts with the monarchist leader, Antonio Goicoechea, was untrue. In response to a question about his involvement with plans for the Falange to rise in Alicante, he replied that it would have been difficult to conspire with so many people visiting him at once – an evident distortion of the truth. To questions from a member of the jury (Ortega), he denied that the Falange had ever planned assassination attempts or that he was in any way responsible for the participation of the Alicante Falange in the rising. To another (Domenech), he claimed that the Falange was participating actively with the military in the Nationalist zone only because he was imprisoned, thereby implying, that if he had been free, he would have prevented it. On 17 November, José Antonio, summing up for the defence, claimed that the Falange was a legally constituted association, and denied that he had any responsibility for Falangist acts of violence or that he had taken part in the preparation of the military coup of 18 July. The three judges deliberated for two hours and returned with twenty-six questions about the Falange for the jury to consider. The jury then retired. After discussing the evidence for four hours, the jury returned at 2.30 a.m. on the morning of 18 November. Their verdict was guilty. The three judges conceded the prosecutor's request for the death penalty for José Antonio Primo de Rivera, life imprisonment for Miguel Primo de Rivera and six years and a day for Margarita

Larios. The trial ended at 3 a.m. on 18 November. The Communist Civil Governor of Alicante, Jesús Monzón, tried to delay the execution. However, before the government had time to call for a pardon or commutation of sentence, the local Comité de orden Público had ordered a firing squad for the morning of 20 November. José Antonio spent most of 18 and 19 November writing his political testament and farewell letters to friends and comrades, all of which were written with great serenity. He was shot at 6.30 a.m. on the morning of 20 November in the prison exercise yard.[130]

Eye-witness accounts testified that he died with courage and dignity.[131] The news of the execution reached Franco's headquarters, the *cuartel general*, shortly afterwards.[132] Franco would make full use of the propaganda opportunities provided by the eternal absence of the hero who could not now be an awkward presence.[133] For two years, he chose, at least publicly, to refuse to believe that José Antonio was dead. The Falangist leader was more use 'alive' while the Generalísimo made his political arrangements. As long as the provisional leadership of the Falange entertained the hope that he might still be alive, they did nothing to create an alternative leadership. In Herbert Southworth's expressive theatrical metaphor, the stage properties, costumes, décor, scripts and *mise en scène* of FE y de las JONS were stolen to mask the doctrinal poverty of Francoism. Certain of Primo de Rivera's writings were suppressed and his designated successor, Manuel Hedilla, was imprisoned under sentence of death. Once the death was officially accepted, Franco used the cult of *el ausente* to take over the Falange.

The execution of José Antonio Primo de Rivera was a significant contribution to Franco's political security. Had his sentence been commuted, and he somehow reached Salamanca *after* the traumatic experience of his trial, it is just possible that he would have worked to bring an end to the carnage. The months in prison, conversations with his jailers, the bloodshed of the war and the louring shadow of his own execution had mellowed the violent figure of only eight months previously. He was open to the idea of national reconciliation in a way that Franco would never be. His testament included the phrase 'would that mine might be the last Spanish blood to be shed in civil strife' (*ojalá fuera mía la última sangre española que se vertiera en discordias civiles*).[134] In his last days in prison, José Antonio was sketching out the possible membership and policies of a government of 'national concord' whose first act was to have been a general amnesty. His attitude to Franco was revealed clearly in his comments on the implications of a military victory which he feared would merely consolidate the past. He saw such a victory as the triumph of 'a group of generals of depressing political mediocrity, committed to a series of political clichés, supported by old-style intransigent Carlism, the lazy and short-sighted conservative classes with their vested interests and agrarian and finance capitalism'.[135] On the other hand, in his testament, he refused to condemn the military for anything done since the uprising.[136]

Had José Antonio been saved, Franco's exploitation of the Falange as a ready-made political base would have been made significantly more difficult. What the role of his friend Serrano Suñer – Franco's principal political adviser – would have been if José Antonio had lived remains an interesting question. However, it takes far too much for granted simply to assume that Franco would not have disposed of Primo de Rivera in the same way as he was to dispose of so many rivals. As José Antonio himself said to Jay Allen, 'I do know that if this movement does win and it turns out to be nothing but reaction, I'll withdraw my Phalanx and I'll . . . I'll probably be back here in this or another prison in a very few months.'[137] None the less, the execution of José Antonio Primo de Rivera was a major political error for the Republic. The trial itself was not illegal. It was a court martial which had followed due process and, José Antonio Primo de Rivera, having been found guilty of military rebellion, was sentenced to death. The sentence went to the Supreme Court and was confirmed. However, he was executed before the cabinet had given final approval. The Republican Prime Minister, Francisco Largo Caballero, along with every member of his government, was outraged.[138] The President of the Republic, Manuel Azaña, also intervened in vain to save the life of José Antonio.[139]

José Antonio cannot be judged for what was done with his memory after his death. Even less can he be judged on the basis of what many of his followers did in the service of Franco. To paraphrase Herbert Southworth once more, 'they sold their shares in the ideals of Falange Española in return for lifetime pensions from Franquismo S.A.' The politics of Spain between 1937 and 1942 provide ample evidence that to think of José Antonio as the great lost opportunity is to underestimate the cunning and ruthlessness of Franco. In this sense, while the remarks of Prieto quoted earlier may be valid as an assessment of the humanity of José Antonio, they have to be seen in the light both of the political context in which they were written and of the enormous difficulties that José Antonio would have had if he had opposed Franco. The Falange which was spawned in the first months of the war owed little to José Antonio. It is impossible to know what authority he would have enjoyed among his erstwhile followers and, even if he had, whether Franco would have permitted him to exercise it. In the eight months since his arrest, the caravan had moved on.

4

Fascism and Flower-Arranging: Pilar Primo de Rivera

Pilar Primo de Rivera y Sáenz de Heredia was one of the most enduring yet enigmatic figures of the Franco regime. A quiet and unambitious woman, she was forced into prominence by the radicalization of politics – and of lives – occasioned by the Spanish Civil War. Her considerable power derived from her position as the sister of the founder of the Falange and head of its women's section for forty years. During that time, she was a crucial player, behind the scenes, in every power struggle within the Falangist establishment. Perceived as the moral heir to her brother, she could lend, or deny, a veneer of Falangist 'legitimacy' to those who jockeyed for influence within the Caudillo's single-party state. General Franco was quick to recognize this and, in consequence, to treat her with exquisite care. Indeed, her acceptance of his leadership in 1937 was to be an important pillar in his survival in power for many years thereafter, helping to deflect much internal discontent. Her influence, however, went far beyond factional politics.

The tentacles of Franco's all-embracing single party, the Falange Española Tradicionalista y de las JONS, or Movimiento, extended into education, work and social relations. From 1937 to at least the mid-1950s, its women's organization, the Sección Femenina, reached into the lives of millions of middle and lower middle-class women. As Jefe Nacional, Pilar Primo de Rivera played a formative role in the social education of two generations of women. She used her great social power, not for self-aggrandizement, but to steer the Sección Femenina towards the formation of women in traditional Catholic values, rearing children and keeping a good home for virile Falangist husbands. Through its Social Service, the Sección Femenina was the conveyor-belt of state policy towards women, constituting both a measure of control and also of rudimentary welfare provision.[1] Despite her enormous influence within a political élite that revelled in the trappings of power, Pilar Primo de Rivera exercised her functions in a self-effacing manner. In consequence, she remained a private, not to say relatively obscure, figure.

Pilar's self-deprecation did not, however, indicate weakness. She was driven by a burning sense of purpose as the heir of her brother and was dogged in her defence of what she considered to be his legacy. The reasons for her determined pursuit of her mission lay buried deep in her own family background. The early life of Pilar took place in a context of frequent death. She and her twin sister, Angela, were born in Madrid on 4 November 1907, the daughters of Casilda Sáenz de Heredia and Colonel Miguel Primo de Rivera y Orbaneja, who was to be dictator of Spain from 1923 to 1930. Their first child, José Antonio, had been born in 1903, the second, Miguel, fifteen months later and the third, Carmen, a year after that. Casilda was exhausted when, barely sixteen months later, she gave birth to twins in a difficult and painful labour. Despite the assistance of wet-nurses, she was obliged to send them to Jérez to be looked after by their paternal grandmother, Inés Orbaneja, and two of their father's sisters. She remained with her three older children and her husband at Algeciras where he was stationed. Casilda had been warned by her gynaecologist that she might die if she had another child. Nevertheless, in the autumn of 1908, she willingly entered upon what was to be a fatal pregnancy, telling a friend that, despite 'the near death sentence, loving each other as we do, Miguel and I cannot live like brother and sister'. Casilda began her final labour in a weakened state, after a pregnancy during which she had had to make a difficult journey to Madrid to look after her own dying mother.[2] Her son Fernando was born on 1 June 1909 and she died of peritonitis on the 9th. The death of her mother for reasons associated with childbirth would profoundly affect the later life of Pilar.[3]

Eighteen months old when Casilda died, Pilar had no memory of her mother.[4] With their father absorbed in his military career, the six children were brought up by their grandmother, and their two aunts, Inés and María Jesús, known as Tía Ma, a quiet and simple woman who devoted her life to the children and grandchildren of her brother.[5] Pilar and her twin sister contracted measles in 1912 and the always sickly Angela died. Shortly after the loss of her sister at the age of five, Pilar had to absorb the blow of her grandmother's death. Deprived of her mother and brought up in a severe and sombre atmosphere, Pilar was a serious child. The Primo de Rivera family was heavily religious, attending mass daily and saying the rosary together. Pilar spent much time with an English nanny. Once promoted to general, her father became an ever more distant figure. She and her brothers and sisters saw him rarely, and always, in the manner of the upper classes of the day, addressed him formally as *usted* and called him 'padre'. Affectionate when he saw them, his principal concern for his children was that they should share his intense patriotism. He also imposed a military timetable on their daily hours, posting a duty roster in the hall on which were listed the times for them to get up, study, eat and sleep.[6]

Imbued with a strict sense of duty and hierarchy, Pilar revered her father. When he died in exile in 1930, she transferred her devotion to her eldest brother, José Antonio, soon to be celebrated as the founder of the Spanish fascist party, Falange Española. As an adult, Pilar would devote her life to the creation, growth and administration of the women's section of the Falange, the Sección Femenina. She was to impose upon it an exclusively female, but implicitly anti-feminist, ideology which advocated the submission of Spanish women to warrior-like menfolk. This reflected the influence of her own family background. There exists a widely reproduced family photograph taken in the 1920s, which gives some indication of this context. The stiffly posed, and rather contrived, portrait features the dictator and his three sons standing in a line while Carmen, Pilar and Tía Ma are seated in front of them. The three women are demurely posed, feet crossed, and hands crossed on their knees, the ethereal delicacy of the girls made possible by the protective wall of men.[7] A lifetime devoted by Pilar to the advocacy of the idea that fragile women were subordinate and at best auxiliary to strong and creative men suggests an extension to the political arena of the conservative values exemplified by the Primo de Rivera family.

The trajectory of Pilar's public life suggested the influence of her appalling early experiences. She manifested a number of traits which implied a rejection of adult sexuality and also of motherhood. Pilar was far from unattractive. She had sad, round eyes and, in a rather timid way, the handsome bearing of her brother. There is, moreover, unanimity about her good nature and engaging shyness. At the same time, she had an obsession with personal cleanliness which might relate to the trauma of her mother's death in premature childbirth or to the early death of her twin. She was most often seen in the utilitarian Sección Femenina uniform of blue shirts and skirts. Out of the public spotlight, she was notorious among her friends for a lack of dress sense and, as she grew older, a deliberately frumpy, twinset-and-pearls style. This was the legacy of her general flight from the feminine norms of her early womanhood, dominated conventionally by the quest for a husband. These characteristics, along with her apparent celibacy and a child-like voice, suggested a rejection of heterosexual carnal relations perhaps in reaction to the fate of her mother. Even at the height of her political eminence, she went about her duties in a rather homely style which many found endearing and proof of her sincerity and lack of personal ambition.[8]

In more relaxed times, it might be supposed that Pilar would have lived a quiet life whose sexual dimension could not easily be predicted. As it was, in the conflictive atmosphere of the Second Republic and the Spanish Civil War, she became a national figure, her ideas useful and agreeable to the reactionary victors of that war. At that time, José Antonio Primo de Rivera was the most charismatic figure on the extreme right. He launched the fascist party, Falange Española, with a celebrated speech in the Teatro de la Comedia in Madrid on 29 October 1933. Pilar attended the meeting accompanied by her elder sister, Carmen, and her cousins Inés and Dolores. Hearing her brother speak at the meeting, Pilar made the decision to dedicate her life to the Falange. Since José Antonio was initially reluctant to admit women because of the dangers involved, Pilar and other upper-class girls who were attracted by the ideas of the Falange were at first incorporated into its student section, the SEU. In June 1934, the Sección Femenina was founded and Pilar herself was appointed the first Jefe Nacional. Sección Femenina officially provided an infrastructure to help imprisoned members of the Falange and the families of those killed in street-fighting. Its members also attended the trials of Falangists accused of breaches of public order and organized disturbances. They made arm-bands and flags and acted as secretaries and message-bearers. The real function of the women at this stage, however, was to provide cover for the violent activities of the Falangist hit-squads. Pilar Primo de Rivera herself admitted in an interview in later life that the women played the role of 'the auxiliaries' of the street-fighting men whose guns they often hid in their dresses. In her memoirs she acknowledged only that, as the men of the organization were jailed for terrorist activities, the women undertook prison welfare visits and charitable activities for their families as well as collecting money and organizing propaganda throughout Spain.[9]

Pilar was to devote her life to the Sección Femenina. The spirit in which she would run the organization derived from her brother's words to some thirty female followers on 28 April 1935 in Don Benito (Badajoz). His statement about the subordinate position of women within the Falange was swiftly printed as fly-sheet and distributed to the Jefes Provinciales with instructions for it to be disseminated as widely as possible as the party line. He told them that the Falange had a particular affinity with women because it rejected both flattery and feminism. He declared 'we are not feminists. We do not believe that the way to respect women is by diverting them from their magnificent destiny and giving them manly functions. Man is a torrent of egoism; woman almost always accepts a life of submission, service and abnegation.'[10] Certainly, Pilar always did. At first a tiny group in a small party, she and the other women of the Sección Femenina happily accepted a subordinate position, devoting themselves to making Falangist blue shirts and embroidering the red yoke-and-arrows emblem, passing the hat at meetings, addressing and stuffing envelopes and selling soap to raise money for the party. In early 1936, she undertook a recruiting drive. First of all, driving her little Morris saloon, and later travelling by second-class rail (not as spartan as third nor as luxurious as first), she carried the Sección Femenina to the provinces of Andalusia, Castille and the north. By the spring, it had about 2000 members in eighteen provincial sections. On 14 March 1936, in the wake of an assassination attempt against the Socialist Luis Jiménez de Asua, José Antonio Primo de Rivera was imprisoned and the Falange declared illegal. In response to the new situation, Pilar organized the members of the Sección Femenina into a network of message-carriers which maintained contact between her brother and the imprisoned leadership and those members of the Falange hierarchy who were still at liberty. In fact, although her brother remained in prison, the Falange was once more permitted to operate as a legal organization as a result of a court decision on 31 May 1936. Thus the women of the Sección Femenina typed, copied and distributed to garrisons and bases around the country José Antonio Primo de Rivera's 'Letter to the Soldiers of Spain'. Written on 4 May, this was an appeal to the army to rise against the Republic.[11]

The outbreak of the Civil War on 18 July 1936 found Pilar in Madrid, in the Republican zone. She had been in hiding since before the military uprising because she had been warned that she was on a black-list of rightists condemned to death by the Communists.[12]

Nevertheless, she was confident that the Nationalist uprising would succeed in a matter of days. She assumed that she would devote her short time waiting to making Falangist blue shirts to be worn when the party militants streamed out into the streets to greet the victorious military rebels. By mid-August, it had become clear that there would be no easy triumph. The Falange was outlawed. As it was dismantled by the Republican authorities, the Sección Femenina organized Auxilio Azul, a network which found hiding places, false papers and food for Falangists and other rightists on the run.

Pilar herself was so well-known that she was obliged to stay in hiding in the houses of various friends until she managed to find refuge in the Argentine Embassy. While there, she received the devastating news of the murder of her younger brother Fernando in Madrid's Cárcel Modelo on 23 August. Finally, with the help of the German and Argentine embassies, she managed to escape. Disguised as the Argentinian wife of a German, and with a German passport, she got to Alicante. Accompanied by Rosario Urquijo, Fernando's wife, and her two children, Miguel and Rosario, Pilar embarked on the *Graf Spee*, which took her to the Franco-held south. Her importance as the sister of Spain's fascist leader accounts for the German readiness to help. Such was her sense of submission and servitude that she spent the journey washing, mending and ironing the clothes of the German sailors. The ship was forced to put in near Seville in order that Rosario Urquijo could be taken ashore to give birth to her daughter, María Fernanda.[13] Once in the Nationalist zone, Pilar briefly took up residence in Seville, before moving in November 1936 to Salamanca because of its greater political importance. Her family connections – and the enforced absence of her brother, José Antonio, imprisoned in a Republican prison in Alicante – quickly ensured that she would acquire a position of moral authority in Falangist circles. Significantly, however, when she was contacted by Falangists trying to arrange the rescue of José Antonio, she advised them to get in touch with Agustín Aznar, the fiancé of her cousin Dolores Primo de Rivera y Cobo de Guzmán. Typically, she referred would-be rescuers to Aznar on the grounds that he was 'the only man in the family'. Aznar was head of the Falangist militias, or 'front line' (Jefe de la Primera Línea).[14]

Once in Salamanca, with the help of her intimate friend, Marichu de la Mora, she resumed her post as Jefe Nacional of the Sección Femenina. She appointed Marichu as Secretaria Nacional Provisional.[15] Like the rest of the Falange, it had swollen in size – from

2000 before the war to nearly 50,000 members. She took over the existing organization of its members as nurses at the front, as secretaries for the Falange and for senior army officers, cooks and washerwomen for the military forces, seamstresses making Falangist and military uniforms. For this, she was always scrupulously careful to seek the permission of the military authorities and of Manuel Hedilla Larrey, the provisional head of the Falange. In the absence of her brother, Hedilla had been elected as Jefe of the provisional Junta de Mando (command council) created in Valladolid at the beginning of September.[16]

A similar function within the Sección Femenina had already been assumed unofficially by Mercedes Sanz Bachiller, the impulsive widow of one of the founders of Spanish fascism, Onésimo Redondo.[17] Despite being the mother of three small children, the energetic Mercedes Sanz worked indefatigably as provincial chief of the Valladolid Sección Femenina. As such, she was subordinate to Pilar but, in her absence, she took initiatives on her own responsibility. Immediately after the death of her husband on 24 July 1936, Sanz Bachiller had moved into the Valladolid headquarters of the Falange, the Academia de Caballería, to organize the collection and distribution of warm clothing for front-line combatants. At the end of October 1936, she had founded Auxilio de Invierno (winter help) in Valladolid. An ecclesiastical city of strong right-wing tendencies, Valladolid had fallen quickly to the military rebels. A savage repression had ensued, largely at the hands of local Falangists. In consequence, the province had many thousands of widows and orphans. Mercedes Sanz organized soup kitchens for the victims of the war. She did so in conjunction with Javier Martínez Bedoya, a Jonsista, who had been a close collaborator of Onésimo Redondo. Having studied in Germany, Martínez Bedoya admired many aspects of Nazism. At the suggestion of a German–Spanish Falangist, Clarita Stauffer, it was decided to copy the name of the Nazi Winterhilfe.[18]

With the authorization of General Mola, the first canteen was established in Valladolid on 30 October 1936. Auxilio de Invierno soon spread to the other provinces of the northern zone under Mola's control.[19] The dynamic widow of Onésimo Redondo seemed not to think twice before impetuously stepping into the position that Pilar Primo de Rivera regarded as her own. Despite her child-like and introverted appearance, Pilar had no intention of being displaced from the leadership of the women's movement in the Nationalist zone. Such was the success of Mercedes Sanz's initiative that the recently arrived Pilar Primo de Rivera regarded it as a challenge to her authority. Her shy exterior hid a stubborn determination. In her extraordinarily oblique memoirs, she refers to this 'problem' and says only that, faced with the 'difficulties' that it posed for the Sección Femenina, she had to employ 'much diplomacy, but, at the same time, an incorruptible tenacity to restore order and put everyone in their correct place'.[20] Pilar was alerted to the scale of her upstart rival's plans when, on 24 December 1936, she attended the inauguration of a canteen in Seville, an area where she had every reason to expect that her influence would be immeasurably greater than that of Mercedes Sanz Bachiller. The point was made even more strongly when, on 5 January, another canteen was opened, this time in her home town of Jérez, albeit with the name of Comedor Pilar Primo de Rivera.[21]

There followed a protracted, and undeclared, power struggle, throughout which the power of Pilar's surname, combined with her own dogged determination, would swing the balance. In addition to the underlying rivalry between the wife of one of the founders of the Juntas de Ofensiva Nacional Sindicalista and the sister of the founder of the Falange, there was a deeper hostility. Beyond any personal jealousy, there was a profound ideological enmity. Pilar's struggle to bring Mercedes Sanz's Auxilio de Invierno under her influence paralleled a campaign by the followers of José Antonio within the wider Falange to tame radical elements in Valladolid. In early 1935, José Antonio had expelled members of the JONS section of the Falange. The outbreak of the Civil War and the assistance provided by Hitler and Mussolini had revived JONS radicalism. The close circle of friends and relatives of José Antonio Primo de Rivera, known as the 'legitimistas', were determined to subjugate the Jonsistas. In early January 1937, that struggle saw Agustín Aznar force the resignation of Andrés Redondo, who had been elected Jefe Provincial by the acclamation of an emotional crowd at the funeral of his brother, Onésimo. Andrés was replaced by the Falangist intellectual, Dionisio Ridruejo, a close friend of José Antonio.[22] The division between Falangists and Jonsistas was expressed within the women's movement by Sanz Bachiller's comment that 'I simply cannot relate to the Sección Femenina's notion of their political activities being only for women.'[23]

With a view to asserting her authority over Mercedes Sanz, Pilar visited Valladolid on 9 December in the company of Manuel Hedilla, the Jefe Provisional. Shortly afterwards, Auxilio de Invierno was formally incorporated into the Falange. At the first Consejo Nacional de la Sección Femenina held in Salamanca and Valladolid between 6 and 9 January 1937, Pilar Primo de Rivera announced the creation of the Delegación Nacional de Auxilio de Invierno with herself as Delegada Nacional, and all the jefas provinciales de la Sección Femenina (provincial heads) as delegadas provinciales de Auxilio de Invierno. Although theoretically under the jurisdiction of the Sección Femenina, Auxilio de Invierno was practically independent. Unlike the Sección Femenina, Auxilio de Invierno was not the exclusive terrain of women and a prominent role was being played by a man, Martínez Bedoya, whose relationship with Mercedes Sanz Bachiller was deepening into something more than political collaboration. Given his friendship with Onésimo Redondo, and his prominence in the Juntas de Ofensiva Nacional Sindicalista, Bedoya was the object of considerable suspicion from Pilar. Moreover, he had left the Falange in January 1935 along with the JONS founder, Ramiro Ledesma Ramos, in protest at the growing power of José Antonio Primo de Rivera.[24]

Martínez Bedoya reacted quickly to counter Pilar's successful intervention with Hedilla. On the day after the Consejo Nacional of the Sección Femenina closed, 10 January 1937, accompanied by Mercedes Sanz, he visited Hedilla in Salamanca. His aim was to have Pilar replaced by Mercedes Sanz as Delegada Nacional and the Auxilio de Invierno transferred from the jurisdiction of the Sección Feminina to become a separate branch or Delegación of Falange Española de las JONS. Aware of the latent hostility of the Primo de Rivera clan towards himself, Hedilla was quickly persuaded that the new movement could be of great value if controlled directly by the Falange's Junta de Mando (command council). He named Bedoya as national secretary of Auxilio de Invierno. However, the considerable influence wielded by Pilar ensured that Auxilio de Invierno remained firmly under the jurisdiction of the Sección Femenina.[25] In the ongoing power struggle, and indeed in maintaining her grip over the Sección Femenina until its dissolution after the death of Franco, Pilar would cite the words of her brother like religious texts. Her link with José Antonio gave her legitimacy and his writings and sayings were elevated by her into the repository of ultimate truth. She gave every indication of feeling that relationship as a religious experience, as if she were part Mary Magdalen and part Virgin Mary in relation to the Master – José Antonio being cast in the role of Christ.

The Falange had been decapitated by the execution of José Antonio

Primo de Rivera on 20 November 1936. The consequent rivalries between the three principal factions were intensified in early 1937 by the likelihood of a takeover by Franco. On the one hand, there was the radical fascist group which centred on Manuel Hedilla. Then, there was the group of recently arrived monarchists and Catholics who were happy to see the entire right united under the leadership of Franco. Finally, there was the patrician group of relatives and close friends of José Antonio known as *legitimistas*. They had acquiesced in the election of Hedilla as Jefe Provisional only to keep open the leadership while they had still hoped for the return of José Antonio Primo de Rivera from prison. Now, aware of the death of their founder and the consequent threat of a Francoist takeover, their aim was to keep open the post of Jefe Nacional until the arrival of José Antonio's friend, executor and Secretary-General of the Falange, Raimundo Fernández Cuesta, at the time imprisoned in Madrid. In this context, with one brother, Fernando, dead and another, Miguel, also still in a Republican prison, Pilar assumed considerable importance as the principal living link with the founder of the Falange.

Social snobs, she and the other *legitimistas* regarded the Hedillistas as vulgar and proletarian. She was also concerned that Hedilla might be easily manipulated by Franco. She visited him frequently between February and mid-April 1937 and told him 'Be careful. The Falange must not be handed over to Franco. Don't give it away!'[26] Ramón Serrano Suñer, who had been a friend of José Antonio, was effectively Franco's political chief-of-staff. He kept a close watch on the manoeuvres of the various right-wing factions in the run-up to Franco's unification of parties in April 1937. He described Pilar as the 'priestess' (*sacerdotisa*) of the 'legitimista' group which used to meet in her house in the Plazuela de San Julián in Salamanca. There, she maintained the sacred flame of her brother's memory. Falangists from all over the Nationalist zone would stop by to receive their instructions from her or to pass on their complaints about the way Franco was not fulfilling the legacy of José Antonio.[27] Pilar had not endeared herself to Franco by opposing the adoption of the royalist yellow and red flag and the Marcha Real, or by distributing a leaflet advocating the red and black flag of the Falange and its hymn 'Cara al Sol' as the national anthem. When some of the things said about him in Pilar's apartment were reported back to the Caudillo, he was furious.[28]

In Salamanca in the second half of April 1937, the Generalísimo hijacked the Falange and the other pre-war rightist forces into a new single-party, the Falange Española Tradicionalista y de las JONS. Pilar eventually collaborated with Franco because, as she put it, she finally realized that 'Franco was right and the war had to be won'. However, during the complex power struggle for control of the Falange, her role was curiously ambiguous. Plans for a takeover of the Falange by the *legitimistas* were hatched with her approval.[29] However, in the machiavellian scenario stage-managed by Franco's *cuartel general* (headquarters staff), the *legitimistas* were initially defeated by the more proletarian group of Manuel Hedilla. When Franco announced the creation of the new movement, which united Falange, the Carlists and other rightists, Hedilla assumed that if the Caudillo became a figurehead Jefe Nacional, he would be the effective head of the new single party as its Secretary General. When the crisis exploded, Pilar was on tour in Galicia and León with Marichu de la Mora. They raced to Salamanca. Hedilla visited Pilar, who blamed him for the unification and urged him to ensure that the ideals of the Falange were safeguarded. When he was offered no more than a place on the Junta Política (executive committee) of the new united FET y de las JONS, as opposed to the leadership position to which he aspired, Pilar sent him a message encouraging him not to accept. In her memoirs, she claims, astonishingly, not to have known that her brother was dead and, for that reason, to have regarded the Unificación as premature. Hedilla rejected the post and became involved in an abortive rebellion against Franco. The Caudillo had him arrested and sentenced to death. Pilar, allegedly to curry favour with those still loyal to Hedilla, interceded with Carmen Polo, Franco's wife, to secure a commutation of the death sentence. Her gesture was unnecessary since Serrano Suñer had already secured his life. Her efforts on behalf of one of Hedilla's supporters, her cousin by marriage, José Luis de Arrese, were altogether more energetic.[30]

In the immediate aftermath of the internecine struggle in Salamanca, Mercedes Sanz and Javier Martínez Bedoya sensed that Pilar's position had been weakened in Franco's eyes by her ambiguous attitude to the unification. They went to Salamanca where they were received by Captain Ladislao López Bassa, an obscure figure, imposed as Secretary of FET y de las JONS by Franco to maintain a vigilant control over internal Falangist politics. They proposed first to him and shortly after to Ramón Serrano Suñer that the name of Auxilio de Invierno be changed to Auxilio Social and that the organization be a separate entity within the new single party. This was successfully implemented on 24 May 1937 with Bedoya as its Secretario General and Mercedes Sanz as its Delegada Nacional – as part of the Falange Española Tradicionalista y de las JONS, parallel to and not subordinate to Sección Femenina.[31] The changes regarding Auxilio Social made political and administrative sense but they were also Franco's response to Pilar's ambiguous role during the murky intrigues of the unification process. Pilar was 'punished' by the strengthening of Auxilio Social and provided with a rival, Mercedes Sanz, as a reminder that she could be cast into the darkness at any moment. At the same time, in a typically convoluted move by Franco, she was brought back into the fold. Needing the endorsement of the Primo de Rivera name for his regime and unwilling to risk outright confrontation with her, Franco appointed her to a place on the Junta Política of the new party. She was also named as first member of the Consejo Nacional de FET y de las JONS created by Franco on 19 October 1937.

The Sección Femenina was probably the only part of the Falange which remained much as it had been before the unification. That was in part because, as José Antonio's sister, Pilar was untouchable by the regime, as long, that is, as she did not become a focus of opposition. In fact, the very submissiveness that she was dedicated to inculcating in women through her organization made that an unlikely eventuality. Nevertheless, in the context of political tension which characterized the immediate aftermath of the unification, Franco and Serrano Suñer had soon realized that they needed the seal of legitimacy provided by the group of *camisas viejas* (old shirts or Falangist veterans) gathered around Pilar. Serrano Suñer was delegated to negotiate with Pilar, Agustín Aznar, Dionisio Ridruejo, José Antonio Girón de Velasco, and others. With seductive subtlety, he did so throughout May and June of 1937. He convinced them that only through collaboration with Franco was there any chance of ever implementing an important part of José Antonio's legacy.[32] Persuaded by his words and, in any case, perhaps perpetually longing for a male authority figure to replace her father and brother, Pilar came willingly into the Francoist fold. She thereby put the enormous authority of her position as José Antonio's sister at the service of Franco's efforts to present himself as the true and legitimate successor. The *legitimistas* still in jail were released, and key, if symbolic, roles were reserved for Pilar and for Raimundo Fernández Cuesta. A prisoner exchange was arranged for Fernández Cuesta in August 1937.[33]

Pilar realized that she could not fight against Franco's authority, as much as it pained her to see him assume her brother's role as Jefe Nacional. In any case, she found little difficulty in respecting the authority of a masculine, and particularly a military, leader. Moreover, she needed the weight of Franco's higher authority in order to impose unity on the newly expanded Sección Femenina. As in the wider Falange, the incorporation of the Carlists, whose female organization was known as the 'Margaritas', required very considerable effort and energy from Pilar. She dutifully alternated Falangists and Margaritas in all the senior positions of national delegates and provincial Jefes and secretaries. It was a task which she undertook with dogged obstinacy, determined as she was to preside over the expansion and not the diminution of her brother's legacy.[34] At the same time, the rivalry between Mercedes Sanz and Pilar would remain latent and burst to the surface at the first sign of weakness on either side. Mercedes Sanz's concept of Auxilio Social advocated the mobilization of women on the basis of a fanciful and idealized notion of the role of women in Nazi Germany. Pilar's ideas reflected those of her brother, influenced more by Italian Fascism than by Nazism, and in fact more by traditions of patrician charity work than by either. Pilar's life's work would tend rather to the demobilization of women back to the home.

In 1937, however, the circumstances of the war favoured Mercedes Sanz. As major Republican cities were captured, occupied and purged, there was a need for an operation much larger than the original canteens of Auxilio de Invierno. The enormity of the social dislocation occasioned by the war went beyond the capacity of the Sección Femenina. To the chagrin of Pilar, the scale of the tasks entrusted to Auxilio Social grew substantially. Fearing that the enthusiasm of volunteers might dry up, particularly after the war, Martínez Bedoya and Mercedes Sanz began to develop the idea of a female equivalent of military conscription to provide the necessary labour for the services they provided. In the early autumn, Mercedes Sanz visited Franco to persuade him of the need for such a service. The Servicio Social de la Mujer was created on 11 October 1937, under the auspices of Auxilio Social. Women were recruited for war work by the Auxilio Social. In theory a voluntary service, it was obligatory for any woman who aspired to a job in the civil service or as a teacher, to acquire a professional qualification in any educational establishment, and to obtain a passport or a driving licence. There were very few exceptions. They included nuns, widows or married women with children, the eldest of eight unmarried siblings or girls who had lost their family at the hands of the left in the Spanish Civil War. These conditions ensured that a high degree of social control could be exercised through the Servicio Social.[35]

This triumph for Mercedes Sanz was bitterly resented by Pilar, who determined to use her influence to recoup the ground lost. In the last resort, the bargain that had been tacitly struck between Pilar and Franco significantly favoured the Caudillo. None the less, the capitulation to Franco brought considerable advantage to Pilar in terms of political influence, although unlike many of the Francoist hierarchy, she never derived material benefit from her situation, living a life of great simplicity and austerity. The Sección Femenina and the late-night political discussions at Pilar's home provided Franco with a harmless safety valve for those *camisas viejas* determined to keep alive José Antonio's memory. The bargain was sealed at the Second Consejo Nacional de la Sección Femenina, held in Segovia and Avila from 15 to 23 January 1938. She embraced the unification with enthusiasm, declaring that only the Army and FET y de las JONS should have any say in the future destinies of the *Patria*. Apart from affirming the undisputed leadership of Franco in terms of religious adoration, Pilar laid out the post-war goals of the Sección Femenina. Picking up on Franco's own notion that the Civil War was merely the first stage of national regeneration and the prelude to imperial greatness, she made it clear that Spanish women were to provide the infrastructure of empire. Ever genteel, she stopped short of the Nazi-style declarations of Auxilio Social that Spanish women must become 'strong and prolific mothers to give us healthy and numerous sons to carry out the imperial wishes of our war dead'. Pilar exhorted women to be as feminine as possible. There was no question of their assuming male dress or functions, let alone those of front-line combatants.[36]

Pilar's capacity for selfless devotion to a male figure focused ever more on General Franco. On 20 November 1938, in Burgos Cathedral, there was held the first official requiem ceremony for José Antonio Primo de Rivera. Pilar accompanied Franco. After his early experiences with Millán Astray, the deranged Francoist, Ernesto Giménez Caballero, had become a regular on the radio. He commentated on the ceremony for Radio Nacional: 'How beautiful she was. She appeared translucent. With an inner beauty, of alabaster and transparent. Submitted with beatific resignation to the tragic destiny of her blood. That blood of the Primo de Rivera family, created by God to serve his greater glory and in the greatest loyalty to Spain. I saw Pilar from time to time turn her ecstatic eyes towards General Franco as if she saw in him the figure of her own father, the figure of her own brother.' By her legitimization of Franco's position within the Falange, she was effectively undermining the possibility of Falangist opposition to the Caudillo.[37] It is difficult to assess whether she did this out of naïvety, out of a basic desire to survive, or because she believed Ramón Serrano Suñer who regularly and eloquently presented a Falangist compromise with Franco as a pragmatically alternative way to salvage at least some of her brother's legacy. Whatever the case, thereafter she enthusiastically adopted the role of the vestal virgin tending the flame of her brother's memory. Her rhetoric was about fulfilling his legacy but she had in fact become part of the machinery whereby the Falange's radical tendencies were tamed and the party simply administered Franco's bureaucratic regimentation of Spanish life. In this regard, she was curiously close to Raimundo Fernández Cuesta, one of the executors of her brother's will, and the most docile of the Francofalangists who helped domesticate the Falange. Her influence played some part in his nomination as Secretario General del Movimiento in Franco's first cabinet of 1 February 1938. Her fondness for Fernández Cuesta seems to have emanated from the fact that José Antonio himself had appointed him to the Falange's first Junta de Mando (command council or politburo) and that he had been arrested with him on 14 March 1936.[38] Later, she would similarly push the candidacy of her cousin by marriage, José Luis de Arrese, to be Secretario-General del Movimiento.[39] However, her devotion to Franco rivalled her dedication to the memory of her brother. In a speech to the VIII Consejo Nacional of the Sección Femenina, held in early 1944 at the Monasterio de Nuestra Señora de Guadalupe in the province of Cáceres, she called on her companions to pray to the Virgin of Guadalupe to grant 'special protection for the Caudillo, our lord on earth who knows how to direct our steps in this age in which perhaps by his works Spain will once more know glory'.[40]

During the latter part of the Civil War, Pilar worked indefatigably for the consolidation of the Sección Femenina, particularly in recently captured areas. The Sección Femenina now claimed 800,000 members. Pilar threw herself into organizing her members to make uniforms, collect cigarettes and food for the troops. To her credit, she opposed the Francoist policy of total annihilation of the enemy, trying to prevent reprisals being taken against the widows of Republican militants.

She occasionally visited the battle front and travelled around Spain with Marichu de la Mora and later with Syra Manteola, her successor as Secretaria Nacional.[41] Behind the public activities, the power struggle with Mercedes Sanz Bachiller rumbled on throughout the war and continued after the end of hostilities. Auxilio Social grew in the immediate aftermath of the war but was brought down by political errors. The organization came under the jurisdiction of the Jefatura de Servicios de Beneficencia (office of welfare services) which was part of the Ministry of the Interior. Based in Valladolid, its principal function was to rebuild some kind of social infrastructure in captured towns. Accordingly, instead of being financed by charity and street collections, Auxilio Social became a charge on state finances. In February 1938, the Minister, Ramón Serrano Suñer, had appointed Javier Martínez Bedoya to head the department – which significantly strengthened the position of Mercedes Sanz. At the end of the war, the Dirección General de Beneficencia and Auxilio Social moved together to Madrid. The task facing Auxilio Social in big cities like Barcelona and Madrid was monumental. It was necessary to deal with mass hunger, refugees, homelessness, broken families, orphaned children. As Auxilio Social and its budget grew, jealousies within the Falange intensified. At the end of the Civil War, for instance, Pilar's friend and ally, Raimundo Fernández Cuesta, the Minister-Secretary of the Falange, humiliated Mercedes Sanz Bachiller when he hijacked her plans to move Auxilio Social into splendid offices in Madrid at Alcalá 44, requisitioning the building as headquarters of FET y de las JONS.[42]

Throughout 1939, the rivalries within the Falange became ever more embittered. Javier Martínez Bedoya threw away the advantages of his position by offending Serrano Suñer, Franco's *eminence grise* and Minister of the Interior. On 26 July, Serrano Suñer had suggested that Martínez Bedoya be made Minister of Labour in a forthcoming cabinet reshuffle. However, his nomination was opposed by both monarchists and the *legitimista* group of the Falange, led by Pilar and Miguel Primo de Rivera. Since Raimundo Fernández Cuesta was being replaced by General Agustín Muñoz Grandes as Minister-Secretary of the Falange Española Tradicionalista y de las JONS, the *legitimistas* complained at the prospect of seeing a Jonsista as the only representative of the old Falange in the government. At the same time, the Chief of the General Staff, General Juan Vigón, told Franco that, in 'the victory government', it would provoke adverse comment in military circles to include Martínez Bedoya, a twenty-four-year-old non-combatant. He was therefore not given the expected ministry nor the under-secretaryship of the Ministry which had been mooted as consolation. In extremely complex circumstances, a furious Martínez Bedoya wrote to Serrano Suñer, resigning his posts as Director General de Beneficencia and member of the Consejo Nacional of FET y de las JONS. He also rashly denounced the new cabinet as '*un triunfo de la CEDA*', that is to say a triumph for the old conservative, Catholic establishment – a great insult to Serrano Suñer, who had been a parliamentary deputy for the CEDA and left it for the Falange.[43]

Martínez Bedoya had played into the hands of the group around Pilar Primo de Rivera which was alert to any opportunity to gain advantage over a rival. He gave a further hostage to fortune when, at the end of the war, he proposed marriage to Mercedes Sanz Bachiller. She hesitated, fearful of the scandal that would be provoked by 'the wedding of a hero of the Crusade with the war barely over'.[44] They married on 3 November 1939. Bedoya thereby 'violated a myth', in the words of Dionisio Ridruejo. Within the value system of the time, much could be made of the contrast between the virginal dedication of the sister of José Antonio Primo de Rivera and the carnal weakness of the widow of Onésimo Redondo. The timing could not have been more unfortunate for Bedoya and Sanz. The news of their wedding became public knowledge as preparations reached their height for the massive commemoration of the third anniversary of the execution of José Antonio Primo de Rivera by the Republicans, on 20 November 1936. In a widely publicized operation, for ten days and ten nights a torchlit procession escorted José Antonio's mortal remains, exhumed in Alicante, in a five-hundred kilometre journey for reburial with full military honours at El Escorial, the resting place of the kings and queens of Spain. An atmosphere of reverential hero-worship which had revived many of the passions of the Civil War provided the perfect context for a campaign of gossip and innuendo against Mercedes Sanz. It bore fruit on 21 December 1939 when Serrano Suñer, keen to secure his own endorsement by the Primo de Rivera clan as legitimate successor to José Antonio, attacked the entire basis of Auxilio Social in his closing speech at its Congress. The wide-ranging radical pretensions of Auxilio Social – and particularly its aim to provide nursery facilities to help working mothers – had provoked the jealousy not only of Pilar Primo de Rivera and the Sección Femenina but also of the traditional charitable establishment, including the Catholic hierarchy. On 28 December 1939, Franco definitively subordinated the Servicio Social de la Mujer to the Sección Femenina. On 9 May 1940, Mercedes Sanz was replaced as Delegada Nacional of Auxilio Social by a man, Manuel Martínez de Tena.[45] This constituted a victory for Pilar and the Falange *legitimistas*. However, the central motivation of the regime was entirely practical and in accordance with its conservative instincts. Women were to be demobilized and returned to the home after the emancipation implicit in their participation in the war. The move away from that glimpse of equality and back towards a submissive, home-making role also fitted better with the predilections of Pilar than with the rhetorical social radicalism of Mercedes Sanz.[46]

After the end of the war, on 30 May 1939, Franco and Pilar Primo de Rivera addressed 10,000 members of the Sección Femenina at Medina del Campo when the organization was formally given the Castillo de la Mota, the castle of Isabel la Católica near Medina del Campo, whose lengthy restoration Pilar painstakingly supervised. In fact, the tone of Francoist architecture was set by Pedro Muguruza, who also played a crucial role in the construction of the Valle de los Caídos. Pilar declared to the assembled women who had courageously participated in the war effort as nurses and ancillary staff near the front-line and worked at social reconstruction in appalling circumstances that they must return to a position of submissive home-making. She announced that 'the only mission assigned to women in the tasks of the fatherland is homemaking [*el hogar*]. Therefore, now in peacetime, we will broaden the task initiated in our Training Schools to make family life so agreeable for men that they will find within the home everything they previously lacked and will thus not need to seek relaxation in taverns or clubs.' It is almost as if she was attempting to put right the deficiencies of her own family, in which it might be imagined that the military members were not assiduously uxorious or home-bound. Be that as it may, a movement committed to producing women who were silent, obedient servants and men who were removed from contact with their peers, and thus from political discussion and bonds of solidarity, fitted well with the ideology of the new regime. For Franco, the purpose of the Sección Femenina was 'to pay homage to our troops and to the Army of Victory'.[47] In general, the attitude of Pilar Primo de Rivera to the men of the Falange was deferential: 'War was for men, and women were for helping men.'[48]

Pilar was too shy to be a good orator.[49] Nevertheless, she made many speeches, in which she made it quite clear that the activism of the Sección Femenina would cease as soon as the Civil War was over. Indeed, in every way, she embraced the notion of the submissiveness of women to men. The symbol of the Sección Femenina was the letter Y, and its principal decoration was a medal forged in the form of a Y, in gold, silver or red enamel according to the degree of heroism or sacrifice being rewarded. The Y was the first letter of the name of Isabel of Castille, as written in the fifteenth century, and also the first letter of the word *yugo* (yoke) which was part of the Falangist emblem of the yoke and arrows. With specific connotations of a glorious imperial past and more generalized ones of servitude, as well as of unity, it was a significant choice of symbol.[50] At the third Consejo Nacional in Zamora in 1939, she claimed that the Falange had converted its female members 'from the frivolous and insubstantial creatures that we were before into women who realized that they could have a use'. She declared that the role of women was merely one of helping men in making the Falangist revolution. Thereafter, women should return to the bosom of the family and thus retreat from the public role imposed on them by the war. Instead, they could teach Falangist women how to inculcate their sons with the ideas of José Antonio Primo de Rivera.[51]

Two years later, in Barcelona at the Fifth Consejo Nacional, Pilar revealed much of herself when she declared that the work of the Sección Femenina should be silent (*callada*) and in complete subordination to the male Falange. 'The Secciones Femeninas must have an attitude of absolute obedience and subordination with respect to their leaders. As is always the role of women in life, of submission to the man'.[52] This message intensified over the years. In Oviedo in 1949, she declared that those, like her, who were forced to play a part in public life 'longed for the sweet peace of a tranquil household' which would release them from 'the torture of having continually to submit their shyness to the blushes of exhibiting themselves publically'. For this reason, the schools of the Sección Femenina insisted on perfection in flower-arranging and taught women always to speak in a low voice and never to interrupt a conversation.[53] Twenty years later, she wrote 'the man is the king; the wife, the children, the servants, just the necessary complements so that the man might reach his plenitude'.[54]

In the post-war period, Pilar Primo de Rivera happily took on the job of justifying the relegation of women to traditional status and roles. Within the legal framework of the Civil Law Code of 1889 which maintained the inability of women to make independent decisions without the permission of their husbands, fathers or brothers, Pilar advocated female obedience and subservience. With Pilar in the vanguard, the Sección Femenina provided a practical ideology for women which not only advocated their exclusion from politics but also trained them in prudent domestic habits well-fitted to times of austerity and rationing.[55] Spain was exhausted after the Civil War. Shortages of food, fuel and household goods of every description intensified dramatically with the outbreak of the Second World War. The consequent privations put good housekeeping at a premium. At the same time, the ideology of a regime deeply influenced by conservative Catholicism ensured the imposition of social norms that were at the furthest extreme from the sexual egalitarianism of the war. Accordingly, an organization predicated on the social submissiveness of women and offering practical classes in cookery, needlework and other domestic skills provided methods of social control which guaranteed the good will of the regime. In her first circular to the Sección Femenina at the end of the war, Pilar wrote 'now comes our silent, continuous work, which will bring us no greater reward than to be able to think that, thanks to the Falange, women are going to be cleaner, children healthier, villages happier and homes brighter'.[56] Franco was delighted to have such an effort dedicated to establishing the hegemony of his ideas in so many Spanish homes.[57] Moreover, after a war which had caused many hundreds of thousands of deaths, the majority of men of marriageable age, a mass organization which demanded spinster status as a pre-requisite of active membership was socially extremely useful.[58] The Sección Femenina effectively provided rudimentary social services on the basis of very cheap voluntary labour. In the aftermath of a bitterly divisive war, these elementary services contributed significantly to the legitimization of the new state. This was particularly the case among the Catholic rural lower middle classes who had supported the Francoist war effort.[59]

During the Second World War, Pilar was involved in the power struggle fought within the regime between segments of the Falange and the military. At first, she was aligned with Serrano Suñer but, when his star began to wane, either out of weakness or cynicism, she sided with Franco. On 1 May 1941, Serrano Suñer had provoked the suspicions of the Caudillo by an attempt to create an independent Falangist press free from all censorship other than that exercised by its own Delegación Nacional de Prensa y Propaganda de FET y de las JONS.[60] On the following day, Serrano Suñer made a violent speech at Mota del Cuervo, calling for all power for a tightly knit Falange. It was regarded by both Mussolini and Ciano as equivalent to the Duce's own declaration of dictatorship on 3 January 1925.[61] The assault on power intensified when Serrano Suñer suggested to Franco that Falangist representation in the cabinet should be increased by creating a Ministry of Labour for the young Falangist fanatic from Valladolid, José Antonio Girón de Velasco. Franco could hardly ignore what seemed like an attempt by Serrano Suñer to gain more power for the Falange and to give it a more clearly fascist and less bureaucratic line. Franco agreed to the promotion of Girón but also took other measures to counter Falangist ambitions, naming his under-secretary of the Presidency, Colonel Valentín Galarza, to take over the Ministry of the Interior, which had previously been under Serrano Suñer's influence through its under-secretary José Lorente Sanz. Another of Serrano Suñer's men, José Finat, the Conde de Mayalde, was removed as Director General de Seguridad. Galarza also rescinded the decree exempting the Falangist press from censorship.[62]

A group of top Falangists, including Serrano Suñer, Dionisio Ridruejo, José Antonio Girón, José Luis de Arrese, Antonio Tovar, Miguel and Pilar Primo de Rivera met at the home of Tía Ma, the aunt who had brought up Pilar. They decided to fight back against this apparent triumph of the military camp. Franco received a letter from Miguel Primo de Rivera resigning as Civil Governor and Jefe Provincial of the Falange in Madrid. This was accompanied by another from Pilar which she had given, signed but undated, to Serrano Suñer to be delivered to Franco when he thought best. Both justified their resignations by citing the way in which the legacy of their brother was not being fulfilled – an implied criticism of the military traditionalists who were opposing the fascist drift of the regime. 'I cannot in all conscience', she wrote, 'continue to collaborate in something that we make people believe is the Falange but which in reality is not.' Claiming to be following instructions sent by José Antonio from his tomb in El Escorial, she alleged that only the Sección Femenina was fulfilling the real mission of the Falange. Her letter reflected the views of Serrano Suñer, lamenting as it did the lack of determined Falangists in key posts within the State apparatus. She wrote to Franco in deeply respectful terms and left the door open to an early reconciliation, mentioning her sorrow at leaving the nearly completed Castillo de la Mota and ending 'if one day Your Excellency needs me again for the service of the Falange you will always find me ready to work with the same enthusiasm as up to now . . .'[63] After the resignations, a savage polemic ensued in the regime press which culminated in the dismissal of Serrano Suñer's men in charge of Press and Propaganda in the Ministry of the Interior. In protest, more of Serrano Suñer's followers submitted their resignations: Girón who had just become Minister of Labour on 5 May, José Luis de Arrese as Civil Governor of Málaga and Serrano Suñer himself as Minister of Foreign Affairs.[64]

There were clashes between the police and Falangists and the hostility between the military and the Falange reached boiling point. There were fatalities after fighting in León. At the suggestion of General Antonio Barroso, Franco made separate deals with Arrese, Girón and Miguel and Pilar Primo de Rivera.[65] In the event, the crisis was finally resolved by a series of cabinet changes which significantly weakened Serrano Suñer's position. Serrano Suñer had resigned in the confidence that he was being seconded by those in the Falange who thought like him that the time had come to bid to implement the legacy of José Antonio Primo de Rivera. He did not discover until later was that several of his 'friends' had already met privately with Franco and accepted offers of senior posts. He found out in time and withdrew his resignation. In the cabinet reshuffle of 19 May, two additional Falangist ministers were appointed, Miguel Primo de Rivera as Minister of Agriculture and José Luis de Arrese as Minister-Secretary of the FET y de las JONS, while Girón remained as Minister of Labour. Delighted with all three appointments, Pilar happily submitted to Franco's insistence that, in such difficult moments for Spain, she must remain as Jefe Nacional of the Sección Femenina.[66] Only Serrano Suñer's faithful friends lost their posts. At the time, the increase of Falangist representation in the cabinet made it seem as though Serrano Suñer had triumphed.[67] The behaviour of Pilar and Miguel, like that of Arrese and Girón, had shown the Generalísimo that the Falange could be bought cheaply.[68] Their elevation did not represent, as many thought at the time, a victory for Serrano Suñer but rather the consolidation of Franco's own power over an ambitious section of the Falange. It was almost certainly in recognition of this that, in June 1942, Serrano Suñer brought Mercedes Sanz back into the political arena by giving her a post on the board of the Instituto Nacional de Previsión, the body responsible for what little provision of social security could be found in Franco's Spain.[69]

A little over a year after the great power struggle, the now fully restored Castillo de la Mota was formally handed over by Franco to the Sección Femenina on 29 May 1942. His speech identified himself with the Spain of Isabel la Católica 'Just as we received Spain, so too did Isabel of Castille, divided and split by petty struggles', and, for the construction of what he called his own 'foundational epoch', he instructed the women of the Sección Femenina to take her 'totalitarian and racist policy' to the four corners of Spain.[70] Pilar wrote a fulsome letter of gratitude to the Caudillo. 'General, after the inauguration of the castle, I want to thank you again for giving us such a marvellous school for training our cadres. I assure you that within its walls, the comrades of the Sección Femenina will truly learn with honour to serve Spain, the Falange and its Jefe Nacional and they will not forget who so generously has made possible their training. Respectfully I salute you with the fascist salute and I remain at your orders.'[71] The Castillo de la Mota became the spiritual headquarters of the Sección Femenina and its principal training school for cadres (Escuela de Mandos). In internal design and furnishings, the Castle was like a medieval convent. The dining-room was a monastic refectory and the daily routine revolved around religious services.

The difference was that Pilar was preparing her nuns for a life of service to José Antonio. The Sección Femenina gained the monopoly of publishing his complete works and each member carried, and referred to, a copy as if it were the Bible. The Sección Femenina had played an important part in the carefully choreographed torchlight procession which in November 1939 accompanied the transfer of José Antonio's mortal remains from his grave in Alicante to El Escorial. Members of the Sección, including Pilar herself, embroidered altar cloths that were used in churches along the way and the black velvet shroud that covered his coffin. Women of the organization referred to themselves as 'the brides [*las novias*] of José Antonio' and there was a curious combination of sexual and religious fervour involved in the cult of the absent one. Having helped pave the way to Franco's absolute power, Pilar became the matriarch of the party – in the words of Serrano Suñer, 'the priestess who offered up sacrifices to the memory, the thought and the grand design of her absent brother'. The Falangist intellectual, Pedro Laín Entralgo, said of her, 'above and beyond her sensitive and cordial manner, which was rather childishly awkward, at times could be perceived her tacit sense of being the greatest and appropriate representative of her much missed brother'.[72] There was also a strong Catholic dimension to the Sección Femenina's daily routine. This was derived in great part from the advice given to Pilar by a Benedictine monk, Fray Justo Pérez de Urbel, whom she had met in Burgos in 1938. A fanatical admirer of Franco, he was an especially belligerent member of a group of militant priests who provided theological justification for the military uprising and the objectives of the Falange. Throughout the 1940s and 1950s, he propagated Franco's burning commitment to maintaining the division of Spain into victors and vanquished. Pérez de Urbel was rewarded in 1957 when the Caudillo named him mitred abbot of the monastery of the Fundación de la Santa Cruz at the Valle de los Caídos, his gigantic monument to his own Civil War dead.[73]

During the Civil War and after, at home and abroad, Pilar was a tireless propagandist for Spanish fascism, regularly undertaking foreign trips on which she met Mussolini, Salazar and Hitler.[74] In the spring of 1938, she had appointed two pro-Nazis to important positions within the Sección Femenina: Clarita Stauffer to deputy headship of the SF's Prensa y Propaganda and Carmen Werner to Head (Regidora Central) of the Youth Organization. In April 1938, Pilar's first visit to the Third Reich was sponsored jointly by the Nazi Auslandorganization, the Berlin branch of the Falange and the Ibero-Amerikanisches Institut, the Nazi propaganda operation directed at the Iberian world.[75] She was received by the Duce in October 1938 and he bestowed on her an autographed portrait. After a visit to Portugal to inspect the Portuguese Organization of Mothers and Feminine Youth, she wrote to request a signed photograph of Antonio Oliveira Salazar.[76] In the autumn of 1942, she headed the Spanish delegation to the First Congress of European Youth organized by the Nazis in Vienna. She argued in favour of a more spiritual and Catholic dimension for fascism, a line entirely in tune with the monastic tone of the Castillo de la Mota.[77] On the occasion of meeting Hitler in September 1941, she presented him with a sword from Toledo.[78]

Pilar's 1941 meeting with Hitler led to aberrant speculation in the fevered brain of Ernesto Giménez Caballero. He hatched a grotesque plan to mate her with the Führer. This erotic fantasy was meant to ensure Spain a major position in the new fascist world order which he expected to come from Hitler's victory in the world war. His idea was to establish a new dynasty which would guarantee the perpetuation of the new order, mitigating the Führer's Teutonic harshness with Pilar's Mediterranean warmth. Ernesto had informed Franco and spoken of the notion to Edith Faupel, wife of General Faupel, who had been German Ambassador to Franco during the Civil War and was now Head of the Ibero-Amerikanische Institut. The plan was to be communicated to Hitler via Magda Goebbels. The opportunity arose when he was invited to Weimar as a Spanish representative to a Congress of the Nazi puppet-organization, the European Writers Federation (Europäische Schriftsteller Vereinigung). It was held between 23 and 26 October 1941 and chaired by Goebbels himself. At a social gathering on the margins of the conference, Giménez Caballero met Magda Goebbels with whom he shared his ideas for Latinizing Hitler. Thereafter, he returned to Madrid and informed both Franco and the Papal Nuncio of his scheme 'to catholicize Hitler'.

Giménez Caballero returned to Germany in December, taking with him a bull-fighter's cape (*capote de luces*) as a Christmas present for the Nazi Minister of Propaganda and Popular Enlightenment. On 23 December 1941, he was invited to dinner at the Goebbels household. The meal was preceded by a bizarre scene in which the gawky surrealist taught the lame Goebbels how to use the bull-fighter's cape. As the dinner drew to a close, Goebbels was called away for an urgent meeting with Hitler. In a scene described by Giménez Caballero in steamily erotic terms, the blonde Magda Goebbels, striking in a black velvet evening dress, led him into a small sitting-room. There, before a wood fire, she warmed a brandy glass in her hands then wet the rim with her lips before passing it to him. His irrepressible optimism inflamed by the statuesque Magda's seductive behaviour, he outlined his scheme in greater detail, naming Pilar as the ideal candidate, 'because of the purity of her blood, her profound Catholic faith and because she would carry with her the entire youth of Spain'. Unfortunately, Magda had bad news for him. She had informed her husband of the scheme in October, only to be told that the scheme was not feasible because Hitler had received a bullet wound in the genitals during the First World War 'which has invalidated him for ever'.[79]

On his return to Madrid, Giménez Caballero informed Franco of the fate of his self-appointed mission. The Caudillo's reaction is not recorded, although Giménez Caballero claimed that 'he understood'. Giménez Caballero also took it upon himself to speak with his ecclesiastical contacts and even with Antón Saenz de Heredia, uncle of José Antonio and Pilar Primo de Rivera.[80] It was long afterwards that Pilar herself was apprised of her 'destiny'. With typical innocence and humility, she commented, 'I was told later by Giménez Caballero himself and I am very grateful to him for having such faith in me. But the fact is that I never even found out about the project, nor would I have agreed to it, because I never felt myself to be worthy of having such an important mission entrusted to me and, in any case, my private life was mine and mine only.'[81]

At that time, Pilar was thirty-four years old. In fact she was never to marry, although there was sporadic speculation about possible partners, including the naval captain, Pedro Nieto Antúnez and the brother of Franco's first Minister of Industry, Juan Antonio Suances. She was briefly courted by Javier Conde, the regime ideologue and inventor of the Francoist equivalent of the *Führerprinzip*, the *teoría del caudillaje*. He even accompanied her on her first visit to Nazi Germany.[82] There was also regime gossip about a possible relationship with Dionisio Ridruejo, the dashing Falangist poet with whom she did indeed maintain a warm friendship.[83] However, the official line was that she was always too busy for men.[84] Where Pilar's sexuality lay is difficult to discern. Everything that is known about her public life suggested a flight from adult sexual responsibility, as a response to the fate of her mother. Certainly, devotion to the memory of her brother left little space for real men.

There were also rumours of lesbianism, both specifically about Pilar and more generally about the Sección Femenina. These may have been no more than expressions of the misogyny typical of an aggressively male society. Serrano Suñer, for instance, commented on the butch and bullying tone of Pilar's general staff.[85] In exile in New York, Constancia de la Mora, the feminist and wife of the Republican airforce chief, Ignacio Hidalgo de Cisneros, spoke bitterly to Herbert Southworth in 1939. She was convinced that her sister Marichu was involved in a lesbian relationship with Pilar Primo de Rivera. They were certainly very close friends but there is no reason to believe their relationship was anything more. Marichu was, for a time, Pilar's private secretary and a prominent member of the Sección Femenina hierarchy. She accompanied Pilar throughout the war. The accusation may simply have derived from the fact that Constancia felt considerable hostility towards her sister because of her radically different political orientation. In fact, three years earlier, in 1936, Constancia had assumed that her unhappily married sister had joined the Falange because of a crush on José Antonio Primo de Rivera.[86]

Dedicated totally to her organization, Pilar permitted herself little in the way of a personal or social life. Throughout the war, Pilar watched Axis progress with avid interest, having put aside the Anglophile traditions of her family. In her view, the Russians were responsible for the murder of her brothers. She was therefore particularly enthusiastic about the despatch in the summer of 1941 of a volunteer force, the Blue Division, to fight on the Eastern Front. Eighty-four women of the Sección Femenina accompanied the Spanish troops as nurses, secretaries and ancillary staff. Within Spain, Pilar ordered Sección Femenina members to be available to fill the jobs left behind by male volunteers. She also organized nation-wide collections in order for the Sección Femenina to be able to give each Spanish volunteer on the Eastern Front a Christmas package with a woollen garment, food, tobacco and a medal of the Virgin Mary. In each province, groups of SF members, known as *madrinas* (bridesmaids), were organized to write letters to the front-line volunteers. Pilar was part of the welcoming committee when the volunteers returned.[87]

In mid-May 1943, Pilar received twelve Bund Deutscher Mädel leaders for a tour of Spain sponsored by the Sección Femenina.[88] To make public her continuing enthusiasm for the Third Reich, she accepted an invitation to visit Germany from the head of the Auslandorganization, Gauleiter Ernst Bohle. On 26 July 1943, accompanied by two fiercely pro-Nazi SF comrades, Clarita Stauffer and María García Ontiveros, she flew to Templehof aerodrome, Berlin. She reached the German capital on the day after the fall of Mussolini. Perhaps for that reason, she was the object of lavish attention from the Germans, received by the Gauleiter of every city on her tour and accommodated at the best hotels. Accompanied by Ingeborg Niekerke, leader of the Berlin branch of the Nazi Women's organization, she visited the Brown House in Munich. Her wide-ranging tour of the country was enthusiastically covered by the Nazi press. She was received by Goebbels and Ribbentrop as well as Gertrud Scholtz-Klink, the national leader (Frauenschaftsführerin) of the women's organization.[89] She maintained close relations with General Faupel, whom she received in Medina del Campo in May and met again in Berlin in June.[90]

When, under Allied pressure, Franco began, rhetorically at least, to talk in terms of withdrawing the Blue Division, Pilar was outraged. She believed that improved relations with the Allies would pave the way to a restoration of the monarchy and the eclipse of the Falange.[91] In the autumn of 1943, she was reported to be in contact with extreme elements of a clandestine group known as the Falange Auténtica and returned veterans of the División Azul who were plotting against Franco.[92] Infuriated by a speech by Arrese in which he stated that Spain was no longer totalitarian, she was planning to demand a meeting of the Junta Política to engineer his removal from office, saying that 'to claim that Spain was not totalitarian was treason against the Falange' and that 'the Falange comes before everything else'. She was also alleged to have argued in favour of Spanish annexation of Portugal. Most of all, under the influence of Ridruejo, she was infuriated by reports of the withdrawal of the Blue Division which she regarded as a betrayal of the Falange and of Germany.[93] In early 1944, with the tide turning against Germany, she recommended contempt for 'the pusillanimous who are timidly distancing themselves from the Falange in case things change'. She urged that note be taken of the names of such traitors in case they wanted one day to return to the fold. She pledged the help of the Sección Femenina to Franco in a difficult period: 'Our life as Falangists is rather like our private life. We have to have behind us all the strength and decision of a man for us to feel more secure, and in exchange for that, we offer the abnegation of our services and never to be the occasion of discord. This is woman's role in life: to harmonize the wishes of others and to let herself be guided by the stronger will and the wisdom of the man.'[94]

After 1945, the Sección Femenina undertook ever more social work, through its responsibility for organizing the Servicio Social de la Mujer, whereby all unmarried women between the ages of seventeen and thirty-five did six months social service. Illiterate women were taught to read although one of Pilar's slogans was 'never be a girl crammed with book learning; there is nothing more detestable than an intellectual woman'. From the 1950s her organization evolved into a cross between the Girl Guides and the Women's Institute, making available to many women sporting facilities, music, theatre, cookery and first aid classes. The greatest and most lasting achievements of the Sección Femenina were the monumental task of collecting Spanish folk songs and dances through the sub-section called Coros y Danzas and the homemaking, and particularly cookery, skills imparted to thousands of women through classes and the massively distributed cookbook, the *Libro de Cocina de la Sección Femenina*. She devoted her life to the organization, in a spirit of adulation of Franco, despite endless disappointments over the never-fulfilled legacy of her brother.

Her hopes flared briefly in 1956 when she believed that the then Minister-Secretary of the Movimiento, José Luis de Arrese, was finally being authorized to make the *revolución pendiente*. Arrese was trying to persuade Franco to accept a new constitution for Spain which would have ensured the dominance of the Falange in every aspect of Spanish life. When, as a result of concerted opposition from military, monarchists and ecclesiastical circles, it did not happen, she swallowed the disappointment as so many times before.[95] On 1 April 1960, the Caudillo rewarded her with the title Condesa del Castillo de la Mota. The various changes of the regime throughout the 1960s saw it taken ever further away from the ideals of José Antonio Primo de Rivera. Loyal to her notions of female submission, she adjusted accordingly, clinging to the idea that José Antonio would probably have adjusted similarly to such eventualities. This involved the dutiful acceptance, in the Ley Orgánica del Estado of November 1966, of the eventual return of the monarchy, and, specifically, in 1969, of the nomination of Juan Carlos de Borbón as Franco's successor.[96] During Franco's final illness in the autumn of 1975, she recommended the members of the Sección Femenina to be calm and place their trust in Franco's arrangements for the continuity of his regime. After his death, she recommended loyalty to Juan Carlos in the struggle against any return of political parties.[97] Having devoted much of her life to the Francoist cause, she remained implacably loyal to the Caudillo. When, in 1976, a law of political reform was presented to the Cortes as part of the process of transition to democracy, she was worried by what she saw as a rejection of everything that she had worked for over the previous forty years. Her nephew, Miguel Primo de Rivera y Urquijo, the son of her murdered brother Fernando, persuaded her that to look forward, as the *reforma política* did, was entirely in tune with the legacy of José Antonio Primo de Rivera. In response to his plea, she hesitantly agreed not to vote against the law. In the historic Cortes session of 16–18 November 1976 which dismantled the Francoist system, Pilar abstained.[98]

Pilar seems to have been able to cope with her political disappointments by lavishing affection on her nieces and nephews. In the later years of the Franco regime, as the Sección Femenina, like the rest of the Movimiento, became an ever more unwieldy bureaucratic apparatus, Pilar sought new causes. While remaining slavishly loyal to Franco, she adjusted to changing social norms by playing a part in trying to liberalize Spanish law in regard to the rights of women to join the professions, and of married women to own property and to inherit.[99] When the Sección Femenina was dismantled in 1977, it was succeeded by Nueva Andadura, the Association of Sección Femenina veterans, which was created on 29 November 1977. Pilar was its honorary president until her death on 17 March 1991.

5

A Quixote in Politics: Salvador de Madariaga

There is a certain artificiality in abstracting from Salvador de Madariaga's dauntingly rich career its political dimension. On the occasion of a tribute organized in Paris on his seventieth birthday, Albert Camus quoted to him Turgenev's death-bed note to Tolstoy, 'I am happy to have been your contemporary'.[1] The formal scale of his achievements may be indicated simply by noting that the universities from which he had received honorary doctorates, including Oxford and Princeton, were legion; that he was a member of the Academies of Political and Moral Sciences of Spain, France and Belgium; and of the Real Academia de la Lengua in Spain; that he was a candidate for the Nobel Peace Prize in 1937 and 1952; and that he was awarded the Hanseatic Goethe Prize of Hamburg University in 1972 and the Charlemagne Prize in 1973. Professor, Ambassador and Minister, he was the author of more than sixty books, with distinguished contributions in international affairs, political philosophy, history, social psychology, literary criticism, novels, poetry and drama. Aristide Briand said that he was one of the ten best conversationalists in Europe, a view which was widely shared.[2] Salvador de Madariaga has never been fully appreciated perhaps because of the difficulty of spanning his works sufficiently well to reach a considered synthetic judgement.[3]

His intellectual formation took place in a Spain dominated by the so-called generation of 1898, the Spanish essayists, philosophers and historians who set out to explain the reasons for defeat in the war against the United States. For that reason, in all his works, the theme of national character was paramount. It is in that theme as he applied it to Spaniards, and therefore to himself, that we can find a key to his kaleidoscopic political and diplomatic enterprises. In one of his earliest books, *The Genius of Spain* (London: Oxford University Press, 1923), he explored the essence of national character which he was to develop to the full in his *Englishmen, Frenchmen, Spaniards* (Oxford, Oxford University Press, 1928). He emphasized the importance of literature as an expression of national spirit and found in *Don Quixote* the quintessence of Spanishness. Don Salvador – as he was known to his readers and pupils – was himself always to have a quixotic streak which was to lead him into his greatest achievements and disappointments, and often to earn him the greatest opprobrium. His role and influence were sometimes less than they might have been precisely because he was idealistic and quixotic. His identification with both Don Quixote and Sancho Panza was total. In the 1920s, his favourite pseudonym was Sancho Quijano, a clear indication of his desire to unite the empirical good sense of Sancho Panza with the idealism of Don Quixote. In his *Don Quixote: An Introductory Essay in Psychology*, he made the point explicitly when he spoke of the 'fraternity of soul which united this strange master and this singular servant. A brother in illusion to Don Quixote, Sancho has to follow him along the road to perfection until death – the death of illusion which is sanity.'[4] His illusion was his quixotic search for a perfect world order based on liberty.

That alone is an indication of the extent to which Madariaga had characteristics which were hardly appropriate for success in the intrigue-ridden politics of the Spanish Republic or within international diplomacy in the fascist era: honesty and directness, idealism and liberalism, open-mindedness and a commitment to a world view, and also a priceless sense of humour. It was after all Don Salvador who first recorded and indeed amplified the story about the international congress held to define the elephant, at which the German contribution was a multi-volumed report on the first steps to towards conceptualizing the elephant; the British, a report on elephant shooting in Somaliland; the Russian, a tortured examination of whether the elephant really existed; the French, a pamphlet entitled *L'Eléphant et l'amour*; the American, a feasibility study entitled *The Elephant: How to Make It Bigger and Stronger* and the Polish, a fevered tract on the Elephant and the Polish Question.

Madariaga's sense of humour, so much in contrast with the Germanic *gravitas* cultivated by the followers of his great contemporary and, to some extent, rival, the philosopher, José Ortega y Gasset, has perhaps prevented his achieving adequate recognition in Spain. However, more than his humour, what was to undo him at times, and yet was at the heart of his creativity, was an impulsiveness of word and deed. He had a habit of saying what he thought without perhaps thinking it through. With disarming honesty, he himself recounted an occasion when at the Vienna Opera house he was introduced to the conductor Felix Weingartner and the pianist Emil Von Sauer. He mischievously gave vent to a diatribe against Liszt and was surprised by the glum faces thus provoked. It was only later that he realized that Weingartner and Sauer were the last, and last living, pupils of Liszt.[5] This outspokenness and rapid judgements were occasionally to lead him astray.

He was born on 23 July 1886 in La Coruña, one of eleven children of Colonel José Madariaga and Maria Ascensión Rojo with whom he enjoyed a happy and uncomplicated childhood. Convinced that Spain had lost the war against the United States in 1898 because of her technological backwardness, the Colonel sent the fourteen-year-old Salvador to France to study engineering in preparation for the traditional family career in the army. His subsequent eleven years at the Collège Chaptal, the Ecole Polytechnique and Ecole Nationale Supérieure des Mines gave him the scientific training which was to provide the implacable logic which lay behind and indeed fed his most quixotic activities. His period in France also took him down the road from being a technician to a humanist, which in turn would become the highway which led him to become the most European Spaniard. In his years in Paris, he acquired a passion for history and he wrote, 'It was then that I began to see Spain from the outside, a perspective which completes the view from within. Moreover, I was starting to acquire an international, or to be more exact, a human and worldwide, stance even with regard to events in Spain.'[6]

After graduating in 1911, instead of taking up the expected military career, he returned to Spain and became an engineer for the railway company Ferrocarriles del Norte. In Madrid, he mixed with the influential intellectuals of the post-regenerationist movement, mostly Republicans, and began to write on political and literary subjects in the Madrid press. To his Francophilia he had added an Anglo-Saxon dimension, visiting England for the first time in 1910 and marrying in 1912 Constance Archibald, a Scottish economic historian whom he had met in Paris. By this time, he had come to be considered part of the group of intellectuals who in later years were to be known as '*los hombres de 1914*'. Led by José Ortega y Gasset and including figures such as Manuel Azaña, the future Republican Prime Minister, the Socialist leader Fernando de los Ríos, and the historian Américo

Castro, they had set up the Liga de Educación Política, out of which was to emerge the journal *España* and eventually the newspaper *El Sol*.[7]

The novelist and journalist Luis Araquistain, one of the most distinguished of these intellectuals, gained financial support for *Espãna* from the Allies, who were anxious that their voice should be heard in the great polemics that divided Spain over the First World War. Araquistain had worked in London for the so-called Wellington House Committee, as the Secret War Propaganda Bureau was known. In 1916, when John Walter, president of the board of *The Times*, appeared in Madrid as a representative of the British government to recruit someone to write pro-Allied propaganda especially tailored for Spain, Madariaga was recommended to him by Araquistain. He gave up his job with the railway company and went to live in London as a full-time writer for the news department of the Foreign Office, producing articles for the Agencia Anglo-Ibérica.[8]

After the war, Madariaga was driven by economic necessity to return to his profession as a mining engineer in Spain. He rapidly found himself bored in Madrid, doing translations and contributing occasional articles to the Spanish and British press, including the *TLS* and the *Manchester Guardian*. He prevailed on a powerful uncle who was a member of the Cortes to recommend him for a post as temporary adviser to the League of Nations Transit Conference being held in Barcelona in the spring of 1921. He made sufficient impression on the Secretary General of the Conference, the Frenchman Robert Haas, and its President, Gabriel Hanotaux, to be offered a permanent post in the press section of the League Secretariat in Geneva from August 1921.[9] His linguistic abilities and his mental agility enabled him to rise quickly to become in 1922 head of the Disarmament Section of the League, a post which he held until 1927.

During these years he developed a truly international outlook. He was bitterly disappointed that the League never became a true world organization, something he attributed to American abstentionism. His *Disarmament*, published by Oxford University Press in 1929, both established his reputation and made a public declaration of his commitment to world government. He aspired to 'a world community which will regulate its life from A to Z on the principle that the world is one, and that there is one common interest which should be disentangled from the knot of conflicting interests and once disentangled, served'. He regarded the United States' refusal to join the League of

Nations as a major obstacle to world peace. Indeed, he was always to remain bitter at what he saw as the betrayal of the ideals of Woodrow Wilson.[10] Madariaga was invited to contribute articles on the world situation to *El Sol*, the great liberal newspaper in Madrid. Because of League regulations, he signed them with the pseudonym Sancho Quijano.

At this time, Spain was living under the dictatorship of the eccentric General Primo de Rivera. As the result of his journalistic activities, Madariaga ran into problems with the dictator's censorship machinery. Partly for that reason, Madariaga came to be considered one of the major Spanish Republican intellectuals in exile from the dictatorship. This was not strictly correct, as it was his post with the League of Nations that kept him abroad. Nevertheless, he had little sympathy for either the military regime or the declining monarchy. In 1926, he met Alfonso XIII in the Paris Embassy and the King struck him as cold, distant and indifferent to problems of foreign policy: 'he left me with the impression that he was no longer number one in Spain, but merely a decorative and historical element in the dictator's regime'. Madariaga believed the King to have committed 'the most monumental blunder of his reign' by supporting Primo de Rivera's coup in 1923. Eventually, he was to come to the conclusion that the King fell because 'he had come down from the impartiality of the throne to the partisanship of the boxing ring'.[11]

He resigned from his post in the League in 1927 in response to a demotion and was fortunate to be offered the newly created Alfonso XIII Chair of Spanish Studies in Oxford through the recommendation and good offices of his friend Henry Thomas, at the time Head of Spanish Books and later Director of the British Museum. His volumes *Shelley and Calderón* and *The Genius of Spain* had already been published by Oxford University Press in 1920 and 1923 and he was asked in 1927 by H. A. L. Fisher, then Warden of New College, to write the volume on Spain in a series that he was editing. The title of his chair caused Madariaga some embarrassment among his political friends in Spain. He was immensely amused that, having been refused a Chair of English at Madrid University because he did not have a doctorate, in Oxford he should be given an MA by decree. He wrote later that 'I seemed doomed to enter professions and institutions through the window; I was apt to become a "great noise" while I remained; and I was evidently destined to leave not very long afterwards, in order to jump through another window that seemed more attractive.' As he put it, when he arrived in the Faculty of Modern Languages, 'I was an upstart, a mining engineer turned man of letters, a humanist with no Greek and little Latin, a professor of Spanish with no standing in philology; finally, I was a total stranger to the ways of Oxford, those subtle forms of behaviour, things taken for granted, items of esoteric knowledge, acquaintances, who's whos, meanings of silence, which shape the human pebble well rounded off by the waters of habit.'[12]

He was perplexed by a social and intellectual ambience which seemed to him to be more appropriate to a monastery of Tibetan lamas:

> In those days, Exeter College was led by a set of old scholars, thoroughly cured by immersion in sherry and port (whose colours still ran in rivulets over their complexions), self-possessed, sure of themselves, their eyes safely set within deep sockets, lit by flashes of wit, disdain, humour, everything but surprise, eyes that had read all there was to be read and could bear no more sadness. They walked slowly, spoke slowly and thought slowly; but they knew everything. Lamas of Tibet, whose gatherings ran in the bed of time like a slow, murmuring river going nowhere.

He was even more shocked by the living conditions in Exeter College, and by the fact that the epoch of one man, one bathroom had not arrived. To avoid the risk of pneumonia either by staying in his room or going in search of a bathroom, he fled to the well-appointed Randolph Hotel. He visited All Souls and was most impressed by the food there. Madariaga enjoyed Oxford and was to return regularly throughout his life but he was never comfortable in the life of a teaching academic, being surprised to discover that it can be both tiring and tedious. Like most autobiographers, indeed perhaps less than most, Madariaga was not in the habit of maligning his subject but with regard to his teaching in Oxford, for once he did. Universally recognized as a brilliant extempore lecturer, he was nevertheless, on his own account, startled by the scale of intellectual energy required for tutorials, regularly turned up late, forgot his obligations and mischievously pretended not to know anything.[13]

Accordingly, as he came to feel that teaching was not his vocation, he also became frustrated because of the failure of his far-sighted efforts to alter the way in which Spanish was taught, wanting to link up language teaching to the study of the country's history, art and politics. In the autumn of 1930, he began a sabbatical consisting of a lecture tour in the United States, Mexico and Cuba. On 14 April 1931 the Spanish monarchy fell and the Second Republic was established. On arriving in Havana on 1 May 1931, he learned from the newspapers that, without being consulted, he had been appointed Republican Ambassador in Washington. Since the bulk of the Spanish diplomatic corps were monarchists, the new Republic turned to some of its more prominent intellectuals: Ramón Pérez de Ayala went to London; Américo Castro to Berlin. Madariaga was somewhat taken aback by his own nomination. However, as a passive opponent of the Primo de Rivera dictatorship, and much impressed by the bloodless transition to the Republic, he accepted despite some reservations about having to serve under the rather shady Minister of Foreign Affairs, Alejandro Lerroux.[14]

Madariaga was to remain in Washington for a total of only seven weeks. Indeed, he had barely presented his credentials, when the notorious incompetence of Lerroux in Foreign Affairs ensured that he was required to represent Spain on the Council of the League of Nations. Lerroux had been made Foreign Minister only because his fellow Republican conspirators at San Sebastián in 1930 believed that it was the Ministry which gave him fewest opportunities for embezzlement. Such was Lerroux's ignorance of international relations that he relied heavily on Madariaga. Effectively, then, Madariaga made a disproportionate contribution to the elaboration of Spanish foreign policy by dint of writing the speeches which Lerroux read out in Geneva in his execrable French. Lerroux's linguistic deficiencies also meant that he could not follow the proceedings.[15] Madariaga's anomalous position as an ambassador in Washington who was almost permanently resident in Geneva was resolved by a transfer to Paris in January 1932.[16]

Madariaga had more influence in Geneva than might have been expected, because many Latin American countries were excited by the fall of the monarchy in Spain. The demise of Catholic, aristocratic and monarchist Spain, associated with the oppressive rule thrown off in the nineteenth century, helped revive the idea of a Spanish motherland. A liberal Spain had more chance of creating something analogous to the British Commonwealth or at least acting as intermediary between Latin America and Europe.[17] Accordingly, the Latin American delegates tended to fall in behind Madariaga and this gave him considerable standing in the League. Moreover, since Lerroux cared little for foreign policy, Madariaga, bereft of specific instructions, had unusual freedom which he used to throw his weight behind any decisions which favoured the position of the League.

During this second period at the League of Nations, the major international event with which he had to deal was the Japanese invasion of Manchuria in September 1931. He believed that Japan was attacking the very concept of a world organization as much as China itself and felt that the supine response of the League was crucial in encouraging later aggression by Hitler. His efforts to organize international action against Japan led his being dubbed by the British Foreign Secretary, Sir John Simon, 'the conscience of the League of Nations' and also earned him the nickname of 'Don Quijote de la Manchuria'. He managed to get the issue brought before the Assembly of the League. However, action against an aggressor needed the agreement of the entire Council of the League and also, in this case, the agreement of the United States, which believed that it was better to leave Japan to deal with the clique of recalcitrant army officers thought to be responsible. Accordingly, Madariaga's efforts came to nought.

The more-or-less autonomous position enjoyed by Madariaga under Lerroux came to an end in mid-December 1931. After forming a new government, Manuel Azaña named Luis de Zulueta as his Foreign Minister. Both Azaña and Zulueta had come to believe by February 1932 that Madariaga 'sees Spain too much as a pawn of the League and he must be slowed down so that we are not thrown into what, from Spain's point of view, are quixotic enterprises'.[18] In March, Zulueta grumbled to Azaña that 'Madariaga forgets at times that he represents our country in the League of Nations and instead he acts like an intellectual'. A month later, Zulueta was complaining again about the effect on Spanish relations with Japan as a result of the positions taken up by Madariaga with regard to Manchuria. 'Madariaga takes up quixotic positions in favour of China which cause us problems with Japan.'[19] Madariaga's fervour for the principles of the League of Nations could not be restrained. In the autumn, Azaña claimed that, as Ambassador in Paris, Madariaga was exceeding his authority in trying to establish ties of solidarity with France. In December, his attacks on Japan in Geneva caused serious problems in terms of Spain's relations with Tokyo. Azaña complained that 'Madariaga goes on in Geneva as if he was the spokesman and the apostle of the League of Nations, forgetting altogether that what he says is said by Spain'. He was reprimanded by Zulueta and Azaña who reminded him sternly that foreign policy was made by the government and not by its agents.[20]

If Madariaga's internationalism was the despair of Azaña, it tended to provoke amusement on the part of British diplomats. When Madariaga suggested, perhaps naïvely, to Sir John Simon that the League should put much greater pressure on Japan, Simon replied by asking if the Spanish fleet would be at the League's side. The Permanent Under-Secretary at the Foreign Office, Sir Robert Vansittart, later wrote that

> Leaguers and pure spirits like Madariaga could not see over their ideals to the nakedness beyond. 'The smaller powers were ready', he declared. With what for what? 'The Spanish fleet will always be by the side of the British fleet' he said to Simon, 'whenever the British fleet will stand by the Covenant'. The Señor had forgotten his Sheridan. 'The Spanish fleet thou canst not see, because / It is not yet in sight'.[21]

Curiously, at about the same time, Azaña remarked in the same vein to the French social commentator Angel Marvaud that Madariaga's activity in Geneva 'would be much more effective if it were backed up by a powerful fleet'.[22]

None the less, his activities in this period at the head of the so-called 'straight eight' of Norway, Czechoslovakia, Sweden, Holland, Belgium, Denmark, Switzerland and Spain effectively put Spain back on the map.[23] There can be little better proof of that than the annoyance caused to Fascist Italy by what was peevishly described as Madariaga's 'fanatismo ginevrino e francofilo'. The Italians especially resented the fact that such a fervent internationalist should be able to act autonomously. Their ambassador in Madrid, Raffaele Guariglia, regularly complained to the Foreign Minister, Zulueta, and later to Lerroux when he became Prime Minister again in late 1933 about Madariaga's 'exclusive monopoly of the conduct of Spanish policy towards the League of Nations' and of 'the control that Madariaga exercised' over successive foreign ministers.[24]

In the summer of 1933, while in Madrid, Madariaga called upon the recently arrived Ambassador of the United States, Claude Bowers. The 'rather small, slender man, with the keenly intelligent face of a professor' made a great impression on the Ambassador. Bowers found him to be 'a charming, scintillating, witty, humourous being, more idealist than realist, a dreamer'. He quickly perceived why the Italians disliked him so much: 'he had set an example in fidelity to the

Covenant (of the League of Nations) that must have been embarrassing to some of his colleagues'. 'He had a capacity for righteous wrath', noted Bowers, 'that shocked the diplomatic world, and when he denounced ammunition makers as manufacturers of wars, the reactionaries of the kept press of Paris, from motives not disinterested, demanded his recall.'[25]

Madariaga remained in Geneva for two years until, in the spring of 1934, he returned to Spain to serve briefly under Lerroux as Minister of Education and even more briefly as Minister of Justice. His political position in Spain was a curious one. He had been elected in the June 1931 elections as deputy for La Coruña for the local left liberal group, Federación Republicana Gallega. He had been chosen as candidate and elected entirely *in absentia*, on the strength of his intellectual prestige. He made enemies on both sides of the Cortes in 1931 by speaking against the trial of Alfonso XIII. During the elaboration of the Constitution, he was prominent in efforts to ensure that it contained the celebrated clause whereby Spain renounced war as an instrument of policy. He had hoped to be made Minister of Foreign Affairs but Azaña offered him the Treasury. He turned it down on the then unheard-of grounds that he knew nothing about the job. He believed, rightly as we have seen, that Azaña had not offered him Foreign Affairs because, knowing Spain's military weakness, he was worried that Madariaga would idealistically and dangerously commit to League initiatives weight which Spain did not have. Madariaga was none the less bitterly disappointed by the appointment as Foreign Minister of the historian Claudio Sánchez Albornoz.[26]

Oblivious to the political implications, Madariaga accepted ministerial office from Lerroux. By dint of his alliance with the Catholic authoritarian CEDA under José María Gil Robles, Lerroux was now loathed by the left. Madariaga, who had no real party affiliations and was something of an outsider in Madrid politics, nevertheless became the Minister of Education on 3 March 1934. He left his Embassy in Paris and took up the post in a spirit of curiosity and enthusiasm. He soon found that he was as unsuited for the day-to-day realities of politics as he had been for those of the academic life. Just as he was coming to grips with the problems of education in a country with a minimal infrastructure of schools, universities and trained staff, he was also asked to take on the Ministry of Justice. It is revealing of his lack of political cynicism that he accepted. However, his tenure lasted barely ten days. At the time, dependent for its survival on the votes of the right-wing CEDA, the government was being impelled to introduce an amnesty which would cover General Sanjurjo, who had been involved in the attempted military coup of 10 August 1932. This led to a split in the Radical Party and the fall of the government on 28 April. Most of this passed Madariaga by, but he was smeared along with others in Lerroux's cabinet as an accomplice of the extreme right.[27] On the day after the government fell, Madariaga called on Bowers 'in a happy, mocking mood, in no sense cast down by his drop from the Ministry, for he retained his post as spokesman of Spain in Geneva, which meant more to him than any place in the government'.[28] He was oblivious to the fact that, if it had not been the case before, the opprobrium of the left was now guaranteed for the rest of his life and he never really realized why this was the case.

Indeed, Madariaga's lack of any sense of when to trim was one of his most likeable characteristics. This was made clear after the failed miners' uprising of October 1934, a rash attempt by the left to stop the establishment of authoritarian government. The uprising against the inclusion of the CEDA in the cabinet had appalled Madariaga. Nevertheless, when the right tried to take advantage of the opportunity given it by left-wing defeat to destroy Manuel Azaña, he was similarly outraged. The new CEDA–Radical coalition government imprisoned Azaña and brought him to trial for complicity in the uprising.[29] In the midst of the campaign against Azaña, Madariaga wrote an extremely courageous article in defence of the left-Republican leader. It ensured that the right would view Madariaga with as much suspicion as did the left. It almost certainly guaranteed that the CEDA–Radical coalition did not make him Spain's permanent representative at the League of Nations, although *faute de mieux*, it continued to use him on an *ad hoc* basis.[30]

It was symptomatic of Madariaga's fatal readiness to blunder into the minefields of politics without a clear right- or left-ward direction that he should write, shortly after leaving office, his book *Anarquía y jerarquía*. It was an implicitly corporativist tract in which he attacked universal suffrage as a form of 'statistical democracy'. He put forward instead a notion of what he called 'organic democracy' in which power would lie with representative bodies composed of various social groups, the family etc. Such ideas were part of the regenerationist ethos and linked him to Joaquín Costa and Luis Araquistain.[31] Unfortunately, his criticisms of democracy were not dissimilar to those which were finding currency among the right-wing opponents of the Second

Republic. To make matters worse, he met General Franco in 1935 at the Hotel Nacional in Madrid and later presented him with a copy. He found the General, then Chief of the General Staff, to be intelligent and cautious.[32] To Madariaga's chagrin, 'organic democracy' – shorn of its genuinely democratic elements – was expropriated and distorted by the Franco regime as a substitute for the parliamentary democracy which it had savagely suppressed. He would have been equally chagrined to know that Mussolini read his *Spain* and said that it helped him to decide to back the Spanish rightists who visited him on 31 March 1934 in search of help.[33] Later in his life, Francoists tried with no little malice to cite Madariaga as an intellectual precursor of the regime. Similarly, in 1959, the dictatorship's propaganda services tried to use Madariaga against the PSOE by publishing sections of *Spain* in an anti-Socialist pamphlet.[34]

Madariaga's views on the problems of inorganic democracy, the demagogy and the corruption implicit in parliamentary electioneering remained firm. In 1955, he was to repeat them in his *De la angustia a la libertad*. In language reminiscent of Ortega y Gasset, he wrote that 'The essence of the contemporary problem lies in the unhealthy excrescence of the mass' which is composed of human units who have lost all their signs of individuality as a result of industrialization, urbanization and centralization. Again he was keen to replace the impersonal institutions of parliamentary or 'statistical' democracy with 'organic' ones emanating from the family and the municipality.[35]

At the same time as writing *Anarquía y jerarquía*, he continued to represent Spain at the League of Nations on an *ad hoc* basis, serving in 1935 as Chairman of the Committee of Five (Britain, France, Poland, Turkey and Spain) which worked in vain to stem Italian aggression in Ethiopia. His fervent efforts to initiate League arbitration in the Ethiopian conflict provoked a certain amount of cynical amusement at what was seen as his obsessively ethical and humanitarian approach. José Antonio Primo de Rivera, the leader of the fascist Falange, referred to Madariaga and those who shared his ideals as *palurdos deslumbrados* (bedazzled yokels). None the less, his efforts to met the British demands for the application of sanctions against Italy earned him the approbation and subsequent friendship of Anthony Eden.[36] He could not have known that detailed reports on his activities were being sent by the junior diplomat, Felipe Ximénez de Sandoval, to José Antonio Primo de Rivera who, in turn, was in touch with the Italians.[37]

Shortly after the victory of the Popular Front in February 1936, Madariaga inadvertently became the object of an acrimonious controversy after the disclosure to the press of a confidential note which he had sent to members of the League over some proposals to reform its structure. He was appalled by the venom of attacks on him, especially those emanating from the Republican and Socialist press. These owed not a little to resentment of his unfortunate tenure of the Ministry of Justice during the Sanjurjo amnesty issue. Accordingly, he announced that he was no longer available for government service and retired to his house (*cigarral*) in Toledo on the banks of the Tajo. As he put it, 'By 1936, I was a liberal European parliamentarian in a world that seemed to have very little time for parliaments, for Europe and for liberty.'[38] Shortly thereafter, the Civil War broke out and it was only with some difficulty that he was able to leave Spain, first for Geneva and then for London. His ability to awaken the ire of the left had become apparent at a most untimely moment. An article in which he had argued that from the point of view of liberty, there was no difference between marxism and fascism, appeared in *Ahora* on 21 July 1936, three days after the military rebellion. He made few friends by refusing to take sides and by taking a stance which he described as 'abstaining' from the Civil War.[39]

Perhaps bitter at the way he had been treated by Republicans he had thought were his friends, Madariaga turned his back on the Republic. He believed that both sides were equally at fault and especially felt that that the Republic had not carried out either agrarian or fiscal reform which he later described as 'the two most scandalous injustices which it had been its duty to correct'.[40] This could have been said only by someone who had spent much of the previous five years out of the country and thus not witnessed the titanic efforts of the Republic to introduce reform against the dogged obstruction of the landed oligarchy. Whatever the justice of his complaints against the Republic, his declaration of neutrality in the Civil War was to provoke more hostility than any other aspect of his career.

Notwithstanding the criticisms of right and left, he threw himself into a commendable, if doomed, attempt to bring peace to Spain. He did so with a mixture of idealism and logic untrammelled by reality, explicable perhaps by the curious combination of birth in the Celtic mists of Galicia and education as a scientist in France. Alongside other mediation efforts by the Uruguayan government and by the Spanish Prime Minister Manuel Azaña, his impetuous efforts were not welcome to either side.[41] Indeed, shortly before he got out of Spain, the Ambassador in London, Sr Julio López Oliván, told Anthony Eden that he was worried for Madariaga's safety because he was 'known to be antipathetic to the Communists'.[42] According to his friend Pablo de Azcárate,

> Carried away by his impulsive temperament . . . he did not realize that his standing in Spain was light years away from what would have been necessary, in terms of political prestige, moral authority and general respect, not just to come out with dignity from the difficult enterprise into which he had so carelessly proposed to launch himself, but even to get it off the ground in the minimal conditions indispensable for it not to be swamped, in the eyes of Spaniards from both sides, in the ridicule which most effectively and irremediably kills off an initiative.[43]

From Geneva, Madariaga wrote to Eden on 18 August 1936 to say that he thought both sides equally balanced and unable to win; that the government's lack of authority over extremist parties had deprived it of the monopoly of legitimacy, that this was not a war for liberty and democracy against tyranny since both sides were in favour of regimes incompatible with liberty and democracy. He argued therefore that Britain should intervene on humanitarian grounds to put an end to the war before full-scale Axis or Soviet intervention got under way.[44] He little realized, it would seem, that over a month previously Hitler had decided to launch *Unternehmen Feuerzauber* (Operation Magic Fire) to help the Nationalists, or that the USSR had no plans at that stage to aid the Republic.[45] Madariaga put himself at Eden's disposal to work for the establishment of a neutral cabinet. When Eden showed the letter to the unhappy Julio López Oliván, he did not share Madariaga's optimism.[46] Nevertheless a great round of minuting by Sir Robert Vansittart, Sir Alexander Cadogan and Sir George Mounsey was provoked in the Foreign Office by Madariaga's letter of 18 August to Eden. All three were in agreement that Madariaga should be encouraged to put forward concrete proposals. This he did on 24 August in a further letter to Eden. He proposed a three-power committee under British chairmanship to organize a humanitarian intervention and to oblige both sides to accept a government of leaders not involved in the monarchy, the Republic or the Burgos Junta; the army and the forces of order would be placed under peace-keeping officers from Britain, Mexico and Argentina. As Foreign Office officials, W. H. Montagu Pollack, Sir Horace Seymour and Sir Alexander Cadogan, were quick to perceive, the chances of such a utopian scheme being accepted by either side were remote in the extreme. Cadogan remarked, 'Señor de Madariaga is always inclined to gallop ahead.'[47] Even if the plan had been adopted by Britain, there were few suitable figures to make up the neutral government except Madariaga himself, although he always denied any such ambition.

In this regard, he was to write on 19 February 1937 to his friend, the Socialist professor, Fernando de los Ríos, of his distress that he was thought to have ambitions 'to make good in Spanish politics at any cost'.[48] At this time, in fact, his energies were directed towards the launching of the World Foundation, an organization dedicated to the fulfilment of his internationalist dream. For that reason, he went to considerable trouble to avoid speaking about the Spanish Civil War.

> My silence on Spain was particularly trying in the United States where I spent three months that winter on a lecture tour and where my audiences, not unnaturally, found it difficult to understand that I should refuse to speak on the Civil War. My reasons were obvious: I could not speak for the Rebels, for they stood against all that I hold true; I could not speak for the Revolutionists, not only because I did not believe in their methods (nor, in the case of some of them, in their aims) but because they did not stand for what they said they stood for. They filled their mouths with democracy and liberty but allowed neither to live.[49]

The corollary of this, however, was that while he was away on lecture tours and trying to get the World Foundation off the ground, he was inevitably being pushed ever further out of touch with events in Spain.

As a consequence, some of his judgements were unsound, especially his belief during the first year of the war that Franco could provide the authority and the reforming impetus to carry forward the changes of which the Republic had proved incapable. On 25 September, he told Lloyd George that Franco would be in Madrid within a month, that Franco was 'able, courageous and clean' and should make concessions to the peasantry. The ideal solution, he believed, would have been 'an understanding between Franco and Prieto, the leader of the moderate Socialists'. 'It is for this I myself am striving,' he said. Lloyd George was sceptical about an immediate Franco triumph. A couple of days later, Madariaga told his friend, the Whitehall insider Dr Thomas Jones, that 'if Franco and Prieto join forces, his own chance, he thinks may yet come'. He described his *Anarquía y jerarquía* to Jones as a constitutional programme which could have avoided civil war. To have thought that Prieto and Franco would be able to come together on the basis of his programme was a fanciful miscalculation.[50]

On 11 October, he published an article in the *Observer* entitled 'Spain's Ordeal', in which he angered many on both sides by depicting Republicans and rebels as equally legitimate. He especially outraged those on the left by expressing the unrealistic view that Franco could save Spain if he could free himself of his reactionary entourage and be a channel for national resurgence.[51] In terms of what was happening in Spain, after the atrocities committed on both sides; with the battle fronts hardening; with a working-class government finally established under Largo Caballero in Madrid and the most hard-line rightists dominant in Burgos; with Soviet aid at last on the way and Axis assistance flooding in, there was little chance of agreements being reached. Nevertheless, five weeks later, on 3 November 1936, Madariaga told Thomas Jones that he remained hopeful of Franco providing a left programme for the peasantry.[52] However, mistaken and misplaced though such notions were, his firm resolve to remain *au-dessus de la mêlée* was to give him an unexpected moral authority in the post-war period.

He continued to press a mediation programme long after it was clear that there was no chance of success. He wrote to Eden on 6 November 1936, outlining a scheme which was minuted by Sir George Mounsey: 'The Madariaga scheme strikes me as quite impracticable', and by Sir Robert Vansittart: 'the Madariaga plan won't work, I fear'.[53] On 7 December 1936, he had lunch with Lord Cranbourne, the Under Secretary at the Foreign Office. He was still hopeful that compromise might be possible between Prieto and Franco, saying 'General Franco himself entered reluctantly into the conflict, is open to moderate counsels'. Madariaga suggested again that, when an armistice had been arranged, there should be a government composed of five representatives each named by the Burgos Junta and the Valencia government under a neutral president, and with the senior posts in the Army handed over to British, Argentinian and Mexican officers. Sir George Mounsey minuted the report on the lunch: 'on every other side from Spaniards as well as foreigners, we have heard that the enmity now prevailing in Spain is too ferocious to allow any sort of intervention'.

Sir Robert Vansittart wrote, 'I much doubt whether Señor Madariaga knows anything about Spain as it is now – or whether indeed he was ever any real authority on his own country'. Like so many of his schemes, it had an intellectual coherence but little relationship to reality.[54]

On 19 July 1937, the first anniversary of the outbreak of the war, he published simultaneously in *The Times*, the *New York Times* and *Le Temps*, an open letter to both sides of tragic insight. In it, he made the point that there could be no victors, that whoever won, Spain would be defeated. The article was quoted by Eden in the House of Commons on the same day and this gave rise to bizarre speculation in some quarters that the British government planned to put Alfonso XIII back on the throne with Madariaga as prime minister. Although Madariaga denied the rumours and although the plan was inconceivable, it is difficult to resist the conclusion that the idea appealed to him.[55] On 31 December 1937, he wrote again to Eden urging British intervention to impose an armistice.[56] Not dismayed by the lack of success, he embarked on a frenetic round of visits. On 6 May 1938, he saw Sir Eric Phipps, the British Ambassador in Paris. He put to him the suggestion that France should press the Republic to remove Soviet advisers as a prelude to an armistice and that Britain should press Italy to impel Franco to the negotiating table. Phipps remained unconvinced that 'the French government would be willing to urge the present Spanish government to commit suicide or to clear out all the elements from Moscow, and whether, even if they were willing to use pressure in this sense, the Duce would be sufficiently convinced of the thoroughness of the Russian "purge" to bring his influence to bear upon General Franco.' When he reported to London on the conversation, Sir George Mounsey minuted: 'Señor Madariaga gives us no solid foundation either for his opinions or his suggestions'.[57]

Madariaga spoke to Daladier and other politicians in Paris, desperately, naïvely, hoping that there might be a way whereby the French might send troops in to stop the war. He had travelled to the United States on the same mission. Back in London, Madariaga visited the Portuguese Ambassador, Armindo Monteiro, aware of his close relationship with Antonio Oliveira Salazar and of his friendship with Anthony Eden. Monteiro, who had last seen him in Geneva in June 1936, was shocked to see Don Salvador 'old and sad', going grey. To Monteiro, Madariaga reiterated his hopes of an Anglo-French intervention to impose peace. Lamenting along the way that he considered Russian aid to the Republic to be a 'calamity', he suggested that substantial French aid to the Republic might permit a peace settlement on equal terms and therefore without reprisals. Monteiro told him that the war would end only with the victory of one side or the other and that foreign intervention would just provoke a general war. As might have been expected from Salazar's representative, he declared that 'to build peace we must start from the victory of General Franco'. Faced with this response, Madariaga turned to talk of his other preoccupation of the day, his great biography of Christopher Columbus.[58] None the less, he continued to seek mediation, both in Europe and in the Americas. In mid-November 1938, with the tide definitively turning against the Republic in the Valley of the Ebro, he approached Monteiro again in the hope that Salazar might be persuaded to mediate. As Monteiro politely told him, things were too far gone.[59]

Madariaga's calculations about the Spanish Civil War and the possibility of a negotiated peace had turned out to be wrong. However, in later years the importance of his remaining outside Spain was to become clear. His role in the subsequent anti-Franco struggle was an important one and far greater than might have been expected. Like many aspects of the resistance against the dictatorship, it is difficult to reconstruct and to quantify. Inside Spain, the defeated Republicans' clandestine opposition faced imprisonment, torture and execution. Outside, the exiles were scattered across the world from Latin America to Eastern Europe. The wartime divisions in the Republican camp, between liberal democrats, Socialists, Communists, Trotskyists and anarchists were intensified by defeat and exile. Weak and divided, the Republicans thought only of overturning the victory of the Nationalists, something which could not be done without the help of the Western powers.[60] In such a context, Madariaga could play a more crucial role than might have been anticipated.

By the end of the Civil War, he had recovered from the sceptical sympathy that he had once shown for Franco. He now felt an aversion for Franco only surpassed by his opposition to communism.[61] From his unique position, he was able to see something to which the bulk of the Republican leadership was blind. The Western powers were loath to help the Republic in exile for many reasons. They believed it to be tainted by communism. Its internal divisions gave no guarantee of stability. Moreover, to support one side necessarily implied a continuation of the Civil War. Accordingly, Madariaga saw the urgent need for a non-partisan alternative to Franco. By having remained outside Spain, and by the fact that he was not linked to any particular faction of the opposition, he was in a remarkable position to help bring it about. After the Civil War, Madariaga was one of the few people with the standing to request and to get an audience at the Foreign Office, the State Department or in the many European institutions to which he had access.

During the Second World War, he devoted himself to the propagation of the Allied cause and to the re-establishment of democracy in Spain. He had lost all his possessions in Madrid, not in the course of the war, but afterwards when the 'forces of order' under Franco arrived in the capital.[62] Madariaga made weekly broadcasts to Latin America in Spanish for the BBC and continued to do so for nine years. He also spoke to Spain for the Spanish service of the Radiodiffusion Française operated by the Free French, as well as to France in French. In the long term, his writings and his broadcasts would have far greater impact in Spain than his efforts to create an alternative government to Franco credible enough to find Allied support.

At the beginning of 1940, however, when British policy-makers were worried that Francoist Spain might decide to pay its debts to the Axis, there was a propitious atmosphere for the establishment of a representative body of moderate elements from the anti-Franco camp which could be held up to Franco as a possible counter-government. In the summer of 1940, with the good will of the British government, such an instrument of pressure was created in the form of the Directory of the Alianza Democrática Española, which was led by Colonel Segismundo Casado, who had rebelled against Negrín and the Communists in the final stages of the war. Madariaga was to be its chief theorist, alongside other anti-communist figures such as the Socialist Wenceslao Carrillo and the anarcho-syndicalist Juan López Sánchez. The moment was brief and the British did not give the initiative the enduring support that it would have needed for success. Madariaga's influence was perhaps less than it might have been at this stage because of the distance that existed between him and the regionalist anti-Francoists. Indeed, both Manuel de Irujo, leader of the Basque exiles in London, and his Catalan equivalent Carles Pi i Sunyer refused to join the Alianza.[63] Somewhat hostile to autonomist aspirations, Madariaga became involved in polemics with the Catalan and Basque leaders exiled in Britain. He believed, not without reason, that the regionalists put their local aspirations before the anti-Franco struggle.

He saw this as one of the most powerful reasons behind the failure of the anti-Franco exile.[64]

At various stages towards the end of the war, there were other paper schemes for governments to replace Franco. Madariaga was usually a fixture in them, along with Ortega and other moderate figures like the liberal intellectual Dr Gregorio Marañón. Such was the case in late 1943 when the leaders of the monarchist opposition, Pedro Sainz Rodríguez and José María Gil Robles, tried to put together a compromise cabinet which they hoped would get the support of the British government. Again in 1946, there was sporadic talk of a government under Colonel Casado and including Madariaga.[65]

Immediately after the end of the war, Madariaga issued an influential book *Victors, Beware* (London, Jonathan Cape, 1945) which called for a united Europe. In it, the dominant themes of the rest of his political life came together: European unity and the re-establishment of democracy in Spain. Franco's Spain was the major obstacle to both. The continuation of Franco in power denied the United States the possibility of giving Spain economic aid. An economically stricken Spain was seen by Madariaga as an open invitation to the Communists to create mischief.[66] By such arguments, he got the State Department to consider the problem. On 10 March 1947, Madariaga had an interview with John Hickerson, Acting Director of the Office of European Affairs, and other senior officials in the State Department. He argued that the continued existence of the Franco dictatorship was only advantageous to the Russians and 'a disaster' for the Western powers. It prevented, *inter alia*, 'the completion of an Atlantic system of security'.

Urging the restoration of the monarchy under Don Juan de Borbón, Madariaga claimed that Franco would go if the USA and the UK were determined that he should. He suggested the use of force if necessary, or at least an embargo on petroleum and cotton exports to Spain. Prior to that, a 'secret emissary' representing the United Kingdom and the USA – he suggested Winston Churchill – should be sent to inform Franco of the decision that he must go. This idea and other details related to it bore a notable resemblance to the American proposal for a joint démarche presented to the British in the course of April 1947, but rejected by Bevin.[67] In fact, Madariaga soon became disillusioned about the possibility of the British government ever seriously trying to remove Franco. At this time, Gil Robles saw Madariaga in Oxford where he spoke to him of his view that the Foreign Office was the major obstacle to anti-Franco action. Gil Robles was struck by the fact that 'his monarchist convictions and his rejection of universal suffrage are greater than ever'.[68]

At this point, Madariaga was called upon to take part in numerous international organizations. His consequent eminence gave a remarkable resonance to his criticisms of Franco. He was first President of the Liberal International from its foundation in 1947 until 1952 when he became its honorary president. He was one of the founders of the Collège d'Europe and its president. He was an active member of UNESCO until he resigned in protest at the admission of Franco's Spain. The first Congress of Europe held at The Hague in 1948 designated him president of its cultural committee, a post he held until 1964. He was given *carte blanche* to recommend possible Spanish delegates and he used his influence in the European Movement to ensure that invitations were issued to the two most powerful leaders of the non-Communist opposition, the Socialist Prieto and the monarchist Gil Robles. In fact, Gil Robles was prevented from attending by the withdrawal of his passport by the Spanish government.[69] Nevertheless, Madariaga was among the first to perceive that agreement between Prieto and Gil Robles was the *sine qua non* of creating a realistic alternative to Franco that might gain the support of the Western powers. At that time, the European Movement was composed of National Councils and international political groupings, of Socialists, Christian Democrats and so on. For countries suffering dictatorship, it was decided to invite councils of exiles and Madariaga set about using this as an opportunity to build a united anti-Franco opposition with a powerful European platform.

He wrote to Prieto of the 'shocking separatist irresponsibility' of both Basques and Catalans, against which he was to campaign for the rest of his life.[70] However, eventually persuaded by Prieto of the impossibility of persuading the Basques and Catalans to restrain their language, Madariaga decided to include both Catalans and Basques in the Spanish Federal Council of the European Movement. It thus became in his words 'what the government of the Republic in exile had not managed to be: the only body in which can be found represented all the colours of the Spanish political rainbow except the totalitarians, communists and fascists'.[71] The Spanish Federal Council never became a plausible alternative, but the publicity that Madariaga generated was a constant thorn in the side of the regime. He organized regular Spanish/European conferences under the auspices of the European Movement, holding meetings in Paris in 1950 and 1952 and in

Toulouse in 1955. In 1957, he threw the weight of the Spanish section of the European movement into condemning, and helping to thwart, an American proposal for the entry of Franco into NATO.[72]

Since he had to make a living, he continued to write. His outspoken book on Simón Bolívar, whom he denounced as 'nothing but a vulgar imitator of Napoleon with dreams of reigning over a South American empire', so outraged Venezuelans that he was hanged in effigy in Caracas. In the post-war period, however, his political activities were devoted to the linked tasks of removing Franco from Spain and fostering European unity. He regularly broadcast against Franco and in so doing reached an enormous audience. He may not have overthrown Franco, but the Caudillo's official biographer referred to him later as 'Franco's enemy no.1'.[73] He also contributed to the exile magazines *Ibérica* and *España Libre* which were published in New York and to Julián Gorkín's *Mañana: Tribuna Democrática Española*.[74] However, his possible impact within an opposition dominated by the Communist Party was diminished because of his determined anti-Communism and his links with the Congress for Cultural Freedom, of which he was for a time an honorary president and in whose journal *Cuadernos*, edited by Gorkín, he was a contributor. He had become a friend of Allen Dulles, the director of the CIA, when Dulles was Secretary General of the United States delegation to the League of Nations and they remained close friends in the 1950s.[75]

His broadcasts had the biggest impact of all, their good sense and humanity contributing to keeping alive inside Spain the ideal of a civilized, humanitarian, democratic Spain. When Madariaga denounced the grey prison of Franco's Spain, he could not be denounced as a simpleton at the service of Moscow. By his stance during the Civil War he had established his credentials as a man of political independence. Typical of this independence, and of his always humourous line of 'third way' opposition to both Communism and the Franco regime, he referred to Spain as Yugoespaña, a marvellous pun which not only associated the Franco dictatorship with that of Tito but by the use of the word *yugo* or yolk characterized the regime and also ridiculed the Falangist symbol of the yolk and the arrows.[76] Apart from his horror at Franco's abuse of power and the elimination of justice in Spain, Madariaga's main complaint against Franco was that he was 'preparing Spain for Communism' by repressive policies which prevented any form of political activity other than the clandestinity which favoured the Communists. 'The regime unwittingly acts as the best recruiting agent for Communism by dubbing as Communist every adversary it wishes to deprive of his liberty.'[77] He abhorred the corruption of 'the drones and locusts of the regime that are eating away at the nation's patrimony'. It might be thought that his journalistic and broadcasting activities had little effect. However, apart from keeping alive world-wide interest in Spain and hostility to Francoism, and maintaining the morale of the democratic opposition, we now have evidence that they seriously needled Franco himself.[78]

Loathing, too, the fact that the dictatorship constituted an obstacle to Spanish entry into Europe and NATO, with remarkable prescience he associated the future democratization of the country with entry into both. He also foresaw the need for a government of the liberal centre after Franco.[79] The biggest contribution that he made to its eventual achievement took place in 1962. In May 1960, in his capacity as President of the Liberal International, he spoke with his opposite number in the Socialist International, Alsing Andersen, about the possibility of a joint meeting to bring together representatives of the democratic anti-Franco opposition from both inside and outside Spain. The idea was to create an 'assembly of notables' with seventy figures from the interior and fifty from the exile and thereby present a democratic alternative to the dictatorship. Madariaga thereby hoped to put an end to the idea the regime had exploited so successfully, that the only choice was between Francoism and Communism. The notion quickly gained adherents and was picked up and developed within Spain by the Asociación Española de Cooperación Europea which was presided over by Gil Robles. The scheme eventually developed into the IV Congress of the European Movement held in Munich from 5 to 8 June 1962 and devoted to discussion of the Spanish situation under the heading 'Europe and Spain'.

Preparations for the meeting coincided with a wave of industrial unrest in northern Spain and caused the paranoid regime considerable alarm. Linking the strikes and Madariaga's planned Munich meeting, the Francoist press announced that to deal with unrest provoked from abroad, martial law would be declared. Inadvertently, the regime was recognizing the symbolic significance of Munich. The exiled opposition was coming to terms both with conservative anti-Francoists and with the new opposition which had grown up in the 1950s. Were it not for the exclusion of the Communists, Munich could be seen in many ways to prefigure the great movement of democratic consensus which was to bear fruit in the 1970s. Monarchists, Catholics and renegade Falangists met Socialists and Basque and Catalan nationalists in Munich. However, without a crucial intervention by Madariaga, the conference might not have taken place. When they met in the Hotel Regina Palace in the afternoon of 4 June, Gil Robles opposed the idea of dialogue between the two sets of delegates. At a dinner organized by Robert van Schendel, the Secretary General of the European Movement, Don Salvador, aided by one of the principal organizers of the meeting, Enrique Adróher (known as 'Gironella'), persuaded Gil Robles to reconsider. It was agreed that there would be two working parties, Comisión A and Comisión B, led respectively by Gil Robles and Madariaga. Since members of both the interior and exterior delegations collaborated in both, it was possible for the two groups to work to produce a joint document which denounced the dictatorial power of Franco, the abuse of human rights in Spain and concluded that 'Either Spain evolves or she will be excluded from European integration.'

The Assembly was closed on 8 June by a moving speech from Don Salvador. 'Europe is not just a Common Market nor the price of coal and steel. It is also above all a common faith and the price of man and his liberty. Is Europe not going to regard it as essential that all its members enjoy a public life? If Madame de Sévigné could write to her daughter: "I feel the pain in your stomach", why cannot Europe say to Spain, "I feel the pain of your dictatorship"?' He ended with the words 'the civil war which began in Spain on 18 July 1936, and which the Regime has maintained artificially through censorship, the monopoly of the Press and the Radio and its victory parades, that civil war ended in Munich the day before yesterday on 6 June 1962'. Nearly one thousand delegates of the European Movement applauded and approved by acclamation the conclusions of the Spaniards and the conditions which the EEC should demand for Spanish entry. The President of the Congress, Maurice Faure, declared that Europe awaited Spain with open arms.[80]

It was a measure of the importance of the Munich Congress that Franco had its sessions monitored closely. He and his Cabinet discussed the perceived threat posed by Madariaga and Gil Robles well into the early hours of the morning of 9 June. The Caudillo ordered his Minister of Information to unleash a ferocious response. The reaction of the Francoist press could hardly have been more hysterical. Madariaga was denounced as a 'decrepit bawd' who organized the union of traitors to the regime. Many of the Spanish delegates were arrested and sent into exile for their part in what came to be known as the *contubernio de Múnich* (the filthy Munich liaison).[81] Franco himself gave vent to his outrage in a series of speeches made in Valencia some weeks later. Denouncing liberalism as weak and rotten, he derided the delegates to Munich 'as the wretched ones who conspire with the reds to take their miserable complaints before foreign assemblies'.[82]

While Spain was a democracy in the 1930s, Madariaga felt able to devote his time in efforts to improve the world situation. Indeed, he tried through his work in the League of Nations to put Spanish democracy at the service of an international ideal. However, his internationalism did not earn him the respect of those who were embroiled in narrow domestic politics. Yet when Spain ceased to be a democracy under Franco, he dedicated his internationalism to the cause of Spanish democracy. His anti-communism deprived him of some of the success that he might otherwise have had in uniting the opposition to the dictatorship. Nevertheless, his achievement in Munich pointed the way to the negotiated transition to democracy that was to take place in the 1970s. It was fitting then that, after Franco's death, Don Salvador de Madariaga should return to Spain in May 1976. He took up the seat in the Real Academia to which he had been elected shortly before the outbreak of war in 1936 and which was denied him by the dictatorship against which he had deployed his most effective efforts in the cause of democracy. He was received by King Juan Carlos and viewed with reserved optimism the possibilities for the building of a constitutional monarchy.[83] In the two remaining years of his life, he was able to watch with great satisfaction the beginnings of the transition to democracy. His death in 1978 prevented him seeing the fulfilment of his most heartfelt wish – the incorporation of Spain into Europe. The following years and his centenary year in 1986 have seen a flowering of interest in his career and a recognition of his achievement as the most European of Spaniards.

6

A Pacifist in War: The Tragedy of Julián Besteiro

In the course of a long and distinguished career within the Spanish labour movement, Julián Besteiro was variously president of the Socialist Party, the PSOE, of its trade union confederation, the Unión General de Trabajadores, and of the Cortes of the Second Republic. As an intellectual – he was an academic philosopher – he was identified unequivocally with the left. In consequence, when the Civil War broke out, he could hardly have been expected to be seen as anything other than a partisan of the Second Republic. That was certainly General Franco's view and, despite, or perhaps because of, his efforts to bring peace to wartime Spain, he died in a Francoist prison. However, his attempts to bring the war to an end suggest that he might properly be considered to belong to the category of the 'third Spain' that stood outside the hatreds of the Spanish Civil War. Friends and enemies alike speak of his personal rectitude, dignity and austerity. In his professional life as a university professor and as a politician, he was irreproachable. His refusal to go into exile out of loyalty to the people of Madrid led to his imprisonment and death at the end of the Civil War. Besteiro was respected by all sections of the political spectrum, except for the extremes of right and left.

His Socialist rival, Indalecio Prieto, commented that 'no Socialist was as ferociously opposed as he was by his own comrades' yet still judged him to have been a 'lay saint' (*santo laico*).[1] The revolutionary left of the PSOE during the Republic vilified him for his reformism. The Francoist right could invent only the most feeble accusations and, to an extent, that is why they hated him. Besteiro could not be dismissed as a cynical rabble-rouser. The Francoist propagandist, Francisco Casares, in his pitiful and nauseating set of portraits of the principal Republican figures, wrote of 'the propriety of Besteiro's language, the moderation of his attitudes, and his gentlemanly dignity' only as a basis for a vicious critique on the lines that 'marxists of Besteiro's type are more dangerous than those who are uneducated fanatics . . . He methodically prepared, theorized, and speculated with, anti-Spanish and revolutionary violence and that is as fraudulent and serious as the actions of those who actually handled the dynamite in 1934.'[2] Casares' words reflect the difficulty that Francoists had in justifying their appalling mistreatment of an incorruptible man of peace who had made significant efforts to stop the slide into violence during the Second Republic and tried during the war itself to bring about a peace settlement.

Everyone who knew Besteiro was struck by the almost aristocratic elegance of his demeanour, by the simplicity and courtesy of his manner, and by his rectitude. Francesc Cambó said once that, when Besteiro took part in a parliamentary debate, he elevated its level.[3] Yet such was the distance Besteiro preserved that few could say that they really knew him. He never permitted anyone outside his family circle to address him in the intimate 'tu' form.[4] His letters to his wife, Dolores Cebrián, show him to have been an exemplary husband, concerned in the worst moments of his imprisonment only with ensuring that she should not suffer. According to his niece, Carmen de Zulueta, he was affectionate, adored children and 'was fun, jolly, he played with us and made up songs and invented games which gave us enormous pleasure'.[5] Others who knew him outside the political arena were entranced by his warmth and simplicity.[6] In contrast, his political colleagues often found him touchy – even, in the case of Prieto, 'very vengeful' – and liable to bear grudges if criticized.[7] For another shrewd Socialist commentator, Antonio Ramos Oliveira, Besteiro had 'a character which was extraordinarily complex, dignified but not humble, very sensitive to personal questions'.[8]

Before 1939, Julián Besteiro was considered to be Spain's leading theoretical marxist.[9] That judgement, which underlay the charges against him at his trial after the Civil War, seems in retrospect astonishing, although it is based on two reasonable premises. The first is that he was a distinguished university philosopher. Besteiro had the highest academic credentials as Professor of Logic in the Universidad Central de Madrid. Moreover, he was one of the few intellectuals in the pre-war Partido Socialista Obrero Español. Secondly, between 1925 and 1931, he was President of both the PSOE and of its union organization, the Unión General de Trabajadores. In those positions, he played an important role in numerous crucial debates, consistently basing his arguments on what he presented as the tenets of classical marxism. However, few if any of his pronouncements extended beyond the limited reformism broadly known as Kautskyism, and none of them could be classified as creative or original marxism. Indeed, his contribution to marxist thought was extremely limited.[10] Moreover, there was an element of moralistic rigidity about much of his thinking on both the tactics and the strategy which he felt ought to be adopted at any given moment by the Socialist Party. The fact remains that his intellectualism, combined with personal austerity and a deep humanity, was the basis of the enormous respect with which he was regarded by many people.

Born in Madrid on 21 September 1870, Julián Besteiro Fernández was the son of a prosperous shopkeeper. He was educated at the freethinking Institución Libre de Enseñanza, where among his classmates could be found the humanist Socialist, Fernando de los Ríos, the poets Manuel and Antonio Machado and Constancio Bernaldo de Quirós, the distinguished criminologist. After studying in the Faculty of Philosophy and Letters in Madrid, he spent periods at the Sorbonne in 1896 and at the Universities of Munich, Berlin and Leipzig in 1909–10. Until his forties, he was a positivist in academic terms and a liberal republican in politics. In 1908, he joined the Partido Radical of the corrupt Republican politician Alejandro Lerroux. As a consequence of his doubts about Lerroux, these first steps in opposition to the monarchy culminated in Besteiro's membership of the Agrupación Socialista Madrileña, to which he was attracted by the morality and decency of the Socialists. In that year, 1912, he gained the Chair of Fundamental Logic in the Faculty of Philosophy and Letters. He quickly became president of the professional workers' section of the UGT. In 1913 he married Dolores Cebrián, a professor of physics and natural science at the teachers' training college in Toledo, who was to be his faithful companion until his death. By 1914 he had been elected a member (*vocal*) of the Comité Nacional of the UGT and at the X Congress of the PSOE, in 1915, vice-president of the party's Comité Nacional.

Besteiro became a national figure in 1917 during the revolutionary general strike of that year. He was tried as a member of the strike committee and sentenced to life imprisonment. In the amnesty campaign which followed, he was elected as a member of the town council (Ayuntamiento) of Madrid. In the general elections of 24 February

1918, he was elected to the Cortes as deputy for Madrid. Thereafter, his positions became progressively less radical. His experiences during the repression which followed the 1917 strike intensified his repugnance for violence. He became aware of the futility of Spain's weak Socialist movement's undertaking a frontal assault on the State. It was no doubt for that reason that he opposed the PSOE's affiliation to the Comintern. During the debates on the Third International, he argued convincingly against acceptance of the twenty-one conditions imposed by Lenin and, without going so far as to condemn the Soviet experience, postulated the inapplicability to Spain of the dictatorship of the proletariat. The essential moderation of his positions was confirmed by a period in England on a scholarship to research the Workingmen's Educational Association. His time there in 1924 confirmed his incipient reformism and he returned to Spain a convert to the ideas of the reformist Fabian Society.

In the meanwhile, Spain was subjected to the dictatorship of General Miguel Primo de Rivera. The Socialist movement was deeply divided over the issue of how to respond to the new regime. While there was broad agreement that it would be foolish to sacrifice the movement in any attempt to re-establish the unlamented constitutional monarchy and its electoral corruption, there was bitter polemic over the Dictator's offer that the UGT participate in his corporative syndical apparatus. Against Indalecio Prieto and Fernando de los Ríos, who argued that the PSOE should join the democratic opposition against the dictator, Julián Besteiro successfully propounded collaboration. He deployed the argument that was always to remain the central plank of his political thought. From the premise that Spain was still a semi-feudal country awaiting a bourgeois revolution, he erected a logic of apparent revolutionary purity, concluding that it was not the job of the Spanish working class to fulfil the tasks of the bourgeoisie. The premise was erroneous since, although Spain had not experienced a political democratic revolution comparable to those in England and in France, throughout the nineteenth century the country had undergone a profound legal and economic revolution which put an end to the remnants of feudalism. Besteiro's conclusion that the working class could stand aside and leave the task of building democracy to the bourgeoisie was thus entirely unrealistic.

Nevertheless, thought Besteiro, while awaiting the moment at which the bourgeoisie would fulfil its historic task, the UGT should seize the opportunity offered by the dictatorship to build up working class strength. This argument – coming from the President of both the PSOE and the UGT – was persuasive and it found an enthusiastic audience in the trade-union bureaucracy eager to reap the benefits of having a monopoly of state labour affairs. The relative success – in the mid-1920s, at least – of the collaboration with the Primo de Rivera dictatorship seems to have contributed to Besteiro's tragically misplaced optimism at the end of the Civil War about the likely nature of the Franco regime. However, as the Primo de Rivera dictatorship became ever more unpopular in the economic downturn at the end of the 1920s, opinion within the PSOE turned against Besteiro.[11] The opposition to the regime grew into the great republican movement which was to sweep away the monarchy in the municipal elections of 12 April 1931. In mid-1930, Besteiro found himself in a small minority in the PSOE in arguing against Socialist collaboration in the broad opposition front established by the Pact of San Sebastián and eventually in the future government of the Republic. He also opposed the participation of the UGT in the general strike planned for 15 December 1930, a reticence which later caused him considerable difficulties within the PSOE.[12] At a joint meeting of the PSOE and UGT executive committees on Sunday 22 February 1931, he felt obliged to resign as President of both the party and the union.[13] Thus began a process of marginalization from his erstwhile comrades. Moreover, his theoretical abstractions about the nature of the historical process through which Spain was passing seem to have given him a sense of knowing better than they did.

When the Republic was established, Besteiro was elected almost unanimously President of the new Cortes Constituyentes (Speaker of the House) by deputies confident that he would be a guarantee of impartiality. His election provoked a eulogy from the monarchist and fiercely anti-Republican newspaper *ABC*.[14] He accepted because he was flattered by the implicit recognition of his superiority and in the rather arrogant belief that it was his duty to put what he considered to be his unique insights at the service of a regime which faced difficult and dangerous tasks. The apparent contradiction with Besteiro's political abstentionism provoked bitter criticisms from his great rival within the party, Francisco Largo Caballero, to whom resentment came easily, especially in the case of the elegant professor. The bluff Prieto was also irritated by Besteiro's elaborate courtesy. According to Azaña, 'Prieto is vexed by thc polite smile and exquisite manners of Besteiro, which he calls "typical of the Institución Libre de Enseñanza"'. The sense of the dignity and importance of his office with which Besteiro conducted his presidential duties convinced Prieto that the post pandered to 'his vanity, of which he has an inexhaustible supply'. At the same time, his taciturnity sometimes appeared supercilious and could hardly endear him to the affable and talkative Prieto.[15] He was considered a rather dry and boring orator. Azaña commented on one of his speeches, 'cold and long. Besteiro does not have the emotion that communicates.' Nevertheless, the seriousness with which he fulfilled his duties helped the Republican Constitution on its difficult passage through the Cortes in the autumn and winter of 1931.[16]

During his period as President of the Cortes, Besteiro began to manifest increasingly conservative views. He spoke in favourable terms of the Civil Guard, a body whose abolition was one of the PSOE's most dearly held objectives.[17] A certain intellectual, if not aristocratic, hauteur was discernible in his relations with his party colleagues. He believed that the collection of deputies who constituted the Cortes were simply not up to the historic task that faced them.[18] He had little to do with the bulk of the PSOE parliamentary group, the *minoría parlamentaria*, commenting 'they are not men of government'.[19] He gave every indication of despising his colleagues. In particular, he was infuriated by the professorial tone of his comrade, Fernando de los Ríos. A distinguished law professor from Granada, successively Minister of Justice, of Education and of Foreign Affairs between 1931 and 1933, De los Ríos was a humanist Socialist, ideologically close to Besteiro, who none the less regarded him as 'a complete nincompoop' (*tonto integral*). Indeed, behind his external appearance as an English gentleman, and his gentle smile, Besteiro could be touchy and bad-tempered. Day after day, his subordinates at the presidential table of the Cortes would hear his muttered expletives and commentaries on what he saw as the inanities of his party comrades. The general feeling among the Socialist deputies was that behind Besteiro's apparent impartiality there was considerable hostility towards them.[20]

It was a view shared by Azaña. After the failed military coup of General Sanjurjo on 10 August 1932, left-wing deputies rallied to the threatened Republic. There was progress again for crucial parliamentary business – particularly the Catalan autonomy statute and the agrarian reform bill – which had been stalled by the obstructive tactics of the Radicals and right-wing agrarians. Azaña, however, believed that Besteiro closed sessions of the Cortes to the detriment of the government either out of physical tiredness, since he was of rather delicate health, or out of a disinclination to help the government, 'to which, it appears, he is no friend. He chairs sessions in the interests of the opposition. Largo and Prieto are very annoyed with him.'[21]

At the XIII Congress of the PSOE from 6 to 13 October 1932, Besteiro was subjected to severe criticism for his restraining role in the strike of December 1930. He did not compete for the presidency of the party, although he still got 14,261 votes against the 15,817 which elected Largo Caballero.[22] The use of the block votes of the union federations controlled by his supporters enabled him to ride more criticisms about the December strike and regained him the presidency of the UGT at its XVII Congress held from 14 to 22 October.[23] Nevertheless, he can have been left in little doubt about the hostility towards his positions emanating from the Largo Caballero wing of the party.

At the XIII PSOE Congress, Besteiro had made it clear that he did not think it wise for the Socialists to leave the cabinet. However, he soon changed his mind. As scandal surrounded the government after the savage repression of anarchist labourers at the village of Casas Viejas in early January 1933, he made little secret of his belief that the Socialists should not continue in the cabinet.[24] At the worst moment for the Republican–Socialist coalition, during the period of parliamentary obstruction by the Radicals in the spring of 1933, Azaña concluded that Besteiro's punctilious behaviour was deeply damaging to the government. Besteiro failed to seize the moments when legislative progress might have been made. He permitted the provocative interruptions and procedural obstructions of the opposition troublemakers. In mid-February, an innocuous law on highways was swamped with amendments. To the delight of his parliamentary colleagues, one Radical deputy alone, Gerardo Abad Conde from Lugo, put down over one hundred frivolous amendments, each of which arbitrarily demanded a different width for each section of highway, some to be eight metres, forty centimetres, others to be eight metres, forty-two centimetres, and so on. This inspired others to propose that the amendments be converted into additional clauses to the law, again aimed at bringing government business to a halt. Azaña called on Besteiro to use his powers to put a stop to this abuse of procedure. To his dismay, Besteiro made it clear that he was not prepared to confront the opposition and he failed to support the government. To make matters worse, even after lengthy discussions and apparent agreement on all sides, Besteiro suspended the parliamentary session on the grounds that decisions on the proposed additional clauses should not be rushed.[25]

'He does nothing to help us', wrote Azaña in his diary on 30 April 1933. 'The slowness with which parliamentary business is conducted and the delay in the passing of several laws is largely the fault of Besteiro. He does not take advantage of opportunities to push the debate along; he permits all kinds of incidents orchestrated by the opposition; he never puts a stop to the excesses of the trouble-makers until it is too late. On many occasions, when the scandals provoked by verbal excesses were at their worst, I have seen him smiling and thoroughly entertained by the show.'[26] However, Besteiro's friend, the Secretary of the Chamber, a member of Azaña's own Acción Republicana, Mariano Ansó, claimed that the antics of the Radicals were at their worst when Besteiro was absent and the sessions chaired by one of the vice-presidents. On such occasions, according to Ansó, the helpless vice-president would have to send for Besteiro to come and he would then impose order by furiously ringing the bell on his table.[27] Azaña believed that Besteiro would happily have used the obstruction to put an end to Socialist participation in government. To this end, on 18 May 1933, he insinuated to Azaña that the government should submit itself to a vote of confidence. When the suggestion was discussed in cabinet, the three Socialist Ministers were furious. Largo Caballero commented, 'he thinks he is a viceroy'.[28]

With the bulk of the PSOE and the UGT eager to use the apparatus of the State to introduce basic social reforms, Besteiro's abstentionist views fell on deaf ears. In fact, the rank-and-file of the Socialist movement was moving rapidly away from the positions advocated by Besteiro. Right-wing intransigence radicalized the grass-roots militants. The conclusion drawn by an influential section of the leadership led by Largo Caballero was that the Socialists should meet the needs of the rank-and-file by seeking more rather than less responsibility in the government. Besteiro continued to argue that this should be avoided since it meant the Socialists carrying out tasks which were properly the historical function of the bourgeoisie. Convinced by his marxism that socialism was inevitable, Besteiro believed that the PSOE and the UGT should conserve their forces until the bourgeois stage of Spanish history had been exhausted and the moment for socialism arrived. Such quietism in the name of strict classical marxism earned him only the accusation from the radicalized Socialist youth of being a Kautskyist traitor. His belief that socialism would come if

Millán Astray embraces Franco: together they imbued the Spanish Foreign Legion with its ethos of ruthless brutality.

RIGHT Ernesto Giménez Caballero: the manic founder of the Spanish surrealist movement.

The philosopher Miguel de Unamuno in his study in Salamanca.

RIGHT Millán Astray's protegée, the Argentinian musical comedy actress, Celia Gámez.

Franco in the Foreign Legion: 'Without Africa, I can scarcely explain myself to myself.'

(*From left to right*) Ramón Serrano Suñer, his wife Zita Polo and her sister, Carmen, Franco's wife.

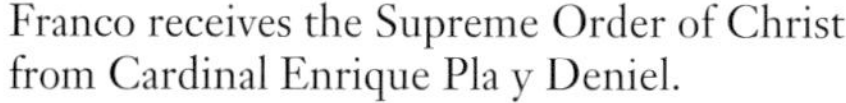

Franco receives the Supreme Order of Christ from Cardinal Enrique Pla y Deniel.

Franco deep-sea fishing on board his yacht *Azor*.

Franco distributed titles as if he were a king. He is seen here, in 1954, at the baptism of his grandson, Francisco Martínez Bordiu, whose name was later changed to Francisco Franco.

On 29 September 1934, to mark his retirement, Miguel de Unamuno *(right)* receives the honorary title of Rector for Life of the University of Salamanca from the President of the Republic, Niceto Alcalá Zamora.

RIGHT: José Antonio Primo de Rivera in conversation with the right-wing journalist, César González Ruano.

José Antonio Primo de Rivera speaking at a Falangist meeting, flanked by Onésimo Redondo (*left*) and Julio Ruiz de Alda.

(*From left to right*) The poet, Antonio Machado, the physician and biographer, Dr Gregorio Marañón, the philosopher, José Ortega y Gasset, and the novelist and diplomat, Ramón Pérez de Ayala, at the foundation of the Agrupaciôn al Servicio de la Repùblica.

José Antonio Primo de Rivera makes a speech on 19 May 1935 distancing the Falange from 'monarchist reaction'.

RIGHT Franco (accompanied by Rafael Sánchez Masas) lays a wreath at a memorial service for José Antonio held in November 1938 in Burgos on the second anniversary of his death.

This celebrated Primo de Rivera family photograph taken in the 1920s features (*from left to right*) Fernando, José Antonio, General Miguel and Miguel with Carmen (*left*) and Pilar (*right*) seated on either side of Tía Ma.

BELOW A Falange meeting in Santander. In the foreground, to José Antonio's right, sits the prominent Sección Femenina activist, Rosario Pereda, and, to his left, sits Manuel Hedilla, who was briefly to be his successor as Jefe Provisional during the first nine months of the war.

BELOW LEFT Mercedes Sanz Bachiller, the energetic and ambitious widow of Onésimo Redondo, and Pilar Primo de Rivera's great rival.

BELOW RIGHT The blue overalls (mono) used by José Antonio in the prison at Alicante.

Salvador de Madariaga, wearing trilby and overcoat, interviewed by journalists while on a mission to the League of Nations.

RIGHT Alejandro Lerroux (*centre with glasses, hat and white moustache*), the wily and corrupt founder and President of the Radical Party.

BELOW Arrested for alleged implication in the Catalan rebellion of October 1934, Manuel Azaña is pictured here while a prisoner on the destroyer *Sánchez Barcaiztegui*. Madariaga wrote a courageous article in Azaña's defence.

Two hundred thousand troops marched past Franco at the sixteen mile-long Victory Parade in Madrid on 19 May 1939. The occasion was choreographed to project Franco as a full-scale partner of the Axis.

Salvador de Madariaga seen at the press conference held on the occasion of his return to Spain in May 1976 after forty years exile. Seated to his right are his second wife, Mimí, and the publisher, Rafael Borrás.

only socialists were well-behaved underlay a disturbing complacency regarding fascism. His failure to understand the real threat of fascism prefigured some of his misplaced optimism about Franco at the end of the Spanish Civil War.[29]

Accordingly, Julián Besteiro opposed the growing radicalization of the Socialist movement and resigned as President of the UGT in January 1934.[30] He was hostile to the participation of the Socialist movement in the revolutionary insurrection of October 1934, as a consequence of which his house in the tranquil Madrid neighbourhood of El Viso was stoned by enraged members of the Socialist Youth. The reaction of other more senior figures ranged from insult to ostracism.[31] Nevertheless, Besteiro took an active part in seeking pardons for those sentenced to death.[32] Thereafter, the radicalizers or self-styled 'Bolshevizantes' within the party saw their first task as to destroy Besteiro's reputation. Their opportunity came in the spring of 1935. On 28 April, at a time when thousands of his comrades were in jail in the wake of the post-October 1934 repression, Besteiro accepted a fellowship of the Academia de Ciencias Morales y Políticas. Election as an Académico de Número involved, according to the Academy's protocol, the delivery of an inaugural lecture which opened with a formal eulogy of the academician's predecessor. Unfortunately for Besteiro, his immediate predecessor had been Gabino Bugallal y Araujo, once an anti-Socialist Minister of the Interior under the monarchy. Bugallal had been President of the Conservative Party which tried to have Besteiro executed after the strike of 1917. Although Besteiro kept his eulogy as brief as possible, it was the object of subsequent ribaldry from his enemies within the PSOE. The central topic of the speech read at the ceremony of his reception into the Academy was 'Marxismo y antimarxismo'. Seemingly oblivious to the menace of fascism, the text provoked a series of sarcastic articles by Luis Araquistain in the journal *Leviatán* which effectively undermined Besteiro's standing within the party hierarchy.[33] In the run-up to the Popular Front elections of February 1936, the Agrupación Socialista Madrileña, now a stronghold of the radicalized followers of Largo Caballero, included him as a candidate only with the greatest reluctance. However, his popularity remained undiminished, and he won the highest number of votes of any candidate in Madrid. There were those who felt that he would have made an excellent President of the Republic after the impeachment of Alcalá Zamora in the spring of 1936. There was little question of that happening, given the revolutionary aspirations of the Caballerista wing of the PSOE.[34]

When the Spanish Civil War broke out on 18 July, Besteiro did not emerge from the obscurity into which he had retreated over the previous months. Indeed, in the course of the war, he behaved in a way which confirmed the suspicion of many within the PSOE that he did not fully understand the great political struggles of the day. Outside of political circles, he reinforced his popularity by refusing numerous opportunities to seek a safe exile.[35] He continued to work in the university, being elected Dean of the Faculty of Philosophy and Letters in October 1936. At the same time, he assiduously fulfilled his duties as a parliamentary deputy, as councillor of the Ayuntamiento de Madrid, to which he had been elected on 12 April 1931, and as president of the Committee for the Reconstruction of the capital (Comité de Reforma, Reconstrucción y Saneamiento de Madrid). His friends tried frantically to persuade him to leave Madrid. Yet, despite, indeed because of, his view that the war would end disastrously for the Republic, he steadfastly refused. His reasons were explained in a letter to Wenceslao Roces, who, as Under-Secretary of the Ministry of Education (Subsecretario del Ministerio de Instrucción Pública y Bellas Artes), had first telephoned and then written to Besteiro to offer him and his family refuge in the Casa de la Cultura in Valencia, which had been created to house intellectuals and artists evacuated from Madrid. On 28 December 1936, Besteiro wrote to Roces: 'I have no post whose duties require my absence from Madrid. On the contrary, having represented this city in parliament without interruption since 1918, I regard myself as being so morally tied to my constituents that I believe it to be my duty to stay with them in the difficult circumstances in which they currently find themselves and which, in all probability, await them.'[36]

On 3 February 1937, he was offered by the Foreign Minister (Ministro de Estado), Julio Alvarez del Vayo, the Spanish Embassy for all of South America, in Buenos Aires. The offer annoyed him since he believed that Largo Caballero, who had formed a government on 4 September 1936, merely wanted to get him out of Madrid because of his well-known, and at the time, inopportune, commitment to a peace settlement. Moreover, like his Prime Minister, Alvarez del Vayo had long resented Besteiro for his opposition to the revolutionary movements of 1931 and 1934. Besteiro wrote to the Minister on 6 February 1937: 'Given that the people of Madrid have helped me consistently by placing their confidence in me, it is little enough for me to help them in these difficult times. Madrid has suffered and still suffers, my dear Alvarez del Vayo, and everyday shows that it has an exemplary spirit. If I were to leave here today, and even more so in order to take up such a prestigious post, but at such a distance, it would produce an anything but comforting effect.'[37] The refusal was made public.[38]

Besteiro's central obsession was an early peace settlement. His chance to do something came in the spring of 1937. As President of the Republic, Azaña had been invited – after some hesitation on the British part – to the coronation of George VI in London on 12 May 1937.[39] Much to the annoyance of Largo Caballero and to the satisfaction of the British Foreign Office, Azaña chose Besteiro as the Spanish representative to go in his place. Since his intention was to entrust to Besteiro a peace mission in London, Azaña did not even consult the Prime Minister, knowing that he would not approve.[40] It was a bad moment for such an initiative. The Nationalists were in the ascendant with their assault on the Basque Country advancing rapidly – in the north, the fall of Bilbao was expected from one day to the next. At the same time, the Republican government was facing significant internal difficulties. In Barcelona, from 3 to 10 May, the forces of the government and the anarcho-syndicalist Confederación Nacional del Trabajo were locked in a bloody struggle for control of the city. Azaña, who had taken up residence near the Catalan capital in October 1936, had feared for his life during 'the May days' and had decided to establish his residence in Valencia. He arranged that, on 7 May 1937, on his arrival at the airport of Manises, he would meet Besteiro who was in transit from Madrid, to Barcelona and then to Paris and London. While the rest of the government waited impatiently, Azaña took Besteiro into a separate office for an hour and instructed him to speak to Sir Anthony Eden and try to secure an early international intervention to bring about the withdrawal of foreign volunteers on both sides in the hope that this might facilitate an eventual suspension of hostilities. Besteiro was, in fact, being sent merely as the private emissary of Azaña but the nearby presence of Largo Caballero and his entire cabinet permitted him to believe that he was the official representative of the government. In fact, as Besteiro should have realized, his mission lacked any significant standing beyond that bestowed by his personal prestige. Its impact would be minimal, at best giving a nudge to a process already in train and, in any case, doomed to failure.

On arrival in London, Besteiro requested the Republican Ambassador, Pablo de Azcárate, to arrange for him to meet Eden. When they met on 11 May, Besteiro found the British Foreign Secretary well-disposed to the Republican cause. However Eden, significantly, asked the Spanish emissary to keep their meeting unofficial and no record of it survives in the Foreign Office documents. Eden did not feel that the two sides in Spain were ripe for peace, although he was prepared to make efforts to get the Great Powers to bring their influence to bear. In fact, two weeks before Besteiro's arrival, draft telegrams to this effect to be sent to the British ambassadors in Germany, Italy, Portugal and the Soviet Union had been drawn up. After discussion, the telegrams were finally despatched on the day that he met Eden, 11 May.[41] The replies from each of the ambassadors, which arrived over the next few days, were to be anything but encouraging.[42] Unaware of any of this, Besteiro returned in good spirits to the Embassy. There, Azcárate threw cold water on his optimism, telling him that Eden's sympathy did not go beyond words and that what they had talked about merely repeated his own conversations with British officials over the previous months.[43] *En route* through Paris, Besteiro also saw Léon Blum who listened attentively but said little.[44]

Besteiro's mission was rendered even more insignificant because, during his absence, the Largo Caballero cabinet fell. Juan Negrín had become Prime Minister on 17 May and had no interest whatsoever in a peace mission that he had not initiated himself. Negrín believed that only a major military triumph by the Republic would bring Franco to the negotiating table. The highly touchy Besteiro perceived an insult in Negrín's understandable failure to follow up on his London trip.[45] Disappointed that his inflated sense of the importance of his own mission was not matched by Negrín, Besteiro began to hatch a fierce grudge against the new Prime Minister. He felt equally betrayed by Largo Caballero when he learned that the meeting with Eden had not been sanctioned by the former prime minister.[46] In terms of the efficacy of the peace mission, it hardly mattered since Eden had made it quite clear that, if Bilbao fell, it would be difficult to impose the withdrawal of volunteers. At best, the Besteiro visit to London had given additional relevance to the correspondence that Eden was already carrying out with his ambassadors in Berlin, Rome, Moscow, Paris and Lisbon.

One of the minor consequences of the fall of the Largo Caballero government in mid-May 1937 was that the Ambassador in France, Largo's faithful follower Luis Araquistain, had resigned in protest.

Besteiro aspired to the Spanish Embassy in Paris in order to be able to seek French mediation in the war, but Negrín's commitment to resistance to the last against Franco made such an appointment an impossible hope. On 3 July, Azaña suggested his name to Negrín and explained why he thought that Besteiro would be more acceptable to the French than the Prime Minister's preferred candidate, the indiscreet conservative, Angel Ossorio y Gallardo. When he expressed his grave misgivings about the nomination of Ossorio, he was told, rather implausibly, by Negrín that Besteiro would not be agreeable to Léon Blum – which was a somewhat disingenuous argument given that, since 22 June, Blum was no longer prime minister.[47]

In the wake of the failure of his peace mission, Besteiro returned to his university post and his position in the Madrid Ayuntamiento where his experiences deepened his admiration for the stoicism of the people of Madrid.[48] Juan Simeón Vidarte, under-secretary of the Ministry of the Interior and a member of the PSOE Executive Committee, claimed that, as a city councillor, Besteiro worked hard on the problems of the besieged capital to the detriment of his health. Vidarte was shocked when he saw him: 'He was a pale spectre, haggard [*ojeroso*], his cheeks caved in, his hair white and dishevelled'. He was so thin that Vidarte wanted to arrange for him to have extra food on grounds of ill-health. He would accept nothing from Vidarte; he refused any more rations than those received by his fellow citizens. He was tortured by the idea that mistakes made in the early 1930s, particularly Socialist participation in government, were responsible for the war. He was also appalled by the violence of the conflict and especially by the sound of firing squads and pistol shots in the night – which he took to be the sounds of political assassinations.[49]

Besteiro's work was extremely discreet. He played no public role because he did not wish to be seen to be lending his support to Republican governments, whether of Largo Caballero or Negrín, of neither of which he approved. He played no part whatsoever in the life of the Socialist Party, attending neither the Agrupación Socialista Madrileña nor the parliamentary group meetings.[50] Henry Buckley, an English journalist in the Spanish capital during the war, wrote later: 'In the most critical days of Madrid I never saw or heard of Señor Besteiro taking any prominent part in any effort to aid or encourage the Madrid people. I never heard of him visiting those who had lost their homes and their parents and friends in air raids, nor addressing gatherings, nor helping in hospital work or relief work. He may have done it. But I lived through all the tense days of Madrid's agony and I never saw or heard of much activity by Sr. Besteiro.'[51] In the same way, his previously steady output of interviews and articles in newspapers dried up completely after the war started.

His stance as a silent but critical spectator of the Republican government puzzled many rank-and-file Socialists. In the last months of the war, a group of Socialist students who were soldiers in the Republican army visited him in the hope of getting some encouragement from him. Among them was the young Enrique Tierno Galván, a future Socialist *alcalde* (mayor) of Madrid. He described their visit to the house in El Viso. As elegantly dressed as ever, a gloomy (*hosco*) Besteiro received them in his neatly ordered study, its polished wood surfaces glistening. He listened silently as the young Socialists expounded their view that it was possible to go on resisting and that, in view of what they heard about the Francoist repression in captured cities, crucial to do so. He responded grudgingly that he did not agree but was not prepared to say any more. When the moment came to speak, then he would speak. His certainty gave Tierno the impression that he believed himself to have a higher purpose.[52] The tenor of Besteiro's remarks suggest the possibility that he was already in contact with the Francoist Fifth Column.

Those fateful links derived from the fact that, over the course of the war, and particularly in the months following his return from London, he had become ferociously anti-Communist. The main target of his obsession was Negrín, whom he frequently accused of being a Communist.[53] His hostility to the Communists was of a piece with his total lack of enthusiasm for the Republican cause. At his trial at the hands of the Francoists, it was claimed in his defence that he had protected several Falangists in the University through whom he eventually made contact with the clandestine Fifth Column in Madrid. Letters to his wife show that Besteiro was happy to have this testimony and he confirmed it with his own extraordinary claim during the proceedings that he 'had been loyal to the Government which combatted the Republic'. In his statement to the court, one of the Francoists who gave evidence on his behalf, Antonio Luna García, a Professor in the Madrid Faculty of Law, spoke of his surprise at the violence with which Besteiro criticized the Republican government. In April 1938, Luna made contact with the clandestine organization of the Falange and was instructed to try to persuade Besteiro to move beyond refusal to work with the government and to try actively to bring the war to an end. Besteiro agreed and lobbied energetically to be permitted to form a cabinet as a preliminary step to peace negotiations.[54]

Indeed, at various times there were rumours of Besteiro being asked to head a government but the strength of his hostility to the Communists made this an unlikely prospect. Nevertheless, a combination of his conversations with Luna García, the Republic's worsening situation and growing divisions within the Socialist Party pulled him out of his self-imposed obscurity in Madrid. The crisis in the Socialist Party became evident between 7 and 9 August 1938, during an important meeting in Barcelona of the Comité Nacional of the PSOE. Prieto delivered a savage denunciation of Negrín, accusing him of being the lackey of the Communists. It was his revenge for having been removed in April 1938 from his position as Minister of Defence. Accused of defeatism, Prieto had been tarred with responsibility for the Nationalist recapture of Teruel and the subsequent offensive which saw Franco's troops reach the Mediterranean and split the Republican zone. His speech was followed by a deathly silence which revealed the impotence of the Party. Prieto's diatribe found no support from the floor – since there was no alternative to the policy being pursued by Negrín, the policy which Prieto himself had followed – but nor did any committee member leap to the defence of Negrín.[55] The implications of this crisis led to Azaña's discussing with Besteiro the formation of a government whose principal task would be to seek peace.

At the August 1938 meeting of the Comité Nacional of the PSOE at which Prieto had launched his attack on Negrín, there was an effort mounted to renew the executive committee in such a way as to contribute to a much sought-after party unity. Since the committee was elected in the spring of 1936, there had been three resignations – of Luis Jiménez de Asúa, Fernando de los Ríos and Anastasio de Gracia because their views were now widely at variance with those of the majority. Jerónimo Bugeda, a solid government supporter, was to be sacrificed in the hope of enticing a representative of one of the dissident groups back into the fold.[56] A candidate list was elaborated and sent to local associations (*agrupaciones*) for their approval. The list contained five proposed *vocales natos* (*ex officio* or honorary members) consisting of three cabinet members, Juan Negrín, as Prime Minister, Julio Alvarez del Vayo as Minister of Foreign Affairs and Paulino Gómez Saez, Minister of the Interior, together with Besteiro and

Largo Caballero, to be included as one-time presidents of the PSOE. The proposed presence of Besteiro and Largo Caballero was intended to provide a symbol of party unity. The new committee was to be presented publicly in the course of a rapidly invented fiftieth anniversary celebration of the Party's foundation. The Committee sent Besteiro a letter inviting him to take part, publishing the candidate list before his reply was received. He eventually declined to take part in the celebrations.[57] He told Julián Zugazagoitia, the editor of *El Socialista*, that he could not take part because 'they wouldn't let me say what I think and feel, that is to say, that we Spaniards are killing one another in a stupid way, for even more stupid and criminal reasons'.[58] Despite his refusal to attend the ceremony and his failure even to accept nomination as a candidate, his election to the Executive was announced.

By now, Besteiro was deeply concerned about the consequences for the bulk of the population of inevitable Republican defeat. He was therefore even more hostile to Negrín because he believed him to be unnecessarily prolonging the war. He was invited by Azaña to Barcelona in mid-November 1938 to talk about a peace government. Besteiro had gone to Barcelona convinced that it was a matter of urgency to seek an armistice but the project did not prosper. In fact, nothing could have come of their meeting since, as Azaña himself admitted, he simply did not have the political support that would permit him to take the essentially defeatist step of asking Besteiro to form a government. Azaña's principal impressions of the encounter were of Besteiro's profound admiration for the people of Madrid and, at the same time, of just how out-of-touch he was with the reality of the situation. Despite the fact that Azaña had nothing to offer him, misplaced rumours flew around about a cabinet including Besteiro, Prieto and Martínez Barrio. In consequence, Besteiro was subjected to virulent attack by the Communist press.[59] Asked by a journalist if he would accept the task of forming a government in order to try ending the war by mediation, Besteiro admitted that it had been suggested to him and that his only condition was that he be given total freedom to choose his ministers. However, it was obvious from his private conversations with Azaña that he knew that it was impossible for him to form a government at such a time. He realized that he did not have the support of the majority of his own Party let alone of Republican Spain as a whole.[60]

Concerned for the safety of Azaña, Besteiro had initially tried to mask the real purpose of his visit with other activities in Barcelona.[61] He stressed to journalists that he was in Catalonia to seek assistance to alleviate the appalling food shortages in the capital.[62] He also attended the PSOE Executive Committee meeting held in Barcelona on 15 November. He was at pains to stress that his participation did not mean that he had accepted membership of the committee but should be considered as merely an opportunity for an exchange of views.[63] His speech to the meeting, like his position in general, was full of contradictions, perhaps reflecting both his Socialist past and his present contacts with the Fifth Column. He acknowledged the practical necessity of Socialist collaboration with the Communist Party, while insisting that he was not part of the group which favoured unity with the PCE. 'Irrespective of what my position with regard to the problem of unity might be, even though I maintained within the Party an attitude of total hostility, and even though I had been opposed to the idea of unity of action between the two parties before the war and I opposed it again after the war started, I believe that a crucial necessity of the war effort is that Socialists and Communists try to present a common front as long as the war lasts.'

However, he took the opportunity to discuss the likely consequences of the Communists being removed from power:

> The war has been inspired, directed and fomented by the Communists. If they ceased to intervene, probably the possibilities of continuing the war would be small. The enemy, having other international support, would find itself in a situation of superiority. I recognize that this [the removal of the Communists] is a grave step at this stage. As you know, this would not affect me personally – other than as something that would have an impact on everyone – because I do not believe that I have had any responsibility for the fact that we have reached this point. I cannot offer you the solution. It is for you to mark out the boundaries and to consider what it is opportune to do at this moment. I see the situation as follows: if the war were to be won, Spain would be Communist. The rest of the democracies would be against us and we would have only Russia with us. And if we are defeated, the future will be terrible.[64]

It was a virtuoso performance of pessimism, defeatism and irresponsibility. He had recognized the inevitability of co-operation with the

Communists yet had remained aloof, determined to keep his hands clean. Now, he denounced collaboration without offering any alternative other than division, defeat and the tender mercies of General Franco.

In the course of his speech, Besteiro returned to what had become an obsessional theme, declaring that Negrín was a Communist who had entered the Socialist Party as a Trojan Horse. Shortly after, he told Negrín himself what he had said, commenting 'Before they tell you anything, I want you to hear from me what I said in the Executive Committee. I regard you as an agent of the Communists.' He told Azaña and others that Negrín was a 'Karamazov', 'a crazed visionary'.[65] On his return to Madrid, a deeply disillusioned Besteiro reported his conversations in Barcelona to his acquaintances in the Fifth Column. He was resigned to the fact that Azaña would not be commissioning him to form a peace government and that, even if the President were to do so, he would be unable to find sufficient political support. However, Antonio Luna García set about persuading him that, if he was unable to fulfil his hopes of forming a peace government with wide political support, he should consider doing so with military backing. The clandestine Falange had already placed agents within the entourage of Colonel Segismundo Casado, the commander of the Army of the Centre. Besteiro enthusiastically accepted Luna García's offer to bring him into contact with Colonel Casado.[66]

The potentially damaging consequences of Besteiro's disaffection were sensed by Tomás Bilbao Hospitalet, Minister without Portfolio in Negrín's government, who visited Madrid at this time. Bilbao found Besteiro irritated and harshly critical of the government. He remained bitterly convinced that his peace mission to London had been torpedoed by Azcárate. He believed the war to be the fatal consequence of the errors committed by the revolutionary elements of the PSOE in the period 1933–6, particularly Largo Caballero. Ironically, Negrín, whom he considered his greatest enemy, agreed totally. Bilbao informed Negrín of his fear that Besteiro, in conjunction with Colonel Casado, might do something dangerous. Negrín did not take the warnings seriously. After all, Besteiro had long made no secret of his view that it was madness to continue resistance when the war was effectively lost.[67]

As things got worse, Besteiro readied himself for action. Barcelona fell on 26 January 1939. On 3 February, through the clandestine organization of the Falange, Besteiro arranged an urgent interview with Casado who recounted to him his plans for peace. According to reports received in Burgos from the Fifth Column, they remained in close contact throughout February.[68] Forced into exile, at the end of the month Azaña resigned as President of the Republic. On 27 February 1939, the British Government announced its recognition of Franco as legitimate leader of Spain. The end was imminent for the Republic. On Sunday 5 March 1939, Besteiro lent his immense prestige to the fiercely anti-Communist Consejo Nacional de Defensa formed by Colonel Casado in the hope of being able to seek an armistice. He did this despite having declared to the PSOE executive three months earlier that abandoning the Communists in order to facilitate peace talks with Franco would merely strengthen the Caudillo.[69]

The Casado coup succeeded because it tapped into deep seems of war-weariness. Hunger and demoralization were rife in the central zone. The consequent desire for an end to the war was often expressed in terms of anarchist and socialist hostility to the Communists, who advocated resistance to the end.[70] While Casado was certainly striking a real chord, there can be little underestimating the importance of Besteiro's contribution. Having stood aside from Republican politics and so carefully nurtured his reputation for rectitude, his participation bestowed a moral legitimacy on the Casado Junta which it would not otherwise have had. It is difficult to know just how aware Besteiro was of the implications of what he was doing – which was to render pointless the bloodshed and the sacrifices of the previous three years by emulating the military coup of 18 July 1936 against an alleged communist danger. His physical privations may have had some impact on his mental health. The exiled ex-Prime Minister, Manuel Portela Valladares, was told by a doctor who had treated Besteiro at the end of the war that the professor was '*gagá*'.[71] For years, Besteiro had fought off tuberculosis and the war years in Madrid, without decent food or warmth in the winter, had taken their toll.[72] On the other hand, his own privations do not explain his wilful ignorance of the Francoist repression.

Besteiro seems to have thought that he could achieve great things in the way of reconciliation. Tierno Galván believed that Besteiro thought himself 'destined to be the moral barrier that could be placed between the victors and the vanquished to avoid reprisals'. He was persuaded that his historic role was to stand between both sides and be the father of the helpless once weapons had been laid down.' Besteiro considered that his own superior moral rectitude and his marginalization during the war would carry weight with the Francoists. It was a view compounded of arrogance and ignorance.[73] The revenge wreaked by the Nationalists in captured Republican cities was well known. Yet Besteiro managed not to know – although it has also been suggested that he was acting on false information about Francoist clemency given him by his Falangist contacts.[74] Antonio Luna García certainly informed him that Franco offered to guarantee the life and liberty of all of those who were guiltless of common crimes and contributed to the bloodless surrender of the Republic.[75] In the basement of the Ministry of Finance during the first hours of Casado's Council of Defence, he asked naïve questions about Negrín which suggested prejudice rather than hard information about the government against which he was rebelling. Witnesses described him as nervous and fidgeting with his hands, chain-smoking, his eyes shining, emanating an air of other-worldliness. According to Eduardo Domínguez, Vice-President of the UGT and Commissar of the Army of the Centre, he was 'infantile, weak and washed-out' (*infantil y desvahído*).[76]

The public announcement of the creation of the Casado Junta was made by Besteiro, who had declined its presidency but accepted the post of Minister of Foreign Affairs. Hunched over the radio microphones, his voice trembling with emotion, he declared that the motives of those involved were 'humanitarian duty and the exigency of the supreme law of the salvation of the innocent masses without responsibility'. His words perfectly summed up his position. Referring to the Negrín government's 'concealment of the truth, its half truths', he denounced its 'policy of catastrophic fanaticism, of complete submission to foreign orders, with a total indifference to the sorrow of the Nation'. 'I speak to you from this Madrid which has known suffering and knows how to suffer its martyrdom with moving dignity ... I speak to you to say that it is in defeat that it is necessary for individuals and nations to show their moral courage. It is possible to lose but with honour and dignity, without denying one's faith, without being crushed by misfortune. I tell you that a moral victory of this type is worth a thousand times more than a material victory achieved by dint of deceit and vilification.' When he finished, he wept.[77]

In the subsequent mini-civil war against the Communists, about 2000 people were killed. Many Communists were left in prison where they were found, and executed, by the Francoists. Troops were withdrawn from the front to fight the Communists. Apparently, this was done in co-operation with the Francoists who undertook not to advance and even to look after the abandoned Republican trenches.[78] During this period, Besteiro was seriously ill and lay on a camp-bed in the cellars of the Ministry. He refused offers to take him home, saying 'I have undertaken to carry out a job with the Council and will carry it out until the last moment.'[79] He had become Foreign Minister precisely in order to be able to negotiate with Burgos but Franco, as was to be expected, refused.

In fact, Besteiro was astonishingly sanguine about the future. On 11 March 1939, Besteiro spoke to the Civil Governor of Murcia, Eustaquio Cañas, who found him 'lying on a hospital bed in the basement, his blue pallor, his emaciated features, his extreme thinness giving him the appearance of a corpse'. To Cañas's utter astonishment, Besteiro confidently assured him that 'those of us who have responsibilities, especially in the union organization, cannot abandon it. I am sure that virtually nothing is going to happen. Let us wait on events, and perhaps we can reconstitute a UGT of more moderate character, something along the lines of the British Trades Unions. Stay at your post as Governor, everything will be fine, I assure you.' Cañas could not credit that a man of Besteiro's intelligence could be so oblivious to the nature of the war.[80] This naïvety may have been the consequence of the illusory optimism which is said to be a symptom of tuberculosis. Equally, it may have been inspired by promises made to him by the Fifth Column or indeed by Casado himself, who had been in touch with friends within the Francoist high command. In later years, Luna García privately expressed his chagrin that Franco, after promising 'life and liberty' to those who helped avoid a massacre, 'went and shot them all'.[81]

Astonishingly, Besteiro seems to have assumed that life for the Socialist movement under Franco would be similar to the privileged existence it had experienced under the dictatorship of Primo de Rivera. His own writings during these days show the remarkable extent to which his fierce anti-communism had fed a bizarre complacency about the Francoists. 'We have been defeated as a nation because we let ourselves be dragged along by the bolshevik line which is perhaps the greatest political aberration known throughout the centuries . . . The reaction against this error . . . is genuinely represented by the Nationalists who, whatever their defects, have fought in the great anti-Comintern crusade.' He fondly believed that the experience of those who had displayed anti-communist attitudes within the Republican zone was something upon which the Francoists would want to draw for the reconstruction of the Spain of the future. He suggested that the contribution of the Casado Junta to shortening the war should be recognized by the victors. The very idea that the victorious half of Spain might set out to destroy the defeated half seemed to him only madness. 'To construct the Spanish character of tomorrow, the victorious Nationalist Spain will have to take into account the experience of those who suffered the errors of the bolshevized Republic . . . The useful Republican masses cannot demand – without losing their dignity – any share of the booty of the war but they can and should demand their post at the constructive labour front.'[82] Franco's firing squads and concentration camps, however, did not limit their work to Communists. Despite Besteiro's naïve hopes, active anti-communists, liberal republicans, Socialists, anarchists, as well as many who were simply non-political, would be victims of the savage repression, as indeed was Besteiro himself.

Besteiro was the only one of the Junta's twenty-eight members to stay in Madrid. On 18 March 1939, he told Regina García, editor of the socialist daily, *La Voz*, 'I will stay with those who cannot save themselves. Of course, we will arrange the departure from Spain of many comrades who have to go, and who will leave by sea, by land or by air; but the great majority, the masses, they can't leave, and I, who have always lived with the workers, will continue with them and with them I will stay. Whatever is their fate will be mine.'[83] He was seemingly unaware of the fact that the Casado coup had in itself severely sabotaged any chance of a properly organized evacuation of those in danger. During those days, he tried to facilitate the escape of others through his lifelong friend and comrade, Trifón Gómez. Gómez, now quartermaster-general of the Republican Army, was in Paris negotiating refuge in Mexico for the Republicans who had to flee.[84] However, Besteiro negated his own efforts by refusing to allow any government resources to be used in getting people out. His logic was that the national wealth was needed in Spain for post-war reconstruction and that Franco would treat those who stayed behind in Spain all the better for having thus safeguarded resources.[85] At his court martial, it was stated that he had done everything possible to facilitate a peaceful handover to the victorious Francoists, in co-operation with the clandestine Falange and the Fifth Column organization known as the Servicio de Información Militar.[86]

He chain-smoked to the end, looking evermore like a skeleton.[87] His faith in Franco's good will sustained him to the end of the war.

On 27 March, he told the anarchist military commander, Cipriano Mera, whom he urged to escape along with Casado, 'I have had no function whatsoever in the war, apart from these last moments when I have tried with you to avoid greater sufferings for our people. The victors can do with me what they please. They will arrest me but perhaps they will not dare to kill me.'[88] In fact, he was virtually the only senior Republican political figure to choose to stay with his constituents rather than escape. It was suicidal to stay yet he did so, with a sense of pride. Just before the end, asked by José del Río, Secretary of the Consejo de Defensa Nacional, if he thought that Franco would have him shot, he replied 'Yes; I accept that possibility and I even desire it. I am not afraid to die, because with my sixty-nine years and my physical ailments, what better service could I lend to the cause of the workers who have been left without a flag and without leaders? If my name could be a flag for them then I would prefer to be shot!'[89] In the appeal against his sentence, however, he claimed proudly, and with a hint of malice, that by staying he was also underlining the contrast between himself and those of his colleagues who had escaped. He had made the same point earlier to the editor of the anarchist newspaper *CNT*, José García Pradas.[90]

Besteiro was captured in the basement of the Ministry of Finance, where he had remained since leaving his home on 5 March. Some hours before the Francoist troops arrived, he was joined by Rafael Sánchez Guerra, Casado's secretary. Besteiro said 'I think it is better to wait to be arrested here to avoid unpleasant scenes for my family.' Referring to his Madrid constituents, he spoke again with a hint of arrogance – 'One cannot abandon those who have put their faith in one. My presence here can prevent much bloodshed; I can prevent many injustices being committed. I will be the wall that holds back the avalanche that is coming.'[91] He was wrong yet his naïve optimism about the new situation continued for some time. On 30 April 1939 he wrote to his wife from prison: 'We will all leave here rather battered, or maybe (who knows?) perhaps we will leave toughened up. I am not pessimistic about our situation. We will have to give up some things but they are things which, given our lifelong habits and our moral exigencies, we are ready to give up. I still hope that we can find a decorous way of making a living, on top of the reparations that are owed us, or certainly to you.'[92]

Nearly sixty-nine years old, on 8 July 1939, he faced a court martial of insurrectionary generals for the alleged crime of 'military rebellion' (*el delito de adhesión a la rebelión militar*). The absurd charges were brought against him despite his efforts for peace and the anti-communism which inspired his participation in the Casado Junta, an act of military rebellion against the government of Juan Negrín.[93] Indeed, his peace mission to London and his links with Casado were among the central accusations against him at his court martial. The prosecutor, Lieutenant Colonel Felipe Acedo Colunga, recognized that Besteiro was an honest man, innocent of any crime of blood, yet he demanded the death sentence. Acedo's long speech made it clear that Besteiro's crime was to have rendered Socialism more acceptable by making it moderate. It is difficult also to avoid the conclusion that the Francoists, unable to try Azaña, Negrín, Largo Caballero and the other major figures of the Republic, poured all their hatred into the trial of Besteiro.[94]

When the time came to appeal against the sentence of life imprisonment, Besteiro wrote a *pliego de descargo* (plea of mitigation) in which it was usual both to confess and excuse oneself. Besteiro wrote:

> Without committing the indignity, which I would never have committed, of going over to the side which, according to my view of things, had to be, at the end of the day, the victor, I could easily have adopted a more cautious position which would have permitted me, either inside or outside Spain, to save my life, my reputation, my interests and those of my family. I did not do so because I understood my duty to be unequivocally to remain in the breach facing all dangers, not to fudge my position nor reduce my influence so as to seek salvation in a kind of political anonymity, but rather to proclaim it clearly and affirm it as much as possible, to make use of the moral force that the adoption of such an attitude might provide me on behalf of my fellow citizens who had been fully put to the test by misfortune, and on behalf of the country in which I was born and to which I wish to belong. I have remained faithful to this rule down to the last moment, a moment in which I have risked everything in order to put an end to an impossible situation and to save the Spanish people greater misfortunes than those which they had already suffered. It is well known that I have had opportunities to leave Spain, not only with ease but with positive advantages both at the time and in the future. But there were two moments

> which illustrated the tenacity with which I have stood by my position. These two moments were 7 November 1936 and 28 March 1939. On the first of those dates, the violence with which the Nationalist troops could have entered Madrid made me fear that I might be one of the victims of the struggle. On the second of those dates, even though it was clear that there would be no attack on Madrid, the news of my removal from my professorial chair and the unjust attacks to which I had been subjected by the Nationalist radio allowed me to have no illusion about the fate which awaited me in the first days. Nevertheless, on both occasions, ignoring advice from all quarters to leave the country, or at least to go into hiding for some time, I decided, without hesitation, to remain at my post. The reasons for my decision are complex: the desire not to re-establish a long-dead solidarity with others who were fleeing; a repugnance both for the very idea of flight, especially since I did not have to flee, and for making a show in foreign parts of the tragedies of my own fatherland; the conviction that I could appear before the most severe judges with my head held high and my conscience clear.[95]

The initial sentence of life imprisonment was commuted to thirty years of hard labour (*reclusión mayor*). He was confined first in the Monasterio de Dueñas in the province of Palencia until the end of August 1939 and then in the prison of Carmona in the province of Seville. In his seventieth year, his health broken by lack of adequate food and medical attention, he was forced to undertake hard physical work, scrubbing floors, cleaning latrines. When his final illness, a fatal blood-poisoning incurred during this latter activity, struck in mid-September 1940, his beloved wife, Dolores Cebrián, travelled immediately to Carmona but was refused permission to see him and was kept waiting eight days until the eve of his death on 27 September 1940.[96] The gratuitous vindictiveness of the persecution of Besteiro was later admitted by Ramón Serrano Suñer, who wrote that 'we must recognize that to let him die in prison was ill-considered and clumsy on our part'.[97]

The sacrifice of submitting himself to the brutal vengeance of Francoist 'justice' was something which his party colleagues did not easily understand. The ever pragmatic Indalecio Prieto admired 'the exemplary greatness of Besteiro's gesture', but believed that 'he could have been more useful giving us his example in exile than suffering in prison'.[98] In any case, the dignity, humanity and courage of his behaviour during the last days of the Spanish Civil War and the injustice of his fate at the hands of the Francoists have to be weighed against the lives lost as a result of the Casado fiasco. Besteiro's comportment throughout the war, first standing aside from the Republican cause then participating in the Casado Junta, was born of a curious mixture of innocence and arrogance. Always thin-skinned behind his dignified exterior, he was deeply wounded by his treatment at the hands of the left during the internal party feuds of 1934–6. His understandable outrage was compounded by his conviction that the left-Socialists were simply wrong in rejecting his definition of the historical moment. His interpretations of practical political issues were often theoretical abstractions elaborated with an olympian detachment from day-to-day realities. This was particularly the case with regard to fascism. His personal sensitivities and his conviction of his theoretical correctness seem to have combined into a sense of overwhelming moral superiority. Out of that sense was born his optimistic belief that his unblemished past would earn him Francoist clemency. Just as he had miscalculated the likely weight of his own intervention with Eden, so his well-meaning, but somewhat self-regarding, views in 1939 stood in stark contrast to the reality of the Caudillo's determination to annihilate all the values of the Republic. Besteiro's case was considered personally by Franco. The fact that he was refused medical treatment or any commutation of his sentence reflected the determination of the Caudillo to destroy him. In the words of his niece, 'the only explanation is that the Caudillo wanted to wipe out the popular figure of Besteiro from Spain's history, making the Spaniards of his epoch forget him and preventing those of future generations knowing that he had ever existed'.[99] Franco was essentially making an example even of a man who had done nothing to oppose the military rising and had done more than most to put an end to Republican resistance. Besteiro's tragedy was that, having lost what little faith that he had in the Republic and his Socialist comrades, he chose instead to place his trust in his executioner.

7

The Prisoner in the Gilded Cage: Manuel Azaña

Late in the evening of 15 August 1936, General Emilio Mola made a broadcast from Radio Castilla in Burgos. He spoke about the military uprising which he had directed less than one month earlier. It was, he declared, intended to free Spain 'from the chaos of anarchy, chaos which since the rise of the Popular Front was being prepared in detail with the cynical support and the morbid complacency of certain members of the government'. The instruments of this anarchy were 'the clenched fists of the marxist hordes' and, for Mola, the blame for unleashing them lay squarely with one man:

> Only a monster of the complex psychological constitution of Azaña could foment such a catastrophe; a monster who seems rather the absurd brainchild of a new and fantastic Dr Frankenstein than the fruit of the love of a woman. When I hear people demand his head, I think they are being unjust. Azaña should be locked away, just that, locked away, so that selected brain specialists might study in him a case of mental degeneration, perhaps the most interesting to have occurred from the times of primitive man to the present day.[1]

Nothing more directly indicates the importance of the service rendered to the Second Spanish Republic by Manuel Azaña than the hatred directed against him by the ideologues and publicists of the Francoist cause. The poisonous slanders to which he was subjected during the Civil War and long after his death are indications that the enemies of the Republic recognized in him one of its greatest bulwarks. As Prime Minister from 1931 to 1933, as architect of the Popular Front in 1935 and President of the Republic from 1936 to 1939, he was the personification of the Second Republic. The reforming achievements of the regime's first two years – the new constitution, the vote for women, divorce, military reforms, the disestablishment of the Church, the Catalan statute, labour legislation and agrarian reform – were considerable. All successfully ran the parliamentary gauntlet and passed into law thanks to the oratorical skills of Azaña. These reforms were all in their various ways substantial challenges to the privileges of the right. At the time, the conservative press vented their spleen against Azaña by means of outrageous political smears and cruel caricatures.

Subsequently, even greater venom was provoked by the great personal sacrifices and tireless efforts made by Azaña for the survival of the democratic regime during the repression which followed the Asturian insurrection of October 1934. A Francoist journalist, Francisco Casares, in discussing the close identification of Azaña and the Republic, referred to him as 'a monster, a congregation of moral vacuums and of formative elements which sum up, concentrate and symbolize all blame and all sins. This amalgam has a personality, that of the person who provided the tone and the sense, the outline and the essence of the Spanish republic.' The reason for such hatred is obvious. In 1935, when the right thought that the Republic was on its knees, Azaña bounced back from his electoral defeat of November 1933 to recreate the regime's greatest bulwark, the republican–Socialist coalition, the so-called Popular Front. He overcame his repugnance for mass politics to provide the inspiration and energy which made possible the creation of the victorious left-wing electoral coalition of 1936. This is what Casares meant when he wrote that 'when the collective impulse knocked him off his pedestal, he, without pity or remorse, without anxieties or doubts, prepared, in the murky waters of his sewer, the new assault'.[2]

Finally, Azaña's courageous determination to remain with the Republic to the bitter end during the Spanish Civil War was a much under-estimated contribution to its struggle against the military rebels. Had he chosen, as many of his one-time Republican collaborators did, to seek safety abroad, the regime's legitimacy in the eyes of the Great Powers would have been fatally diminished. The psychotically hostile description of Azaña made by Franco's friend and propagandist, Joaquín Arrarás, is extremely revealing in this respect: 'bastard freak elevated to the highest office of an abject Republic by a corrupt and corrupting pseudo-democratic vote. Let us say to be accurate that Azaña was the abortion of masonic lodges and Internationals who deserved the presidency of the Republic of the Popular Front, a repulsive caterpillar of the red Spain of killings and chekas, of refined satanic cruelties.'[3]

The vitriol directed by Franco's propagandists against Azaña reflected the Caudillo's own hatred. It was also a reflection of the intense fear provoked in the Spanish right by the man whom, as early as 1932, Giménez Caballero called 'the father of the Republic'. Azaña came to personify the Second Republic and with it to challenge the existence of the *ancien régime* in Spain. According to Salvador de Madariaga, an acute judge who had little reason to be grateful to Azaña,[4] Don Manuel was 'the Spaniard of greatest stature discovered by the brief Republican period'; 'in his own right, the man of greatest value in the new regime, simply because of his intellectual and moral superiority' and 'the most distinguished parliamentary orator ever known in Spain'. Salvador de Madariaga rightly insisted on 'the ethical dimension of Azaña'.[5] No other politician, with the possible exception of Indalecio Prieto, perceived as did Azaña the need for the modernization of the state apparatus in Spain and in particular of its relationship with powerful institutions tied to the old regime. He was committed to three principal goals: to modernizing Church–State relations, to modernizing the Army both technically and in terms of its political subordination to the civilian government and, finally, to introducing rationality and dialogue into political and parliamentary life. He acted on the basis of a belief that laws change reality, that great reforms are made by the passing of the relevant law. Azaña conceived the exercise of power as the practice of virtue; he had reason, he convinced with words and he acted by making laws. Unfortunately, he was to discover that legal, verbal and rational power was insufficient against the massed forces of the Army, the Church, the Spanish oligarchy and their German and Italian allies. Nevertheless, outraged by their assault on the legality that he cherished, he stood by 'his' Republic. His programme for the creation of a modern Spain was not to be implemented until after the death of Franco.

His background suggested anything but the morally degenerate revolutionary or mentally defective monster of Francoist propaganda. Manuel Azaña Díaz was born on 17 January 1880 in the small sleepy town of Alcalá de Henares, thirty kilometres from Madrid. His father, a prosperous businessman and landowner, Esteban Azaña y Catarineu was mayor and historian of Alcalá, the birthplace of Miguel de Cervantes. His mother, Josefina Díaz Gallo Muguruza, was an intelligent and exceptionally well-read woman. The young Manuel was brought up in a large book-filled house which was diagonally across the narrow Calle de la Imagen from the house where it is believed that Cervantes had lived. His mother died when he was nine, his father when he was ten. Manuel, his brother Gregorio and his sister Josefa were then looked after by their maternal grandmother, Concha de Catarineu. In the huge family house, he was often alone. Highly intelligent but shy, he withdrew into a world of books, voraciously devouring Spanish classics and popular literature of the time, particularly the works of Jules Verne. In later life, his solitary bookishness would easily be interpreted by his enemies as arrogance.

Manuel inherited his parents' love of literature and his father's interests in politics and civic affairs. He was educated in Alcalá de Henares until the age of thirteen when he went to the Augustinian Real Colegio de Estudios Superiores in the monastery at El Escorial. An élitist institution for the sons of the *haute bourgeoisie*, it was the first of his gilded cages. He referred to his fellow students as 'fellow prisoners' (*compañeros de presidio*). His experiences there would be the basis of his exquisite novel, *El jardin de los frailes*.[6] In 1898, on the basis of his studies in El Escorial, he successfully presented himself for the examinations for a law degree at the University of Zaragoza. Two years later, he wrote a doctoral thesis in Madrid on 'the responsibility of the multitudes'. He gained, as number two in his year, the highly competitive administrative post of legal counsel in the Registry Section of the Ministry of Justice ('letrado de la Dirección General de los Registros y del Notariado'). It was a mark of his intellectual distinction that, in 1902, he was invited to deliver a lecture on 'The Freedom of Association' to the Academia de Jurisprudencia in Madrid. A respectable bureaucrat, he devoted most of his time to intellectual activities centred on the Ateneo de Madrid. In 1911–12, with a grant from the élitist body for fostering academic research, the Junta de Ampliación de Estudios, he studied at the Sorbonne in Paris. It was the beginning of a lifetime empathy with French liberal and legal ideas. During the First World War, he visited the Austro-Italian battle fronts and campaigned throughout Spain in favour of the Allies. As secretary of the great liberal club, the Ateneo de Madrid, as a collaborator in the journal *España* and the newspapers *El Sol* and *El Imparcial*, and as founder with José Ortega y Gasset of the Liga de Educación Política, he exercised a significant role in the culture of the period. In the mid-1920s, he became fascinated by the liberal nineteenth-century

Andalusian novelist, Juan Valera. His biography, *Vida de don Juan Valera*, won the Premio Nacional de Literatura in 1926. He entered politics, joining the Partido Reformista of Melquíades Alvarez in 1912 only to leave in 1924 to found Acción Republicana.[7]

By the time that he was becoming known in Madrid literary and political circles, Azaña had developed the relatively unprepossessing appearance that was to be the occasion of later rightist insults. Salvador de Madariaga described him as having 'a seriously unfriendly face' (*una cara de pocos amigos*). His shyness made him seem stand-offish. His acute intelligence made him intolerant of fools and adulators, to whom he came across as short-tempered. He was not effusively talkative but not taciturn. As Madariaga acutely put it, 'his countenance was complex: the lower part of the face, sulky; but in his eyes and eyebrows there lurked an almost pathetic appeal for sympathy'. His pale complexion and a tendency to obesity were accentuated as he got older.[8] This was the basis of right-wing caricature – particularly, in 1932 and 1933, in the satirical magazine *Gracia y Justicia* – as 'a toad, a frog, a salamander, a snake – anything slimy or untouchable, but most especially a snake – the stealthy, hissing, vengeful danger, and with the additional implication of femininity'.[9]

Azaña's training for public life was unprecedented in an active Spanish politician. As a child of 1898, he had studied and written on Spanish literature, on the problems of Spain, on militarism and on *caciquismo* (the corrupt clientelist system). Through constant reading and meditation, he developed a thorough conception of the rational reform of Spain. What perplexed and infuriated the right in general, and Franco in particular, was that this intellectual vision should attract sufficient popular support to make it a threat. Through books and travel, Azaña had reached the conclusion that the modernization of Spain required the apparatus of the State to impose its will upon both militarism and the religious orders. He also had unequivocal ideas on the necessity for agrarian reform, not as a revolutionary but out of a humanitarian concern that landless labourers should not die of hunger in the countryside. These ideas would have remained innocuous had Azaña not leapt from obscurity to being Minister of War in April 1931 and Prime Minister in mid-October 1931 as a result of his intervention in the debate over the religious articles of the constitution.[10]

It should not be thought that Azaña was driven by ambition or a burning sense of mission. Throughout his career, he frequently took refuge in obscurity. His early political life saw him playing only a modest role in the Partido Reformista of Melquíades Alvarez from 1913 to 1923. During the early years of the Primo de Rivera dictatorship, he was living a solitary existence, writing his novel *El jardín de los frailes*, which was published in 1927. In that same year, he met and fell in love with Dolores, the youngest sister of his closest friend, Cipriano Rivas Cherif. Since Dolores was twenty-four years his junior, Azaña was tortured with doubts about the propriety of their relationship. However, his feelings were reciprocated and, after overcoming the reservations of her family, on 27 February 1929 they were married. It was an unlikely union between a witty and attractive young woman and a lugubrious and solitary writer, but one which was to be enduringly happy. On returning from their honeymoon in Paris, Azaña resumed his incipient involvement in the republican opposition to the monarchy and the dictatorship.[11]

Azaña's activity in Alianza Republicana and the various republican committees which finally developed into the Pact of San Sebastián of August 1930 and the provisional government of 14 April 1931 was the result of the prodding of a friend, Enrique Martí Jara. Reflecting on this period some years later, saddened by the premature death of Martí Jara, he wrote in his diary:

> I believe that solitude led me into error – the solitude and the total lack of ambition that I've always had – a facility to be happy with the present and not to believe that I have a right to anything more or indeed to anything at all. I wonder if it is the restraint that comes from indolence? It was Martí Jara who took me, virtually dragging me, to the first meetings to set up Alianza Republicana . . . by dint of pushing me, Martí Jara got me out of my shy seclusion, pushing me into taking part in political committees and councils which were plotting the overthrow of the monarchy . . . Thanks to Martí Jara, I joined the executive committee of the alliance and out of that came my presence at the Pact of San Sebastián and the fact that I was made a member of the revolutionary council which was later to become the provisional government of the Republic.[12]

On 12 December 1930, news reached Madrid of the failure of the premature Republican rising in the remote Aragonese town of Jaca. Azaña, who was at a performance of Mussorgsky's *Boris Godunov*, fled the Teatro Calderón when police came for him.[13] He went into hiding at his father-in-law's house, and began to write a novel. Until 14 April 1931, with no confidence in his capacity to influence events, he did little or nothing to help bring about the Republic.

Indeed, Azaña never concerned himself with the issues to which the politically ambitious are normally deeply sensitive: the need for an electoral machine, a party, an organization. Having been dragged into the Pacto de San Sebastián by Martí Jara, Azaña was made Minister of War in the first Republican–Socialist cabinet in recognition of his talents and, specifically, of his interest in military politics. In 1918, he had published a major study of the military policy of the French Third Republic.[14] He was determined to eradicate the problem of militarism from Spain, which he regarded as 'a noisy and disorderly' obstacle to rational politics. It was a problem which he equated with the fact that, as a legacy of her imperial past, Spain had an Army completely disproportionate to her economic possibilities, overmanned and under-equipped. Thus the Army was pulled away from its proper task of defending Spain and inclined instead to intervene in domestic politics. The urgency with which Azaña set about his task caused great dismay within the officer corps. This, together with his determination to eliminate where possible the irregularities of the dictatorship of Primo de Rivera, account for the fierce hatred felt towards him by prominent officers who had been promoted by the dictatorship.[15]

Azaña's military reforms of the spring and summer of 1931 were cleverly manipulated by the rightist press in order to propagate the notion that Army officers, along with landowners and clerics, were the object of persecution by the new regime. That was a deliberate distortion of Azaña's intentions. By a decree of 22 April 1931, Army officers had to take an oath of loyalty to the Republic just as previously they had to the monarchy. According to the decree, to stay in the ranks, an officer simply had to make 'a promise to serve the Republic faithfully, obey its laws and defend it by arms'. A officer's refusal to give the promise would be taken as an application to resign his commission. For many, the promise was just a routine formula without special significance and was made by a large number whose real convictions were anti-Republican.[16] After all, few had felt bound by their oath of loyalty to the monarchy to spring to its defence on 14 April. On the other hand, although a reasonable demand on the part of the new Minister and the new regime, the oath was perceived by the more partisan officers as an ideologically motivated attack on their dearest convictions. The right-wing press easily generated the impression that Azaña was maliciously forcing into penury those whose convictions prevented them from swearing the oath.[17] In fact, that was untrue: those who opted not to swear were automatically transferred to the reserve and continued to receive the appropriate pay.

An even greater cause of outrage to the more right-wing officers was the decree announced on 25 April, which came to be known as the *Ley Azaña*. By this decree, Azaña offered voluntary retirement on full pay to all members of the officer corps, a generous and expensive way of trying to reduce its size. However, the decree stated that after thirty days, any officer who was surplus to requirements but had not opted for the scheme would lose his commission without compensation. This caused massive resentment and further encouragement of the belief, again fomented by the rightist press, that the Army was being persecuted by the Republic.[18] Since the threat was never carried out, its announcement was a gratuitously damaging error on the part of Azaña or his ministerial advisers.

The smouldering hatred of Azaña beginning to be felt by many officers was intensified by what was known as the 'responsibilities' issue. This concerned the trials of officers for misdemeanours committed under the monarchy. General Dámaso Berenguer had been arrested on 17 April, for alleged offences in Spain's Moroccan colony, as Prime Minister and later as Minister of War during the summary trial and execution of the Jaca rebels, Captains Fermín Galán and Angel García Hernández.[19] General Mola was also arrested on 21 April for his police work against the Republican movement as Director General of Security under Berenguer.[20] These arrests and subsequent trials were part of a symbolic purge of significant soldiers and politicians for acts of political and fiscal abuse and corruption carried out during the Dictatorship and after, the greatest of which was considered to be the execution of Galán and García Hernández. The campaign 'for responsibilities' helped keep popular Republican fervour at boiling point in the early months of the regime but at a high price in the long term. Azaña rightly believed that the Responsibilities Commission was dangerously damaging to the Republic.[21] In fact, relatively few individuals were imprisoned or fled into exile but the 'responsibilities' issue created a myth of a vindictive and implacable Republic – a myth wrongly identified with Azaña. The 'responsibilities' campaign increased the fears and resentments of powerful figures of the old regime, inducing them to see the threat posed by the Republic as greater than it really was.[22] The trials of Berenguer and Mola were to provide the Africanistas with a further excuse for their instinctive hostility to the Republic. Ironically, Azaña, who became the focus of right-wing resentment for the issue, had tried, along with other moderate members of the government, to bury it.[23]

More than the 'responsibilities' and even the *Ley Azaña*, the issue which most inflamed military sensibilities was Azaña's decree of 3 June 1931 initiating the so-called *revisión de ascensos* (review of promotions) whereby some of the merit promotions given during the Moroccan wars were to be reconsidered. This reflected the determination of Azaña and his liberal military advisers to reverse some of the arbitrary promotions made by Primo de Rivera. The announcement raised the spectre that, if all of those promoted during the *Dictadura* were to be affected, many influential right-wing generals – including Francisco Franco – would go back to being colonels, and many other senior Africanistas would be demoted. Since the commission carrying out the revision did not report for more than eighteen months, it was to be at best an irritation, at worst a gnawing anxiety for those affected. Nearly one thousand officers expected to be involved, although in the event only half that number had their cases examined.[24]

The right-wing press and specialist military newspapers mounted a ferocious campaign alleging that Azaña had declared that his intention was to *triturar el Ejército* (crush the Army).[25] Azaña never made any such remark, although it has become a commonplace that he did. He made a speech in Valencia on 7 June in which he praised the Army warmly and declared his determination to *triturar* the power of the corrupt bosses who dominated local politics, the *caciques*, in the same way as he had dismantled 'other lesser threats to the Republic'. This was twisted into the notorious phrase.[26] What especially infuriated the Africanistas was the belief that Azaña was being advised by a group of Republican officers known among his rightist opponents as the 'black cabinet'. In fact, one of Azaña's informal military advisers, Major Juan Hernández Saravia, complained to a fellow-officer that Azaña was too proud to listen to advice from anyone. Moreover, far from setting out to persecute monarchist officers, Azaña seems rather to have cultivated many of them, such as General José Sanjurjo, whom he left in the key position of Director of the Civil Guard, or General Enrique Ruiz Fornells, whom he kept on as his under-secretary. Indeed, there were even some leftist officers who took retirement out of frustration at what they saw as Azaña's complaisance with the old guard. Moreover, the offensive and threatening language which Azaña was accused of using against the Army is difficult to find. Azaña, although firm in his dealings with officers, spoke of the Army in public in respectful terms.[27] However, the conservative newspapers read by most Army officers, *ABC*, *La Época*, *La Correspondencia Militar*, presented the Republic as responsible for Spain's economic problems, mob violence, disrespect for the Army and anti-clericalism.

It was Franco who was to bear Azaña the deepest grudge of all and it was his resentment which set the tone for the anti-Azaña venom of Nationalist propaganda from 1936 onwards. The principal cause of his chagrin was Azaña's order of 30 June 1931 closing the Academia General Militar de Zaragoza of which Franco was Director and which he had imbued with the violent ethos of the Foreign Legion. The future Caudillo had loved his work there and he would never forgive Azaña and the so-called 'black cabinet' for snatching it from him. Franco's outrage could be perceived in his farewell address to the cadets at the Academy on 14 July 1931. In that speech, he made an oblique reference to the Republican officers who held the key posts in Azaña's Ministry as 'a pernicious example of immorality and injustice'.[28] Azaña issued a formal reprimand (*reprensión*) in Franco's service record for this speech.[29]

Just as, with the aid of a ferociously hostile right-wing press, Azaña became the target of military resentment, a similar thing happened with Catholics. The position of organized religion in society was challenged in Article 26 of the new Constitution drafted in August 1931. This concerned the termination of state financial support for the clergy and religious orders; the dissolution of orders, such as the Jesuits, that swore foreign oaths of allegiance; and the limitation of the Church's right to wealth. The attitude to the Church of Azaña and most Republicans was based on the belief that, if a new Spain was to be built, the clerical stranglehold on many aspects of society must be broken. Religion was not attacked as such, but the Constitution aimed to put an end to the government's support for the Church's privileged position. This was presented by right-wing deputies in the Cortes, and by the Catholic newspaper network at the heart of which stood *El Debate*, as virulent anti-clericalism. As a result, opponents of any kind of reform could hitch their reactionism to the cause of religion. When the debate was reaching a cul-de-sac, Azaña made a speech in the Cortes on 13 October 1931.[30] The speech was a magisterial statement of common sense and flexibility. However, one phrase – 'Spain has ceased to be Catholic' – created unnecessary alarm among Catholics. Although a reasonable sociological observation, it earned him the enmity of some right-wing Republicans and the fierce hostility of much of the clergy. Azanã's remark was perceived as the satanic war-cry of a vengeful lay inquisitor, yet his attitude to the Church was altogether more reasonable and his speech persuaded the left-wing majority not to push for the complete dissolution of the religious orders. Nevertheless, it came to seem as though he was the arch-enemy of the Catholic Church. In fact, the cordial relations of Manuel Azaña, and other prominent Republicans such as Luis de Zulueta, Jaume Carner and Luis Nicolau d'Olwer with liberal churchmen such as Cardinal Vidal i Barraquer belied the cries that the Church was being mercilessly persecuted.[31]

As a result of Azaña's intervention on 13 October, the Constitution was saved. However, a cabinet crisis was precipitated because the senior Catholics in the government, the Prime Minister, Niceto Alcalá Zamora, and the Minister of the Interior, Miguel Maura, felt obliged to resign. Azaña's performance, and the prolonged applause with which it was greeted, had made him the obvious person to become prime minister. In the cabinet meeting to discuss the issue, he rejected the idea as premature: 'I refused resolutely and almost with violence. For a while, I thought that I would have the strength to convince them or to maintain a non-negotiable *no*. The scene was dramatic, at times. And eventually, just too much for me.' His reaction was indicative of his lack of ambition – 'I was really upset and in a black mood, even desperate.' He was incredulous – 'and I went home, saying to myself, I'm prime minister but I don't feel any different, I don't even believe it.' When one of his proposed cabinet, José Giral, was reluctant to accept a ministry, Azaña persuaded him, 'citing what they had done to me'.[32]

Thereafter, Azaña showed a curious mixture of energetic determination and a depressive tendency to throw in the towel. Already in the late summer of 1931, he had written in his diary, 'I am in serious need of a dose of leisure and solitude'.[33] Within six months of assuming the presidency of the Council of Ministers, Azaña wrote in his diary on 14 March 1932, of his desire to 'send politics packing and immerse myself in books' – although his black mood could have been the effect of a visit to the Teatro Español earlier that evening to see a Russian company present *Crime and Punishment*.[34] With or without the influence of Dostoevsky, he was frequently depressed. On 25 June 1932, disheartened by the slow progress of the Catalan statute and by a sense of having to do everything himself, he wrote: 'I can scarcely find anyone with whom to have a dialogue. This impression, which I get time and again, depresses me, and since today I feel physically frail, everything seems black and a lost cause.'[35] A little over a week later, on 3 July 1932, he outlined the contradictions between his intellectual formation and his political duties, writing, 'I am too inclined to find reasons for elevation and pleasure inside myself; I have educated myself in twenty-five years of voluntary seclusion, in contemplation and in contempt. There's no cure for me. La Morcuera [a mountain pass to the north of Madrid] interests me more than my parliamentary majority and the trees in the garden more than my party.'[36]

He constantly displayed a readiness to withdraw from politics in order to read and meditate. It was with healthy irony that he said in a speech to the Acción Republicana branch in Santander on 30 September 1932, 'no matter how hard I try, every now and again I remember that I am prime minister'. In his last speech to the Cortes Constituyentes, on 3 October 1933, Azaña recalled that he had been obliged by the pressure of his government colleagues to accept the presidency of the Council of Ministers in 1931: 'At that moment, I made the biggest sacrifice of my life.' The notion of impersonal and disinterested service of the public good permeates all of his writings and speeches. He asked Lerroux in the Cortes, 'if I were ambitious, does the honourable gentleman really think that I would have spent years in a library writing books which are no interest to anyone, even to me who wrote them?' In the same speech, he explained his view of political activity: 'Out of discipline and duty, I have swallowed my personal feelings, my inclinations and my most intimate devotions, sacrificing them on the altar of public service.' A brutally realistic assessment of his achievements and of his deficiencies ended with the words: 'the fact is that since I aspire to nothing, nor wish to be anything, nor plan to be anything, I have no reason to ask for anyone's help to get anything ... I know my horoscope; it's been done by an expert, and as I'm a credulous and rather timid person, I believe it: in opposition, I signify nothing.'[37]

It was not that Azaña was incapable of exercising authority – he often did so with decision and determination. In January 1932, he had not shown the slightest hesitation in ordering troops to extinguish the anarchist uprising in the Alto Llobregat. When the trials of those responsible came, he opposed executions, declaring: 'I have no wish to shoot anyone. Someone has to stop shooting people left and right. I will start.'[38] A similar incident took place, after the military uprising led by General José Sanjurjo on 10 August 1932. Plutarco Elías Calles, the Mexican President, sent a message to Azaña, 'If you wish to avoid widespread bloodshed and make the Republic live, shoot Sanjurjo.' Azaña refused.[39] Curiously, during the *Sanjurjada*, Azaña, who was often accused of cowardice by his enemies, stood on the balcony of the Ministry of War smoking a cigarette, as a sign to the rebels shooting at the building that their cause was lost.[40]

The difficulties faced by the Republic throughout 1932 and 1933 saw the pace of reform slow down to a crawl. Although Azaña had faced anarchist insurrectionism and an attempted military coup with determination, he was exhausted by the process of attrition. In particular, he invested massive reserves of energy into ensuring the passage of the Catalan Autonomy Statute, delivering three major speeches in the course of the spring and summer of 1932.[41] He was particularly saddened and embittered by the attacks to which he was subjected after the massacre perpetrated by the forces of order at Casas Viejas, in the province of Cádiz, during the repression of the anarchist insurrection of January 1933. On Thursday 23 February 1933, there was a debate in the Cortes during which he was attacked savagely from the right and accused of ordering the massacre. He wrote in his diary that same night:

> The session has been a repugnant spectacle. They have voraciously hurled themselves on the blood, churned it up and tried to smear us with it. The Radicals, especially, showed terrible viciousness. Discovering the rot that underlies this manoeuvre ended up turning my stomach and I left the chamber because I couldn't take any more . . . I am under no obligation to put up with being accused in the Cortes of deceiving my fellow party members and the deputies . . . It is hateful to have to sit expressionless on the government benches putting up with the hypocritical clamour of people who simply want to hunt down the Republic or do damage to the Republic. If they were disinterested and fair, they would be happy to co-operate in establishing the truth and then, afterwards, in punishing whoever happens to have been at fault.[42]

That sense of attrition and disappointment at the breakdown of the reform process was most bitterly felt within the Socialist Party. The blame was directed, particularly by Largo Caballero and his followers, against the Socialists' Republican allies. There was a long-standing distrust of the Republicans within the Socialist ranks – a distrust from which only Azaña was immune. He himself was aware of the lack of reforming zeal among many of the Republic's important functionaries.[43] The consequence of Socialist frustrations was the decision prior to the elections of November 1933 to break the 1931 electoral coalition, a fateful decision which made possible the period of the politics of revenge and reprisal, the so-called *bienio negro* ('black two years') from November 1933 to November 1935. Until the last moment, Indalecio Prieto, the voice of pragmatic moderation within the PSOE, maintained the hope that Largo Caballero might change his mind. When that proved impossible, he did the only thing he could, which was to include both Azaña and the Radical-Socialist leader nearest to the PSOE, Marcelino Domingo, in the Socialist electoral list presented for Vizcaya.[44] The results nationally were a disaster for both the PSOE and the left Republicans. After gaining 116 seats in the 1931 elections, the PSOE representation in the Cortes now dropped to 58. The left Republicans, that is to say Azaña's Acción Republicana, the Radical Socialists, Esquerra Catalana and the Organización Regional Gallega Autonoma, fell from their 1931 total of 139 deputies to a mere 40.[45]

Azãna's left Republicans were virtually wiped out and he had a seat in the Cortes thanks only to the perspicacity of Prieto. The Socialists were bitterly disappointed that, going it alone, their 1,627,472 votes had given them only 58 deputies, as against the 104 seats which the Radicals, in coalition with the rightist CEDA, had earned with a mere 806,340 votes.[46] Pushed by the Caballero faction, the Socialist Party now lurched to the left. In part, Caballero hoped that rhetorical revolutionism might inhibit the right from dismantling the social advances which the Republic had made or even frighten the President into calling new elections. Azaña was appalled because he realized that Caballero's verbal extremism would just intensify an already dangerous process of political polarization. The Caballeristas' naïvety was to be exploited skilfully by right-wing governments which provoked a series of strikes in order to justify repressive actions against the UGT.[47] While the PSOE dabbled with revolutionary plans, Azaña began the first of his several efforts to prevent the total radicalization of Spanish political life. In the first instance, this meant an unwelcome burden. At a point when all he wanted was to withdraw from public life, the task of rebuilding the Republican–Socialist coalition fell upon his shoulders.

It was an enormous task which was to see him imprisoned, publicly vilified and involved in a political campaign in which, against his inclinations, he was to address hundreds of thousands of people. Despite a widespread belief to the contrary, Manuel Azaña was not a personally ambitious man. His first reponse to being out of power was a sense of relief at being able to return to his books and to escape from the aridity of politics:

> Ever since I was a boy, I have always loved being at home. To return there signified for me to enter an atmosphere of calm. To wake up from a nightmare. Profound repose after a long walk. Silence after so much uproar. How I enjoyed breathing in my freedom! It was as if the air was purer when I thought that not only during that first day, but the next, and all the next month and many more, at my leisure, I could be the person I used to be, master of my own interior life, within a comforting, soft, domestic happiness, a haven for a pilgrim! I had worked and toiled so much for others; my most elevated projects had been received with such barbarity, that it was easy to excuse my temporary abandonment of what has so pompously been called an exigent civic duty, and forgive myself for retreating from the public arena in order to relax, so to speak, in the suburbs . . . And so, I recovered my dealings with books and papers. I gorged myself with reading. A thirst long built-up. A regime intended to correct a dangerous deformation. Because nothing narrows the mind, switches off the imagination, and sterilizes the spirit more than active politics and government . . . In order to be able to work in politics and the government, I have had to write off and leave unused three quarters of my powers, for lack of something for them to do, and, at the same time, develop the other part . . . One of the harshest things about politics is the aridity, the dryness, the sad spiritual narrow-mindedness of the world in which one is buried.[48]

This fragment of his diary was written near la Pobleta, his refuge near Valencia, at the height of the Spanish Civil War on 4 July 1937, and his retrospective account of how he felt in the winter of 1933 was perhaps influenced by his disillusionment at the time of writing.

Nevertheless, his comments indicate the extent to which he understood politics as a duty and often, as was soon to be the case, as a duty which only he could fulfil. In his speech in Santander on 30 September 1932, he had declared:

> I don't think of politics like a personal vocation nor even as a profession in which one has to take positions because of the simple passing of time and which is exercised sometimes in power and sometimes out of power, having periods of adversity or prosperity according to the ups and downs of politics. I don't think of it like that. I conceive of it as an ever steeper and more difficult climb towards power, towards the leadership of the country, towards the implementation by convincing public opinion of the ideas which move us and seem best to us, as long as public opinion accepts them, approves them and sustains them. And on this climb . . . what one has to do is exhaust oneself, yield the greatest utility, and, when the party or oneself is exhausted or sterilized, the best thing to do is to go away and end one's life where one will not be a nuisance, letting others occupy the post.[49]

He made it clear that this was a duty which was far from pleasant, remarking that the recent parliamentary recess 'has allowed me to travel around various Spanish provinces and to carry out a project rarely possible for those in government, which is to make intimate, direct and personal contact with the popular masses, hear what they have to say, speak with citizens and generally escape from the cold confinement of a ministerial office rarely reached in their full warmth even by favourable and happy realities'.[50] It was only half in jest that he declared 'the head of the government has no friends in politics and nor does he want any. Friendship ends before politics or begins after politics.'[51] In the winter of 1933–4, his withdrawal into private life was only in small part a reaction to the realization that it would be difficult to overcome the hostility of the left wing of the PSOE towards the Republicans.

Azaña returned to politics in 1934 only because he felt that the Republic was in serious danger. In general, he was regarded as an exception within the general Socialist perspective of contempt for the Republican betrayal, guilty of no more than what Largo Caballero's intellectual spokesman, Luis Araquistain, prophetically called 'Azaña's noble error, his beautiful Republican utopia: thinking that that it was possible to construct and govern a State that was not a class State'.[52] Nevertheless, there was considerable tension between the left-wing Socialists and Azaña. In 1937, he wrote in his diary, 'I maintained contact with some Socialists, like Prieto and Besteiro, Fernando de los Ríos, and others, who had always been friends of mine. I also still had a certain popularity among the masses, as was proved by the public meetings that I organized – a popularity and a prestige which did not go down well with the pontiffs of revolutionary extremism. But the predominant "caballerista" tendency in the party was hostile to us.'[53]

Accordingly, Azaña's efforts in early 1934 were confined to attempts to facilitate the re-grouping of left Republican forces and to warn those Socialists with whom he had contact that the PSOE's rhetorically revolutionary line could lead to disaster. Azaña was fully aware of the need to rebuild the Republican–Socialist coalition. On 30 September 1932, in his speech in Santander, he had declared, 'I believe, and I say it here and I'll repeat it wherever necessary, that I don't know whether the presence of the Socialists in the government brings them any benefit or not. It doesn't matter to me. However, I will say that the presence of the Socialists in the government, I repeat, has been one of the most vital services – a contribution so important that it was indispensable – that could possibly have been rendered to the Republican regime.'[54] Azaña's awareness of the need for Republican–Socialist collaboration was strengthened by the disaster of November 1933. Even before the elections, he had hinted at the catastrophic consequences of going divided into the electoral contest.[55] After Prieto made the public announcement of the termination of the Republican–Socialist coalition, Azaña declared in the Cortes on 2 October 1933: 'the government is finished, collaboration is at an end; you are taking another road, we follow the republicans' route; but what will always remain between us is that invisible bridge of our shared emotions and our common service to the Spanish nation.'[56] Now, in early 1934, realizing that there was little possibility of overcoming Largo Caballero's distrust, Azaña confined himself to the immediately urgent and realizable tasks of restructuring the shattered Republican camp and giving sound advice to those Socialists who would listen.

Azaña was fully informed of the Socialist belief that threats of revolution might restrain the Radical–CEDA coalition through messages from Prieto passed to him by their mutual friend, the Radical-Socialist Marcelino Domingo, and through his own direct contacts with Fernando de los Ríos. With the permission of the PSOE executive committee, De los Ríos had passed on to him a copy of the Socialists' proposal for revolutionary action. On 2 January 1934, Azaña informed De los Ríos in extremely strong language that an uprising was doomed to be smashed by the Army and that it was the duty of the Socialist leadership to control the impulses of the rank-and-file. 'I said terrible things to him', Azaña noted in his diary, 'I don't know how he put up with them'. Although De los Ríos was personally moved by what Azaña had said and passed it on to other members of the Socialist executive, it had little effect.[57] Given the ferocity of the rightist attacks on the working class, even Prieto was in no mood to listen to reason and almost certainly seduced by the possibility of revolutionary action. Years later, speaking in the Círculo Pablo Iglesias in Mexico City, he blamed himself for his participation in the revolutionary movement which was to break out in Asturias in October 1934.[58] The painfulness of Prieto's position was perceived by Azaña at the time.

He had taken the opportunity of coinciding with Prieto in Barcelona during the campaign for the Catalan municipal elections to renew his warnings about the dangers of continued left-wing disunity. This was the theme of his speech in the Barcelona bull-ring on 7 January, but it seems to have had little effect on Prieto, with whom he lunched on the following day at the Font del Lleó restaurant on the Tibidabo.[59] Nevertheless, Azaña continued to try to re-establish contact with the Socialists. On 4 February, Prieto, appalled by the rightist onslaught against the working class, went along with the Caballeristas and threatened that a revolutionary uprising would take place. Exactly seven days later, Azaña, speaking as Prieto had done in the Teatro Pardiñas de Madrid, made a long speech warning against the frivolous resort to revolutionary solutions but also recognizing how the government's contempt for social justice was provoking the Socialists. It was a reasoned appeal for unity and moderation, but the Socialists were not yet ready to pay him heed.[60]

Azaña had rather more success in his self-appointed task of attempting to unify the fragmented and demoralized left-Republican parties. His hope was that 'out of the remnants of the three small parties there will almost certainly emerge a nucleus which will be quite important simply by dint of the merger of the three, which will start off with enough strength and authority to attract many other republicans and grow rapidly'. After overcoming petty rivalries and distrust between the groups, Azaña secured on 2 April 1934 the unification of Marcelino Domingo's Partido Radical Socialista Independiente, Santiago Casares Quiroga's Organización Regional Gallega Autónoma and his own Acción Republicana into Izquierda Republicana.[61] Azaña became the new party's president and Marcelino Domingo its vice-president. While the formation of Izquierda Republicana did not lead to the reunification of the entire Republican camp, it did begin a major process of rationalization. When the liberal wing of the Radicals broke away from Lerroux in May 1934, under the leadership of Diego Martínez Barrio, it was not long before it was in contact with the rump of the Radical Socialist Party of Félix Gordón Ordás which had been left somewhat isolated by the union of Domingo and Azaña. Negotiations throughout the summer of 1934 led to the foundation on 11 September of Unión Republicana.[62] This was to facilitate considerably Azaña's plans for a broad concentration of the moderate left.

The other front of Azaña's activities, relations with the Socialists, was not progressing so smoothly. In a desultory fashion, the PSOE revolutionary committee organized by Largo Caballero played at making preparations for the forthcoming rising. The sheer unreality of the committee's activities suggests that Caballero, at least, hoped that it would never be necessary to put its plans to the test. Prieto, against the hostility of Largo Caballero, tried on a number of occasions throughout 1934 to have Azaña and Domingo apprised of the preparations being made. Perhaps Prieto hoped to subject Largo Caballero to the cold reason which Azaña would inevitably have brought to the proceedings. However, at a joint meeting of the executive committees of the PSOE and the UGT in mid-March 1934, Largo declared that there would be no collaboration with the Republicans either in the revolutionary movement or in the subsequent provisional government.[63]

It was hardly surprising that when Azaña made an initiative for renewed Republican–Socialist collaboration in June he should be rebuffed by Largo Caballero. The meeting took place at the home of José Salmerón, secretary-general of Izquierda Republicana. Salmerón, Marcelino Domingo and Azaña represented their party. Largo Caballero, Enrique de Francisco and a third Socialist (probably Juan-Simeón Vidarte, who was like De Francisco one of the revolutionary committee's secretaries) represented the PSOE. Azaña spoke for an hour about the need for unity and the profound effect that the announcement of such unity would have on the political situation. He was absolutely right. The CEDA leader, Gil Robles, had already begun his very successful tactic of periodically withdrawing support from the Radicals in order to provoke cabinet crises and thus a gradual break-up of Lerroux's party. At each crisis, when consulted by the President of the Republic, Azaña recommended a dissolution of the Cortes and the calling of elections. There would have been far more chance of Alcalá Zamora agreeing, and thereby resolving the acute problems of the day without violence, if there had existed a united block of left Republican and Socialist forces. Largo Caballero, however, was not interested and said that he had attended the meeting merely 'out of deference to those who had called it'. In the hope that circumstances might change, Azaña concluded the meeting with a formula which left the door open to future contacts: 'each one will remain alert in case circumstances advise a change of position.'[64]

Largo Caballero declared at that meeting that he could not be seen by the Socialist masses to be entering into an agreement with the Republicans for fear of being 'materially and morally diminished'. Largo's determination to be seen to be as militant as his UGT rank-and-file was the greatest obstacle to Azaña's plans for rebuilding the Republican–Socialist coalition. That he was fully aware of this had been made clear in his speech 'Grandezas y miserias de la política' given in the Bilbao liberal club El Sitio on 21 April 1934. In a speech of great sadness and vision, Azaña again made clear that politics was a burden which he shouldered only with the greatest reluctance. He had also warned, with an eye to the provocatively revolutionary lines being followed by the PSOE and by the Catalan Republicans of the Esquerra Catalana, against the dangers of being carried along by the crowd.[65] Largo Caballero's remarks at the meeting held in Salmerón's house suggested that Azaña's warnings had been ignored. However, at the end of September, Don Manuel made one last try to get the Socialists to see reason. On 26 September 1934, Jaume Carner, the wealthy Catalan Republican who had been Azaña's Minister of Finance, died. Azaña went to the funeral along with numerous other Republican figures. In fact, he had been in Barcelona less than a month previously and had made a speech calling for the reconquest of the Republic. Now, at the end of September, Azaña coincided again with Prieto and De los Ríos at the funeral of Carner. Catalan friends of all three organized a luncheon for them at the Font del Lleó. Azaña lamented the lack of agreement between the Socialists and the left Republicans. More urgently, he took the opportunity to warn them in desperate terms against the radicalization of the Socialist rank-and-file.[66]

The realism of what Azaña had to say could hardly affect the position of either Prieto or De los Ríos since they were unable to influence attitudes within a PSOE dominated by Caballero and the militant youth. As Azaña himself noted, Prieto was now opposed to the Caballerista plans for a revolutionary insurrection but went along out of party discipline.[67] During his stay in Barcelona, Azaña also talked to several members of the Generalitat, including Joan Lluhí Vallesca, to all of whom he reiterated his view that violence was not the answer to the provocation to which they were being subjected by the government. He pointed out to them that, as members of the autonomous regional government, it was absurd for them to become involved in an insurrection against the central state.[68] Despite his efforts, when three ministers of the CEDA entered the cabinet on 4 October, the ill-prepared rising broke out in Madrid, Catalonia and Asturias. At one level, this represented the defeat of Azaña's efforts to bring the Spanish left to reason. At another, by galvanizing Prieto into joining him in a quest for a great electoral union of the left, it constituted the starting point for his greatest triumph: the electoral victory in the so-called Popular Front elections of February 1936.

The repression of the PSOE and the UGT following the defeat of the left in Asturias was ferocious. From this, Largo Caballero decided that a more 'bolshevik' line should be adopted. In contrast, Prieto believed that the left should endeavour to regain power legally. Accordingly, throughout 1935 Prieto would put his considerable influence and authority within the Socialist movement at the service of Azaña's efforts to rebuild the 1931 electoral coalition of the left. Azaña threw himself into that task after his traumatic experiences during the events of October 1934. He had been arrested in Barcelona on 8 October at the beginning of the events and imprisoned on a ship in Barcelona harbour until the end of December 1934. Subjected to vilification by the right-wing press, he became a symbol for all those in Spain who were suffering from the authoritarian politics of the Radical–CEDA coalition. His arrest, and the contemptuous violence with which he was treated by the Assault Guards who carried it out, were frightening and humiliating experiences for him. While he was detained, his brother, Gregorio, died in Zaragoza. Azaña believed that his arrest had aggravated his brother's heart condition.[69] Although thousands of telegrams of support were sent to him, the authorities tried to break his spirit by informing him at one point that he had received only seven. Azaña was also distressed by the fact that neither the President of the Republic, Niceto Alcalá Zamora, nor the President of the Cortes, Santiago Alba, did anything to ensure the implementation of his immunity as a parliamentary deputy, let alone as ex-prime minister. This was all the more galling since not only was Azaña innocent of the charge of subversion but he was also someone who had dedicated his life to building respect for the State.[70]

He was intensely embittered by the experience, which he described vividly in his best-selling book *Mi rebelión en Barcelona*. However, he was also inspired by the popular support that he received during his persecution to redouble his efforts to defend the Republican ideal. In prison, he finally received the masses of letters of support sent to him by intellectuals and politicians and collective letters signed by hundreds of ordinary Spaniards. One, which was published, was signed by 87 leading personalities from the literary and academic worlds including Fernando de los Ríos, the doctor and writer Gregorio Marañón, the left-wing Catholic writer José Bergamín, the historians Américo Castro and Manuel Núñez de Arce, the poets Federico García Lorca, Juan Ramón Jiménez and León Felipe, and the novelist Ramón del Valle Inclán.[71] Azaña wrote to Prieto from prison on 25 December 1934, 'I get hundreds and hundreds of letters, in all of which there is a recurrent theme: now more than ever . . . And everyone speaks of a "left-wing reaction which gets bigger by the day". I don't want to discourage anyone. They also say that there is more "Azañaism" than ever, "even among people who aren't on the left".'[72]

Azaña had committed no crimes and eventually the charges against him were dropped. He was freed on 28 December 1934 and recuperated from his ordeal with his wife, Dolores, and brother-in-law, Cipriano Rivas Cherif, at a friend's house in Barcelona. His release coincided with his saint's day and Izquierda Republicana invited all those who sympathized with him to send a card or telegram of congratulation. The messages of support arrived at the party's Madrid headquarters by the hundreds of thousands. A member of the Izquierda Republicana Youth described the scenes:

> the postmen could not cope with the delivery of the cards and telegrams, bearing bulging postal sacks for which there was soon no room in the party's branch offices. An endless queue of citizens, both men and women, endlessly delivered their personal congratulations and wound around the block, through the Puerta del Sol and down the Calle del Arenal.

> That spontaneous demonstration of hope by the Madrileños and from Spaniards from the furthest confines of the country was a surprise for all of us, even the initiators of the idea.

While Izquierda Republicana headquarters dealt with the avalanche of post, Azaña, his wife and Cipriano Rivas Cherif were dealing with another mountain of letters in Barcelona.[73]

When Azaña came out of prison, the last thing that he wanted to do was to take on single-handed the task of rebuilding the electoral force necessary to bring back the Republic of 1931. Yet, despite himself, he was reclaimed by the ordinary people of Spain and pushed to undertake that task by the popular support which he received during his persecution. Azaña was clearly moved by these demonstrations of popular esteem and what he took to be enthusiasm for a return to the Republic of 1931–3. On 16 January 1935, he wrote to Prieto who was in exile in Belgium: 'a movement of optimism and hope has been produced here, simply by the fact of my liberation, and for that reason I have been the object of an almost plebiscitary demonstration by all the forces and organizations of the left in Spain'.[74]

While urging Prieto to work for the creation of a political alliance which would allow the winning of the next elections, Azaña himself worked to consolidate the Republican unification begun in the previous spring. In the late summer of 1934, he had used his influence to ensure that the new party Unión Republicana would drop its anti-Socialist leanings. After his release from prison, he renewed his contacts with Unión Republicana and also with the conservative Felipe Sánchez Román's Partido Nacional Republicano. This bore fruit in the joint declaration issued on 12 April 1935 listing the minimum conditions which they regarded as essential for the reconstruction of political co-existence in Spain. The seven conditions were: the prevention of torture of political prisoners; the re-establishment of Constitutional guarantees; the release of those imprisoned for the events of October 1934; an end to discrimination against left-wing and liberal functionaries; the readmission to their jobs of workers dismissed after the October strike; the legal existence of trade unions and the reinstatement of the town councils overthrown by the government.[75] This programme was the potential basis of a renewal of the Republican–Socialist electoral coalition.

In order to achieve the implementation of these conditions, an electoral victory was clearly essential and the repression after October had imposed sufficient realism on many of the left to make it a viable prospect. On the basis of this minimal agreement, Azaña and Prieto worked together to recreate the electoral coalition. From his exile, Prieto's task was to seek areas of agreement between the Republican camp and moderate Socialists and, even more importantly, to neutralize the irresponsible extremism of the Caballeristas, which inevitably earned him their virulent hostility.[76] Azaña's role was even more crucial. It consisted of the massive effort of publicity and propaganda which not only took the idea of a resuscitated electoral coalition to hundreds of thousands of Spaniards, but also, more importantly, demonstrated to the left wing of the PSOE the immense popular support for an electoral agreement.

Azaña undertook the campaign of 'open-air speeches' (*discursos en campo abierto*) with some initial distaste. It began on 26 May at the Campo de Mestalla in Valencia. Before more than 100,000 spectators, he announced that Izquierda Republicana was working with other parties on an electoral platform and a future plan of government which would eventually be submitted to the approval of groups further to the left. Then on 14 July, he spoke to an even larger crowd at the Campo de Lasesarre in Baracaldo near Bilbao, provoking intense enthusiasm when he called for new elections and defended the necessity of an electoral coalition. These were not well-organized meetings but rather totally spontaneous demonstrations of popular support for the man and for the regime which he personified. People travelled from all over Spain in enormous numbers. The culmination and the most spectacular event of his campaign came on 20 October 1935 at Comillas, on what in those days were the outskirts of Madrid. Azaña was thoroughly aware of the wider implications of his campaign. On the day before he was due to speak, he visited Comillas by car; somewhat surprised by the size of the venue, he asked the members of the organizing committee, 'Do you really think that this will be filled? Because if not, we are going to look ridiculous.' In the event, nearly half a million arrived to hear him elaborate his projected programme of government.[77]

The English journalist Henry Buckley wrote of the occasion:

> more than half the spectators could not even see the stand from which the former Prime Minister addressed them. The loudspeakers functioned only partially and therefore tens of thousands not only saw nothing but they heard nothing either.

> This meeting had not been widely advertised. It was frowned upon by the authorities and in some cases the Civil Guard turned back convoys of trucks carrying spectators. All vehicles bringing people from afar were stopped some miles outside Madrid, thus causing endless confusion and forcing weary men and women to trudge a long distance after a tiring ride. Admission was by payment. The front seats cost twelve shillings and sixpence and the cheaper ones ten shillings and half a crown. Standing room at the back cost sixpence. No one was forced to go to that meeting. Presence there, in fact, was much more likely to bring the displeasure of employer or landlord ... From the furthest points of Spain there were groups who had travelled in some cases six hundred miles in rainy cold weather in open motor lorries.[78]

At the end of his speech, Azaña called the huge crowd to total silence. Like an Old Testament prophet, he ended with a moving condemnation of the repressive policies of the ruling Radical–CEDA coalition; of the crushing of the unions; the closing down of the *casas del pueblo* (workers' clubs); of the thousands of political prisoners: 'The silence of the people declares its grief and indignation; but the voice of the people can sound as terrifying as the trumpets of the day of judgement. Let my words not rebound against frivolous hearts but penetrate your hearts like darts of fire. People, for Spain and for the Republic, unite!' His listeners burst into a frenetic ovation and thousands of clenched fists flowered. Azaña did not return the salute.[79] It was a revealing moment in his political career. The support which he was capable of inspiring would be the basis of the Popular Front, capable of persuading even the blindest of the Socialist left that there was popular backing for a broad electoral alliance. Yet it clearly worried Azaña. Like the sorcerer's apprentice, the mild liberal politician was taken aback by the fervour of the proletarian passion he had unleashed. His responding passivity presaged a withdrawal into isolation during the Civil War. None the less, not only did the display of discipline by those who attended seriously disturb the right, but the sheer size of the crowd and its enthusiasm helped resolve remaining doubts among those who still opposed the creation of the electoral front.

Meanwhile, the PSOE was undergoing bitter internal conflict over its future electoral tactics. Prieto seized the initiative. He had been in correspondence on the subject with Azaña since late 1934. Convinced that Largo Caballero's notion of an exclusive workers' block facing the electorate without Republican allies would guarantee electoral defeat, Prieto advocated a much wider 'circumstantial alliance'. Secure in the knowledge that important sectors of the party were with him, Prieto published an article on 14 April 1935 in his paper *El Liberal* calling for Socialist collaboration with the broad front of Republicans being forged by Azaña and Martínez Barrio. The article had a huge impact. Nevertheless, with Prieto still in exile, the job of carrying the call to the masses was undertaken by Azaña. On 7 August, three weeks after his huge public meeting at Baracaldo, replete with *¡Vivas!* for Prieto, Azaña wrote to him: 'I believe that you have won, not only within public opinion, but also inside the mass of your own party. This is not just my opinion but that of many people, Socialists and non-Socialists.'[80] The theoretical polemics of the PSOE left had little impact on the rank-and-file and Prieto continued to work confidently for union, meeting Azaña in Belgium in mid-September to discuss the programme of the projected coalition. On 14 November 1935, Azaña wrote formally to Enrique de Francisco of the PSOE executive committee proposing an electoral understanding.[81] Impelled by the evidence of the popular support enjoyed by Azaña in his campaign of *discursos en campo abierto* and by the change of tactics adopted by their Communist allies, the Caballeristas reluctantly came around to Prieto's point of view.

A complex process of negotiation over the Popular Front programme remained, carried forward by Amos Salvador of Izquierda Republicana, Bernardo Giner de los Ríos of Unión Republicana, and Manuel Cordero and Juan Simeón Vidarte for the UGT and PSOE and in representation of the other working-class groups.[82] The adherence of Largo Caballero would not have been possible without the efforts of the Communists. They were fully aware of the hostility felt towards them by Azaña and Prieto and were anxious to see Largo Caballero join the Front not least because his preference for a more proletarian union would guarantee their presence. Accordingly, they worked hard to get him to drop his opposition, even sending the prominent French Communist Jacques Duclos to try to persuade him. Nevertheless, the fact remains that the core of the Popular Front was the Republican–Socialist electoral coalition recreated by the efforts of Azaña and Prieto. No one, not even Prieto, worked harder than Azaña to ensure the electoral success of the Spanish left in February 1936. Indeed, if anything swayed the doubting Largo Caballero, it was almost certainly the evidence of popular endorsement for the idea of union displayed during Azaña's propaganda campaign. The victory of the Popular Front was ultimately the victory of Manuel Azaña, born both of his diplomacy behind the scenes and his massive popularity in the country as a whole.

In the wake of the elections of 16 February 1936, General Franco was involved in various efforts at military intervention to prevent a hand-over of power to the Popular Front.[83] The intimidated outgoing Prime Minister, Manuel Portela Valladares, insisted on handing over power to Azaña immediately. Azaña had no desire to assume the post of prime minister and would have preferred it to go to Diego Martínez Barrio, the leader of Unión Republicana. However, both he and Martínez Barrio realized that, after the enormous success of the *discursos en campo abierto* and the electoral campaign, the masses would not have understood. Accordingly, Martínez Barrio had advised the President, Niceto Alcalá Zamora, that he should offer the government to Azaña. As he wrote in his diary, 'whether I like it or not, it has been imposed by the logic of events'. Nevertheless, he was annoyed to be told by a panic-stricken Portela on the afternoon of 19 February, 'I have no role to play here, the provincial governors are resigning one after another and no one pays me any attention. You must take charge of this immediately.' Azaña reminded him in vain that the proper procedure was for him to resign at the first meeting of the new Cortes. With Largo Caballero adamant that the Socialists should play no part in the cabinet, Azaña assembled in a matter of hours a ministerial team consisting exclusively of left Republicans. Azaña's difficulties were exacerbated by the fact that Portela did not inform him of the full extent of his conversations with Franco until well after, saying only, 'About the army, I know nothing.' Franco was therefore not punished for transgressing his authority and was in a position to play a crucial role in the military rebellion of July 1936.[84]

Azaña returned to power with 'the desire that the hour has struck in which Spaniards stop shooting each other'. It was a vain hope. After the stark polarization of the previous two years, he faced a massive task of pacification and reconciliation. The festering divisions within the Socialist Party had serious implications for his own government since they cast considerable doubt on the stability of its parliamentary backing. Prieto was ready to support Azaña but Largo Caballero, determined never again to carry out bourgeois policies in a coalition government with Republicans, was merely waiting for the fulfilment of the Popular Front programme before pushing for an all-Socialist cabinet. At the same time, Mola and the other military plotters had already begun to prepare for the July rising and their work would be greatly facilitated by any sign of government uncertainty or a breakdown of law-and-order. Azaña wrote of his 'black despair' at church burnings and attacks on right-wingers – manifestations of left-wing rejoicing at the electoral victory and of revenge for the sufferings of the *bienio negro*.[85] Nevertheless, throughout the last week of February, all of March and early April, he appeared to be on top of the situation, behaving decisively, energetically, satisfying all elements of the parliamentary coalition that kept him in power and presenting himself convincingly as the guarantee of law and order, social peace and moderation.

At this point in the spring of 1936, he was deeply aware of the threat of civil war but he was still optimistic. This was evident from his magisterial speech to the Cortes on 3 April: 'my principal concern as a citizen, as a Spaniard and as a republican, as long as I have responsibility for leading the government of the Popular Front, is to project the policies of the Popular Front.' It was a message of hope to his supporters and an attempt to calm those on the right who opposed him but who were susceptible to reason. He spoke in arrogantly confident terms, despite – or perhaps because of – his awareness of the dangers facing Spain: 'I have been aware, since before the elections, of the massive difficulties waiting to trip up the government but they don't frighten me . . . it is my intention to govern with right on my side: my hands are full of reasons for doing so . . . We govern with just cause and with laws. Ah! He who steps outside the law has lost all justification for what he does.' The scale of his apparent confidence was a rallying cry to supporters and a challenge to those who were working against the Republic. They hardly sounded like the words of a man who was contemplating a resignation from active politics. On the other hand, there was always an element of Azaña's screwing up his courage when duty called. That did not mean that his personal preference would not have been to withdraw into the security of private life. Nonetheless, his combative speech to the Cortes, and to the nation, made it clear that he knew that there could be no second chances this time around; no room or time for mistakes to be rectified. The speech ended on a spine-chilling note: 'if we do not triumph over those whose interests we are going to damage, we will have lost the last legal, parliamentary and republican chance to face the problem head on and solve it with justice . . . we are ready to do our duty with the cold tenacity of those who are convinced that we are playing the last card.' 'I would go so far as to observe that these are, perhaps, the last opportunities we have, not only for the peaceful and normal functioning of republican politics, but rather for the definitive and pacific establishment of the republican regime in Spain, and also for the parliamentary regime.'[86]

An apparent opportunity to strengthen the government for the tasks outlined in his speech arose out of the weakness of the President of the Republic, Alcalá Zamora. Article 81 of the Republican Constitution gave a President the power to dissolve the Cortes twice during his mandate. To prevent a President being deprived of the essential power to call new elections, Article 81 further required that, in the case of a second dissolution during the mandate of a single president, the subsequently elected Cortes investigate the necessity and validity of the decree which dissolved its predecessor. In the event of the Cortes deciding that the previous decree of dissolution had been unnecessary, the President would be obliged to resign. A broad majority of the Cortes welcomed this opportunity to get rid of Alcalá Zamora. The parties of the left had never forgiven him for permitting the entry of the CEDA into the government in October 1934 and the parties of the right were furious that he had not handed power to Gil Robles in December 1935. Azaña and Prieto too did not trust Alcalá Zamora and saw in Article 81 an opportunity to remove him and so consolidate the new government. Azaña, in particular, was frustrated by the President's frequent interference in cabinet meetings and his barely concealed hostility. Their relationship had become increasingly difficult. Azaña had begun to speak of Alcalá Zamora, who was from Priego in Córdoba, as *el maleficio de Priego* (the curse of Priego). He could not forgive the President for acquiescing in his persecution after October 1934. Most recently, at a cabinet meeting on 2 April, Azaña and Alcalá Zamora had had a wild slanging match, based on their mutual repugnance. Azaña wrote to Rivas Cherif: 'I told the ministers that I would not return to the presidential palace with that man.' He seems to have reached the conclusion that it was necessary to get rid of Alcalá Zamora, although an element of passionate personal resentment may have influenced what should have been a cold political decision. Now, Azaña was impelled to act by credible rumours that Alcalá Zamora hoped to sidestep his fate by forcing the resignation of Azaña's cabinet before Article 81 was discussed.[87] Azaña hesitated for fear of military intervention but, after lengthy deliberations, he concluded that 'I could not carry the responsibility of leaving the Republic's worst enemy in the presidency. If everyone now regretted having voted for him in 1931, I did not not want to have to repent having elected him again in April 1936, because that's what missing Tuesday evening's opportunity would mean.'[88]

Alcalá Zamora was duly impeached and the need for a new President opened possibilities to strengthen the Republic. Azaña wrote to his brother-in-law, 'once the vacancy arose, I thought that there would be no other solution but for me to take it'. He had long thought that it would benefit the Republic more if the 'wave of Azañaism' (*oleada del azañismo*) of the previous summer were used to strengthen the regime by his occupancy of the presidency rather than worn away by the attrition to which he was subjected as prime minister. There was, however, an ambiguity about his position. On the one hand, he was driven as always by a sense of duty and a belief that only he could solve certain problems. At the same time, he was exhausted by the exertions of the previous eighteen months. It is also possible that he wanted to be in a position of influence to counteract what he knew to be the plans of Largo Caballero. The Socialist leader had made it clear that the left Republicans were supposed to exhaust themselves in preparation for an exclusively Socialist government.[89] The presidency not only constituted an unavoidable duty but it also offered an apparent opportunity to escape from the debilitating daily round of politics. In the subsequent public and private discussion of the merits of Azaña, Prieto argued convincingly that Azaña was the only plausible candidate and did more than anyone to ensure that he would be Alcalá Zamora's replacement.[90]

Not everyone agreed. The bulk of Azaña's colleagues in the leadership of his party were appalled at the thought of losing him as prime minister and of Izquierda Republicana being decapitated. Largo considered it ludicrous to transfer Azaña from where he was doing an essential job to what Vidarte called the 'gilded cage of the Presidency'. Curiously, although the newspaper of the PSOE left, *Claridad*, railed against Azaña and Prieto, the Caballeristas did not produce their own candidate.[91] Prieto was gambling rashly on being able to follow Azaña as prime minister. If he failed, there would be no one else capable of leading the government at a time of intensifying rightist hostility.

Prieto and Azaña were probably the only two politicians with the skill and popularity to stabilize the ever more polarized situation of the spring of 1936. Working in tandem, they might have been able to introduce sufficient reform to satisfy the militant left while showing the determination to crack down on the extreme right. Even if they could not have attracted the moderate right, Prieto and Azaña might have been able to stop the fascist provocations and the leftist responses to them which were preparing the ground for a military coup. That required Azaña in the presidency and Prieto as prime minister. As things turned out, the impeachment of the President and his replacement by Azaña ensured that neither could lead the cabinet.

At no time during the Second Republic was there a greater need for strong and determined government than in the spring of 1936. Military conspirators were plotting the overthrow of the regime. The youthful activists of right and left were clashing in the streets. Unemployment was rising and social reforms were meeting dogged resistance from the landowners. The problem had become particularly acute after the elevation of Azaña to the presidency on 10 May. The new President immediately asked Prieto to form a government. When summoned by Azaña on 11 May, Prieto told him of his plans to restore order and accelerate reform. It was a programme of government capable of preventing civil war but it required the strong parliamentary backing of all Republican forces, including the PSOE, and Prieto was doubtful that he could count on the votes of the left wing of the PSOE.[92] On the following day, when he informed the deputies from the PSOE's parliamentary group of Azaña's offer, Prieto was defeated.

There is no hard evidence that Azaña mounted the operation in order to form a powerful political team with Prieto. It has been a widespread assumption based on the facts that Prieto virtually acted as Azaña's campaign manager for the presidency through his newspaper *El Liberal* and that, once president, Azaña offered power to Prieto. However, years later, Prieto claimed that 'I never had any possibility of leading the government'. According to Prieto, Azaña had always intended to appoint Santiago Casares Quiroga. He regarded it as most irregular that, at his interview with the new President on 11 May, he was accompanied by Casares. Azaña knew full well that the Caballerista majority of the PSOE would never permit Prieto to form a government. 'Azaña wanted a kitchen cabinet and I'm no good for domestic service, which meant that I, implicitly, was already excluded by him, even though on the following day, he called me to the Palace to invite me officially to form a government, but in the certainty that I couldn't or shouldn't accept.'[93] If Prieto's recollection and interpretation are accurate, it would appear that Azaña aimed initially at controlling the cabinet through the pliable (and virtually unknown) Casares. In the event, that is not what happened. The consumptive Santiago Casares Quiroga gave no indication of being controlled by Azaña. Certainly, oblivious to the threat of military conspiracy, he was no match – as Prime Minister and Minister of War – for the problems that he was called upon to solve. Accordingly, Azaña himself was accused by the PSOE left of simply fleeing from his responsibilities. To be sure, once he became President, he spent the early summer of 1936 in a country retreat just outside Madrid, the Quinta del Pardo, which he had restored in 1932. There he rested after his exertions in taking the Popular Front to power and took great interest in the fate of the roses in its gardens. He took immense delight in his ceremonial, especially diplomatic, functions, in the restoration of official buildings, in the decoration of the presidential apartments in the old Palacio Real and in becoming a patron of the arts.[94] The euphoria of the President and his Prime Minister was entirely misplaced. By May 1936, the military conspiracy was well under way. On 16 July, barely thirty-six hours before the outbreak of war, he and his wife moved from La Quinta to the lugubrious lower apartments of the Palacio Real, described by Prieto as 'a pantheon'.[95]

The military uprising of 18 July 1936 and the explosion of revolutionary violence which it provoked appalled Azaña. The actions of soldiers and revolutionaries alike were far removed from his vision of rational and moral politics. Throughout that first day of war, Azaña received streams of political figures in a frantic endeavour to find a solution to the crisis. It became ever more apparent to him that the irresolute Casares Quiroga was totally paralysed and incapable of dealing with the situation. One of his staff told Julián Zugazagoitia, the editor of *El Socialista*, that the Ministry of War was 'a mad-house, and the Minister is the craziest of the lot'. Azaña's response was to try to put together a broad-based coalition, a national government 'made up of all those who accept the Constitution from the republican right to the Communists'. He telephoned the conservative Republican, Miguel Maura, to seek his collaboration. It was not an idea that could prosper without the collaboration of Largo Caballero, however, and for that, it would have been necessary to accede to Largo's insistence that there was no option but to arm the workers. Both Azaña's instincts and his sense of international opinion made him recoil before the suggestion of arming the revolution in order to defeat the counter-revolution.

Nevertheless, the gravity of the situation was such that, three hours later, Casares was obliged to resign. Hoping to open negotiations with the rebels and to preclude the possibility of proletarian revolution, Azaña called on the moderate centre Republican Diego Martínez Barrio to form a broad coalition government. At 11.00 p.m., Largo Caballero rejected Martínez Barrio's invitation, brought by Prieto, for Socialist participation in his new cabinet because the proposed coalition would also include groupings to the right of the Popular Front. Believing that the absence of the PSOE might facilitate talks with the military rebels, in the early hours of the morning of 19 July, Martínez Barrio finally formed a government composed exclusively of Republicans. Downcast, Azaña said 'It's too late!' Nevertheless, with the explicit permission of the President, Martínez Barrio began immediately to telephone military garrisons and spoke twice to General Mola who spurned compromise and dismissed his assurances that his government would pursue a more right-wing policy and re-impose law and order. To Azaña's horror, rumours of the conciliation attempts led to mass protest demonstrations in the streets of Madrid. By midday on 19 July, Martínez Barrio had been forced to resign.[96]

Azaña had tried a conservative cabinet in the hope of compromise with the rebels. The only remaining option was to fight and that meant arming the workers. Already unhappy about the working-class radicalism manifested during the spring of 1936, Azaña contemplated such a prospect with alarm. The quest for compromise was abandoned but he had little choice. He was still reluctant to grant power to Largo Caballero who believed that the military uprising meant that the Republicans must now make way for an all-Socialist cabinet. Azaña finally replaced Martínez Barrio with the Minister for the Navy, a chemistry professor, José Giral, virtually the only one of his left-Republican followers prepared to grasp the nettle. His cabinet was hardly distinguishable from that of Casares Quiroga which had shown so little urgency and initiative before the threatened coup. It was a government that was not up to the tasks which faced it.[97] Prieto was to be the real power behind the throne, working tirelessly as principal adviser to Giral who quickly took the dramatic step of authorizing the distribution of arms to the workers. That decision was to be crucial in the defeat of the rebellion in many places, but it meant that the Republican legality to which Azaña was devoted had essentially been replaced by the spontaneous actions of the working class.

Azaña's frenetic efforts to seek a solution of conciliation had been defeated when he had to acquiesce in Giral's opening of the arsenals. Thereafter, he virtually withdrew from public life except to work for peace. There was no place in the Spain of the Civil War for Azaña, a man of reason who was repelled by violence. His despair was the consequence of coming to terms with the fact that the right would unleash mass bloodshed rather than permit the fulfilment of his vision. At the same time, the revolution in the loyalist zone deprived the Republic of legitimacy, drove a wedge between Azaña and his beloved democratic regime and, eventually, rendered him impotent. In his fictionalized dialogue about the war, *La velada en Benicarló*, he wrote of the 'collapse of the Republic: it succumbed in the last weeks of July, when it could not defeat the rebellion within a few days, and then, to save itself and to save us all from military tyranny, opened the gates to, or let them be knocked down by, the chaotic impetus of the people, thereby recognizing its own impotence.' With the outbreak of war, everything that he had worked for was besmirched: 'the religious tolerance imposed by law on a country of bigots, the freedom of conscience and of worship, have all been wiped out by the murder of priests, by the burning of churches, by the conversion of cathedrals into warehouses, on one side; and by the shooting of freemasons, protestants and atheists, on the other.'[98] The consequence of this loss of faith for Azaña was, in the words of his friend, Angel Ossorio y Gallardo, that 'he never believed that we could win'.[99]

In the first days of the war, Azaña was devastated by the news that his beloved nephew, Gregorio Azaña, had been murdered in Córdoba.[100] On 23 August 1936, an attempted mass escape by political prisoners in the Cárcel Modelo in Madrid led to a massacre. Rivas Cherif found a horrified Azaña completely beside himself. In his shock and indignation, he was almost unable to speak. 'They've murdered Melquíades!' he said, fell into a silence and then, 'This cannot be, this cannot be! I am sickened by the blood. I have had as much as I can take; it will drown us all.'[101] He felt 'despair', 'horror', 'dejection', 'shame', and considered resigning.[102] In *La velada en Benicarló*, almost certainly drawing upon his own experience, Azaña has one of his characters hear the screams of agony of political prisoners being shot at night in a cemetery.[103] With Franco's forces bearing down on the capital, he was bereft of hope. On 18 October 1936, he attended a showing of the Soviet film *The Sailors of Kronstadt* at the Cine Capitol. While still at the cinema, he was informed by Giral that Largo Caballero's government had decided to leave the capital. On the instructions of the Prime Minister, he left the Palacio Nacional on the following day to take up residence in Barcelona. Three weeks later, in extremely confused circumstances, and without offering any explanation to Azaña, Largo Caballero decided to establish the government not in Barcelona but in Valencia. Although deeply saddened by the contemptuous way in which he was ignored by Largo Caballero, Azaña was happy to be in the Catalan capital because he felt that his presence there might inhibit any attempt at a Catalan break-away from the Republic.[104]

At first, he and Dolores were installed in the Palacio de las Cortes Catalanas in the Parque de la Ciudadela near the docks in Barcelona. However, when the opportunity arose to move to a more tranquil setting, at the remote Abadía de Montserrat with its beautiful cloisters, he seized it gratefully. On 2 November, he took up residence in the monastery – reinforcing the impression of many in Spain and elsewhere that he was a prisoner of the government.[105] Carles Gerhard, the Generalitat's representative, found him 'aged, downcast and embittered'. Azaña was appalled by the excesses of the anarchists. Gerhard commented later: 'I was deeply affected by his bitterness, the severity of judgement which, behind an amiable façade of courtesy, still ran through the words of our president. I was strangely disturbed by the fact that, from his elevated vantage point, it was possible to have a panoramic view of the sheer scale, the sheer depth of the disaster.'[106] With the government in Valencia, residence in the Catalan capital intensified Azaña's isolation from day-to-day politics although there was little that he could have done to influence a hostile government presided over by Largo Caballero and containing representatives of the anarcho-syndicalist Confederación Nacional del Trabajo. After two months, the dangers and difficulties of a daily sixty-kilometre drive to and from Barcelona to fulfil his official functions impelled him to move once more. His official residence was established at the Palacio de Pedralbes, in what was then a suburb of Barcelona.

Azaña did not flee the country as so many of his Republican friends did, but his presence was as a symbol rather than as an active politician. His sense of duty kept him in Spain but his mood was one of despair. On 21 January 1937, in a speech in Valencia, he spoke in terms which revealed the unutterable sadness that afflicted him: 'to make war is always hateful, and more so if it is between compatriots, when it becomes baneful, even for the victor. To make war requires a moral justification of the highest, most irreproachable, kind.' His speech ended with a judgement on a possible Republican victory: 'Victory will be impersonal because it will not be the triumph of any of you, nor of our political parties, nor of our organizations . . . It will not be a personal triumph, because when one suffers the pain as a Spaniard that I have in my soul, it is impossible to triumph over compatriots. And when your president lifts the victory trophy, his Spaniard's heart will break, and no one will ever know who has suffered most for the liberty of Spain.'[107]

During the state of virtual civil war in Barcelona in the early days of May 1937, Azaña was besieged in the Palacio de las Cortes Catalanas. His despair was intensified by what he called the 'revolutionary hysteria' and he was outraged that Largo Caballero kept him in total ignorance of what was happening. Later, he railed at the 'ineptitude of the leaders, immorality, cowardice, scandals and shootings when one union was set against another, the vanity of upstarts, the insolence of separatists, treachery, deceit, the hot air of losers, exploitation of the war for private gain, the refusal to organize a proper army, paralysis of operations, little independent power centres run by local dictators . . .'[108] The terrible anxieties suffered during those days saw him decide to transfer his residence to 'La Pobleta', a house on the outskirts of Valencia. It was on his arrival at the airport of Manises in Valencia that he entrusted Julián Besteiro with his peace mission in London.[109] Shortly after, when Largo Caballero resigned on 17 May, Azaña was to experience his last glimmer of hope. The President had not been alone in his distress at the substitution of working-class committees for the organs of the state. For different reasons, the Prieto-led right wing of the PSOE, the Communists and the Republicans were keen to see the removal of Largo Caballero and the CNT from the cabinet. Confident therefore of wide support, Azaña was able to exercise his presidential functions and invite the moderate Socialist, Juan Negrín, to form a government.[110]

In fact, it would not be long before he realized that Negrín shared neither his deep distrust of the Communists nor his hope to see the war ended by mediation. His differences with the energetic and determined Negrín led to further marginalization. Their mutual incompatibility, the one decorous and respectable, the other a sybarite of gargantuan energy and appetites, intensified Azaña's isolation. He felt a degree of chagrin that Negrín's government, like Largo's before, never invited him to visit the battle fronts.[111] He perceived himself as impotent, something which was reflected in a remarkable conversation he had with Negrín on 22 April 1938. 'Ever since 18 July 1936, I have been a political cashed cheque. Since November 1936, a president without a presidency. When you formed a government, I thought I would be able to breathe a sigh of relief and that at least my opinions would be heard. It hasn't been like that. I'm the only one whose feelings can be violated with impunity, by simply presenting me with one *fait accompli* after another. I put up with this because of the sacrifices made by the real combatants, which is the only thing worthy of respect. All the rest isn't worth a damn.'[112] His sense of duty and debt to those who had died on the battlefields was a sign of Azaña's dedication to his ideals and of his essential nobility.

Established at La Pobleta, he spent his time there writing his diaries, until in December 1937, he returned to Barcelona, living in a country house, La Barata, near Tarrasa. Disgusted by the bloodshed, profoundly anguished, he nevertheless remained in the presidency because he feared that his resignation might damage the Republic. He had plenty of opportunity to resign, go abroad and join other one-time friends and colleagues, such as Madariaga, who felt that they had to distance themselves from both extremes in the war. He was harsh in his judgements of those of his friends who thus tried to flee to the 'Third Spain'. He told his ambassador in Brussels, Angel Ossorio, 'As for the Republicans who have fled, if one of them tells you that he did so on my advice, just tell him he's a liar . . . They have all gone without my consent, without even seeking my advice, and some of them [and he named them], actually lied to me.' It was an issue that caused him some bitterness: 'I made many of them out of nothing and I got them all afloat again, after the shipwreck of 1933, and I made them members of parliament, ministers, ambassadors, under-secretaries, etcetera etcetera. They all had the obligation to serve the Republic until the last minute.'[113]

Azaña, although he suffered greatly in consequence, fulfilled his duty to stay with the Republic until the last moment. He had overcome fear and stayed on despite the massacres of August 1936, the incorporation of the anarcho-syndicalist CNT into the government in November 1936, the terrors he experienced during the May Days of 1937 and the unavoidable evidence of Franco's inexorable triumphs after the fall of Teruel in February 1938.[114] His bitterness at being left alone by the majority of his one-time Republican comrades was intense. In August 1937, he was visited by the historian Claudio Sánchez Albornoz, who had been briefly Ambassador in Lisbon and then spent nearly a year in Paris. Azaña reproached him severely for his 'deplorable example': 'to be afraid is only human, and if you press me, I would say normal in intelligent men. But it is our obligation to overcome fear when there are public duties to fulfil.'[115]

Despite his despair and pessimism, Azaña never doubted that the first such duty was that of standing up against the outrage of the military uprising. A life devoted to the rule of law and a democratic ideal could not be betrayed by flight. In his resounding condemnation of the rebels and their 'horrendous crime', in a broadcast on 23 July 1936, he had undertaken to see the struggle through to the end.[116] In his speech in Valencia, he spoke of his duty as 'to oppose the military rebellion by every means. It is not possible to compromise with a rebellion and remain in power with dignity.' By staying, he gave the Republic legitimacy in the international arena: 'my presence in this place signifies and denotes the continuity of the legitimate Republican State, which has, in the President of the Republic, in the present responsible cabinet and in the Cortes, the supreme bodies of representative democracy and of government.'[117] He stayed on without any real faith in eventual victory, working actively in search of international mediation to end the war.[118]

In his conversation with Negrín on 22 April 1938, Azaña protested against the death sentences imposed on forty-five officers accused of conspiracy, giving legal, humanitarian and political reasons against what he called an atrocity. In stark contrast with Franco's diatribes against an enemy that had to be annihilated, Azaña declared: 'hatred enrages and leads only to bloodshed. No. The generosity of the Spaniard is capable of distinguishing between guilty criminals, those who have been forced and those who have gone astray. This distinction is crucial because once again on both sides we have to get used to the idea – and it is a frightening notion but unavoidable – that no matter how many of the twenty four million Spaniards are killed in this war, there will still be many survivors and they will have the need and the obligation to go on living together so that the nation does not perish.' Spain had to wait for thirty-six years after the end of the Civil War, and thirty-five years after the death of Don Manuel, for his vision to be fulfilled.

Azaña's humanity contrasted with Franco's cold-blooded ruthlessness: Azaña desperate to bring the slaughter to an end; the Caudillo ready to kill half the population if necessary. Azaña declared in Valencia on 18 July 1937: 'it is not possible to base any political system on the decision to exterminate the adversary, not only – and that alone is plenty – because morally it is an abomination, but because it is also materially impossible; and the blood shed out of hatred, with the aim of extermination, is reborn, revives and bears fruit in a curse; a curse, not, unfortunately, on those who shed the blood but on the very country which as the height of its misfortune has soaked up that blood.'[119]

As the Republic was defeated by instalments throughout 1938, Azaña held on, appalled by the lack of understanding between the government in Valencia and the Generalitat in Barcelona. Aware that soldiers were throwing down their arms before the Francoist advance, a horrified Azaña – virtually abandoned by the Republican authorities – witnessed the fall of Catalonia. On 22 January 1939, he and his family embarked on a dreadful journey to Figueras near the French border. On Sunday, 6 February, after Negrín had tried to persuade him to return to Madrid, he finally chose exile. He described the manner of his departure some months later in a letter to his friend Angel Ossorio. He was to leave at dawn, with the President of the Cortes, Diego Martínez Barrio, in a small convoy of police cars. Martínez Barrio's car broke down and Negrín, who was present, tried to push it out of the way. The President had to cross the frontier on foot.[120] At the beginning of the war, he had predicted to his wife, 'We will leave Spain on foot.'[121] He reached Paris on 9 February, resisting pressure from Negrín to return to Madrid. Instead, he worked to support British proposals for mediation. Britain and France recognized the government of General Franco on 26 February 1939 and, on the following day, he resigned the presidency. Manuel Azaña died in Montauban on 3 November 1940. He had finally escaped from the gilded cage of political pre-eminence.

'One hundred years from now, most people won't know who Franco and I were', said Manuel Azaña to Julio Alvarez del Vayo.[122] That modesty on the part of the President of the Second Republic, so often thought to be arrogant, contrasted dramatically with the view of Francisco Franco regarding his own place in posterity – expressed in his constant refrain that he was 'responsible before God and before History'. The difference may be seen starkly even today in their final resting places. For Franco, there is the pharaonic Valle de los Caídos, the immense challenge to posterity through which the Caudillo sought to emulate 'the grandeur of the monuments of old, which defy time and forgetfulness'.[123] For Don Manuel, there is the simple tomb in Montauban, whose only inscription is *Manuel Azaña (1880–1940)*.

8

A Life Adrift: Indalecio Prieto

There are few Spanish politicians who so single-mindedly sacrificed their lives to the cause of democracy as Indalecio Prieto. He did more than any other individual to create the Second Republic, to sustain it in power, to defend it in war and, in exile and old age, to continue working for the re-establishment of democracy in Spain. It is hardly surprising that Francoist propagandists set out to denigrate him. In fact, their worst accusations were of cowardice and of being 'a vulgarian, a rude man, full of resentments and passions'.[1] In fact, despite severe intellectual reservations, he risked his life on behalf of the Socialist Party and the Spanish Republic in 1917, in 1930, in 1934 and during the Spanish Civil War. Like Azaña, although tormented by doubt, he never shied away from what he perceived as his duty. It is a tribute to his talents and to his humanity that his defeats in no way diminished his devotion to public service.[2] As for his vulgarity, he was an easy target. He was very much a man of the people, highly approachable, easily recognized. His corpulence, which made him the delight of politicial cartoonists, derived in part from his legendary knowledge of the restaurants and of the gastronomical delights of the various regions of Spain although, like his glaucoma, it was probably more related to diabetes.[3] Indalecio Prieto was affable, good-natured and witty, an inveterate raconteur, and his jokes, like his language in private, were often obscene. He used to delight in shocking his prim ally, the professor Fernando de los Ríos, as if he were a maiden aunt.[4] Prieto's sharpness, wit and humour made him immensely popular but they concealed a deep insecurity.

Ironically, while 'Don Inda' (as friends and public alike called him) radiated confidence and success he knew more than his share of pessimism and defeatism. Prieto's passionate convictions could unleash bottomless reserves of energy yet he could also slump into despair. This was noted by the most acute of observers, Manuel Azaña, who wrote of him, 'he is violent, and when he is not driven by some passion or other, he hibernates . . . in Prieto, there is to be found distrust in everyone and everything, most of all in himself. He is shy and pessimistic, and a kind man, which is perhaps his least recognized quality.'[5] The conservative politician, Miguel Maura, wrote of him: 'I have met few, very few, people more unselfish, readier to sacrifice themselves for their friends, more given to compassion, more generous, in a word, more decent, than Indalecio Prieto.'[6] Despite the most humble beginnings, Prieto's career was crowned with success as a businessman and as a journalist, yet he devoted his life to politics. Prieto was a brilliant and biting journalist, and he never gave up the use of his pen even when he had become a newspaper proprietor or a parliamentary deputy. He was also one of Spain's greatest parliamentary orators, as sarcastic, effective and witty as in his newspaper articles. On re-reading them today, it is impossible not to be struck by his spontaneity, his lack of doctrinaire theory, his love of things concrete. His down-to-earth realism reflected a constant questioning of his own abilities and a humility entirely rare among politicians.

Self-doubt lay at the heart of Prieto's political trajectory. It was to be seen in his constant efforts to resign as Minister of Hacienda (Treasury) during 1931 on the extremely unusual grounds (for a politician) that he felt himself incompetent to deal with the great problems of the day. It was seen again, perhaps most tragically, in May 1936 when he failed to combat the opposition of his jealous rival, Francisco Largo Caballero, to his becoming President of the Council of Ministers. Above all, it could be seen in his pessimism during the Civil War. The humility went hand-in-hand with a lack of ambition. 'I don't know how to smile. I don't want to know. I never made the slightest effort to alter my character in order to make myself more agreeable. But, in my conduct, I have always been demanding of myself. And, even though it might not be very democratic, I will say that the opinion of others never mattered to me.' Yet for all that he was devoid of personal aspirations, as he also recognized, he was a thoroughly political animal, throwing himself body and soul into public life.[7] His readiness to remain in the shadows partly explains why, within the PSOE, Prieto inspired such loyalty and admiration. Except, that is, in the case of Largo Caballero, who wrote of him: 'Prieto has been envious, arrogant, proud; he thought he was better than everyone else; he never permitted anyone to overshadow him.'[8] Apart from projecting many of his own shortcomings on to his rival, Largo Caballero was conveniently forgetting that Prieto's personal style was that of a man who has known the humiliations of poverty.

Indeed, Prieto's early life was one of tragedy and harshness. His father, Andrés Prieto Alonso, a respectable town-hall official, was fifty-nine when his son was born. His first wife, Josefina Martínez Orvid, had died at the age of sixty in December 1881. Barely one year later, to the intense chagrin of the rest of his family, Andrés Prieto married the twenty-six-year-old and four-months pregnant, Constancia Tuero, who had been the family's maid. She had already given him an illegitimate son, Ramón. Five months after their marriage, Indalecio Prieto Tuero was born in Oviedo on 30 April 1883. Within eighteen months, his brother, Luis-Beltrán was born. The maid became the lady of the house and herself employed a maid, testimony to the fact that they lived comfortably.[9]

Everything changed dramatically when Indalecio was five and a half years old, with the death of his father on 11 August 1888. Andrés Prieto died without savings and, after the funeral was paid for, there was nothing left. His family turned their backs on his widow, punishing her for the extra-marital relationship with him. Indalecio wrote in 1930: 'He bequeathed his children an honourable name. I have since found out through my own experience the tremendous drawbacks of receiving a legacy which consists only of an honourable name.' Furniture was sold and the entire family was obliged to move from their respectable apartment into a nearby garret. As he put it himself, 'While the application for a widow's pension wended its weary way through the bureaucracy – an endless journey – we orphans were distributed amongst various relatives. But the relatives soon got tired of us, or we of them. I confess that I have always been handicapped by pride. Doubtless that was what impelled me to hit a cousin with the very boot that he had just ordered me to clean for him. I turned to the garret which was to be our new home.' His mother tried briefly and unsuccessfully to make ends meet by running a *pensión* (boarding-house). She was ruined after three months of keeping a circus troupe who never paid. To the unconcealed delight of their erstwhile maid, Constancia herself then had to find work as a servant. Shortly afterwards, driven by the social shame of their fall, she undertook the hazardous step of moving the family to Bilbao. *En route*, everything of value in their luggage was stolen. Indalecio's childhood was the fount of his acute sense of social justice, his rectitude and his abhorrence of corruption. He was especially affected by the ridicule to which he was subjected by the maid who had mocked him over the change in his circumstances.[10]

The family arrived penniless in Bilbao just as a series of violent labour conflicts was intensifying. Finding a home in the squalid slums known as the *barrios altos*, his mother scraped together a living by selling cotton-reels, lace and trinkets from a street stall. Unable to afford school fees, the young Indalecio attended classes given by the London Bible Society and was thus brought up as a protestant. At the age of eight, he witnessed bloody confrontations in the streets. He would never be an ideologue, in part because he always had too much of a sense of humour, but even more so because the intensity of his childhood experiences left him with a basic realism that was impatient of theory. What he saw of the violent repression of working-class struggles on the streets of Bilbao at the turn of the century impelled him, aged fourteen, to join the local Centro Obrero (workers' centre) of the Socialist Party. He commented later, 'I went in with the same reverence as in a church for the red flags which hung from the walls. I heard the vibrant hymns of the Socialist choir, I listened to the debates in the assemblies and concentrated on the speeches at meetings. That was my faculty of sociology.' Without formal education, he read voraciously, despite a recurrent eye infection which often left him nearly blind. He earned his living hawking boxes of matches, newspapers and fans, selling penny serialized novels (*entregas*) and singing as an extra in the chorus of *zarzuelas*, a genre of which he became a connoisseur. He also learned much by devouring the newspapers that he was supposed to be selling. He found work packing at the local Socialist journal, *La lucha de clases* (The Class Struggle) where he learned stenography. He later called his time there his salvation, since it opened to him the doors of the daily, *La Voz de Vizcaya*, where his job taking down the great parliamentary speeches of the day was an education in oratory. He quickly rose to become a journalist at the age of seventeen. A year earlier, fired by a burning conviction, he had formally joined the Partido Socialista Obrero Español. By the age of twenty, he had helped found the Juventud Socialista and become a member of its executive committee.[11] At the age of twenty-one, on 9 April 1904, he married Dolores Cerezo González, daughter of a Socialist town councillor in Bilbao. Two days later his son, Luis, was born. Thereafter, they would have three daughters, Blanca (1906),

Concha (1909), and Marina (1910) who died aged only two months.[12]

In his early career, when the PSOE was politically isolationist, committed to the view that the workers' party should struggle for workers' interests, Prieto recognized the prior need for the establishment of liberal democracy and therefore fought for an electoral alliance with local middle-class republicans. His experiences in Bilbao had shown that, alone, the Socialists could do little while, with the Republicans, they could secure election.[13] The establishment of the Conjunción Republicano-Socialista in 1909 opened up the prospect of electoral success. In April 1911, Prieto was elected as a deputy to the provincial assembly (Diputación Provincial) of Vizcaya. Within the Socialist Party, he was unusual in that he did not have a trade union behind him. His advocacy of a Republican–Socialist electoral alliance brought him into conflict with local leaders such as Facundo Perezagua, who advocated an exclusively syndical strategy of confrontational strike action. After a long and bitter struggle within the Federación Provincial Socialista de Vizcaya, Prieto eventually defeated Perezagua and thereafter Bilbao became a stronghold of Republican–Socialist collaboration. That was enough to earn Prieto the lifelong hostility of the UGT vice-president, Francisco Largo Caballero, who shared Perezagua's distrust of bourgeois republicans. The rancour of Largo Caballero would bedevil Prieto's existence and, eventually, have devastating consequences for Spain. Prieto was re-elected to the Diputación in 1915 but the election was declared void. However, in the same year he was elected to the town council of Bilbao. In early 1917, he abandoned Basque politics and moved to Madrid to take a post with the Compañía Ibérica de Telecomunicaciones and also become the correspondent in the capital for a series of northern newspapers, *El Liberal* of Bilbao, *La Voz de Guipúzcoa* of San Sebastián and *El Cantábrico* of Santander. In Madrid, he entered into contact with Pablo Iglesias, the leader of the PSOE.[14]

During the First World War, the economy experienced a boom as neutral Spain exported to both sets of belligerents. However, the consequence was massive inflation and shortages, both of which severely affected working-class living standards. In the summer of 1917, a revolutionary general strike against rapidly crumbling living standards was being prepared. Iglesias ordered Prieto to return to the Basque Country where he underwent some prophetic experiences. Although the idea of the strike seemed to him 'absurd and mistimed', he obeyed out of a sense of duty to the PSOE. The strike of August

1917 took place in a context of military protest about pay and promotion conditions and a bourgeois rebellion against a central government run in the interests of the landed oligarchy. The maximum aims of the Socialists were the establishment of a provisional republican government, the calling of elections to a constituent Cortes and vigorous action to deal with inflation.[15] Despite its pacific character, the strike was easily and savagely repressed by the government.

In Madrid, the strike committee consisting of Largo Caballero, the PSOE vice-president, Julián Besteiro, the editor of *El Socialista* and leader of the printers' union, Andrés Saborit, and the secretary-general of the railwayworkers' union, Daniel Anguiano, was arrested. All four were very nearly subjected to summary execution. They were finally sentenced to life imprisonment and spent several months in prison until they were freed on being elected to the Cortes in 1918.[16] Although not a member of the national strike committee, Prieto's reputation as an orator was such that, when the strike was defeated, he was pursued by the authorities as the ring-leader of the Basque strikes. He took to the hills and lived as a fugitive for a month before managing to escape into France. He lived in Hendaye and Paris until April 1918, when his name was put forward as a candidate for Bilbao in the general elections. He returned clandestinely to Spain and organized his campaign from hiding. He was successful in part because of electoral fraud. He proclaimed: 'I consider myself as much the parliamentary representative of the Republicans as of the Socialists.' His entry into the Cortes was painful. He was a diabetic and the privations suffered during his exile had damaged his health and in particular his eyes, provoking ulcers on the cornea.[17]

The repression of 1917, which was most brutal in the areas where Prieto's influence was strongest – Asturias and the Basque Country – polarized the Spanish Socialist movement. Many moderates, including Prieto, together with the bulk of the national leadership of the UGT, were traumatised, determined never again to risk their legislative gains and the movement's property in a direct confrontation with the State. There were others, particularly in the industrial areas affected by the industrial collapse which followed the end of the First World War boom who, inspired by the events in Russia and stimulated by the insurrectionary line adopted by the anarcho-syndicalists, began to adopt more revolutionary positions. As a concession to the radical left, the Conjunción Republicano–Socialista was rescinded. Prieto opposed the radicalization, commenting in January 1920 on the 'puerilities' of the anarchists and lamenting 'the worst thing is that many of our own party are blinded by the light [of the Russian Revolution]'.[18] In 1918, he had become a member of the PSOE's executive committee.[19] He was thus able to witness the bitter debate which divided the party over the next three years. The ostensible issue at stake was the PSOE's relationship with the Comintern. In fact, in the wake of its defeat in the revolutionary strikes of 1917, the issue being worked out was whether the PSOE was to be legalist and reformist or violent and revolutionary.

It was obvious to Prieto that the corrupt politics of the constitutional monarchy were no longer an adequate mechanism for defending the economic interests of the ruling classes. However, his solution was to seek reform through the electoral victory of a broad front of democratic forces. Without hesitation, throughout the Socialist debates on the Comintern, he opposed any acceptance of the discipline of Moscow. At the cost of some unpopularity with some sections of the party, he maintained that the PSOE should remain in the Second International. Shortly before the third of the three Congresses convened – in December 1919, June 1920 and April 1921 – to discuss the issue, Prieto gave a lecture in Bilbao with the title 'Freedom, the essential basis of socialism'. He told his listeners 'I am a socialist because I am a liberal' and declared that 'for the Socialist Party to submit to the conditions imposed from Moscow would, to my mind, constitute the total negation of the liberal essence of the party'. He told the press that he would leave the PSOE if it joined the Third International.[20] In a closely fought struggle, the pro-bolshevik tendency was defeated and left to form the Spanish Communist Party.[21] Prieto wrote confidently, 'I am convinced that the schism which began last night will have the most minute impact.' The essential moderation that he had advocated was thus consolidated. The PSOE turned aside from the syndical battles which raged elsewhere and, with Prieto in the vanguard, turned to the parliamentary campaign against the Moroccan war and the King's alleged reponsibility for the army's disastrous performance. Prieto identified the monarchy with inefficiency and corruption and set about building an alliance of all democratic forces.[22]

Following the military disaster at Annual near Melilla in July 1921, the military position in the eastern part of Morocco completely collapsed.[23] Prieto travelled to North Africa in September 1921. He toured the area indefatigably for seven weeks, interviewing survivors, accompanying the troops, witnessing the most gruesome sights. Since the fighting was still in progress, and given the fact that he was regarded with suspicion by the local military authorities, this took no little courage. His series of twenty-eight articles, published in *El Liberal*, were a vivid account of conditions after Annual which provided the first reliable account of the magnitude of the disaster. They were written with objectivity and some sympathy for the military on the ground. They were widely reproduced by other newspapers.[24] When a national debate began as a result of the official enquiry led by General Picasso, Prieto was singularly well-equipped to take the lead. He did so with several powerful speeches, the first of which was delivered eight days after his return from Morocco, highlighting government incompetence and military corruption. He denounced the government for not issuing figures for the number of dead, which he put at eight thousand, commenting 'Eight thousand corpses give us the right to demand that those responsible face the consequences.'[25] Eventually, Picasso's report would put the casualties at more than 13,000. Prieto returned to the charge on 4 May 1922, making his most devastating intervention in response to the final Picasso report presented on 14 November. Prieto spoke passionately to the Cortes over two days on 21 and 22 November 1922.[26] The implacable nature of his fulmination perhaps reflected the desolation that he felt at the painful death from cancer of his wife Dolores on 19 August 1922.[27]

In the spring of 1923, Prieto was arrested and briefly imprisoned for an explosive attack on the King at the Ateneo de Madrid.[28] Indeed, one of the objectives of General Primo de Rivera's coup of 13 September 1923 was to silence Prieto. Speaking at the PSOE's XII Congress in 1928, without referring to his own role, Prieto declared that the imposition of the Dictatorship 'was intended to strangle the debate on the responsibilies for Annual; its purpose was to destroy parliament at the very moment when it gave the first sign of its sovereignty and independence'.[29] Accordingly, during the Dictadura his commitment to parliamentary democracy obliged him, along with Fernando de los Ríos, to oppose the majority of his party who, led by Largo Caballero, opted for collaboration with the regime. Ironically, both Prieto and the collaborationists adopted their respective positions for equally reformist reasons. For Prieto, the closure of the Cortes was a vicious blow against efforts to reform the political system. For Largo Caballero, above all a trade-union bureaucrat, the first priority was always the protection of the union, its property and its members.

With political struggle suspended, Caballero accepted the Dictator's invitation for the UGT to become the regime's trade union organization, both to protect the union and in the hope of aggrandizing it at the expense of the banned anarcho-syndicalist CNT. On the first anniversary of the military coup, Caballero joined the dictatorship's Council of State. Prieto was aghast at such opportunism, rightly fearing that it would be exploited by the Dictator for its propaganda value. He wrote to the PSOE executive, reiterating his view that 'it is indispensable that there be clear distance established between party leaders and the generals in power'. The PSOE executive committee replied, disingenuously, that Caballero's nomination was a UGT matter. As a result, Prieto resigned from the committee.[30] Although Prieto played down rumours of schism within the party, declaring publicly that the discrepancies were tactical and did not affect the cordiality and unity among the party's leaders, thereafter Largo Caballero's already festering personal resentment of him was intensified.[31]

Four years of labour unrest gradually brought the Socialist movement in line with Prieto's stance. The growth of Socialist opposition to the Dictatorship was shown clearly at the XII Congress of the PSOE, held from 9 June to 4 July 1928. Prieto and his close friend and lifelong political associate, the delegate of the Federación Socialista de Asturias, Teodomiro Menéndez, defended a line of outright resistance. Although the majority remained in favour of collaboration, the scale of support for Prieto impelled Largo Caballero to begin reassessing his attitude to the regime. An intensification of strike action throughout 1929 alerted Caballero to the counter-productive consequences of association with the Dictatorship. Prieto was in constant contact with the disparate opposition of intellectuals, republicans, renegade monarchists and, increasingly, disgruntled army officers from the more professional artillery and engineering corps whose cherished promotions system had been attacked by Primo de Rivera. The growth of rank-and-file hostility to the regime pushed Caballero reluctantly to embrace Prieto's advocacy of a broad front against the monarchy in alliance with the republicans.[32]

After the resignation of the Dictator on 28 January 1930 and his replacement by General Dámaso Berenguer, Prieto became probably the most inspirational figure of the nascent republican movement. He had built a wide network of civilian and military contacts during the responsibilities campaign after the Annual disaster and had maintained them in the opposition to the Dictatorship. With the full support of the Agrupación Socialista de Bilbao and of the Federación Socialista Vascongada, he threw himself into the task of creating a wide front in favour of the Republic. On 9 February 1930, he spoke at the meeting held to welcome home from exile the philosopher, Miguel de Unamuno.[33] Largo Caballero was infuriated by Prieto's involvement in the republican movement and the pre-eminence and popularity that it brought him. Caballero demanded that the PSOE censure Prieto for a series of acts in support of the growing opposition: for congratulating the conservative José Sánchez Guerra on his participation in a failed military coup against the monarchy; for attending a banquet at which Sánchez Guerra announced his lack of faith in the King; for publishing pro-republican declarations in France and Argentina; for organizing a meeting to celebrate the return to Spain of the republican Eduardo Ortega y Gasset.[34] It was the very energy which so distressed Caballero that led Miguel Maura to the judgement that 'Prieto was, by far, the principal figure of this epoch in the history of Spain . . . Prieto's most notable characteristic was always his political realism. He never let himself be carried away by romantic idealism or ideological vagueness. He always had an accurate vision of things, and above all, of people, and of the objective that might be achieved at any given moment.'[35]

This was made clear in his lecture on 25 April 1930 at the Ateneo of Madrid, entitled 'El momento político'. He told an enthusiastic and influential audience that the six years of rule by General Primo de Rivera was merely 'the first dictatorial period' and that rule by Berenguer was simply 'a more covert, more subtle, velvet-gloved dictatorship'. He roundly denounced the corruption of the Dictatorship and the fortunes made by friends of the King on the back of its public works and telephone communications programme and through the concession of monopolies. Finally, he posed the stark alternative '*o con el Rey o contra el Rey*' (the choice is with the King or against the King). In proclaiming that men of good will should unite to cut the knot of the monarchy, Prieto clearly set the agenda for the next year. Prior to that time, most of the Republicans and the principal Socialist leaders, Largo Caballero and Besteiro, had little sense of strategic direction. They were looking forward passively to some evolutionary solution, hoping for a vote of censure for the responsibility for Annual in a future parliament. Prieto had now established unavoidably both the urgency of the situation for the future of Spain and the need for the unity of all anti-monarchical forces in a revolutionary movement to sweep away the King.[36]

Having made his rallying cry in the spring, Prieto was a central figure in the organization of the great Republican coalition known as the Pact of San Sebastián which was cemented in mid-August 1930 at a historic gathering held in the Hotel Londres in the Basque resort. Given the attitudes of Largo Caballero and Besteiro, he and Fernando de los Ríos attended the meeting in a personal capacity. Shortly afterwards, he travelled with Maura and Azaña to Madrid to clinch the participation in the Pact of the Unión General de Trabajadores. On the way, they survived a car crash in which Prieto manifested considerable sang-froid. By that time, the growing number of strikes was convincing Caballero that, if he were not to be left behind by rank-and-file militancy, he would have to align himself with Prieto. In October 1930, he joined Prieto and De los Ríos in successfully overcoming Besteiro's opposition to the acceptance of three ministries for the PSOE in a future cabinet. Largo was unable to conceal his irritation at seeing Prieto in the limelight. Nevertheless, soon after his conversion to republicanism, Largo was matching Prieto in enthusiasm.[37] During the organization of the revolutionary movement intended to bring the provisional government to power, Prieto's extraordinary network of contacts was invaluable. Maura commented.

> Once we had clinched the agreement of the Socialists, the republican block was compact and efficient. Moreover, the security represented by being able to count on Prieto and the elements that he had been accumulating on his own account for months represented an enormous relief for the rest of us. Indalecio, who knew the most heterogeneous and picturesque characters, was a truly exceptional judge of men. When he spoke with someone twice, he knew exactly what to expect in terms of their moral fibre and, without the slightest euphemism, he passed judgement once and for all. Time after time we were to find out just how accurate his assessment had been![38]

The participants of the Pact of San Sebastián met in Madrid in September 1930 to arrange the creation of a provisional government. There was unanimous agreement that the prime minister should be the moderate conservative Niceto Alcalá Zamora, a choice meant to reassure middle-class opinion. The debate then turned to the Ministry of the Interior. Maura suggested Prieto, on the grounds of his knowledge of the masses and his political dexterity. However Largo

Caballero was so hostile that Prieto thought it better not to seek the post. At first, he was allotted the Ministry of Public Works (Fomento), but later, the Treasury (Hacienda). He put up a stiff resistence.[39]

The opposition leaders then turned to the elaboration of a scheme for a revolutionary general strike with which they hoped to overthrow the monarchy. Prieto was given responsibility for Asturias and the Basque Country. There the strike was widespread but was called off once it became clear that the promised military support had not materialized. Alerted when local republicans in the remote Aragonese town of Jaca jumped the gun, the police tried to arrest all the conspirators. Prieto escaped arrest in Bilbao and managed to get across the French frontier disguised as monk. He almost gave himself away when a frontier guard at Irún stood on his bare, sandalled foot at which the foul-mouthed Prieto gave out a series of obscene expletives, to the amazement of the rather dim *carabinero*. He lived on a shoestring in Paris, where his eyes deteriorated as a consequence of a vitamin deficiency. He was ordered by his doctor to eat fruit but could not afford to buy oranges. He returned to Spain on 16 April 1931 and took part in the first cabinet meeting of the new Republic.[40]

The man who had done so much to overthrow the previous regime had no doubts that the new Republic needed Socialist support for its consolidation. Besteiro argued that the Socialist movement should not collaborate with the new regime, lest it be burnt out in pursuing what he perceived to be a bourgeois task. An extraordinary Congress of the PSOE to debate the issue of participation in government was held from 10 to 12 July. Prieto carried a majority of 10,607 to 8326 for a proposal that 'it is a fundamental obligation of the Partido Socialista Obrero Español to defend the Republic and to contribute, by all means possible, to its definitive consolidation' and that the party would continue to be represented in the government until the Constitution was approved. He skilfully left the way open for the PSOE ministers to remain in the government by the suggestion that 'the parliamentary group, although directly responsible for its actions to the Congresses of the Party, in cases of exceptional importance in which its stance might impose a new and decisive direction on Spanish politics, will appeal to the Executive Committee for a joint resolution'. This left the decision in the hands of men more likely to be sympathetic to Prieto's views. It opened the way to a full collaboration and clearly implicated the PSOE in the success or failure of the Republic. However, the relative narrowness of Prieto's victory suggested that the issue of participation in the government of the Republic was potentially divisive.[41]

In the first months of the Republic, Prieto was, according to Miguel Maura, the real source of energy and direction in the Republican–Socialist cabinet.[42] As so often in his career, energetic dedication went hand-in-hand with pessimistic insecurity. Without really analysing them, Azaña noticed Prieto's mood swings from dynamic bursts of energy to bouts of despairing paralysis: 'what happens with Prieto is a result of his flippancy and recklessness. He imagines that some problem is going to be resolved in a day and he lacks the political tact and the diplomacy to deal with people.'[43] In fact, in his diaries for 1931 and 1932 Azaña had little respect for Prieto and treated him patronizingly, frequently ridiculing his pessimism and defeatism – 'whenever he's depressed, he takes on a plebeian tone, like a domestic servant working herself up about some bloodthirsty fairground murder'. He often cruelly described a morose Prieto 'plunged in his own blubber, his myopic eyes half-closed'.[44]

Prieto never stopped struggling to overcome his own depressive tendencies. He approached his role as Ministro de Hacienda with a great sense of responsibility and a total lack of confidence in his own ability. His first act was to meet the distrustful representives of the banking world and reassure them that all the debts of the Dictadura would be recognized by the new regime.[45] He also went to considerable trouble to ensure that the royal family was given time and adequate facilities to have its belongings properly collected and packed for shipping from the Palacio Real.[46] He was appalled as, despite his efforts at conciliation, large sums of capital were spirited out of the country and the peseta collapsed. He spent large sums, to little avail in the short term, in an effort to maintain the value of the currency as well as pursuing a deflationary, high-interest policy in the hope of enticing a repatriation of funds. However, he flinched from adopting the full-scale stabilization measures which might have boosted the value of the peseta but undermined economic activity. During his time at the Ministry, the peseta fell by 22 per cent against the US dollar which, by favouring Spanish exports, inadvertently diminished some of the effects on Spain of the world crisis.[47] His impatient determination to eradicate corruption earned him the hostility of the business community. With what has been called his habitual 'verbal incontinence', he threatened and insulted bankers to whom he regularly referred as 'thieves'.[48] On 13 November 1931, in the Cortes, when the name of

Juan March Ordinas, the millionaire smuggler came up, he shouted from the government benches, 'They should have hanged him in the Puerta del Sol. And I would have happily swung on his feet.'[49] He was equally indiscreet in making no secret of his own lack of confidence. Prieto's under-secretary, Isidoro Vergara, told Azaña that 'the Ministry is getting on top of him and he just cannot get the hang of its problems'.[50] At the end of July, he wrote, 'I am aware that I amount to much less than I thought I would before I became a Minister'. To the despair of Azaña, Prieto told journalists and anyone else who would listen that he was 'convinced of his incapacity for the Finance portfolio because of his total lack of preparation'.[51] He believed, not unreasonably, that the functionaries of his ministry were sabotaging his measures. He had taken on a conservative adviser, Antonio Flores de Lemus, who lost no opportunity to show, in the most malicious terms, his dislike and contempt for the Minister.[52]

The problems, in a context of international depression and inherited budgetary deficit, were enormous. The Second Republic was committed to a policy of public works, educational reform and the voluntary retirement on generous terms of superfluous army officers. At the same time, recessionary pressures were diminishing the revenue base. It was hardly surprising that, as a result of the despair shown by Prieto in a cabinet meeting on 7 August, Azaña could comment that 'his morale is at rock-bottom, he says, he considers himself a failure, although he has no major errors on his conscience and he does not want, faced with the rapid fall of the peseta, to preside over the collapse of Spain's Exchequer'. In early August, Prieto again wanted to be replaced and talked of dying. Six weeks later, at a cabinet meeting on 22 September, he made it clear that 'he has no faith in anything or anyone'. When Maura complained about the hostility of the banks to the Republic, Prieto told his fellow-ministers that he was 'a failure' and announced his resignation, threatening that 'if you hassle me over this, I'll go immediately to the chamber and I'll announce it from the government benches'. He withdrew his threats after his colleagues pleaded with him – De los Ríos even went down on his knees, only to be told by Prieto, 'Get up, you're creasing your trousers.'[53] He was acutely aware that the Banco de España was far more concerned with its own profits than with the fiscal health of the State. Accordingly, he introduced a new Ley de Ordenación Bancaria (law of banking regulation) in October 1931, which led to a press campaign against Prieto financed by the Bank itself.[54] In fact, despite his pessimism, his policies of stabilizing the peseta and imposing control on the Banco de España eventually bore fruit.[55]

Prieto's martyrdom in the Ministerio de Hacienda came to an end with Azaña's elevation to the presidency of the council of ministers. Azaña's great parliamentary speech on 13 October secured the passage of the constitution and ensured the resignations of Maura and Alcalá Zamora. With the enthusiastic support of Prieto, who had long since asserted that he should be prime minister, Azaña formed a government on 14 December. Azaña's nomination as prime minister was a reflection not only of his remarkable political talents but of a deadlock between the two largest parties in the Cortes, the PSOE and Alejandro Lerroux's Radicals. The Socialists did not aspire to head the government themselves, but they were determined that it should not be headed by someone that they despised for his corruption. Prieto, in particular, considered Lerroux to be a criminal (*facineroso*). Accordingly, thwarted of the presidency, Lerroux stood down and passed into a fierce opposition directed at the presence of the Socialists within the government. The long-term consequence would be the creation of a broad, albeit disunited, front of anti-PSOE opposition from the agrarian right, via the Radicals, to the anarcho-syndicalist CNT, outraged by the Socialists' determination to crush their syndical radicalism.[56]

The new cabinet had to be re-shuffled slightly to permit Santiago Casares Quiroga to move from the Naval Ministry to the Ministry of the Interior to replace Maura. Prieto continued in Hacienda but still spoke frequently of his determination to resign. This frustrated Azaña who wrote: 'it's all verbal violence, then nothing'. Only the difficulty of finding a successor stood in the way of removing Prieto from Hacienda. When Azaña found a suitable candidate in the form of the Catalan nationalist businessman Jaume Carner Romeu, he informed Prieto that he wished him to be Minister of Public Works. Prieto was not pleased and proclaimed that he would rather leave the government altogether in order to try and put together a package to save *El Liberal*, the Bilbao newpaper to which he contributed and which was owned by his friend Horacio Echevarrieta. It took a reminder of party discipline from Largo Caballero to persuade him to agree.[57] Nevertheless, after the new cabinet met on 14 December 1931, he was disarmed by Carner's honesty and competence and he did everything possible to support him.[58]

He continued to have problems with his eyes and, in March 1932, he suffered severe chest pains in the course of a cabinet meeting, leading Azaña to worry that he might have arteriosclerosis. The widowed Prieto did not look after himself, particularly where diet was concerned.[59] In the Ministry of Public Works, despite poor health, he was a daring and dynamic Minister from 14 December 1931 to 8 September 1933. He set about trying to use his Ministry as the instrument for the eradication of Spain's social and economic backwardness. He saw it as an opportunity to put the state machine at the service of the modernization of Spain through civil engineering projects, favouring labour-intensive plans in order to reduce unemployment. With the assistance of the distinguished civil engineer Manuel Lorenzo Pardo, Prieto completed many of the hydro-electrical projects initiated by the Primo de Rivera dictatorship. At the same time, he pushed through with considerable energy many of the large-scale irrigation schemes for which the Franco regime was to take credit after the war. He instituted a series of plans which were the basis of the modern expansion of Madrid: the extension of its central boulevard, the Castellana; the creation of a local railway network with a central north-south underground axis; the building of a complex of ministerial buildings, the so-called 'Nuevos Ministerios', and the creation of a public transport network with the surrounding countryside to facilitate excursions for the population of the capital. He put into place a major road-building programme. After his experience in Hacienda, he was deeply sensitive to the costs of public works programmes, declaring in the Cortes on 7 January 1932, 'not one kilometre, not a single kilometre more of railway for the moment'. He risked the enmity of the steel industry and of the railwayworkers' and metalworkers' unions by cancelling a number of expensive railway extensions, preferring to concentrate resources on the electrification of lines joining major cities.[60] Typically, he was outraged to discover that there was a market in free passes for the railways and set out to eradicate it.[61]

With many Socialist hopes running up against the intransigence of the right, the issue of continued government participation was raised again at the PSOE and UGT congresses held in Madrid in October 1932. The XIII Congress of the PSOE opened on 6 October. Since the previous year's extraordinary congress, Besteiro had considerably modified his position. Prieto put forward a motion in favour of continued ministerial participation and Besteiro spoke in its support. Prieto's ambiguous wording saw the Congress agree to 'put an end to the Socialist Party's participation in the government as soon as circumstances permit it to do so without damage to the consolidation and strengthening of the Republic'. The proposal was passed by 23,718 votes to 6356. The main issue debated in the congress was the failed strike of December 1930 and the debate, highlighting Besteiro's lukewarm stance at the time, severely damaged his prestige. The XIII PSOE Congress represented the last major Socialist vote of confidence in the efficacy of governmental collaboration.[62]

The early months of 1933 saw the Republican–Socialist coalition subjected to serious attrition from right and left. The repression of an anarcho-syndicalist uprising in January was especially bloody at the village of Casas Viejas in Cádiz. Anarchists and rightists alike seized on the opportunity to attack the government. In fact, the responsibility lay with local units of the Civil Guard. However, before the details reached Madrid, all three Socialist ministers, and Prieto in particular, had conveyed to Azaña their approval of the repression of the anarchists.[63] Throughout the early months of 1933, government business was brought to a halt by a deliberate campaign of parliamentary obstruction mounted by the Radicals and the right. Combined with an efficacious employers' boycott of Socialist legislation in the countryside, the parliamentary obstruction brought the Socialists face-to-face with the cost of collaboration in the government. Prieto contined to believe that the benefits of parliamentary democracy justified the sacrifice of some credibility with the Socialist masses. This was a view which Largo Caballero still shared, although his conviction was wavering. To boost the confidence of the government, Prieto organized a banquet in Madrid on 14 March 1933 which was attended by two thousand people. Speaking of the sacrifices which the PSOE had made in order to give a solid base to the Republic, Prieto declared that the Socialists considered themselves 'committed to co-operating in government only as long as Azaña considers our collaboration to be necessary'. He made this commitment without seeking the authorization of the PSOE executive committee. However, when it met on 4 April to discuss the situation, after an energetic speech by Prieto, the executive reaffirmed support for remaining in the cabinet.[64]

In late May of 1933, the Catholic President of the Republic, Alcalá Zamora, hoped to use the rising tide of opposition to Azaña's government as an excuse not to ratify the 'Ley de Congregaciones' which confirmed the secular nature of the Spanish state. The opportunity arose at the beginning of June 1933, when Azaña had to replace Jaume Carner, terminally ill with cancer. When he proposed a wider cabinet re-shuffle, Alcalá Zamora responded that he would have to consult with the heads of the major political parties. Prieto said 'this is tantamount to withdrawing confidence from the government' and Azaña resigned.[65] Alcalá Zamora then invited Besteiro to form a government. He refused, but was obliged by the PSOE executive to make it clear that he did so on a purely personal basis. The President had no choice but to extend his offer to Prieto, who first secured the approval of the PSOE executive. He then gathered together the outgoing cabinet and asked if Azaña or any other minister would think him disloyal if he tried to form a cabinet. With Azaña's encouragement, he accepted the President's offer. He asked Azaña to join the cabinet, making it clear that he had 'no illusions about his aptitude to be prime minister' and that without Azaña's 'moral authority' he would abandon the effort to form a cabinet. Delighted as always to be able to return to private life, Azaña felt considerable reluctance. However, as he told his own party, Acción Republicana, he did not want to appear to be the principal obstacle to the formation of a government. His acceptance of a place in the putative cabinet greatly moved Prieto, who had set out to create the widest possible Republican–Socialist coalition. However, his effort failed when in both the PSOE's parliamentary group and Comisión ejecutiva, Largo Caballero refused to contemplate collaboration with Lerroux's Radicals. After informing Alcalá Zamora, Prieto advised him to call Azaña again, which he did, shortly before midnight on 11 June. All three Socialist ministers agreed to return to the cabinet.[66]

Alcalá Zamora would return to the charge four months later. In the meanwhile, Largo Caballero's followers had begun to advocate that the PSOE end its collaboration with the Republicans. This was apparent in a speech made by Caballero on 23 July, while still a Minister. Speaking in the Cine Pardiñas in Madrid to the radicalized youth movement, the Federación de Juventudes Socialistas, he declared that the Socialists should seek power alone.[67] Prieto replied in a speech given at the FJS summer school at Torrelodones near Madrid. He defended Socialist participation in the government, pointing out that he had not had the 'infantile optimism' to have expected the Republic to produce instantaneously the social transformations desired by Socialists. He reminded his young audience of the context of disastrous economic depression in which the Repubic had been established. He called upon them to consider whether the Socialists had the capacity to challenge the immense economic power which still remained in the hands of the upper classes. An exclusively Socialist government was not a realistic aspiration, said Prieto; 'our kingdom, as far as Spain is concerned, is not of this instant'. Dismissing the comparisons between Spain in 1933 and Russia in 1917 made by the Caballerista radicals, Prieto commented prophetically: 'If Spain, in whatever circumstances ... could establish a fully socialist regime, would bourgeois Europe impose a blockade on Spain, besiege her?' It was a skilful speech, accepting the moral justification of radicalism, but rejecting the notion that there should be a dramatic change of party policy. Realistic as it was, the speech was not what Prieto's youthful listeners wanted to hear.[68]

Replying some days later, Largo Caballero pleased the same audience by speaking of the impossibility of implementing truly Socialist legislation within a bourgeois democracy.[69] To a certain extent, Caballero was warning the President against replacing the Republican–Socialist coalition with a government under Alejandro Lerroux, but this is precisely what he did on 11 September. To prevent his new cabinet facing a parliamentary defeat, Lerroux simply kept the Cortes closed. The social legislation of the previous two years was totally ignored. On 19 September, the PSOE executive decide to break its understanding (*compromisos*) with the left-Republicans.[70] On 2 October, Prieto dutifully undertook the painful task of announcing the end of the Republican–Socialist coalition to which he had dedicated much of his life. In an electoral system which favoured wide coalitions, the Socialists were rashly going alone into new elections. Bilbao, where Prieto insisted on including Azaña in the Socialist list, was one of the very few places where the left-wing vote was not damagingly split. In the elections of 19 November 1933, the Socialists suffered a considerable defeat, falling from 116 seats in 1931 to a mere 58.[71]

The left-Republicans were virtually wiped off the electoral map and the Socialists had far fewer deputies than their numerical vote seemed to them to justify. Their 1,627,472 votes had given them 58 deputies, while the 806,340 votes gained by the Radicals had secured them 104 seats.[72] Although this was the consequence in part of the Socialists' failure to utilize an electoral system which they had helped to elaborate, it was taken as further proof of the falsity of bourgeois democracy. For a variety of reasons, the Socialist Party now took a dramatic turn to the left. To bitterness about the paucity of thoroughgoing social reform between 1931 and 1933 was added a fear that the Socialist rank-and-file might pass to the more militant CNT or the

Communist Party if its radicalization did not find some echo among the PSOE leadership. Above all, there was hope that verbal revolutionism might frighten the right into moderating its assault on those social advances which the Republic had made, or else scare the President into calling new elections. Such rhetorical extremism could only accelerate the political polarization set in motion by the distorted electoral results. Moreover, the radicalization of the Socialist movement was to be exploited skilfully by the right in order to permit the progressive repression of various sections of it througout 1934. Strike after strike was provoked and section after section of the UGT was emasculated.[73] Prieto opposed the revolutionary line, yet out of the unwavering loyalty to the Socialist Party which usually dictated his conduct, he fulfilled his role more thoroughly than many allegedly convinced revolutionaries. It extended even to the extent of buying a boatload of guns and being involved in the risky adventure of trying to get them ashore in Asturias.[74]

While Prieto drew up plans for a post-revolution government and made arrangements for arms purchases, Azaña had already assumed the burden of rebuilding the Republican–Socialist coalition. Years later, speaking in the Círculo Pablo Iglesias in Mexico, Prieto made a devastating self-criticism:

> Before my conscience, before the Socialist Party and before all of Spain, I plead guilty to participation in that revolutionary movement. I declare it as guilt, as a sin, not as glory. I was not guilty of the genesis of that movement but I take full responsibility for my part in its preparation and development . . . I took on missions which others avoided because they feared not only to lose their liberty but also their honour. I, in contrast, took them on. I threw myself into that mission with all my soul and I felt, it is time to confess it, horribly violated.[75]

Prieto seemed to be paralysed by a sense of party discipline. When Azaña met him in Barcelona in late September 1934 and reproached him for the PSOE's reluctance to enter into alliance with the left-Republicans, 'Prieto maintained a stony silence throughout the discussion. Probably, everything we said seemed otiose and perhaps he wasn't wrong. I felt sure that Prieto was equally opposed to the proposals for armed insurrection but he took part in them out of fatalism, because he felt they were unstoppable and out of party discipline.' Years later, Azaña was told by the railwayworkers' leader, Trifón Gómez, 'when as a result of Caballero's influence, the lunacy of the insurrection went ahead, Prieto, in some executive committee meetings, was beside himself and he even cried. He wanted to strangle Caballero. Besteiro said to him: "Don't go on like that and don't take it so badly. Just resist him."'[76]

In the event, Prieto did not resist the Caballeristas. Their bluff was called and the revolutionary movement of October 1934 was brutally repressed.[77] The Socialist movement was badly scarred by the events of October. The insurrection may have been an 'objective victory', but it remained a terrible immediate defeat. Most prominent Socialists were either in prison or else in exile, mostly in France or Russia. Prieto hid in the apartment of a family friend known for her Catholic piety. Then he managed to escape from Madrid – astonishingly, given his substantial girth – hidden in the boot of a Renault car guided through police check-points by the Spanish air attaché to Italy, Ignacio Hidalgo de Cisneros. Lerroux told Alcalá Zamora that he knew about Prieto's hiding-place and escape plan but decided to turn a blind eye.[78]

The tragic events of Asturias in October 1934 finally galvanized Prieto into joining Azaña in a quest to recreate the great electoral coalition of 1931. The impact of Asturias on the PSOE and the UGT was catastrophic: imprisonment and torture for many militants, exile for others, the closing of Casas del Pueblo, the harassment of trades unions, and the Socialist press silenced. From this disaster, the Prietista and Caballerista wings of the movement drew entirely different conclusions. Caballero was advised by members of the radicalized Juventud Socialista, with whom he was imprisoned, several of whom, including Santiago Carrillo and Amaro del Rosal, were later to join the PCE. He concluded that an even more revolutionary stance should be adopted. Prieto argued, much more rationally, that the first priority was to regain power in order to put an end to the sufferings of the working class at the hands of the CEDA–Radical coalition. He was able to take this stand with enormous credibility because, whereas the revolutionary movement had been a fiasco in areas controlled by the Caballeristas, there had been effective action by the workers precisely in those areas dominated by Prietistas – Asturias and the Basque Country. Moreover, since, in order to defend themselves against right-wing persecution, the bolshevizers denied their participation in the events of October, they virtually handed the legacy of October to Prieto.

Throughout 1935, Don Inda was to use that legacy to ensure massive working-class backing for initiatives deriving from Azaña. Azaña's campaign of 'open-air speeches' (*discursos en campo abierto*) would carry the idea of a reborn Republican–Socialist coalition to hundreds of thousands of Spaniards and, at the same time, demonstrate to the left-wing of the PSOE the gigantic popular backing that existed for an electoral understanding. From his position in exile, Prieto would assume the equally important tasks of widening the areas of coincidence between the Republican camp and moderate Socialists and of neutralizing the rhetorical extremism of the Caballerista wing. This ensured that Prieto would bear the brunt of the bolshevizers' most virulent criticisms. Despite the abuse to which he was subjected by relative newcomers to his own party, Prieto continued undeterred to work for the rebuilding of the electoral coalition.

In the wake of Asturias, the PSOE was in turmoil over any future electoral tactics. The first initiatives came from Prieto. He had been in correspondence on the subject with Azaña since late 1934. His ideas were shared by the party secretary, Juan-Simeón Vidarte, who visited the Cárcel Modelo in the middle of March 1935 to put them to Largo Caballero. Largo was as hostile as ever to the idea of a coalition but he authorized Vidarte to ask Prieto to outline his ideas more fully. This he did, and Prieto wrote from Paris on 23 March 1935 a long letter to be used as a memorandum for discussion by the PSOE executive committee. He was at pains to point out that the idea of a workers' block defended by Largo Caballero would almost certainly lead to a repetition of the electoral defeat of November 1933. Instead, Prieto advocated 'a circumstantial alliance that should extend to our left and to our right'. For Prieto, the key issue was to ensure a vote which would put an end to the the abuses committed by the CEDA–Radical coalition and that was unlikely with an exclusively proletarian alliance. In fact there was no guarantee of working-class unity, given the anarchists' suspicions of what they saw as Socialist imperialism. Prophetically, Prieto also pointed out that to hitch the wagon of the PSOE to the horses of the PCE and the CNT would be dangerous. On the basis of Prieto's letter, Vidarte drew up a circular which was widely distributed within the Socialist movement. It led to intense debate and finally revealed a considerable rank-and-file majority in favour of concrete action to put an end to the rule of Gil Robles and Lerroux.[79]

On 31 March 1935, Prieto had received a letter from Ramón

González Peña, the hero of Asturias, supporting his position.[80] Confident that important sectors of the party were with him, Prieto published an article on 14 April 1935 in his newspaper, *El Liberal*, calling for Socialist collaboration with the broad front of Republicans being forged by Azaña. His argument was overwhelming: another electoral victory for Gil Robles would mean the end of democracy in Spain. Although these views struck a chord in the hearts of the rank-and-file who had suffered the daily brutality of life under the CEDA–Radical coalition, they infuriated the 'bolshevizing' Socialist Youth. Attacks were launched on Prieto by Carlos Hernández Zancajo, Santiago Carrillo and Amaro del Rosal through the medium of a pamphlet, *Octubre – segunda etapa* (October – second stage), published in April, and by Carlos de Baraibar, in the form of a book entitled *Las falsas 'posiciones socialistas' de Indalecio Prieto*, published in June. This was a reply to a pamphlet by Prieto entitled *Del momento: posiciones socialistas* which collected together five of his articles originally published in *El Liberal* of Bilbao, *La Libertad* of Madrid and several provincial Republican newspapers. Together, the five articles constituted a reasoned defence of the need for an electoral alliance. His pamphlet enjoyed far wider distribution and far deeper influence than the rather insubstantial polemic of Baraibar. As far as the Caballeristas were concerned, Prieto was working to save a doomed bourgeois democracy. They resented him for this, as well as for his wit, for his air of bon vivant, for his rejection of marxism.[81] Largo Caballero wrote later: 'As far as I am concerned, Indalecio Prieto has never been, in the real sense of the word, a socialist, either in his ideas or in his actions.'[82] Prieto understood why the left felt disappointed by the Republic, but he had a far more realistic view of the real relation of forces in Spain. The strength of the oligarchy was such as to make threats of revolution seem utopian. Thus he believed it to be essential that, in the uneven fight between the oligarchy and the labour movement, the workers at least had the machinery of the State on their side. The repressive policies of the Radical–CEDA government had ensured that the revolutionary rhetoric of the Caballeristas had found an echo among the rank-and-file. Even more, however, the memory of the Asturian October, the continued existence of thousands of political prisoners, and the desire to remove Gil Robles and Lerroux ensured a sympathetic mass response to Prieto's call for unity and a return to the progressive Republic of 1931–3.

While Prieto remained in exile, the task of taking the call to the masses was successfully undertaken by Azaña. The theoretical polemics of the left had little impact on rank-and-file opinion and Prieto continued to work confidently for the alliance, meeting Azaña in Belgium in mid-September to discuss the programme of the projected coalition. Eventually, impelled by the evidence of the popular support enjoyed by Azaña and by pressure from their Communist allies, the Caballeristas came around to Prieto's point of view in November 1935. A fierce battle was still to be fought over the programme of the Popular Front but the most important victory was Prieto's. The electoral success of the Popular Front in February 1936 was yet another of his services to the PSOE and to democracy in Spain, gained at the cost of great personal sacrifice and singleness of purpose.

Prieto realized quickly that the heterogeneous nature of the alliance of reformists and revolutionaries would bring difficulties. The central difficulty derived from Largo Caballero's dogged opposition to Socialist participation in a truly Popular Front cabinet. He insisted that the Republicans govern alone, albeit with Socialist support in parliament. He was confident that they would soon exhaust their possibilities and be replaced by an all-Socialist government. Within two months, Prieto told the PSOE secretary, Juan-Simeón Vidarte, 'this Popular Front is a pipe-dream that should already have been dissolved'.[83] During the early spring of 1936, there was a break-down of law-and-order as popular jubilation at the electoral victory often turned into sporadic church burnings and land seizures in revenge for the sufferings of the *bienio negro*. At the same time, there was an orchestrated wave of right-wing violence aimed at provoking left-wing reprisals. In March, Prieto worked hard as chairman of the committee set up to verify the validity of the February elections. He was concerned to ensure that the right should not be able to claim that it was not fully represented in the Cortes. He thus conducted the proceedings fairly and even turned a blind eye to right-wing abuses of the system. Prieto eventually resigned from the committee partly because he felt that it would have been politically more prudent not to pursue the expulsion of senior right-wing figures, however justified it might have been, considering it safer to have them in parliament rather than conspiring outside. He also resented pressure from Alcalá Zamora to approve the particularly shady election of one of his cronies in Pontevedra and from Azaña to turn a blind eye to corruption in La Coruña, examination of which would have endangered the seat of his Minister of Public Works, Santiago Casares Quiroga.[84]

In April 1936, anxious as ever to strengthen the Republic, he collaborated with Azaña in bringing about the removal of the President Niceto Alcalá Zamora. Both perceived the President to be hostile to the Popular Front and there was a valid pretext in that Alcalá Zamora had exceeded his presidential power to call early elections in 1933 and 1935. On 7 April, Alcalá Zamora suffered a humiliating parliamentary defeat when Prieto raised the issue of the validity of his dissolution of the previous Cortes. It was a dramatic act, undertaken in the hope of saving the Republic.[85] Convinced that Azaña was the only plausible replacement – a view shared by Azaña – Prieto threw his weight behind his candidacy. The loss of Azaña as a strong prime minister would only be justifiable if he were replaced by Prieto. Although there could be no guarantee of success, the last chance for the survival of the Republic seemed to be that Azaña, as an efficacious president, would work in tandem with Prieto. Together, they might have been able to maintain a pace of reform which would have satisfied the left while decisively cracking down on military conspiracy and the fascist provocation and left-wing reprisals which provided its justification. Effectively, Prieto was gambling on being able to do so, despite being aware of the personal and ideological reasons why Largo Caballero would do everything in his power to stop him.[86]

On 1 May, in a statesmanlike speech at Cuenca, where there was a by-election, he had essentially laid out the case for becoming prime minister. He went to Cuenca 'worried about an imminent fascist uprising about which I have been making warnings to no avail other than to bring upon myself abuse and contempt. According to the small-town mistrust of many, narrow political ambition lay behind my insistent dire predictions.' Even as he arrived in Cuenca, ashes were still blowing about from the burning of the local right-wing club (*casino*). He had to be accompanied by a bodyguard of faithful young Socialists known as the 'Motorizada'. Speaking of the dangers of a military uprising, he pointed prophetically to General Franco, who had recently withdrawn as a candidate for the Cuenca by-elections, as the likely leader. Commenting on the rightist accusations that the Popular Front was the *antipatria*, he made a passionate declaration that could serve as his epitaph: 'I feel ever more profoundly Spanish. I feel Spain in my heart and I carry her in the very marrow of my bones. All the struggles, all the enthusiasm, all the energy which I have prodigally squandered to the detriment of my health, I have consecrated "to Spain".' He laid out a plan of government which was an extension of his programme at the Ministry of Public Works, a plan for 'the internal conquest of Spain', for social justice based on well-planned economic growth. He denounced right-wing provocation and left-wing disorder: 'what no nation can sustain is the attrition of its government and of its own economic vitality while being forced to live with unease, nerves and anxiety'.[87] His words earned Prieto the praise of a wide range of politicians, from Juan Negrín on the right of his own party to José Antonio Primo de Rivera.[88]

Many shared the assumption that a combination of a strong president of the Republic and an equally strong prime minister was the only way to defend the Republic against military subversion. According to Miguel Maura, 'there was a solemn undertaking by the principal statesmen of the Republic with Azaña on the eve of his presidential election that this [the nomination of Prieto as prime minister] would be the direction to take'.[89] Azaña certainly claimed later that that was what he had planned.[90] Prieto later cast doubt on this.[91] Whatever Azaña's real intention, on 11 May Prieto was told by the newly elected President that he was going to ask him to form a government. Prieto then made the tactical error of twice consulting the PSOE parliamentary group of which Largo Caballero was president. On the evening of 11 May, he posed in general terms the question of a possible Socialist participation in a wide coalition government, and the group reaffirmed Largo Caballero's commitment to an all-Republican cabinet. On 12 May, when Prieto returned with Azaña's commission to form a cabinet, Largo Caballero and his followers opposed him again, determined not to see him breathe life into a moribund Popular Front. He capitulated quietly. He did not raise any of the arguments that he might have used in favour of a strong, broadly based cabinet and those deputies who supported him remained silent. Prieto could have formed a government against Largo's opposition, using the parliamentary support of the Republican parties and about a third of PSOE deputies. However, he was not prepared either to split the PSOE or to seek parliamentary support further to the right. When Vidarte offered to mediate with Largo Caballero, a livid Prieto choked out 'Let Caballero just fuck off'.[92]

One year later, Vidarte told Azaña that 'the executive committee was certain that, if Prieto had accepted, with our support and that of the National Committee, and a Congress of the Party was then called, it would have approved of what we had done. He didn't see it that way, he wanted the unequivocal support of the parliamentary group.' Azaña replied, 'I always believed that his courage had failed him when it came to taking charge of the government – his inveterate pessimism!'[93] If, instead of requesting the permission of the PSOE's parliamentary group, where he knew he was in the minority, Prieto had simply accepted Azaña's commission, then the onus would have been on the Caballeristas to block the formation of a government which would have had considerable popular backing. On the long road to the Spanish Civil War, Prieto's failure to form a government was probably the decisive moment. Tragically, Prieto, in deciding not to fight Largo Caballero, must bear some part of the responsibility. A combination of his depressive pessimism and his blind loyalty to the party discipline of the PSOE was his undoing. After all, he knew before helping to remove Alcalá Zamora from the presidency and accepting Azaña's offer of the premiership that Largo Caballero would oppose him. If he did not have the certainty of being able to overcome that opposition, then it would have been better to leave Azaña as prime minister.[94]

The prevention of a government led by Prieto effectively destroyed the last chance of avoiding a military uprising.[95] Prieto realized, as Largo Caballero apparently did not, that attempts at revolutionary social change would only enrage the middle classes and drive them to fascism and armed counter-revolution; he was convinced that the answer was to restore order and accelerate reform. He had plans to remove unreliable military commanders, reduce the power of the Civil Guard and disarm the fascist terror squads. He also was anxious to promote massive public works, irrigation and housing schemes and speed up agrarian reform. It was a project which, pursued with energy and will, might have prevented civil war.[96] Largo Caballero, however, ensured that Prieto's vision would not be realized. That the strongest party of the Popular Front was not therefore able to participate actively in using the apparatus of the State to defend the Republic was all the more tragic in the light of the inefficacy of Casares Quiroga, the new Prime Minister, who was no match for the problems he was called upon to solve. Prieto wrote later: 'My mission was thus reduced to constantly issuing warnings about the danger, making people aware of it, and trying to ensure that, within our camp, naïve and blind obstinacy, typical of a lamentable revolutionary infantilism, did not go on creating an atmosphere favourable to fascism because that was all that absurd acts of disorder brought about.' Caballero was confident that a fascist rising, though inevitable, would easily be crushed by the left. One of his followers told Vidarte, 'All this about a possible military insurrection is no more than blackmail by Prieto to overcome Caballero's opposition to his forming a government.' The Prime Minister seemed to have even less appreciation of the gravity of the situation, irritably shrugging off Prieto's frequent warnings about military plotters. On one occasion in late May, he dismissed him with the comment, 'Look, Prieto, if you cannot, or do not want to, govern, at least be kind enough to let the rest of us run the government. I am not prepared to have anyone laying out the direction for me to follow. If you and your followers are not happy with my policy, then defeat me in the chamber, but I am not prepared to put up with your menopausic hysteria.'[97]

In the two months before the outbreak of the Spanish Civil War, the revolutionary activities of the Caballerista wing of the PSOE went no further than passively awaiting what they assumed would be the inevitable exhaustion of the Republican government. However, their demagogic rhetoric intensified middle-class fears. The deterioration of the political situation brought many Socialists around to the view that Prieto's realistic moderation made more sense than the utopianism of Largo Caballero. By the end of May, Prieto was encouraged by their support to begin the fight to take back initiative within the PSOE. This took the form of a bitter campaign for elections to renew the PSOE executive.[98] On 31 May, he and other candidates for the executive were greeted with a hail of bullets, stones and bottles from members of the Caballerista youth at a meeting in Écija in Seville. Only the prompt action of his pistol-bearing friend, Dr Juan Negrín, and the *motorizada* ensured that they got out safely.[99] In the battle over the executive, the Prietista candidacy claimed the victory, although the ensuing verbal battle was silenced only by the outbreak of war. Prieto's revenge on Largo Caballero would not be implemented for another ten months. That bitterness was eating him up is evident from an article that he published on 26 June 1936. He wrote 'I have had to swallow a large portion of live toads. It is disgust that defeats me. My capacity for repugnance is exhausted.'[100] In the meanwhile, throughout July, Prieto publicly repeated in *El Liberal* the private warnings that Casares had ignored.[101] A few days before the military uprising, along with Alcalá Zamora and Alejandro Lerroux, he received reliable information that it was imminent and a warning to leave Spain. The ex-president and the Radical leader quickly sped across the frontier. When Calvo Sotelo was assassinated on 13 July, Prieto was in Pedernales near Bilbao. He could have collected his family and been in France in a matter of hours. Instead, he returned to Madrid to help defend the Republic. Once there, he was astonished to find Casares still treating the rising in Morocco as an isolated incident and refusing to believe that it was part of a wider coup.[102]

When war broke out, the Republican state collapsed. Largo Caballero's prediction that a military uprising would be crushed by a workers' revolution came only partly true. The military rebellion was undefeated in half of Spain but, within the Republican zone, the principal functions of government – production, supply, security, defence, communications and transport – fell into the hands of the unions, for a time at least. The indecision of the Republicans in the first thirty-six hours of the rebellion saw another opportunity missed for Prieto to be named prime minister. At first, many had assumed that the error of May was about to be remedied at any moment. However, the ongoing confrontation within the PSOE made it impossible for Prieto to lead a moderate Republican–Socialist coalition. Prieto controlled the new party executive, and enjoyed considerable support within the party, however the popular revolution had strengthened Largo Caballero's hand as well as underlining the implicit hostility between middle-class republicans and the revolutionary left. Largo Caballero, calmly taking a tram into Madrid on the morning of 19 July, had made it clear that he would not countenance Socialist participation in a government led by the conservative Republican Diego Martínez Barrio.[103] Accordingly, Azaña, anxious not to alarm international opinion, commissioned his Izquierda Republicana colleague, José Giral, to form an exclusively Republican government. Prieto effectively became prime minister in the shadows while apparently serving merely as advisor to Giral's cabinet from 20 July to 4 September. From a large office in the Ministerio de la Marina, he overcame his own pessimism and his contempt for the impotence of Giral's cabinet. He worked unceasingly to impose order and direction on the shambles that was the government.[104]

The exiled Italian Socialist, Pietro Nenni, wrote in mid-August,

> I've been watching Indalecio Prieto for the last few days. It could be said that, more than just a man, he is a prodigious work machine. He thinks about a hundred things at once. He

> knows everything, he sees all. Within the space of a few minutes, he receives a group of socialists, he runs twenty times to pick up the telephone . . . Belarmino Tomás takes him to one side to speak about dynamite, ammunition and cannons. Professor Negrín takes him by the arm to report on the latest developments in an important diplomatic issue. In his short sleeves, sweating and breathing heavily, Indalecio goes from one to another, gives orders, signs papers, takes notes, shouts on the telephone, bawls out one and smiles at another. He is nothing; he isn't a minister; he's just a member of a parliament that is in recess. And yet he is everything: the heart and soul and co-ordinator of all government activity.[105]

Although his pessimism was compensated by his tireless labour, it still created a contagious depression among even his closest collaborators. Ramón Lamoneda, secretary-general of the PSOE executive, wrote: 'we members of the Executive Committee who visited him every day in the Navy Ministry during the early months of the war eventually had to give up going for fear of dying of pessimism and because we used to come out so depressed. He didn't give a cent for Republican resistance yet it lasted three years. On the other hand, he worked like a donkey in practical things and with supreme intelligence in intellectual things.'[106]

By late August, with Franco's columns rapidly moving north eastwards to Talavera de la Reina and Mola's troops on the verge of capturing Irún, Giral was convinced that a change to a more broadly based government was essential. Largo Caballero demanded both the Ministry of War and the premiership as his price for co-operation. On 26 August, Prieto was interviewed by the Soviet journalist Mikhail Koltsov and spoke frankly about his feelings regarding his rival: 'Our political differences lie at the heart of the struggle within the Spanish Socialist Party in recent years. And, despite everything, at least today, Caballero is the only man, rather is the only appropriate name, to head a new government. I am ready to take part in that government, to take any post and work at Caballero's orders doing whatever is necessary. There is no other outlet for Spain nor for me, if I want to be of use to the country.'[107]

Prieto had informed Azaña that Largo Caballero was the only prime minister likely to be capable of bringing the anarcho-syndicalist CNT into a concerted war effort. Eventually, Caballero was brought round to Prieto's view that the survival of the Republic required a cabinet backed by both the working-class organizations and the bourgeois Republicans.[108] On 4 September, a true Popular Front government was formed under Largo Caballero, who took over the Ministry of War, with Prieto as Navy and Air Force Minister. Unlike Prieto in May, Largo did not seek the approval of the party executive or of the parliamentary group. Prieto overcame his scruples about Caballero and swallowed his disappointment at being deprived of directing the war effort, telling the PSOE executive, 'Now is not the time for haggling or recrimination. It is a time of the gravest responsibility. I am not avoiding responsibility by not accepting the Ministry of War. On the contrary, Largo Caballero insists, and I can see the logic of it, that it should be him, given that he is becoming prime minister, who should take responsibility for the direction given to the Ministry of War.' On behalf of the PSOE executive, Prieto chose two ministers in the cabinet, Dr Juan Negrín, as Minister of Finance, and Anastasio de Gracia, as Minister of Industry and Commerce.[109]

Despite his reservations about the political bankruptcy of the Caballeristas, Prieto hoped that Largo Caballero, with his totally undeserved reputation as the 'Spanish Lenin', might serve to contain the revolution. In fact, Caballero was soon forced to recognize that to improve the economic and military position of the Republic, the workers' militias and collectives had to be brought under central control. Although by inclination anti-Communist, Prieto realized, as Largo Caballero did not, the importance of collaboration with the PCE. He saw that the Republic's international isolation required cordial relations with the Soviet Union and thus with the PCE which was the channel through which Soviet aid would be distributed. Prieto, like Azaña, agreed with the Communists' assertion that the first priority had to be the winning of the war and that, to this end, the popular revolution should be extinguished. This reflected his hostility to the anarchists and also to the PSOE left. For the Communists, the crushing of the revolution was closely related to the foreign policy needs of the Soviet Union, whose goal of alliance with the Western democracies was threatened by association with a revolutionary Spain. Prieto was even driven briefly to contemplate the ultimate sacrifice of merging the PSOE with the Communist Party.[110] In any case, he was impressed by the competence, discipline and efficiency of the Communists in comparison with the disorganized spontaneity of the anarchists and other revolutionaries. In fact, Caballero's cabinet made some progress towards reasserting the power of the central state. In terms of the war effort, however, his government was unwieldy, divided and ineffective. Out of pessimism or party discipline, Prieto did nothing to oppose Largo and simply got on with running his Ministry. He was bitterly depressed by his incapacity to provide the aircraft needed to counter the Francoist threat to the Basque Country and Asturias.[111] By the spring of 1937, he and the Communists were united in a belief that Caballero must be replaced.[112]

Caballero's hesitations during the clashes between Communists and anarcho-syndicalists in Barcelona in May 1937 led to the cabinet crisis which clinched his fate. Prieto collaborated in the protracted process whereby the Prime Minister was ousted by the Communists and shed no tears when he was replaced, on 17 May, by Juan Negrín.[113] When Azaña asked the PSOE executive to propose a new prime minister, he expected that Prieto would be the nominee. Prieto's colleagues on the executive were unanimous in wanting to put forward his name. However, he categorically refused, on the grounds that he was disliked by the anarcho-syndicalists, the Communists and the Caballeristas. His inclination was, as before, to stay in the shadows, taking overall charge of the war effort in a new Ministry of National Defence created by the merger of two crucial ministries, those of War and of Navy and Air.[114] Azaña was not displeased to have to invite Negrín to form a government: 'The public expected that it would be Prieto but Prieto was better left to run the combined military ministries for which there was no one, other than him, remotely suitable. As prime minister, the ups and downs of Prieto's moods, his sudden impulses, might have been a real disadvantage.'[115]

In every respect, the new government seemed to be Prieto's in all but name. Negrín himself was a close collaborator of Prieto and the important Ministry of the Interior was occupied by another Prietista, Julián Zugazagoitia. At the first cabinet meeting, Negrín asked Prieto to make a broadcast to the people. He refused, 'since, in order to do so, it is necessary to have faith in our victory and I simply do not have it; anyone else would make a better job of speaking to the Spanish people'.[116] From the first, Prieto faced difficulties. Largo Caballero refused to hand over formally and bring him up-to-date on the great issues that he left pending in the Ministry. Nevertheless, despite his black pessimism, he dug deep into his reserves of energy. To hold back the Francoist descent on Bilbao, he launched a diversionary attack on Segovia. He even suggested, as a reprisal for the shelling of Almería by the warship *Deutschland*, a bombing attack on the German Mediterranean fleet in the hope of precipitating an international incident and subequent mediation. The idea was turned down by his alarmed colleagues.[117] His manic energy was to no avail – within two weeks of taking over the Ministry, he had to watch the fall of the Basque Country. He was inconsolable and told Zugazagoitia: 'I have been so embittered and I have judged myself so severely for my own responsibility that, not only did I send the prime minister a letter of resignation, but I also contemplated suicide. I became obsessed with the idea and I had my pistol ready.' Negrín insisted that he remain at the Ministry of National Defence.[118]

At that point, Prieto informed Azaña that the best hope was that the Nationalists would throw their energies into conquering the rest of the north rather than launching an assault through Aragón, which he regarded as 'totally disorganized and inadequately manned' despite the considerable quantities of weaponry sent there.[119] In the hope of slowing down the Nationalist advance in the north, he put Colonel Vicente Rojo, who had masterminded the defence of Madrid, in charge of the General Staff. With Rojo, Prieto launched the beleaguered Republic's three most successful operations, the diversionary offensives of Brunete in July 1937, Belchite in August 1937, and Teruel in December 1937.

Discussing the early planning of the Brunete offensive with Azaña, he told him that the Republican army of the Centre was the Republic's best hope of ultimate success. The President asked him what would happen if, in the case of things turning out badly, he reached the conclusion that the war was lost. Prieto replied, 'There's no choice but to hang on until all this goes down the drain. Or until we start thumping one another which is how I have always believed that this will end.' Having reinforced each other's pessimism, Prieto left, 'with the hesitant walk of the short-sighted and fat, swaying from side to side'.[120] Despite his lack of hope, Prieto threw himself into overseeing in minute detail the Brunete operation which was launched on 6 July.[121] The attack by more than eighty thousand troops on the Nationalist besiegers of the capital achieved initial surprise but the deficiencies of Republican junior officers were exposed. As Rojo had hoped, Franco's eternal determination not to give up an inch of territory impelled him to turn away from his northern campaign. He sent two Navarrese brigades plus the Condor Legion and the Italian Aviazione Legionaria to Madrid, determined, at whatever human cost, to hammer home to

Republican Spain the message of his invincibility. By 18 July, the battle had begun to swing the Nationalists' way, thanks above all to Axis air support.[122] Prieto was plunged into even deeper pessimism because of the shortage of reliable officers and of aircraft and airmen. By 26 July, the Nationalists had recaptured Brunete.[123]

Prieto grimly watched, during the rest of the summer, the Nationalist advances against Santander and then, in the autumn, Asturias. Perceiving every defeat as somehow his fault, he again offered to resign and again Negrín refused.[124] From the fronts, he received an endless flow of depressing news of poor morale and lack of modern equipment.[125] To relieve the pressure in the north, he and Rojo conceived another desperate diversionary attack. With the situation in Santander beyond hope, on 24 August 1937 they launched another offensive westwards from Catalonia in an attempt to encircle Zaragoza. It was meant to gain time for the defence of Asturias. The ferocious Republican assault was concentrated on the small fortified town of Belchite to the south-east of Zaragoza. This time, however, Franco did not take the bait as he had at Brunete and he did not delay his assault on Asturias. Although he sent some reinforcements, the Caudillo conceded ground that was of little strategic value. To the despair of Prieto, the Republican advance was, as before, initially successful. But, after the exhausting effort of Brunete, it was insufficiently supported by reserves and petered out in the appalling heat against fierce Nationalist defence. By 6 September, Belchite had fallen but Franco was able to see that the Republic's broad strategic attack on Zaragoza had failed.[126] The bloodshed of Belchite had not saved Santander, which fell on 26 August. Just as he did after the Brunete advance had petered out, Prieto complained of the lack of speed, precision and improvisation, which he attributed to the poor quality of the officer corps. After reports of mutinies and reluctance to fight among Republican conscripts, he told Azaña that he could see no way in which the Republic could resist another attack on the scale of that suffered in the northern provinces.[127]

In the winter of 1937, with Largo Caballero long since removed from the equation, the marriage of convenience between Prieto and the Communists was beginning to break down. They had been united by their opposition to the revolutionism of Caballero and the anarchists, seeing in each other the means to further their own particular interests. Prieto had always been suspicious of the Communists yet had permitted them to place key personnel in both the Ministries of Defence and of the Interior. To reduce the prominence of the Communists, he had soon set about a profound reform of the Ejército Popular (People's Army), aiming at its depoliticization and the reaffirmation of the role of professional officers. Since this involved the elimination of the political commissars and prohibited political proselytism in the ranks, the Communists' enmity was guaranteed. Within a month of taking up the Ministry of Defence, he had told Azaña that the policy of the Communists 'consists of taking over all the influential positions in the State. The decree which I have published prohibiting political affiliations within the Army will have infuriated them.' He resisted Communist pressure to withdraw his order although it took its toll on his already depleted morale.[128] He was outraged by a speech made in the Cortes on 1 October 1937 by Dolores Ibárruri, which he perceived as an attack on his stewardship of the Ministry of Defence.[129] He was, in any case, his own most unrelenting critic. The fall of Asturias on 21 October 1937 affected him profoundly. Nevertheless, he continued to work hard. Azaña wrote in his diary: 'Prieto, in the face of the gigantic difficulties that he has to confront, has grown and achieved greatness. He sustains himself now by digging deep into the reserves of the best features of his character. He is one of the very few – one can count them on one hand and have fingers to spare – who today are worth more than they were before the war.'[130]

In the late autumn of 1937, Franco planned to complete the encirclement of Madrid with an army of more than 100,000 men gathered for an attack near Guadalajara and a subsequent push towards Alcalá de Henares.[131] Prieto had reached the conclusion that the Republican army had little offensive capability, yet he ordered Vicente Rojo, recently promoted to General, to prepare another diversionary offensive on 15 December in the hope of turning Franco away from Madrid. It was directed against Teruel, capital of the bleakest of the Aragonese provinces.[132] Once again, complete surprise was achieved. The Nationalists, caught unawares, found their aeroplanes grounded by the weather. This allowed the Republican forces to press home their initial advantage and, in the first week, to close a pocket of one thousand square kilometres and, for the first time, to enter an enemy-held provincial capital.[133] Although Teruel had little strategic significance, Franco took the bait. To the delight of General Rojo, he pulled forces away from the capital and towards Teruel.[134] However, the Caudillo poured in ample forces to counter the Republican attack.

Not only did he recapture Teruel on 22 February 1938 but he also seized the opportunity to destroy a large body of the Republic's best troops.[135]

Throughout the winter of 1937–8, Prieto overcame his own despair and worked feverishly at the Ministry. Azaña wrote: 'Prieto is more serious and laconic than ever. He senses, better than any other politician – he is after all the shrewdest of the lot – the difficulty of the situation and the responsibilities which weigh on him. His case is truly extraordinary. His radical scepticism, bleak and disillusioned, does not prevent him working hard and fulfilling his duty as well or better than anybody.'[136] Not all of his feverish work was as productive as it might have been, since he insisted on dealing with every minor detail even to the extent of personally examining journalists' applications for visits to the front. His secretary, Cruz Salido, simply referred everything back to Prieto.[137] Moreover, frenetic work could not prevent an unhappy Prieto coming increasingly to share Azaña's long-held conviction that all was lost and that a negotiated peace was necessary to avoid the senseless loss of more lives. In May 1937, he had approached Léon Blum with a request that he seek mediation by the United States.[138] The deterioration of his health led Prieto to tell Azaña that, 'as soon as the war is over, however that may come about, I am determined, if I save my skin, to put an end to my political life, for ever. I will be on board the first boat which leaves for the most distant Spanish-speaking country.'[139]

In fact, frenetic work was Prieto's entire life and, when he was eventually forced to give it up, great bitterness would fill his days. From early in the morning to late at night, Prieto was at his desk despite his poor health. He stopped working only when the pain from his heart condition rendered it impossible. Zugazagoitia, who saw him nearly daily in the first months of 1938, wrote: 'He often forces himself to his office by dint of a desperate act of will and he stays there, immobile in an armchair, wrapped in blankets, combatting the cold with an electric fire and killing the pain with injections given him by Dr Fraile.' Occasionally, he would cheer up and dazzle his companions with his astonishing knowledge of the *zarzuela*. After the Nationalist recapture of Teruel, the blackest despair descended on him. The experiences of Brunete, Belchite and Teruel, in which an initial Republican advance was eventually driven back by superior Nationalist forces, confirmed him beyond any possible doubt in his long-held view that the Republic could not win the war. Yet his belief that defeat

After the general strike of August 1917, Julián Besteiro was sentenced to life imprisonment. Seen here with the other members of the strike committee and their lawyer, from left to right are, standing, Francisco Largo Caballero and the lawyer Luis de Zulueta, and seated, Besteiro, Andrés Saborit and Daniel Anguiano.

On 14 July 1931, during the inaugural session of the Constituent Cortes, Julián Besteiro was unanimously elected President of the Chamber. He is seen here in the carriage of the President of the Republic, Niceto Alcalá Zamora (*to his left*), arriving for a gala occasion at the Cortes.

On 5 March 1939, Besteiro, speaking from the cellars of the Ministry of Finance, makes the radio broadcast announcing the creation of the anti-Communist Junta de Defensa. Standing to his right is the President of the Junta, Colonel Segismundo Casado.

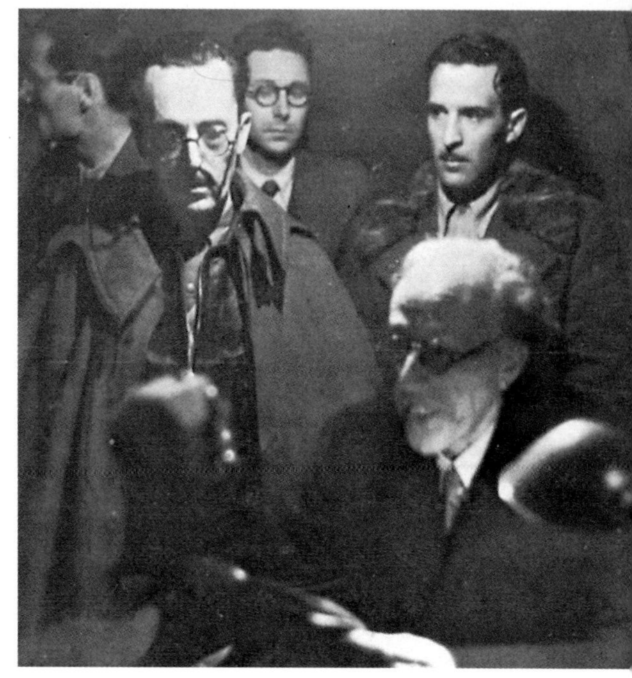

LEFT Besteiro (*seated*) in 1940 in the prison at Carmona accompanied by another prisoner, Carmelo Antomás, who had volunteered to look after him.

LEFT Azaña casts his vote in Madrid during the elections for the Constituent Cortes.

BELOW LEFT: Azaña in La Coruña on 21 September 1932. A shifty-looking Franco who was military commander of the town claimed later that he had tried to avoid being photographed with the Prime Minister.

BELOW Azaña seen with the Papal Nuncio, Monsignor Federico Tedeschini.

General Franco, as Chief of General Staff, accompanies José María Gil Robles, the Minister of War, during manoeuvres in Asturias on 22 July 1935.

LEFT Azaña addresses his follows after the victory of the Popular Front in the elections of February 1936.

Prieto, (*centre foregound*), in conversation with an affable Manuel Portela Valladares.

Número Extraordinario

El Día Gráfico
diario de la mañana

DIEZ CÈNTIMOS

Barcelona, 13 de Septiembre de 1923

GOLPE DE ESTADO MILITAR

El Ejército se pronuncia contra el Gobierno.-Al frente del movimiento figura el Excmo. Sr. Capitán general de Cataluña, marqués de Estella.-Las demás regiones secundan el movimiento.-Manifiesto al pais.-El estado de guerra en Cataluña.

Nos lanzamos a la calle en un ansia informativa meramente y para calmar la natural inquietud del público.

En los grandes momentos de la vida de los pueblos la misión altísima de la Prensa se manifiesta de una manera soberana. Si siempre el periódico es el amigo fiel del ciudadano, lo que lo liga con el ambiente general y lo convierte en parte integrante de un todo armónico humano, en los instantes de culminación social y política, el periódico es el instrumento indispensable para encauzar la opinión y mantenerla dentro los justos límites de la verdad, o al menos, los partidos y los gobernantes, levantamos el clamor de nuestra protesta y predecimos que la marcha de los acontecimientos nos llevaría fatalmente o a un desastre irreparable o a una reacción violenta y salvadora.

La vida política española de estos últimos años—principalmente desde 1921—nos debia llevar a lo que ocurre. Si el movimiento se dirige, como parece, al mantenimiento de los grandes principios vitales en que descansa la vida y el honor de los pueblos, si tiende, como expresan sus directores, a la defensa de la vida de la hacienda, la producción y el trabajo nacionales, nosotros, que te-

Al País y al Ejército

ESPAÑOLES:

Ha llegado para nosotros el momento más temido que esperado (porque hubiéramos querido vivir siempre en la legalidad y que ella rigiera sin interrupción la vida española) de recoger las ansias, de atender el clamoroso requerimiento de cuantos, amando la patria, no ven para ella otra salvación que libertarla de los profesionales de la política, de los hombres que en una u otra razón nos ofrecen el cuadro de desdichas e inmoralidades que empezaron el año 98 y amenazan a España con un próximo fin trágico y deshonroso. La tupida red de la política de concupiscencias ha cogido en sus mallas, secuestrándola, hasta la voluntad real. Con frecuencia parecen pedir que gobiernen los que na limpia, pura y patriótica que se nos ponga en contra, anunciamos que la fe en el ideal y el instinto de conservación de nuestro régimen, nos llevará al mayor rigor contra los que lo combatan.

Queremos vivir en paz con todos los pueblos y merecer de ellos para el español hoy la consideración, mañana la admiración por su cultura y virtudes. Ni somos imperialistas, ni creemos pendiente de un terco empeño en Marruecos el honor del ejército, que con su conducta valerosa a diario lo vindica. Para esto, y cuando aquel ejército haya cumplido las órdenes recibidas (ajeno en absoluto a este movimiento, que aun siendo tan elevado y noble no debe turbar la augusta misión de los que están al frente del enemigo) buscaremos al problema de

Newspaper headlines announce the military coup of Miguel Primo de Rivera on 13 September 1923. A principal aim of the coup was to silence Prieto's accusations of military incompetence.

Dolores (*left*) and José Díaz (the secretary general of the PCE) watch Jesús Hernández (*standing*). After the war, Hernández accused her of being involved in the murder of the POUM leader, Andreu Nin.

Andreu Nin, leader of the Partido Obrero de Unificación Marxista, murdered by Stalinist agents for 'Trotskyist deviations'.

Cover of a Communist pamphlet containing a speech by Dolores Ibárruri in Toulouse on 20 July 1947.

In the spring of 1936, (*from left to right*) Santiago Casares Quiroga, Manuel Azaña and Indalecio Prieto.

BELOW Franco, as military commander of the Balearic Islands, escorts the then Minister of War, Diego Hidalgo, during military manoeuvres in Mallorca.

RIGHT Dr Juan Negrín, Prime Minister from May 1937 until the end of the civil war, was an energetic war leader. He clashed with Prieto over the latter's pessimism and the subsequent hostility between them poisoned the Socialist movement for many years.

ABOVE LEFT During the war, Dolores Ibárruri was tireless, visiting the front, making speeches to raise the morale of civilians and soldiers alike and, seen here, digging trenches.

ABOVE The simplicity and approachability of Pasionaria made her immensely popular and permitted her to give voice to the fears and aspirations of many ordinary citizens of the Republic.

Having been separated from her husband for more than six years, a rejuvenated Dolores Ibárruri took a twenty-seven-year-old lover, Francisco Antón. (*left foreground*). He was fifteen years younger than Pasionaria which provoked malicious gossip within the Communist Party.

was only a couple of months away did nothing to diminish his rhythm of work.[140]

On 16 March 1938, at the Palacio de Pedralbes in Barcelona, a cabinet meeting was chaired by Azaña who wanted to raise the possibility of a mediated peace. To counter his proposal, Negrín, together with the Communists, had organized a huge mass demonstration in the surrounding park in favour of continued resistance. Prieto was outraged, not least because he claimed to have heard shouts of 'Down with the Minister of Defence!' It was the beginning of an irrevocable enmity between Prieto and his one-time protégé.[141] At the heart of the split lay Prieto's ever more poisoned relations with the Communists. They had used the defeat at Teruel to put pressure on him to resign. Behind a pseudonym, one of his cabinet colleagues, Jesús Hernández, the Communist Minister of Education, attacked him in two newspaper articles entitled 'Pesimista impenitente' (unrepentant pessimist) and 'El silencionismo' (systematic silence). The military situation was worsening by the day after the collapse of the Aragón front. Two weeks after the Pedralbes confrontation, at another cabinet meeting on 29 March 1938, Prieto spoke aloud the simple truth that the war effort could not be sustained and that Franco's post-Teruel offensive was about to reach the Mediterranean and cut the Republic in two. This intervention, according to Negrín, 'completely demoralized our government colleagues by describing events in a tone of bleak despair and presenting them as fatal'. Negrín was aware that he needed Prieto in his cabinet but not, after he had let his defeatist views become common knowledge among senior military staff, at the Ministry of Defence.[142]

Negrín was worried about the effect of Prieto's pessimism becoming widespread – 'if it was expressed only by him, it would lack importance since he is capable of making it compatible with passionate and indefatigable labour'. Prieto was aware of his own pessimism and it irritated him, as Lamoneda put it, 'as much as the hump irritates the hunchback' but he denied that it impeded his efficacy. He was prepared to take over the Ministry of Finance, with a view to preparing the way for an eventual republican exile. This was unacceptable to Negrín for whom the primordial mission of the Ministry was to find the funds for the purchase of arms. After a lengthy exchange of views, through the mediation of Zugazagoitia, Negrín suggested that Prieto become minister in charge of public works and railways. Prieto felt deeply wounded by what he saw as a humiliating demotion and resigned from the cabinet on 5 April 1938, despite appeals to remain from the PSOE executive and a delegation of CNT leaders. When Negrín arrived to take charge of the Ministry of Defence himself, he told Prieto, 'I want to be able more directly to command the Army by taking personal charge of the Ministry of War because I want whoever is in charge there to be someone who sees and resolves problems of the war effort with personal faith in the results and Señor Prieto, because of overwork, sees everything with scepticism and doubt.' A visibly annoyed Prieto replied, 'I am not ill and nor am I a pessimist, nor do I see things with little faith, no do I feel exhausted by work. It is certainly true that I have worked more than fifteen hours per day for many months without taking a rest but I have more than enough energy to remain at the head of this Ministry for however long the war lasts.' He left without taking his leave of Negrín. Prieto told a delegation from the PSOE executive, 'there's no point in fighting it, the Communists want my skin and against them nothing can be done by Negrín, by you or by me.'[143]

In the immediate aftermath of his departure from the cabinet, Prieto's attitude to Negrín was apparently cordial. Negrin praised Prieto's work; Prieto spoke of 'the warm friendship which ties me to Negrín' and promised to be 'a determined collaborator of the government'.[144] However, on the evening of 5 April, Zugazagoitia asked Prieto, 'Do you feel liberated from a heavy burden? No, he replied, I would have liked to continue in the government with dignity.' Despite having told Azaña of his desire to escape from political responsibilities, he felt lost without his ministerial duties. He was soon to be heard saying bitterly 'they've thrown me out with a kick in the . . .'[145] He could not believe that, despite his tireless efforts, he had been removed because of his pessimism. Whereas he had contained with dignity the bitterness he felt when Largo Caballero blocked his way to power, now it was to fester into full-blown hatred of Negrín, perhaps because the Prime Minister had been his friend. The consequent feud between them was to guarantee a legacy of harsh and sterile division within the Socialist Movement. The new cabinet was a return to a broad Popular Front line-up, including one minister each from the PCE, the CNT and the UGT. Prieto portrayed the cabinet crisis as not to do with his defeatism but as a plot by the Communists with Negrín as their lackey. In fact, Prieto had been a willing accomplice in placing Communists in important positions and turned against them as a scapegoat for his own humiliation.[146] The National Committee of the

PSOE met on 9 August 1938 to discuss the cabinet crisis of April. Negrín repeated his view that Prieto's belief that the war was lost made it impossible for him to stay in the Ministry of Defence. Prieto replied with a savage three-hour long accusation that Negrín had acted on the orders of the Communists. His intervention was greeted by a stunned silence from his colleagues. Since there was no alternative to the policies pursued by Negrín, which were more or less those of Prieto anyway, the speech constituted little more than a personal settling of scores.[147] Thereafter, Prieto took no further part in the war effort.[148] In December 1938, he went to Chile as a special envoy to attend the inauguration of a new president. He never returned to his fatherland, which he missed deeply for the remaining twenty-two years of his life.

In exile in South America after the Civil War, he earned his living by journalism. On 2 August 1941, starting a lengthy relationship with the Mexican newspaper, *Excélsior*, he wrote revealingly: 'Even though the bright lights of politics may have lit up my figure, at times in an unpleasant way, I have always been, above all, a journalist.'[149] Nevertheless, he still devoted his life to politics. Finding once more the audacity and daring of his younger days, Prieto managed to gain control of the funds taken out of Spain on the yacht *Vita*. He knew he was taking a risk – 'I might end up to my neck in shit' – but was determined to help Spanish refugees. Even his enemies recognized that he made no personal profit from the *Vita*.[150] Despite his unequivocal identification with the Second Republic, after the Civil War, Prieto quickly accepted the need for national reconciliation.[151] He was one of the very few leaders in exile who realized that to make a fetish of a restoration of the Republic was to guarantee the hostility of the Western democracies to any plans for removing the Franco dictatorship. Thus he returned to Europe and, in October 1947, led the PSOE into a dialogue with his erstwhile monarchist enemies under the auspices of the British government. He did so in the hope of finding an alternative coalition government to Franco which the Allies might accept. As it turned out, the monarchists ultimately preferred to make an arrangement with Franco for the eventual restoration of the crown, thereby undermining Prieto's project.

Ever honourable, always the servant of his party, Prieto felt obliged by the failure of his rapprochement with the monarchists to resign as both president of the PSOE and vice-president of the UGT. He was demoralized and discredited by the negotiations on which he had staked so much. He wrote, in his letter of resignation on 6 November 1950, 'My failure is complete. I am responsible for having induced our party to trust in the powerful democratic governments who do not deserve that trust.'[152] He returned to Mexico, where he spent the rest of his life actively pursuing the interests of the PSOE and writing the brilliant newspaper articles which have to serve us instead of the unfinished autobiography which he planned to entitle *Una vida a la deriva* (a life adrift). It may have been, as he wrote then, that 'frequent tempests blew me from one place to another through stormy seas without direction ever being imposed by the rudder of my will-power, the hinges of which are rusted over by apathy.'[153]

He lived out his Mexican exile in intense sadness, homesick for Spain. The agonies of absence from his homeland were eloquently expressed in articles and speeches. In 1939, he wrote 'I have faith in our Spain, in the destinies of the immortal fatherland [*Patria*] and we all long to return!' In 1940, in a speech in Mexico, he stated 'nothing would make me take part in any project which might undermine the unity of Spain. I will never join anything that contributes to breaking up Spain; not for anything in the world.' In 1941, he wrote 'Señor Alfonso Alamán says of me that I am Spanish to the marrow [*medularmente español*]. He is absolutely right. Spanish above all else. That is the quality of which I am proudest.'[154] In the last months of his life, confined to a wheelchair, he would occasionally asked to be taken to the airport in Mexico City to watch the Iberia planes coming in from Spain.[155] After a series of heart attacks, he died on 11 February 1962. His life had been an example of dedication to a party, the PSOE, and to a cause – democracy in Spain. It was a life of sacrifice: 'I have no feeling for politics; it disgusts me, fills me with loathing . . . Every day I want to get away from the political life . . . but then I hear of some injustice and I line up with the rest of the humbugs to chant slogans . . .'[156] He made sacrifices to bring the democratic republic to Spain, to defend its existence against the attacks of both the right and the radicalized left of his own party and, during the Civil War, he worked himself to a standstill despite his own pessimism. He made mistakes, some of them enormous; he knew defeats, some of them devastating. In 1930, he wrote, in relation to his own lack of ambition, 'a politician without ambition is unimaginable. He has to have ambition. His motives are either profit, vanity or a desire for glory or immortality.'[157] Yet it remains an indication of his authentic stature that, even taking into consideration the mistakes and the defeats, he remains one of the great political figures of the century. As Miguel Maura wrote prophetically a decade and a half before the death of Franco: 'let nobody doubt that the figure of Indalecio Prieto will be respected by the Spaniards of tomorrow more, much more, than so many, many false big shots of the Spain of the years of the autocracy.'[158]

9

Pasionaria of Steel: Dolores Ibárruri

For her admirers, especially among Communists, Dolores Ibárruri was both the inspirational heroine of the Spanish Civil War and a universal earth-mother figure. Rafael Alberti summed up this attitude in a poem which referred to the death of her son, Rubén Ruiz, in the defence of Stalingrad: 'Good mother, strong mother, who for the sake of life itself, gave a son to Death'. In the 1940s and 1950s her birthdays were turned into great ceremonies of the personality cult. Songs, odes, elegies and sonnets would be trotted out with religious fervour. A party publication declared that 'Dolores Ibárruri is the symbol and the incarnation of a better tomorrow, she is the far-seeing guide who leads the people to the goal of victory.' Even Jorge Semprún, later bitterly anti-Communist, wrote a poem while still a party member which ended with the words 'You were shaking hands, you smiled and the spring burst forth'.[1] This was not just the product of a Communist cult of personality. There is little doubt that for many, veneration of Pasionaria was spontaneous and sincere.

In contrast, for her enemies among Spanish Nationalists, she was a terrifying virago whose blood-thirsty rhetoric unmanned the right-wing parliamentary deputies in the Cortes of the Popular Front. The popular Nationalist perception of her reflected the bizarre invention of the French right-wing newspaper, *Le Gringoire*: 'An ex-nun, she married a defrocked monk. Hence her hatred of the religious. She became famous when she hurled herself upon an unfortunate priest and ripped open his jugular vein with her bare teeth.'[2] It was an indication of the fear that she provoked on the right that the principal accusation against her was of being both manly and a whore who advocated free love: 'she is more intelligent, more energetic, more manly than the majority of her comrades. Especially more manly . . .

and where there should be a woman's sensitivity, there is only a hyena's instinct.' For the right, her crime was to have encouraged women to abandon the serene servility which was considered the proper attitude of womankind, the attitude advocated by Pilar Primo de Rivera and the Sección Femenina of the Falange:

> Nothing in the past could equal the scale and the horrendous magnitude of the role played by the women of the lower classes of Madrid and elsewhere, when they renounced all human feeling and sensitivity to take part in the orgies of resentment and of wild marxist revenge. Having said that, among these women, as a protagonist and as one who urges on the others, as a leader and as a symbol, the most ferocious, the most passionate, the one with the lowest instincts and the least sensibility was this ex-domestic servant from Vizcaya, with the desires of a butch female and the whiff of renegade piety.[3]

Such attitudes reveal more about the sexual and social fears of Spanish right-wing men than they do about Dolores Ibárruri. None the less, the vehemence of such insults is an indication of her historical importance. To this day, her role in raising the morale of the defenders of Madrid, her much-quoted words to the women of the beleaguered city, her immortal farewell speech to the International Brigades have not lost their capacity to move those who sympathized with the Republican cause. Nevertheless, those familiar images of Pasionaria portray precisely the passionate fire-eater of both communist legend and anti-communist demonology. They give a picture which is not false but is certainly partial and fails to capture the warmth, the humanity and the complexity of Dolores Ibárruri. In both her private life and in the political arena, the essential characteristics of Pasionaria were empathy with the sufferings of others, a fierce determination to correct injustice, strength, realism, flexibility, and, as the years passed, a touch of cynicism and an obsession with the unity of the Spanish Communist Party. During the hard years of exile and the struggle against Franco, a cool and dispassionate Pasionaria developed who differed considerably from the Civil War stereotypes.

Dolores Ibárruri was born on 9 December 1895 in Gallarta, an iron-ore mining village in Vizcaya. She was the eighth of eleven children. Her father, Antonio Ibárruri, was a miner and a Carlist. Her mother was Dolores Gómez, a devoutly Catholic Castilian, who had also worked in a mine before her marriage. 'I am of pure mining stock. Granddaughter, daughter, wife and sister of miners . . . I have forgotten nothing.'[4] She was a rebellious child. Until the age of twenty, she was a devout Catholic and even thought that she had a religious vocation. Because of delicate health, and thanks to the relative prosperity of her family, she attended the village school until she was fifteen, which awoke hopes of entering the Escuela Normal de Maestras (teachers' training college). These hopes were to be frustrated: 'All those illusions of youth faded away when faced with the harsh economic reality. Studies, travel, food, clothing, books constituted more expense than my family could afford.' After school, she attended a dress-making academy which permitted her to find work as a domestic servant with a local middle-class family. The work was harsh, she had to rise at 6.00 a.m. and did not get to bed until 2.00 a.m. the following morning.[5] At the age of twenty, on 15 February 1916 in the Church of San Antonio de Padua in Gallarta, she married a Socialist miner, Julián Ruiz.

To say that her marriage was not a happy one is a cruel understatement. In moving pages of her autobiography, she wrote of the desperation that she experienced as a married woman:

> a domestic slave with no rights . . . In the home, the wife lost her personality; she gave herself, by dint of sheer necessity, to a life of sacrifice. She bore the brunt of work, of privations, slogging in every way to make the lives of her children, and of her husband, more pleasant, less harsh, less difficult, until she had annihilated herself, eventually turning herself into 'the old girl' who 'doesn't understand', who just gets in the way, who at best is a servant for the young ones, a nanny for the grandchildren . . . when my first daughter was born, I had lived in less than a year an experience so bitter that only the love of my little one kept me hanging on to life. And I was terrified not only by the present, hateful and unbearable as it was, but by the future which I could foresee as appallingly painful and inhuman.

Her marriage brought her not the slightest glimmer of happiness:

> The crude reality, the bare truth, hit me as it did every woman, with its unforgiving hands. A few short, fleeting days of illusion and afterwards . . . In my own experience, I learned the harsh truth of the popular saying 'Mother, what does it mean to be

married? Daughter, it means to sew, to give birth and to cry' . . . To cry, to cry over our misfortunes, to cry over our powerlessness. To cry over our innocent children, to whom all we had to offer was our caresses soaked with tears. To cry over our pain-filled lives, without prospects, with no way out. Bitter tears, with a permanent curse in the heart and a blasphemy on the lips. A woman blaspheme? A mother blaspheme? And what is so strange about that since our lives were worse than those of the damned.[6]

The hardship of life as a miner's wife might have been ameliorated by some tenderness from her husband. In fact, the basic *machista* attitudes of Julián Ruiz drove Dolores to seek diversion in reading, principally in the marxist literature provided first by her husband and then by the library of the Casa del Pueblo in Somorrostro where they lived. Grinding poverty together with the proselytizing zeal of her husband turned the previously Catholic wife into a leftist. Julián was arrested after the revolutionary strike of August 1917. Left alone with a young baby, Esther, who had been born on 29 November 1916, she received the news of the Russian Revolution in October 1917 as a beacon of hope. In 1918, when she was asked to write an article for the miners' newspaper, *El Minero Vizcaíno*, she used the pseudonym *Pasionaria* (passion flower) by which she would be known for the rest of her life. The choice of a flower that bloomed in spring was nothing to do with her character but rather a reference to the fact that the article was published at Easter. In 1921, when the Partido Comunista de España was founded, both Dolores Ibárruri and Julián Ruiz were among the Basques who abandoned the Socialist Party to join. She was soon elected to the provincial committee of the PCE in Vizcaya, the dominant section of the party in the Basque region.

Throughout the 1920s, the human costs of her own, and more particularly her husband's, militancy in the Communist Party intensified the appalling hardship of Dolores' life. With Julián in and out of prison, she was left to bring up a family with little money. After her husband was released, she was often pregnant. Her second child, and only son, Rubén, was born on 9 January 1920. Later that year, Esther died, a victim of their poverty. In July 1923, Dolores gave birth to triplets, Amaya, Amagoya and Azucena. It was a difficult labour and she was looked after by her neighbours. Amagoya died after few days, Azucena lived only for two years. A fifth daughter, Eva, was born in

1928 and lived only for two months. Inability to pay for adequate medical care and nourishment for her children had contributed to the deaths of four of her daughters. Her grief and outrage intensified her determination to fight injustice, and she worked hard for her family as well, growing vegetables to supplement the family income, taking in sewing work from a local tailor. In the surviving photographs of this period, she is always wearing an apron.[7] With astonishing determination, and despite the burden of looking after her family, she remained politically active, addressing meetings, writing articles, organizing demonstrations, yet also quite capable of darning the socks of a comrade or cooking for them. She was an archetypal mother-figure to the miners, teaching them to read, yet she was also an early feminist, passionately advocating the inclusion of women in the party's activities. One day, she led a group of women to the local tavern in Somorrostro to protest about men arriving home drunk and penniless. On another occasion, she organized the women of the district to stop a train taking young conscripts to the war in Morocco. Her growing significance within the Communist Party was recognized at a clandestine party conference, known for security reasons as the Conferencia de Pamplona, but in reality held in Bilbao in early March 1930. Dolores was elected to the Central Committee of the PCE.[8]

In the campaign for the municipal elections of 12 April 1931, which would bring the Second Republic to Spain, Dolores came to prominence as an orator. She was reluctant to speak in public – indeed, even when she had become famous as one of the world's greatest speakers, she felt nervous before a speech.[9] She enjoyed writing and always wrote her own speeches; both the text and her manner of delivery gave them an enormous emotional power. Her oratorical and journalistic abilities, together with her rarity value as a woman, brought her to the attention of the Comintern leadership. Her devotion to the Bolshevik revolution was a considerable bonus. She was introduced in Bilbao to a Comintern agent, Mikhail Koltsov: 'in a working-class slum of Bilbao, in a little tavern on the banks of the River Nervión, some comrades introduced me to a tall, thin woman of few words. Like all Spanish lower-class women, she was dressed entirely in black despite the torrid heat. She remained locked inside herself, rather shy; she listened avidly to the conversation but hardly spoke; she watched us all with her big, clear, black eyes. And it was quite obvious from those eyes that she was carefully mulling over every word of the conversation.' Koltsov was quick to see that 'the woman in the simple black dress constituted an enormous acquisition for the Party'.[10]

Having been noticed by Moscow, it was hardly surprising when she was called to Madrid at the end of September 1931 to work as a journalist for *Mundo Obrero* under the editorship of one of the Party hard-men, Vicente Uribe. Her principal Party task was to oversee the women's section. The move to the capital coincided with the final break-down of her marriage. She left her children with her sister Teresa in Sestao so that they would not be abandoned in the event of her being arrested. It was a wise precaution. One evening in September 1931, on leaving the offices of *Mundo Obrero*, Dolores Ibárruri was detained and jailed with common thieves and prostitutes. She was eventually charged with hiding a Communist comrade on the run from the Civil Guard. After being held in Madrid for two months, she was taken at the end of November 1931 to the prison at Larrínaga in Bilbao. For lack of evidence against her, she was released at the beginning of January 1932.[11]

On her return to Madrid, she was accompanied by her twelve-year-old son, Rubén. From 17 to 23 March 1932, the IV Congress of the PCE was held in Seville. Dolores was made a member of the Party secretariat with responsibility for women. On her return from Seville, she was again arrested, this time on the charge of having 'insulted the government' at a political meeting in January. To make her situation more unbearable, on hearing the news of her arrest, the family with whom she and Rubén were lodging began to mistreat him. He found his way to the women's prison and she managed to arrange for Party comrades to look after him until he could be taken back to the Basque Country. In the meantime, he visited her every day. This situation caused her the most intense emotional suffering, 'tears of blood'. Every new day tortured her with doubts about the incompatibility between her political activities and her maternal instincts: 'This brought me unbearable pain because I felt powerless to protect my son, who had nobody to look after him.' She was detained for seven months in Madrid, then at the beginning of November, she was again transferred to the Larrínaga prison in Bilbao. She was finally released in January 1933.[12]

In prison, she had been absent from dramatic events within the PCE. At the time, the Comintern line was of 'class against class', according to which the party should oppose the Second Republic as a decadent bourgeois regime. The party leadership, under José

Bullejos, was critical of Moscow's instructions, believing that the Republic should be given working-class support. This led to considerable tension with the delegates of the Comintern. Matters came to a head when, on 10 August 1932, Bullejos supported the revolutionary general strike against General Sanjurjo's coup. The Kremlin's representative, the Italo-Argentinian Víctor Codovilla, replaced Bullejos and the rest of the leadership with a new secretary-general, the virtually unknown José Díaz Ramos from Seville. Once a prominent member of the anarcho-syndicalist bakery workers' union, Díaz had been converted to communism during a spell in prison in the mid-1920s. Like Pasionaria, he was in prison during the party crisis.[13] Dolores Ibárruri, still imprisoned, avoided expulsion by dint of her proven loyalty to Moscow and an *autocrítica*. This took the form of an article which can be interpreted as ingenuous or cynical: 'I and, with me, all those of us who made up the Central Committee . . . share the responsibility for having been weak, for having been cowards, for having let ourselves be passive followers of the sectarian Executive Committee.'[14]

On her release from prison at the beginning of 1933, she returned to Madrid, finally bringing Rubén and Amaya with her. In November 1933, however, she had to leave them behind once more as she was invited to make her first trip to the Soviet Union as a delegate to the XIII Plenum of the Comintern. Pasionaria was invited to stay on to speak at the XVII Congress of the CPSU in February 1934, at which her oratory impressed Stalin. In the three months that she was able to travel in the Soviet Union, she was dazzled by what she saw. Moscow 'for me, and I saw it with the eyes of my very soul, was the most marvellous city on earth'. She visited Leningrad and met Sergei Kirov, secretary of the Leningrad Party, who was assassinated shortly afterwards. She also toured the celebrated Putilov works. Her network of international contacts widened when she was invited to organize the Spanish women's branch of the World Committee against War and Fascism, known as the Unión de Mujeres Antifascistas. In August 1934, she attended the Comité's first World Congress.[15]

On that occasion she was accompanied, among others, by Irene Falcón. As a middle-class intellectual, she was the very antithesis of the proletarian Dolores, yet they became close friends. On their return to Spain, Irene began to work with Dolores in the Comisión Femenina del PCE and the Unión de Mujeres Antifascistas. A deeply intelligent woman, devoted to the Communist cause, Irene was to become Dolores's life-long companion and helper both in Spain and in exile.[16]

Tiny and unassuming, Irene was to put her considerable talents into being Pasionaria's right hand. Born Irene Lewy Rodríguez in Madrid in 1907, the daughter of a middle-class Polish Jewish father, Siegfried Lewy Herzberg, she was educated at the German school in Madrid, spoke several languages and had worked as librarian for the Nobel Prize-winning biologist, Santiago Ramón y Cajal. As a teenager, she met and married the Peruvian revolutionary journalist, César Falcón, with whom she founded an ultra-leftist group – the Izquierda Revolucionaria y Anti-Imperialista – which was merged with the PCE in 1933. Her marriage to César Falcón foundered on his compulsive womanizing and she devoted her life to party work in the service of Dolores.[17]

Through the organization of Mujeres Antifascistas, Dolores Ibárruri played a major role in welfare work to combat the effects of the brutal repression which followed the workers' uprising in Asturias. The PCE and the Unión de Mujeres Antifascistas were declared illegal. She acted with remarkable courage and not a little foolhardiness since it was dangerous work, the mining districts being occupied by troops. Working with the Comintern delegate, the Italian Vittorio Vidali, who used the pseudonym 'Carlos Contreras', she was principally concerned to organize the evacuation of the children of miners who had been killed in the fighting or imprisoned. The children were taken in by workers' families in other parts of Spain or in the Soviet Union. In November 1934, she was arrested returning to Oviedo after organizing an evacuation of 150 children from the mining valleys. In early April 1935, she undertook a hazardous journey across the Pyrenees on foot to speak at a meeting in Paris for the victims of the repression in Asturias.[18]

As her children were unable to attend school and were often left alone all day while she was engaged in her political work, the PCE suggested that she send them to Russia. The decision caused her intense pain and guilt. At first it was assumed that it would be for just a few months but the political turmoil of the spring of 1936 followed by the Civil War meant that she would not see them again for several years. The fifteen-year-old Rubén went to work as an apprentice mechanic at the Stalin car works in Moscow. Twelve-year-old Amaya was placed in a home for the children of foreign communists in the textile town of Ivanovo. Separated from each other and from their mother, in a strange country, they found life bitterly hard. Dolores was able to visit them in July 1935, undertaking the same mountain journey this time *en route* to Moscow. Along with José Díaz, she was a delegate to the VII Congress of the Comintern, at which the Popular Front policy was adopted. Once more she met Mikhail Koltsov, who recalled that 'she listened attentively to the speeches of the delegates, taking notes with great care in a notebook and herself intervened with a brilliant, passionate and ambitious speech'. Díaz was given a seat on the Comintern Executive and Pasionaria was also elected as an alternate member (*suplente*). She had an eventful journey back to Spain in the 'borrowed' yacht of Juan Ignacio Luca de Tena, the owner of *ABC*. She lived clandestinely, moving from one apartment to another to evade police vigilance.[19]

In January 1936, she organized a further evacuation of 200 from Asturias. No sooner had she distributed the children among the waiting families at Madrid's Estación del Norte than she was arrested. She spent one month in prison before being freed to take part in the campaign for the Popular Front elections. The success of her activities in Asturias was such that she had been chosen by the PCE as a candidate in the Popular Front slate for the region.[20] She played a major part in the election campaign and the left won thirteen out of the seventeen seats for Asturias. Pasionaria was elected as one of the two Communist deputies for the region. On the day after the elections, there was agitation among political prisoners demanding amnesty. She immediately visited the jails of Gijón and Oviedo. In Oviedo, she prevented a bloodbath. Huge crowds had gathered to demand the release of political prisoners and, in response, the prison governor set up machine-guns to prevent a break-out by the prisoners. Pasionaria calmed the crowds by promising them that she would secure the release of the prisoners, then imposed her authority on the governor by telling him that she, as deputy for the region, would take full responsibility for releasing the prisoners. Not without an element of demagoguery, her precipitate action captured the popular mood.[21] Her return to Madrid was a triumphal progress, and her arrival at the capital was met by a huge demonstration quickly mounted by the PCE in order to capitalize on her new-found celebrity. For the remainder of the spring of 1936 she was increasingly in the limelight, campaigning for amnesty for prisoners, advocating revolution at mass rallies and supporting strikers. She did this most notably on behalf of miners in Sama de Langreo, threatening to stay down the Cadavio mine with the strikers until their demands were met. Similarly, she helped a group of tenants evicted for non-payment of rent to break into their own apartments. On another occasion, she obliged a maternity hospital to take back two women in advanced pregnancy who had been thrown onto the street for refusing to pray. Every day, ordinary people brought their problems to the Cortes and the Communists made a point of being available to listen. In incident after incident Dolores took risks, in part because of the propaganda value but also because of her burning commitment to social justice. On every occasion, she demonstrated her unfailing empathy with the poor.[22]

In April 1936, Santiago Carrillo, the one-time follower of Largo Caballero who had just betrayed his mentor by taking the Federación de Juventudes Socialistas into a merger with the Communist Youth to create the Juventud Unificada Socialista, was permitted to attend a meeting of the PCE Central Committee. Years later he spoke of the impact of seeing Dolores for the first time:

> I was moved. She was wearing rope-soled sandals, a huge shawl of pretty colours and, as always, dressed in black. Despite this simplicity, she seemed to me like a queen. There emanated from her a dignity, a majesty that is so often found in the women and men of our people . . . What seduced me, apart from her beauty, was her extraordinary charm when she laughed or spoke. In those days, in the Party, she was the great tribune who mobilized the multitudes, because she had a voice which grabbed you by the throat and extraordinary gifts as an orator. Above all, she had political instinct, an always correct instinct about how to position herself and play her cards in any situation. Certainly, where tactics were concerned, she could sometimes go too far, carried away by the passion and sincerity of her character . . . People came up to touch her as they would a saint.[23]

Dolores was also a great success as a parliamentary deputy. Her speeches were media events because of the way in which she broke with the Cortes tradition of ornate oratorical performance. She attacked the right with passion and directness. Indalecio Prieto wrote a warm tribute in *El Liberal* after her first speech. Despite the enormous political difference that would always separate them, their shared ties with both Asturias and the Basque Country ensured that he always had a soft spot for her. He once asked her after one of her parliamentary speeches where she had learned to speak so well, and she replied, 'Attending your meetings'.[24] In the notorious Cortes session of 16 June, she replied magisterially to the Catholic authoritarian leader, José María Gil Robles and the ultra-rightist, José Calvo Sotelo. Gil Robles, in the guise of an appeal for moderation, made a lengthy justification of the rising that was being prepared. With cold-blooded exaggeration, he read out a long list of murders, beatings, robberies, church-burnings and strikes, a catalogue of disorder for which he placed the responsibility on the government. Calvo Sotelo virtually called for an uprising, saying, 'I would consider to be a madman any officer who, faced with his destiny, was not ready to rise for Spain and against anarchy.' The Prime Minister, Santiago Casares Quiroga, replied that, after Calvo Sotelo's provocation, he would hold him responsible for whatever might happen. The subsequent intervention by Pasionaria began with an elegantly sarcastic demolition of Gil Robles's rhetorical deviousness: 'I trust my right honourable friend will allow me to expose his double game, that is to say, the manoeuvres of the right, who while they carry out provocations in the streets, send men here who, with the faces of innocent children [laughter], come to ask the government what is going on and where it will all end [applause].' She then went on to unleash a powerful denunciation of the atrocities in Asturias 'because today's storms are the consequence of yesterday's winds'. She also accused Pilar Primo de Rivera – without naming her – of organizing Falangist terror squads. Her passionate recital of the post-Asturias tortures led to the deputies of the Popular Front interrupting her with a standing ovation. 'And if there are little reactionary generals who, at a given moment, worked up by elements like Señor Calvo Sotelo, can make an uprising against the State, there are also soldiers of the people who can keep them under control.' From that speech grew the Francoist myth that Pasionaria had threatened Calvo Sotelo and therefore bore some part of the responsibility for his assassination on 13 July. In fact, no threat of any kind appears in the text of her speech reproduced in the parliamentary record, the *Diario de Sesiones*.[25]

The military uprising quickly revealed the capacity of Dolores Ibárruri both to inspire and give voice to the popular mood. On 19 July 1936, speaking from the Ministry of the Interior, she made a broadcast on behalf of the Communist Party. She was nervous as she started to read the sheets she had rapidly scribbled. Once she began to speak, however, she forgot her nerves and passion took hold of her. The veins stood out on her neck as her voice rang out powerfully. In a rousing appeal to every man, woman and child of all the regions of Spain, she coined the phrase 'The fascists shall not pass! ¡*No pasarán*!'[26]

The words 'They shall not pass!' had originally been used by Marshal Pétain during the siege of Verdun in 1916 and repeated by journalists of *Mundo Obrero* over the previous two years. Heard in Casas del Pueblo, in cafés, in the heightened atmosphere of Madrid at the begining of the Spanish Civil War, the phrase became the Republican battle-cry. The impact on her listeners was recalled by the Republican Isabel de Palencia: 'Her voice haunted me for months afterwards.'[27] Two days later, as popular outrage against the uprising resulted in the burning of churches and businesses, she made an appeal for order and discipline which was to be the keynote of Communist Party policy: 'We understand your indignation at the crimes of the rebels, but do not let yourselves be dragged along by those who want to lead you down the road of destruction, of shameful robbery and of arson.'[28]

In the early days of the rising, there were several military units in Madrid which had been confined to barracks and had still not defined their stance in relation to the rising. The Communist Party ordered its militants in each area to make contact with party members in each garrison to try to clarify the situation. On 23 July, together with Enrique Líster, Dolores Ibárruri was sent to address soldiers of the Regimiento Wad-Ras No. 1 stationed at the garrison in the Pacífico district of Madrid near Vallecas. There were large numbers of Civil Guards in the garrison who greeted the Communists with hostility. Showing great courage in a dangerously tense situation, Dolores stood on a chair and talked the soldiers out of rebelling against the Republic. Having turned their hesitations into an enthusiastic commitment to the Republic, she and Líster organized a convoy of lorries and cars to take them to the front to the north of Madrid. On arrival at the village of Guadarrama, they were astonished by the lack of concern of the officer in charge, who ordered them to settle down in the village square. It took a protest from Pasionaria before the local military authorities would agree to the recently arrived troops being taken up to the front.[29]

Throughout much of August, she worked hard visiting active fighting units, consolidating the morale of the troops. Her arrival at a particular unit would always lift spirits. Her courage and concern for the conditions of the troops guaranteed her a warm welcome:

> everyone knows Dolores, they wave to her from afar, the soldiers give her bread, with wine from their canteens, they try to persuade her to stay longer, to sit down, not to go on

> further . . . [When there is enemy fire] the soldiers urge her to duck but she takes no notice and runs, like everyone else, upright with her head slightly inclined . . . She plays hell with the cooks about the quality of the food. When she discovers that the column has gone two days without vegetables, she uses the field telephone to contact some organizations and somehow gets a lorry-load of water-melons and tomatoes.[30]

Her energy inspired those around her. Stalin's agent, Mikhail Koltsov, described her work within the leadership of the PCE where she provided a link with the life in the streets outside the smoke-filled rooms:

> To the severe, masculine atmosphere of the Politburo, excessively dominated by the rule-book, the presence of Dolores brought warmth, joy, a sense of humour or of passionate anger. She was particularly hard-line when it came to keeping promises. Dolores would arrive with her joyful spirit, with her happy, mischievous smile, well turned-out, elegant even, despite the simplicity of her dress, always black. She would sit down, put her hands on the table and slightly bending her large and beautiful head, listen in silence to the conversation. At other times, dead tired, struck with sorrow by something, depressed, her face grey like stone, looking old, she would slump heavily into a chair by the door, in a corner, and also say nothing. Then, suddenly, she would interrupt something someone was saying and then it would be pointless to try to stop her until, without pausing for breath, she had poured out her long tirade, which could be happy, funny, ingenious, and triumphant or gloomy, angry, almost plaintive, full of pained reproaches, of accusations, of protests and of threats against the obvious or hidden enemy of the day, against the bureaucrat or the saboteur who had prevented arms or food being sent to the militias at the front, or who had offended the workers or who was involved in intrigue from outside or inside the Party.[31]

Her greatest impact came from the many major public speeches in which she appealed to the civilian population to support the militias and to the rest of the world to support the Republic. Although her tone was broadly Republican not narrowly Communist, the PCE derived enormous benefit and prestige from her emergence as the single most representative figure of the Republic. The pressure on her was intense and she worked herself to exhaustion. The Austrian sociologist Franz Borkenau was present when she spoke to 50,000 people at Valencia on 23 August 1936. As an ex-Communist, he described the scene with a certain objectivity:

> what is touching about her is precisely her aloofness from the atmosphere of political intrigue: the simple, self-sacrificing faith which emanates from every word she speaks. And more touching even is her lack of conceit, and even her self-effacement. Dressed in simple black, cleanly and carefully but without the slightest attempt to make herself look pleasant, she speaks simply, directly, without rhetoric, without caring for theatrical effects ... At the end of her speech came a pathetic moment. Her voice, tired from endless addresses to enormous meetings since the beginning of the civil war, failed her. And she sat down with a sad waving gesture of her hands, wanting to express: 'It's no use, I can't help it, I can't say any more; I am sorry.' There was not the slightest touch of ostentation in it, only regret at being unable to tell the meeting those things she had wanted to tell it. This gesture, in its profound simplicity, sincerity, and its convincing lack of any personal interest in success or failure as an orator, was much more touching than her whole speech. This woman, looking fifty with her forty years, reflecting, in every word and gesture, a profound motherliness ... has something of a medieval ascetic, of a religious personality about her. The masses worship her, not for her intellect, but as a sort of saint who is to lead them in the days of trial and temptation.[32]

It was hardly surprising that the ordinary people of Republican Spain whose lives had been turned upside down by the war should find a powerful mother-figure so appealing. Every day brought losses of loved ones, food shortages, bombing raids and the constant anxiety of Nationalist terror. The strength and concern emanating from Pasionaria was a beacon of certainty in a sea of insecurity. Her simplicity and sincerity created a rapport which enabled her to become the mouthpiece for the fears and hopes of many working-class people in the Republican zone. Every day, she was inundated by letters from ordinary people and soldiers, asking her to solve some problem or other. The Spanish Ambassador in Moscow, Marcelino Pascua Martínez, complained that, such was the scale of correspondence which arrived for her at the Embassy, he spent more time as Pasionaria's secretary than on his official duties.[33]

On 8 September 1936, she formed part of a Republican delegation which visited France to try to mobilize French public opinion against the government decision not to sell arms to Spain. Addressing a huge crowd in the Paris Velodrome d'Hiver, she coined another ringing phrase: 'the Spanish people would rather die on its feet than live on its knees'. Her powerful speech seemed to be understood even by those who did not speak Spanish. Indeed, when she paused for an interpreter to translate, the crowd shouted him down so that Pasionaria could continue without interruption. According to one eye-witness, 'the people around me could not speak Spanish but they all understood her. Her eloquence came from the depths of her soul and therefore needed no translation.' She ended with a disturbingly prophetic warning: 'And do not forget, and let no one forget, that if today it is our turn to resist fascist aggression, the struggle will not end in Spain. Today it's us; but if the Spanish people is allowed to be crushed, you will be next, all of Europe will have to face aggression and war.'[34] When the delegation visited Léon Blum to request arms supplies, she made the same point. Blum, to her contempt, snivelled, his nose running. Tears dripped down onto his scraggy beard as he refused to help the Republic, repeating over and over, 'Je ne peux pas, Madame, je ne peux pas.'[35]

After the meeting, she met the twenty-year-old Manuel Azcárate, a member of the Juventud Comunista and son of the future Republican Ambassador to London: 'Meeting Dolores had a profound impact on me. Despite the gravity of the moment, there is an infectious joy in her laugh. She has a response for everything.' As she herself was aware, that trip to Paris established her worldwide as the symbol of the Republican war effort. She was applauded by the customers in a working-class restaurant where she went to eat.[36] Her eloquent speeches pleading for aid were reproduced in newspapers, magazines and pamphlets. She represented perfectly the besieged Republic, a mother who could speak for the children being threatened by fascism.

She came to even greater prominence during the siege of Madrid. Her own courage was on display every day, boosting the morale of others. While bombs fell at the front, without the slightest flicker of fear, she sauntered upright along the tops of the trenches calling for courage and determination in the face of the enemy.[37] She despised Largo Caballero's weak conduct of the war. She was particularly contemptuous of the fact that he was afraid even to issue a decree forcibly ending a strike by the Madrid construction workers for fear of losing UGT members to the CNT. He insisted on keeping normal office hours and was in bed at nine, leaving instructions that he was not to be disturbed.[38] In *Mundo Obrero* on 25 September, Pasionaria called for a total mobilization of the population of the capital:

> Madrid must be militarized and, along with Madrid, all of loyalist Spain. And when I speak of militarization, I'm not speaking of externals, the obligation to wear a uniform, whether it's a *mono* [the workingmen's blue overalls worn by the militias] or battledress, but of the content, of what is meant by the obligation of conscientious work, of a sense of responsibility, of discipline, of adaptation to the needs of the moment, of submission to the impositions of the war . . . Militarization: obligatory labour; rationing; discipline; exemplary punishment for saboteurs. In a word, it is necessary to feel the war, it is necessary to make war.[39]

On 4 October, she had been made an honorary major (*comandante*) in the crack Fifth Regiment, the PCE's well-organized militia. At the ceremony, she made a belligerent speech: 'This is not the moment to weep for our dead but to avenge them. The raped women, the murdered militiamen demand vengeance and justice; vengeance and justice are what we owe them and vengeance and justice is what we will impose on the executioners of the people.'[40] In the first days of the war, she had participated in the creation of the Quinto Regimiento under the command of Enrique Castro Delgado. One of its battalions was named after her. Thereafter, she became a passionate advocate of the creation of a professional army for the Republic along the lines of the Quinto Regimiento.[41] She was the visible expression of the Communist Party line which was expressed in a manifesto issued on 2 November 1936, 'We must do miracles of organization to convert Madrid into an impregnable fortress.' On that same day, she headed a demonstration of 200,000 women calling for the mobilization of the entire population for the defence of Madrid. She also found time to write an article for *Pravda*.[42]

Along with her public speeches, her frequent radio broadcasts were also a major contribution to the maintenance of Republican morale.

As the African columns neared Madrid, she turned panic and fear into hope and a determination to fight. Something about her strong voice as it filled rooms throughout the capital restored people's faith in themselves. From her efforts to raise the morale of the women of Madrid came perhaps the most famous of her battle cries: 'It is better to be the widows of heroes than the wives of cowards!'[43] The first time that she used the phrase was in addressing a demonstration in Madrid in mid-October in which she criticized the Largo Caballero government for what she regarded as the lack of seriousness with which he was approaching the war effort: 'We cannot shut our eyes when faced with a somewhat frivolous atmosphere in the capital. In Madrid, people are not fully aware of the war . . . the government has decided to militarize the militias but this is not enough. The entire population must be militarized!' She protested that the building trade was still functioning normally in civilian pursuits. 'What we need at this moment are blockhouses, bunkers, parapets, trenches, to make Madrid impregnable.'[44] Invariably accompanied by photographers and reporters, her every action had an impact on morale and a propaganda dimension. She was regularly seen digging trenches, haranguing the troops, consoling soldiers who had lost their comrades and mothers who had lost their children.[45]

At the end of October, the distinguished British reporter, Geoffrey Cox, witnessed an extraordinary scene. A demoralized unit, the heart torn out of it by constant shelling and aerial bombardment, was revitalized by the arrival of Dolores Ibárruri. 'Shattered, retreating, dispirited, they wanted leaders who would help them.' 'La Pasionaria walked up the road to towards the line. In the growing darkness, broken only by a fiery sunset glow on the horizon, man after man crowded after her. But there was a note of tragedy over the scene. For all her eloquence and courage, what could La Pasionaria do at this late hour to check the retreat?'[46] At other times, she stopped panic withdrawals by shaming the fleeing soldiers into returning to the trenches.[47]

At the beginning of November, a young Communist political commissar, Santiago Alvarez, came across a group of Party leaders between Seseña and Valdemoro and told them that the front was crumbling:

> The first to react was Dolores Ibárruri. 'What? *Milicianos* in retreat. I'm going with you immediately!' Dolores grabbed her bag and went out onto the road. As a group of retreating

> *milicianos* came near to us, Dolores climbed onto the granite wall of the bridge and harangued them: 'Soldiers, comrades! Where are you going? Why are you fleeing from the front? Surely you're not cowards? So, who is going to defend Madrid? What will your wives, your girlfriends, your mothers think of you? Don't you love the cause of the workers, the cause of freedom, your cause? . . . You must fight to stop Madrid falling into the hands of the fascists!' Her black figure, standing proudly erect on the wall, her voice of steel, whose resonance cut the air of the sunlit morning, her reproaches to those who had abandoned the front, her words of encouragement, her mere presence there at that moment, had the effect of turning the retreating soldiers to stone. Suddenly, as if shot from a spring, the nearest group turned around as one man and set off back to the front. Some of them were crying. The remainder followed their example. The retreat was stopped. The militiamen, soldiers once more, returned to the front.[48]

Pasionaria was tireless, hurrying around the city's defences, in one place stopping to deliver an impromptu speech, in another undertaking to do something about the lack of supplies. She also found time to seek out suitable premises and welfare work for one group of nuns that had been detained for their own protection and for another that had been discovered in hiding.[49] Sure that Madrid would fall, the Republican government left for Valencia on 6 November, and placed the protection of the city in the hands of a Defence Junta presided over by General Miaja. Dolores Ibárruri was outraged. The Communist Party representatives in Largo Caballero's cabinet, Jésus Hernández (Education) and Vicente Uribe (Agriculture), had argued in October that the defence of Madrid and the evacuation of the government were not incompatible objectives. Despite Dolores' hostility to the move, a meeting of the Politburo of the PCE had decided that she and José Díaz should accompany the government to Valencia. Vittorio Vidali wrote: 'I remember her tearful and furiously angry on that night of November 6, 1936, when I accompanied her out of the capital, then in mortal danger.' 'That night I accompanied Dolores and saw her weep bitterly; she had fought to stay in Madrid and her departure seemed to her like running away.'[50] Vidali was mistaken about the date. Dolores Ibárruri did not leave Madrid until later in November and then only briefly.[51] The manner in which the government left Madrid created a very poor impression among the beleaguered population. It allowed the Communist Party to dominate the Junta de Defensa and effectively assume the lead in defending Madrid, and thereby to enhance its own prestige. It was an important step along the path to its ultimate take-over of the whole Republican war effort.

On 8 November, in a terror-stricken Madrid, she addressed an enthusiastic meeting in the Cine Monumental, barely one kilometre from the front. The superhuman efforts of the previous weeks had taken their toll. A colleague from *Mundo Obrero*, Eugenio Cimorra, was struck by how thin she had become. Koltsov, who was also present, was equally shocked: 'she has lost weight, she is pale; now she seems even taller, more imperious and, also in a way, younger. As always, dressed in black, and, despite the simplicity of her dress, elegant.' She was greeted enthusiastically and her speech giving thanks for Soviet aid raised spirits enormously.[52] This was not just a recital of the party line – Dolores was genuinely moved by the Russian assistance to the Republic. Her office was dominated by large portraits of Lenin and Stalin and a gigantic bunch of flowers, as well as piles of detective novels.[53] In a similar way, she was especially affected by the arrival of the International Brigaders on 6 November to help defend Madrid. Without thought for her own safety, she shared the same risks as they did in her efforts to help boost their morale. In the cellars of the Faculty of Architecture in the University City on the northern outskirts of Madrid, full of woman and children sheltering from the Nationalist bombardment, she addressed the brigaders on 15 November. Having to make herself heard over the sound of artillery shells and machine-guns, she once more emphasized the international significance of the Spanish struggle: 'You fight and make sacrifices for the freedom and independence of Spain. But Spain is sacrificing herself for the whole world. To fight for Spain is to fight for freedom and peace in the whole world.'[54]

By 23 November, Franco had to accept that the frontal assault on Madrid had been beaten back. He moved to a policy of trying to encircle the capital and simultaneously mop up some of the periphery. Pasionaria would never again be as directly involved in the war effort but her role in maintaining morale remained as crucial as ever. Celia Seborer, an American who worked as an assistant to the surgeon, Norman Bethune, attended a rally in Valencia in mid-February 1937 at which Dolores spoke. She wrote of that experience: 'I knew that she was a dramatic and inspiring speaker, but was quite unprepared for the beauty and warmth of her voice. It has a rich, enveloping quality that makes one feel that her arm is about one's shoulder, and she is talking directly to one. Her gestures are few, simple and direct, but her spirit, courage and human warmth are contagious.'[55] John Tisa, an American International Brigader, described her speaking to a congress of writers in Madrid in July 1937 during an air raid. The strength and confidence of her voice dissipated the fears of her audience and kept them transfixed for an hour.[56]

She was infuriated by the fall of Málaga in February 1937, for which she held Largo Caballero largely responsible. On 4 March, at a meeting in Valencia, she launched a barely veiled attack on Largo Caballero's under-secretary of Defence, General José Asensio Torrado: 'We want an army without generals who cavort in brothels and sinks of iniquity while the people and the soldiers fight with heroism, while, on the roads out of Málaga, our women and children are machine-gunned by the fascist airforce.'[57] She would play an important role both publicly through her speeches and privately in the campaign to remove Largo Caballero. An opportunity arose after the infamous May Days, when the anti-Stalinist Communists of the POUM and the anarcho-syndicalist CNT rebelled against the Republic in Barcelona. Dolores visited Azaña with José Díaz and complained about Largo Caballero, his ineptitude, his lack of control, his timidity with regard to the CNT and the pernicious influence of his personal entourage.[58]

In large part because of Communist pressure, Largo Caballero was replaced on 17 May by the Minister of Finance, Dr Juan Negrín. The change of government came too late to help the Basque Country. The fall of Bilbao on 19 June was a devastating blow to Dolores and she expressed her rage in an eloquent article: 'German and Italian armies, hordes of mercenaries, legions of professional assassins, have invaded the ancient Basque Country, after razing to the ground its villages and towns, profaning its soil with their bloody jackboots. Euzkadi weeps tears of blood for this horrendous sacrilege.' Her pain, however, did not prevent her from drawing the political lesson and making implicit criticisms of both Largo Caballero and of the Basque Government; 'the loss of Euzkadi has been a terrible lesson for those who refused to understand something fundamental: The Basques had no regular army. They had only brave and heroic militiamen – whether Basque nationalists, Socialists or Communists. They fought bare-breasted; their courage was irresponsibly squandered. But there was no organized army. There were no commanders. There were no commissars – those valiant and devoted commissars who are the soul of the Popular Army.'[59]

In 1937, among Dolores' many tasks was that of meeting visiting foreign dignitaries. The impact of her great warmth was invariably positive. The Duchess of Atholl, who was chairwoman of the British National Joint Committee for Spanish Relief, met her in 1937. She compared her with the great Italian actress, Eleonora Duse: 'She had Duse's wonderful grace and voice, but she was much more beautiful, with rich colouring, large dark eyes, and black wavy hair. She swept into the room like a queen, yet she was a miner's daughter . . . I could understand nothing that she said, and she talked with great rapidity, but to look and to listen was pleasure enough for me.'[60] Charlotte Haldane, an English writer working to raise money for the families of International Brigaders, met Dolores in 1938: 'she had a matronly but magnificent figure, and bore herself with that unselfconscious nobility and dignity that is so characteristic of certain Spaniards, irrespective of birth or class. Her features were regular, aquiline; her eyes dark and flashing. She had splendid teeth, and her smile was young and feminine. The voice that in public meetings could enthral thousands was, in private conversations, low and melodious, though still decisive.'[61]

Dolores never ceased visiting the front and gained the affection and respect of the troops precisely because of her courage in doing so. It appears that for this woman in her early forties, the exhilaration of war was a rejuvenating experience. Shortly before the battle for Brunete at the beginning of July 1937, Dolores visited the front accompanied by the political commissar for the Madrid front, Francisco Antón, and some war correspondents. The troops enthusiastically rushed to see her.[62] The diversionary attack on the besiegers of Madrid at Brunete was planned to pull Nationalist troops away from their successful campaign in the north. To that extent it worked, although at enormous cost in casualties. The Republican attackers were subjected to incessant bombing for three weeks in the sweltering summer heat of Castilla. After the battle, Pasionaria returned to visit the surviving troops who were camped alongside the River Guadalix near the village of Fuente del Fresno. Many of them were swimming and decided to play a prank on her. When she was near the edge of a deep pool, they grabbed her and threw into the water. She walked out of the pool, wiping back her hair. Grinning broadly, she just said, 'How warm the water is!' She stood there wet and laughing, her clothes revealingly clinging to her body, much to the delight of the soldiers. She took the incident in good part, in the knowledge of what these troops had suffered and what they needed to restore their morale.[63]

She fervently supported the diversionary attack of Brunete and that of Belchite which followed it on 24 August because of her desperate anxiety about the war in the north. In an article published in *Mundo Obrero* on 18 October 1937, three days before the fall of Gijón, she paid tribute to the heroic resistance in Asturias. Her impotent rage at the short-sightedness of the Western democracies was expressed in a heartfelt article published in *Mundo Obrero*: 'We have appealed to the proletariat of the entire world to come to our aid. We have shouted until we were hoarse at the doors of the so-called democratic countries, telling them what our struggle meant for them; and they did not listen.'[64]

In the atmosphere of the wartime Republic, relationships were in flux. Separated from her husband for more than six years, Dolores Ibárruri had taken a lover, the twenty-seven-year-old Francisco Antón. Early in the war, he had been secretary of the PCE provincial committee for Madrid. Slightly built, darkly handsome, Antón was soon made commissar for the Quinto Regimiento, then Comisario-Inspector for the entire Madrid front. He and Dolores were constantly thrown together. There was no reason why she should not have some human warmth in her personal life but the relationship caused her difficulty with some members of the PCE leadership. That was partly because of the puritanical ethos in the party and also because it was regarded as politically useful to be able to proclaim that her husband was at the front.[65] It also reflected jealousy from her rivals. According to one of them, Jesús Hernández, Dolores' relations with José Díaz were soured because of his criticisms of her affair with Antón.

Hernández's poisonous account has to be treated with great care. Party propaganda had converted Antón into one of the heroes of the defence of Madrid yet Hernández later alleged that José Díaz had commented, 'he had never dirtied his boots in the mud of a trench'. Certainly, Antón was always elegantly turned out, his trousers sharply pressed. However, Hernández was surely inventing when claimed that Antón ran the corps of commissars 'by dint of sending out circulars and receiving the delegates from the front at their comfortable house in Ciudad Lineal [on the outskirts of Madrid] decked-out in his magnificent, perfumed silk pyjamas'. The malicious gossip within the party was that Antón, fifteen years younger than his lover, was using her for his political ambitions. Hernández claimed that Díaz had said to her, 'I don't give a damn about your private life but since I have to be the pimp covering your love affair (which I do because if the facts got out, your prestige would plummet and we have turned you into the moral standard-bearer for revolutionary women) then I want you to know that I feel as much contempt for Antón as I feel respect for Julián' (her husband).[66]

However the affair with Antón might have damaged Pasionaria's standing with the narrow-minded and provincial Spanish leadership, it did not affect her good relations with the rather more cosmopolitan delegates of the Comintern. They were inclined to raise her up as the principal figurehead of the party. Given her proven loyalty to Moscow, she had especially good relations with Palmiro Togliatti and Boris Stepanov, the Comintern advisers. Togliatti lived in her house in Valencia and shared his meals with Dolores and Antón. In mid-September 1937, Togliatti wrote to Dimitrov and Manuilsky praising her as a potential leader of the party.[67] Nevertheless, the affair with Antón was not without wider political ramifications. In the autumn of 1937, Prieto issued a decree that political commissars of military age should serve at the front, a decree which directly affected Antón. For reasons not entirely unconnected with Dolores, enormous pressure was put on Prieto by the PCE to have the decree rescinded. Prieto refused and Antón was demoted from a position in which he commanded the commissars in three army corps to that of Brigade-Commissar on the Teruel Front. He simply failed to report for duty at his new headquarters and was dismissed by Prieto from the Cuerpo de Comisarios. He then appeared in Madrid, without Prieto's permission, as a civilian attaché to General Vicente Rojo, the Republican Chief of the General Staff.[68]

Dolores' admiration for the Bolshevik experience was total and her loyalty to the Soviet Union unquestioning.[69] With complete conviction, she wrote denunciations of Trotskyism.[70] In her memoirs, she refers to the POUM as 'anarcotrotskistas fascistas'.[71] Hernández tried to implicate her in the murder of Andreu Nin, claiming that she and Codovilla authorized the arrest on 16 June of Nin and the leadership of the POUM behind the back of the proper judicial authority, the Minister of the Interior, Julián Zugazagoitia, as well as of both Díaz and Hernández himself.[72] That is probably not the case but there can be little doubt that she approved of the liquidation of the POUM. Her attitude to Trotskyism may have reflected the influence over her of the hard-line Victorio Codovilla. In fact, on 25 November 1937, Togliatti would write to Moscow about what he considered to be the excessive nature of that influence.[73]

In the summer of 1937, in fact, Andreu Nin was far from Dolores' principal preoccupation. With José Díaz profoundly ill, she was carrying out many of the functions of the secretary-general. She was working day and night, constantly importuned by problems, papers to read and authorize, visitors to receive. Over the days just before and after the arrest of Nin, she was preparing her report to the plenum of the PCE held in the Conservatorio in Valencia on 18 June 1937, at which she would make the case for a merger of the PCE and the PSOE.[74] Although that was the principal objective of her report, she also justified the assault on the POUM. Accusing the Trotskyists of being a worse enemy than the fascists, she declared 'No measures taken to purge the proletarian camp of the poisonous growth of Trotskyism can ever be considered excessive . . . The activities of the Trotskyists in our country – not to mention the monstrous criminal deeds committed by the Trotskyists in the Soviet Union – should sound the alarm to keep the proletariat vigilant to repel the despicable ends pursued by the Trotskyists.'[75] Given her faith in Moscow, it would have been easy for her to see Nin as a provocateur.[76] Her powerful report in favour of Socialist-Communist unity would be met with some suspicion by the Largo Caballero wing of the PSOE.

On 13 October 1937, Dolores Ibárruri formed part of a delegation which visited President Azaña to argue against the proposed move of the government from Valencia to Barcelona. Acting as the spokeswoman for the group, she went out of her way to be agreeable to the President. Azaña said frivolously, 'I imagine that you have put off for a little while that business of the dictatorship of the proletariat', to which she replied submissively, 'Yes, Mr President, because we have common sense.' The delegation argued that a move of the government to Barcelona would demoralize the population. They also claimed that it would be disastrous if the Nationalists were to cut off Catalonia from the rest of Spain. Azaña pointed out that such an eventuality would mean defeat for the Republic whether the government was in Valencia or Barcelona. Pasionaria agreed, 'Sí, señor. That would be to lose the war, without doubt, and then it would be a question of seeing what we could salvage.'[77]

After the conflict over political commissars, Pasionaria's relations with Prieto were irrevocably damaged, but it was not just the question of Antón which came between them. Given her intense commitment to the war effort, she was infuriated whenever the frequent pessimistic remarks of Prieto were reported to her. Within a week of the loss of Teruel, she launched a savage attack on Prieto in a speech on 27 February 1938 to the PSUC in Barcelona: 'Who are those who at this moment sow the seeds of defeatism, and speak of the incapacity of our army? They are those who have always been in the rearguard, those who live off the war and not for the war. They are those who have never felt in the back of their throats the acrid aftertaste of gunpowder at the battlefront. They are the useless ones and the cowards . . .'[78] Then, on 16 March, she led a mass demonstration organized by the PCE and the PSUC at the Palacio de Pedralbes to bring pressure to bear on the cabinet against the inclination of Azaña and Prieto to seek international mediation. The entire event was stage-managed. As part of the orchestration of the event, Negrín left the cabinet meeting in order formally to receive Pasionaria. She presented him with the demonstration's demands for commitment to continued resistance, with which he fully agreed.[79]

On 23 May 1938, in the absence of the now seriously ill José Díaz, Pasionaria delivered the main report to the plenary meeting of the Central Committee of the PCE held in Madrid. The American journalist, Vincent Sheean, was introduced to Dolores by the French Communist Georges Soria: 'I saw a deep-bosomed Spanish woman of about forty or a little more, with a hearty laugh and a firm hand . . . There was a splendid earthy quality about her laugh, but her face was very sad in repose.' Her three-and-a-half-hour speech impressed Sheean by dint of its extraordinary delivery. Although the speech was the official party line, and, he presumed, drafted in committee,

> it became wholly her own by virtue of the phrasing and above all by means of her extraordinary voice, face, hands, personality. The voice was not what is usually called 'musical' – that is, it had no melodious tones and little sweetness. It was a little higher and lower than the average, had a greater range, but that was all . . . Where it became quite unlike any other voice I have ever heard was in the effect of passionate sincerity. This expressive gift abides in Dolores' voice throughout, in her slightest remark as in the great sweeping statements, with the result that it is impossible to disbelieve anything she says while she is actually saying it.[80]

Five weeks earlier, the forces of Franco had reached the Mediterranean, split Republican Spain and cut off Catalonia. It was the situation which she had conceded to Azaña meant the inevitable defeat of the Republic. Perhaps for that reason, her report to the Central Committee was brutally frank, making no effort to minimize the gravity of the situation: 'The military defeats that we have suffered in recent months have left us in such a state that we have to declare, without any kind of exaggeration, that, at this moment, the liberty and independence of our country is more directly and seriously threatened than ever before.' She went on to make a bleak assessment of the international situation, of the difficulties likely to face the central zone and of the ongoing problem of defeatism. She ended with a rousing call for greater unity and discipline behind the programme of Dr Negrín as the basis of resistance.[81] According to Sheean:

> Sometimes she gave it to them so straight and hard that you could hear the gasp of the whole audience. Her purpose was, of course, to make such failures and mistakes rarer in the future. She criticized the government not at all, but her own and the other revolutionary parties came in for some terrific lashings. And then, having frightened the audience into breathlessness by her picture of disaster, she set out to prove that victory was possible, and on what conditions . . . To an ordinary American journalist in the front row of the hall it seemed that she was asking these people to stop being Communists altogether, at least until the war was won. [Although the audience was shaken by her message,] the genius of Dolores – her unquestionable genius as a speaker, the most remarkable I ever heard – worked upon them its customary miracle, and she had the whole audience cheering with enthusiasm when she finished.[82]

On 26 July 1938, she spoke in a similar spirit at a demonstration organized at the Velodrome d'Hiver in Paris by the Rassemblement Universel pour la Paix. She appealed for help for the starving Republican zone. She also took time to denounce the POUM as responsible for Franco's successful burst to the Mediterranean, asserting that the Communists 'are fighting to clean our land of poisonous weeds'. Most powerfully, she again denounced talk of a mediated peace: 'Who are those who dare speak of armistice, of mediation or of capitulation? They are not the men who every day face death. They are not the workers who exhaust their strength in the factories. They are not the women who offer their sons and their menfolk for the war. They are the carrion crows of defeatism, those who have never had faith in our people, those who, far from the battle-front, who lend themselves to the manoeuvres and intrigues of the enemy.'[83] It was a clear reference to Azaña, Besteiro and Prieto.

John Tisa saw her in Barcelona in November 1938. He described her as 'a striking woman of about thirty-five years of age . . . she parts her hair on the right side, black hair mixed with thick threads of gray, and pulls it back and neatly knots it on the back of her well-shaped head. With her fine aquiline nose and smooth skin and features, she is a strong and handsome woman.' A few days later, he came across her again amidst a group of children in a Barcelona street:

> Today her black and steel-gray hair is pushed to the back of her head in a roll and held together by a coffee-coloured comb. Her eyes are deep-set under black eyebrows and a smooth, high forehead. Though heavy in body, with high, full breasts, she looks well proportioned. Her beautifully chiselled face exposes an unconquerable personality; she radiates warmth and confidence; there is nothing artificial about her. Her voice is deep and of full resonance, almost masculine. When she applauds, which is frequently, her clap is loud and her long-fingered hands come together continuously and smoothly like well-oiled pistons. I am told that she is annoyed because someone who is supposed to be here with gifts for the children has not yet arrived. What innate quality does she possess that makes a roomful of people suddenly halt what they're doing and stare at her with awe, admiration, and affection?[84]

During the Munich crisis, Negrín proposed the withdrawal of the International Brigades in the hope that it might tip British and French sentiment in favour of the Republic. Although she understood the political reasons behind the decision, Pasionaria was devastated by the implications. She had always seen the presence of the brigaders as the ultimate symbol that the Spanish Republic did not have to face fascism alone. The official farewell parade was held in Barcelona on 29 October. In the presence of many thousands of tearful, but cheering, Spaniards, Dolores Ibárruri wept as she gave an emotional and moving speech:

> Comrades of the International Brigades! Political reasons, reasons of state, the good of that same cause for which you offered your blood with limitless generosity, send some of you back to your countries and some to forced exile. You can go with pride. You are history. You are legend. You are the heroic example of the solidarity and the universality of democracy . . . We will not forget you; and, when the olive-tree of peace puts forth its leaves, entwined with the laurels of the Spanish Republic's victory, come back! Come back to us and here those of you who have no homeland will find a homeland, those who are forced to live without friends will find friends, and all of you will find the affection and the gratitude of the entire Spanish people who today and tomorrow shout with enthusiasm: 'Long live the heroes of the International Brigades!'

It was in many respects her finest moment, her words had captured the emotions of the defeated. Under the mournful gaze of President Azaña, the brigaders then marched past as the onlookers threw flowers.

At the end of the war, Dolores escaped to Algiers and from there to France, whence she was recalled to Moscow.[86] The escape from Spain and the journey to Russia was traumatic in the extreme. Exiled in Moscow and totally dependent on Russian charity, the PCE leadership could hardly be anything but the most hard-line orthodox Stalinists. Gratitude for haven in the Soviet Union and for Soviet help during the Civil War obliged Pasionaria and the other Spanish party leaders to support the Nazi–Soviet Pact of 23 August 1939. Dolores Ibárruri and José Díaz silenced their own profound experience of fascist aggression. In the interests of Soviet policy and therefore of the Third Reich, they denounced the imperialist ambitions of the democracies and urged exiled Spaniards in Europe not to get involved in resistance struggles.[87] It is possible that this caused Dolores more distress than she would have been prepared to show. Fred Copeman, an International Brigader and a member of the Central Committee of the Communist Party of Great Britain, visited Moscow at about this time. He met Dolores Ibárruri at the Hotel Luxe, where officials of the Comintern stayed: 'no longer the fiery orator of the Madrid defences – a quiet, dark-haired woman with a kindly face, yet very practical'. Copeman had the impression that she was under some form of arrest:

> My meeting with Pasionaria hurt me deep down and I did not like it. I expected to find her on the stage at the Bolshoi

> Theatre, holding the hand of Stalin, and being introduced as one of the greatest living Communists. I found her alone in a little room closely guarded by units of the Red Army . . . If any living creature had the right to everything we had, to me it was Pasionaria. She had never given up the struggle for the Spanish people. She took her chances with the men in the line. She was the mother of a family which had made great sacrifices, and one of her sons had given his life. She was a worker born of the working classes, and her loyalty and integrity was beyond doubt, yet at this moment, she was far from happy . . . Spain to the Soviet Union had become an embarrassment. The Brigade was beginning to pass into history. Future Soviet policy would wish to forget it. Her new-found friends had no time for Pasionaria. The Soviet–Nazi Pact had already become an immediate possibility. This woman, with her deep convictions and loyalty to principles, was likely to become a political problem.[88]

In fact, the Nazi–Soviet Pact was to work in favour of Dolores. At the end of the Civil War, the PCE sent Francisco Antón to France where he was captured by the Gestapo after the German invasion. Dolores was devastated by the news, spending hours locked in her office, neither speaking nor smiling. According to various renegade Communists, she finally intervened with Georgy Dimitrov who, in turn, intervened with Stalin. One of them, Enrique Líster, claimed many years later that Stalin commented, 'Well if Juliet can't live without her Romeo, we'll get him for her, since we're bound to have a German spy we can swap for Antón.' Her friend and companion Irene Falcón, however, categorically insisted that, given Dolores' character, it is inconceivable that she would ever have made a personal request for Antón to be rescued. In fact, during the period of the Pact, there were substantial numbers of agents exchanged and it was quite normal that Antón would have been one of them. The Soviet Embassy in Paris made many deals with Otto Abetz, Hitler's Ambassador to France. In one of them, Antón was released from the concentration camp at Le Vernet, provided with a Soviet passport and escorted through Germany by a Soviet diplomat. Understandably, she was delighted to be informed by Dimitrov that Antón was being brought to the USSR. Once in Moscow, Antón was given the job of overseeing the studies of Spanish Communists attending political and military academies.[89] He formed part of Dolores' entourage, along with Irene Falcón and a highly intelligent young party functionary, Ignacio Gallego. Deeply depressed by the defeat of the Republic, Dolores withdrew into this small circle. Contact with her had to be arranged through Irene Falcón. The situation contributed to the isolation and sanctification of Dolores as a kind of queen mother of the party.[90]

In exile, she became unwillingly involved in a battle for the succession to José Díaz. Despite her lack of appetite for the struggle, she was eventually to emerge victorious. That triumph was the fruit of her skill in tacking to the prevailing winds of the Kremlin, no simple task in wartime Moscow. Her tactical flexibility was revealed at the first meeting of the secretariat of the Comintern which dealt with the situation inside Spain. With Díaz, she optimistically described the Spanish Party as strong and about to overthrow Franco. When the report was bitterly criticized by her arch-rival Jesús Hernández and the senior Comintern leaders, Georgy Dimitrov and Dimitry Manuilsky, she allegedly changed sides and launched a fierce attack on José Díaz, who commented afterwards, 'What a hurry she's in'.[91] In 1941, Moscow was evacuated and Dolores, along with the other senior functionaries of the Comintern, undertook the hazardous nine-day train journey to new quarters far to the east in Ufa in the Republic of Bashkiria.[92] Towards the end of his long battle with stomach cancer, doctors had recommended that José Díaz be moved to the warmer climate of Georgia. There, isolated, in pain, without medicines, he committed suicide by hurling himself from a balcony in Tbilisi (Tiflis) on 21 March 1942.

In the vicious power struggle within the PCE leadership which had started before his death, Pasionaria's relationship with Antón was used as ammunition against her by her principal rival Jesús Hernández and his allies, Enrique Líster, Juan Modesto and Enrique Castro Delgado. They nicknamed Antón 'Godoy', a reference to the favourite of the wife of Carlos IV. Castro Delgado alleged that she prevented him from writing a book about the Spanish Civil War for fear that it might undermine her efforts to present Francisco Antón as the hero of the battle for Madrid.[93] Hernández claimed implausibly that she arranged for her lover to lead a life of luxury as a playboy in Moscow. In his vicious and malicious account, he wrote that 'Pasionaria's was one of those senile infatuations that are so out of control that they leap any obstacle in their way'.[94] In the dislocation of the Soviet Union during the war, the power struggle went on from 1940 until the end of 1943, with Antón acting as campaign manager for Dolores. For a time, a substantial section of the party supported Hernández and he seemed to have the backing of Dimitrov and Manuilsky. While Hernández spent time with the exiled rank-and-file militants, Dolores tended rather to cultivate her relationship with top Kremlin figures. In fact, her interest in the power struggle was dramatically curtailed when, on 3 September 1942, she was shattered to be told by Nikita Khrushchev of the death of her son Rubén at Stalingrad. Having always considered that, as a mother, she had let Rubén down, her sorrow was tinged with guilt. Dolores withdrew for nine months into even greater detachment.[95]

It was not until the early summer of 1943 that she was able to begin to shake herself free of her grief-stricken isolation. She broke irrevocably with Antón, perhaps as a consequence of that same grief or because she realized that it was the pre-requisite of her eventual success in the power struggle. Santiago Carrillo's version claims that she had decided to renounce all personal life after the abuse to which she was subjected by the Hernández–Castro alliance. She took up again the reins of leadership, began to occupy herself with the multiple problems of the exiles and made pithy broadcasts to Spain from the transmitter known as Radio Pirenaica. Her eventual victory was evident in the autumn of 1943, when Jesús Hernández was permitted to go to Mexico, indicating that the Kremlin did not favour his candidacy. His vain hope was to muster support among the exiles in Latin America. Significantly, he was accompanied – and watched – by Antón who remained on friendly terms with Dolores.[96] In May 1944, Hernández was expelled from the party in Mexico for sectarianism and 'fractional activity'.[97] Thereafter, Dolores assumed the post of Secretary General.

Shortly before the end of the Second World War, confident that she would soon return to Madrid in triumph, Dolores Ibárruri undertook a hazardous journey through Iran, Syria and Egypt to France to take over leadership of the PCE. Before she left Moscow, on 23 February 1945, she spoke at length with Stalin, who pledged his support.[98] She had long advocated a wide anti-francoist unity, although the PCE line in this regard was simply to require all other groups to accept its leadership by joining the Communist-dominated front known as Unión Nacional.[99] Her initial optimism that Franco would share the fate of his German and Italian allies soon faded. In the immediate aftermath of the Potsdam Conference, she had moderated her position somewhat to a readiness to contemplate the need for a national coalition against Franco, although she was still thinking in terms of the restoration of the Second Republic.[100] On her return to France, she addressed a plenum of the PCE in Toulouse on 5 December 1945, calling for a national coalition to organize a democratic plebiscite. She condemned the government-in-exile of José Giral as insufficiently representative and called for the inclusion of the PCE.[101] From 1944, the centrepiece of PCE policy inside Spain was a guerrilla war against the dictatorship inspired by hopes of restoring the defeated Republic. By 1948, however, the guerrilla groups were increasingly on the defensive in their isolated struggle against the police, the Civil Guard and the Army. Their immediate objective had been to prepare a national uprising to coincide with Allied intervention against Franco. With the intensification of the Cold War, not only was that clearly not going to take place but Stalin was loath to risk an international incident over Communist activity in Spain.

Accordingly, in the early summer of 1948, a delegation of Dolores Ibárruri, Santiago Carrillo and Francisco Antón was summoned to the Kremlin. They were met by Stalin, Molotov, Voroshilov and Suslov. Stalin strongly advised them to withdraw the *guerrilleros* and to begin a long-term policy of infiltration into legal syndicates and other organizations within Spain.[102] A corollary of the abandonment of violence was a heightened commitment to the view that the dictatorship could be overthrown only by a broad alliance of opposition forces. With the rest of the Spanish democratic forces widely influenced by the Cold War atmosphere of anti-communism and still experiencing smouldering resentment of PCE high-handedness during the Civil War, the creation of a wide front obliged the Communists to mount a show of credible moderation. And that would eventually involve a degree of destalinization, a process which Dolores was to handle astutely. In the meantime, however, some of the worst effects of Stalinism were to hit the PCE. At the height of the Cold War, the PCE, like many other European Communist parties, was profoundly affected by the series of trials arising from Stalin's deep paranoia about Jews, doctors and foreigners.

In late 1948, poor health obliged Dolores to return to Moscow. She caught pneumonia after a gall-bladder operation in 1949 and nearly died, spending six months in hospital where she was visited by Stalin. Her convalescence was long and slow, and marked the beginning of the end of her effective leadership of the PCE.[103] Despite her weakness, she was soon obliged to deal with severe problems within the party. The focus of the crisis was to be Francisco Antón. After their separation, Antón had continued to enjoy prominence in the party. After the Second World War, he had shared, with Carrillo, Uribe and Mije, the leadership of the Paris operational centre. One of the central problems was the ill-tempered bullying and disorganization of the senior figure, Vicente Uribe. Things remained manageable while Dolores was still in France to keep him in check but, after she returned to Moscow, they became impossible. Antón and Carrillo tried to reform the party by marginalizing Uribe. This required the sanction of Dolores. Accordingly, Antón went to Moscow in 1951 to put their case to her.

To his utter surprise, she was cold and hostile, attacking him violently. He returned with some trepidation to Paris where, with her approval, Uribe drew up a document accusing him of fractional activity and authoritarian methods. Pasionaria even accused him of being a police agent. A senior official of the Spanish Party in Moscow at the time, Fernando Claudín, suspected that behind her extreme hostility was the news that Antón was living in Paris with Carmen Rodríguez, a pretty young Party militant. Santiago Carrillo, however, believed that, in the murderous atmosphere of suspicion which was beginning to take hold in Moscow, Dolores was protecting herself and others. Antón was the most suitable target for attack precisely because her earlier relationship with him could be seen as a dangerous debility. He was subjected over nearly two years – from mid-1952 to mid-1954 – to relentless accusations and interrogations in Paris. In theory, Antón could simply have walked away from the Party, but it never occurred to him to do so. The PCE was his whole world. He 'admitted' his petit-bourgeois deviations in a series of humiliating confessions in the drafting of which Dolores provided a guiding hand. At the end of the long process, psychologically destroyed, he was ordered to leave Carmen Rodríguez, now his wife, and his children, in Paris and go to Warsaw where he was to live and work in isolation, even prohibited from making contact with PCE exiles. He was offered work in publishing by the Polish authorities. He chose instead martyrdom and redemption through work in a motorcycle factory. Eventually joined by his wife and two children, he remained in Warsaw until 1964 when an extremely discreet rehabilitation began.[104]

Pasionaria's uncharacteristically vindictive part in the Antón affair overlapped with, and may have part of its explanation in, another tragic case. The fate of Francisco Antón and the role of Dolores Ibárruri therein cannot be understood other than as part of the Spanish dimension of a cycle of purge trials which affected the Communist movement in the years immediately preceding the death of Stalin. A series of trials was mounted in the aftermath of the disappearance in Prague of the head of the American Unitarian Welfare Service in Geneva, Noel Field. In the autumn of 1949, the Hungarian Foreign Minister, Laszlo Rajk, was tried and executed on charges of contact with Field who, it was alleged, was an American intelligence agent. Similar purges took place in the Bulgarian, Polish, Rumanian and other dependent parties. Throughout 1950, fourteen senior Czechoslovak Communists, including Rudolf Slansky, former Secretary General of the Czech Communist Party, and the deputy Foreign Minister, Artur London, were arrested. Eleven of the accused were Jews, most had fought as International Brigaders in the Spanish Civil War, and all were accused of Trotskyism. At the end of 1952, they were tried and eleven were executed. Among them was Bedrich Geminder, head of the department of international relations of the Central Committee of the Czech Communist Party.[105] Geminder, a close collaborator of Georgy Dimitrov in the Comintern in Moscow in the early 1940s, had been director of the foreign language broadcasts of Radio Moscow. His arrest had implications for Dolores Ibárruri because he had been the partner of Irene Falcón from 1935 to 1936 and from 1939 until Irene went with Pasionaria to France in 1945. Geminder had left Moscow and returned to Czechoslovakia in 1948. Broken by torture, Geminder 'confessed' to contacts with Field and with Trotskyists as well as to being a 'Jewish Nationalist' and other bourgeois capitalist deviations.

Irene Falcón now became *persona non grata* to the Stalinist authorities. She was removed from her post in Radio Pirenaica. That worse did not happen was thanks to the discreet protection of Dolores Ibárruri, who was herself taking a risk in doing so. Both Irene Falcón and her sister Kety were prevented from working. When her son, Mayo, was prevented from joining the CPSU, she appealed to Fernando Claudín who was officially in charge of the Spanish community in Moscow. He replied coldly, 'other families are already in Siberia'. Finally, Dolores was able to get work for both Irene and her sister in Radio Pekin. Since all subordinate Communist parties had to go along with Moscow, mount similar trials, and produce sacrificial victims, the PCE threw up three who were at least not likely to be shot in an

Eastern bloc jail cell. They were Antón and Manuel Azcárate in Paris and Jesús Monzón, who was already in a Francoist prison in Spain. Both Monzón and Azcárate had been helped by Field during the Second World War while they were working in the French resistance. Years later, all those involved in the Rajk–Slansky trials were exonerated when the Soviets recognized that Field was an anti-fascist and not an American agent.[106] It is in this context that Dolores Ibárruri's attack on Antón must be assessed. The vehemence with which she apparently turned on him may have reflected her bitterness at the perceived rejection implicit in his relationship with Carmen Rodríguez, but its coincidence with the Slansky trials strongly suggests the need both for her own self-preservation and for the protection of Irene Falcón. The extent to which Dolores might have been affected by the psychosis and paranoia of Moscow at the time is impossible to calculate with any exactitude.

The death of Stalin in March 1953 profoundly shocked Dolores.[107] It was a symptom that her epoch was passing. In the immediate aftermath, only the most slow and grudging effort was made to liberalize the PCE. Within eighteen months, the party held its Fifth Congress in Prague. The proceedings there revealed a willingness to change but also indicated how painfully gradual destalinization was likely to be. As PCE Secretary General, Dolores Ibárruri presented a long report whose main theme was the need for democratic unity against the Francoist clique. There were several aspects of it that were unlikely to seduce the Socialists, Republicans and Anarchists with whom unity was proposed. Not only did she accuse them of responsibility for Franco's victory in 1939 but she also implied that they were lackeys of American imperialism. A previous attempt at unity, the Alianza Nacional de Fuerzas Democráticas, sponsored by them in 1944, was maliciously dismissed as a police creation.[108] She used language reminiscent of the Stalinist purges to denounce 'degenerate' elements within the PCE itself. Like the victims of the Rajk and Slansky trials, they were accused of contact with Noel Field. If such references preoccupied Socialists, Republicans and Anarchists, their effect was hardly minimized by reiterated admiration for Eastern bloc countries and declarations of intent to follow the example of the CPSU.[109]

Pasionaria's report resounded with the Politburo's conviction that the leaderships of the other left-wing groups could be by-passed and their rank-and-file members simply absorbed into the PCE.[110] On the other hand, by comparison with the virulent sectarianism which had characterized the Communist attitude to Socialists and Anarchists since the departure of the PCE from the Republican government-in-exile in August 1947, Dolores Ibárruri's language represented a significant effort at moderation. Indeed, she spoke at length of the need to eliminate sectarian attitudes within the party. However, her tentative steps towards liberalization were surpassed by those of the PCE's organization secretary, Santiago Carrillo. He disagreed with the basic position of Dolores and the other 'historic' leaders that the object of a broad anti-Franco front had as its principal objective the restoration of the Second Republic. In late 1955, with the bulk of the party leadership in Bucharest for Pasionaria's sixtieth birthday celebrations, the Paris operational centre was being run by Santiago Carrillo, Fernando Claudín and Ignacio Gallego. News came in that the United Nations, including the Soviet Union, had voted in favour of the entry of sixteen new members, including Franco's Spain. The reaction of the PCE's Paris group was positive. In fact, the Russian vote had secured the entry of Hungary, Bulgaria, Rumania and Albania into the UNO. The Paris PCE group saw Spain's inclusion as more than a mere tit-for-tat and as part of the post-Stalin quest for peaceful co-existence. An inevitable recognition of the reality of the Franco regime's stability, it was a gesture to the West. In contrast, Dolores and the old guard denounced the United Nations for admitting Spain.

Carrillo sent Jorge Semprún to put the case for the 'young lions'. Semprún travelled to Czechoslovakia and then accompanied Pasionaria on a special closed train from Prague to Bucharest. He was astonished by the scale of the luxury in which senior party officials lived. He was impressed to note that Dolores, when presented with a cornucopia of delicacies, took only a glass of mineral water. He found her ready to listen but hostile. Anxious not to precipitate a major split in the Party, she said that she would consider his views.[111] Plans were then made to divide the Paris group. Claudín was included, with Uribe, Mije, Líster and Pasionaria, in the PCE delegation to the Twentieth Congress of the CPSU in February 1956. The intention was to 'recuperate' him prior to denouncing Carrillo for social democratic reformism and opportunism. Claudín had, however, agreed with Carrillo that they would go down together in the fight to renovate the party. In the intervals of the sessions of the Moscow Congress, Claudín resisted the blandishments of the old guard and forcibly put to Dolores Ibárruri his group's views on the poor showing of the PCE in the interior. At first, she sided with Uribe and things looked bleak for the liberalizers. Then suddenly, having had a preview of Khrushchev's secret report denouncing Stalinism, she decided that the views of Claudín and Carrillo were in line with the new currents of liberalism emanating from the Kremlin. Carrillo was sent for. He arrived in Bucharest unaware of Dolores' change of mind, wrongly convinced that he was about to receive the same treatment as Antón before him and, like Antón, meekly ready to accept the fate that the Party reserved for him, even if it meant being sent to Siberia. Mije and Líster saw what was happening and Uribe, who according to Vittorio Vidali seemed 'to be living in another world', was isolated. Shortly afterwards, he was replaced as director of the Paris centre by Carrillo, who was now virtually acting Secretary General.[112]

During the proceedings of the Twentieth Congress of the CPSU, Vittorio Vidali met Dolores in the corridors of the Kremlin and was struck by the consequences of her illness: 'How she had changed! I had always remembered her as she was when I knew her during the period of illegality when she had helped me in aiding the political prisoners and their families after the rising in Asturias, and during the Spanish Civil War: beautiful, majestic, now joyous, now sad; intelligent and a splendid impromptu speaker; her beautiful face had been marked by illness and her glance was less bright, but her voice was still the same and rang like a silver bell.' She spoke at the Congress, as she did at many important Soviet public occasions but, for Vidali, she was 'the most tragic figure at the congress', worn down by seventeen years of exile.[113] Even if she had suspected much of what was revealed in Khruschev's report, it came as bitter shock. She revered Stalin and the Soviet system. They had been central to her political activities for nearly thirty years. Khrushchev's demolition of all her certainties in some way diminished her will to fight on.[114]

The first fruit of the February 1956 revelations was an unprecedented flexibility in the PCE Politburo which led to the elaboration of the policy of national reconciliation. Free of the Stalinist stranglehold, Carrillo and the Paris leadership moved to meet the demands of the interior for efforts to find common ground with the new opposition to Franco emerging among students and Catholics. The denunciation of the Stalinist cult of personality had removed the halo of saintliness and the aura of infallibility from the PCE's own Secretary General. Dolores was not only depressed by the loss of Stalin but increasingly isolated and deprived of news by the Paris group.[115] After lengthy discussions during the spring of 1956, and cleverly playing on the implications of Khrushchev's speech, the Parisian young lions prevailed over Dolores and the PCE issued a major declaration in favour of burying the wartime hatreds fostered by the dictatorship. The new policy not only expressed Communist readiness to join with monarchists and Catholics in a future parliamentary regime but also indicated a commitment to peaceful change.[116] In August 1956, a plenum of the central committee was held near Berlin to ratify the new policy. It was to witness a dramatic extension of the process of liberalization tentatively begun at the PCE's Fifth Congress.

The two principal reports were presented by Dolores Ibárruri and Santiago Carrillo. They both reflected a desire to emulate the post-Stalinist example of the CPSU, a further indication of the influence of Moscow over the PCE's democratization. Nevertheless, the two reports also heralded important changes in the party's methods. Dolores Ibárruri, although temperamentally attached to the idea of the violent overthrow of Franco and the re-establishment of the Second Republic, was also sympathetic to the idea of a wide programme of pacific national reconciliation. In her report, Pasionaria paid tribute to the CPSU for its courage in publicly recognizing its errors and for pointing the way to different roads to socialism. She went on to speak of the need for alliances with conservative and liberal forces inside Spain in order to secure a peaceful transition to democracy.[117] This clearly represented a new departure from past sectarianism, but it was mild by comparison with what Carrillo had to say. His report was an intensely critical survey of the defects of the party leadership which clearly meant Dolores Ibárruri. Pungent and lucid, it indicated his ambition and his resolve to complete the process begun in 1954. He began by denouncing the cult of personality in the PCE, albeit absolving Dolores Ibárruri of complicity therein. He criticized the exiled leadership for subjectivism, sectarianism and isolation from the realities of the interior. Carrillo, as head of the operational centre of the PCE in Paris, was now Secretary General in all but name. When Dolores Ibárruri opposed his initiative for a peaceful nationwide general strike for 18 June 1959, he refused her protests. Although the strike was a failure, she ignored the opportunity to attack Carrillo. She knew that her day had now passed and, as she approached her sixty-fifth birthday, seemed content to accept the fact.[118] Carrillo asserted his authority and the PCE officially proclaimed that the strike had been a success. He put his case to a meeting of party leaders held at the end of July 1959 at Uspenskoie, near Moscow. Only Claudín opposed his interpretation of the strike.

The shock of the meeting was Dolores Ibárruri's announcement of her resignation as Secretary General. It is probable that, faced with the strength of Carrillo's position, she had decided to put an end to a false situation in which she was Secretary General in name only.[119] In fact, Khrushchev's report at the Twentieth Congress of the CPSU had already undermined her faith in the cause and made her readier to give up the leadership of the party. At the PCE's Sixth Congress, held from 28 to 31 January 1960, in Prague, Carrillo was formally confirmed as Secretary General and Dolores Ibárruri 'elevated' to the newly created post of Party President.[120] Her resignation was an impressive demonstration of her sense of realism and the fact that she put the Party above her own interests. She was also happy to withdraw into private life, looking after her grandchildren, Rubén, Fyodor and Dolores, on whom she lavished the love that she had been unable to give her own children. Faced with the harsh fact of the strength which Carrillo had accumulated during his many years as organization secretary, Pasionaria had no wish to destroy the Party with a fratricidal struggle. Carrillo's inexorable concentration of power continued, eliminating in 1964 his erstwhile allies Claudín and Semprún. Dolores played little part in that polemic other than, on their expulsion, to describe Claudín and Semprún more in sorrow than anger as 'bird-brains' (*cabezas de chorlito*).[121] The woman who had lived for so many years in Moscow, who knew more than anyone in the Party what power struggles were really about, thereby expressed her sadness at the tactical naïvety of Claudín and Semprún.

In her later years, Pasionaria's obsessions were loyalty to the PCE apparatus and Party unity. That was starkly revealed during the Russian invasion of Czechoslovakia in 1968. Despite her instinctive sympathies for the Russians, on 21 August 1968 Pasionaria went to the Kremlin to present the Spanish condemnation of the Soviet action. It took great courage to do so, bearing in mind that she still lived in Moscow. Indeed, in the presence of Luigi Longo and Giancarlo Pajetta of the Italian Communist Party, Mikhail Suslov brutally reminded her and Carrillo of the PCE's dependence on the Russians. In 1969, Brezhnev and Kosygin berated Dolores and Carrillo for two hours to change their critical line. Her standing in official circles in Moscow was never the same again. However, her prestige was too great for her to be openly attacked in the Soviet Union.[122] The Russians took their revenge by sponsoring a pro-Soviet break-away Communist Party under the Civil War General Enrique Líster. Even greater resolve was shown by Pasionaria, who backed Carrillo when he began the fight against these Stalinist elements. Despite having no desire to fight her old friends and comrades, she knew that the long-term survival of the PCE inside Spain required that it be distanced from Moscow. She was also influenced by her experience in Moscow of the first signs of the break-up of the system in terms of corruption, the black market, and the emergence of a mafia.[123]

The beginning of the end of her long exile was marked by the death of Franco. She greeted it with a broadcast on Radio Pirenaica. Putting aside the sordid internecine party struggles, her speech recaptured some of her old fire, her deep love for Spain and her capacity to give voice to the hopes of millions: 'Franco is dead but Spain, the eternal Spain, the Spain of democracy and freedom, the Spain which gave life to a new world, lives on in her wonderful people, capable of any achievement . . . In Spain, the dawn is beginning to break again, and today's dawn, breaking with the darkness of the past, is the dawn of a Spain in which the people will be the principal protagonists, in which once more human rights will be recognized along with those of the peoples of our multi-national and multi-regional fatherland.'[124] Two weeks later, her eightieth birthday was celebrated in Rome. In the Palace of Sport, a rejuvenated Dolores enthused a cheering crowd of 20,000 with an oratorical performance reminiscent of her great moments of the past. It was a nostalgic speech, looking back over nearly sixty years of militancy. Yet, after recalling 'the roads of blood and terrible sacrifices' made by the left in the struggle for democracy, she ended prophetically citing Cardinal Enrique y Tarancón who, on 27 November, had said, 'For Spain to advance along her way, the co-operation of all in a spirit of respect for all will be necessary.' Dolores Ibárruri said: 'With all the strength of my Communist convictions, I call for national reconciliation to put an end to the martial law and the divisions imposed on our country by the war and a Francoist dictatorship built on one million dead.' She took her leave with the words, 'I won't say goodbye but see you soon in Madrid!'[125] Six months later, on 13 May 1977, after nearly four decades in exile, she returned to Spain to play a significant role in the transition. The most successful parties were emphasizing their break with the past and it was felt that her identification with the Spanish Civil War might do some electoral damage to the PCE. It thus caused some chagrin to local activists when Carrillo imposed Dolores as a candidate for Asturias in the elections. Nevertheless, she campaigned energetically both locally and nationally. She was successfully elected.[126] For a brief period in the first parliament of the new democracy, she acted as Presidente de las Cortes, an astonishing symbol of national reconciliation.

Once more in 1977, she was called upon to stand up against her erstwhile Soviet friends when Carrillo was attacked by the Soviet journal *New Times* and by Anatoly Krasikov in *Pravda* in response to the publication of his book *Eurocommunism and the State*. She felt enormous reservations with regard to Eurocommunism, but kept her doubts to herself out of the same sense of realism, of horror at a possible division of the Party and of loyalty. She again supported Carrillo against the Soviet criticisms. She was to do the same in the mid-1980s, supporting the young Gerardo Iglesias when she saw that Carrillo's opposition to more change was leading the Party to disaster. There was no shortage of comments to the effect that this was her final revenge for thirty years of humiliations suffered at Carrillo's hands. That is as maybe. What is more crucial is to note that her participation in the latest crisis of the PCE showed once more that beyond the fiery public orator, there was a politician who, far from being carried away by passion, was cool and calculating and had both short-term tactical skills and long-term strategic vision. Both the public and private Dolores shared remarkable personal courage, wisdom and an iron loyalty to the Communist Party.

In August 1977, she felt the beginnings of heart problems and had a pace-maker fitted. She lived for another twelve years, to witness the consolidation of democracy and the collapse of the PCE. After a battle with pneumonia, she died on 12 November 1989, aged 93. Her body lay for three days at party headquarters and over 70,000 people came to pay their respects. At her funeral on 16 November in Madrid her coffin, draped in the Party's red flag, was drawn through crowds of many thousands of people. After many tributes, a recording of her last speech was played and the crowd sang *La Internacional.* The woman who had come to maturity as the Bolshevik revolution was taking place died as holes were being knocked in the Berlin Wall and the Soviet Union itself was collapsing. Yet neither that, nor the fact that Franco's victory in 1939 had obliged her to spend nearly forty years in wretchedly nostalgic exile, meant that she had been a failure. During the Spanish Civil War, she had progressed from being the mother of her party to a maternal symbol for large swathes of the population in the Republican zone. Throughout her life, her stature had grown commensurately with the scale of the problems with which she had to deal. She consistently met challenges with courage and was not diminished by defeat. In exile, just as they had done during the Civil War, her speeches and broadcasts helped to keep alive the spirit of resistance to the dictatorship and of the struggle for democracy in Spain.

Epilogue: The Three Spains of 1936

Since the return of democracy to Spain, commemoration of the Civil War has been muted. The silence was partly a consequence of the legacy of fear deliberately created during the post-war repression and by Franco's consistent pursuit of a policy of glorifying the victors and humiliating the vanquished.[1] It was also a result of what has come to be called the *pacto del olvido* (the pact of forgetfulness). An inadvertent effect of Franco's post-war policies was to imbue the bulk of the Spanish people with a determination never to undergo again either the violence experienced during the war or the repression thereafter. Stronger than any longing for revenge, this provided the basis for a new civic consciousness. Deliberately fomented by politicians and the majority of the press, it was manifested as a collective resolution to ensure a bloodless transition to democracy by renunciation of any settling of accounts after the death of Franco.[2]

A curious side-effect of the *pacto* has been a proliferation of interest in 'men of peace', the once-excoriated neutrals and those on both sides who put their efforts into diminishing the violence around them. Both personal and national tragedies are involved in the stories of all who died in the struggle between the two Spains. However, there were victims of the war who were neither the perceived enemies of the left murdered in the Republican zone nor the liberals and leftists imprisoned and executed by the Francoists. Those men who vainly attempted to bring peace to Spain – a crime for which some lost life or liberty and others lost fatherland and livelihood – have come to be known as *la tercera España* (the third Spain). During the Civil War and after, there were many who suffered in the cause of their moderation. There were some – Salvador de Madariaga, Niceto Alcalá Zamora, Cardinal Vidal i Barraquer, Miguel de Unamuno, José Ortega y Gasset, to name but a few of the more celebrated – whose neutrality earned them ostracism and internal or external exile. There were other men of peace whose material and moral sufferings at the hands of the Francoists were more considerable.

This book grew out of interconnected reflections. One, discussed in the prologue, concerned the relationship between individuals and historical processes more often examined in terms of collectivities. The second, largely inspired by the work of the Catalan monk, Dom Hilari Raguer, concerned the third Spain. In February 1998 the Spanish edition of my book, entitled *Las tres Españas del 36*, received Spain's biggest non-fiction literary prize, 'Así fue – la Historia rescatada'. As a consequence, it received considerable attention in the media. Apart from very substantial review coverage, there were several television and radio debates and a number of newspaper editorials on the subject of 'the three Spains'.[3] The attention given to the book was the result of the fact that the title struck a particular chord at a particular moment. The title was, to a large extent, a literary conceit: the book might more properly have been called 'the many Spains of 1936'. I believe that it had such resonance because it had emerged from the two sets of reflections mentioned above. The book looked at individuals of left, right and centre and tried to do so with some empathy for human frailty. The war of 1936–9 destroyed the lives of millions of people. Many of those who lived through the war, irrespective of their ideology, and many members of subsequent generations have struggled to make sense of what seemed an unutterably senseless episode of national self-destruction. The book perhaps helped them to see that most of the nine protagonists, and, by extension, many other individuals, were overwhelmed by extreme situations and tried to make the best of them. The consideration of a much amplified, if rather loose, definition of that third Spain which was not responsible for the bloodthirsty extremisms of the far left and the far right, struck a chord with a Spanish audience perhaps because it made it possible to think about the Civil War not in terms of good and evil but in terms of human weakness.

Although prior to the publication of *Las tres Españas del 36* there had been recognition of the extent to which there were at least three Spains rather than the two monolithic antagonists of Franco's rhetoric, it had tended to be confined to indisputable neutrals. The classic cases were individuals such as Salvador de Madariaga and the philosopher José Ortega y Gasset, who refused to take part in the war. Madariaga was subjected to considerable criticism because he spent much of the war trying to arrange a negotiated peace – a possibly misguided effort which nonetheless involved considerable courage and sacrifice. The object of contempt on the left, where he was regarded as having abandoned the Republic, Madariaga was similarly excoriated within the Nationalist zone. Others who took no part in the war included Centrists such the conservative ex-President of the Republic, Niceto Alcalá Zamora, and the leader of the Radical Party, Alejandro Lerroux. They were not welcome in either zone. However, 'abstaining from the war', to use Madariaga's phrase, was a luxury permitted to only a tiny minority of intellectuals and politicians. Madariaga and Ortega and some other exiles belonged to the 'Third Spain' but they were not the only ones.

Inspired by the work of Father Raguer, and going some way beyond it, *Las tres Españas del 36* endeavoured to widen the concept of the Third Spain from a narrow group of wartime exiles to embrace large segments of both sides in the Spanish Civil War. There were others who suffered in various ways, at the hands of both left and right, for their moderation. A typical case was that of Manuel Portela Valladares, the moderate conservative who had been Centrist prime minister from the end of 1935 until the elections of February 1936. He had refused to give legal sanction to an attempt by General Franco, at the time Chief of the General Staff, to use the army to prevent the implementation of the election results.[4] Portela was a wealthy man, with widespread interests in banking and newspapers, married to an aristocrat, la Condesa de Brías. The military rising found him in his palatial mansion between the Diagonal and the Paseo de Gracia in Barcelona. Aware that he was in danger from the anarchists, with the help of the Catalan regional government, the Generalitat, he crossed the city disguised as a woman, reached the port and took ship for France. He was no more welcome in Nationalist Spain. In both zones, his properties were confiscated and his houses ransacked. In exile, he suffered considerable difficulties in Vichy France during the Second World War as Franco tried to have him extradited to face trial in Spain.[5]

Another exile from Barcelona was the Catalan politician Joan Baptista Roca i Caball, one of the founders of the Catholic Catalan Nationalist party, Unió Democràtica de Catalunya. During the campaign for the elections of February 1936, Roca had refused an offer from the Catalan President, Lluis Companys, of two places on the electoral list of the Popular Front on the grounds that a party which affirmed its

Christian inspiration could not enter an electoral list containing marxists. When the war started, the hostility of the extreme anarchist group, the Federación Anarqista Ibérica, to this devout Catholic forced him to leave Barcelona. He went to Paris where he worked with the Catholic philosopher Jacques Maritain in the Comité pour la paix civile en Espagne. As a Catalanist, he was *persona non grata* in Franco's Spain. When he was eventually permitted to return, years after the war, he was not, of course, allowed to recover his confiscated property.[6]

A much worse fate befell Roca Caball's friend and party colleague, Manuel Carrasco i Formiguera, a prominent Catalanist who happened also to be a deeply pious Catholic. He was a conservative of common sense and humanity who worked in the early months of the war as a legal adviser to the Finance Ministry of the Generalitat – efforts which would be used by the Francoists to justify his execution. His Catholic beliefs, however, provoked the outrage of the anarchists and a denunciation of his conservative past by the newspaper *Solidaridad Obrera* was effectively an invitation for him to be assassinated. He was forced to flee his beloved Catalonia. He undertook a mission to the Basque Country on behalf of the Generalitat. He returned to Barcelona to collect his family and, on 2 March 1937, he set off with his wife and six of his eight children through France. The final part of the journey to Bilbao was from Bayonne by sea. The steamer *Galdames* on which they were travelling was shelled and then captured by the Nationalist battlecruiser, *Canarias*. His wife and children were imprisoned in four separate prisons. The pious Catholic Carrasco was tried and executed by firing squad on Easter Saturday, 9 April 1938, because he was a Republican and a Catalanist.[7]

Similar contradictions determined the fate of the most prominent progressive in the Spanish Church, the Archbishop of Tarragona, Cardinal Francesc Vidal i Barraquer. At the beginning of the Spanish Civil War, despite enormous popularity and friendship with many prominent Republicans, he was arrested in Tarragona by militiamen of the FAI. The Generalitat – which worked hard to save many religious from the anti-clerical fury of the anarchists – managed to secure his release and, for his safety, secure his passage to Lucca in Italy where he spent the rest of the war in various efforts to bring about a mediated peace. In punishment for this, Franco never permitted him to return to Spain.[8]

The fate of many moderate Basque Catholics was equally harrowing. Fourteen Basque priests were executed by the Francoists in the autumn of 1936 because of their Basque nationalist views. After the fall of the Basque Country in the summer of 1937, several hundred secular and regular clergy were imprisoned, exiled or transferred out of the region.[9] In the Republican zone, the scale of the atrocities committed against innocent religious was far greater. There were many nuns and monks who had tended the sick, instructed the ignorant, fed the hungry, clothed the naked and visited the imprisoned. They had been doing something which the ecclesiastical hierarchy regarded as controversial but that did not save more than 6000 of them from death at the hands of anti-clericals during the Civil War.[10]

Another lamentable, if hardly so tragic, case was that of Mateo Múgica y Urrestarazu, Bishop of Vitoria, who claimed to support the military rebels yet suffered at the hands of Franco. He had been expelled by the Republic in 1931 for his outspoken hostility to the regime. As a Basque nationalist, however, he was the victim of frequent humiliations and death threats at the hands of Francoist officers and Falangists. He had reason to believe that the ruling military Junta de Burgos planned to have him executed. The Archbishop of Valencia, Prudencio Melo y Alcade, hearing this, intervened and warned the military authorities of the international repercussions of doing so. It was decided instead to summon Múgica to Burgos. His crime was to havc proclaimed that Basque nationalists were every bit as Catholic as those professing Spanish nationalism. He was to be murdered along the way and thus appear as just another casual victim of the war. The attack was to be carried out by a Falangist hit-squad led by Ramón Castaños, the Jefe Provincial of the Falange in Alava. Múgica refused to go. Múgica was then informed by Cardinal Isidro Gomá that he must leave Spain. He was expelled from Francoist Spain and forced into exile in Italy. There he denounced the bombing of Guernica to the Vatican, as a result of which Franco determined that he would never be permitted to return to his diocese. Although he always maintained his general support for the Francoist cause, Múgica refused to sign the Spanish hierarchy's Collective Letter in favour of the Nationalists, 'To the Bishops of the Whole World', published on 1 July 1937. Explaining his decision to the Vatican, he wrote, 'According to the Spanish bishops, justice is well served in Franco's Spain, and that is just not true. I have bulging lists of devout Christians and exemplary priests murdered with impunity, without trial and without any juridical formality.'[11]

The persecution of moderates was not confined to Catalonia and the Basque Country. Luis Lucia was another who fell foul of both sides. Lucia was a devout Catholic and leader of the Christian Democrat party, the Derecha Regional Valenciana, a component of the Catholic authoritarian party, the CEDA, the Confederación Española de Derechas Autónomas. At the beginning of the war, he issued a statement condemning violence and affirming his commitment to Republican legality. Nevertheless, given his prominence as a right-wing politician, he went into hiding from the left. Lucia was concealed in various farmhouses in the north east of Castellón and Teruel until captured by anarchists in February 1937. He spent nine months in various prisons in Valencia and was then transferred to Barcelona. For two years, he awaited trial as a right-wing Catholic then, on 25 January 1939, the day before the Francoists took the Catalan capital, he managed to escape. He was arrested on 12 February by the Francoist authorities and, in a summary trial two weeks later, he was tried and sentenced to death for the alleged offence of military rebellion. In fact, his crime was to have denounced the uprising and to have sought a political solution to the crisis of July 1936 by proposing a centre government to negotiate with the military rebels. In early March 1939, his sentence was commuted to thirty years in prison.[12]

The middle-class liberals of the Valencian republican party, the Partido de Unión Republicana Autonomista, were also caught between the two sides in the Civil War. Several prominent members of the party were murdered at the beginning of the war by left-wing militiamen, their crime being their parliamentary support for right-wing governments in 1934 and 1935. The PURA's leader, Sigfrido Blasco, son of the novelist Vicente Blasco Ibáñez, went into hiding and eventually managed to escape to Italy. He then went into exile in France along with other members of the PURA. At the end of the war, as a punishment for his Republican past, his property was confiscated by the Francoist authorities. He remained in exile until Franco's death.[13]

The Valencians Lucia and Blasco at least did not lose their lives for their beliefs. More horrendous were the cases of Besteiro, Carrasco y Formiguera and of a Catalan soldier, General Domingo Batet. In 1934, Batet was the general commanding one of Spain's eight military regions, the so-called División Orgánica IV (Catalonia), the post which before the coming of the Second Republic was the Capitanía General de la Cuarta Región Militar. When the President of the Catalan regional government, the Generalitat, declared independence on 6 October in an attempt to forestall revolution, Batet responded by employing common sense and moderation to restore the authority of the central government and thereby prevented a potential bloodbath. Franco, masterminding the repression of the rebellions of Asturias and Catalonia, was infuriated by Batet's failure to impose savage punishment on the Catalans like that inflicted by Lieutenant Colonel Yagüe on the miners of Asturias. In June 1936, Batet was placed in charge of the VI División Orgánica, whose headquarters were in Burgos, an area of military reaction and one of the nerve centres of the uprising of 18 July. Faced with the virtually unanimous decision of his officers to join the rising, Batet bravely refused to join them. His commitment to his oath of loyalty to the Republic guaranteed his trial and execution. Franco deliberately and maliciously intervened in the supposedly independent judicial process to ensure that Batet would be executed.[14]

There were many other cases of soldiers who were punished, if not for their equidistance from both sides, for their failure to manifest the requisite degree of commitment to one cause or another. A curious example is that of General Miguel Campins, Franco's one-time friend and second-in-command at the Academia General Militar de Zaragoza. Campins was tried on 14 August in Seville for the crime of 'rebellion'. As military commander in Granada, he had delayed two days before joining the rising. Campins was sentenced to death and shot on 16 August.[15] Campins was hardly a partisan of the Republic. He was simply a victim of the fanatical extremism of General Gonzalo Queipo de Llano who ran a virtually independent fief in the south of Spain. Another general who met an appalling fate was Eduardo López Ochoa. He had been charged with the repression of the Asturian rebellion of October 1934 and, in consequence, was criticized by the left as the instrument of repression and by hard-line rightists, including Franco, for his failure to apply exemplary terror. At the beginning of the war, López Ochoa was under arrest in Madrid, charged with excesses carried out after the insurrection in Asturias. He was dragged from the military hospital at Carabanchel by a mob and murdered.[16]

There are also innumerable cases of individuals who loyally served one side or the other but suffered considerable embarrassment because they could not meet the requisite levels of fanaticism. A notable case on the nationalist side was the able leader of the Catholic authoritarian party, the CEDA, José María Gil Robles, who was insufficiently extremist for the tastes of Franco's coterie. At the beginning of the war, he had taken refuge in the southern French resort of Biarritz.

He announced that he was totally committed to the rising but could help it better from abroad. Expelled from France, he proceeded to Portugal, where he helped Franco's brother Nicolás to establish an unofficial Nationalist embassy or 'Agency of the Burgos Junta' in the Hotel Aviz in Lisbon. Gil Robles played a vital role in organizing the purchase of arms and other supplies, propaganda and financial assistance for the rebel cause. However, on several visits to rebel Spain, notably at the end of July, in late August, in mid-September 1936 and May and July 1937, he found himself increasingly unwelcome. He was accused of being responsible for the Civil War, because his tactic of 'accidentalism' or working within parliamentary legality during the Second Republic had delayed the necessary annihilation of the left. In consequence, he had to be protected by the military from hostile Falangists.

Despite the fact that, throughout the war, his public statements were those of the Caudillo's eager subordinate, Gil Robles became *persona non grata* in the Nationalist zone. He welcomed Franco's forced unification of the various Nationalist political groupings. His party was dissolved, its leadership and middle-rank functionaries absorbed into the Francoist Movimiento. Several of the CEDA's leaders found preferment under Franco but Gil Robles was not one of them. He was still derided as having delayed the inevitable war against corrupt democracy. It served for nothing that he accepted the unification. In the charged atmosphere of war, Gil Robles's legalist stance during the Republic had no place. Indeed, as the catastrophist groups which had worked to overthrow the Republic became more enmeshed in the killing, the more inclined they were to see Gil Robles and his 'accidentalism' as simply treacherous. This experience at the hands of his co-religionaries contributed to Gil Robles's post-war evolution into a democratic monarchist opponent of the Franco regime.[17]

The discomfit of the erstwhile Socialist philosophy professor, Julián Besteiro, was of a different order. Believing naïvely that he was helping to avoid the division of Spain, he had entered into contact with the Nationalist Fifth Column within the Republican zone. He was informed by his contact, the Professor of International Law, Antonio Luna García, that 'the Generalísimo guaranteed the life and freedom of all those who, without having committed common crimes themselves, contributed to the surrender without bloodshed of the reds. These conditions, which were transmitted directly to the military by me personally, were also extended to include the civilians who collaborated with them.'[18] These circumstances applied fully to Besteiro and no one did more than he (to the extent of betraying many of his erstwhile comrades) in an effort to bring about a Republican surrender. Yet he was imprisoned and left to die without adequate medical assistance. In the late 1960s Antonio Luna, by then Ambassador to Austria, was visiting a Jesuit residence at the University of Innsbruck and told a Spanish priest that 'On behalf of Franco, I promised them life and freedom if they avoided a massacre at the end of the war. They accepted, kept their word and then they were almost all shot.'[19] That Besteiro's own essential honesty led him to take Franco's word is a sad commentary on the Caudillo.

It can plausibly be argued that these individuals – Lucia, Carrasco i Formiguera, Roca i Caball, Batet, Vidal i Barraquer, Múgica, Portela Valladares, Besteiro – all belong to the Third Spain. They all suffered because of the extremism of one or both sides. Having said that, it does not mean that they were in some way morally superior to those who loyally served one side. Only two of the individuals studied in this book – Madariaga and Besteiro – fit easily into the conventional definition of the Third Spain as that of the neutrals. On the other hand, only three – Franco, Millán Astray and Dolores Ibárruri – categorically fit into the general assumptions about extremism. Even then, although she never wavered in her commitment to the victory of the Republic, the Communist leader never manifested the bloody cruelty that was an everyday habit for the two generals. General Millán Astray was probably the person who contributed most to the early brutalization of Franco and the wartime propagandistic exaltation of violence on the Nationalist side. Ultimately, the scale of his violence was overshadowed by that of his erstwhile assistant. Interviewed in Tangiers on 28 July 1936, General Franco revealed that he had learned the lessons of the founder of the Spanish Foreign Legion. He told the American war correspondent, Jay Allen, 'Shortly, very shortly, my troops will have pacified the country and all of this will soon seem like a nightmare.' Allen responded, 'that means that you will have to shoot half Spain?', at which a smiling Franco said, 'I repeat, at whatever cost.'[20]

The partisan callousness was entirely at odds with Azaña's all-embracing patriotism; the single-minded Caudillo determined to redeem the nation by blood, Azaña the man of reason and peace tormented by doubts. On the very day, 18 July 1937, that Azaña dissociated himself from any ambition to exterminate the adversary, on the grounds that to do so would be a moral abomination,[21] Franco enthused over his own 'glorious epic' in which he praised his bloodiest victories 'the assault on Badajoz' and 'the capture of Málaga'. He described the Spaniards against whom these triumphs were achieved as 'rabbles of murderers', 'assassins and thieves'.[22]

If Julián Besteiro belonged to the Third Spain, then could a case be made for Azaña, who remained at his post although horrified by the war and the killing on both sides? Or even for Prieto, whose sentiments were hardly different? It might be stretching the definition too far, but the fact remains that Azaña and Prieto, even the imprisoned José Antonio Primo de Rivera, hardly fall into the conventional categories of extremism. The 'Third Spain' was the Spain of democratic dialogue and understanding, and embraced a wide spectrum of the population. Prieto wrote at the end of 1938, 'The philosophical statement that there is a grain of truth in all ideas goes way back. It comes to mind because of the manuscripts which José Antonio Primo de Rivera left in the prison at Alicante. Perhaps in Spain we have not calmly compared the respective ideologies to find the coincidences, which are perhaps fundamental, or to measure the divergences, which are probably secondary, with a view to finding out if they were worth resolving on the battlefield.'[23] In fact, long before the war began, the humanity and patriotism which underlay Prieto's words had been revealed often, most notably perhaps on 1 May 1936, in the celebrated speech made during the campaign for the re-run election at Cuenca. His words had earned Prieto the praise of, amongst many others, José Antonio Primo de Rivera.[24] That is not so surprising. In 1935, rather flippantly but with some insight, Miguel de Unamuno wrote of José Antonio Primo de Rivera, 'He is too fine, too much of a gentleman and, deep down, too shy to be a leader, let alone a dictator.' Whatever he did before, José Antonio Primo de Rivera had undergone a considerable ideological and intellectual evolution between his arrest on 14 March 1936 and his execution on 20 November 1936.[25] A case could be made to the same end for Dolores Ibárruri and Pilar Primo de Rivera. Neither questioned the rectitude of their cause but neither indulged in the kind of bloodlust associated with the atrocities and revenge killings.

It is hardly surprising that Azaña tried to save the life of José Antonio Primo de Rivera.[26] Like Prieto, the President of the Republic could not have been more devastated by the outbreak of the war. It provoked a depression from which he would never recover.[27] The resort to war signified the destruction of his lifetime project of rationalizing the politics of Spain. His patriotic outrage can be sensed in his broadcast to the people of Spain on the night of 23 July 1936:

> And those who are responsible for this destruction, those who bear the guilt of the horrendous crime of having ripped apart the heart of the nation, those who carry the horrendous blame of so much bloodshed and so much destruction, are they not yet convinced that their undertaking has failed? How long will they persist in their ambition? How long are they going to scandalize the world, bringing shame on the name of Spaniards and making us all shed tears of pain for the victims they have caused, the innocent victims of their ambition and their crime?[28]

Speaking in the Ayuntamiento de Valencia on 21 January 1937, he said, 'We are waging a terrible war, a war on the body of our own fatherland; but we make war because they make war on us.' 'Peace will come and I hope that it will fill you all with joy. But not me. Allow me to make a terrible confession because, for me as President, these circumstances can harvest nothing but terrible suffering, the torture of my Spanish soul and of my Republican sentiments . . . it is impossible to triumph over compatriots.'[29] The same sense of outrage and despair enveloped Prieto. Just as Azaña, despite his despair, maintained the dignity of his office, Prieto, who was hardly less desperate and even more pessimistic, mobilized immense reserves of energy for the Republican war effort.

Azaña spoke in Barcelona on the second anniversary of the outbreak of the Spanish Civil War. His words were a moving epitaph for those who had died on both sides and a terrible indictment of the policy of the victors:

> I am not going to apply to this Spanish drama the simple doctrine of the old adage that 'it's an ill wind . . .' It is not true, it is not true. But it is a moral obligation, above all for those who suffer war, when it ends, as we hope it will end, to draw from its lesson and from its warning the greatest benefit possible. And when the torch passes to other hands, to other men, to other generations, may they remember, if some day their blood boils with anger and once more the Spanish temper is infuriated with intolerance and with hate and with the appe-

> tite for destrution, let them think of the dead and hear their warning; the lesson of those men who fell bravely in the battle, fighting generously for a grandiose ideal and who now, locked in the embrace of mother earth, have no more hatred, have no more resentment and who send us, with the glimmers of their light, tranquil and remote like that of a star, the message of the eternal fatherland which says to all its children: paz, piedad y perdón (peace, pity and forgiveness).[30]

It would be thirty-nine years before Azaña's message of reconciliation was implemented in the peaceful transition to democracy. A vengeful repression had to be suffered by the defeated who remained in Spain and a painful exile by those forced from their homes. Prieto and Salvador de Madariaga spent much of the rest of their lives trying to bring about Azaña's plea for 'paz, piedad y perdón'. Prieto had been dead for four months when his and Madariaga's efforts came near to fruition. Monarchists, Catholics and repentant Falangists from inside Spain – led by Gil Robles – met exiled Socialists and Basque and Catalan nationalists – led by Madariaga – in Munich at the IV Congress of the European Movement from 5 to 8 June 1962. The Munich conference was in many respects a rehearsal for the later transition to democracy. It was hardly surprising, therefore, that Franco should denounce it in the most venomous terms. In fact, his repressive regime would survive for a further fourteen years. However, the message of Munich was one that would be reflected in the political behaviour of the mass of the Spanish population in the years following 1976. Traumatized by the horrors of sectarian extremism witnessed during the Civil War and the postwar repression, most Spaniards rejected political violence and the legacy of Franco, his deliberate policy of maintaining the divisions between victors and vanquished. Dolores Ibárruri returned to Spain and took part in the first elections since the Civil War, elections conducted in a spirit of national reconciliation. In that sense, the two Spains which fought between 1936 and 1939 had become the Third Spain of democratic consensus prefigured in Azaña's Barcelona speech.

NOTES

PROLOGUE: In Extremis

1 [Franco Bahamonde, Francisco], *Palabras del Caudillo 19 abril 1937–31 diciembre 1938* (Barcelona: Ediciones Fe, 1939) p. 273.
2 [Franco Bahamonde, Francisco], *Franco ha dicho . . . recopilación de las más importantes declaraciones del Caudillo desde la iniciacion del Alzamiento Nacional hasta el 31 de diciembre de 1946* (Madrid: Editorial Carlos-Jaime, 1947) pp. 252–3.
3 Conversation of the author with Miquel Roca i Junyent. See also Martin Blinkhorn, *Carlism and Crisis in Spain 1931–1939* (Cambridge: Cambridge University Press, 1975) p. 260.
4 I am grateful to Fernando Urbaneja who recounted this anecdote to me.
5 Ronald Fraser, *Blood of Spain. The Experience of Civil War* (London: Allen Lane, 1979) p. 167; Rafael Abella, *La vida cotidiana durante la guerra civil* (Barcelona: Planeta, 1978) pp. 61–8.

1 The Bridegroom of Death: Millán Astray

1 Paul Preston, *Franco: A Biography* (London: HarperCollins, 1993) pp. 91–2, 186, 250–1.
2 Carlos de Silva, *General Millán Astray. El Legionario* (Barcelona: AHR, 1956) pp. 39–43.
3 Silva, *Millán Astray*, pp. 46–7, 52–64.
4 David S. Woolman, *Rebels in the Rif: Abd el Krim and the Rif Rebellion* (Stanford: Stanford University Press, 1969) p. 66. On José Millán Astray senior, see Carlos Rojas, *¡Muera la inteligencia! ¡Viva la muerte! Salamanca 1936. Unamuno y Millán Astray frente a frente* (Barcelona: Planeta, 1995) pp. 72–80.
5 See an anonymous article based on interviews with Millán Astray's daughter, Peregrina, 'Militar y caballero. José Millán Astray', *El Figaro*, 28 January 1995, p. 58.
6 Silva, *Millán Astray*, pp. 67–85.
7 Silva, *Millán Astray*, pp. 91–106.
8 Silva, *Millán Astray*, p. 108.
9 José Millán Astray, 'Prólogo', Comandante Franco, *Marruecos: Diario de una Bandera* (Madrid: Editorial Pueyo, 1922) p. 7; General Millán Astray, *Franco. El Caudillo* (Salamanca: M. Quero y Simón, 1939) pp. 9–12.
10 Silva, *Millán Astray*, pp. 109–18.
11 Silva, *Millán Astray*, pp. 120–35.
12 Arturo Barea, *La forja de un rebelde* (Buenos Aires: Losada, 1951) p. 315; Franco, *Diario*, pp. 18–19.
13 *Tauima Legión*, No.20, enero de 1954, p. 3; Silva, *Millán Astray*, pp. 124–30, 150; Carlos Blanco Escolá, *La Academia General Militar de Zaragoza (1928–1931)* (Barcelona: Labor, 1989) pp. 86–9; Julio Busquets, *El militar de carrera en España* 3ª edición (Barcelona: Ariel, 1984) pp. 100–1.
14 Millán Astray, *Franco*, pp. 171–2; Silva, *Millán Astray*, pp. 143–7; Woolman, *Rebels in the Rif*, p. 66.
15 Inazo Nitobé, *Bushido. The Soul of Japan. An Exposition of Japanese Thought* (New York: G. P. Putnams, 1905). In his prologue to the Spanish version – *El Bushido* (Madrid: Gráficas Ibarra, 1941) – Millán Astray describes himself as the translator although elsewhere

mention is made of the collaboration of Luis Alvarez de Espejo. See also Ernesto Giménez Caballero, *Memorias de un dictador* (Barcelona: Planeta, 1979) p. 275; Silva, *Millán Astray*, p. 144.

16 Francisco Franco Salgado-Araujo, *Mi vida junto a Franco* (Barcelona: Planeta, 1977) p. 42; Silva, *Millán Astray*, p. 146.

17 Barea, *La forja*, p. 315.

18 Arturo Barea, *The Struggle for the Spanish Soul* (London: Secker & Warburg, 1941) pp. 30–1.

19 Ramón Garriga, *La Señora de El Pardo* (Barcelona: Planeta, 1979) p. 40; José Martín Blázquez, *I Helped to Build an Army: Civil War Memoirs of a Spanish Staff Officer* (London: Secker & Warburg, 1939) p. 302; Herbert R. Southworth, *Antifalange: estudio crítico de 'Falange en la guerra de España: la Unificación y Hedilla' de Maximiano García Venero* (Paris: Ruedo Ibérico, 1967) pp. xxi–xxii; Guillermo Cabanellas, *La guerra de los mil días* 2 vols (Buenos Aires: Grijalbo, 1973) II, p. 792.

20 Preston, *Franco*, pp. 27–34.

21 Claude Martin, *Franco, soldado y estadista* (Madrid: Fermín Uriarte, 1965) pp. 129–30.

22 Mijail Koltsov, *Diario de la guerra de España* (Paris: Ruedo Ibérico, 1963) pp. 88–9; John Whitaker, 'Prelude to World War: A Witness from Spain', *Foreign Affairs*, Vol. 21, No. 1, October 1942, pp. 105–6.

23 Barea, *La forja*, pp. 315–16.

24 Barea, *Struggle for the Spanish Soul*, p. 23.

25 Hilari Raguer, *El general Batet. Franco contra Batet: Crónica de una venganza* (Ediciones Península, Barcelona, 1996) p. 331.

26 Silva, *Millán Astray*, p. 38.

27 Eugenio Vegas Latapie, *Los caminos del desengaño: memorias políticas II 1936–1938* (Madrid: Tebas, 1987) p. 173.

28 Juan de la Cierva y Peñafiel, *Notas de mi vida* (Madrid: Instituto Editorial Reus, 1955) p. 281; Niceto Alcalá Zamora, *Memorias* (Barcelona: Planeta, 1977) pp. 76–7; Carolyn P. Boyd, *Praetorian Politics in Liberal Spain* (Chapel Hill: University of North Carolina Press, 1979) p. 192.

29 Giménez Caballero, *Memorias*, p. 43.

30 Julián Zugazagoitia, *Guerra y vicisitudes de los españoles* 2ª edición, 2 vols (Paris: Librería Española, 1968) I, p. 85.

31 Franco Salgado-Araujo, *Mi vida*, pp. 52–3.

32 Millán Astray, *Franco*, p. 17.

33 Silva, *Millán Astray*, pp. 165–9.

34 Torcuato Luca de Tena, *Franco, Sí, pero . . .* (Barcelona: Planeta, 1993) p. 31.

35 Silva, *Millán Astray*, p. 229.

36 José María Pemán, *Mis almuerzos con gente importante* (Barcelona: Dopesa, 1970) p. 138.

37 Dionisio Ridruejo, *Sombras y bultos* (Barcelona: Destino, 1977) pp. 110, 112.

38 Rafael Abella, *Por el imperio hacia Dios. Crónica de una posguerra (1939–1955)* (Barcelona: Planeta, 1978) pp. 171–2.

39 Ridruejo, *Sombras y bultos*, p. 110.

40 Boyd, *Praetorian Politics*, p. 214. The dispute between Millán Astray and the Junteros led to the publication of a short book, Francisco Madrid, *El ruidísimo pleito de la juntas de defensa y Millán Astray* (Barcelona: Gráficos Costa, 1922).

41 Boyd, *Praetorian Politics*, pp. 225–6.

42 Boyd, *Praetorian Politics*, pp. 228–9; De la Cierva, *Notas*, p. 281; Joaquín Arrarás, *Historia de la Cruzada española* 8 vols (Madrid: Ediciones Españolas, 1939–43) I, p. 121; Silva, *Millán Astray*, pp. 169–76; Stanley G. Payne, *Politics and the Military in Modern Spain* (Stanford: Stanford University Press, 1967) pp. 182–3.

43 Franco Salgado-Araujo, *Mi vida*,

pp. 63, 67–8; Blanco Escolá, *La Academia General Militar*, p. 99; Silva, *Millán Astray*, pp. 175–84.

44 Carlos Navajas Zubeldia, *Ejército, Estado y sociedad en España (1923–1930)* (Logroño: Instituto de Estudios Riojanos, 1991) p. 56; Francisco Franco Salgado-Araujo, *Mis conversaciones privadas con Franco* (Barcelona: Planeta, 1976) p. 361; Silva, *Millán Astray*, pp. 184–91, 243.

45 Gabriel Maura Gamazo, *Bosquejo histórico de la Dictadura. I 1923–1926* (Madrid: Tipografía de Archivos, 1930) p. 217.

46 Franco Salgado-Araujo, *Mi vida*, p. 75; Blanco Escolá, *La Academia General Militar*, pp. 12, 99–100; Guillermo Cabanellas, *Cuatro generales* 2 vols (Barcelona: Planeta, 1977) I, pp. 93, 140.

47 Blanco Escolá, *La Academia General Militar*, pp. 87–9, 102–22.

48 Franco Salgado-Araujo, *Mi vida*, p. 97.

49 Manuel Azaña, *Obras completas*, 4 vols (Mexico DF: Oasis, 1966–8) IV, p. 226.

50 Franco Salgado-Araujo, *Mis conversaciones*, p. 499; Luis Galinsoga & Francisco Franco-Salgado, *Centinela de occidente (Semblanza biográfica de Francisco Franco)* (Barcelona: Editorial AHR, 1956) p. 158; Silva, *Millán Astray*, p. 196.

51 Manuel Portela Valladares, *Memorias. Dentro del drama español* (Madrid: Alianza, 1988) p. 184.

52 Alejandro Lerroux, *La Pequeña historia. Apuntes para la Historia grande vividos y redactados por el autor* (Buenos Aires: Editorial Cimera, 1945) p. 346; Franco Salgado-Araujo, *Mi vida*, p. 113.

53 He figures in group photographs of the senior commanders and the Ministers reproduced in Ricardo de la Cierva, *Francisco Franco: un siglo de España* 2 vols (Madrid: Editora Nacional, 1973) I, pp. 394, 407.

54 Ministerio de la Guerra Estado Mayor Central, *Anuario militar de España. Año 1936* (Madrid: Imprenta y Talleres del Ministerio de la Guerra, 1936) p. 361.

55 Millán Astray, *Franco*, p. 27; Cabanellas, *Cuatro generales* I, pp. 431–2; José Ignacio Escobar, *Así empezó* (Madrid: G. del Toro, 1974) p. 166; Silva, *Millán Astray*, pp. 233–5.

56 Cabanellas, *Cuatro generales* II, pp. 424, 431.

57 *ABC* (Sevilla) 18 August 1936; Franco Salgado-Araujo, *Mi vida*, p. 190; Vegas Latapie, *Los caminos*, p. 173.

58 José P. San Román Colino, *Legislación del Gobierno Nacional, 1936 segundo semestre* (Avila, SHADE, 1937) pp. 93–5, quoted by Herbert Rutledge Southworth, *Guernica! Guernica!: A Study of Journalism, Propaganda and History* (Berkeley: University of California Press, 1977) p. 411.

59 *ABC* (Sevilla), 14 August 1936.

60 *ABC* (Sevilla), 15, 16 August 1936; Antonio Bahamonde y Sánchez de Castro, *Un año con Queipo: memorias de un nacionalista* (Barcelona: Ediciones Españolas, 1938) pp. 34–5; Cabanellas, *Cuatro generales* II, pp. 253–4.

61 Jaime del Burgo, *Conspiración y guerra civil española* (Madrid: Alfaguara, 1970) pp. 158–9.

62 Pedro Laín Entralgo, *Descargo de conciencia (1930–1960)* (Barcelona: Barral Editores, 1976) pp. 178–9.

63 See, in this regard, Millán Astray, *Franco*, p. 19, where he writes 'Franco, with our martyr Goded, and the present writer, managed to oppose the fearful path on which Spain was embarked'.

64 Giménez Caballero, *Memorias*, p. 90. His book *Franco. El Caudillo* is an uninterrupted hymn of praise for Franco.

65 Cabanellas, *Cuatro generales* II, p. 330; Rafael Abella, *La vida cotidiana durante la guerra civil. 1)*

La España nacional (Barcelona: Planeta, 1978) pp. 57–8.
66 Vegas Latapie, *Los caminos*, p. 89.
67 Alfredo Kindelán Duany, *Mis cuadernos de guerra* 2ª edición (Barcelona: Planeta, 1982) pp. 103–5.
68 See *Franco*, pp. 174–89; Cabanellas, *Cuatro generales* II, pp. 330–3.
69 Broadcast of 4 October 1936, reprinted in Millán Astray, *Franco*, pp. 41–4.
70 Pilar Franco Bahamonde, *Nosotros los Franco* (Barcelona: Planeta, 1980) p. 54; Ramón Garriga, *Nicolás Franco, el hermano brujo* (Barcelona: Planeta, 1980) pp. 128–30. On Hammaralt and his activities in the laboratories, see also Angel Alcázar de Velasco, *Siete días de Salamanca* (Madrid: G. del Toro, 1976) pp. 120–1.
71 Abella, *La España nacional*, p. 109. On Aguilera, see Preston, *Franco*, pp. 190–1.
72 Charles Foltz, Jr., *The Masquerade in Spain* (Boston: Houghton Mifflin, 1948) p. 80.
73 Luis Portillo, 'Unamuno's Last Lecture', Cyril Connolly, *The Golden Horizon* (London: Weidenfeld & Nicolson, 1953) p. 398.
74 Luis Moure Mariño, *La generación del 36: memorias de Salamanca y Burgos* (La Coruña: Ediciós do Castro, 1989) p. 70.
75 Moure Mariño, *La generación del 36*, p. 71.
76 Antoni Pelegrí, *Catalans entre la Falç i les fletxes* (Barcelona: Oikos-Tau, 1996) p. 215.
77 Franco Salgado-Araujo, *Mi vida*, pp. 190–1.
78 Franco Salgado-Araujo, *Mi vida*, p. 201.
79 Ridruejo, *Sombras y bultos*, p. 110.
80 Moure Mariño, *La generaciõn del 36*, pp. 73–9; Portillo, 'Unamuno's Last Lecture', pp. 397–403; Carlos Rojas, *¡Muera la inteligencia! ¡Viva la muerte!* pp. 134–9; Preston, *Franco*, pp. 191–2; Abella, *La España nacional*, pp. 110–12.
81 Moure Mariño, *La generación del 36*, p. 82.
82 Franco Salgado-Araujo, *Mis conversaciones*, p. 431.
83 Silva, *Millán Astray*, p. 200.
84 Almirante Juan Cervera Valderrama, *Memorias de guerra (1936–1939)* (Madrid: Editora Nacional, 1968) p. 33.
85 Franco Salgado-Araujo, *Mi vida*, p. 219.
86 Millán Astray, *Franco*, pp. 61–2.
87 Philippe Nourry, *Francisco Franco: la conquête du Pouvoir* (Paris: Denoël, 1975) p. 542.
88 Giménez Caballero, *Memorias*, pp. 88–90; Moure Mariño, *La generación del 36*, p. 69; Vegas Latapie, *Los caminos*, p. 175.
89 Giménez Caballero, *Memorias*, pp. 88–92; Millán Astray, *Franco*, pp. 47–52.
90 Del Burgo, *Conspiración*, pp. 730–2; Ronald Fraser, *Blood of Spain. The Experience of Civil War, 1936–1939* (London: Allen Lane, 1979) p. 207.
91 Del Burgo, *Conspiración*, pp. 870–1.
92 Giménez Caballero, *Memorias*, p. 106.
93 Torcuato Luca de Tena, *Papeles para la pequeña y la gran historia. Memorias de mi padre y mías* (Barcelona: Planeta, 1991) p. 264.
94 Millán Astray, *Franco*, pp. 47–50, 77–9, 161–5.
95 Millán Astray, *Franco*, pp. 229–37.
96 Cabanellas, *Cuatro generales* II, pp. 424, 431; del Burgo, *Conspiración*, p. 885. On the service in Burgos, see Cervera, *Memorias*, p. 167 and Antonio Ruiz Vilaplana, *Doy fe . . . un año de actuación en la España nacionalista* (Paris: Éditions Imprimerie Coopérative Étoile, n.d. [1938]) pp. 121–2.
97 Maximiano García Venero, *Falange en la guerra de España: la Unificación y Hedilla* (Paris: Ruedo Ibérico, 1967) p. 295.
98 Olao Conforti, *Guadalajara: la prima sconfitta del fascismo* (Milan: Mursia, 1967) pp. 34–5.

99 García Venero, *Falange/Hedilla*, p. 404.
100 Millán Astray, *Franco*, pp. 193–201.
101 Millán Astray, *Franco*, p. 209.
102 Ridruejo, *Sombras y bultos*, pp. 110–12.
103 Abella, *La España nacional*, pp. 146–7; Silva, *Millán Astray*, pp. 204–22.
104 Manuel Valdés Larrañaga, *De la Falange al Movimiento (1936–1952)* (Madrid: Fundación Nacional Francisco Franco, 1994) p. 134.
105 On Iniesta, see Preston, *Franco*, pp. 734, 761–7.
106 Carlos Iniesta Cano, *Memorias y recuerdos* (Barcelona: Planeta, 1984) pp. 132–4.
107 Dr Julio González Iglesias, *Los dientes de Franco* (Madrid: Fénix, 1995) pp. 164–72.
108 Laín Entralgo, *Descargo de conciencia*, p. 208.
109 Galeazzo Ciano, *Diario 1937–1943* a cura di Renzo De Felice (Milano: Rizzoli, 1980) p. 143. On the encounter with Delcroix, see J. A. Giménez Arnau, *Memorias de memoria. Descifre vuecencia personalmente* (Barcelona: Destino, 1978) p. 101 and Serrano Suñer, *Memorias*, p. 159. On Delcroix, see Philip V. Cannistraro, editor, *Historical Dictionary of Fascist Italy* (Westport, Connecticut, Greenwood Press, 1982) p. 161. Like Millán Astray in relation to Franco, Delcroix was a fanatical propagandist and publicist for Mussolini.
110 Pemán, *Mis almuerzos*, p. 138. Millán Astray was obsessed with the fact that Franco worked fourteen hours per day, so much so that he reprinted the same speech on the subject twice in his collected speeches, see Millán Astray, *Franco*, pp. 65–8, 187, 187–90. On his efforts to speak Italian, see also Giménez Arnau, *Memorias*, p. 101.
111 Millán Astray, *Franco*, pp. 135–6.
112 Pemán, *Mis almuerzos*, p. 137.
113 González Iglesias, *Los dientes*, p. 172.
114 Moure Mariño, *La generación del 36*, p. 71; Franco Salgado-Araujo, *Mi vida*, p. 238; Fraser, *Blood of Spain*, p. 207; Vegas Latapie, *Los caminos*, p. 173.
115 Giménez Caballero, *Memorias*, p. 93.
116 Millán Astray, *Franco*, pp. 135–6.
117 Pemán, *Mis almuerzos*, pp. 135–6, gives an extremely expurgated version of this story which was current in Madrid at the time. On Celia Gámez, see *El País*, 11 December 1992.
118 Hilari Raguer, *La Unió Democràtica de Catalunya i el seu temps (1931–1939)* (Barcelona: Abadía de Montserrat, 1976) pp. 307–8. See also Ricardo de la Cierva, *Francisco Franco: biografía histórica* 6 vols (Barcelona: Planeta, 1982) IV, p. 232.
119 José Martínez Esparza, *Con la División Azul en Rusia* (Madrid, Ediciones del Ejército, 1943) pp. 26–7; Gerald R. Kleinfeld & Lewis A. Tambs, *Hitler's Spanish Legion: The Blue Division in Russia* (Carbondale, Southern Illinois University Press, 1979) pp. 26, 187.
120 Alessandro Cova, *Graziani. Un generale per il regime* (Roma: Newton Compton, 1987) p. 280; Silva, *Millán Astray*, pp. 238–41.
121 Ricardo de la Cierva, *Historia del franquismo: I orígenes y configuración (1939–1945)* (Barcelona: Planeta, 1975) p. 251.
122 Franco Salgado-Araujo, *Mi vida*, pp. 323–6.
123 See the anonymous article based on interviews with Peregrina Millán Astray, 'Militar y caballero. José Millán Astray', *El Figaro*, 28 January 1995, p. 58.
124 *ABC*, 2 January 1954; Franco Salgado-Araujo, *Mi vida*, p. 335.
125 *Tauima Legión*, No.20, enero de 1954, p. 2.
126 *ABC*, 3 January 1954.

2 The Discreet Charm of a Dictator: Francisco Franco

1 Franco speech in the Museo del Ejército, 7 March 1946, Carlos Fernández, *Antología de 40 años* (La Coruña: Libros de las Hespéridas, 1983) p. 170; *Arriba*, 8 March 1946.

2 Testimony of P. Bulart, María Mérida, *Testigos de Franco: retablo íntimo de una dictadura* (Barcelona: Plaza y Janés, 1977) p. 36.

3 Jaime de Andrade, *Raza anecdotario para el guión de una pelicula* (Madrid: Ediciones Numancia, 1942). For an acute commentary, see Román Gubern, *'Raza' (un ensueño del General Franco)* (Madrid: Ediciones 99, 1977).

4 George Hills, *Franco: The Man and His Nation* (New York: Macmillan, 1967) pp. 107, 132.

5 Rogelio Baón, *La cara humana de un Caudillo* (Madrid: Editorial San Martín, 1975) p. 117.

6 Ramón Serrano Suñer, *Entre el silencio y la propaganda, la Historia como fue: memorias* (Barcelona: Planeta, 1977) p. 169.

7 *Palabras del Caudillo 19 abril 1937–31 diciembre 1938* (Barcelona: Ediciones Fe, 1939) p. 204.

8 Mérida, *Testigos*, pp. 22, 139.

9 Manuel Vázquez Montalbán, *Los demonios familiares de Franco* (Barcelona: Dopesa, 1978) pp. 90–1.

10 Pilar Franco Bahamonde, *Nosotros los Franco* (Barcelona: Planeta, 1980) p. 28; Pedro Sainz Rodríguez, *Testimonio y recuerdos* (Barcelona: Planeta, 1978) p. 335; José María Gil Robles, *La monarquía por la que yo luché: páginas de un diario 1941–1954* (Madrid: Taurus, 1976) p. 270.

11 Pedro Theotonio Pereira, *Memórias postos em que servi e algumas recordações pessoais* 2 vols (Lisbon: Verbo, 1973) II, p. 59.

12 Pereira to Salazar, 6 July 1940, *Correspondência de Pedro Teotónio Pereira para Oliveira Salazar* 4 vols (Lisbon: Presidência do Conselho de Ministros, 1987–1991) II, p. 59.

13 Francisco Franco Salgado-Araujo, *Mi vida junto a Franco* (Barcelona: Planeta, 1977) p. 337.

14 John Whitaker, 'Prelude to World War: A Witness from Spain', *Foreign Affairs*, Vol.21, No.1, October 1942, p. 116.

15 Harold G. Cardozo, *The March of a Nation* (London: The Right Book Club, 1937) p. 141.

16 William Foss & Cecil Gerahty, *The Spanish Arena* (London: The Right Book Club, 1938) p. 62.

17 Georges Rotvand, *Franco Means Business* (London: Paladin Press, n.d. [1937]) p. 20.

18 S. F. A. Coles, *Franco of Spain* (London: Neville Spearman, 1955) p. 71.

19 Ramón Soriano, *La mano izquierda de Franco* (Barcelona: Planeta, 1981) pp. 60, 76, 155.

20 'Declaraciones de S. E. a Manuel Aznar', 31 December 1938, *Palabras del Caudillo 19 abril 1937–31 diciembre 1938*, p. 314.

21 Arturo Barea, *The Struggle for the Spanish Soul* (London: Secker & Warburg, 1941) p. 21.

22 Joaquín Arrarás, *Franco*, 7ª edición (Valladolid: Librería Santarén, 1939) pp. 131–3.

23 On his attitude to funerals in general, Franco, *Nosotros*, p. 159. On Jordana's death, Abel Plenn, *Wind in the Olive Trees – Spain from the Inside* (New York: Boni & Gaer, 1946) pp. 96–7; Sir Samuel Hoare, *Ambassador on a Special Mission* (London: Collins, 1946) pp. 269–72.

24 Eugenio Vegas Latapie, *Los caminos del desengaño: memorias políticas II 1936–1938* (Madrid: Tebas, 1987) pp. 74–5.

25 John F. Coverdale, *Italian Intervention in the Spanish Civil War* (Princeton NJ: Princeton

University Press, 1975) pp. 191–2; Ramón Garriga, *La España de Franco: las relaciones con Hitler* 2ª edición (Puebla, Mexico: Cajica, 1970) pp. 207–9.

26 J. Boor [pseud. Francisco Franco], *Masonería* (Madrid: Gráficas Valera, 1952) p. 10.

27 José Antonio Ferrer Benimeli, *Masonería española contemporánea* 2 vols (Madrid: Siglo XXI, 1980) II, pp. 168–70; José Antonio Ferrer Benimeli, 'Franco contra la masonería', *Historia 16*, año II, no. 15, julio de 1977, pp. 37–51; Manuel de Paz, 'Masonería y militarismo en el norte de Africa', Cursos de Verano, El Escorial, 1988, *La masonería y su impacto internacional* (Madrid, Universidad Complutense, 1989) pp. 114–17; Francisco Franco Salgado-Araujo, *Mis conversaciones privadas con Franco* (Barcelona: Planeta, 1976) p. 152; Soriano, *La mano*, p. 128.

28 See speeches by Franco on 24 August 1942, *Palabras del Caudillo 1937–1942* (Madrid: Ediciones de la Vicesecretaría Popular, 1943) p. 279, 14 May 1946, 19 October 1946, 28 March 1950, 13 June 1958, 2 October 1961, 1 April 1964 quoted in Agustín del Río Cisneros, editor, *Pensamiento político de Franco* 2 vols (Madrid: Ediciones del Movimiento, 1975) I, pp. 78–93; letter of Franco, 12 May 1942, to Don Juan de Borbón, reprinted in Alfredo Kindelán, *La verdad de mis relaciones con Franco* (Barcelona, Planeta, 1981) pp. 42–6.

29 Speech in Lugo, 21 August 1942, *Palabras del Caudillo 1937–1942*, p. 273; Fernando Valls, *La enseñanza de la literatura en el franquismo 1936–1951* (Barcelona: Antoni Bosch, 1983) p. 67.

30 Testimony of Ramón Serrano Suñer to the author, Madrid, 21 November 1990. The priest in question seems to have been Don Manuel Fidalgo Alonso, who according to the parish records of San Cucao, was the parish priest between 1928 and 1932. Since the Asturian diocesan records were destroyed during the Civil War, it is impossible to be sure.

31 José Antonio Vaca de Osma, *Paisajes con Franco al fondo* (Barcelona: Plaza y Janés, 1987) pp. 158–9.

32 Manuel Azaña, *Obras completas* 4 vols (Mexico D. F.: Oasis, 1966–8) IV, p. 35.

33 Roberto Cantalupo, *Fu la Spagna. Ambasciata presso Franco. Febbraio–Aprile 1937* (Milan: Mondadori, 1948) pp. 230–3; Paul Preston, 'General Franco as Military Leader', *Transactions of the Royal Historical Society* 6th Series, Vol. 4, 1994, pp. 21–41.

34 Baón, *La cara humana*, p. 143.

35 The first comment on this came from the pen of Miguel de Unamuno in a letter written on 13 December 1936 to Quintín de Torre, reproduced in Luciano González Egido, *Agonizar en Salamanca: Unamuno julio–diciembre 1936* (Madrid: Alianza Editorial, 1986) pp. 226–8.

36 José María Pemán, *Mis encuentros con Franco* (Barcelona: Dopesa, 1976) p. 130.

37 Francisco Franco, *Textos de doctrina política. Palabras y escritos de 1945 a 1950* (Madrid: Publicaciones Españolas, 1951) p. 229.

38 Francisco Franco, *Discursos y mensajes del Jefe del Estado, 1955–1959* (Madrid: Publicaciones Españolas, 1960) pp. 496–7.

39 Francisco Franco, *Discursos y mensajes del Jefe del Estado, 1960–1963* (Madrid: Publicaciones Españolas, 1964) pp. 263–4.

40 Angel Bayod, *Franco visto por sus ministros* (Barcelona: Planeta, 1981) pp. 151–2.

41 Rafael Calvo Serer, *La dictadura de los franquistas: el 'affaire' del 'Madrid' y el futuro político* (Paris: El Autor, 1973) pp. 67–70.

42 Mariano Sánchez Soler, *Villaverde:*

fortuna y caída de la casa Franco (Barcelona: Planeta, 1990) pp. 39–51, 92–4, 122–4, 131–9; Coles, *Franco*, p. 29.
43 Sánchez Soler, *Villaverde*, p. 127.
44 Ramón Garriga, *La Señora de El Pardo* (Barcelona: Planeta, 1979) p. 11.
45 Plenn, *Wind in the Olive Trees*, p. 146; Heleno Saña, *El Franquismo sin mitos. Conversaciones con Serrano Suñer* (Barcelona: Grijalbo, 1982) pp. 365–8; Franco, *Nosotros*, pp. 31, 227–8; Jaime Sánchez Blanco, *La importancia de llamarse Franco: el negocio inmobiliario de doña Pilar* (Madrid: Edicusa, 1978) *passim*.
46 On Nicolás's business deals, see Ramón Garriga, *Nicolás Franco, el hermano brujo* (Barcelona: Planeta, 1980) pp. 171–84, 306–20; on his private life, pp. 269–91.
47 See, for instance, the business interests of Admiral Nieto Antúnez listed in Equipo Mundo, *Los noventa ministros de Franco* (Barcelona: Dopesa, 1970) p. 323.
48 Thomas J. Hamilton, *Appeasement's Child: The Franco Regime in Spain* (London: Gollancz, 1943) pp. 121–31; Plenn, *Wind in the Olive Trees*, p. 138.
49 Ramón Garriga, *Franco-Serrano Suñer: un drama político* (Barcelona: Planeta, 1986) p. 178.
50 See the comments of his brother-in-law and of his cousin and aide-de-camp, Serrano Suñer, *Memorias*, p. 230; Franco Salgado–Araujo, *Mis conversaciones*, pp. 19, 37, 56–8, 83, 178.
51 I am obliged to Tristan Garel-Jones for locating the first occasion on which Franco said this. Luis Suárez Fernández, *Francisco Franco y su tiempo* 8 vols (Madrid: Fundación Nacional Francisco Franco, 1984) I, p. 8; José Ignacio Escobar, *Así empezó* (Madrid: Gregorio del Toro, 1974) p. 151; Vicente Pozuelo, *Los últimos 476 días de Franco* (Barcelona: Planeta, 1980) p. 46.
52 Franco Salgado-Araujo, *Mis conversaciones*, p. 80.
53 Testimony of Manuel Fraga to the author, Madrid, February 1983.
54 José María de Areilza, *Diario de un ministro de la monarquía* (Barcelona: Planeta, 1977) pp. 73–6.
55 Franco Salgado-Araujo, *Mis conversaciones*, p. 214.
56 *Cambio 16*, No.278, 10 April 1977, p. 13.
57 Vaca de Osma, *Paisajes*, pp. 155–6, 178, 183; Pemán, *Mis encuentros*, pp. 52, 123–6; Suárez Fernández, *Franco*, I, p. 61; Pereira, *Memórias* II, pp. 58–9; Mérida, *Testigos*, pp. 168, 173–4; Coles, *Franco*, p. 74.
58 Vegas Latapie, *Los caminos*, pp. 74–5, 257; Guillermo Cabanellas, *Cuatro generales 1) preludio a la guerra civil* 2 vols (Barcelona: Planeta, 1977) p. 56.
59 Francesc Cambó, diary entry for 8 May 1944, *Meditacions: dietari (1941–1946)* (Barcelona: Editorial Alpha, 1982) p. 1449.
60 Sainz Rodríguez, *Testimonio*, p. 335.
61 Testimony of Ramón Serrano Suñer to the author, 21 November 1990.
62 Saña, *Franquismo*, p. 190.
63 Pereira to Salazar, 7 November 1940, *Dez anos de política externa (1936–1947) a nação portuguesa e a segunda guerra mundial* vol. VII (Lisbon: Imprenta Nacional, 1971) pp. 580–1; Lequio to Ciano, 27 January 1941, *I Documenti Diplomatici Italiani*, 9ª serie, vol. VI (Rome: Libreria dello Stato, 1986) p. 506.
64 Pilar Jaraiz Franco, *Historia de una disidencia* (Barcelona: Planeta, 1981) pp. 156, 162–3, 174, 205.
65 Jaraiz Franco, *Historia*, pp. 163–7.
66 Pemán, *Mis encuentros*, p. 9.
67 Suárez Fernández, *Franco*, I, p. 55. Franco, *Nosotros*, pp. 163–4, claims that Franco's daughter possesses the full text of his memoirs.
68 Francisco Franco, *'Apuntes' personales sobre la República y la*

guerra civil (Madrid: Fundación Nacional Francisco Franco, 1987) *passim*; Pozuelo, *Los últimos 476 días*, pp. 79–102.

69 On the alchemist, see Franco, *Nosotros*, p. 54; Garriga, *Nicolás Franco*, pp. 128–30. On Hammaralt and his activities in the laboratories, see also Angel Alcázar de Velasco, *Siete días de Salamanca* (Madrid: G. del Toro, 1976) pp. 120–1. On von Filek, see Preston, *Franco*, p. 348.

70 Giuliana di Febo, *La santa de la raza: un culto barroco en la España franquista (1937–1962)* (Barcelona: Icaria Editorial, 1988) pp. 63–71.

71 Franco, *Apuntes*, pp. 42–5; Soriano, *La mano*, pp. 61–2, 154–5.

72 *Palabras del Caudillo 19 abril 1937–31 diciembre 1938*, pp. 309–10.

73 Vegas Latapie, *Los caminos*, p. 400.

74 Franco Salgado-Araujo, *Mis conversaciones*, p. 67.

75 Vegas Latapie, *Los caminos*, p. 400. On Alfonso XIII's ability to talk knowledgeably about many subjects in several languages, see José Calvo Sotelo, *Mis servicios al Estado. Seis años de gestión: apuntes para la Historia* (Madrid: Imprenta Clásica Española, 1931) pp. 113–14.

76 Franco Salgado-Araujo, *Mi vida*, p. 116; Sainz Rodríguez, *Testimonio*, pp. 331–3; testimony of Ramón Serrano Suñer to the author; Soriano, *La mano*, pp. 57, 155.

77 José María Fontana, *Franco: radiografía del personaje para sus contemporáneos* (Barcelona: Ediciones Acervo, 1979) p. 47.

78 Sainz Rodríguez, *Testimonio*, p. 341.

79 *Palabras del Caudillo 1937–1942*, pp. 253, 267.

80 Speech in Lugo, 21 August 1942, *Palabras del Caudillo 1937–1942*, p. 273.

81 José María Pemán, *Mis almuerzos con gente importante* (Barcelona: Dopesa, 1970) p. 138.

82 Soriano, *La mano*, p. 108.

83 Interview with López Rodó in Bayod, *Franco visto*, p. 167; Raymond Carr, 'The legacy of Francoism' in José L. Cagigao, John Crispin and Enrique Pupo-Walker, editors, *Spain 1975–1980: The Conflicts and Achievements of Democracy* (Madrid: Ediciones José Porrúa Turanzas, 1982) p. 136; Coles, *Franco*, p. 29.

84 Coles, *Franco*, p. 63; Franco Salgado-Araujo, *Mi vida*, p. 319.

85 Serrano Suñer, *Memorias*, pp. 207–8; Pemán, *Mis encuentros*, p. 92. A brilliant satire on Francoist hunting, *Escopeta Nacional*, was produced in 1978 by Luis García Berlanga.

86 Maurice Peterson, *Both Sides of the Curtain* (London: Constable, 1950) p. 224.

87 Federico Sopeña, *Escrito de noche* (Madrid, 1985) p. 133.

88 Franco Salgado-Araujo, *Mi vida*, p. 345; Soriano, *La mano*, pp. 87–8; Pozuelo, *Los últimos 476 días*, pp. 35, 109, 178.

89 Vicente Gil, *Cuarenta años junto a Franco* (Barcelona: Planeta, 1981) pp. 84–5; Carlos Fernández Santander, *El futbol durante la guerra civil y el franquismo* (Madrid: Editorial San Martín, 1990) pp. 196–7.

90 Vegas Latapie, *Los caminos*, pp. 79–80.

91 Jaraiz Franco, *Historia*, p. 77.

92 Mérida, *Testigos*, p. 21; Coles, *Franco*, p. 30.

93 Mérida, *Testigos*, p. 31.

94 Vaca de Osma, *Paisajes*, pp. 158, 198–9.

95 Testimony of P. Bulart, Mérida, *Testigos*, p. 33; Franco, *Nosotros*, p. 66.

96 *Estampa*, 29 May 1928.

97 Coles, *Franco*, p. 26; Brian Crozier, *Franco: A Biographical History* (London: Eyre & Spottiswood, 1967) pp. 46, 50–1; Hills, *Franco*, 105, 157; Franco, *Apuntes*, p. 6.

98 Crozier, *Franco*, p. 46, (quoting Franco's friend and early biographer, Joaquín Arrarás); Coles, *Franco*, p. 77.

99 *Estampa*, 29 May 1928; Baón, *La cara humana*, p. 93.
100 Pemán, *Mis encuentros*, pp. 68–9. *Marina*, written in 1855, was the work of Emilio Arrieta y Corera (1823–1894), see Gilbert Chase, *The Music of Spain* 2nd edn (New York: Dover, 1959) pp. 142–3.
101 Pemán, *Mis encuentros*, p. 88. On Juan Carlos's presence at the première, see Margarita Rivière, *La generación del cambio* (Barcelona: Planeta, 1984) p. 19.
102 See the reproductions in *Interviu*, No.39, 21–27 December 1983; Pozuelo, *Los últimos 476 días*, between pp. 176–7.
103 See the pictures reproduced in Julio Rodríguez Martínez, *Impresiones de un ministro de Carrero Blanco* (Barcelona: Planeta, 1974) pp. 144–7.
104 Franco Salgado-Araujo, *Mi vida*, p. 71.
105 Pemán, *Mis encuentros*, p. 119; testimonies of Padre Bulart, Pilar Franco, Max Borrell, Mérida, *Testigos*, pp. 33, 92, 226.
106 Jaraiz Franco, *Historia*, pp. 101, 105; Franco, *Nosotros*, pp. 69–70; Pemán, *Mis encuentros*, pp. 85–8; Soriano, *La mano*, p. 156.
107 Franco Salgado-Araujo, *Mi vida*, pp. 36–7.
108 Franco Salgado-Araujo, *Mi vida*, p. 340.
109 Vaca de Osma, *Paisajes*, p. 190.
110 Testimony of Ramón Serrano Suñer to the author, 21 November 1990.
111 Niceto Alcalá Zamora, *Memorias* (Barcelona: Planeta, 1977) p. 114.
112 Hugh Thomas, *The Spanish Civil War* 3rd edn (London: Hamish Hamilton, 1977) p. 414.
113 Serrano Suñer, *Memorias*, p. 164.
114 Whitaker, 'Prelude', p. 116.
115 Willard L. Beaulac, *Franco: Silent Ally in World War II* (Carbondale: Southern Illinois University Press, 1986) p. 45.
116 Plenn, *Wind*, pp. 74–5.
117 Coles, *Franco*, p. 161.
118 Ramón Garriga, *El Cardenal Segura y el Nacional-Catolicismo* (Barcelona: Planeta, 1977) pp. 294–6.
119 Testimony of Manuel Fraga, Mérida, *Testigos*, p. 82.
120 Franco, *Nosotros*, p. 139.
121 *Hitler's Table Talk 1941–1944* (London: Weidenfeld and Nicolson, 1953) 5 September 1942, p. 693.
122 Pereira to Salazar, 10 June 1940, *DAPE*, VII, pp. 115–16.
123 Pemán, *Mis encuentros*, pp. 116, 152; Hamilton, *Appeasement's Child*, pp. 87–8.
124 Willard L. Beaulac, *Career Ambassador* (New York, 1951) p. 179.
125 Franco Salgado-Araujo, *Mis conversaciones*, pp. 79, 105.
126 Franco Salgado-Araujo, *Mis conversaciones*, p. 395.
127 See the interviews with Máximo Rodríguez Borrell recounted in Mérida, *Testigos*, pp. 217–27 and Coles, *Franco*, pp. 13–15. Vaca de Osma, *Paisajes*, p. 186.
128 Daniel Sueiro, *El Valle de los Caídos: los secretos de la cripta franquista* (Barcelona: Argos Vergara, 1983) p. 177.
129 Pemán, *Mis encuentros*, p. 117; Mérida, *Testigos*, p. 24.
130 Franco, *Discursos y mensajes 1955–1959*, pp. 478–9.

3 The Absent Hero: José Antonio Primo de Rivera

1 José María Amado, *Via crucis* (Málaga, Editorial Dardo, 1938).
2 Maximiano García Venero, *Falange en la guerra de España: la Unificación y Hedilla* (Paris: Ruedo Ibérico, 1967) p. 38; Ramón Serrano Suñer, *Entre Hendaya y Gibraltar* (Madrid: Ediciones y Publicaciones Españolas, 1947) pp. 365–7; Ramón Serrano Suñer, *Política de España 1936–1975* (Madrid: Editorial Complutense, 1995) p. 81.
3 Francisco Bravo, *José Antonio: el*

hombre, el jefe, el camarada (Madrid: Ediciones Españolas, 1939) p. 7.

4 Primo de Rivera to Julián Pemartín, 2 April 1933, in Sancho Dávila & Julián Pemartín, *Hacia la historia de la Falange: primera contribución de Sevilla* (Jerez: Jerez Industrial, 1938) pp. 24–7.

5 Ramiro Ledesma Ramos, *¿Fascismo en España?* 2ª edición (Barcelona: Ariel, 1968) pp. 178–9.

6 *Ahora*, 19 April 1935, quoted by Carlos Rojas, *¡Muera la inteligencia! ¡Viva la muerte! Salamanca, 1936. Unamuno y Millán Astray frente a frente* (Barcelona: Planeta, 1995) p. 25.

7 Indalecio Prieto, *Convulsiones de España* 3 vols (Mexico D.F.: Ediciones Oasis, 1967–9) I, pp. 127–33.

8 On the Falangist role in the repression, see García Venero, *Falange/Hedilla*, pp. 227–37; Herbert Rutledge Southworth, *Antifalange; estudio crítico de 'Falange en la guerra de España' de Maximiano García Venero* (Paris: Ruedo Ibérico, 1967) pp. 3–4; Dionisio Ridruejo, *Escrito en España* 2ª edición (Buenos Aires: Losada, 1964) p. 83; Antonio Bahamonde y Sánchez de Castro, *Un año con Queipo* (Barcelona: Ediciones Españolas, n.d. [1938]) pp. 89–136.

9 The most vivid short portrait of José Antonio Primo de Rivera is to be found in Dionisio Ridruejo, *Casi unas memorias* (Barcelona: Planeta, 1976) pp. 53–62. See also Pilar Primo de Rivera, *Recuerdos de una vida* (Madrid: Ediciones Dyrsa, 1983) p. 20.

10 Claude Bowers, *My Mission to Spain* (London: Gollancz, 1954) p. 28; Henry Buckley, *Life and Death of the Spanish Republic* (London: Hamish Hamilton, 1940) p. 127.

11 *Textos de doctrina política: Obras de José Antonio Primo de Rivera* edited by Agustín del Río Cisneros, (Madrid: Sección Femenina, 1966) pp. 3–13. See also Hugh Thomas, 'The Hero in the Empty Room: José Antonio and Spanish Fascism' in *Journal of Contemporary History*, Vol.1, No.1, 1966, pp. 174–82.

12 Bravo, *José Antonio*, p. 76.

13 Gabriel Jackson, *The Spanish Republic and the Civil War* (Princeton NJ: Princeton University Press, 1965) pp. 178–80; Stanley G. Payne, *Falange: A History of Spanish Fascism* (Stanford: Stanford University Press, 1961) pp. 24–30; Hugh Thomas, 'The Hero in the Empty Room: José Antonio and Spanish Fascism' and his introduction to *José Antonio Primo de Rivera: Selected Writings* (London: Jonathan Cape, 1972) pp. 11–16; Hugh Thomas, 'Spain' in S. J. Woolf, editor, *European Fascism* (London: Weidenfeld & Nicolson, 1968) pp. 289–96.

14 Felipe Ximénez de Sandoval, *'José Antonio' biografía* 2ª edición (Madrid: Gráficas Lazareno-Echaniz, 1949) pp. 41–2, 90; Ian Gibson, *En busca de José Antonio* (Barcelona: Planeta, 1980) pp. 189–207; Raimundo Fernández Cuesta, *Testimonio, recuerdos y reflexiones* (Madrid: Ediciones Dyrsa, 1985) p. 31; Southworth *Antifalange*, p. 4; Ramón Garriga, *La España de Franco: las relaciones con Hitler* 2ª edición (Puebla, Mexico: Cajica, 1970) pp. 15–18; Guillermo Cabanellas *La guerra de los mil días* 2 vols (Buenos Aires: Grijalbo, 1973) pp. 166–7.

15 Ximénez de Sandoval, *'José Antonio'*, p. 15.

16 Interview with Ramón Serrano Suñer in *Dolor y memoria de España en el segundo aniversario de la muerte de José Antonio* (Barcelona: Ediciones Jerarquía, 1939) p. 204; Fernández Cuesta, *Testimonio*, p. 32; Gibson, *En busca de José Antonio*, pp. 196–7.

17 Pedro Sainz Rodríguez, *Testimonio y recuerdos* (Barcelona: Planeta, 1978) p. 222.

18 Gibson, *En busca de José Antonio*, p. 206.
19 Ximénez de Sandoval, *'José Antonio'*, pp. 252–4.
20 Gibson, *En busca de José Antonio*, pp. 201–2.
21 Most eloquently by Manuel Cantarero del Castillo, *Falange y socialismo* (Barcelona: Dopesa, 1973) which uses the writings of José Antonio Primo de Rivera to establish 'the socialist vocation of the Falange' (p. 9), 'the Falangist negation of the Right' (pp. 177–200), 'Falangist revolutionism' (pp. 211–22), 'the predominant leftism of the Falange' (pp. 237–51) and the influence of Marx and Engels on José Antonio Primo de Rivera (pp. 254–6). See also Miguel Ramos González, *La violencia en Falange Española* (Oviedo: Ediciones Tarfe, 1993) pp. 19–58; Carlos Rojas, *Prieto y José Antonio: socialismo y Falange ante la tragedia civil* (Barcelona: Dirosa, 1977).
22 Ximénez de Sandoval, *'José Antonio'* pp. 12–13.
23 On José Antonio's naturally aristocratic bearing, see Javier Martínez Bedoya, *Memorias desde mi aldea* (Valladolid: Ambito Ediciones, 1996) pp. 72, 77.
24 *FE*, 18 January, 22 February 1934; Ernesto Giménez Caballero, *Memorias de un dictador* (Barcelona: Planeta, 1979) pp. 74–5; Eugenio Vegas Latapie, *Memorias políticas: el suicido de la monarquía y la segunda República* (Barcelona: Planeta, 1983) pp. 194–6; Ximénez de Sandoval, *'José Antonio'*, p. 24.
25 Ximénez de Sandoval, *'José Antonio'*, pp. 23, 573; Southworth, *Antifalange*, pp. 267–8; Ridruejo, *Memorias*, pp. 54–5.
26 Ximénez de Sandoval, *'José Antonio'*, pp. 92–108; Sainz Rodríguez, *Testimonio*, p. 196; Bravo, *José Antonio*, pp. 18–22; Sheelagh Ellwood, *Prietas las filas. Historia de Falange Española, 1933–1983* (Barcelona: Editorial Crítica, 1984) pp. 22–5.
27 Ernesto Giménez Caballero, *España y Franco* (Cegama, Guipúzcoa: Ediciones 'Los Combatientes', 1938) p. 31.
28 Ismael Saz Campos, *Mussolini contra la II República: hostilidad, conspiraciones, intervención (1931–1936)* (Valencia: Edicions Alfons el Magnànim, 1986) pp. 97–101; Manuel Pastor, *Los orígenes del fascismo en España* (Madrid: Túcar Ediciones, 1975) pp. 24–37; Enrique Selva Roca de Togores, 'Giménez Caballero en los orígenes ideológicos del fascismo español', *Estudis d'Història Contemporània del País Valencià*, No.9, 1991, pp. 183–213.
29 For a list of his publications, see Dr Albiñana, *Confinado en las Hurdes (una víctima de la Inquisición republicana)* (Madrid: Imprenta El Financiero, 1933) pp. 7–10. The manifesto of the PNE is printed in José María Albiñana, *Después de la dictadura: Los cuervos sobre la tumba* 2ª edición (Madrid: CIAP, 1930) pp. 252–9. See also Saz, *Mussolini contra la II República*, pp. 95–7; Pastor, *Los orígenes*, pp. 38–61; Southworth, *Antifalange*, pp. 29–30.
30 Ledesma Ramos, *¿Fascismo?*, pp. 77–81; Tomás Borrás, *Ramiro Ledesma Ramos* (Madrid: Editora Nacional, 1971) pp. 216, 248–50; Herbert Rutledge Southworth, 'The Falange: An Analysis of Spain's Fascist Heritage' in Paul Preston, editor, *Spain in Crisis: The Evolution and Decline of the Franco Regime* (Hassocks: Harvester Press, 1976) p. 6.
31 *Onésimo Redondo Caudillo de Castilla* (Valladolid: Ediciones Libertad, 1937) pp. 18–37; Ledesma Ramos, *¿Fascismo?*, p. 99; Payne, *Falange*, pp. 15–18.
32 Raffaele Guariglia, *Ambasciata in Spagna e primi passi in diplomazia 1932–1934* (Naples: Edizioni Scientifiche Italiane, 1972) pp. 288–9.

33 José María Pemán, *Mis encuentros con Franco* (Barcelona: Dopesa, 1976) pp. 14–16; Ramón Garriga, *La Señora de El Pardo* (Barcelona: Planeta, 1979) pp. 57–9; Ramón Serrano Suñer, *Entre el silencio y la propaganda, la Historia como fue. Memorias* (Barcelona: Planeta, 1977) pp. 54–6.

34 *FE*, 22 February 1934; Ledesma Ramos, *¿Fascismo?*, pp. 104–8; Guariglia to MAE, 24 febbraio 1933, in Guariglia, *Ambasciata*, pp. 263–4; Juan Aparicio, 'Mi recuerdo de José Antonio' in *Dolor y memoria*, pp. 255–6; Ximénez de Sandoval, '*José Antonio*', pp. 124–6; Alejandro Corniero Suárez, *Diario de un rebelde* (Madrid: Ediciones Barbarroja, 1991) p. 42; Saz, *Mussolini contra la II República*, pp. 105–8; Gibson, *En busca de José Antonio*, pp. 43–56.

35 *FE*, 22 February 1934; Ximénez de Sandoval, 'José Antonio', pp. 130–4; Gumersindo Montes Agudo, *Pepe Sainz. Una vida en la Falange* (Barcelona?) Ediciones Pallas de Horta, [1959?] pp. 24–8; Gibson, *En busca de José Antonio*, pp. 56–64.

36 Southworth, *Antifalange*, pp. 15–19, 39–53; Ernesto Giménez Caballero, *Genio de España* (Madrid: Ediciones Jerarquía, 1939) note to p. 276.

37 Southworth, *Antifalange*, p. 50; José María de Areilza & Fernando María Castiella, *Reivindicaciones de España* (Madrid: Instituto de Estudios Políticos, 1941) pp. 48–52.

38 Ximénez de Sandoval, '*José Antonio*', p. 412.

39 On the anti-democratic and nationalistic tendencies of Ortega y Gasset, see Antonio Elorza, *La razón y la sombra: una lectura política de Ortega y Gasset* (Barcelona: Anagrama, 1984) pp. 191–213; Andrew Dobson, *An Introduction to the Politics and Philosophy of José Ortega y Gasset* (Cambridge: Cambridge University Press, 1989) pp. 95–105. On Frente Español, see Elorza, *La razón*, pp. 213–24.

40 José Antonio Primo de Rivera, 'Homenaje y reproche a Don José Ortega y Gasset' in *Textos de doctrina política*, pp. 745–9; 'El Gran Inquisidor', 'Autos de F. E.: Antifascistas en España Don José Ortega y Gasset' in *FE*, 7 December 1933, p. 12.

41 José María de Areilza, *Así los he visto* (Barcelona: Planeta, 1974) pp. 92–4; Saz, *Mussolini contra la II República*, pp. 109–12; Ledesma Ramos, *¿Fascismo?*, pp. 122–3. On Ledesma's motorcycle, see Sainz Rodríguez, *Testimonio*, p. 220. On Areilza's links to the JONS, see *JONS*, May, September 1933, and Martínez Bedoya, *Memorias*, pp. 57, 60–1. Onésimo Redondo travelled to meetings in the side-car of a Harley Davidson, ibid., p. 70.

42 The only reliable contemporary report of this agreement is Guariglia to MAE, 1 settembre 1933, in Guariglia, *Ambasciata*, pp. 304–5. There is confusion about the date of the agreement – see Saz, *Mussolini contra la segunda República*, pp. 111–12, Sainz Rodríguez, *Testimonio*, pp. 220–2; José María Gil Robles, *No fue posible la paz* (Barcelona: Ariel, 1968) pp. 442–3. There is also doubt as to whether the money was actually handed over, see Juan Antonio Ansaldo, *¿Para qué . . . ? (de Alfonso XIII a Juan III)* (Buenos Aires: Editorial Vasca Ekin, 1951) p. 89.

43 Guariglia to MAE, 24 novembre 1933, Guariglia, *Ambasciata*, pp. 323–4; Primo de Rivera, *Textos*, pp. 53–5; Raffaele Guariglia, *Ricordi 1922–1946* (Naples: Edizioni Scientifiche Italiane, 1949) pp. 203–5; Saz, *Mussolini contra la II República*, pp. 113–18.

44 Bravo, *José Antonio*, p. 68; Ximénez de Sandoval, '*José Antonio*', p. 138.

45 Corniero, *Diario*, pp. 47–50, 66–8.

46 José Antonio Primo de Rivera, 'Discurso de la fundación de Falange Española' in *Textos*, pp. 61–9.
47 Southworth, *Antifalange*, pp. 27–9; Ximénez de Sandoval, *'José Antonio'*, pp. 204–5, 210–12, 316–17, 358, 437–40.
48 Ximénez de Sandoval, *'José Antonio'*, p. 166.
49 Martínez Bedoya, *Memorias*, p. 69; Fernández Cuesta quoted by Ximénez de Sandoval, *'José Antonio'*, p. 151.
50 Undated letter of García Valdecasas to Sainz Rodríguez, in Sainz Rodríguez, *Testimonio*, p. 221; Ledesma Ramos, *¿Fascismo en España?*, pp. 136–7.
51 Bravo, *José Antonio*, pp. 31–2.
52 Saz, *Mussolini contra la II República*, pp. 120–1.
53 Bravo, *José Antonio*, pp. 64–6; Ximénez de Sandoval, *'José Antonio'*, pp. 218–30; Payne, *Falange*, pp. 46–7.
54 Southworth, 'The Falange', p. 6
55 Martínez Bedoya, *Memorias*, p. 67.
56 Ledesma Ramos, *¿Fascismo?*, pp. 159–60, 164–5; Ximénez de Sandoval, *'José Antonio'*, pp. 564–74.
57 Angel Viñas, *La Alemania nazi y el 18 de julio* (Madrid: Alianza Editorial, 1974) pp. 155–60, 496–9; Ximénez de Sandoval, *'José Antonio'*, pp. 288–91.
58 Saz, *Mussolini contra la II República*, pp. 121–2; Guariglia to MAE, 20 marzo, 26 aprile 1934, Guariglia, *Ambasciata*, pp. 349, 372; Giménez Caballero, *Memorias*, p. 74.
59 Corniero, *Diario*, pp. 72, 74. According to Ledesma Ramos, *¿Fascismo?*, pp. 167–8, between May 1933 and the merger in February 1934, the JONS had had 12,000 pesetas to cover all of its activities including propaganda and publications. The Falange had been significantly more prosperous having 150,000 pesetas at its disposal in the three months between its foundation and the fusion. After the merger, the monthly needs of the new party were 40,000 pesetas per month.
60 Corniero, *Dairio*, p. 96; Ximénez de Sandoval, *'José Antonio'*, pp. 364, 369–70; Southworth, *Antifalange*, pp. 81–2; Saz, *Mussolini contra la II República*, pp. 122–3.
61 Ledesma Ramos, *¿Fascismo?*, pp. 161–2; 169–71, 173–80; Ansaldo, *¿Para qué?*, pp. 84–6; Bravo, *José Antonio*, p. 57; Ximénez de Sandoval, *'José Antonio'*, pp. 577–82; Ramos González, *La violencia*, pp. 75–80.
62 *FE*, 12, 19 July 1934; Ledesma Ramos, *¿Fascismo?*, pp. 175–87; Ansaldo, *¿Para qué?*, pp. 86–7; Martínez Bedoya, *Memorias*, pp. 74–5; Bravo, *José Antonio*, pp. 58–9, 75; Payne, *Falange*, pp. 59–61.
63 Alejandro Salazar, *Diario*, in Rafael Ibáñez Hernández, *Estudio y acción: la Falange fundacional a la luz del Diario de Alejandro Salazar (1934–1936)* (Madrid: Ediciones Barbarroja, 1993) p. 34.
64 Gibson, *En busca de José Antonio*, pp. 63, 208–9. On Ledesma as orator, see Martínez Bedoya, *Memorias*, p. 68.
65 Primo de Rivera, *Textos*, pp. 297–300; Francisco Franco Bahamonde, *'Apuntes' personales sobre la República y la guerra civil* (Madrid: Fundación Nacional Francisco Franco, 1987) p. 9.
66 Alejandro Lerroux, *La Pequeña historia. Apuntes para la Historia grande vividos y redactados por el autor* (Buenos Aires: Editorial Cimera, 1945) pp. 314–15; Martínez Bedoya, *Memorias*, pp. 76–7.
67 Gumersindo Montes Agudo, *Vieja guardia* (Madrid: Aguilar, 1939) pp. 217–36; Corneiro, *Diario*, pp. 87–8; Ledesma Ramos, *¿Fascismo?*, p. 188; Bravo, *José Antonio*, pp. 78–81; Ibáñez Hernández, *Estudio y acción*,

pp. 65–8; Manuel Suárez Cortina, *El fascismo en Asturias (1931–1937)* (Gijón: Silverio Cañada, 1981) pp. 164–6.

68 Fernández Cuesta, *Testimonio*, p. 37; Corniero, *Diario*, pp. 41, 93–4.

69 Saz, *Mussolini contra la II República*, p. 122.

70 García Venero, *Falange/Hedilla*, pp. 52–6; Francisco Bravo, *Historia de la Falange* 2ª edición (Madrid: Editora Nacional, 1943) pp. 77–80.

71 Ledesma Ramos, *Fascismo*, pp. 197–8; Bravo, *José Antonio*, pp. 182–3; Southworth, *Antifalange*, pp. 80–1; Martínez Bedoya, *Memorias*, pp. 79–80.

72 Saz, *Mussolini contra la II República*, pp. 123–4; Ibáñez Hernández, *Estudio y acción*, pp. 74–5.

73 Bravo, *José Antonio*, pp. 82–4; Ximénez de Sandoval, *'José Antonio'*, pp. 373–6; Ibáñez Hernández, *Estudio y acción*, pp. 75–6; Martínez Bedoya, *Memorias*, pp. 80–1.

74 'Las JONS rompen con FE. Manifiesto de las JONS', *La Patria Libre*, No.1, 16 February 1935; undated letter of Ledesma Ramos to Francisco Bravo, in Bravo, *José Antonio*, p. 83; Ramiro Ledesma Ramos, *Discurso a las juventudes de España* 2ª edición (Bilbao: Ediciones Fe, 1938) p. 6; Ledesma Ramos, *¿Fascismo?*, pp. 200–2.

75 Ximénez de Sandoval, *'José Antonio'*, p. 377; José María Sánchez Diana, *Ramiro Ledesma Ramos: biografía política* (Madrid: Editora Nacional, 1975) pp. 210–13; Bravo, *José Antonio*, pp. 82–4; Corniero, *Diario*, p. 102.

76 Fernández Cuesta, *Testimonio*, p. 44.

77 *Arriba*, 21 March 1935.

78 *La Patria Libre*, 2 March 1935.

79 *Arriba*, 11 April 1935; Corniero, *Diario*, p. 109; García Venero, *Falange/Hedilla*, pp. 265–8.

80 Interview of the author with Serrano Suñer, Madrid, 1993. See also Serrano Suñer, *Política*, p. 34; Suárez Cortina, *El fascismo en Asturias*, pp. 156–7.

81 Ledesma Ramos, *¿Fascismo?*, pp. 199–200; Fernández Cuesta, *Testimonio*, p. 44.

82 Correspondence between Celso Luciano, Capo Gabinetto di SE il Ministro per la Stampa e la Propaganda, and Amadeo Landini, press attaché at the Italian Embassy in Paris, Archivio Centrale dello Stato, Ministero Cultura Popolare, Busta 170 bis, fasc.36. The pioneering account of this episode is by Viñas, *La Alemania nazi* pp. 152–5. The definitive version is by Saz, *Mussolini contra la II República*, pp. 138–45. See also John F. Coverdale, *Italian Intervention in the Spanish Civil War* (Princeton NJ: Princeton University Press, 1975) pp. 57–8; Max Gallo, *Spain Under Franco: A History* (London: George Allen & Unwin, 1973) pp. 48–9.

83 Bravo, *José Antonio*, pp. 100–2.

84 Bravo, *José Antonio*, pp. 159–65; Corniero, *Diario*, p. 120; Fernández Cuesta, *Testimonio*, pp. 51–2; Montes Agudo, *Pepe Sainz*, pp. 56–7; García Venero, *Falange/Hedilla*, p. 66; Ibáñez Hernández, *Estudio y acción*, pp. 98–101. There has been speculation that generals such as Franco, Mola and Goded had been contacted – Joaquín Arrarás, *Historia de la Cruzada española* 8 vols, 36 tomos (Madrid: Ediciones Españolas, 1939–43) II, pp. 358–9. However, it is likely that the idea derived from a *post factum* desire to stress the links between the Falange and the Army. The uprising was allegedly to have been started by Captain José Luna, Jefe Provincial of Cáceres, who was later involved in the violence at Begoña in 1942. See Gibson, *En busca de José Antonio*, pp. 130–4.

85 Salazar, *Diario*, in Ibáñez Hernández, *Estudio y acción*, p. 36.

86 Antonio Cacho Zabalza, *La Unión*

Militar Española (Alicante: Egasa, 1940) pp. 24–5.

87 Primo de Rivera, *Textos*, pp. 567–70.

88 *Arriba*, 21 November 1935; Primo de Rivera, *Textos*, pp. 705–22.

89 Southworth, *Antifalange*, p. 95.

90 Primo de Rivera, *Textos*, pp. 651–9.

91 Primo de Rivera, 'A los maestros españoles', *Textos*, pp. 815–16.

92 The versions of all the protagonists coincide in broad lines but differ in detail. For Moscardó's accounts, see García Venero, *Falange/Hedilla*, p. 66 and Benito Gómez Oliveros, *General Moscardó* (Barcelona: Editorial AHR, 1956) p. 104. Fernández Cuesta's version appears in a letter to Felipe Ximénez de Sandoval, 9 February 1942, in Ximénez de Sandoval, '*José Antonio*', pp. 209–10, and Fernández Cuesta, *Testimonio*, pp. 52–3. See also Montes Agudo, *Pepe Sainz*, pp. 57–62. There are excellent accounts in Southworth, *Antifalange*, pp. 91–4, and Gibson, *En busca de José Antonio*, pp. 136–41, which included testimonies from both Alfaro and Fernández Cuesta.

93 Franco, *Apuntes personales*, pp. 21–2.

94 Serrano Suñer, *Memorias*, p. 56. As part of the political operation undertaken in 1937 to link the names of Franco and José Antonio, Arrarás gives a version of this interview, placing it in early March and portraying the two protagonists as decisive colaborators in the preparations for the rising, Joaquín Arrarás, *Franco* 7ª edición (Valladolid: Librería Santarén, 1939) p. 228.

95 *Arriba*, 19 December 1935.

96 Gil Robles, *No fue posible la paz*, pp. 444–6; Ximénez de Sandoval, '*José Antonio*', pp. 624–6.

97 Ridruejo, *Memorias*, p. 60.

98 Saz, *Mussolini contra la II República*, p. 121.

99 Gil Robles, *No fue posible la paz*, pp. 573–5, 688; Southworth, *Antifalange*, pp. 113–17; Paul Preston, *The Coming of the Spanish Civil War: Reform, Reaction and Revolution in the Second Republic 1931–1936* 2nd edition (London: Routledge, 1994) pp. 256–7; Payne, *Falange*, pp. 104–5; Rafael Valls, *La Derecha Regional Valenciana 1930–1936* (Valencia: Edicions Alfons el Magnànim, 1992) pp. 227–31; Serrano Suñer, *Entre Hendaya y Gibraltar*, p. 25.

100 Interview with Ramón Serrano Suñer in *Dolor y memoria*, p. 204; B. Félix Maíz, *Mola, aquel hombre* (Barcelona: Planeta, 1976) pp. 206–7, 238. On the generals' meeting of 8 March, see Gil Robles, *No fue posible la paz*, pp. 719–20; Arrarás, *Cruzada*, II, p. 467; B. Félix Maíz, *Alzamiento en España: de un diario de la conspiración* 2ª edición (Pamplona: Editorial Gómez, 1952) pp. 50–1; Felipe Bertrán Güell, *Preparación y desarrollo del alzamiento nacional* (Valladolid: Librería Santarén, 1939) p. 116.

101 Ximénez de Sandoval, '*José Antonio*', pp. 706–8; Corniero, *Diario*, p. 150; Southworth, *Antifalange*, p. 95; Juan-Simeón Vidarte, *Todos fuimos culpables* (Mexico DF: Fondo de Cultura Económica, 1973) pp. 66–7; Ansaldo, *¿Para qué?*, pp. 115–19; Julio Gil Pecharromán, *José Antonio Primo de Rivera. Retrato de un visionario* (Madrid: Temas de Hoy, 1996) pp. 439–41, 461.

102 Ximénez de Sandoval, '*José Antonio*', pp. 745–55.

103 Testimonio de Miguel Primo de Rivera, reproduced in Miguel Primo de Rivera y Urquijo, *Papeles póstumos de José Antonio* (Barcelona: Plaza y Janés, 1996) p. 212; Fernández Cuesta, *Testimonio*, pp. 59–62; Ximénez de Sandoval, '*José Antonio*', pp. 709–10, 728.

104 Bravo, *Historia de la Falange*, pp. 164–8.

105 Ximénez de Sandoval, '*José Antonio*', pp. 724–5, 733–4; Southworth, *Antifalange*, pp. 101–2; Sainz Rodríguez, *Testimonio*, p. 222.
106 Arrarás, *Cruzada* II, p. 511; Maíz, *Mola*, p. 158; García Venero, *Falange/Hedilla*, pp. 197–8.
107 Bravo, *José Antonio*, pp. 96–9; Corniero, *Diario*, p. 155.
108 Arrarás, *Cruzada* III, p. 275; Southworth, *Antifalange*, p. 106.
109 Southworth, *Antifalange*, pp. 108, 131–3; García Venero, *Falange/Hedilla*, pp. 141; Montes Agudo, *Pepe Sainz*, pp. 62–76.
110 Maíz, *Alzamiento en España*, p. 129.
111 Gil Robles, *No fue posible la paz*, pp. 561–2; Maximiano García Venero, *El general Fanjul: Madrid en el alzamiento nacional* (Madrid: Ediciones Cid, 1967) pp. 208–12.
112 Gil Robles, *No fue posible la paz*, pp. 563–72; García Venero, *Fanjul*, pp. 226–8; Serrano Suñer, *Memorias*, pp. 56–8.
113 See Paul Preston, *Franco: A Biography* (London: HarperCollins, 1993) pp. 127–8; Franco, *Apuntes personales*, pp. 34–5.
114 Primo de Rivera, *Textos*, pp. 925–9; García Venero, *Falange/Hedilla*, p. 49; Southworth, *Antifalange*, p. 76.
115 Ansaldo, *¿Para qué?*, p. 121.
116 Reproduced in Bravo, *José Antonio*, p. 130. See also Ximénez de Sandoval, '*José Antonio*', pp. 757–8.
117 Testimonio de Miguel Primo de Rivera, Primo de Rivera y Urquijo, *Papeles póstumos*, pp. 219–21; José Antonio Primo de Rivera, to Onésimo Redondo, 17 June 1936, José Antonio Primo de Rivera, *Textos inéditos y epistolario* (Madrid: Ediciones del Movimiento, 1956) p. 502; José María Mancisidor, *Frente a frente (José Antonio Primo de Rivera frente al Tribunal Popular) (Texto taquigráfico del Juicio Oral de Alicante) Noviembre 1936* 2ª edición (Madrid: Editorial Almena, 1975) pp. 69, 102, 146, 150; Gibson, *En busca de José Antonio*, pp. 149–51.
118 Primo de Rivera to Giménez Caballero, 12 July 1936, reproduced in Bravo, *José Antonio*, pp. 135–6; Primo de Rivera to Mola, 15 July 1936, Primo de Rivera, *Textos inéditos y epistolario*, p. 513; Gibson, *En busca de José Antonio*, pp. 151–6; Gil Pecharromán, *José Antonio Primo de Rivera*, pp. 494–7. His brother Miguel later claimed that, two days earlier, José Antonio had given his sister a similar letter for transmission to Mola, containing the question 'Does the assassination of a member of parliament on government orders justify and excuse all violence?' There is, however, no corroborating evidence of the existence of this letter while a fragment from the one carried by Mayalde has been published. See 'Testimonio de Miguel Primo de Rivera', Primo de Rivera y Urquijo, *Papeles póstumos*, pp. 221–3.
119 Testimonio de Miguel Primo de Rivera, Primo de Rivera y Urquijo, *Papeles póstumos*, pp. 224–34; Gibson, *En busca de José Antonio*, pp. 156–9; el último manifiesto, Primo de Rivera, *Textos*, pp. 951–2; Francisco Bravo, *José Antonio ante la justicia roja* (Madrid: Ediciones de la Vicesecretaría de Educación Popular, 1941) pp. 32–5.
120 *Homenaje a Diego Martínez Barrio* (Paris: Imprimerie La Ruche Ouvrière, 1978) pp. 185–9; Gibson, *En busca de José Antonio*, pp. 250–3.
121 Some of José Antonio Primo de Rivera's prison writings are reproduced by Prieto, *Convulsiones* I, pp. 137–44. A heavily censored version, which omits his projected government of conciliation, is reproduced in Primo de Rivera, *Textos*, pp. 951–7. The definitive edition is Primo de Rivera y Urquijo, *Papeles póstumos*.
122 Prieto, *Convulsiones de España* I,

pp. 145–6; Bravo, *José Antonio frente a la justicia roja*, pp. 41–3.

123 Primo de Rivera, *Textos*, pp. 933–8; Prieto, *Convulsiones* I, pp. 136–7.

124 Bravo, *José Antonio*, p. 104.

125 Julián Zugazagoitia, *Guerra y vicisitudes de los españoles* 2 vols (Paris: Librería Española, 1968) I, pp. 256–9.

126 Zugazagoitia, *Guerra y vicisitudes* I, pp. 176–7.

127 Ximénez de Sandoval, '*José Antonio*', pp. 784–5; Angel Viñas, *Guerra, dinero, dictadura: ayuda fascista y autarquía en la España de Franco* (Barcelona: Editorial Crítica, 1984) pp. 69–97; taped testimony of Hans Joachim von Knobloch to Sheelagh Ellwood; García Venero, *Falange/Hedilla*, pp. 200–7.

128 *News Chronicle*, 24 October 1936; Gibson, *En busca*, pp. 161–70; Southworth, *Antifalange*, pp. 144–8.

129 Claude G. Bowers to Acting Secretary of State, 20 November 1936, *Foreign Relations of the United States 1936* II (Washington: US Government Printing Office, 1954) p. 568.

130 Bravo, *José Antonio frente la justicia roja*, pp. 73–82, 88–123; Mancisidor, *Frente a frente*, pp. 29–263. The interrogation of José Antonio, pp. 47–83, his summing-up, pp. 195–200.

131 See affidavit by a member of the firing squad reproduced in Southworth, *Antifalange*, pp. 162–3.

132 García Venero, *Falange/Hedilla*, p. 255.

133 Southworth, *Antifalange*, pp. 164–5.

134 Primo de Rivera, *Textos*, p. 955.

135 Facsimile of letter from José Antonio Primo de Rivera to Serrano Suñer and Fernández Cuesta, 19 November 1936, Angel Alcázar de Velasco, *Serrano Suñer en la Falange* (Madrid/Barcelona: Patria, 1941) between pp. 166–7; Zugazagoitia, *Guerra* I, pp. 256–64; Prieto, *Convulsiones de España* I, pp. 130–53; Southworth, *Antifalange*, p. 203; Serrano Suñer, *Memorias*, pp. 483–4; Primo de Rivera, *Papeles póstumos*, p. 143.

136 Mancisidor, *Frente a frente*, pp. 274–5; Southworth, *Antifalange*, p. 148.

137 *News Chronicle*, 24 October 1936.

138 Francisco Largo Caballero, *Mis recuerdos* (Mexico D. F.: Editores Unidos, 1954) pp. 208–9.

139 Manuel Azaña, *Apuntes de memoria inéditos y cartas 1938–1939–1940* (Valencia: Pre-Textos, 1990) p. 20.

4 Fascism and Flower-arranging: Pilar Primo de Rivera

1 Helen Graham, 'Gender and the State: Women in the 1940s' in Helen Graham & Jo Labanyi, *Spanish Cultural Studies: An Introduction. The Struggle for Modernity* (Oxford: Oxford University Press, 1995) pp. 182–94.

2 Julio Gil Pecharromán, *José Antonio Primo de Rivera. Retrato de un visionario* (Madrid: Temas de Hoy, 1996) pp. 35–7.

3 All biographies of José Antonio Primo de Rivera, following an error in the first, by Felipe Ximénez de Sandoval, give the date of the death of his mother as 9 June 1908. The correct date, 9 June 1909, was confirmed to me by Fernando's son, Miguel Primo de Rivera y Urquijo (12 September 1997). See also his book *Papeles póstumos de José Antonio* (Barcelona: Plaza y Janés, 1996) pp. 47–8.

4 Pilar Primo de Rivera, *Recuerdos de una vida* (Madrid: Ediciones Dyrsa, 1983) p. 16.

5 I am grateful to Miguel Primo de Rivera y Urquijo for sharing with me his memories of Tía Ma.

6 Primo de Rivera, *Recuerdos*, pp. 17–21.

7 Primo de Rivera, *Recuerdos*, p. 40.

8 Dionisio Ridruejo, *Casi unas memorias* (Barcelona: Planeta, 1976)

p. 52. I am also indebted for information about Pilar to Kathleen Richmond who interviewed many affiliates of the Sección Femenina who knew Pilar well and to Mabel Marañón and Marisa Laporta Girón.

9 María Teresa Gallego Méndez, *Mujer, Falange y franquismo* (Madrid: Taurus, 1983) pp. 26–7, 44–5; Shirley Mangini, *Memories of Resistance. Women's Voices from the Spanish Civil War* (New Haven: Yale University Press, 1995) p. 91; Primo de Rivera, *Recuerdos*, pp. 60, 65.

10 *Arriba*, No.7, 2 May 1935. The printing of the fly-sheet in Luis Suárez Ferñandez, *Crónica de la Sección Femenina y su tiempo* (Madrid: Asociación Nueva Andadura, 1993) p. 39.

11 Primo de Rivera, *Recuerdos*, p. 71; Francisco Bravo Martínez, *Historia de Falange Española de las JONS* 2ª edición (Madrid: Editora Nacional, 1943) p. 141; Suárez Fernández, *Crónica*, pp. 34–6, 43–5; Gallego Méndez, *Mujer, Falange y franquismo*, pp. 40–1.

12 Primo de Rivera, *Recuerdos*, p. 70; Suárez Fernández, *Crónica*, pp. 34–6, 43–5, 47.

13 Testimony of Miguel Primo de Rivera y Urquijo to the author; Primo de Rivera, *Recuerdos*, pp. 75–9; Suárez Fernández, *Crónica*, pp. 50–4.

14 Maximiano García Venero, *Falange en la guerra de España: la Unificación y Hedilla* (Paris: Ruedo Ibérico, 1967) pp. 205–6.

15 García Venero, *Falange/Hedilla*, p. 272.

16 García Venero, *Falange/Hedilla*, pp. 282–4, 304, 314.

17 They were married on 12 February 1931 in Valladolid, see José Luis Mínguez Goyanes, *Onésimo Redondo 1905–1936. Precursor sindicalista* (Madrid: Editorial San Martín, 1990) p. 23.

18 Ridruejo, *Casi unas memorias*, pp. 82–3; Mónica Orduña Prada, *El Auxilio Social (1936–1940). La etapa fundacional y los primeros años* (Madrid: Escuela Libre Editorial, 1996) pp. 23–5, 32–8; Javier Martínez Bedoya, *Memorias desde mi aldea* (Valladolid: Ambito Ediciones, 1996) pp. 85–90, 108–9.

19 Martínez Bedoya, *Memorias*, p. 105–6; Orduña Prada, *El Auxilio Social*, pp. 40–1.

20 Primo de Rivera, *Recuerdos*, p. 103; Ridruejo, *Casi unas memorias*, p. 82. Pilar's memoirs were ghosted by a journalist on the basis of interviews with her (conversation of the author with Miguel Primo de Rivera y Urquijo).

21 Orduña Prada, *El Auxilio Social*, pp. 42–3.

22 Martínez Bedoya, *Memorias*, pp. 101, 107; José Antonio Girón de Velasco, *Si la memoria no me falla* (Barcelona: Editorial Planeta, 1994) p. 43; Stanley G. Payne, *Falange. A History of Spanish Fascism* (Stanford: Stanford University Press, 1961) pp. 122–5.

23 Martínez Bedoya, *Memorias*, p. 104.

24 Francisco Bravo, *José Antonio. El hombre, el jefe, el camarada* (Madrid: Ediciones Españolas, 1939) pp. 82–4; Rafael Ibáñez Hernández, *Estudio y acción. La Falange fundacional a la luz del Diario de Alejandro Salazar (1934–1936)* (Madrid: Ediciones Barbarroja, 1993) pp. 75–6; Martínez Bedoya, *Memorias*, pp. 80–1, 120, 127–8.

25 Martínez Bedoya, *Memorias*, pp. 107, 109; García Venero, *Falange/Hedilla*, p. 283; Herbert Rutledge Southworth, *Antifalange; estudio crúico de 'Falange en la guerra de España' de Maximiano García Venero* (Paris: Ruedo Ibérico, 1967) pp. 171–3; Heleno Saña, *El franquismo sin mitos: conversaciones con Serrano Suñer* (Barcelona: Grijalbo, 1982) pp. 84–5; Orduña Prada, *El Auxilio Social*, pp. 46–8;

Ridruejo, *Casi unas memorias*, p. 82.

26 García Venero, *Falange/Hedilla*, pp. 339–48.

27 Ramón Serrano Suñer, *Entre Hendaya y Gibraltar* (Madrid: Ediciones y Publicaciones Españolas, 1947) p. 42; Saña, *El franquismo*, p. 153: García Venero, *Falange/Hedilla*, p. 290; Primo de Rivera, *Recuerdos*, p. 100.

28 Ramón Serrano Suñer, *Entre el silencio y la propaganda, la Historia como fue. Memorias* (Barcelona: Planeta, 1977) pp. 170–2; Ridruejo, *Casi unas memorias*, p. 77.

29 *Actas del último Consejo Nacional de Falange Española de las JONS (Salamanca, 18–19–IV–1937) y algunas noticias referentes a la Jefatura nacional de prensa y propaganda*, edited by Vicente de Cadenas y Vicent, (Madrid: Gráficas Uguina, 1975) pp. 65–6.

30 García Venero, *Falange/Hedilla*, pp. 402–3, 424–5; Ridruejo, *Casi unas memorias*, p. 99; Primo de Rivera, *Recuerdos*, pp. 109–10; Paul Preston, *Franco: A Biography* (London: HarperCollins, 1993) pp. 248–74.

31 Martínez Bedoya, *Memorias*, p. 110; Orduña Prada, *El Auxilio Social*, pp. 58–9.

32 Serrano Suñer, *Entre Hendaya y Gibraltar*, p. 42; Primo de Rivera, *Recuerdos*, p. 102; Ridruejo, *Casi unas memorias*, p. 102; Stanley G. Payne, *The Franco Regime 1936–1975* (Madison: University of Wisconsin Press, 1987) pp. 174–5.

33 Primo de Rivera, *Recuerdos*, pp. 110–11; Raimundo Fernández Cuesta, *Testimonio, recuerdos y reflexiones* (Madrid: Ediciones Dyrsa, 1985) pp. 107–34.

34 Gallego Méndez, *Mujer, Falange y franquismo*, pp. 58–9.

35 Martínez Bedoya, *Memorias*, pp. 116–17; Suárez Fernández, *Crónica*, pp. 68–9, 90–1; Orduña Prada, *El Auxilio Social*, pp. 202–8; Gallego Méndez, *Mujer, Falange y franquismo*, pp. 59–66, 91–5; Rosario Sánchez López, *Mujer española, una sombra de destino en lo universal. Trayectoria histórica de Sección Femenina de Falange (1934–1977)* (Murcia: Universidad de Murcia, 1990) pp. 35–40.

36 Pilar Primo de Rivera, *Discursos, circulares, escritos* (Madrid: Sección Femenina de FET y de las JONS, n.d. 1950) pp. 14–21; Suárez Fernández, *Crónica*, pp. 73–6; Geraldine M. Scanlon, *La polémica feminista en la España contemporánea 1868–1974* 2ª edición (Madrid: Akal, 1986) pp. 314–16.

37 Conferencia de Ernesto Giménez Caballero, *Dolor y memoria de España en el II aniversario de la muerte de José Antonio* (Barcelona: Ediciones Jerarquía, 1939) pp. 49–50; Daniel Sueiro & Bernardo Díaz Nosty, *Historia del franquismo* 2 vols, 2nd edition (Barcelona: Argos Vergara, 1985) I, pp. 176–7.

38 Ramón Garriga, *La España de Franco: las relaciones con Hitler* 2ª edición (Puebla, Mexico: Cajica, 1970) p. 41.

39 Garriga, *La España de Franco: las relaciones con Hitler*, p. 326.

40 Primo de Rivera, *Escritos*, p. 62.

41 Primo de Rivera, *Recuerdos*, p. 129.

42 Martínez Bedoya, *Memorias*, p. 120; Orduña Prada, *El Auxilio Social*, pp. 64–9, 293–303.

43 Martínez Bedoya, *Memorias*, p. 134–9; Girón de Velasco, *Si la memoria*, pp. 52–6; Orduña Prada, *El Auxilio Social*, pp. 69–73.

44 Martínez Bedoya, *Memorias*, p. 128.

45 Martínez Bedoya, *Memorias*, pp. 141–6; Ridruejo, *Casi unas memorias*, p. 79; Orduña Prada, *El Auxilio Social*, pp. 73–7, 145–6.

46 Orduña Prada, *El Auxilio Social*, pp. 106.

47 Pilar Primo de Rivera, *Discuros, circulares, escritos* (Madrid; Sección Femenina de FET y de las JONS, n.d. [1950]), pp. 152–3; [Francisco Franco Bahamonde], *Palabras del Caudillo 19 abril 1937–7 diciembre 1942* (Madrid: Ediciones de la

Vice-Secretaría de Educación Popular, 1943) pp. 111–14; Primo de Rivera, *Recuerdos*, pp. 145–7, 157–8. See also Gallego Méndez, *Mujer, Falange y franquismo*, pp. 88–90.

48 Interview with Pilar quoted by Mangini, *Memories of Resistance*, p. 92.

49 Primo de Rivera, *Recuerdos*, p. 105.

50 Suárez Fernández, *Crónica*, pp. 81, 101.

51 Pilar Primo de Rivera, *Escritos*, pp. 22–4.

52 Pilar Primo de Rivera, *Escritos*, p. 109.

53 Pilar Primo de Rivera, *Escritos*, p. 109.

54 Pilar Primo de Rivera, *La mujer en casa* (Barcelona: Ediciones del Congreso de la Familia Española, 1963) cited by Sueiro & Díaz Nosty, *Historia del franquismo*, I, p. 363.

55 Carmen Martín Gaite, *Usos amorosos de la postguerra española* (Barcelona: Editorial Anagrama, 1987) p. 56.

56 Pilar Primo de Rivera, *Escritos*, pp. 270–1.

57 Gallego Méndez, *Mujer, Falange y franquismo*, pp. 73–6.

58 Gallego Méndez, *Mujer, Falange y franquismo*, p. 106.

59 I am indebted to Dr Helen Graham both for this point and for her constructive criticism of the entire chapter.

60 Memorandum of conversation between Serrano Suñer and Bernard Malley, autumn 1945, undated, PRO FO371/49663, Z13272/11696/41. For the decree, *Boletín Oficial del Estado*, 4 May 1941.

61 *Arriba*, 3 May 1941; Ciano to Serrano Suñer, 4 May 1941, Galeazzo Ciano, *L'Europa verso la catastrofe* (Milan: Mondadori, 1948) pp. 658–9; Galeazzo Ciano, *Diario 1937–1943* a cura di Renzo De Felice (Milan: Rizzoli, 1980) p. 509.

62 *ABC*, 6, 8 May; *El Alcázar*, 6 May; *Arriba*, 10, 11 May; *Boletín Oficial del Estado*, 10 May 1941; Xavier Tusell & Genoveva García Queipo de Llano, *Franco y Mussolini: la política española durante la segunda guerra mundial* (Barcelona: Editorial Planeta, 1985) pp. 131–2.

63 Pilar Primo de Rivera to Franco, undated, Miguel Primo de Rivera to Franco, 1 May 1941, Serrano Suñer to Franco, 5 May 1941, *Documentos inéditos para la historia del Generalísimo Franco* 4 vols (Madrid: Fundación Nacional Francisco Franco, 1992–1993), II–2, pp. 139–45; Girón de Velasco, *Si la memoria no me falla*, p. 76; Southworth, *Antifalange*, p. 217.

64 Saña, *El franquismo*, pp. 160–2.

65 Testimony of Ramón Serrano Suñer to the author, 21 November 1990.

66 Lequio to Ciano, 15 May 1941, *I Documenti Diplomatici Italiani, 9ª serie, vol. VII (24 aprile – 11 dicembre 1941)* (Roma: Istituto Poligrafico e Zecca dello Stato/ Libreria dello Stato, 1987) pp. 107–8.

67 *Arriba*, 21, 22 May 1941.

68 Ramón Serrano Suñer, *Entre el silencio y la propaganda, la Historia como fue. Memorias* (Barcelona: Editorial Planeta, 1977) pp. 200–1.

69 Martínez Bedoya, *Memorias*, p. 174.

70 [Franco], *Palabras del Caudillo 1937–1942*, pp. 211–16.

71 Pilar Primo de Rivera to Franco, 1 June 1942, *Documentos inéditos*, III, p. 545.

72 Serrano Suñer, *Entre Hendaya y Gibraltar*, p. 42; Pedro Laín Entralgo, *Descargo de conciencia (1930–1960)* (Barcelona: Barral Editores, 1976) pp. 200–1.

73 Daniel Sueiro, *El Valle de los Caídos: los secretos de la cripta franquista* 2ª edición (Barcelona: Argos Vergara, 1983) pp. 166–82; José Andrés-Gallego, *¿Fascismo o Estado católico? Ideología, religión y censura en la España de Franco 1937–1941*

(Madrid: Ediciones Encuentro, 1997) pp. 43, 94, 153–4; Suárez Fernández, *Crónica*, pp. 79–80, 113–14.

74 Primo de Rivera, *Recuerdos*, pp. 210–11.

75 Wayne Harold Bowen, *Spaniards and Nazi Germany: Collaboration in the New Order* Ph.D. dissertation (Ouachita Baptist University, Arkadelphia, Arkansas, January 1997) pp. 61, 67.

76 *Correspondência de Pedro Teotónio Pereira para Oliveira Salazar* 4 vols (Lisbon: Presidência do Conselho de Ministros, 1987–1991) II, p. 119

77 Amando de Miguel, *La herencia de Franco* (Madrid: Editorial Cambio 16, 1976) pp. 131–2; Suárez Fernández, *Crónica*, pp. 150–1.

78 Primo de Rivera, *Recuerdos*, p. 210; Suárez Fernández, *Crónica*, p. 147.

79 Ernesto Giménez Caballero has given two accounts of the fate of his scheme, in *Genio de España* 7th edition (Madrid: Doncel, 1971) pp. 218–23 and in *Memorias de un dictador* (Barcelona: Planeta, 1979) pp. 148–52.

80 Giménez Caballero *Memorias*, p. 154.

81 Primo de Rivera, *Recuerdos*, p. 210.

82 Giménez Caballero, *Memorias*, p. 198; Primo de Rivera, *Recuerdos*, p. 209.

83 *Documentos inéditos para la historia del Generalísimo Franco* IV (Madrid: Fundación Nacional Francisco Franco, 1994) pp. 502–3.

84 Primo de Rivera, *Recuerdos*, p. 101.

85 Saña, *El franquismo*, p. 83.

86 The accusation was communicated to me privately by Dr Southworth. On Marichu de la Mora in the Sección Femenina, see Primo de Rivera, *Recuerdos*, pp. 103, 105, 109, 110, 129, 285; Southworth, *Antifalange*, p. 200; García Venero, *Falange/Hedilla*, p. 402. For her relationship with her sister, see Constancia de la Mora, *In Place of Splendour. The Autobiography of a Spanish Woman* (London: Michael Joseph, 1940) *passim* and especially pp. 211, 241.

87 Gerald R. Kleinfeld & Lewis A. Tambs, *Hitler's Spanish Legion: The Blue Division in Russia* (Carbondale: Southern Illinois University Press, 1979) pp. 184, 187; Primo de Rivera, *Recuerdos*, p. 290; Suárez Fernández, *Crónica*, pp. 139–42.

88 *Arriba*, 21 May 1943.

89 Archivo General de la Administración, P. SGM 54 'Informe del viaje de la Delegada Nacional de la Sección Femenina a Alemania, Delegación Nacional de la Sección Femenina, Servicio Exterior.'

90 Ramón Garriga, *La España de Franco: de la División Azul al pacto con los Estados Unidos (1943 a 1951)* (Puebla, Mexico: Cajica, 1971) p. 17; Bowen, *Spaniards and Nazi Germany: Collaboration in the New Order*, pp. 254–6, 268–9.

91 Suárez Fernández, *Crónica*, pp. 157–8, 161.

92 *Documentos inéditos* IV, p. 502.

93 *Documentos inéditos* IV, pp. 506–9.

94 Pilar Primo de Rivera, *Escritos*, pp. 64–9.

95 José Luis de Arrese, *Una etapa constituyente* (Barcelona: Planeta, 1982) pp. 159–71; Preston, *Franco*, pp. 650–64; Suárez Fernández, *Crónica*, pp. 306–12.

96 Suárez Fernández, *Crónica*, pp. 331–2, 363–4, 393–6, 405–8, 421–2.

97 Suárez Fernández, *Crónica*, pp. 484–5.

98 Information provided to the author by Miguel Primo de Rivera y Urquijo; *El País*, 18, 19 November 1976.

99 Primo de Rivera, *Recuerdos*, pp. 194–5; Sánchez López, *Mujer española*, pp. 42–6; Suárez Fernández, *Crónica*, pp. 314, 343, 346–9.

5 A Quixote in Politics: Salvador de Madariaga

1 *La Voz de Galicia*, 24 July 1986.
2 Josep Trueta, *Surgeon in War and Peace* (London: Victor Gollancz, 1980) p. 211; conversation of the author with Manuel Azcárate who knew Madariaga in Geneva.
3 One specialist authority wrote of being overwhelmed by 'the breadth of the poetic *oeuvre*'. Damáso Alonso, *Salvador de Madariaga, poeta* (La Coruña: Ayuntamiento, 1979) p. 1.
4 Salvador de Madariaga, *Don Quixote: An Introductory Essay in Psychology* (Oxford, Oxford University Press, 1934) pp. 96, 111.
5 Salvador de Madariaga, *Memorias (1921–1936) Amanecer sin mediodía* (Madrid: Espasa Calpe, 1974) pp. 445–6. Henceforth *Memorias*. There exists a slightly truncated version in English, from which translations have been taken, *Morning Without Noon Memoirs* (Westmead: Saxon House, 1974). On the musicians concerned, see Eric Blom, editor, *Grove's Dictionary of Music and Musicians* 5th edition (London: Macmillan, 1954) Vol.7, p. 419; Vol.9, p. 243.
6 Salvador de Madariaga, *Memorias de un federalista*, 2nd edition (Madrid: Espasa Calpe, 1977) pp. 227, 232. Henceforth *Federalista*.
7 Enrique Montero, 'Luis Araquistain y la propaganda aliada durante la Primera Guerra Mundial', *Estudios de Historia Social*, No.s 24–25, Enero–junio 1983, p. 245; Manuel Tuñón de Lara, *Medio siglo de cultura española (1985–1936)* 3rd edition (Madrid: Tecnos, 1973) p. 145.
8 Montero, 'propaganda aliada' pp. 246–9; *Federalista*, pp. 237–8; *Memorias*, p. 328.
9 *Memorias*, pp. 18–23.
10 *Memorias*, pp. 35–9.
11 *Memorias*, pp. 119, 208, 216.
12 *Memorias*, p. 158–9, 184.
13 *Federalista*, pp. 253; *Memorias*, pp. 184–9; cf. Roser Caminals Gost, *Salvador de Madariaga and National Character*, unpublished Ph.D thesis (University of Barcelona, 1986) p. 11.
14 *Memorias*, pp. 227–9, 248.
15 Azaña, diary entry for 9 October 1931, Manuel Azaña, *Obras completas* 4 vols (Mexico DF: Oasis, 1966–8) IV, p. 163. Henceforth *OOCC*. On Lerroux, see Francisco Largo Caballero, *Mis recuerdos* (Mexico: Editores Unidos, 1953) p. 121; Henry Buckley, *Life and Death of the Spanish Republic* (London: Hamish Hamilton, 1940) pp. 186–7.
16 For details of Madariaga's diplomatic career, see Jesús Riosalido, 'El expediente diplomático personal del Embajador Don Salvador de Madariaga', *Salvador de Madariaga 1886–1986* (La Coruña: Ayuntamiento de La Coruña, 1987) pp. 89–96.
17 See Francisco Fernández Ordóñez, 'Homenaje a un Europeo de España', *Salvador de Madariaga 1886–1986*, pp. 145–7.
18 Azaña, diary entry for 22 February 1932, *OOCC* IV, p. 336.
19 Azaña, diary entries for 19 March, 19 April 1932, *OOCC* IV, pp. 356, 373.
20 Azaña, diary entries for 8 September, 8 December 1932, Manuel Azaña, *Diarios, 1932–1933 'Los cuadernos robados'* (Barcelona: Grijalbo, 1997) pp. 60–1, 95–6.
21 Lord Vansittart, *The Mist Procession* (London: Hutchinson, 1958) p. 438.
22 Azaña, *OOCC* IV, p. 609.
23 *Memorias*, pp. 282–300; Thomas Jones, *A Diary With Letters 1931–1950* (London: Oxford University Press, 1954) p. 63; Caminals, p. 17.
24 Raffaele Guariglia, *Primi passi in Diplomazia e Rapporti dall 'Ambasciata di Madrid 1932–1934*

(Naples: Edizioni Scientifiche Italiani, 1972) pp. 294, 317, 329, 340.

25 Claude Bowers, *My Mission to Spain* (London: Victor Gollancz, 1954) pp. 71–2.

26 *Memorias*, pp. 262–8, 368, 394, 400, 616–23. He seems to have believed that Lerroux wanted him to take over the leadership of the Radical Party, pp. 285–6, 531.

27 Paul Preston, *The Coming of the Spanish Civil War: Reform, Reaction and Revolution in the Second Spanish Republic 1931–1936* 2nd edition (London, Routledge, 1994) pp. 145–7.

28 Bowers, *My Mission*, p. 87.

29 Paul Preston, 'Azaña y el Frente Popular' in Vicente Manuel Serrano & José María San Luciano, *Azaña* (Madrid: Edascal, 1980) pp. 282–3. The best account of the persecution of Azaña remains his own *Mi rebelión en Barcelona* (Madrid: Espasa Calpe, 1935).

30 *Ahora*, 20 March 1935; Salvador de Madariaga, *Spain A Modern History* (London: Jonathan Cape, 1971) p. 434; Henceforth *Spain*. *Memorias*, pp. 409, 417, 422.

31 Raul Morodo, 'Madariaga', *El País*, 23 May 1986.

32 *Memorias*, p. 532.

33 Guariglia, *Ambasciata*, p. 376.

34 See Rafael Calvo Serer, *La literatura universal sobre la guerra de España* (Madrid: Ateneo, 1962) p. 63; Gonzalo Fernández de la Mora, *Los teóricos izquierdistas en la democracia orgánica*, cited by Morodo, 'Madariaga'. *¿Qué pasa en España? El problema del socialismo español* (Madrid: Cedesa, 1959) pp. 23–88; cf. Francisco J. Bobillo, 'El pensamiento político', *El País*, 28 July 1986.

35 Salvador de Madariaga, *De la angustia a la libertad* 2nd edition (Madrid: Espasa Calpe, 1977) pp. 51–2, 101, 161.

36 Earl of Avon, *Facing the Dictators* (London: Cassell, 1962) pp. 114–15; Bowers, *My Mission*, pp. 154–5; Felipe Ximénez de Sándoval, *José Antonio. Biografía* 2nd edition (Madrid: Gráficas Lazareno-Echaniz, 1949) p. 406.

37 Ximénez de Sándoval, *José Antonio*, pp. 413–14.

38 *Memorias*, p. 566.

39 Isabel de Madariaga, 'Salvador de Madariaga et le Foreign Office' in *Revista de Estudios Internacionales* Vol.4, No.2, abril–junio 1983 p. 230. (Henceforth 'SMFO'). Letter of Thomas Jones to Abraham Flexner, Jones, *Diary*, p. 239; *Federalista*, p. 272; *Memorias*, pp. 558–62.

40 *Memorias*, p. 552.

41 Antonio Marquina Barrio, 'Planes internacionales de mediación durante la guerra civil', *Revista de Estudios Internacionales*, Vol.5, No.3, Julio–septiembre 1984.

42 Mr Eden to Sir Henry Chilton, 24 July 1936 (W6893/3694/41), *Documents on British Foreign Policy 1919–1939*, Vol. XVII *Western Pact Negotiations: Outbreak of the Spanish Civil War June 1936–January 1937* edited by W. N. Medlicott & Douglas Dakin (London: HMSO, 1979) pp. 19–20. (Henceforth *DBFP*.)

43 Pablo de Azcárate, *Mi embajada en Londres durante la guerra civil española* (Barcelona: Ariel, 1976) p. 58.

44 FO371/20553, W9656/62/41.

45 Angel Viñas, *La Alemania nazi y el 18 de julio* 2nd edition (Madrid: Alianza, 1977) pp. 321–70; Denis Smyth, '"We Are With You": Solidarity and Self-Interest in Soviet Policy Towards Republican Spain, 1936–1939' in Paul Preston & Ann Mackenzie, editors, *The Republic Besieged: Civil War in Spain 1936–1939* (Edinburgh, Edinburgh University Press, 1996).

46 I. de Madariaga, 'SMFO' pp. 231–2; Eden to Chilton, 20 August 1936 (W9248/62/41), *DBFP*, pp. 140–1.

47 Avon, *Facing the Dictators*, p. 405; I. de Madariaga, 'SMFO', pp. 233–7.
48 *Memorias*, pp. 724–5.
49 Madariaga, *Spain*, pp. 692–3.
50 Jones, *Diary*, pp. 269–71. Madariaga had had some contact with Prieto before the war broke out. See the exchange of letters between them in *Memorias*, pp. 719–23.
51 Azcárate, *Mi embajada*, pp. 260–1; I. de Madariaga, 'SMFO', p. 239.
52 Jones to Lady Grigg, 3 November 1936, in Jones, *Diary*, p. 280.
53 FO371/20548, W15838/62/41.
54 FO371/20535, W17694/62/41; cf. I. de Madariaga, 'SMFO', pp. 241–53.
55 Madariaga, *Spain*, pp. 693–5.
56 FO371/22659, W172/86/41.
57 FO371/22659, W5836/86/41.
58 Monteiro to Salazar, 15 June, 12 July, 1938, *Dez anos de política externa (1936–1947). A nação portuguesa e a segunda guerra mundial* Vol.V (Lisbon: Imprensa Nacional, 1967) pp. 323–7, 350–1.
59 Monteiro to Salazar, 19 November 1938, *Dez anos de política externa* pp. 537–41.
60 On anti-Francoist opposition, see Paul Preston, 'The Anti Francoist Opposition: The Long March to Unity' in Preston, editor, *Spain in Crisis: The Evolution and Decline of the Franco Regime* (Hassocks: Harvester Press, 1976); Sergio Vilar, *Historia del antifranquismo 1939–1975* (Barcelona: Plaza & Janés, 1984); Xavier Tusell, *La oposición democrática al franquismo 1939–1962* (Barcelona: Planeta, 1977).
61 Trueta, *Surgeon*, p. 211.
62 *Memorias*, p. 165.
63 Hartmut Heine, *La oposición política al franquismo* (Barcelona: Crítica, 1983) pp. 34, 284.
64 Trueta noted a tendency to anti-Catalanism in Madariaga. When Trueta was involved in successful BBC Catalan language broadcasts to Barcelona, Madariaga 'pressed the British authorities to suspend the broadcasts on the grounds that "they would only bring about increased military and Francoist intolerance towards Catalonia"'. Trueta, *Surgeon*, pp. 172, 160, 211; *Federalista*, pp. 279–80, 294–306, 310.
65 Heine, *Oposición*, p. 328; José María Gil Robles, diary entries for 26 November 1943 & 7 August 1946, *La monarquía por la que yo luché* (Madrid: Taurus, 1976) pp. 69, 188.
66 Salvador de Madariaga, 'Prospects in Spain', *The Spectator*, 8 February 1946; 'The Problem of Franco Spain', *Contemporary Review*, CLXX, September 1946.
67 Memorandum by Hickerson, 10 March, and subsequent correspondence between the State Department and the US Embassy in London, 7–25 April 1947, *Foreign Relations of the United States 1947* (Washington: Government Printing Office, 1972) Vol. III, pp. 1062–75. I am indebted to Professor Qasim Ahmad of the Universiti Sains Malaysia of Penang for drawing my attention to this incident.
68 Gil Robles, diary entry for 13 July 1947, *La monarquía*, p. 228.
69 *Federalista*, p. 310; Gil Robles, diary entry for 18 April 1948, *La monarquía*, p. 259; Tusell, *La oposición democrática*, p. 384.
70 Madariaga to Prieto, 31 May 1948; Prieto to Madariaga, 30 June 1948; Madariaga to José Antonio Aguirre, 20 October 1952, 10 November 1952, 28 December 1959; to Josep Batista i Roca 30 July 1957, and to Josep Tarradellas 22 November 1952, 6 June 1963, *Federalista*, pp. 311, 337–45, 482–99.
71 *Federalista*, p. 311; *Spain*, p. 601.
72 Tusell, *La oposición democrática*, pp. 384, 386.
73 Ricardo de la Cierva, *Francisco Franco: biografía histórica* 6 vols (Barcelona: Planeta, 1984) VI, p. 300.

74 Elías Díaz, *Pensamiento Español 1939–1973* (Madrid: Edicusa, 1974) pp. 208–9.
75 *Memorias*, pp. 121–2. On Gorkín, see Herbert R. Southworth, 'The Grand Camouflage: Julián Gorkín, Burnett Bolloten and the Spanish Civil War' in Paul Preston & Ann Mackenzie, editors, *The Republic Besieged: Civil War in Spain 1936–1939* (Edinburgh: Edinburgh University Press, 1996) pp. 261–310.
76 Salvador de Madariaga, *General, márchese usted* (New York: Ibérica, 1959) pp. 107–11.
77 *Spain*, pp. 630, 634.
78 Francisco Franco Salgado-Araujo, diary entries for 21 July 1962, 2 March 1963, 11 October 1969, *Mis conversaciones privadas con Franco* (Barcelona: Planeta, 1976) pp. 348, 376, 549–50.
79 *Spain*, pp. 630–7, 646.
80 Ignacio Fernández de Castro & José Martínez, editors, *España hoy* (Paris: Ruedo Ibérico, 1963) pp. 235–56. An indispensable collection of documents and interviews with protagonists of the Munich conference is to be found in Joaquín Satrústeguí et al., editors, *Cuando la transición se hizo posible. El 'contubernio de Múnich'* (Madrid: Tecnos, 1993). See also Tusell, *La oposición democrática*, pp. 388–432; Pedro Sainz Rodríguez, *Un reinado en la sombra* (Barcelona: Planeta, 1981) pp. 54–6; José María Gil Robles, *Marginalia política* (Barcelona: Ariel, 1975) pp. 121–4.
81 Paul Preston, *Franco: A Biography* (London: HarperCollins, 1993) pp. 702–5.
82 Francisco Franco, *Discursos y mensajes del Jefe del Estado 1960–1963* (Madrid: Publicaciones Españolas, 1964) pp. 412, 423–4, 427.
83 'Les Grands Témoins: Salvador de Madariaga', *Réalités* (Paris) No.369, November 1976.

6 A Pacifist in War: The Betrayal of Julián Besteiro

1 Indalecio Prieto, *Convulsiones de España. Pequeños detalles de grandes sucesos* 3 vols (Mexico: Ediciones Oasis, 1967–9) III, pp. 331, 337.
2 Francisco Casares, *Azaña y Ellos: cincuenta semblanzas rojas* (Granada: Editorial Prieto, 1938) pp. 185–6.
3 Ramón Serrano Suñer, *Entre el silencio y la propaganda, la Historia como fue. Memorias* (Barcelona: Editorial Planeta, 1977) p. 76.
4 Salvador de Madariaga, *Españoles de mi tiempo* (Barcelona: Planeta, 1974) p. 87.
5 Carmen Zulueta, 'Introducción' to Julián Besteiro, *Cartas desde la prisión* (Madrid: Alianza, 1988) p. 13.
6 I am enormously grateful to two people who shared their memories of Besteiro with me – Shevawn Lynam, who knew Besteiro during her time at the Instituto Escuela in Madrid during the Second Republic, and Isabel de Madariaga, who knew him well as both neighbour and close family friend.
7 Manuel Azaña, *Obras completas* 4 vols (Mexico: Oasis, 1968–8) IV, pp. 226–7.
8 Antonio Ramos Oliveira, *Politics, Economics and Men of Modern Spain* (London: Gollancz, 1946) p. 646.
9 Andrés Saborit, *El pensamiento político de Julián Besteiro* (Madrid: Seminarios y Ediciones, 1974) pp. 254, 328–9; Emilio Lamo de Espinosa & Manuel Contreras, *Política y filosofía en Julián Besteiro* 2nd edition (Madrid: Sistema, 1990) pp. 278–319.
10 Paul Heywood, *Marxism and the Failure of Organised Socialism in Spain 1879–1936* (Cambridge: Cambridge University Press, 1990) pp. 90–1, 117–18.
11 Paul Preston, *The Coming of the Spanish Civil War: Reform Reaction

and Revolution in the Second Spanish Republic 1931–1936 2nd edition (London: Routledge, 1994) pp. 14–34.

12 The resentment affected a wide swathe of the party, from Prieto in the centre to Alvarez del Vayo on the left. Azaña, *Obras* IV, p. 62; Julio Alvarez del Vayo, *The Last Optimist* (London: Putnam, 1950) pp. 198–203, 210–11. See also Partido Socialista Obrero Español, *Convocatoria y orden del día para el XIII Congreso ordinario* (Madrid: Gráfica Socialista, 1932) pp. 74–7.

13 *El Socialista*, 22, 24 February 1931; PSOE, *Convocatoria*, pp. 77–83; Andrés Saborit, *Julián Besteiro* (Buenos Aries: Losada, 1967) pp. 200–3.

14 *ABC*, 15 July 1931.

15 Azaña, *Obras* IV, pp. 62, 226–7, 524.

16 Azaña, *Obras* IV, pp. 48, 154, 165, 167, 264.

17 Azaña, *Obras* IV, p. 294.

18 Niceto Alcalá Zamora, *Memorias* (Barcelona: Editorial Planeta, 1977) p. 175.

19 Azaña, *Obras* IV, p. 302.

20 Azaña, *Obras* IV, pp. 354–5; Mariano Ansó, *Yo fui ministro de Negrín* (Barcelona: Editorial Planeta, 1976) p. 230; Alcalá Zamora, *Memorias*, p. 198.

21 Manuel Azaña, diary entry for 4 September 1932, *Diarios, 1932–1933. Los cuadernos robados* (Barcelona: Grijalbo-Mondadori, 1997) p. 58.

22 *El Socialista*, 7, 8, 9, 10, 11, 12, 13, 14 October 1932; Saborit, *Besteiro*, pp. 227–8.

23 *El Socialista*, 14, 15, 16, 17, 18, 19, 20, 21, 22, 23 October 1932; Saborit, *Besteiro*, pp. 227–8.

24 Azaña, *Obras* IV, p. 508.

25 Azaña, diary entry for 21 February 1933, *Diarios, 1932–1933*, p. 183.

26 Azaña, diary entry for 30 April 1933, *Obras* IV, p. 500. On the obstruction and the work generated, see the memoirs of the Secretary to the Chamber, Ansó, *Yo fui ministro de Negrín*, pp. 43–6.

27 Ansó, *Yo fui ministro de Negrín*, pp. 230–1.

28 Azaña, *Obras* IV, p. 530–1, 533.

29 Preston, *The Coming of the Spanish Civil War*, pp. 113–15.

30 *El Socialista*, 25, 26, 28, 30 January 1934; *Boletín de la Unión General de Trabajadores*, February 1934; Gabriel Mario de Coca, *Anti-Caballero: una crítica marxista de la bolchevización del Partido Socialista Obrero Español* (Madrid: Ediciones Engels, 1936) pp. 137–42. See also Preston, *The Coming of the Spanish Civil War*, pp. 137–8.

31 Saborit, *Besteiro*, p. 251; Prieto, *Convulsiones* III, pp. 331–2.

32 Alcalá Zamora, *Memorias*, p. 301.

33 The inaugural lecture was published as Julián Besteiro, *Marxismo y anti-marxismo* (Madrid, 1935). The text is reprinted in Julián Besteiro, *Obras completas* 3 vols (Madrid: Centro de Estudios Constitucionales, 1983) III, pp. 227–334. The subsequent polemic may be consulted in Luis Araquistain, 'El marxismo en la Academia', 'Un marxismo contra Marx', 'La esencia del marxismo', *Leviatán*, Nos. 13–15 (May–July 1935); Julián Besteiro, 'Leviatán: el socialismo mitológico', 'Mi crítico empieza a razonar', *Democracia*, 15 June, 6 July 1935. See also the commentaries by Heywood, *Marxism*, pp. 158–9 and Preston, *The Coming of the Spanish Civil War*, pp. 221–2.

34 Ansó, *Yo fui ministro de Negrín*, p. 232; Lamo de Espinosa & Contreras, *Besteiro*, p. 107.

35 Julián Zugazagoitia, *Guerra y vicisitudes de los Españoles* 2 vols (Paris: Librairie Espagnole, 1968) I, p. 182.

36 Saborit, *Besteiro*, p. 270.

37 Saborit, *Besteiro*, pp. 269, 271–2; Julio Alvarez del Vayo, *Freedom's Battle* (London: Heinemann, 1940)

p. 292; Alvarez del Vayo, *The Last Optimist*, pp. 198–203, 210–11.

38 *ABC*, 20 February 1937.

39 On British reluctance, see minutes by various Foreign Office Officials, 28 January – 4 February 1937, PRO FO372/3233, T2443/1/379 & T2541/1/379.

40 Francisco Largo Caballero, *Mis recuerdos: cartas a un amigo* (Mexico DF: Editores Unidos, 1954) p. 199; Juan-Simeón Vidarte, *Todos fuimos culpables. Testimonio de un socialista español* (Mexico DF: Fondo de Cultura Económica, 1973) p. 760. On 24 March 1937, Sir George Mounsey told Azcárate that 'we were much gratified by the selection of Sr Besteiro for the mission', FO372/3234, T4371/1/379.

41 Minutes by Mounsey & Eden, 29 April, texts of telegrams to ambassadors sent on 11 May 1937, FO371/21333, W9306/7/41.

42 Eden to Phipps (Paris) 11 May 1937 (and to ambassadors in Berlin, Rome, Lisbon and Moscow) 11 May 1937, *Documents on British Foreign Policy 1919–1939* Second Series, Vol. XVIII (London: HMSO, 1980) pp. 732–3; Leche (Valencia) to Eden, 12 May, *British Documents on Foreign Affairs* (Washington: University Publications of America, 1993) p. 108. See also Henderson (Berlin) to Eden, 12 May; Wingfield (Lisbon) to Eden, 13 May; Drummond (Rome) to Eden, 14 May; Chilston (Moscow) to Eden, 15 May; *DBFP 1919–1939* 2, XVIII, pp. 740–2, 750–2.

43 Azaña, *Obras* IV, pp. 588, 833; Pablo de Azcárate, *Mi embajada en Londres durante la guerra civil española* (Barcelona: Ariel, 1976) pp. 64–7; Enrique Moradiellos, *La perfidia de Albión. El Gobierno británico y la guerra civil española* (Madrid: Siglo XXI de España, 1996) p. 171.

44 Azaña, *Obras* IV, pp. 655–6; Henry Buckley, *Life and Death of the Spanish Republic* (London: Hamish Hamilton, 1940) pp. 362–3.

45 Gabriel Jackson, *The Spanish Republic and the Civil War 1931–1939* (Princeton, NJ: Princeton University Press, 1965) pp. 441–2.

46 Largo Caballero, *Mis recuerdos*, p. 200; Zugazagoitia, *Guerra y vicisitudes* II, pp. 144–5.

47 Ansó, *Yo fui ministro de Negrín*, pp. 190–1; Azaña, *Obras* IV, p. 655.

48 Azaña, *Obras* IV, pp. 895–6.

49 Vidarte, *Todos fuimos culpables*, pp. 758–60. See also Jackson, *The Spanish Republic*, pp. 470–1.

50 Ramón Lamoneda, *Posiciones políticas, documentos, correspondencia* (Mexico D.F.: Roca, 1976) p. 95.

51 Buckley, *Life and Death*, p. 363. Buckley's view was shared by the Socialist commentator Antonio Ramos Oliveira, *Politics, Economics and Men*, pp. 645–6.

52 Enrique Tierno Galván, *Cabos sueltos* (Barcelona: Bruguera, 1981) pp. 26–7. On Tierno, who had much in common with Besteiro, not least as a university professor who enjoyed consdierable popularity in Madrid, see Elías Díaz, *Ética contra política. Los intelectuales y el poder* (Madrid: Centro de Estudios Constitucionales, 1990) pp. 131–87 and Raúl Morodo, *Tierno Galván y otros precursores políticos* (Madrid: Ediciones El País, 1987) pp. 157–267.

53 Ansó, *Yo fui ministro de Negrín*, pp. 220–2; Zugazagoitia, *Guerra y vicisitudes* II, p. 145.

54 'Declaración del testigo don Luis de Sosa y Pérez' & 'Declaración de don Antonio Luna García' in Ignacio Arenillas de Chaves, *El proceso de Besteiro* (Madrid: Revista de Occidente, 1976) pp. 188–96. See also ibid., pp. 240, 323–8; Besteiro, *Cartas*, pp. 128, 138; Lamo de Espinosa & Contreras, *Besteiro*, pp. 113–16; Ricardo de la

Cierva, *1939. Agonía y victoria (El protocolo 277)* (Barcelona: Editorial Planeta, 1989) pp. 49–52.

55 'Informe ante el Comité Nacional del Partido Socialista Obrero Español', reproduced in Prieto, *Convulsiones* I, pp. 27–70; Helen Graham, *Socialism and War: The Spanish Socialist Party in Power and Crisis, 1936–1939* (Cambridge: Cambridge University Press, 1991) pp. 136–45; Vidarte, *Todos fuimos culpables*, pp. 844–54; Santos Juliá Díaz, *Historia del socialismo español (1931–1939)* (Barcelona: l'Avenç/ Conjunto Editorial, 1989) pp. 273–5.

56 On the reshuffled candidate list and the reasons for it, see Graham, *Socialism and War*, pp. 115–17, 153–4.

57 Actas de la Comisión Ejecutiva, September 1938, Fundación Pablo Iglesias, AH-20–5; Dolores Ibárruri et al., *Guerra y revolución en España* 4 vols (Moscow: Editorial Progreso, 1967–77) IV, pp. 139–40; Besteiro, *Cartas*, p. 127; Juliá, *Historia del socialismo*, pp. 276–7; Graham, *Socialism and War*, pp. 151–5.

58 Zugazagoitia, *Guerra y vicisitudes* II, pp. 173, 178.

59 Azaña, diary entry for 19 November 1938, *Obras* IV, pp. 895–6; Palmiro Togliatti, *Opere* IV (Rome: Editori Riuniti, 1979) pp. 352, 356.

60 Zugazagoitia, *Guerra y vicisitudes* II, p. 141; Cipriano de Rivas Cherif, *Retrato de un desconocido: vida de Manuel Azaña (seguido por el epistolario de Manuel Azaña con Cipriano de Rivas Cherif de 1921 a 1937)* (Barcelona: Grijalbo, 1980) p. 437.

61 See his concluding statement at his trial, Saborit, *Besteiro*, p. 285; Azaña, *Obras* IV, p. 895.

62 Zugazagoitia, *Guerra y vicisitudes* II, p. 190.

63 Actas de la Comisión Ejecutiva, 15 November 1938, FPI, AH-20-5; Lamoneda, *Posiciones políticas*, p. 96.

64 Actas de la Comisión Ejecutiva, 15 November 1938, FPI, AH-20-5; Ibárruri et al., *Guerra y revolución* IV, p. 166; Lamoneda, *Posiciones políticas*, p. 96.

65 Azaña, *Obras* IV, p. 895; Rivas Cherif, *Retrato de un desconocido*, p. 394; Ansó, *Yo fui ministro de Negrín*, p. 222; Saborit, *Besteiro*, p. 285; Zugazagoitia, *Guerra y vicisitudes* II, pp. 190–1.

66 'Declaración de don Antonio Luna García' in Arenillas, *El proceso*, pp. 192–3; ibid., p. 241; La Cierva, *1939*, pp. 54–6; José Manuel Martínez Bande, *Los cien últimos días de la República* (Barcelona: Caralt, 1973) pp. 119–21.

67 Zugazagoitia, *Guerra y vicisitudes* II, pp. 195, 270; Ansó, *Yo fui ministro de Negrín*, p. 230.

68 La Cierva, *1939*, pp. 79–80, 91, 110, 118, 120–1. Cf. Segismundo Casado, *The Last Days of Madrid* (London: Peter Davies, 1939) p. 276.

69 Lamoneda, *Posiciones políticas*, p. 96.

70 Togliatti, 'Relazione del 21 maggio 1939', *Opere* IV, pp. 343–410; Graham, *Socialism and War*, pp. 234–5.

71 Manuel Portela Valladares, *Dietario de dos guerras (1936–1950). Notas, polémicas y correspondencia de un centrista español* (La Coruña: Ediciós do Castro, 1988) p. 152.

72 Jackson, *The Spanish Republic*, p. 471.

73 Tierno Galván, *Cabos sueltos*, pp. 26–7, 34; Cf. Gabriel Morón, *Política de ayer y política de mañana. Los socialistas ante el problema español* (Mexico DF: Talleres Numancia, 1942) pp. 142–3.

74 Lamo de Espinoa & Contreras, *Besteiro*, p. 116.

75 'Declaración de don Antonio Luna García' in Arenillas, *El proceso*, p. 193.

76 Eduardo Domínguez Aragonés, *Los vencedores de Negrín* (Mexico DF: Roca, 1976) pp. 150, 154–5; F. Ferrandiz Alborz, *La bestia contra*

España. Reportaje de los últimos días de la guerra española y los primeros de la bestia triunfante (Montevideo: CISA, 1951) p. 73.

77 For the text of his speech, *El Socialista*, 7 March 1939; the description of Besteiro, José García Pradas, *Como terminó la guerra de España* (Buenos Aires: Ediciones Imán, 1940) pp. 71–2, 131.

78 According to Wenceslao Carrillo, Minister of the Interior in the Consejo de Defensa Nacional. See the unpublished report by Eustaquio Cañas, 'Marzo de 1939. El último mes', in Fundación Pablo Iglesias, ARLF-172-30, p. 28.

79 Cipriano Mera, *Guerra, exilio y cárcel de un anarcosindicalista* (Paris: Ruedo Ibérico, 1976) p. 209.

80 Cañas, 'Marzo de 1939', FPI/ ARLF-172-30, pp. 29–30.

81 Private information. See pp. 328–9 and note 19 of the Epilogue.

82 Besteiro, *Obras* III, pp. 435–7.

83 Regina García, *Yo he sido marxista, El cómo y porque de una conversión* 2ª edición (Madrid: Editora Nacional, 1952) pp. 330–1.

84 Casado, *The Last Days*, pp. 290–1; La Cierva, *1939*, p. 266; Ferrandiz Alborz, *La bestia*, p. 74.

85 Domínguez, *Los vencedores de Negrín*, p. 213.

86 'Declaración de don Antonio Luna García' in Arenillas, *El proceso*, p. 195.

87 García Pradas, *Como terminó la guerra*, p. 131.

88 Mera, *Guerra, exilio y cárcel*, pp. 224–5.

89 José del Río, 'Besteiro, martir', *El Socialista*, 24 September 1959. See also Jackson, *The Spanish Republic*, p. 471, who speaks of 'the notion of vicarious sacrifice, the hope that his imprisonment and death might lighten the burden of reprisals against others.'

90 García Pradas, *Como terminó la guerra*, p. 131.

91 Saborit, *Besteiro*, p. 300.

92 Besterio, *Cartas*, p. 121.

93 Elías Díaz, *Los viejos maestros. La reconstrucción de la razón* (Madrid: Alianza, 1994) pp. 61–2.

94 Prieto, *Convulsiones* III, pp. 334–7.

95 In Saborit, *Besteiro*, pp. 293–5.

96 On the imprisonment and death of Besteiro, see 'Notas de Dolores Cebrián' in Besteiro, *Cartas*, pp. 177–202; Saborit, *Besteiro*, pp. 301–15.

97 Serrano Suñer, *Entre el silencio y la propaganda*, p. 76.

98 Prieto, *Convulsiones* III, p. 331.

99 Zulueta, 'Introducción' to Besteiro, *Cartas*, p. 23.

7 The Prisoner in the Gilded Cage: Manuel Azaña

1 Emilio Mola Vidal, *Obras completas* (Valladolid: Librería Santarén, 1940) p. 1178.

2 Francisco Casares, *Azaña y ellos* (Granada: Librería Prieto, 1938) pp. 26, 34.

3 Joaquín Arrarás, preface to *Memorias íntimas de Azaña* (Madrid: Ediciones Españolas, 1939) p. 6.

4 On the tensions between them, see the chapter 'A Quixote in Politics' in this volume.

5 Salvador de Madariaga, *Españoles de mi tiempo* (Barcelona: Planeta, 1981) pp. 230–3.

6 Manuel Azaña, *El jardin de los frailes* (Madrid: Sáez Hermanos, 1927).

7 Cipriano Rivas Cherif, *Retrato de un desconocido. Vida de Manuel Azaña* (Barcelona: Grijalbo, 1980) pp. 21–174; Frank Sedwick, *The Tragedy of Manuel Azaña and the Fate of the Spanish Republic* (Ohio: Ohio State University Press, 1963) pp. 3–81; José María Marco, *Azaña* (Madrid: Mondadori, 1990) pp. 9–116.

8 See Madariaga's acute foreword to Sedwick, *Azaña*, pp.vii–x.

9 Sedwick, *Azaña*, pp. 21–2.

10 Manuel Tuñón de Lara, 'El proyecto político de Manuel Azaña en la coyuntura de la República y la Guerra', *Historia Contemporánea*, 1, 1988, pp. 11–31.

11 Manuel Azaña, diary entry for 10 July 1927, *Obras completas* 4 vols (Mexico D. F.: Oasis, 1966–8) III, p. 893; Rivas Cherif, *Retrato*, pp. 145–7, 155–6; Santos Juliá, *Manuel Azaña: una biografía política, del Ateneo al Palacio Nacional* (Madrid: Alianza, 1990) pp. 51–2.

12 Azaña, diary entry for 18 August 1931, *Obras* IV, pp. 85–6.

13 Juliá, *Azaña*, p. 86.

14 Manuel Azaña, *Estudios de política francesa. I: La política militar* (Madrid: Saturnino Calleja, n.d. [1918]). For a commentary, see Michael Alpert, 'Azaña y la política militar francesa', *Revista de Extremadura*, 19, segunda época, enero–abril 1996, pp. 33–42.

15 Ramón Salas Larrazábal, *Historia del Ejército popular de la República* 4 vols (Madrid: Editora Nacional, 1973) I, pp. 7, 14, 22–3; Juliá, *Azaña*, pp. 98–106.

16 Antonio Cordón, *Trayectoria (recuerdos de un artillero)* (Paris: Ebro, 1971) p. 196; Salas Larrazábal, *Ejército popular*, I, pp. 5–6; Juliá, *Azaña*, p. 106.

17 Michael Alpert, *La reforma militar de Azaña (1931–1933)* (Madrid: Siglo XXI, 1982) pp. 125–31; *ABC*, 24 April; *La Época*, 24 April 1931.

18 Mola, *Obras*, pp. 1056–8; Alpert, *La reforma militar*, pp. 133–50; Mariano Aguilar Olivencia, *El Ejército español durante la segunda República* (Madrid: Econorte, 1986) pp. 65–75.

19 Dámaso Berenguer, *De la Dictadura a la República* (Madrid: Editorial Plus Ultra, 1946) p. 407.

20 Mola, *Obras*, pp. 879–80; José María Iribarren, *Mola, datos para una biografía y para la historia del alzamiento nacional* (Zaragoza: Librería General, 1938) pp. 39–40.

21 Azaña, diary entry for 2 September 1931, *Obras* IV, pp. 115–16.

22 Carolyn P. Boyd, '"Responsibilities" and the Second Republic, 1931–1936' in Martin Blinkhorn, ed., *Spain in Conflict 1931–1939: Democracy and its Enemies* (London: Sage Publications, 1986) pp. 14–39.

23 Boyd, '"Responsibilities"', pp. 22–3.

24 Alpert, *La reforma militar*, pp. 216–28; Azaña, diary entry for 20 July 1931, *Obras* IV, p. 35.

25 *La Correspondencia Militar*, 18 June, 17, 31 July 1931; Mola, *Obras*, pp. 1045–65. Cf. Cordón, *Trayectoria*, p. 194.

26 The speech is reproduced in full in Eduardo Espín, *Azaña en el poder: el partido de Acción Republicana* (Madrid, Centro de Investigaciones Sociológicas, 1980) pp. 323–34. See p. 330. On the injustice of the accusation, see Alpert, *La reforma militar*, pp. 293–7, whose account is slightly flawed by his acceptance of the misquoted version of the speech given in Miguel Maura, *Así cayó Alfonso XIII* (Mexico D.F.: Imprenta Mañez, 1962) p. 227. Stanley G. Payne, *Politics and the Military in Modern Spain* (Stanford: Stanford University Press, 1967) p. 275, accepts that Azaña said the offending phrase. Hugh Thomas, *The Spanish Civil War* 3rd ed (London: Hamish Hamilton, 1977) p. 92, accepts Maura's version.

27 Cordón, *Trayectoria*, pp. 192–3, 197; Juliá, *Azaña*, pp. 101–2.

28 'Discurso de despedida en el cierre de la Academia General Militar', *Revista de Historia Militar*, Año XX, No.40, 1976, pp. 335–7.

29 Azaña, diary entries for 16, 22 July 1931, *Obras* IV, pp. 33, 39. See also 9 December 1932, *Memorias íntimas de Azaña* (Madrid: Ediciones Españolas, 1939) pp. 307–8. Franco's service record in [Franco Bahamonde, Francisco] *Hoja de servicios del Caudillo de España, Excmo. Sr. Don Francisco Franco Bahamonde y su genealogía*, edited by Esteban Carvallo de Cora (Madrid: Autor, 1967) pp. 82–3.

30 The full text is reproduced in Azaña, *Obras* II, pp. 49–58.
31 Exchange of letters between Cardinal Vidal i Barraquer and Luis Nicolau d'Olwer on 22 November 1931, between Cardinal Vidal and Manual Azaña on 24 and 25 November 1931, and between Cardinal Vidal and Cardinal Pacelli, recounting a conversation with Azaña, on 28 November 1931, Arxiu Vidal i Barraquer, *Esglesia i Estat durant la segona República espanyola*, 4 vols in 8 parts (Barcelona: Monastir de Montserrat, 1971–90) II, pp. 48–9, 158–63, 168, 179–80.
32 Azaña, diary entry for 14 October 1931, *Obras* IV, pp. 183–6.
33 Azaña, diary entry for 4 September 1931, *Obras* IV, p. 120.
34 Azaña, *Obras* IV, p. 351.
35 Azaña, *Obras* IV, p. 412.
36 Azaña, *Obras* IV, p. 424.
37 Azaña, *Obras* II, pp. 862–74.
38 Azaña, *Obras* II, p. 141.
39 Julio Alvarez del Vayo, *The Last Optimist* (London: Putnam, 1950) p. 228.
40 Angel Ossorio, *Mis memorias* (Buenos Aires: Losada, 1946) p. 226.
41 Azaña, Cortes speeches on 27 May, 2, 3 June, *Obras* II, pp. 248–309.
42 Manuel Azaña, diary entry for 23 February 1933, *Diarios, 1932–1933. Los cuadernos robados* (Barcelona: Grijalbo–Mondadori, 1997) p. 186.
43 Azaña, *Obras* IV, pp. 644, 648.
44 Juan Simeón Vidarte, *El bienio negro y la insurrección de Asturias* (Barcelona: Grijalbo, 1978) p. 21. See also the minutes of the meetings of the PSOE executive committee, Actas de la Comisión Ejecutiva del PSOE, held at the Fundación Pablo Iglesias, Madrid, 24, 25, 27, 31 October, 22, 29 November 1933.
45 It is difficult to arrive at absolutely accurate party loyalties of deputies in the Republican Cortes. See Enrique López Sevilla, *El Partido Socialista en las Cortes Constituyentes de la segunda República* (Mexico D.F.: Ediciones Pablo Iglesias, 1969); Jesús Lozano, *La segunda República: ímagenes, cronología y documentos* (Barcelona: Acervo, 1973) pp. 445–62.
46 Francisco Largo Caballero, *Discursos a los trabajadores* (Madrid: Gráfica Socialista, 1934) pp. 163–6.
47 Paul Preston, *The Coming of the Spanish Civil War: Reform Reaction and Revolution in the Second Spanish Republic 1931–1936* 2nd edition (London, Routledge, 1994) pp. 120–60.
48 Azaña, *Obras* IV, p. 661.
49 Azaña, *Obras* II, pp. 433–4.
50 Azaña, *Obras* II, p. 430.
51 Azaña, *Obras* II, p. 431.
52 Luis Araquistain, 'La utopía de Azaña' in *Leviatán*, 5, September 1934, pp. 18–30.
53 Azaña, *Obras* IV, pp. 643–4.
54 Azaña, *Obras* II, p. 434.
55 Azaña, *Obras* II, pp. 833–42.
56 Azaña, *Obras* II, pp. 849–50.
57 Azaña, *Obras* IV, pp. 649–52; Vidarte, *Bienio negro*, pp. 90–7.
58 Indalecio Prieto, *Discursos en América con el pensamiento puesto en España* (Mexico D.F.: Federación de Juventudes Socialistas, n.d. [1945]) pp. 102–3.
59 Azaña, *Obras* IV, pp. 659–60: II, pp. 901–10.
60 *El Liberal*, 6 February 1934; Azaña, *Obras* II, pp. 911–44 and especially pp. 926–7; Vidarte, *Bienio negro*, pp. 98–100.
61 Azaña, *Obras* IV, pp. 660–1.
62 Manuel Ramírez Jiménez, 'La formación de Unión Republicana y su papel en las elecciones de 1936' in *Las reformas de la segunda República* (Madrid: Túcar, 1977) pp. 125–69.
63 Preston, *The Coming*, pp. 155–60; Vidarte, *Bienio negro*, pp. 113–14, 141, 184–5, 210; Manuel Benavides, *La revolución fue así* (Barcelona: Imprenta Industrial, 1935) pp. 9–20.

64 Azaña, *Obras* IV, pp. 653–4.
65 Azaña, *Obras* III, pp. 5–21, especially pp. 11–13.
66 Rivas Cherif, *Retrato*, p. 294.
67 Azaña, *Obras* IV, pp. 667–8.
68 Rivas Cherif, *Retrato*, pp. 299–300.
69 Azaña to Prieto, 25 December 1934, *Obras* III, pp. 589–90.
70 Rivas Cherif, *Retrato*, pp. 297–9.
71 Juliá, Azaña, pp. 388–90. The public letter is in Azaña, *Mi rebelión*, pp. 5–8.
72 Azaña to Prieto, 25 December 1934, Azaña, *Obras* III, pp. 589–90.
73 A. C. Márquez Tornero, *Testimonio de mi tiempo (memorias de un español republicano)* (Madrid: Editorial Orígenes, 1979) p. 115; Rivas Cherif, *Retrato*, pp. 298–303.
74 Azaña, *Obras* III, pp. 591–3.
75 *La Libertad*, 13 April 1935; Diego Martínez Barrio, *Orígenes del Frente Popular español* (Buenos Aires: Patronato Hispano-Argentino de Cultura, 1943) pp. 24–31; Juliá, *Orígenes*, pp. 31–3.
76 For Prieto's role, see Preston, *The Coming*, pp. 215–38; Santos Juliá, *La izquierda del PSOE (1935–1936)* (Madrid: Siglo XXI, 1977) pp. 53–111; Vidarte, *Bienio negro*, pp. 387–514.
77 Azaña, *Obras* III, pp. 229–93; Márquez Tornero, *Testimonio*, pp. 118–21.
78 Henry Buckley, *Life and Death of the Spanish Republic* (London: Hamish Hamilton, 1940) pp. 182–3.
79 Sedwick, *Azaña*, p. 152.
80 Azaña to Prieto, 7 August 1935, Azaña, *Obras* III, pp. 603–4.
81 Letter from Azaña to De Francisco, 14 November 1935, in Fundación Pablo Iglesias, Madrid, (AH, 24–9).
82 Vidarte, *Bienio negro*, pp. 493–514; Preston, *The Coming*, pp. 231–8.
83 Paul Preston, *Franco: A Biography* (London: HarperCollins, 1993) pp. 115–19; Juan Simeón Vidarte, *Todos fuimos culpables* (Mexico DF: Fondo de Cultura Económica, 1973) pp. 40–55; Azaña, *Obras* IV, p. 563.
84 Rivas Cherif, *Retrato*, pp. 320–2. Azaña, diary entry for 19 February 1936, *Obras* IV, pp. 563–7. See also Azaña to Rivas Cherif, 16 March 1936, reprinted in *Retrato*, pp. 662–5.
85 Azaña to Rivas Cherif, 17 March 1936, in Rivas Cherif, *Retrato*, pp. 665–6.
86 Azaña, *Obras* III, pp. 297–307.
87 Rivas Cherif, *Retrato*, pp. 323–4; Azaña to Rivas Cherif, Rivas Cherif, *Retrato*, pp. 662–79.
88 Azaña to Rivas Cherif, 10 April 1936, Rivas Cherif, *Retrato*, pp. 675–7.
89 In this regard, see Juliá, Azaña, p. 486.
90 Azaña to Rivas Cherif, 14 May 1936, Rivas Cherif, *Retrato*, pp. 680–2; Vidarte, *Todos fuimos culpables*, pp. 96–7.
91 Azaña to Rivas Cherif, 14 May 1936, Rivas Cherif, *Retrato*, pp. 682–4; *Claridad*, 9, 10, 11, 12, 22 April 1936; Vidarte, *Todos fuimos culpables*, pp. 97–9; Francisco Largo Caballero, *Escritos de la República* (edición, estudio preliminar y notas de Santos Juliá) (Madrid: Editorial Pablo Iglesias, 1985), pp. 299–300; Francisco Largo Caballero, *Mis recuerdos* (Mexico DF: Editores Unidos, 1954) p. 155; Julián Zugazagoitia, *Guerra y vicisitudes de los Españoles* 2 vols (Paris: Librairie Espagnole, 1968) I, p. 20.
92 Vidarte, *Todos fuimos culpables*, pp. 115–18.
93 Indalecio Prieto, *Cartas a un escultor. Pequeños detalles de grandes sucesos* (Buenos Aires: Losada, 1961) pp. 44–5.
94 Azaña to Rivas Cherif, 14, 18 May, 5 June, Rivas Cherif, *Retrato*, pp. 679–92; Manuel Azaña, *Apuntes de memoria inéditos y cartas 1938–1939–1940* (Valencia: Pre-Textos, 1990) pp. 17–18.
95 Azaña, *Apuntes*, p. 18.
96 Azaña, diary entry for 7 August

1937, *Obras* IV, pp. 714–16; Diego Martínez Barrio, *Memorias* (Barcelona: Planeta, 1983) pp. 356–68; Largo Caballero, *Mis recuerdos*, pp. 166–8, 181; Vidarte, *Todos fuimos culpables*, pp. 263–86; Zugazagoitia, *Guerra y vicisitudes*, I, pp. 57–65; Luis Romero, *Tres días de julio* 2° edición (Barcelona: Ariel, 1968) pp. 158, 193, 614–15.

97 Emilio González López, *Memorias de un diputado republicano en la guerra civil española (1936–1939)* (La Coruña: Ediciós do Castro, 1990) pp. 21–2.

98 Azaña, *Obras* III, pp. 434–5.

99 Ossorio, *Mis memorias*, p. 226.

100 Rivas Cherif, *Retrato*, p. 381.

101 Rivas Cherif, *Retrato*, pp. 344–7.

102 Azaña, *Apuntes*, p. 19.

103 Azaña, *Obras* III, p. 395.

104 Rivas Cherif, *Retrato*, pp. 356, 359. A minute and painstaking account of Azaña's departure from Madrid may be found in Enrique de Rivas, *Comentarios y notas a 'Apuntes de memoria' de Manuel Azaña y a las cartas de 1938, 1939 y 1940* (Valencia: Pre-textos, 1990) pp. 79–83.

105 Rivas Cherif, *Retrato*, pp. 362–3.

106 Carles Gerhard, *Comissari de la Generalitat a Montserrat (1936–1939)* (Montserrat: Publicacions de l'Abadia de Montserrat, 1982) pp. 383–92, 410–32.

107 Azaña, *Obras* III, p. 341.

108 Azaña, diary entry for 20 May 1937, *Obras* IV, pp. 575–88.

109 See pp. 177–8 of the chapter on Besteiro in this volume.

110 Santos Juliá, 'Presidente por última vez: Azaña en la crisis de mayo de 1937', in *Manuel Azaña: Pensamiento y acción* edited by Alicia Alted, Angeles Egido and María Fernanda Mancebo (Madrid: Alianza Editorial, 1996) pp. 240–4; Helen Graham, *Socialism and War: The Spanish Socialist Party in Power and Crisis, 1936–1939* (Cambridge: Cambridge University Press, 1991) pp. 99–101.

111 Rivas Cherif, *Retrato*, p. 403.

112 Azaña, diary entry for 22 April 1938, *Obras* IV, p. 877.

113 Azaña, diary entry for 17 June 1937, *Obras* IV, pp. 623–4.

114 Juliá, 'Presidente por última vez', pp. 240–4.

115 Azaña, diary entries for 28 June, 19 August 1937, *Obras* IV, pp. 634–5, 742–3.

116 Azaña, *Obras* III, pp. 607–9.

117 Azaña, *Obras* III, pp. 330, 336.

118 See, for instance, the chapter on Besteiro in this volume.

119 Azaña, *Obras* III, p. 355.

120 Azaña to Ossorio, 28 June 1939, *Obras* III, pp. 535–54.

121 Rivas Cherif, *Retrato*, p. 415.

122 Alberto Reig Tapia, *Violencia y terror. Estudios sobre la guerra civil española* (Madrid: Akal, 1990) p. 171.

123 *ABC*, 1, 2, 3 April 1940.

8 A Life Adrift: Indalecio Prieto

1 The most virulent accusation of cowardice can be found in the malicious commentary to the collection of Prieto's writings tendentiously assembled by the Francoist propagandist, Mauricio Carlavilla, Indalecio Prieto, *Yo y Moscú* (Madrid: Editorial Nos, 1955) p. 63. See also Francisco Casares, *Azaña y ellos* (Granada: Editorial y Librería Prieto, 1938) pp. 149–60.

2 In this respect, the tribute of an erstwhile enemy is particularly pertinent, Santiago Carrillo, *Juez y parte. 15 retratos españoles* (Barcelona: Plaza y Janés, 1996) p. 56. See also Miguel Maura, *Así cayó Alfonso XIII* (Mexico DF: Imprenta Mañez, 1962) pp. 216–22.

3 Alfonso Carlos Saiz Valdivieso, *Indalecio Prieto. Crónica de un corazón* (Barcelona: Planeta, 1984) pp. 243–4.

4 Salvador de Madariaga, *Españoles de mi tiempo* (Barcelona: Planeta,

1974) p. 273; Azaña, diary entries for 15 July 1931, 19 April 1932, Manuel Azaña, *Obras completas* 4 vols (Mexico DF: Oasis, 1966–8) IV, pp. 31–2, 374; Manuel Azaña, diary entry for 25 August 1932, *Diarios, 1932–1933. Los cuadernos robados* (Barcelona: Grijalbo–Mondadori, 1997) p. 44; Santiago Carrillo, *Juez y parte*, p. 56.

5 Azaña, diary entry for 13 November 1931, *Obras* IV, p. 222.

6 Maura, *Así cayó Alfonso XIII*, p. 217.

7 An autobiographical essay written by Prieto in 1930, reprinted as Indalecio Prieto, 'La fascinación de la política', *Revista del Ministerio de Obras Públicas y Urbanismo*, No.305, December 1983, pp. 6–8; Juan Pablo Fusi, *El País Vasco. Pluralismo y nacionalidad* (Madrid: Alianza Universidad, 1984) pp. 103–4.

8 Francisco Largo Caballero, *Mis recuerdos* (Mexico DF: Editores Unidos, 1954) p. 153.

9 Antonio Masip, *Indalecio Prieto y Oviedo* (Oviedo: Baraza Oviedo, 1981) pp. 5–8.

10 Prieto, 'La fascinación de la política', p. 6; Masip, *Prieto*, pp. 12–13. See also Saiz Valdivieso, *Indalecio Prieto*, pp. 17–18. On his rectitude, see Maura, *Así cayó Alfonso XIII*, pp. 217–18.

11 Prieto, 'La fascinación de la política', pp. 6–8; Indalecio Prieto, *Palabras al viento* (Mexico DF: Ediciones Oasis, 1969) pp. 14–15; Saiz Valdivieso, *Prieto*, pp. 21–6; Fusi, *El País Vasco*, pp. 103–4.

12 Valdivieso, *Prieto*, pp. 29–33.

13 Fusi, *El País Vasco*, p. 105.

14 Juan Pablo Fusi, *Política obrera en el País Vasco* (Madrid: Ediciones Turner, 1975) pp. 333–58; Santos Juliá Díaz, 'Gobernar ¿para quién? Debilidad de partidos y representación de intereses en la II República', *Revista de Derecho Político*, No.12, winter 1981–2.

15 Saiz Valdivieso, *Prieto*, pp. 48–50; Juan Antonio Lacomba, *La crisis española de 1917* (Madrid: Editorial Crítica 1970) pp. 213–55; Carlos Forcadell, *Parlamentarismo y bolchevización: el movimiento obrero español 1914–1918* (Barcelona: Editorial Crítica, 1978) pp. 237–50; Manuel Tuñón de Lara, *El movimiento obrero en la historia de España* (Madrid: Taurus, 1972) ch.10.

16 Largo Caballero, *Mis recuerdos*, pp. 55–8; Julián Besteiro, *Cartas desde la prisión* (Madrid: Alianza Editorial, 1988) pp. 29–113.

17 Saiz Valdivieso, *Prieto*, pp. 50–3; Fusi, *Política obrera*, pp. 377–82; Prieto, 'La fascinación de la política', pp. 9–10.

18 Fusi, *Política obrera*, p. 429.

19 José Carlos Gibaja Velázquez, *Indalecio Prieto y el socialismo español* (Madrid: Editorial Pablo Iglesias, 1995) p. 13.

20 Fusi, *Política obrera*, pp. 429–35; Gibaja Velázquez, *Indalecio Prieto*, pp. 14–16.

21 Gerald H. Meaker, *The Revolutionary Left in Spain, 1914–1923* (Stanford: Stanford University Press, 1974) pp. 225–384; Paul Heywood, *Marxism and the Failure of Organised Socialism in Spain 1879–1936* (Cambridge: Cambridge University Press, 1990) pp. 62–83; Manuel Tuñón de Lara, *El Movimiento obrero en la historia de España* (Madrid: Taurus, 1972) pp. 681–717.

22 Fusi, *Política obrera*, p. 478.

23 David S. Woolman, *Rebels in the Rif: Abd el Krim and the Rif Rebellion* (Stanford: Stanford University Press, 1968) pp. 83–102.

24 The articles were reprinted in Indalecio Prieto, *Con el Rey o contra el Rey* 2ª edición, 2 vols (Barcelona: Editorial Planeta, 1990) I, pp. 11–138. See also Saiz Valdivieso, *Prieto*, pp. 76–7.

25 Prieto, *Con el Rey* I, p. 141–209.

26 Reprinted as Dictamen de la Minoría Socialista, *El desastre de Melilla: dictamen formulado por Indalecio Prieto como miembro de la*

Comisión designada por el Congreso de los Diputados para entender en el expediente Picasso (Madrid: Sucesores de Rivadeneyra, 1922) and in Prieto, *Con el Rey* II, pp. 37–126.

27 Saiz Valdivieso, *Prieto*, pp. 82–3.

28 Indalecio Prieto, *Convulsiones de España. Pequeños detalles de grandes sucesos* 3 vols (Mexico DF: Oasis, 1967–9) I, pp. 53–5.

29 PSOE, *XII Congreso del Partido Socialista Obrero Español, 28 de junio al 4 de julio de 1928* (Madrid: Gráfica Socialista, 1929) p. 154.

30 PSOE, *Convocatoria y orden del día para el XII congreso ordinario del Partido Socialista Obrero Español* (Madrid: Gráfica Socialista, 1927) pp. 103–4; PSOE, *XII Congreso*, pp. 140–53.

31 *El Socialista*, 13 December 1923; Francisco Largo Caballero, *Presente y futuro de la Unión General de Trabajadores* (Madrid: Javier Morata, 1925) pp. 42–7; Largo Caballero, *Mis recuerdos*, pp. 90–2.

32 Paul Preston, *The Coming of the Spanish Civil War: Reform Reaction and Revolution in the Second Spanish Republic 1931–1936* 2nd edn (London: Routledge, 1994) pp. 19–27.

33 Ricardo Miralles, *El socialismo vasco durante la II República* (Bilbao: Universidad del País Vasco, 1988) pp. 133–6.

34 Gabriel Mario de Coca, *Anti-Caballero. Crítica marxista de la bolchevización del partido socialista* 2ª edición (Madrid: Ediciones del Centro, 1975) pp. 30–1; PSOE, *Memoria: Convocatoria y orden del día para el XIII Congreso ordinario* (Madrid: Gráfica Socialista, 1932) pp. 68–9.

35 Maura, *Así cayó Alfonso XIII*, p. 58.

36 The text is reprinted in Prieto, *Con el Rey* II, pp. 155–77.

37 Preston, *The Coming*, pp. 29–33; Andrés Saborit, *Julián Besteiro* (Buenos Aires: Editorial Losada, 1967) p. 191; Prieto, *Convulsiones* I, p. 61.

38 Maura, *Así cayó Alfonso XIII*, pp. 69–75.

39 Maura, *Así cayó Alfonso XIII*, pp. 83–4, 92; Prieto, *Convulsiones* I, p. 62.

40 Henry Buckley, *Life and Death of the Spanish Republic* (London: Hamish Hamilton, 1940) p. 168; Isabel de Palencia, *I Must Have Liberty* (New York: Longmans, Green & Co., 1940) p. 191; Maura, *Así cayó Alfonso XIII*, pp. 104, 107.

41 *El Socialista*, 11, 12 July 1931; PSOE, *XIII Congreso*, pp. 126–35; Gabriel Morón, *La ruta del socialismo en España* (Madrid: Editorial España, 1932) pp. 39–48; Santos Juliá, *Manuel Azaña, una biografía política. Del Ateneo al Palacio Nacional* (Madrid: Alianza, 1990) pp. 111–21.

42 Maura, *Así cayó Alfonso XIII*, pp. 209, 217–19. The speeches of 18 and 23 May 1934 are reprinted in Indalecio Prieto, *Dentro y fuera del Gobierno. Discursos parlamentarios* (Mexico DF: Oasis, 1975) pp. 11–64.

43 Azaña, diary entry for 31 May 1932, *Obras* IV, p. 392.

44 Azaña, diary entries for 24 March, 25, 26 May 1933, *Obras* IV, pp. 477, 544–5, 548.

45 Maura, *Así cayó Alfonso XIII*, pp. 209–10; Jordi Palafox, *Atraso económico y democracia. La segunda República y la economía española, 1892–1936* (Barcelona: Crítica, 1991) p. 180.

46 Maura, *Así cayó Alfonso XIII*, pp. 209–10, 219–21.

47 Juliá, *Historia del socialismo*, p. 44; Palafox, *Atraso económico*, pp. 155, 192–3, 209; Maura, *Así cayó Alfonso XIII*, p. 201.

48 Santos Juliá Díaz, *Historia del socialismo español (1931–1939)* (Barcelona: Conjunto Editorial, 1989) p. 43; Azaña, diary entry for 9 January, 11 May 1932, *Obras* IV, pp. 302, 382.

49 Azaña, diary entry for 13 November 1931, *Obras* IV, p. 227.

Curiously, Prieto knew March and had a cordial personal relationship to the extent, on the day after the meeting at which the Pact of San Sebastián was agreed, of suggesting jokingly to him that he might like to give money to the revolutionary committee as a sort of insurance policy – Azaña, diary entry for 3 April 1932, *Obras* IV, p. 367.

50 Azaña, diary entries for 5 & 7 July 1931, *Obras* IV, pp. 13, 18.

51 Azaña, diary entries for 28 & 31 July 1931, *Obras* IV, p. 49; Palafox, *Atraso económico*, pp. 290, 294.

52 Azaña, diary entries for 10 August, 8 September, 13 November 1931, *Obras* IV, pp. 76–7, 121, 222.

53 Azaña, diary entries for 7 August and 22 September 1931, *Obras* IV, pp. 68–70, 140–5; Prieto, *Convulsiones* I, pp. 101–3.

54 Azaña, diary entries for 1 & 4 September, 9, 29 October, 14 November 1931, *Obras* IV, pp. 112, 118, 171, 204–5, 230.

55 Joseph Harrison, *The Spanish Economy in the Twentieth Century* (London: Croom Helm, 1985) pp. 99–102.

56 Juliá, *Historia del socialismo*, pp. 65–8.

57 Azaña, diary entries for 11, 12, 13 December 1931, *Obras* IV, pp. 269–75. Prieto bought *El Liberal* on 30 January 1932, see Saiz Valdivieso, *Prieto*, pp. 134–5 and Joaquín Arrarás, *Memorias íntimas de Azaña* (Madrid: Ediciones Españolas, 1939) p. 86.

58 Azaña, diary entries for 12 January, 11 May 1932, *Obras* IV, pp. 308, 382.

59 Azaña, diary entry for 13 March 1932, *Obras* IV, p. 350.

60 Prieto explained his policies in the Ministerio de Obras Públicas in three great parliamentary speeches, on 30 November 1932, 16 August 1933 and 23 February 1934. See Prieto, *Dentro y fuera del Gobierno*, pp. 87–192. See also Manuel Díaz Marta, 'Indalecio Prieto en Obras Públicas: una gestión intensa y acertada', *Revista del Ministerio de Obras Públicas y Urbanismo*, No. 305, December 1983, pp. 11–15; Palafox, *Atraso económico*, pp. 204–5; Juliá, *Historia del socialismo*, pp. 45–6.

61 Azaña, diary entry for 8 June 1932, *Obras* IV, p. 400.

62 *El Socialista*, 8 & 9 October 1932; Juan-Simeón Vidarte, *Las Cortes Constituyentes de 1931–1933* (Barcelona: Grijalbo, 1976) pp. 485–93; Coca, *Anti-Caballero*, pp. 62–5.

63 Azaña, diary entry for 13 January 1933, *Memorias íntimas*, p. 208.

64 Azaña, diary entry for 14 April 1933, *Obras* IV, pp. 484–5; Vidarte, *Las Cortes Constituyentes*, pp. 508–35.

65 Azaña, diary entries for 6, 7, 8 June 1933, *Diarios, 1932–3*, pp. 332–41; Santos Juliá, *Manuel Azaña, una biografía política. Del Ateneo al Palacio Nacional* (Madrid: Alianza Editorial, 1990) pp. 258–63.

66 Azaña, diary entries for 9, 10, 11, 12 June 1933, *Memorias íntimas*, pp. 259–91; Juliá, *Azaña*, pp. 264–70.

67 *El Socialista*, 25 July 1933.

68 Indalecio Prieto, *Discursos fundamentales* (Madrid: Ediciones Turner, 1975) pp. 160–80. Prieto's commentary on the audience reaction in Indalecio Prieto, *Cartas a un escultor* (Buenos Aires: Losada, 1961) p. 83–91.

69 *El Socialista*, 13 August 1933.

70 *El Socialista*, 20 September 1933; Juliá, *Historia del socialismo*, pp. 78–81.

71 Preston, *The Coming*, pp. 115–24.

72 Francisco Largo Caballero, *Discursos a los trabajadores* (Madrid: Gráfica Socialista, 1934) pp. 163–6.

73 Preston, *The Coming*, pp. 122–55.

74 Prieto, *Convulsiones* I, pp. 109–12.

75 Indalecio Prieto, *Discursos en América con el pensamiento puesto en España* (Mexico DF: Ediciones de la Federación de Juventudes

Socialistas de España, 1944) pp. 102–3.

76 Azaña, diary entry for 26 November 1938, *Obras* IV, p. 900.

77 Preston, *The Coming*, pp. 161–80.

78 Ignacio Hidalgo de Cisneros, *Cambio de rumbo* 2 vols (Bucharest: Ebro, 1964 & 1970) II, pp. 95–101; Niceto Alcalá Zamora, *Memorias* (Barcelona: Planeta, 1977) p. 299.

79 Vidarte to Prieto, 20 March 1935, Prieto to the PSOE executive committee, 23 March and 26 April 1935, *Documentos socialistas* (Madrid: Indice, 1935) pp. 17–26.

80 Letter from Ramón González Peña to Prieto, 31 March 1935, and replies by González Peña to a questionnaire sent to him by the Madrid branch of the Socialist Youth Movement, *Documentos socialistas*, pp. 143–55.

81 Conversation of the author with Santiago Carrillo in 1976; see also Carrillo, *Juez y parte*, p. 56.

82 Largo Caballero, *Mis recuerdos*, p. 145.

83 Vidarte, *Todos fuimos culpables*, p. 99.

84 *Diario de las sesiones de Cortes, Congreso de los Diputados, comenzaron el 16 de marzo de 1936*, 20, 24, 31 March 1936; Indalecio Prieto, 'Prólogo', Luis Romero Solano, *Vísperas de la guerra de España* (Mexico D.F.: El Libro Perfecto, n.d. [1947]) pp. 3–8; Juan-Simeón Vidarte, *Todos fuimos culpables* (Mexico D.F.: Fondo de Cultura Económica, 1973) pp. 71–2; Preston, *The Coming*, pp. 245–50.

85 Vidarte, *Todos fuimos culpables*, pp. 72–81; Preston, *The Coming*, pp. 251–2.

86 Preston, *The Coming*, pp. 252–73, 261–4.

87 Prieto, *Discursos*, pp. 255–73; Prieto, *Cartas a un escultor*, pp. 92–110.

88 Vidarte, *Todos fuimos culpables*, pp. 107–8; José Antonio Primo de Rivera, *Textos de doctrina politica* 4th edn (Madrid: Sección Femenina, 1966) pp. 933–8; Prieto, *Convulsiones* I, pp. 136–7.

89 Maura, *Así cayó Alfonso XIII*, pp. 221–2.

90 Azaña, diary entry for 7 August 1937, *Obras* IV, p. 714.

91 Prieto, *Cartas a un escultor*, pp. 44–5 and pp. 225–6 of this book.

92 Vidarte, *Todos fuimos culpables*, pp. 117–27; Prieto, *Discursos en América*, pp. 29–31; Preston, *The Coming*, pp. 261–5.

93 Vidarte, *Todos fuimos culpables*, p. 664.

94 Prieto raised this issue in a speech in Mexico on 21 April 1940, saying that he would never act against party discipline, *Discursos en América*, pp. 29–13.

95 Coronel Jesús Pérez Salas, *Guerra en España (1936 a 1939)* (Mexico D.F.: Imprenta Grafos, 1947) pp. 77–9.

96 Vidarte, *Todos fuimos culpables*, pp. 115–18.

97 Prieto, *Cartas a un escultor*, pp. 57, 93; Vidarte, *Todos fuimos culpables*, pp. 93–5, 99–100, 146–7. Casares was equally dismissive of Communist warnings, Dolores Ibárruri, *El único camino* (Madrid: Editorial Castalia, 1992) p. 349.

98 *El Socialista*, 26 May, 1, 2 July 1936; *Claridad*, 26 May, 1 June, 30 June, 1, 2, 13 July 1936; Helen Graham, *Socialism and War: The Spanish Socialist Party in Power and Crisis, 1936–1939* (Cambridge, 1991) pp. 36–50; Vidarte, *Todos fuimos culpables*, pp. 192–6, 205–8; Preston, *The Coming*, pp. 271–4.

99 Prieto, *Convulsiones* III, pp. 159–60; Vidarte, *Todos fuimos culpables*, pp. 199–200, 859–61.

100 Gibaja Velázquez, *Prieto*, p. 124.

101 Gibaja Velázquez, *Prieto*, p. 132.

102 Prieto, *Cartas a un escultor*, pp. 61–2; Prieto, *Convulsiones* I, pp. 184–7; Julián Zugazagoitia, *Guerra y vicisitudes de los españoles* 2 vols (Paris: Librería Española, 1968) I, pp. 30–1, 39.

103 Largo Caballero, *Mis recuerdos*, pp. 165–8; Graham, *Socialism and War*, pp. 53–6.
104 Mijail Koltsov, *Diario de la guerra de España* (Paris: Ruedo Ibérico, 1963) p. 55; Vidarte, *Todos fuimos culpables*, p. 476. Prieto regarded Giral as 'aburrido', (boring), Azaña, diary entry for 28 March 1932, *Obras* IV, p. 363.
105 Pietro Nenni, *La guerra de España* (Mexico DF: Ediciones Era, 1967) p. 105.
106 Ramón Lamoneda, *Posiciones políticas-documentos-correspondencia* (Mexico DF: Roca, 1976) p. 228.
107 Koltsov, *Diario*, p. 55.
108 Koltsov, *Diario*, pp. 64–5.
109 Prieto, *Convulsiones* II, p. 28; Vidarte, *Todos fuimos culpables*, pp. 481–3.
110 Vidarte, *Todos fuimos culpables*, pp. 618–23; Graham, *Socialism and War*, pp. 131–4.
111 See the interchange of letters between Prieto, Largo Caballero and the Basque Government in José Antonio Aguirre, *El informe del Presidente Aguirre al Gobierno de la República* (Bilbao: La Gran Enciclopedia Vasca, 1978) pp. 351–62.
112 Graham, *Socialism and War*, pp. 58–68.
113 Graham, *Socialism and War*, pp. 94–103.
114 Vidarte, *Todos fuimos culpables*, pp. 661–3, 666–7, 678–9.
115 Azaña, diary entry for 20 May 1937, *Obras* IV, p. 602.
116 Prieto, *Convulsiones* II, p. 29.
117 Prieto, *Convulsiones* II, p. 29.
118 Zugazagoitia, *Guerra* II, p. 14; Aguirre, *Informe*, p. 177; Prieto, *Convulsiones*, II, p. 44.
119 Azaña, diary entries for 24, 29 June 1937, *Obras* IV, pp. 634, 637.
120 Azaña, diary entry for 29 June 1937, *Obras* IV, pp. 638–40.
121 Azaña, diary entry for 15 July 1937, *Obras* IV, p. 678.
122 Ramón Salas Larrazábal, *Historia del Ejército popular de la República* 4 vols (Madrid: Editora Nacional, 1973) pp. 233–44.
123 Azaña, diary entry for 22 July 1937, *Obras* IV, pp. 687–8, 691.
124 Zugazagoitia, *Guerra* II, pp. 38–43; Prieto, *Convulsiones* II, p. 44.
125 Azaña, diary entry for 23, 24 August 1937, *Obras* IV, pp. 744, 749.
126 General Vicente Rojo, *España heroica: diez bocetos de la guerra española* 3ª edición (Barcelona: Ariel 1975) pp. 103–15; Servicio Histórico Militar (Coronel José Manuel Martínez Bande), *La gran ofensiva sobre Zaragoza* (Madrid: Editorial San Martín, 1973) pp. 78–167; Luis María de Lojendio, *Operaciones militares de la guerra de España* (Barcelona: Montaner y Simón, 1940) pp. 346–9; Salas Larrazábal, *Ejército* II, pp. 1287–330; Manuel Aznar, *Historia Militar de la guerra de España (1936–1939)* (Madrid: Ediciones Idea, 1940) pp. 499–516.
127 Azaña, diary entries for 31 August, 8 September 1937, *Obras* IV, pp. 759–60, 768.
128 Azaña, diary entries for 29 June, 15 September 1937, *Obras* IV, pp. 638, 785–6.
129 Dolores Ibárruri, *En la lucha. Palabras y hechos 1936–1939* (Moscow: Editorial Progreso, 1968) pp. 176–85; Azaña, diary entry for 3 October 1937, *Obras* IV, p. 810.
130 Azaña, diary entry for 1 November 1937, *Obras* IV, p. 842.
131 Aznar, *Historia militar*, p. 535–41.
132 Azaña, diary entry for 6 November 1937, *Obras* IV, p. 849; Rojo, *España heroica*, pp. 117–19; Aznar, *Historia militar*, pp. 543–4.
133 Rojo, *España heroica*, pp. 119–125; Servicio Histórico Militar (Coronel José Manuel Martínez Bande), *La batalla de Teruel* 2ª edición (Madrid: Editorial San Martín, 1990) pp. 52–64; Aznar, *Historia militar*, pp. 545–54; Salas Larrazábal, *Ejército* II, pp. 1637–49; Lojendio, *Operaciones militares*, pp. 365–7.

134 Rojo, *España heroica*, pp. 125, 128–9.
135 Claude Martin, *Franco, soldado y estadista* (Madrid: Fermín Uriarte, 1965) p. 293; Aznar, *Historia militar*, pp. 551, 622; Ramón Garriga, *El general Yagüe* (Barcelona: Planeta, 1985) pp. 139–40.
136 Azaña, diary entry for 8 September 1937, *Obras* IV, p. 769.
137 Buckley, *Life and Death*, pp. 336–7.
138 *Documents on German Foreign Policy* Series D (London: HMSO, 1951) III, p. 294.
139 Azaña, diary entries for 15, 24 September 1937, *Obras* IV, pp. 786, 803.
140 Zugazagoitia, *Guerra* II, pp. 50–1, 75–7, 82; Louis Fischer, *Men and Politics: An Autobiography* (London: Jonathan Cape, 1941) p. 400.
141 Zugazagoitia, *Guerra* II, pp. 87–92; Vidarte, *Todos fuimos culpables*, pp. 823–7.
142 Prieto, *Convulsiones* II, pp. 41–2; *Epistolario Prieto y Negrín* (Paris: Imprimerie Nouvelle, 1939) pp. 8–9, 23–7; Vidarte, *Todos fuimos culpables*, pp. 827–9.
143 Vidarte, *Todos fuimos culpables*, pp. 827–32; Lamoneda, *Posiciones*, pp. 227–8; Zugazagoitia, *Guerra* II, pp. 94–106; Prieto, *Convulsiones* II, pp. 28, 42–51; Palmiro Togliatti, *Opere 1935–1944* (Rome: Editori Riuniti, 1979) pp. 313–19. On the Prieto–Negrín friendship, see Zugazagoitia, *Guerra* II, pp. 50–1.
144 Gibaja Velázquez, *Prieto*, p. 180.
145 Zugazagoitia, *Guerra* II, p. 108.
146 Graham, *Socialism and War*, pp. 134–6; Gabriel Morón, *Política de ayer y política de mañana (Los socialistas ante el problema español)* (Mexico D.F.: Author, 1942) pp. 91–107.
147 Prieto's report to the National Committee is reprinted in Prieto, *Convulsiones* II, pp. 27–70. For accounts of the meeting, see Vidarte, *Todos fuimos culpables*, pp. 844–58; Zugazagoitia, *Guerra* II, pp. 114–15; Graham, *Socialism and War*, pp. 142–55.
148 Morón, *Política*, p. 55.
149 Prieto, *Palabras al viento*, p. 13.
150 Saiz Valdivieso, *Prieto*, p. 218; Carrillo, *Juez y parte*, p. 72.
151 Prieto, *Palabras al viento*, p. 252.
152 Gibaja Velázquez, *Prieto*, pp. 445–7.
153 Prieto, *Palabras al viento*, pp. 9–10.
154 The articles in Prieto, *Palabras al viento*, p. 209; the speech in Prieto, *Discursos en América*, pp. 42–3.
155 Manuel Cantarero del Castillo, *Tragedia del socialismo espanol* (Barcelona: Dopesa, 1971) p. 262.
156 Saiz Valdivieso, *Prieto*, p. 68.
157 Prieto, 'La fascinación de la política', p. 10.
158 Maura, *Así cayó Alfonso XIII*, p. 217.

9 Pasionaria of Steel: Dolores Ibárruri

1 Jorge Semprún, *Autobiografía de Federico Sánchez* (Barcelona: Planeta, 1977) pp. 18–24.
2 Dolores Ibárruri, *El único camino* (Madrid: Editorial Castalia, 1992) pp. 444, 535–6. The idea that she was an ex-nun was still current in Francoist circles in the mid-1980s, Luis Suárez Fernández, *Francisco Franco y su tiempo* 8 vols (Madrid: Fundación Nacional Francisco Franco, 1984) II, p. 10.
3 Francisco Casares, *Azaña y ellos* (Granada: Editorial y Librería Prieto, 1938) pp. 241–3.
4 Ibárurri, *El único camino*, p. 113; Andrés Carabantes & Eusebio Cimorra, *Un mito llamado Pasionaria* (Barcelona: Planeta, 1982) p. 17.
5 Ibárruri, *El único camino*, pp. 139–40.
6 Ibárruri, *El único camino*, pp. 141–2.
7 Andreu Claret Serra, *Pasionaria. Memoria gráfica* (Madrid: Ediciones PCE, 1985) pp. 17–25.
8 José Bullejos, *La Comintern en España* (Mexico DF: Impresiones Modernas, 1972) pp. 98–100; Joan Estruch, *Historia del PCE (1920–*

1939) (Barcelona: El Viejo Topo, 1978) pp. 57–8.

9 Manuel Vázquez Montalbán, *Pasionaria y los siete enanitos* (Barcelona: Planeta, 1995) pp. 72–3; Carabantes & Cimorra, *Un mito*, p. 48.

10 Mijail Koltsov, diary entry for 17 June 1937, *Diario de la guerra de España* (Paris: Ruedo Ibérico, 1963) pp. 412–13.

11 Ibárruri, *El único camino*, pp. 198–218.

12 Ibárruri, *El único camino*, pp. 222–7, 244–7; Carabantes & Cimorra, *Un mito*, p. 69.

13 María Victoria Fernández Luceño, *José Díaz Ramos. Aproximación a la vida de un luchador obrero* (Sevilla: Universidad de Sevilla, 1992) pp. 41–65, 110–22.

14 Dolores Ibárruri, 'Contestación a una carta abierta al camarada Hurtado y a todo el Partido', *Mundo Obrero*, 5 December 1932; Bullejos, *La Comintern*, pp. 123–208; Rafael Cruz, *El Partido Comunista de España en la II República* (Madrid: Alianza Editorial, 1987) pp. 142–57.

15 Ibárruri, *El único camino*, pp. 257–8, 265–8; Irene Falcón, *Asalto a los cielos. Mi vida junto a Pasionaria* (Madrid: Temas de Hoy, 1996) pp. 130–2.

16 Falcón, *Asalto a los cielos*, pp. 95–9.

17 Falcón, *Asalto a los cielos*, pp. 53–87; Gregorio Morán, *Miseria y grandeza del Partido Comunista de España 1939–1985* (Barcelona: Planeta, 1986) p. 71.

18 Ibárruri, *El único camino*, pp. 269–73; Vittorio Vidali, *Diary of the Twentieth Congress of the Communist Party of the Soviet Union* (Westport, Connecticut: Lawrence Hill, 1984) p. 11.

19 Koltsov, diary entry for 17 June 1937, *Diario*, p. 413; Ibárruri, *El único camino*, pp. 269–303; Falcón, *Asalto a los cielos*, pp. 128–9.

20 Ibárruri, *El único camino*, pp. 317–18.

21 Paco Ignacio Taibo II, *Historia general de Asturias, vol. 8, Octubre 1934: la caída* (Gijón: Silverio Cañada, 1978) pp. 213–24; Ibárruri, *El único camino*, pp. 321–8.

22 Ibárruri, *El único camino*, pp. 329–41.

23 Santiago Carrillo, *Demain l'Espagne: entretiens avec Régis Debray et Max Gallo* (Paris: Éditions du Seuil, 1974) pp. 105–6.

24 Falcón, *Asalto a los cielos*, p. 375; Carabantes & Cimorra, *Un mito*, p. 36. Cf. Palmiro Togliatti, *Opere 1935–1944* (Rome: Editori Riuniti, 1979) p. 314.

25 *Diario de las sesiones de Cortes, Congreso de los Diputados, comenzaron el 16 de marzo de 1936*, 16 June 1936. For the alleged threat, see Suárez Fernández, *Franco*, II, p. 36.

26 Dolores Ibarruri, *En la lucha. Palabras y hechos 1936–1939* (Moscow: Editorial Progreso, 1968) pp. 36–7; Carabantes & Cimorra, *Un mito*, pp. 114–17.

27 Isabel de Palencia, *I Must Have Liberty* (New York: Longmans, Green, 1940) p. 230.

28 Ibárruri, *En la lucha*, p. 39.

29 Ibárruri, *El único camino*, pp. 382–5; Enrique Líster, *Nuestra guerra* (Paris: Colección Ebro, 1966) pp. 35–6; Juan Modesto, *Soy del Quinto Regimiento (Notas de la guerra española)* (Paris: Colección Ebro, 1969) pp. 24–5.

30 Koltsov, diary entry for 20 August 1936, *Diario*, pp. 42–3.

31 Koltsov, diary entry for 22 August 1936, *Diario*, pp. 478.

32 Franz Borkenau, *The Spanish Cockpit* 2nd edn (Ann Arbor, University of Michigan Press, 1963) pp. 120–1.

33 Falcón, *Asalto a los cielos*, p. 138.

34 Ibárruri, *En la lucha*, pp. 44–5; Santiago Carrillo, *Juez y parte. 15 retratos españoles* (Barcelona: Plaza y Janés, 1996) p. 114; Manuel Azcárate, *Derrotas y esperanzas. La República, la guerra civil y la*

resistencia (Barcelona: Tusquets Editores, 1994) p. 115; author's conversation with Pierre Vilar.

35 Ibárruri, *El único camino*, pp. 423–5.

36 Azcárate, *Derrotas y esperanzas*, p. 115.

37 Antonio Candela, *Adventures of an Innocent in the Spanish Civil War* (Penzance: United Writers, 1989) pp. 56–7.

38 Dolores Ibárruri et al., *Guerra y revolución en España 1936–39* 4 vols (Moscow: Editorial Progreso, 1966–77) II, pp. 136–7; Koltsov, *Diario*, p. 330.

39 *Mundo Obrero*, 25 September 1936, reprinted in Ibárruri, *En la lucha*, pp. 54–6.

40 *Milicia Popular Diario del 5° Regimiento de Milicias Populares*, 6 October 1936.

41 *Milicia Popular*, 12 August 1936; Juan Andrés Blanco Rodríguez, *El Quinto Regimiento en la política militar del PCE en la guerra civil* (Madrid: UNED, 1993) pp. 31–42; Modesto, *Soy del Quinto Regimiento*, pp. 25–6; Santiago Alvarez, *Memorias II La guerra civil de 1936/1939. Yo fui Comisario Político del Ejército Popular* (La Coruña: Ediciós do Castro 1986) p. 46; Ibárruri, *El único camino*, pp. 403–6; Ibárruri et al, *Guerra y revolución* I, p. 273.

42 *Mundo Obrero*, 2 November 1936, quoted in Ibárruri, *Guerra y revolución* II, pp. 149–51; Koltsov, diary entry for 2 November 1936, *Diario*, pp. 170–1.

43 Constancia de la Mora, *In Place of Splendour* (London: Michael Joseph, 1940) p. 272; Ibárruri, *En la lucha*, p. 65.

44 Ibárruri, *En la lucha*, pp. 59–65.

45 *Milicia Popular*, 29 October 1936; *Estampa*, 7 November 1936; Koltsov, diary entry for 26 October 1936, *Diario*, p. 156; *Pasionaria Memoria gráfica*, pp. 52–80; Ilya Ehrenburg, *Corresponsal en España* (Gijón: Ediciones Júcar, 1979) p. 70; Carabantes & Cimorra, *Un mito*, p. 133.

46 Geoffrey Cox, *Defence of Madrid* (London: Victor Gollancz, 1937) pp. 16–17.

47 Carrillo, *Demain l'Espagne*, p. 106.

48 Alvarez, *Memorias II*, pp. 74–5.

49 Ibárruri, *El único camino*, pp. 437–44; Falcón, *Asalto a los cielos*, p. 429. To her immense amusement, a delegation from the convent told her, after she returned to Spain in 1977, that, in thanks, they had prayed for her every night since – letter to the author from Professor Christopher Cobb, recalling his own interview with Dolores Ibárruri, 26 April 1998.

50 Vidali, *Diary*, p. 12.

51 Conversation of the author with Irene Falcón, 24 November 1997. See also Dan Kurzman, *Miracle of November: Madrid's Epic Stand, 1936* (New York: G.P. Putnam's, 1980) p. 234.

52 Ibárruri, *En la lucha*, pp. 66–7; Carabantes & Cimorra, *Un mito*, p. 136; Koltsov, diary entry for 6 November 1936, *Diario*, pp. 211–13.

53 Enrique Castro Delgado, *Hombres made in Moscú* (Barcelona: Luis de Caralt, 1965) pp. 297–302.

54 Luigi Longo, *Le brigate internazionali in Spagna* (Roma: Editori Riuniti, 1956) p. 74; Carabantes & Cimorra, *Un mito*, p. 137.

55 *Women's Voices from the Spanish Civil War* edited by Jim Fyrth & Sally Alexander (London: Lawrence & Wishart, 1991) p. 159.

56 Diary entry for 6 July 1937, John Tisa, *Recalling the Good Fight: An Autobiography of the Spanish Civil War* (Massachusetts: Bergin & Garvey, 1985) pp. 116–17.

57 Ibárruri, *El único camino*, pp. 495–6, 502–4. Communist distrust of Asensio was long-standing, see Koltsov, diary entry for 23 October 1936, *Diario*, p. 152.

58 Manuel Azaña, diary entry for 20 May 1937, *Obras completas* 4 vols

(Mexico D.F.: Oasis, 1966–8) IV, p. 592.
59 Ibárruri, *En la lucha*, pp. 152–4.
60 Fyrth & Alexander, *Women's Voices*, p. 252.
61 Fyrth & Alexander, *Women's Voices*, p. 307.
62 Alvarez, *Memorias II*, pp. 221–2.
63 Candela, *Adventures* pp. 96–7; Alvarez, *Memorias II*, pp. 231–2.
64 Ibárruri, *En la lucha*, pp. 182–5.
65 See the open letter to her son, Rubén, 2 October 1936, Dolores Ibárruri, *Speeches & Articles 1936–1938* (Moscow: Foreign Languages Publishing House, 1938) pp. 26–7.
66 Jesús Hernández, *Yo fui un ministro de Stalin* (Madrid: G. del Toro, 1974) pp. 142–5. According to Irene Falcón, in conversation with the author, this is inconceivable, both because Dolores had excellent relations with Díaz and because Díaz was far more concerned about the womanizing of Hernández himself.
67 Togliatti, *Opere 1935–1944*, pp. 273–5.
68 Indalecio Prieto, *Convulsiones de España* 3 vols (Mexico D.F.: Oasis, 1968) II, pp. 34–5: Ronald Fraser, *Blood of Spain: The Experience of Civil War 1936–1939* (London: Allen Lane, 1979) pp. 461–2.
69 Ibárruri, *Speeches & Articles*, pp. 42–5, 76–7; *En la lucha*, pp. 68–70.
70 Ibárruri, *Speeches & Articles*, pp. 60–2.
71 Ibárruri, *El único camino*, p. 515.
72 Hernández, *Yo fui ministro de Stalin*, pp. 145–6.
73 Togliatti, *Opere 1935–1944*, pp. 288, 291.
74 Koltsov, diary entry for 17 June 1936, *Diario*, p. 412.
75 Dolores Ibárruri, *Nuestra Bandera*, No.1, 15 July 1937, pp. 17–26.
76 Falcón, *Asalto a los cielos*, pp. 143–4.
77 Azaña, diary entry for 13 October 1937, *Obras* IV, pp. 819–21.
78 Ibárruri, *En la lucha*, p. 249.
79 Julián Zugazagoitia, *Guerra y vicisitudes de los españoles* 2 vols (Paris: Librería Española, 1968) II, pp. 87–92; Juan-Simeón Vidarte, *Todos fuimos culpables* (Mexico D.F.: Fondo de Cultura Económica, 1973) pp. 823–7.
80 Vincent Sheean, *Not Peace But A Sword* (New York: Doubleday, Doran, 1939) pp. 183–4.
81 Reprinted in Ibárruri, *En la lucha*, pp. 264–317.
82 Sheean, *Not Peace*, pp. 185–7.
83 Ibárruri, *En la lucha*, pp. 331–41.
84 Diary entries for 12 & 17 November 1938, Tisa, *Recalling the Good Fight*, pp. 194–6.
85 Ibárruri, *En la lucha*, pp. 354–6.
86 Falcón, *Asalto a los cielos*, pp. 183–5.
87 José Díaz & Dolores Ibárruri, *España y la guerra imperialista: llamamiento del PCE a la emigración española* (Mexico D.F: PCE, 1939) pp. 5–12; Morán, *Miseria y grandeza*, pp. 29–34.
88 Fred Copeman, *Reason in Revolt* (London: Blandford Press, 1948) pp. 167–71. Copeman dates the meeting in November 1938 at a time when Dolores Ibárruri was still in Spain. There is little doubt that his memory was at fault given his reference to the death of Dolores's son Rubén who did not die until September 1942. The meeting must have taken place in 1939, although the reference to the Nazi–Soviet pact suggests that it might have been earlier than November.
89 Enrique Castro Delgado, *Mi fé se perdió en Moscú* (Barcelona: Luis de Caralt, 1964) p. 85; Enrique Líster, *Así destruyó Carrillo el PCE* (Barcelona: Planeta, 1983) p. 95; Azcárate, *Derrotas y esperanzas*, p. 232; Manuel Tagüeña Lacorte, *Testimonio de dos guerras* (Mexico DF: Oasis, 1973) p. 390; conversation of the author with Irene Falcón.
90 Tagüeña, *Testimonio*, p. 411; Morán, *Miseria y grandeza*, p. 71; conversation of the author with Santiago Carrillo, 11 December 1997. According to Morán, Ignacio

Gallego briefly courted her daughter, Amaya. This was categorically denied to the author by Santiago Carrillo, Irene Falcón and Santiago Alvarez.

91 Castro Delgado, *Mi fé*, pp. 86–90.

92 Dolores Ibárruri, *Memorias de Pasionaria 1939–1977. Me faltaba España* (Barcelona: Planeta, 1984) pp. 61–3.

93 Castro Delgado, *Mi fé*, p. 84.

94 Hernández, *Yo fui un ministro de Stalin*, p. 144. He claimed absurdly that the relationship with Antón caused the deaths of both Rubén and Julián Ruiz, who did not in fact die until 1977.

95 Ibárruri, *Memorias*, pp. 64–8; author's conversations about Dolores in Moscow with Ignacio Gallego, Fernando Claudín and Irene Falcón.

96 Tagüeña, *Testimonio*, pp. 411, 439–40, 456, 465–78; Falcón, *Asalto a los cielos*, pp. 212–17, 227–32; Jesús Hernández, *Yo fui un ministro de Stalin*, pp. 99–100; Santiago Carrillo, *Memorias* (Barcelona: Planeta, 1993) p. 358; Fernando Claudín, *Santiago Carrillo. Crónica de un secretario general* (Barcelona: Planeta, 1983) pp. 70–2.

97 Santiago Alvarez, *Memorias III* (La Coruña: Ediciós do Castro, 1988) pp. 319–21.

98 Ibárruri, *Memorias*, pp. 89–90.

99 Dolores Ibárruri, 'Deberes de la hora actual', *Nuestra Bandera* No.2, Toulouse, June 1945, pp. 3–6.

100 Dolores Ibárruri, 'Por un Gobierno de Coalición Nacional', *Nuestra Bandera* No.3, Toulouse, September 1945, pp. 4–10.

101 Dolores Ibárruri, 'Informe ante el Pleno del Partido Comunista de España, celebrado en Toulouse el 5 de diciembre de 1945', *Nuestra Bandera* No.4, Toulouse, January/February 1946, pp. 13–14.

102 Claudín, *Santiago Carrillo*, pp. 95–7; Carrillo, *Demain l'Espagne*, p. 100; Morán, *Miseria y grandeza*, pp. 137–8.

103 Falcón, *Asalto a los cielos*, pp. 261–2; Vázquez Montalbán, *Pasionaria*, p. 125.

104 Claudín, *Santiago Carrillo*, pp. 101–2; Carrillo, *Memorias*, pp. 428–37; Morán, *Miseria y grandeza*, pp. 194–207; Vázquez Montalbán, *Pasionaria*, pp. 127–8; Vidali, *Diary*, p. 50. In conversation with the author, Santiago Carrillo explained Antón's meek acceptance of his fate as not unusual: 'at that time, we were like a medieval military order'.

105 Artur London, *On Trial* (London: Macdonald, 1970), *passim*.

106 Falcón, *Asalto a los cielos*, pp. 135–7, 140, 239–41, 276–84, 340–1; London, *On Trial* pp. 147–51, 196–8, 215, 245–6; Azcárate, *Derrotas y esperanzas*, pp. 274, 324–31; Semprún, *Autobiografía*, pp. 141–2; Claudín, *Carrillo*, pp. 65, 93; Morán, *Miseria y grandeza*, pp. 157–8, 203–7.

107 Ibárruri, *Memorias*, p. 149.

108 Dolores Ibárruri, *Informe al Comité Central al 5° Congreso del PC de España* (n.p., n.d. [Paris: PCE, 1955]), pp. 10, 20, 70–91.

109 Ibárruri, *Informe*, pp. 8, 11, 16–17, 81–5, 116.

110 Ibárruri, *Informe*, pp. 71, 99–104.

111 Semprún, *Autobiografía*, pp. 218–23.

112 Semprún, *Autobiografía*, pp. 217–24; conversations of the author with Jorge Semprún and Santiago Carrillo; Vidali, *Diary*, p. 6.

113 Vidali, *Diary*, pp. 11–12, 52.

114 Ibárruri, *Memorias*, p. 149.

115 Líster, *Así destruyó Carrillo el PCE*, pp. 124–5.

116 Partido Comunista de España, *Declaración por la reconciliación nacíonal, por una solución democrática y pacífica del problema español* (n.p., n.d. [Paris: PCE, 1956, pp. 3, 5, 29–31, 37–40; Santiago Carrillo, *La situación en la dirección del partido y los problemas del reforzamiento del mismo* (Paris: PCE, 1956), pp. 23–4; Semprún, *Autobiografía*, p. 38;

Morán, *Miseria y grandeza*, pp. 263–80; Claudín, *Santiago Carrillo*, pp. 111–20.

117 Dolores Ibárruri, *Por la reconciliación de los españoles hacia la democratización de España* (Paris: PCE, 1956), pp. 39–42, 83–9, 94–7.

118 Luis Ramírez, *Nuestros primeros veinticinco años* (Paris: Ruedo Ibérico, 1964), pp. 169–71; Fernando Claudín, *Las divergencias en el partido* (n.p., n.d. [Paris: author, 1965]) pp. 21–7; Semprún, *Autobiografía*, pp. 44, 79–80.

119 Semprún, *Autobiografía*, pp. 7–9; Líster, *¡Basta!*, pp. 187–9.

120 Falcón, *Asalto a los cielos*, pp. 304–12; Ibárruri, *Memorias*, pp. 153–4.

121 Conversations of the author with Fernando Claudín and Francesc Vicens in 1978; Ibárruri, *Memorias*, pp. 154–8.

122 Carrillo, *Juez y parte*, p. 121; Falcón, *Asalto a los cielos*, pp. 349–52, 359–62; Vázquez Montalbán, *Pasionaria*, p. 174.

123 Carrillo, *Juez y parte*, pp. 120–1; Paul Preston, 'The PCE's Long Road to Democracy 1954–1977' in *In Search of Eurocommunism*, edited by Richard Kindersley (London: Macmillan, 1981) pp. 55–8.

124 Ibárruri, *Memorias*, p. 201.

125 *Mundo Obrero*, 17 December 1975.

126 Falcón, *Asalto a los cielos*, pp. 391–5; Carabantes & Cimorra, *Un mito*, p. 11–13, 319–23.

EPILOGUE: The Three Spains of 1936

1 Paul Preston, *The Politics of Revenge: Fascism and the Military in Twentieth Century Spain* (London: Unwin Hyman, 1990) pp. 30–52.

2 Juan Luis Cebrián, 'Para una nueva cultura política' in *El País, La guerra de España 1936–1939* (Madrid: El País, 1986) *passim*; Paul Preston, 'Introduction', *The Republic Besieged: Civil War in Spain 1936–1939* edited by Paul Preston and Ann Mackenzie (Edinburgh: Edinburgh University Press, 1996) pp. v–viii.

3 See, for example, Manuel Jiménez de Parga, 'La tercera España', *ABC*, 20 March 1998; Manuel Vázquez Montalbán, 'Cinco, seis Españas', *Interviu*, 20 April 1998; Hilari Raguer, 'Paul Preston i les tres Espanyas', unpublished lecture given at the Escola d'Estiu de Unió Democràtica de Catalunya, Platja d'Aro, 3 July 1998.

4 Paul Preston, *Franco: A Biography* (London: HarperCollins, 1993) pp. 115–19.

5 Indalecio Prieto, *De mi vida* (Mexico D.F.: Ediciones 'El Sitio', 1965) pp. 299–300. See also the introductory essays by José Antonio Durán in Manuel Portela Valladares, *Dietario de dos guerras (1936–1950)* (La Coruña: Ediciós do Castro, 1988) pp. 11–17, 147–50, and in Manuel Portela Valladares, *Memorias* (Madrid: Alianza Editorial, 1988) pp. 11–47.

6 Hilari Raguer, *Divendres de passió. Vida i mort de Manuel Carrasco i Formiguera* (Barcelona: Publicacions de l'Abadia de Montserrat, 1984) pp. 240–1; Hilari Raguer, 'Joan B. Roca i Caball i la tercera Espanya', unpublished paper.

7 Raguer, *Divendres de passió*, pp. 250–78, 334–46, 373–90. See also Carrasco's correspondence with his wife written from prison, Manuel Carrasco i Formiguera, *Cartes de la presó* edited by Hilari Raguer (Barcelona: Abadia de Montserrat, 1988).

8 Ramón Muntanyola, *Vidal i Barraquer, el cardenal de la paz* (Barcelona: Laia, 1974) pp. 277–303; Hilari Raguer, *Salvador Rial, vicari del Cardenal de la pau* (Barcelona: Publicacions de l'Abadia de Montserrat, 1993) pp. 207–14; Josep María Tarragona, *Vidal i Barraquer. De la República al franquisme* (Barcelona: Columna Assaig, 1998) pp. 196–201.

9 Anastasio Granados, *El Cardenal Gomá: Primado de España* (Madrid: Espasa Calpe, 1969) pp. 145–6;

María Luisa Rodríguez Aisa, *El Cardenal Gomá y la guerra de España: aspectos de la gestión pública del Primado 1936–1939* (Madrid: Consejo Superior de Investigaciones Cientificas, 1981) pp. 61–5; José M. Sánchez, *The Spanish Civil War as Religious Tragedy* (Notre Dame, Indiana: University of Notre Dame Press, 1987) pp. 79–81.

10 Frances Lannon, *Privilege, Persecution, and Prophecy: The Catholic Church in Spain 1875–1975* (Oxford: Clarendon Press, 1987) pp. 75–80; Josep M. Solé i Sabaté & Joan Villarroya i Font, *La repressió a la reraguardia de Catalunya (1936–1939)* 2 vols (Barcelona: Publicacions de l'Abadia de Montserrat, 1989) I, pp. 169–79; Vicente Cárcel Orti, *La persecución religiosa en España durante la segunda República (1931–1939)* (Madrid: Ediciones Rialp, 1990) pp. 198–262; Antonio Montero Moreno, *Historia de la persecución religiosa en España 1936–1939* (Madrid: Biblioteca de Autores Cristianos, 1961) *passim.*

11 Juan de Iturralde (pseudonym of Juan José Usabiaga Irazustabarrena), *La guerra de Franco: los vascos y la Iglesia* 2 vols (San Sebastián: Publicaciones 'Clero Vasco', 1978) pp. 198–205, 242, 248, 412–15.

12 Rafael Valls, *La Derecha Regional Valenciana 1930–1936* (Valencia: Edicions Alfons el Magnànim, 1992) pp. 235–6, 241–2, 246–8.

13 Vicente R. Alós Ferrando, *Reorganización, supremacia y crisis final del Blasquismo (1929–1936)* (Valencia: Ajuntament de València, 1992) p. 269.

14 Hilari Raguer, *El general Batet. Franco contra Batet: Crónica de una venganza* (Barcelona: Ediciones Península, 1996) pp. 154–86, 211–37, 239–41.

15 Ian Gibson, *Queipo de Llano. Sevilla, verano de 1936* (Barcelona: Grijalbo, 1986) pp. 101–5.

16 Guillermo Cabanellas, *Los cuatro generales* 2 vols (Barcelona: Planeta, 1977) p. 416.

17 Paul Preston, *The Coming of the Spanish Civil War: Reform Reaction and Revolution in the Second Spanish Republic 1931–1936* 2nd edn (London: Routledge, 1994) pp. 277–81.

18 Ignacio Arenillas de Chaves, *El Proceso de Besteiro* (Madrid: Revista de Occidente, 1976) p. 193.

19 I am grateful to Dom Hilari Raguer i Sunyer who gave me this information. After the publication of the Spanish edition of this book, it was confirmed by the priest in question, Father Jesús María Alemany, in a letter to Raguer of 11 May 1998.

20 *News Chronicle*, 29 July 1936.

21 Manuel Azaña, *Obras Completas* 4 vols (Mexico D.F.: Oasis, 1966–8) III, p. 355.

22 *Palabras del Caudillo* (Barcelona: Ediciones Fe, 1939) pp. 24–5.

23 Indalecio Prieto, *Convulsiones de España. Pequeños detalles de grandes sucesos* 3 vols (Mexico D.F.: Oasis, 1967–9) I, 152. Cf. Miguel Primo de Rivera y Urquijo, *Papeles póstumos de José Antonio* (Barcelona: Plaza y Janés, 1996) p. 10.

24 Prieto, *Convulsiones de España* I, p. 391; José Antonio Primo de Rivera, *Textos de doctrina política* 4th edn (Madrid: Sección Femenina, 1966) pp. 933–8.

25 Ian Gibson, *En busca de José Antonio* (Barcelona: Planeta, 1980) p. 271; Primo de Rivera, *Papeles póstumos*, p. 11.

26 Manuel Azaña, *Apuntes de memoria inéditos y cartas 1938–1939–1940* (Valencia: Pre-Textos, 1990) p. 20.

27 Alberto Reig Tapia, 'La tragedia de Manuel Azaña', *Historia Contemporánea*, No. 1, p. 49.

28 Azaña, *Obras* II, p. 608.

29 Azaña, *Obras* II, pp. 331, 341.

30 Azaña, *Obras* III, p. 378.

INDEX